"THIS IS AN EMERGENCY . . .

This is not a test . . . repeat . . . this is disaster . . . This is no dream!"

Hanna looked at the displays but she could not see the enemy. She cried out and tried to run. All the others aboard were dead, yet still they screamed in her mind. They took too long to die and dragged her down, down, and death ate at her. Smoke of burning flesh, ship metal screeching, and beyond the enemy she knew, beyond the true-human foe, something evil and unseen hunted through the darkness. Closer, closer it came, deadly, unknowable, unstoppable— and reaching out to claim only her!

THE
D'NeeraN
FACTOR

Novels of Science Fiction
by Terry A. Adams:

THE D'NEERAN FACTOR
(*Sentience* | *The Master of Chaos*)

BATTLEGROUND*

*Coming soon from DAW Books

THE
D'NEERAN
FACTOR

SENTIENCE

THE MASTER OF CHAOS

TERRY A. ADAMS

DAW BOOKS, INC.
DONALD A. WOLLHEIM, FOUNDER
375 Hudson Street, New York, NY 10014
ELIZABETH R. WOLLHEIM
SHEILA E. GILBERT
PUBLISHERS
www.dawbooks.com

First Printing, July 2013
1 2 3 4 5 6 7 8 9

DAW TRADEMARK REGISTERED
U.S. PAT. AND TM. OFF. AND FOREIGN COUNTRIES
—MARCA REGISTRADA
HECHO EN U.S.A.

PRINTED IN THE U.S.A.

Author's Note

The two novels that make up *The D'neeran Factor* had their origin in one question: What would life be like if people really, really knew what others were thinking? Science fiction seemed the most appropriate venue for exploring the question. Of course, the joy of writing science fiction—which is all I've ever wanted to write, really—lies in that *What if...?*

I try to keep the science reasonably on track, allowing for conventions of the genre (speedy interstellar travel and the ability to manipulate gravity, for instance). I'm not trained in any science. I read a lot of science for the non-scientist, but not in any disciplined way, and recognize that our perceptions and descriptions of the universe keep changing. (Even in our own little neighborhood. Pluto got demoted. Maybe it wasn't an asteroid that caused the Cretaceous–Paleogene extinction after all.) Scientists, come to think of it, are always asking, "What if?" too. And I bet they have as much fun with it as I do. Only, I'm allowed to be fuzzy about it, and they aren't.

Out of all this reading and writing, three personal axioms have emerged.

The first is that the universe absolutely can produce anything I can imagine, and more besides.

The second is that human nature hasn't changed since the indefinable day when "hominid" became "human," so it's not likely to change in the next thousand years. (I read about history and prehistory, too. Also without discipline.)

The third blossomed at the moment I became a writer. That wasn't when I completed the first few pages of *Sentience*.

It was when I looked at those pages and said: This could be a lot better.

The axiom is: It can *ALWAYS* be better.

Peace.
Terry Adams

SENTIENCE

Affectionately dedicated to
Lynn Brunner Carlson, Robin Brunner, and Leveda Smith
With special thanks to
Barry Fierst.

Prologue

The millefleurs sang a melody of ending. Clouds of twilight dimmed their thousand colors; rainbows faded into grayness, peace and longing mingled and black was there. Singing into silence:

Hallucination, she thought. Desperate battle to think. *Oxygen loss.*

She struggled for breath and lost the thought in Tirane's screams.

But he was dead—the strength of that ego, to survive in memory still!

Dorista leaned close and said aloud, "Not lack of air."

Shock made Hanna stupid. "But—?"

"The flowers. They're Gabriel dying."

Dorista wept. Hanna felt hot wetness, tasted salt. Tears of the living: Dorista, Martin, Antonia, Roly, Hanna herself. She knew these few were alive because she saw them here in Auxiliary Control.

There were also the tears of the dead.

She thought of getting up and decided against it, remembering dimly how a few minutes ago she had struggled to pick herself up off the floor and regain her seat. With clearing eyes she saw that Auxiliary Control was untouched, even though something like the heart of a star had smashed into the corvette *Clara Mendoza* and rammed it through space without effort. Pretty *Clara* with her rainbow passages, garlanded for battle: she had never had a chance against the Nestorian cruisers, nor had any of her mates.

(I want to go home oh please I'm lost lost alone and it's dark—)

Dark-eyed Pamir. Dying too, his final thoughts echoing in her mind.

Hanna lifted her right hand and brought it down hard on the edge of the console before her. The surface was curved but she hit it with all her strength and the sharp personal pain filled her and blotted out the ghosts. In the reprieve she began calling Main Control. No voice answered. Gabriel of the millefleurs faded. Had anyone survived?

"Smashed. It was smashed." Dorista still wept. "There can't even be any bodies."

"Gabriel's, anyway." The personal essence disappearing from the cooling flesh . . . the strongest took hours to go.

Voices rose round Hanna. Instinctively they were reverting to speech, the old way, the true-human way. To enter each other's thoughts was to lose their way in the mental chaos of the injured, the dead, and the dying. Not many left injured, not now. The second assault had finished the patients from the first, along with sickbay and the medics and the drugs for pain and the drugs for dying. The third had finished everything.

"Report," Hanna said over her shoulder, but nobody did. She turned and screamed at them, "Report!"

(Agony staggered them and stopped. They put a name to it. Don trying to keep pain to himself so it would not defeat them. Half the ship was crushed between them and he said: *Don't even try—*)

"I am—"

(Ash, dead or dying, mourned the son he would not have—)

Hanna said through the wave of darkness, "I'm the senior officer. If Main Control is gone, I must be. Report! *Concentrate!*"

Ghosts moved among them, nearly visible: scraps of childhood, loving faces, the detritus of ebbing consciousness. She gave them something to concentrate on: white hatred of Nestor. *Nestor, Nestor!* she cried to them, and shaped the images, fanning hate. The crazed old general, the bleak warrens of an ill-managed colony world. The Polity worlds had closed ranks and done nothing for Nestor, and it was the ancient story: find an outside enemy to hate. D'neerans were easy to hate, telepaths; true-humans considered them only quasi-human. And D'neera was a peaceful world. With more love for flowers than for defenses.

Hanna kept her mind—

(*Oh God, I'm so afraid, his blood, oh God, oh God—*)

"Who's—?" someone said.

She said over the swelling panic, "Alia. Not even hurt. Roly, find her and calm her down. It's clear to Engineering." —kept her mind on the reports.

Main Control gone. She knew that. The few secure modules of *Clara* were on local life support. The reactor heat wasted into space, irretrievable; soon the cold of space would creep in. Of the twelve ships D'neera had been able to muster, only two answered now, and they were fighting, falling back. They could not come to *Clara's* aid. The guns were out. Such as they were. And the shields. And Hanna's head was spinning and her stomach lurched; gravity was erratic, it would be free fall soon.

"They want surrender," Martin said. He snatched the link from his ear as if it had caught fire.

"Give me the link."

But it fell to the floor as a mental howl from somewhere stopped them, and somewhere a failing heart stopped.

"Willi!"—that was Martin—"Willi!"

Hanna was stuck in a nightmare where nothing could be done. Through dimming eyes she saw Martin crawling, his frantic fear for Willi (but too late for fear; time for grief) heavy as her head.

I told them. The slow thought ticked over. I told them no lovers on the same—

The mental weight suddenly lifted. Martin sobbed and collapsed. The arm Hanna had stretched out to him hurt. She snatched up the link, fumbling it, put it to her ear and picked out the words that meant disaster.

Surrender. Immediate. Destroy.

Enough. It was too much effort to sort out the Standard words from the uncouth Nestorian accent.

"Let me see them. Tonia, what can you get?"

Her head was empty and quiet now. She supposed the living were unconscious or calming themselves. Roly had not gone after Alia; she assumed Alia had fainted. She risked a thought to Tonia that took in every sensor the *Clara* possessed, and an order to Dorista to evaluate their

chances of escape through the unspace of Inspace. And an
order to Roly to count, if he could, the living. For hand-to-
hand fighting, if it came to that.

*You know we're all there is you're good at this too good
as true-human,* Roly said, and it was hateful, a signal for a
purely D'neeran catfight. There was no time for one. She
stared him down and he bowed his head and started the
hopeless job, dropping into himself and reaching out.

Tonia said unsteadily, "No visual. Nothing."

"What about the rest?"

"I think—wait."

Smoke began to drift through the ventilators with, oh
God, the smell of burning meat.

Hanna clipped off her own horror and made them do it
too.

"This is bad," Dorista muttered.

Hanna looked at the computer's relentless judgment.
Not just bad. Fatal. Inspace systems were working, in a manner of speaking. They could Jump out of here. But incoming
space-time data was getting garbled somewhere in the system, and if they Jumped—

Dorista's vision was almost soothing. Particles fanning at
random through infinity like fine gray dust . . .

"We'll have to surrender," Tonia said.

"You don't want to surrender," Hanna said, and Roly
came out of the silence where silence should not be and
stabbed her with a picture of herself as the quintessential
soldier, fighting mindlessly to the end.

"Giving up is better than dying," Tonia said.

"Come on! They want to question us. They want to find
out what can hit them from the surface. And it's an all-male
army, Tonia."

Roly looked at her blankly, the two women with growing
unease. Innocent, innocent, Hanna thought in despair, how
innocent we are! We feel one another's pain and cannot
harm each other. And are helpless before our brothers who
are our enemies.

Tonia had forgotten the sensors. She was examining
things caught from Hanna's mind, shocking lessons in
events that had happened in places that were not D'neera.
Third-hand memories, fourth-hand; they had not happened
to Hanna. She had only brushed against them, and imag-

ined how it would be. But they made Tonia tremble. Giving up did not look so good.

Hanna got up and went to her and pushed her aside. There were faults in the pictures the sensors drew, colors changing for no reason, lines flickering and re-forming. But Hanna said, *"What's that?"*

Her hands worked at Tonia's controls. She knew two of the shapes—Nestorian cruisers, not as fast as *Clara* in real-space but bigger, better shielded, better armed, and scarcely damaged. *Clara* was their prey. But something new was there, and when the mass readout came she looked at it with disbelief.

"Data error," Roly whispered.

"No." She coaxed the library for a guess.

"Cit—" its vocal circuit said, and expired.

Citybuster, said the legend on the screen.

Gravity rocked and they fell against each other.

"It's not after us," Hanna said, single-minded. The others did not speak but watched the lumpy thing grow as sensors built up a pseudo-visual pattern.

"Havock," the library said suddenly. *"N.S Havock* commissioned ST 2808 drydocked . . . ST 2809 . . . under . . . terms . . ." It sighed and died again.

"You could stuff a hundred *Claras* into that," Dorista said.

"Uh-huh. More than that. And look at those shields."

Hanna sank into Tonia's seat. Weight flux or defeat tore at her stomach, and she might have been watching herself go through the motions of command from a distance. She had never taken Defense as lightly as most of her comrades, who thought danger meant pirates and knew the existence of their elegant little fleet was deterrent enough. The news that Nestor would attack had not surprised her—nor should defeat; yet defeat did not seem real.

And we are all so young, she thought. Parents cannot serve . . . I should have had Max's baby when he asked me.

Roly mumbled, "I don't believe it. Mass sensors would've warned us."

Hanna presented him with her memory of the third and last assault. Every alarm on *Clara* had been screaming, and even those sounds were dim; the voices in their minds, the soundless terror, had drowned them out.

The cruisers were beginning to move toward them. They did not have much time.

"We took them on," Dorista said suddenly. "We did that, anyway."

Her palpable pride annoyed Hanna. "Too little and too late," she said.

She got up and turned away and paced the tiny chamber, leaving them to stare at *Havock*. She felt resentment spreading through them at the unfairness of this giant's coming when they could do nothing to it. It felt better than Alia's panic, anyway. It did not occur to her that her own control strengthened them.

The lights in the room seemed dimmer. She did not bother to check the power.

Dorista said, "What are they going to do?"

Hanna looked around, remembering the others had not heard the ultimatum. She told them, but she added, "I think it's bluff. I still think they want prisoners. They won't put that buster in place till they're sure we're finished. That—" She pointed at a signal for an incoming message; it had been flashing since she threw the link down. "That's probably an order to stand by for boarding."

"We can't," said Tonia. "I won't. I'll kill myself first. I'll kill them."

There was an overtone of wonder in what she said, as if she could not believe it of herself. Hanna looked at her thoughtfully.

"Me too," she said. "Dorry?"

Dorista hesitated. Faint voices, visions, the traces of death, but in their minds. Dorista and Don had been friends. Don was still conscious and paralyzed with his back broken and the fire coming close. The reeking smoke had begun to choke him.

Dorista said, "I want to fight. I want to kill one for him."

"Roly?"

He opened his mouth and shut it. He had liked Defense exercises; he had liked free fall and riding the clouds and the little band's camaraderie. He had never expected to fight. He did not want to fight anymore and he was ashamed of not wanting to. He let them see it and Tonia touched him sympathetically, accepting it.

"Doesn't matter," Martin said. He pulled himself up and

set his back against the wall. His grief for Willi filled the room, the world, the universe, and then he shut it in again.

"Oh, Martin," Dorista said, and went to him and took him in her arms.

"I guess we don't give up," said Roly, looking sick. "But what's the use?"

"No use," Hanna admitted. She wandered back to her place, veering here and there as gravity wavered. It was safer sitting down. She got into her seat and stared at the outline of the city buster. D'neera had nothing dangerous on the surface. Nestor would find that out soon enough. And then this thing would move into orbit, ungainly, unbalanced, but efficient enough in space. It could blanket fifty square kilometers with fast or slow death. Its presence would guarantee there would be no resistance.

She said softly, "The Polity's got good intelligence. They must have known Nestor refitted that thing."

"Why didn't they tell us?" Roly said. He was cross. He could not get used to what had happened or what was coming, and with the end nearly here he could only be querulous.

"I don't know. Yes, I do. They only told us to prepare for an attack. They thought we'd ask for help and then, you see, when they had us where they wanted us, they'd tell us all the rest. I don't think they were even going to tell us where the strike force was coming into realspace without an agreement. But they did. Somebody must have thought the ambush was our only chance. It was, too."

Don's control broke in a wave of death-fear that stopped breath and thought. Hanna clung to her seat and her sanity, riding it out. It lasted only an instant before the smoke knocked him out, and when it ended the others were choking. Alia was awake and screaming in their heads.

"Roly! Will you go shut that bitch up!"

"Yes. Yes." He stumbled into a wall and righted himself and made it out the door on the second try.

"She's too dumb to get out of Engineering," Dorista muttered.

"Why'd we put her there anyway? Never mind. At least there's air there," Hanna said, and rubbed her face with weary hands. After the first two attacks they had been spread too thin to be selective.

They waited in silence. Alia modulated to shock and pain and was still. It was like having a siren turned off, something that squawked just at the end when you touched the switch.

"Sharp right to the jaw," Hanna said.

I think I'll stay here, Roly said to her, half-present. *To be here when Alia wakes up. For the end.*

He felt acquiescence and let the mind link go, and Hanna forgot him. She ought to be thinking of sidearms, some form of futile deployment, but she could not stop staring at the citybuster. There was something at the back of her mind and she could not dig it out, and it was getting harder to think, to go on trying. Roly and Martin were passive dead weight, the future another weight of apprehension. *Clara* had set out with a crew of thirty-six and the survivors had died, in effect, thirty times in these last hours. The dead spoke to them still with ghostly voices their ears would not hear again. Perhaps the voices were even real. To let herself and the others believe so would reduce them to shadows for Nestor to take with ease.

And she could not keep from thinking of how she would die. Small-arms fire if they boarded, perhaps. A single blast of heat and radiation if they didn't. If she were taken alive there would be the half-world of stripdope, irresistible. And other indignities; but perhaps she would be drugged and would not care; and perhaps she would live and someday get revenge.

The patterns before her eyes grew and shrank and burgeoned again as the computers adjusted for real motion. They had settled on red and yellow, and the lines that showed the cruisers coming in on *Clara's* flanks were lengthening. When they met the uncertainty would end. The thought had a kind of seductiveness.

"H'ana," said Dorista from the floor. She still held Martin's hand. He looked indifferently at nothing; with Willi gone he waited patiently to die.

"H'ana?"

Wildfire, whispered her thought, the intimate image that meant Hanna in happier times, laughing and ready and reckless. It woke Hanna, a little.

"What?"

"They tried this once with Lancaster, didn't they?"

"I think so . . ." She was not good at history, recent or not. "Years ago. About the time they built *Havock*, I guess."

"And the Polity stopped them."

"Must have. Lancaster's got fewer defenses than we have. Than we had."

"Why didn't they stop it now?"

Hanna said wearily, "They thought we'd ask for help. We didn't ask."

"Why?" Dorista sounded merely curious, but behind Hanna's eyes she floated the shadow of D'neera encased in implacable stupidity.

"The magistrates couldn't agree. Stiff-necked as usual. That's all."

Hanna saw that her hands were unsteady. It made her angry. She knew, distantly, that Alia was conscious and huddled in Roly's arms. Tonia sat unspeaking near the door; she had caught Martin's mood of relinquishment. Only Hanna and Dorista on this dying ship were thinking, and Hanna did not know how much longer her own endurance would hold. She was a D'neeran, after all, though she knew D'neera's faults better than most. D'neerans gave and took comfort freely, and readily believed against all evidence that wrongs could be cured with love. They were stubborn and joyous anarchists who could not make a common move without arguing the direction for years, and they did not like emergencies, did not know how to meet them. There were men and women still alive and vigorous who remembered the time when D'neera had nothing to do with the rest of the human species. Many wished it were still that way. They had argued too long about asking for help.

The cruisers were closing in, in no hurry. Perhaps they thought everyone on *Clara* was dead. The *Havock* was closer too; *Clara* could not hold herself steady, and she would drift near but not into the monster's path. Hanna put her chin on her hand and watched the course and mass displays, resisting an impulse to let herself sink into the pretty colors. The idea was coming by itself. Think of something else and let it be born.

Dorista said in a desultory way, "They wanted to help, didn't they."

"Umm-hmm. One of the commissioners talked to the magistrates personally. Jameson of Heartworld, in fact. Isn't that funny?" The ghost of a smile twitched at her mouth. "Of all people."

"What did he say? Did Lady Koroth tell you?"

"There wasn't time for much. She thought he was angry because she was the only one who'd listen."

"They'd listen now."

"It's too late."

"To call for help now? Why? Even if we're finished, the Interworld Fleet would just come in and kick Nestor out of the system."

"It would take too long for the Fleet to get here. By that time the buster would be in place. Over Koroth, probably. It's got the biggest city and its House has the best ties with the Polity. Then—well. City Koroth alone gives Nestor two hundred thousand hostages."

Dorista sighed and did not speak again. Hanna watched the citybuster coming closer. She thought of City Koroth with its fountains and its ever-blowing wind and the slow clean river rolling toward the sea, and its white splendid House gleaming in the sun, and how in winter the scarlet stoneveins grew up its walls from the snow. She thought of the sky as she had seen it last, so crisp a blue she could almost touch it, and how this abomination would dirty it with threat.

The idea was there, born whole.

Suicide.

What wasn't?

Dorry! Hanna said, showing it to her all at once. They were almost close enough to *Havock* to make it work. Closer would be better.

Fear and approval wrestled in Dorista. This was different from deciding to fight; no human being believes in his death, and there is always a chance of winning if he fights.

But look, Hanna said, concentrating on *Havock*'s end, displaying it: yes, only dust left of *Clara* and, yes, her people dust too, but also much of *Havock,* the rest crumpling and folding like soft plastic and a fireball at the end—

Hanna looked at her friend. "Well?" she said.

Dorista hung back. But the logic was irresistible. With *Havock* gone Nestor would find it hard to press the Polity for terms of occupation.

"Yes," Dorista said.

Martin focused on Hanna and smiled.

Tonia sighed and got up. "Where do we start?" she said. She added, "Don't ask the others."

"I have to," Hanna said. "Start figuring it out, Dorry."

The ghosts sang to her more loudly: Come to us. I am not doing this, she thought, it is against nature; but her hands moved, her voice was clear, even Roly somehow did not hear the ghosts. Roly was relieved. He did not mind dying so much, only fighting. The picture Hanna showed him comforted him: *Clara* drifting helpless, harmless, near *Havock.* A last burst of conventional power to throw them straight at *Havock,* crashing with luck right through its shields. And a last Jump to anywhere shredding *Clara* and *Havock* together through all of space-time. Roly would not have to fight. He would just be here, and then not here; and he settled on what his death would buy with a fixity of purpose that shamed Dorista's hesitation. And Alia took courage at last, took it from him.

"Are you smiling?" Tonia asked. She looked at Hanna strangely.

"It's everything they warn us about," Hanna said. "Random terminus, undescribed mass, we're not clearing dimensional topography for any point—we're doing it all wrong. Every last thing."

They had had the same solemn instructors, and Dorista smiled too.

For a while they worked very hard, sabotaging failsafes and destroying *Clara's* automatic inhibitions against what they were going to do. They worked with an air of astonishment at themselves and also, because they were D'neerans, some of the pleasure of clever children getting away with the forbidden. Hanna fixed on the pleasure to keep her thoughts from other things. She would key the Jump herself. There was no time to program the computers for every contingency, and they might be unreliable in any case. She thought about the final key, the last thing she would touch. She pushed the dead away so the others would not hear, and went machinelike through her tasks. Past a crystal wall the shadows waited, urging her to farewells. Farewell to sun and sea of youth, the lure of stars and strangeness, to the bright future, to so much, so much wasted—

(You are our future, Lady Koroth said. The white faces of a non-human emerged from the past. The F'thalian Hierar-

chus had chuckled at humanity's useless squabbles. *You were right, Progenitor,* she said. *But did you see my only own end?)*

"Ready," Dorista said, but something in her wavered. Hanna put aside her memories and the alien Hierarchus diminished into the past. She had strength for Dorista and steadied her. Where did the strength come from? The ghosts, perhaps. In a kind of exultation she saw the wills of her friends as separate threads and took them in her hand. H'ana ril-Koroth faded with the ghosts. She had become an instrument.

She drew a lever through its course, and *Clara* shuddered and began to move.

And the cruisers moved fast; but not toward *Clara.*

"*What the hell?* What have they got up their sleeves?"

Hanna stood up suddenly. She felt very light; gravity had stabilized, but not at norm. She pushed at her hair and rubbed her hands, too nervous to keep still.

"They're heading out," Tonia said.

"Where? What to? There's nothing out that way. Why aren't they defending *Havock*?"

Clara picked up speed. Dorista said, "Maybe *Havock*'s going to finish us off and they're getting out of the way."

"Busters don't track moving targets. They depend on warships for defense. *Clara* masses enough to get through its shields. Get us more speed, Roly."

One of the cruisers started back in a wide turn.

"That's for us," Hanna said. "That was a command error before. Why? What happened?"

"Now," Tonia said suddenly.

"What?"

"I can't get the evasion program going. They're going to fire and it'll catch us before we do it."

"I want to be closer."

"There isn't time!"

Hanna's hand crept toward the key. She said, "A second. A few seconds. Marty, can you hear what they're saying? Let us hear."

The loop was still going, mindless. On another band someone shouted at them to halt. The same on still another.

They were close enough to *Havock* and the cruiser would fire. Now. Now.

A new voice boomed out in clear strong Standard, not at them.

"This is Commander Andre Tirel of the Interworld Fleet Warship *Willowmeade*. You are ordered to lay down your arms and vacate the stellar system of D'neera at once. Do not attack. We will return fire—"

Dorista caught at Hanna's moving hand. She looked at Hanna's face, slipped in front of her, and set about changing course. *Clara* responded slowly, pulling up, up, on a course that would clear *Havock*. The calm voice went on.

"Any hostile act directed toward a D'neeran vessel will be considered an act of war against the Interworld Polity and we will take appropriate action—"

Martin shut off *Willowmeade*. "We could get them on sensors," he said.

Tonia's fingers flew. "There they are." Her voice shook. "We weren't looking there. What's the other one?"

After a minute Martin said, "*St. Petersburg*."

"There's more. What happened?"

"They must have been waiting. They must have been close. For days maybe. Waiting for the magistrates to yell."

Dorista said, "H'ana? H'ana. Are you all right?"

Hanna slowly took her eyes from the shifting forms. The cruiser was not coming after them. Sweet ballistic curves of life. She said thickly, "All right."

All right but wounded. All right; but there was no joy. Shock held them silent and guilt gnawed at them already. Others who deserved to live were dead. The world was changed and they were changed forever. They could not yet know how. Hanna felt them touch her, seeking comfort and offering it. She did not want comfort. She did not know what had happened to her. It seemed she had pressed the button after all; that the decision had been the reality and all of them were ghosts, chattering in the dust, and the fireball which she saw vividly, sharp-edged and real, in the lesser reality of this crippled chamber.

She moved at last, slowly. Dorista had canceled the Jump order; but she looked once at Hanna, and checked it again.

Hanna said, her voice dragging, "Get *Willowmeade*, Marty."

The choice came unconsciously from memories of Willow. She had been met courteously there.

"Got it," Martin said.

She did not bother to identify herself. "Polity force," she said, "we need help."

She put her head down and thought about darkness. Dorista took over.

PART I

Chapter 1

The art of personal combat, like every other human endeavor, is transmuted on D'neera. Combatants abstain from the use of telepathy, presumably in order to retain the element of surprise; but in compensation, by a curious inversion of logic, each movement is announced before it is made by the tiniest of gestures, nearly subliminal, so that no one is hurt unless he is incompetent or undisciplined or distracted.

Hanna nearly got hurt; she was unexpectedly flat on her back, looking up at Master Ling through the indignation of pain, the sun-warmed boards of the studio floor very hard beneath her. The big dusty space swung round her once and stopped.

Ling thought: *Soldiers!*—a piercing image of destructive, undisciplined children. "They send me," he said aloud, "soldiers, who of all human animals are least suited to this art."

Hanna sat up and carefully rubbed her spine. She did not point out that D'neera's tiny defense establishment hardly qualified as an army, or that its handful of part-time fighters had, on the whole, a profound distaste for the job, or that if it were not for them Ling might have been blown to atoms a few months ago. He knew all that; he was only relieving his dissatisfaction with her performance.

"I was thinking of other matters," she said humbly.

"That is more than enough for today," Ling said, permitting himself a sharp edge of sarcasm.

"Yes," said Hanna, still aching. She got to her feet and went to the railing that in summer was the only thing separating the studio from the space over City Koroth. Ling's next student sat cross-legged near the edge, meditating; he had not seen her fall, nor had he seen anything for some time except the non-images deep in his own soul, where, according to Ling, all the universe was discernible. Hanna had never seen the boy before. She leaned over the railing to let the summer breeze dry her sweating skin and wondered if Ling had arranged for the stranger to be present as a lesson to her. She had been coming to Ling for four Standard years, and for four years he had been scolding her because of her—

"Youth," she said. "That's all. Consider what distracts me, Master. Travel and sex and curiosity—maybe in forty years, or a hundred and forty, I'll be an apt pupil."

"You are facetious," said Ling, whose worst fault in Hanna's eyes was his lack of humor. "I teach children who are less easily distracted."

"Yes," Hanna said submissively, but she was distracted again, looking out over City Koroth.

Ling had his studio on the fourteenth floor of the tallest building in City Koroth. The child H'ana Bassanio, occasionally towed here by her mother from the little seaside town of Serewind, had looked up, it seemed forever, at this structure with its sometimes transparent, sometimes vanished walls, where artists played in the sunshine and Ling (not much younger then) taught something that might be combat or dance, and at the very top in a space as bare as this, the Development Committee argued the future. The committee had now withdrawn to more comfortable quarters—after fighting about it for years—and to the woman H'ana ril-Koroth, who had traveled, who had seen the cloud-piercing towers of Earth and the spires of alien F'thal, this box of a building was very small. But not many D'neerans had traveled, and to most of her compatriots it was still tall.

Ling came up behind her and laid his hands on her bare shoulders. He knew what she was thinking, and would not be drawn into it.

"Nevertheless, you have what is necessary to become Adept," he said. She shivered a little in the sunlight, caught in his vision of the precise, inhuman control of the Adept.

"To what end?" she said.

"The no-end of the inward journey, which is the beginning of all others," he said.

"I haven't the time," Hanna said, "or the patience," but that was as close as a D'neeran could get to a lie or an evasion, and the rest of the truth was as visible to Ling as if it stood before them: the silver spaceship and the starclouds.

Ling's hands tightened for a moment and withdrew.

"Go," he said. "You are impatient for news. Pursue it."

Hanna turned from the railing, drew her small figure upright, and made him a formal bow. He returned it courteously.

"We meet again in three days' time," he said.

"In three days, Master," she said. But she hoped, and he knew it, that soon she would be nowhere near D'neera.

The bathing rooms of Ling's establishment were uncompromisingly bare. It was a condition of working with Ling that on his premises, at least, his students share his asceticism. Hanna stood under a fall of cold water until she felt clean—it did not take so long to feel clean in winter, when the water was icy—cupped some of it in her hands and drank to ease her dry throat, dressed and left quickly. It was a considerable walk to her House, and she was eager to be there.

The answer's got to come today, she thought. This morning. But it's midnight at Polity Admin. But no, dammit, he's not even on Earth, I don't know what time it is where he is. Why doesn't he make up his mind?

Much of her way was uphill and the day was growing hot, but she was in superb condition and City Koroth seemed to flow backward around her. City Koroth: first city of D'neera, center of the first province, site of the first governing House. The founders leaving ravaged Luna had sworn not to repeat history's mistakes. They had favored beauty over utility, trees over convenience, flowers—a tiny side street caught Hanna's eye, and she glanced appreciatively at its blaze of blossoms—flowers over almost everything. Sometimes the ground trembled under her feet as heavy machinery moved beneath it, but the ground itself, in this stretch, was surfaced with beautifully painted and well-maintained tiles. It was true that the midyear sun heated them so they stung her bare feet; but the next part of her way was through a shade garden where birds swooped low and sang piercingly and snatched at her ears until she thought soothing shoo-away thoughts at them. And how odd, she thought, looking at their tiny paws, that we call them "birds." When first I saw true-birds on Earth I said no, that can't be a *bird . . . !*

After the garden there were neighborhood markets which sold, absurdly, flowers. She bought one with her good name and tucked it into her coiled dark hair. There were cool thick-walled dwelling places, a place for the manufacture of clothing—she skidded to a stop and looked through the open door in astonishment. A woman passing by inside wheeled and came toward her, already angry.

"It's just," Hanna said weakly, "that last week they grew foodstuffs here."

But the woman only met her with a vast certainty that none of the too-numerous regulations were being broken, nothing was being polluted, and not even the House of Koroth—here her finger waggled emphatically in the hot breeze; Hanna's head began to ache—could find anything wrong!

But the produce balance, said Hanna, trying to remember whether the ponics people had reported a move and if so to where, but the woman was having none of it, and took her rather forlorn thought that she would have to check into it as a threat.

Hanna left, and ran the next block or two.

Governing any part of D'neera was not easy.

There were more gardens, including a stark patch of desert which she circled carefully because it grew spikes which would hurt her feet. There were plenty of people about, many noisy children and their quieter adults, but snatches of song and the music of fountains came to her plainly on the wind. A child came with her for a time, chattering confidentially and practicing his budding faculty for projection until her head ached again from his efforts. When he grew tired of walking she handed him over to the nearest willing adult; when he was ready to go home, someone would make sure he got there. Once she passed an adolescent boy and girl leaning together against a tree, eyes closed, barely touching, deep in that mutual inner exploration which for a season obscures all other concerns. Likely enough they had forgotten where they were and would begin making love right here, unless they got hungry first. No one would disturb them. Hanna was twenty D'neeran or twenty-four Standard years old and she had not felt this sort of attraction, as of particles of opposite charge, since adolescence; and in spite of her protest to Ling, even the purely sensual encounters were increasingly far between. I'm getting old, she thought in a moment's panic, and I'm still young. A hundred and fifty years to go, and already no time for love! There was too much else to think about: produce reports, facilities-use reports, the New City being built past the wilderness, the aftermath of war. And, when she could manage it, her private work in exopsychology, shabbily neglected. And the decision in the far-away Polity. And its consequences. If it came out the way she wanted it; she and the Lady of Koroth.

She reached a wide stone avenue that broke up at the end into greensward, and beyond it the white walls of the House rose into the clear blue sky. There was not much traffic to the House today, though as she ascended the final hill she met a freight carrier, festooned with banners and piloted by two men deep in half-spoken, half-thought conversation. On Earth the machines drove themselves. Was that what she wanted for D'neera someday? The machines thinking and the people tending to them? Towers founded on crystal and held up by aggies? Anti-gravity mansions in the sky, anchored by fragile-seeming cables and swaying— but only for effect—with the wind . . .

"But I didn't really like it there," she said a little guiltily, and plucked a handful of many-scented millefleurs and carried them with her the rest of the way to the House, holding them as if they were a talisman against change.

When she passed into the House its ambience closed over her like water, cool and dim in the summer's fierce heat. The walls and floors and ceilings and furnishings testified to a peculiarly D'neeran passion for the decorative arts, and the whole vast warren always smelled deliciously of flowers and baking. But its essence was the people who lived and worked here. There was always an undercurrent of activity, less a matter of sound than the hum of many brains thinking all at once, and the flavor was decidedly female; this House was traditionally female, and had been since Maria Koroth started building it six hundred years ago. A hundred and fifty people worked here (when they felt like it), and all but a handful of them lived here. There was room for all of them; the House had been growing by

fits and starts for hundreds of years, and Hanna still could
get lost in it after five years of residence.

She did not have to ask for news. Cosma ril-Koroth, who,
like Hanna, stood high in the house, sensed her presence
and met her in a scarlet-draped hallway with a shake of the
head. They made faces at each other, sharing disappointment in silence, and Hanna went on to her workspace. The
first thing she saw when she came into the room—plainer
than most, by her choice—was a message from Iledra, Lady
Koroth, winking at her from a computer terminal:

"The Design Arbitration Committee at the New City
site has failed to settle the Central Garden question within
the lawful ninety-day negotiation period. I intend to invoke
magistrate's privilege. Will you go there tomorrow and settle the matter? Choose a design that appeals to you and *do
not* let them persuade you to grant an extension of the arbitration period. This project *must* be started this year. At
least half the committee members, to my certain knowledge, are expectant parents. Ask them where they think
their children will live if we do not build ..."

Hanna stared at the message for a little while. Grimly,
trying to ignore disappointment, she rearranged her
thoughts. She had hoped to disinter her notes on Girritt
tomorrow, and try to make sense out of them. But perhaps
it was just as well; perhaps she would never make sense of
them without the Polity archives. And the archives were
closed to her, unless ...

She thought of the silver spaceship, the library it would
carry, the ancient eyewitness accounts of the first contacts
with Girritt and F'thal and the Primitives. Surely the evidence she needed was there. Without it how could she
prove to contemporary true-humans that they were wrong?
How could she show them that the charming, monkeylike
Girrians had not knowledgeably rejected high technology
but were simply incapable of thinking past a certain level of
abstraction in technical matters? True-humans would have
it that Girrians lived as they did for noble motives. They had
passed into the mythologies of certain religious and social
movements as the embodiment of non-technocrat virtue—
and the Girrians fostered the myth, having learned to enjoy
the respect it brought them from the smooth-skinned beings called humans. But they did not understand telepathy,

either, and had permitted Hanna to examine the contents
and blank spaces of their minds (so many and such very
large blank spaces!) with the generosity of naïveté. True-
humans would take a lot of convincing, however—and
more and more it looked as if Hanna would never have a
chance to convince them.

She sighed and sat down and wiped Iledra's message,
and called up the ever-growing list of questions to answer,
tasks to perform, reports to read and write, requests to fulfill, disputes to arbitrate. Two landkeepers of Riverine Sector were quarreling over a stand of falseoaks on their
common border, which one wished to fell. A nearby village
had entered the dispute. I will have to stop seeing Ling,
Hanna thought, I just don't have the *time*—

The Lady of Koroth came into the room without a sound.
She had a trick of making unexpected entrances, and Hanna
jumped at this one, seeing herself without warning through
Iledra's eyes—

*(Brown-skinned and blue-eyed and growing into beauty
but always too thin since the war, too apt to see the shadows
beyond sunlight, hear silence in the intervals of music—)*

"Stop it," Hanna said. Her hands made fists on the keyboard. A trace of shadow lingered for a moment, and the
intrusive presence withdrew. Hanna said without turning
around, "I wish you wouldn't think such things, Lee. Not at
me, anyway."

"A week ago your nightmare woke half the House from
sleep. Must I order you to visit the mindhealers?"

"You already did. They've done little enough for other
survivors. I don't want to talk about it, Lee."

"Very well," Iledra said. Her composure was unaltered;
Hanna thought of it as unalterable. She said without a
change of tone, "You know I've heard nothing from Jameson?"

"Cosma told me."

Hanna tapped a familiar sequence on her keyboard. The
opening page of what had become a large file flashed onto
the screen. "The *Endeavor* Project," said the title page. "A
proposal for renewing the organized search for sentient life
on the borders of human space." At the head of the list of
names of those who had prepared the document it said:
"Starr Hollin Jameson VI, Commissioner-Heartworld.

Chairman, Committee on Alien Relations." Near that was a
flamboyant, illegible signature. The proposal was dated a
Standard year before, and Hanna knew it by heart.

She said, "I have to get on that ship. I just have to."

"Heart's desire," Iledra murmured.

"Yes. Oh, yes."

"It never pays to have them," Iledra said.

She moved at last to Hanna's side, and Hanna looked up
a little apprehensively. Iledra was well into her sixties, but
she looked only a little older than Hanna; D'neera's first
concern upon reopening relations with the Polity a century
before had been to appropriate, with unbecoming eagerness, every available advance in anti-senescence techniques.
On that score there had been scarcely a dissenting voice.
The tall Lady of Koroth, smooth-skinned, gray-eyed,
golden-haired, was proof of their efficacy. Hanna could not
imagine anything changing her. At some time in the past
Iledra had unbent sufficiently to give birth to a daughter,
and afterward had given the golden child to its father and
forgotten it. Once, when Hanna asked her about that time,
she had tried with D'neeran honesty to answer, but she
could remember little about so brief and unimportant a
contretemps. She had been Koroth's Lady for twenty years
and might be Lady a hundred more. She spoke sometimes
of the advisability of early retirement, and was fond of
pointing to the stagnation of true-human societies as evidence that the young-seeming old gripped power too tightly
and too long; but Hanna rather thought that "early" would
always be a point somewhere in the future.

Iledra looked over Hanna's shoulder at the *Endeavor*
proposal. She said, "I think we should begin giving more
attention to alternative ways of proving our usefulness to
true-humans."

"That's what you were doing before this came up. It
didn't get you anywhere."

"True. But the choice is not ours."

"I don't want to keep plowing away at something I know
is hopeless."

"You know no such thing." She touched Hanna's shoulder and the girl looked up again, rebellious and reluctant.
"Patience," Iledra said softly. "Patience is everything. . . ."

Behind the gentle words were images of many rivers, of

waters flowing, shifting, changing, slight perturbations repeated for centuries and gradually changing the contours of earth and sky till the whole mighty network was changed. Continents and climates shifted. Hanna rode the imaginary waters—and shook her head as if it were wet, came back breathless to the quiet cool room, and said loudly, "All the same. The data I need so— And to have a telepath at a first contact. They must see what it could mean!"

"They do," Iledra said. "But they would rather put it off for a century or two . . . Here is the ring."

She never bothered canvassing subjects she felt had been sufficiently discussed. Hanna was used to it. She looked at the gem in Iledra's hand and said hesitantly, "I'm still not sure."

"It is not an absolute commitment. It is an honor, however, and the formality gives, well, some weight to one's authority. I remember that when Penelope gave it to me I found those I dealt with were suddenly more cooperative. It is one thing to defy an administrator-delegate of the House, even knowing what she is likely to become. It is another to quarrel with its acknowledged heir."

The ring that lay in her white palm was a plain gold band set with a blue stone. After a minute Hanna took it and slipped it onto her hand.

Iledra glided to the door, unhurried. Hanna stared at the Heir's Ring of Koroth, but when she spoke it was not about the ring. She said, "Lee? Why hasn't Jameson called you?"

"Rudeness," Iledra said succinctly.

"What?"

"The privilege of power. We have no power. We need the Polity, but it does not need us. Whatever courtesy a commissioner shows us is ours by his sufferance." She gave Hanna a long gray look and said, "I would like to see that change before I die."

Hanna, left alone, looked at the ring's blue fire. The bauble felt heavy on her hand.

Stanislaw Morisz went to see Starr Jameson about the *Endeavor* project a day or two later. He did not know that the House of Koroth had given up its hopes of participating in the project. If he had known he would not have cared; he had other things to think about. Jameson made Morisz nervous, and Morisz was finding out to his consternation that even approaching Jameson's residence was enough to produce the symptoms.

"I thought," he said, "this was all wilderness," and looked out the window of the aircar again at the great fields brown with stubble in the weak afternoon light. He felt lost.

The flier who had come to meet him at Arrenswood's only outport said, "No wilderness here. Farther on."

"Where does Commissioner Jameson live, then? Closer to the forest?"

"No. Here's Starrbright," said the man, and the aircar dove to the left and down. There was a knot of trees there and in the center half a dozen structures that grew rapidly as they went down. They went down fast. Evidently, Morisz thought, Jameson required speed from his subordinates when he was at home just as he did on Earth. They talked less here, however, if this pilot was a sample.

Morisz stood a little helplessly by the aircar when it landed, not sure of the protocol. You might or might not be expected to carry your own luggage, depending on where you were on which world and also on who you were. He did not know how Heartworld's respect for status applied to him; Jameson's status was very high indeed, and presumably so was that of his guests. On the other hand Morisz was a subordinate of any commissioner from a Polity world, and Terrestrials were not highly regarded here.

But the pilot began getting the bags out without a glance in his direction, and Morisz had a chance to look around. He had been on Heartworld before, even in Arrenswood province, but only in the cities, which were grim. This was a little grim too, he thought: windswept prairieland, further flattened to increase the efficiency of machines.

Morisz was a man of crowded Earth, not used to being far from centers of population even though his job had sometimes required it before he moved into Polity Administration. He was not sure how far the aircar had brought him, but he knew he was some distance from any town. Beyond the trees, fields stretched to the horizon. Everything he could see would belong to Jameson; the term "landed family of Heartworld" suddenly took on new meaning.

The main house was made of brick, and no doubt the bricks were handmade, though somewhere, probably underground, there must be agricultural robots of great size and power. The house was three stories tall, shingled with wood—shingled? Yes—and also trimmed with wood. It was gaunt as the bare trees surrounding it. Nothing about it suggested it was the product of a star-traveling civilization. On the other hand it did not have the patchwork look of settlements on poorer planets, none of which were Polity worlds. The latter fact was largely due to Heartworld; its representatives to the Coordinating Commission of the Polity made a good case against letting underdeveloped societies enjoy Polity perquisites. Jameson had been the commissioner from Heartworld for eight years. And after all, Morisz thought, why should he want to sell the produce of these fields for less than the market would bear to customers who had nothing to offer but money?

He was still looking out over the fields, fallow in the dying year, when he heard a footfall behind him and realized his status was settled; Starr Jameson had come out to meet him in person. He turned a little hesitantly. Morisz was director of Polity Intelligence and Security, and knew more about Jameson than almost anyone else did. He rather liked the man, but did not understand him and had never seen him in this setting. He thought Jameson might be different here.

But the only difference he saw was that Jameson was smiling, the rare sunburst of a smile Morisz had seldom seen.

"Stan. Glad to see you," Jameson said, and they shook hands and Morisz relaxed. There was no difference. It was just like Polity Admin on Earth, except for the smile and also that this was partly a social occasion.

Morisz, not thinking socially, said, "I thought you'd be glad. This is it, isn't it?"

Jameson seemed not to have heard him. He said, "You've come prepared for big game, I hope?"

"I don't know," Morisz said cautiously. "How big?"

"Medium, I should say. Earth import. Nothing difficult."

"I thought of bringing a combat laser," Morisz said a little wistfully.

"Not here. Here you hunt with spears or bows or not at all. It'll be good for you, Stanislaw. Come on up to the house."

Morisz wondered if he should pursue the matter of the report he carried or wait for Jameson to bring it up again. Well, that was like Admin too. He supposed ambiguity was a sort of immutable attribute, which Jameson practiced with guests as well as professional associates.

The house had a great central hall that made Morisz look around in wonder. The floor was made of polished wood. Of course; Heartworld was famous for its exotic woods. It would require a great deal of human, not robot, care, and Morisz was sure Jameson did no polishing. The rugs scattered on it would be handwoven. He stared at a gleaming brass chandelier and Jameson followed his gaze.

"F'thalian glowpods," he said. "It only looks incandescent."

"Doesn't that spoil the authenticity?" Morisz was surprised into bluntness.

"The Authenticist movement is very vocal but very small. And its spokesmen travel in aircars."

He took Morisz to a room where a fire blazed in a stone hearth. Morisz did not like open fires but sat near it anyway. He took the drink Jameson handed him and without making a display of it stole a more careful look at the other man's face. Was he spaced? Did he, on vacation at home, indulge himself as he did at his leisure on Earth, with whatever interesting drug the purveyors to Polity VIPs might provide? With, of course, the tacit consent of Earthside Enforcement officials who did not like to antagonize men like Jameson.

But Jameson sat down with a sigh, said, "How does the roster shape up, Stan?" and Morisz might have been back in the big riverside office on Earth, preparing to report in the ordinary way.

He took a cassette from a locked pouch under his shirt. It was wafer-thin and almost weightless in his hand, and it held the final I&S reports on the proposed crew of the exploration vessel *Endeavor*. It contrasted so sharply with its surroundings that Morisz suddenly wondered if there were a reader in the house to put it in.

"It's not a bad list," he said. "I question a couple of the names."

"You've already had one shot at it," Jameson said.

Morisz smiled faintly. "You're still showing a couple I could do without."

"I know," Jameson said. He brought a reader from a drawer built into the wall, reassuring Morisz, and slipped the cassette into it. He said, "Make yourself comfortable. This might take a while," and began reading.

Morisz was not comfortable. The room was too quiet, except for the fire, which made distressingly irregular sounds. The place was full of light that seemed warmer than glowpod luminescence; presumably the shades around the pods accounted for the golden cast. The shades were made of glass. Glass? Yes. Morisz had not been to Jameson's Earthside home. He had heard it was something like this; not nearly so extreme, however. He would bet this house didn't even speak. It was free from the subliminal sounds of machines and the energy transformations that ran them, and it felt too much as if it had a life of its own. Occasionally human voices sounded through it; one was a woman's, and Morisz wondered who she was. Jameson's recent companion in Namerica, a spectacular creature, was still there, which was not to say Jameson had no companions during his rare visits home. But Morisz knew of none at present, and he would know. No doubt whoever it was was at home here. Jameson had relatives nearby, a steward to manage the great estate, a housekeeper—the whole arrangement reminded Morisz that Heartworld's first families still had things pretty much their own way, especially in Arrenswood.

Jameson glanced up at Morisz once, his face expressionless, and went back to reading. Morisz watched him covertly. Jameson was a big man whose face seemed to have been put together without regard for consistency. There might be Amerind blood in the jutting bones and dark hair, but his eyes and skin were incongruously light. His mouth was sensitive when he let it be, the strong face surprisingly pleasant when he smiled; but he did not smile often. By Standard count he was forty-six and, Morisz thought, aging well. Rapidly, but well. He looked—

Morisz hesitated, wondering not for the first time about standards for judging age. Jameson stubbornly kept trying all the usual anti-senescence procedures, and probably looked younger than the forty-six of earlier centuries; but he seemed older than Morisz, who was near eighty but might have been an untreated thirty-five. Today Jameson also looked pale and very tired—unexpected in a man supposed to have been vacationing for eight weeks. He's tried A.S. again, Morisz thought, and it hit him hard. He looks like hell. And now he's waiting for the rest of the verdict.

Presently Jameson put the reader aside with an economical, final-seeming motion. Morisz came to attention.

Jameson said, "The alternate for Liuku. That's the only change."

Morisz estimated his chances of prevailing and found them small. *Endeavor's* crew list had been thrashed out over several months by the Coordinating Commission, the Interworld Fleet, Alien Relations, and all the other components of a living bureaucratic network whose separate parts had their own goals to consider. I&S probably had exercised all its options. Nonetheless Morisz said, "Liuku's a hell of an Inspace technician. I'd rather see her out there than the alternate."

"She's a Technocrat," Jameson said. Without giving the word special emphasis, he managed to make it sound distasteful. Morisz was a man of moderate views, and he did not care for Earth's Technocrat enclaves either. Their children were machined and augmented to something more or less than human, and they came out of the enclaves slightly or severely bent. But Liuku had bent in the not-uncommon direction of becoming a superb technician. Morisz's report said so, but now he said so again, emphatically.

Jameson said, "I know. But any person on the *Endeavor,* including the engineering staff, might have to talk to whatever's out there. How do you think a Technocrat would get along with something like a Girrian?"

"Heartworld prejudice," Morisz said.

"Possibly. But I won't risk it. Liuku's out," Jameson said, and Morisz knew he had lost.

He hesitated, wondering if he should bring up his personal reservations about the man who would command *Endeavor.* Their sum, however, was only that at thirty-nine—half Morisz's age—Erik Fleming was too young. You never got anywhere arguing age with Jameson, and in any case it was Jameson who had bullied and cajoled Fleet into leapfrogging a handful of young officers upstairs.

Morisz decided to skip Fleming and move on to surer ground.

"The D'neeran woman," he said. "Hanna Bassanio. Ril-Koroth. Whatever they call her."

Jameson leaned back and put the tips of his long fingers together. He said politely, "Yes?"

"I think she's a very unwise choice."

"I know you do. I believe she is the only person you strongly protested who will be making the voyage."

It was a pointed reminder that Morisz had gotten nearly everything he wanted, but he said anyway, "They're erratic. D'neerans in general, I mean. This one's reckless. You saw what she almost did against Nestor?"

"Courageous," Jameson remarked.

Morisz eyed him doubtfully, wondering just how much Jameson knew about it. He certainly knew the basic facts of D'neera's half-day war with Nestor—the only war in D'neeran history. There would have been no D'neeran defense force to fight it if Jameson, unofficially and personally, had not talked the D'neeran magistrates into creating one when Nestor's militarism had begun concentrating on the despised telepaths. It was supposed to be coincidence that D'neera was lush and prosperous, while Nestor's settlements were bleak and tired. Morisz believed in that coincidence just about as much as he believed the Interworld Fleet's timely intervention in the incident meant that the Coordinating Commission had acted on a wave of spontaneous, unanimous altruism. Jameson surely had been behind that too. But the official record included only a bare outline of Hanna ril-Koroth's part in the engagement, and there was no reason for Jameson to know the details.

Morisz said, "Let me tell you what really happened. This woman was left in command of the—the—"

He hesitated, searching his memory. Jameson's eyelids drooped; he looked half-sleep, or bored. He murmured, "The D'neeran corvette *Clara Mendoza.*"

"Uh—yes. She was in command because she was the only rank left among the survivors. The *Clara*'s arms and shields were out, life support was half-gone, gravity was fluxing, the thing could just barely wallow around in real-space. She's called on to surrender. She decides not to. What does she decide to take on?"

It was a rhetorical question. Jameson said, however, "She goes after a citybuster. The *N.S. Havock.*"

Morisz knew he had made a mistake. "Right," he said.

Jameson said sleepily, "The *Clara* appeared to be drifting into *Havock*'s path. She was not considered a threat. It seems to have occurred to Lady Hanna, however, that a switch into Inspace mode and a random Jump at the point of closest approach would take *Havock* out. It would have worked, Stanislaw. It would have worked, you know."

"And killed everybody on the *Clara*. It wasn't smart," said Morisz, who believed in the wisdom of living to fight another day. "Not even so brave. Just crazy. They were all half-crazy on that ship. Your typical D'neeran doesn't like violence. He starts talking about how he's too empathic to stand it. Then he gets stomped. That won't go over with the Fleet personnel."

"It's an experiment," Jameson said mildly. "Let's give her a chance, shall we? Naturally there will be personnel changes at the end of the first year."

"A year's a long time," Morisz said. "Something might—"

He stopped, but too late. Jameson looked at him narrowly and said, "Something might happen sooner. Was that what you were going to say?"

Morisz did not answer. He was half-ashamed of his interest in *Endeavor*'s projected route. There had been unexplained communications blips for centuries. The experts said the last few years' reports from Sector Amber were not really disproportionate. Officially they had no connection with *Endeavor*'s course through Amber. Officially the name was arbitrary too. Not amber for caution. Just Amber.

Jameson said casually, "Amber's out in the direction some church used to fulminate about, isn't it? The Church of the Coming from the Stars, I believe. Quite a mouthful. What do the brethren think of the project?"

"I wouldn't know," Morisz said. He felt his face getting hot. He was too honest to expunge anything from his own I&S file, and anyway his life so far had been blameless. But if his youthful fling with that nutcult disappeared from the record by itself, he wouldn't reinsert it.

Embarrassed into silence, he watched Jameson pick up the reader and a stylus, note Liuku's replacement and sign the report. He had entirely forgotten Hanna ril-Koroth; when he remembered it was too late. He had been smoothly, ruthlessly diverted for just long enough.

Jameson handed back the cassette without a sign of smugness. "Behind schedule," he said, "but close enough. How about a drink and early dinner? We've got a long flight in the morning. Have you ever hunted with a spear?"

"No," said Morisz, wishing he hadn't come.

"You'll be learning the hard way, then. It's the only way to learn, however."

"What are we hunting, anyway?"

"Tigers," Jameson said, and almost smiled.

Chapter 2

The exploration vessel *Endeavor,* carrying a crew of two hundred, left terrestrial orbit on the first day of March in the year ST 2835. There were ceremonies. Starr Jameson appeared in the *Endeavor*'s common room and made a practiced and inspiring speech about mankind's destiny to seek new horizons. With him was Commissioner Andrella Murphy of Willow, who looked at everything about her with an air of friendly interest and spoke to no one except Jameson. The commissioners from Colony One and Co-op were not there. Their schedules did not permit them to attend: not by accident. Katherine Petrov, Earth's voting commissioner, made a few formal remarks in a flat voice and disappeared—literally; she was a holo projection.

Jameson and Murphy were real, however. Hanna stood unsteadily on tiptoe to see them from the rear of a too-dense crowd. She wished she could catch a glimpse of their thoughts, but without prior personal knowledge of an individual's "flavor," it was impossible with so many people about. She liked Murphy's looks, but not Jameson's. When he was not exerting himself he looked, she thought, cold and indifferent; but she could not see anything very well. The ceremonial circle included Erik Fleming, and Hanna knew he must look like a model officer in his forest-green Fleet uniform, because he always did. He also was admirably handsome—a golden-haired sunchild, Hanna thought, though she was not given to poetic flights. Partly because of this she was favorably disposed toward Fleming, and in the hectic month of training before launch, they had become more than friends. This had advantages besides the obvious ones; for one thing it smoothed Hanna's way with her crewmates, who did not know what to do with D'neerans, but knew how to behave toward their captain's friend.

After the formal leavetaking *Endeavor* proceeded to Alta at the edge of human space, a passage that took it an infinitesimal distance into the spiral arm that was Earth's home. The journey took many more days than such a routine trip required, and every minute was used for systems testing. There would be no help near if anything went wrong after Alta.

At Alta, the monks came up to bless them. Hanna was fascinated. It was her first experience with one of the little splinter colonies founded on religious principles, and she imagined penitents stuffing their robes into spacesuits and performing rituals in free fall, firing little globules of blessed liquid that would splat on *Endeavor*'s sensitive hull. Or perhaps they would use a pressurized stream of it?

They did not. They went round *Endeavor* in a vessel begged, borrowed, or stolen from whatever secular government Alta had and shook holy water in the general direction of the ship as it drifted in orbit. Hanna found them prosaic.

Afterward the abbot drank wine with Erik Fleming in the captain's quarters.

"A peculiar experience," Erik said to Hanna later.

"What did you talk about?"

"You, among other things."

He said it teasingly, but Hanna, not mind-listening, missed the overtone. Her sketchy knowledge of history was biased toward the paranoid. The genetic experiments that had created D'neera's founders had been prohibited and outlawed everywhere. There were dreadful tales of what the founders had fled, and some of the nastiest concerned measures taken in the name of holiness.

She said with some alarm, "Is this one of those groups that thinks D'neera is demons' work?"

"Oh, no, he thinks you're all right. He's a very intelligent man, actually. He said he was looking forward to further revelations of God's glory."

But Erik had a quizzical expression, and Hanna, sprawled ungracefully on the lounge that was the only visible luxury in the captain's spartan suite, said, "But?"

"He seems to have some idea that Inspace transit is a

matter of being picked up by God's hand and thrown across space."

"Well, that's as reasonable as some of the other theories. I lean to the one that says there's no such place as 'Inspace,' myself."

"Why not?" said Erik, and went off to approve another checklist. No space captain was so unimaginative that he did not wonder how he annihilated space and time without himself being annihilated; but meanwhile there were checklists.

Even on the customary routes, space travel required caution and, past Alta, the last human outpost in the direction *Endeavor* now took, there were no customary routes. One could go from Earth to Alta in a matter of two Standard days, the actual transits taking no measurable time but data processing requiring a good deal. The equivalent distance through unexplored space would take weeks or months. In a comfortable room on a long-settled world it was easy to speak of great Jumps "through" Inspace that gobbled light years. Alone in immensity you thought instead of limitations: one unsuspected gravity well in your (theoretically nonexistent) path, one unsuspected wrinkle in space, and you would not be heard of again. Under these circumstances you did not gobble space but nibbled at it, felt your way with probes, and concentrated on looking very, very carefully for what might be between you and where you wanted to go. If you got there, others could follow at speed; but someone had to be the plodding first, and out here *Endeavor* was the first.

Hanna settled rather cautiously into shipboard routine. As an exopsychologist she would not be needed until and unless *Endeavor* found intelligent life, and meanwhile she was assigned to Navigation. Unknown-space techniques were familiar to her in theory, new in practice. She was entrusted with little responsibility and did not expect much. Mostly she helped with preliminary studies that would be checked and re-checked and double-checked and checked again. The work was tedious, the sense of community she remembered from D'neeran spacecraft was missing—or at least withheld from her—and at the end of each six-hour shift her ears rang with the constant noise of true-humans who communicated only out loud. Her only wish at those times was to escape to the quiet of her tiny cabin, where she measured the gap between herself and her companions and thought it might be unbridgeable.

Nonetheless, the spacegoing experience was priceless. In these times there were few ways to learn the navigational skills of space exploration. The worlds of the Polity, concerned with internal development and consolidation, had done little exploration for three hundred years. Other human settlements, a scattered fringe marking the outer limit of the first wave of expansion through space, had many problems, little money, and no reason to move on. The roughly spherical volume of the universe known as human space was still limited in content. There were the Polity worlds—Earth, Willow, Co-op, Colony One, and Heartworld—five jewels of prosperity. There were D'neera and Lancaster, which were doing well enough, and a handful of settlements like Nestor which were not. There were many apolitical or quasi-political units like Alta or its infamous converse, Valentine, for the most part single-purpose colonies carved out of hostile environments and barely maintaining themselves. They did not matter much to the Polity, or to anyone except their more or less wretched inhabitants, and if they had any curiosity about what lay past human borders, they could not afford to satisfy it.

Also inside human space, though collectively called Outside, were F'thal and Girritt and two worlds that were home to species of uncertain status known as Primitives A and B. Hanna's personal interest in the *Endeavor* lay with the beings Outside. By the time the ship left Alta, she had investigated its library and found that it contained masses of material she had never seen before on all four species. There were minor works and papers and reports from countless governments and scholarly projects, all written during the centuries of D'neera's isolation, all archival matter considered so obsolete or unimportant that it had never been collected in one memory before. There were long-defunct journals, autobiographies of forgotten researchers, obscure essays, operational holos of rituals no human had attended for hundreds of years. There was data on the F'thalians, the only star-traveling species humanity knew of besides itself, whose existence Hanna had not suspected, accessible now because it was newly declassified to this ex-

pedition. Much of it was poorly organized, having been
poured into *Endeavor*'s memory with no attempt to order
the chaos of centuries; but before the first Jump into unknown space, three weeks into mission, Hanna already had
seen—not how the data would combine with her own observations, but that somehow it would.

This was exactly what she had hoped for, and she began
to spend all her free time reading. She had perhaps one
Standard year for research, and she would not waste it. Research was what she had come here to do. To be present
when *Endeavor* made a contact was, she thought, a dream,
Iledra's dream; space was too vast, full sentience too rare,
for contact to come soon. Her presence here was enough to
set a precedent so that when *Endeavor* achieved its goal,
one D'neeran or another would be there.

What she thought she could do with the archives was of
more immediate interest.

Sentience showed different faces to true-humans and to
D'neerans—more precisely, to Hanna. If she could synthe-
size them, the achievement would do more for D'neeran
status in the community of man than the whole last century
of tentative rapprochement had done. This was her reason
for being here, and all the rest—token participation in true-
human society, navigational skills, even the slight chance of
a first contact— was insignificant beside it. She was so absorbed in her own concerns that she hardly noticed when
Endeavor made its first halt to signal a likely star system,
three months into mission. Later she knew she ought to
have paid attention, because that was when the dreams began.

A loudspeaker said: This is an emergency this is not a test.
Repeat. This is disaster. This is no dream.

She looked at the displays but she could not see *Havock*
because the displays looked back at her with great yellow
eyes. She cried out and tried to run from them. Tirane was
dead and screaming and all the others too. They took so
long to die and dragged her down, down, and death ate her.
Smoke of burning flesh sucked at her knees and tripped her.
Metal screamed: the *Clara Mendoza*'s dying wails. Death
and more death and *Havock* waited with her to die in a life
become night. The Nestorian cruisers stalked her and she

could not move. Something huge hunted behind them in the dark. Closer. Closer. The smoke choked her screams.

She woke up snorting and struggling, tangled in sheets smooth as water.

Managed to sit up. Couldn't remember the voice code for light. Fumbled with numb fingers until she found a switch and light blazed. Her heart thudded brutally and her muscles were weak.

"Erik," she said. He didn't stir.

"Erik. Wake up. Please."

She shook him once and rubbed his chest. Her brown hand, tremulous, looked alien against the white skin and coarse gold hair. He opened his eyes and smiled, then reached up and pulled her down to him.

"No. No. That's not it, Erik. That's not what I want."

She struggled again and he let her go. The smile faded. He was puzzled and vaguely annoyed.

"What's wrong?" he said.

Her heart quieted.

"The dream. Something after me."

She showed him what she could—not the immediate horror, because the dream was receding after the fashion of dreams, but the residual fear she knew would not let her sleep again soon. Before she broke the quick contact she felt a flash of anger. He did not like telepathy, like most true-humans, and she had given him no warning this time.

She lay down and put her head on his chest. She wanted him to put his arm around her. Instead he said, "You ought to get some help."

She looked from a pool of light into darkness and thought of Iledra's advice, stubbornly ignored.

"But the other dreams stopped," she said. "It's different this time."

He said after a minute's silence, "If you say so. But talk to Peng tomorrow, will you? That's what he's here for."

"It won't help."

"Hanna. . . ." He patted her shoulder finally. His voice was carefully tolerant. "I'm getting a little tired of this."

She was instantly guilty, and resentful too. And she could not show him her resentment without angering him again. And she did not know how to tell him about it. She had never learned to filter emotion through words. That was a true-human skill.

She eased off the bed, feeling a tug at her stomach as she slipped from its half-gee field into normal gravity. She had discovered long ago where the disciplined officer liked his luxuries: right here. She was one of them.

"I'll see you tomorrow," she said inaccurately, since it was well past ship's midnight.

"Turn out the light before you go," he said.

Hanna's pullover and pants and sandals were scattered between the suite's outer door and the bed. She put them on and slipped out into a quiet corridor. Its lights were dimmed in deference to the arbitrary hour. More doors led to other officers' suites, and she hesitated outside one of them. Tamara — but she knew communications chief Tamara Hweng well enough to know that Tam was not inside.

She began walking, not toward her own room but drawn by an intangible thread toward the woman she sought. Not even Erik could quell the D'neeran impulse to seek understanding, and gentle Tamara at least would listen. The aftermath of the dream oppressed her. She finally found Tamara sipping coffee in the crew's mess hall, not alone. Heads turned casually and away again. Hanna was used to being ignored, almost unseen.

Tamara waved at her. "Sit down," she said. The man with her, Ludo Brown, did not look pleased.

Hanna sat, sharply sensitive to Brown and feeling like an unwelcome child.

"I had another one of those dreams," she said.

Even as she spoke, Hanna saw that Tam looked tired and preoccupied.

"Was it the same thing?" Tamara said.

"The same as it's been lately, yes. Not like the ones I used to have."

"Well, I can't tell the difference, from what you say," Tamara said, but Hanna felt her quick sympathy. She patted Hanna's hand. "You had an awful experience and you still dream about it. You ought to talk to Peng about it. You really ought to. You'll get over it quicker if you ask him to help."

"But it's not *like* that, Tam. It's not just living it over. It's like there's really something out there."

Brown, to her astonishment, looked at her sharply. "What is?" he said. "Out where?"

"Out—" She stared at him, taken aback. "I don't know. Out there."

"Well?" he said not to Hanna but to Tam.

"No. Ludo, don't be silly." Tamara began to laugh.

"Is she talking about the same thing?"

"It's not the same thing at all. She's been having bad dreams. What we've got is something else. Prob'ly means less than a dream. I mean, it's altogether different."

Hanna might as well not have been there. She looked from one to the other doubtfully and said, "What are you talking about?"

"Spooks," Tamara said. "An incoming Inspace signal. Very erratic. We've been debugging and defogging all night and we can't get rid of it. *I* think the last relay we planted is defective."

Hanna, distracted, considered it. Communications through so-called inner space were subject to the same uncertainties as travel and could not be maintained without closely spaced signal relays. A tenuous chain of them now connected *Endeavor* with the established networks of human space.

"Is it a message?" she said.

"No, it's not. Random energy, random timing. That's what makes it so frustrating. If there were some structure we could use for diagnosis—but there's not. And Mister Imagination here keeps telling me it's not in the system."

Brown looked up and grinned at Tam. Hanna wished he liked her better, because she liked him. She liked looking at him, too. There were many D'neerans of Hanna's coloring and some who were darker, but Brown's rich darkness was rare where she came from. But he did not like her, because he did not like D'neerans, and he only tolerated her for tolerant Tamara's sake.

"All the same," Brown said, "you can't get away from it. They think there might be something out here. You can't help thinking about it."

"I can," Tamara said, and Hanna said again, "What are you talking about?"

"The Amber signals," Tam said. "We pick them up sometimes around Alta. They don't say anything, they don't mean anything, and, Lord knows, they're not focused on Alta. They're ordinary glitches, only more of 'em. They're nothing. Some natural source we haven't pinned down yet."

"Or maybe not," Brown said. "That's why we're out here, isn't it? And not out past, say, Heartworld?"

"I don't understand this," said Hanna, beginning to feel desperate. It would be so clear if she could just peek into Brown's thoughts. But that wasn't polite, and his native human faculty for projection, the foundation of her own ability but uncontrolled, was not operating at the moment.

"There's nothing to understand," Tamara said, but Brown said simultaneously, "They told us to track down the spooks. You know they did, Tam."

Tamara raised her fingers to her lips in a comic shushing gesture and breathed, "Unofficially. . . ." She added, "The relay's defective. If we can't eliminate the noise we'll have to censor it. Or go back and replace the relay module. I'll talk to the captain, but I'm sure he'll go for the censor."

"We could do it through the DeCastro program—"

They were going to start talking shop. Hanna stood up and said. "Well, good night."

"Good night," they said without even looking up.

She tried talking to the true-human psychologist Peng, as she had been advised. He said laughingly that he could hardly succeed where D'neeran mindhealers had failed. Were they not supposed to achieve remarkable results with trauma victims? Even with soft psychology?

Hanna gathered this meant they did not use biochemical intervention. She thought she felt a trace of condescension.

She said apologetically, to Peng's amusement, that she had expected the matter to take care of itself.

He approached his task with some enthusiasm, but Hanna was so inarticulate that she did not have to read his thoughts—just his face—to see his enthusiasm wane as quickly as it had come.

He gave her a little flask of something called Dreamdust and told her how to instruct herself to dream that the dead were at peace and the hunters vanquished. It was, he told her, all a matter of suggestion.

Hanna looked at the flask doubtfully and said, "But what if there's another source of suggestion?"

Peng beamed at her and said, "There can't be. That's the beauty of it. Dreams are entirely your own creation. It all comes from inside you."

"But I'm a telepath."

"Oh," said Peng. He frowned.

"We'd never dream—I mean, think of using something like this. We don't project when we're sleeping, unless we're very sick or very drugged or it's enormously stressful, but things creep in."

"You mean," Peng said after a pause, "you dream other people's dreams?"

"It's been known to happen."

"Well," he said after a further pause, "try it."

She tried it. The Dreamdust was effective, all right, but the effect was that the thing hunting behind the cruisers was bigger and closer than ever. She could almost see it. She *would* see it. She had to see it, this thing of terror, though she trembled in reality as well as in the dream. But it was shrouded in cloud and when she crawled trembling into the cloud, every instinct screaming for retreat, it solidified before her and was an impenetrable wall behind which the thing faded and was gone.

She didn't want to see it anyway.

There was nothing about peace or vanquishing at all.

She gave the Dreamdust back to Peng and told him she would not trouble him again.

The dreams receded to their former level of tolerable horror, and she was no nearer understanding their significance than she had been before.

Hanna was not on duty when the excitement began. She must have felt it sweep through the ship, but she got it mixed up with her own enthusiasm. She had discovered "Enchanted River: Notes on a Non-Terrene Evolutionary Process." The work was seven hundred years old, but she had seen that river, and Marshall Ho, dead half a millennium, spoke to her as to a contemporary. Her mind was not on *Endeavor*'s quest but in a steaming forest on the world of Primitive A, where the hot thick air lay heavy on her hair and mud squelched at every step and a fault in her breathing mask would mean death.

She had never learned to whom she owed the privilege

of being so uncomfortable. Her request for Polity permission to visit A had been turned down repeatedly, and then one day was granted. She had gone to the planet at once, before They could change Their minds again. A bored Fleet guardian hovered at her shoulder and thought about patting her behind. She watched the sinuous leathery A creatures for days without seeing a single piece of behavior to support her conviction, immediate and direct, that they had already entered the gray area between bestiality and sentience.

"Enchanted River" was a treasure.

Ho, working under the auspices of a rough coalition of Earthly nations, had been unhampered by the stringent regulations developed later by the Polity. He had gotten right down in the beings' midst, and at considerable personal risk watched every detail of their lives for months. He thought their intelligence was on a level with that of certain extinct terrestrial primates, and he held out great hopes for their future.

No one paid much attention even then. Colony One and Co-op had just been established, and there were enough strange things in places where the air was safe to breathe. The contact with F'thal came a few years later, and Ho's ambiguous pets were forgotten. The infant Polity remembered to interdict the place—after the Co-opers decimated a population of potentially future-sentient mammals on their own planet—but the act was neither necessary nor daring, since no one wanted anything on A. Marshall Ho became a footnote in the history of exploration, and then disappeared altogether. "Enchanted River" was never translated into Standard. Hanna did not know why; the translation program was still available, and she had done the job herself by pushing a button. She supposed no one had ever been interested enough to push the right buttons.

She skimmed the work in a couple of hours, her attention so concentrated that when she was done she could have repeated long passages from memory. Then, just to be sure, she ran a search for any mention of something she had seen on A. There was nothing.

("When did they start building dams?" she said to the Fleet sentinel.

"They've always made 'em. Instinct. Read Rutherford.

*Twenty-six fifties," he said, looking longingly at her breasts.
It was a long and lonely tour of duty out here, and he was
nearly at the end of it.*

*"I've read Rutherford. I've seen his pictures. What they
were building then wasn't as sophisticated. And it was confined to a limited area."*

"That's very interesting," he said, edging closer.

*She never had to hit him. Her blast of anger straight into
his head was enough; and taught her for the first time what
true-humans thought of telepathy. It was all mixed up together in memory: the discomfort and his bitter resentment
and the—pups, she supposed she must call them—learning
to build. The vague stirrings of extension of the learning skill
to other things. Inchoate, as yet. Unrealized. When need
called it would happen. But no telepath had gone there before, and no one else could have sensed it.)*

The dams created quiet deep pools where the beings
lounged and played. Ho described their environment in ex-
haustive detail; but he did not mention dams. His photo-
graphs showed no dams. Now the structures were
everywhere, wherever the A Primitives lived.

It was negative evidence. It was better than saying: I am
a telepath and I know. But would it be enough?

She had been still for so long that her muscles were
cramped. She got up and the heat and stench faded. Her
memory of sunlight filtered through leaves vanished, and
her cabin seemed cold and dark. It was standard issue; she
had brought little with her from D'neera, and regretted the
omission. It seemed noisy, as if many voices were talking
very loudly nearby.

After a minute she realized there were no voices. But
somewhere on *Endeavor* were some very excited people.

She went out into the corridor and followed her instinct
toward the source of excitement—Communications. The
suggestion of noise grew stronger as she focused her attention. The walls seemed to carry it like a vibration, and the
unsound pricked at her scalp. Something was happening,
something important. People stood in clusters talking about
it, but she did not ask them what it was. She went on toward
Communications, moving faster, her breath short for no
reason.

It was controlled, crowded chaos inside, but everyone's

attention was focused on instrument readings and— something else: something mind-conjured yet so shapeless, shadowy, hidden in cloud that her dream came upon her in a great rush and she drew in her breath harshly, for an instant thinking all of it a dream, and almost turning to run.

Nearby Brown called, "Tamara! Hey, Tam!"

Tamara looked across bent heads. Brown said, "Secondary traces negative. Exclusion from the relay pipeline confirmed."

Tamara said, "Check it again." She plunged back into conversation with Erik.

Hanna was shivering. She was not dreaming, but still everything seemed faintly unreal. She looked for someone to talk to. De Assis, the linguist, was speaking with animation to McCarthy of exobiology; but Marte Koster, chief of exopsychology, stood silent and a little apart. Hanna went to her, picking her way carefully through a larger crowd than the space was designed to handle. Koster was a pudgy woman who made Hanna think of an ill-tempered duck, but her face, Hanna saw with shock, was transfigured, and she caught at Hanna's arm with plump hands.

"It's wonderful! Wonderful!" she said. A clean pure note of excitement made her almost likable.

Hanna said—with an edge of reluctance that made no sense—"What is it?"

"You haven't heard?"

"No. No. I was busy. Heard what?"

"Contact! A first contact!"

"What?" Hanna said. Koster kept talking, but Hanna did not hear her. She looked at Koster's shining eyes, at the bustle around them, as if all of it would collapse now, immediately, any second. Humankind knows one star-traveling race and that is F'thal. Elementary knowledge, you knew it before you knew what stars were—

She stood perfectly still. Koster patted at her nervously. "It's a shock, I know. I don't believe it yet myself. But it's true. It's true!"

Hanna said with an effort, "What happened?"

"They got a message a few hours ago. They're still checking to make sure it's not of human origin. It's a series of prime numbers and a location. Clearly intelligent."

"From the system they've been signaling?"

"Where else?"

"But there's no power generation there!"

"You mean not that we recognized. No heat or radiation. We've got to find out how they do it. Think of it!"

Koster was ecstatic; more than ecstatic—bordering on hysteria. "Don't," Hanna said, trying to soothe her. "Don't. For heaven's sake—" She felt giddy. Everyone seemed to be shouting, but that was an illusion; it was only that they could not help projecting. She shut them out as well as she could and tried to think sensibly.

"That's the location they gave? That system?" she asked.

"No. No. The rendezvous is a week away, I think. In deep space."

"Why?"

"Who knows?" But the questions calmed Koster. She took a deep breath and said quite rationally, "I don't suppose you've felt anything, have you?"

"Felt—?"

"Felt anything telepathically that might have come from them."

"I wouldn't. There are too many people on this ship. The aliens would have to—"

She stopped abruptly. Koster said, "They'd have to what?"

"I was going to say, they'd have to be telepaths themselves. But if they touched us I wouldn't necessarily know it was them."

"You let me know if there's anything. Anything at all. Any slightest possibility."

"I will," Hanna said, but she was glad Koster was not looking at her too closely when she said it, because she did not want to be questioned about possibilities. She did not want to talk about the one that had just occurred to her, which was preposterous anyway, but then it was all preposterous. It was too new, she could not believe in aliens yet and half these busy people could not either. History was being made but it wasn't, for those making it, real. Not yet. So the possibility wasn't real either, and besides she did not even want to think about it because—thinking about it made her afraid, and if she thought about it she would have to do something about it; the fear would not go away until she knew she was wrong.

Chapter 3

Endeavor came to the appointed place nine days later, and found no one there.

The journey ought to have taken longer, and Hanna, like everyone else in Navigation, was tired when the push for speed was over. She was not at once concerned with the silence that answered *Endeavor*'s homing beacon, nor were any of the others. Species X had not specified a time for rendezvous. Perhaps the aliens were still on their way. If this area of space was familiar to them, they might have started for it later, underestimating *Endeavor*'s pace through unknown space. They might think less like humans than like F'thalians, who were universally tardy. As long as the creatures were an enigma, there was no point in speculating about their punctuality or their notion of a timely tryst.

Besides, there was the micro factor to consider. From the macroscopic point of view, an interstellar location could be pinpointed with high accuracy; but on the scale of two small ships seeking each other in perpetual night, there was room for error in even the most precise equations. The *Endeavor*'s beacon had its limitations, too. Inspace signals did not travel, but came into existence more or less at the point of reception, the more or less being a matter of probability. The beacon therefore consisted not of one Inspace signal but of billions, fired in a series run at subatomic speed to an array of points within a radius of one light-year in any direction from *Endeavor*. This left sizable gaps in the reception pattern, so it was customary to shift the whole thing in space for each repetition of the sequence of signals. If you were in a crack at the beginning, you had only to wait until a point in the pattern was close enough to register on reasonably sensitive instruments.

Of course, the aliens would not know that; but as the days wore on and stretched into a week of silence, the fear that grew on the crew of the *Endeavor* and the project's Earth-based managers was that they did not care.

Starr Jameson watched the conference and doodled.

He had positioned himself so that he could see past the video screen that showed a dozen members of *Endeavor*'s complement at their conference table, and look instead at the brilliant June afternoon outside. He had gone even farther than his Heartworld predecessors in making his Central Admin quarters at least appear utterly unguarded, though the appearance was deceptive. This room had no visible outer wall, so that the broad river running past the administration complex lapped at its edges, and he could walk straight off the thick carpet into the water if he chose. He never would; a Polity commissioner did not do such things, and in any case Jameson would not have done it because he had seldom done an impulsive thing in his life. But sometimes he thought about it, especially at times like this.

In front of the conference screen floated a smaller screen which displayed the conferees' words as they spoke. Jameson had lowered the volume of the dialogue. He kept half an ear on it and half an eye on the readout, and in his lap he held a notepad and stylus. He would appear to the *Endeavor* personnel, and to the other Earth-based participants whose disembodied voices joined in from time to time from Admin and other locations, to be taking studious notes. He never took notes, but a lifetime of conferences had taught him the necessity of doodling to have something to do besides look at interchangeable faces and listen with diminishing concentration to interminable voices going on and on.

This meeting had been going on half an hour and he had already filled and wiped the notepad's screen once before something on the readout caught his attention.

He leaned forward and said, "One moment, please."

All the voices stopped immediately. He said, "Lieutenant Hweng, back up a moment, please. What did you say about confirmation of the source of the original signal?"

Tamara Hweng said without hesitation, "It took some time to refine the parameters of transmission, sir, probably because of equipment incompatibility, and we've only just pinned down the ambiguity margin. The signal we received didn't originate in the target stellar system. It came from perhaps a third of that distance from *Endeavor*. Unless you accept the possibility of our being directly in line with an established relay system, that means they answered us from a spacecraft."

"Thank you," Jameson said. He waited for the voices to take up their theme before he leaned back and considered the news. It must fit into a pattern somewhere; but there were not yet enough facts to form a discernible pattern. There were only the signal to a distant new world, the answer from a spacecraft close at hand, a meeting set for an unspecified hour—then nothing.

He appreciated the irony of the situation. All the laws of chance and logic argued the impossibility of *Endeavor*'s first effort drawing an answer. Hundreds or thousands of efforts with no answer had been the likely scenario. The impossible had most gratifyingly happened, however—and now was slipping out of reach.

Why had species X not answered from the system that received the signal? To draw *Endeavor* away from it? To avoid being caught on the ground? If they had answered from a spacecraft, why had they not simply made physical contact with *Endeavor* at its original, well-described position?

The readout said: "—suppose we scouted the target system just went there maybe used one of the shuttles or—"

Jameson said, "No."

The speaker was McCarthy. He was a Heartworlder and not over-fond of Jameson. He looked up and said with a familiarity most of the others would not have dared, "Why not?"

"You have no shuttles with Inspace capability, Harry," Jameson said. "You'd have to take the *Endeavor* into the gravity complex. If you took nine days to get to your present location, in deep space and working flat out, you would need—how long, Captain Fleming, to chart a safe path to and through the target system?"

Fleming nodded. He said, "At a guess—and this is just a guess—a month. At least. Probably longer."

"Yes. And you would relinquish the chance of contact where you are."

First Officer Ito Hirasawa said, "What about getting a smaller Inspace vessel out from the closest base? We could stay where we are while somebody else charts a course."

Jameson said, "We don't know yet that they don't consider one ship an invasion. We don't want them worrying about two. Gentlemen and ladies, we have no idea what we're dealing with. It has been seventeen days since Signal Alpha. Seventeen days may be only a moment to these beings. I suggest maintaining your position for a time. There are other reasons, but at present let's just assume that your time can be best employed in waiting."

Marte Koster said rather plaintively, "But how long, Commissioner?"

She looked woebegone. Jameson did not like her expression, and he did not like Koster. Sheer weight of Fleet seniority had earned her this choice assignment. There had been no valid reason to reject her, and he had not tried to do so. But he did not like her. He said, "I don't know how long you should wait. But as an exopsychologist you're certainly aware that curiosity is a prime trait of sentient life. They'll come take a look at you sooner or later."

She tapped the table restlessly and said, "It might speed them up if we gave them more information. We could add to the beacon content."

One of the disembodied voices—an I&S man from Morisz's office—said immediately, "No!" There was a pause during which he must have considered how his haste looked—a little too paranoid, perhaps—and he added more smoothly, "I'm not an exopsychologist, but surely what we've already told them is enough to stir up any reasoning creature's curiosity. What if we got a message out of nowhere from somebody identifying himself as an intelligent, oxygen-breathing biped? I know how we'd react. Wouldn't we, ma'am?"

Koster said, "You can't generalize—" and was quickly interrupted. Jameson listened long enough to be sure the I&S man was carrying his point, and tuned out again.

The conference started to disintegrate, its business done. Jameson began to think of the long cool evening ahead, of catching up on his endless reading in the sweet-scented garden of his nearby home. Presently Henriette would come to be beautiful and compliant over drinks at twilight, and later all warmth in the dark.

But once he looked again at Marte Koster, and wondered if she were making any use of the D'neeran girl who was somewhere on *Endeavor*. A long time ago he had given Koster a gentle hint of the possibilities there. Too gentle perhaps; but his was a very private experiment.

Heartsong of the beast. We are (it sings) intelligent star-yearning star-earning. . . .
We know. And knew. Eversought since one day's seeking. . . .
Here. Here. Give no warning.
Wait . . .

"What?" Hanna said.

"Umm?"

"Did you say something?"

"Heaven knows. I don't think so."

"I thought you said something about—" Hanna fumbled uneasily. Water? Waiting? "Never mind," she said.

"Good," said Tamara. "Don't ask me to remember anything I said two seconds ago. Please."

She sat on Hanna's bunk with her capable hands, a little unsteady, wrapped around a mug of steaming coffee. There were hollows under her brown eyes, and the lids drooped from watching too many readouts that did not change. Signal Alpha now was twenty-four days in the past. Tamara had told Hanna that her ears were even wearier than her eyes; that she listened always for an audible voice, although it was absurd; that in her rest periods she lay still and awake because she could not stop listening. It had become her habit to meet Hanna in her short breaks from Communications, because Hanna knew little of the field. With Hanna, Tam could, she said, stop listening.

Hanna said, "They set the damn meeting place. They've got to be close."

She sipped tea and waited for Tamara to say the next thing; they had had this conversation before.

Tamara said inevitably, "Well, maybe they're not."

"Huh?"

"Not close."

"And if they're not we either did something wrong or—"

"Or they never meant to show up at all."

"Which is ridiculous."

"Ridiculous."

Tamara got up with a sigh. She said, "I guess it's time to go back and make sure we're set up for the conference."

"What conference?" Hanna said with half-hearted curiosity.

"Alien Relations. At sixteen hundred hours. Another session with The Man himself listening to every word and jumping on anything he doesn't like. I'm not used to operating on that level, Hanna."

Hanna frowned at her. "What man?"

"What?"

"Wait a minute." Hanna sorted it out. True-humans sometimes used a verbal shorthand that seemed to make up for the vivid images D'neerans exchanged to supplement language, and she was not good at it. "You said the man listens to every word. What man?"

"The commissioner."

"Which commissioner?"

"Jameson," Tamara said patiently.

"Oh. I see. Alien Relations. Erik won't let me in on those meetings, you know."

"I know," Tam said, but she left without saying anything else. There was nothing more to say. Hanna had told her all about it: the bitter argument, the truth coming out at last that even Erik thought her not quite human, a threat, a freak to be kept away from important *human* work.

"You're lucky to be here at all," he had said, and that had been the end of it. She had done as she was told. Erik was the captain and orders were orders; the implications would not be self-evident on D'neera, but there were no other D'neerans here. So she had stayed in her place in Navigation, downing stimulants and working endless hours like everyone else, with little room in her mind for anything else; the stimdope she and the rest of the crew were taking had given her no choice, because they concentrated your mind on whatever task was set it. Her head was filled with mathematical symbols that danced around each other in closed circles and ran together until they made no sense. She was stuffed with them and befogged by them, and her baffled crewmates made another fog around her. Their search went round and round in circles too.

She wouldn't think about it any more. She couldn't bear to. There was no way out of the fog, but at least she could sleep and forget about it for a little while.

She yawned and hovered a moment behind someone's eyes in the command module with its bright displays and tell-tales and the human beings monitoring a sleek machine whose trillion nerve endings made it a nearly living thing. She drifted, soothed, through the ordinary detritus of humankind, a hundred separate universes of greater or lesser charm, self-contained though admirably bridged. Her tension eased. For after all, though D'neeran she was human, at home, at rest among the—

Beasts, said a whisper in her head. She whimpered but the whispering went on without words; she struggled to move limbs that had no strength; she was trapped in the smoke again, and the first flicker of apprehension swelled into fear. The whisper crept closer and called her. Wrong, wrong, no good at all; dark and ashes and an eye like the sun watching pitiless and the shadow looming without mercy, new, new, something new and terrible and that was all she knew, that was all she would ever know but it knew *her.*

I come. I come to you—

She heard herself with terror. *N.S. Havock* filled her eyes. Her hand moved toward a key and Roly, who did not want to die, cried, "You're too good at this!" But still her hand crept on to the last thing she would ever touch. "You're mad!" Dorista said and seized the dreaming hand but it seemed she had gone on: dust of *Clara* and, yes, her people dust—what waited past that end? The whisper said: *We wait.*

She shouted and the shout woke her up. She sat up shakily, sweating.

("But you were saved," Peng said reasonably. "The Interworld Fleet, wasn't it?"

"Yes. Heavy cruisers. *The* Willowmeade *under Tirel—I remember* Willowmeade—"

"These dreams, then. Do you want to die?"

"Me?" she said with disbelief.

"What else?"

"If they come from outside—"
"They don't come from outside," he said.)
She said out loud, "It's the drugs."
The words fell into the cabin's dead air without conviction.

She turned over and pushed her face into the thin blanket that covered her bunk. Her thoughts shot off in all directions: the numbers danced in the puzzled fog and Erik's fear and unkindness underlay it all. If only she could talk to Iledra— really *talk* to her, not record a message that would be censored anyway and wait for a reply to clear Earth. Or to her mother; but Cassie had taken up with a mood poet and gone to live on a beach in the tropics.

The thing that pulled her thoughts in all directions was something she did not want to think about. It had been easy to avoid, with the dreams gone and the stimulants at work.

Suddenly she wanted very badly to go to the conference, to find out what somebody else thought. The heads out here were numbed with drugs and anticlimax. What would the outsiders say? What did the omnipresent Jameson think of the mire his pet project had gotten into? Maybe he knew what was going on. Maybe somebody would say something that would make it unnecessary for her to think about her scraps of surmise. If she went, would Erik throw her out in front of all those important people? What would be the harm in just listening?

She reached out and turned out the light, and sought the greenish glow of a chronometer across the room.

The conference would begin in thirty minutes.

In forty she would go.

... and knew. Found today
found yesterday
found at last
tomorrow ends
today ...
Wait.
Watch.
Wait ...

It was more than an hour before she stood outside the door and stared at it as if she could see through it.

She had fallen asleep again, just for a little while, and waked feeling profoundly uneasy. Had she had the dream, or not? She couldn't have; she hadn't had it since *Endeavor*'s frustrating chase began; but in her fitful nap it had returned to memory at least, and now it haunted her and teased her as if something known yet not known hovered waiting for a word to make it real.

The polished door showed her nothing but her own reflection: thinner than ever, the dark blue eyes too big, her hair a shaggy mane. She ran both hands through it to tame it, but she did not move yet to open the door. She heard nothing behind it and reached through the wall into mist. There were too many people thinking unfocused thoughts; they slipped from her grasp like the dreams' unseen thing.

Finally she touched the switch that controlled the door, and it opened.

The room beyond was dark, but in a central blaze of light that seemed to float without foundation, Erik sat at the end of a long table whose other end she could not see. Hirasawa sat at his right and Tamara at his left, and Koster and Brown were in her line of sight. She sensed other presences and all of them, seen and unseen, looked at something hidden by a jutting corner at her left.

She edged into the dark edge of the room, feeling like a spectator at a drama arranged by an invisible director. The wall at her side made an alcove from which she watched in shadow. But what were the actors watching?

A male voice she had never heard before was saying, "—your point, of course, but the project calls for keeping on the move unless you have definite results. You've got too much ground to cover to waste time. You're off course and stretching optimum scheduling now."

Hanna felt a jolt of anxiety. Marte Koster's. She knew what Koster would say before the woman spoke, her voice more tranquil than her heart.

"We might stay on course twenty more years without results. Either of the other options would be more acceptable to me than giving up."

The others murmured programmed agreement—Hanna shook off the thought in irritation.

(The white faces of a F'thalian Hierarchus emerged from

the past. The thought of the Hierarchus soared and dipped and dizzily she caught at the flashes of light which were scintillating nodes of intersection, though she could not follow his spirit's flight.

Observe the water-breathers, he had said. Move a leaflet, so, and they rush eagerly to feed, though on this world to which they were not born they have no prey that moves so. Yet they do it, and their offspring will do it, and thus with all their generations. Thus with thee, Little One—)

She shoved the Hierarchus back into memory with an effort. Damn the drugs, they weren't working as they were supposed to work, she was more and more easily distracted and divided. Erik was saying, "—a combination of efforts. I think we could do it that quickly; it's a matter of refining Communications' data. But you said, sir, that you were opposed to that course of action on grounds other than the time it would require?"

She had heard the voice that answered once before. It was deep and precisely inflected and instantly recognizable. Starr Jameson said, "The likelihood that this system is the home of a star-traveling species is small, gauged by chance alone. The absence of any sign of artificial power generation settles the matter, to my mind."

Koster said, "We signaled it and somebody answered. Somebody who was breathing down our necks."

"Quite." Jameson again. "You were then two and one-half light-years away from—let's be specific and say from the life-bearing planet of that system. Your data on the planet itself, therefore, is two and one-half years old. Certainly no native species has developed Inspace techniques in that time. The beings who responded to you therefore came from elsewhere—"

"Yes," Hanna muttered, and froze: how had she known that? She stood in the dark and heard the voice going on, a deep music without meaning, her thoughts paralyzed. She made herself breathe again, and think of what it meant. She knew it; never mind how, for now. She *knew* it. It meant something—

"—should say they prefer to keep their business there to themselves since they invited you to a meeting not in that stellar system but some distance in an opposite direction. I still agree with Kwomo that you ought not to spend time visiting the system. You might do something with an unmanned probe, if you can do it quickly enough—"

Hanna slid without volition into Koster's frustration. Marte reached out, reached out, for something unseen she saw slipping away. Her need for comfort was so strong that Hanna moved forward automatically. Her eyes were drawn to the end of the room, visible now, where most of the wall was a video screen that showed Starr Jameson and two other men bigger than life, dominant and unreal. The little group of spectators was tense.

Something nagged at the back of her mind. She ignored Koster, with difficulty, and stopped and dug for it in silence.

Koster was talking again: "—backtrack to our original point of contact? If we got our signals mixed up and they're looking for us somewhere else, they'll go back too. There's been a mistake."

"Assuming they exist," said one of the strangers on the screen. "Lieutenant Hweng, are you sure the signal's source was nearby? Couldn't it actually have originated within the system, maybe an automatic device set in place long ago? Something important might have been where you are now and be long gone."

Tamara said with absolute conviction, "There has been no mistake. The margin of ambiguity was too tight for the origin to be in the system. It was far more clear than ours must have been at reception."

Koster said, "Then there's been some kind of accident. We've missed each other. They must want to meet us as much as we want to meet them."

She expanded on the theme, but Hanna was not listening anymore. The receding shadow stood for an instant in the light.

"Oh, they don't," Hanna said out loud. "They don't want us to see them. They don't."

After one frozen instant all the heads turned in her direction at once. Someone said from the video screen, "Who is that?"

Hanna did not move. She did not even feel the eyes; she was looking inward, watching pieces slot into place: the dreams and the tracking shadow always just outside her perception, the Dreamdust experiment whose results had reflected no suggestion of hers, the conviction that she had already known Jameson's theory to be true without knowing, until she heard it, that she knew it. It fit together so simply. It was as simple as—

—as killing *Havock* would have been.

She shivered and looked up.

Jameson said across fifty light-years, "Would you come into view, please? And identify yourself?"

She stood on the edge of light and saw that Erik's face was scarlet. His anger was a tangible barrier she would have to push through. Tam watched her with surprise and approval. She concentrated on Tam; the barrier vanished and she stepped into the light.

Erik said tightly, "I'm very sorry for this interruption. Ms. Bassanio wasn't supposed to be here."

Jameson said, "The proper title is 'Lady Hanna,' is it not? Is that correct?"

She turned to face the screen. She did feel the eyes now, and someone was thinking with sarcasm of her kludge of a title, and someone else was thinking *GO AWAY*. The faces borrowed from Earth were not half so unfriendly. The man in the center knew exactly who she was. That was odd, but she could not spare much thought for the oddness, because she was still thinking hard and she was frightened. She was not good with words, and she was willing to make a fool of herself by being wrong, but it would be terrible to do it by being right and not being able to explain. *WE DON'T WANT YOU*, somebody thought, and it stabbed her. Jameson had asked her something but she could not remember what it was and could not answer. Now he was saying, "Would you repeat your remark?" She took a deep breath, trying to tell herself this was no worse than the Arbitration Committee. But it was.

"I said—" She fastened her attention on the video screen. She couldn't remember what she had said. "I meant maybe Marte is wrong. Maybe they don't really want to meet us."

"Nonsense!" Marte Koster said so violently that Hanna jumped. Her hands trembled with self-consciousness, with fatigue, with the impact of Koster's hostility. She felt an urge to hit Koster's puffy face.

But Jameson did not look hostile. He did not even look surprised. She concentrated on him with a kind of gratitude.

"It's not nonsense," she managed to say. "There's something wrong about the whole thing. What were the odds against making a contact so soon? I know—I've heard—there's a reason we came this way. I'm not a statistician, but still it only makes sense if they were looking for us too."

"That's what I said!" Koster almost rose in her frustration. Hanna would not look at her but felt the movement in her own limbs, which jerked in unwilled sympathy.

She said, "No. No. It's not the same thing. They might—they might want to do other things besides meet us. They might just want to know where we are. They might want to study us. They're watching us. I think they're watching us."

She did not take her eyes off Jameson. She had never seen so guarded a face in her life. He might have been thinking anything. She waited for him to say something, but it was one of the strangers at his side who said with open skepticism, "Do you have any evidence to support this—this very remarkable hypothesis?"

Hanna glanced at him, but then she looked back at Jameson and said, "I think I do. It's not objective. It's not on a readout anywhere. It's all inside my head. But I started, I started feeling it about the time we sent the first transmission. And it's come and gone and it's taken different forms, but I think it's real."

She waited for a response. Nothing, for a few seconds that seemed much longer. *GET RID OF HER,* Koster thought. Then Jameson said, "Go on," and just as she relaxed in relief, "Please be brief."

She tried, but it seemed to go on for a long time. It was hard to keep it in order, hard to put it all in words, and she could not show the Polity's men directly what she meant. They watched her without expression as she talked. Jameson moved only once, to put down the notepad he held, and Hanna stumbled because she heard Koster think savagely: *NOT WORTH TAKING NOTES ON!* On the wall in faraway Namerica there was a lambent glow as of sunlight reflected from water, and when she noticed it she faltered again. All the *Endeavor*'s clever design tricks failed, and she was vividly aware that she inhabited a metal container lost in darkness. But she recovered and went on.

She finished, "It has occurred to me that they might be telepaths. If the things I've noticed are significant, they have to be. I'm not a telepathic Adept. I couldn't possibly be aware of a distant non-telepathic presence when I'm surrounded by so many people and—I don't think even an Adept would be, unless he were deliberately reaching out to something and had a pretty clear idea what it was. That means they must be touching us in some way, though I'm the only one equipped to feel it strongly."

She thought of Tamara listening always for the voice that did not come, of the goal at the edge of Marte's sight. She added, "Maybe some of the others feel it a little. But if that's true, the only possible interpretation is that they have, have gone partway toward contact and are avoiding completing it. For some reason. I don't have any idea why they would do that. I don't—I don't know why it would take the form of something from my own experience. Yes, I do. I mean, that's because I pattern it unconsciously, because I don't have the, the templates of their experience. But why it should be *that*—"

She stopped abruptly, unwilling to approach the question more closely. She had said everything she had to say. There was no reason to go on.

They were waiting for more, however. They waited until Erik said, "Thank you, Ms. Bassanio."

It was a dismissal, and his voice was rough. He had only gotten angrier while she talked. She looked at him uncertainly.

Jameson said, "Lady Hanna."

"Yes?"

She looked back at the wall with some anxiety. Nobody up there looked inviting, but it was a better view than Erik's fury.

"Do you think it would be worthwhile importing an Adept?"

"Why—I don't know. They've got skills I haven't, of course, but on the other hand. . . ." She pondered.

She must have thought about it too long, because Jameson said patiently, "On the other hand what?"

"Oh. I'm sorry. Adepts don't have my training. My experience. I mean, I think I'm the only D'neeran who's been to F'thal, for example, Adept or not. The Adepts I know, they'd have some very interesting mystical things to say about aliens, but it wouldn't be much use from your point of view.

There's something I could try," she said, and regretted it instantly.

It was too late, however. Jameson said, "What is that?"

She said unwillingly, "I could try to touch them without the interference. I'd have to be separated from the ship."

Jameson moved abruptly. No, not abruptly; it was just that her attention was caught because he had been so still until now. He said, "Telepathic reception is not a matter of proximity, I understand."

"Not really. But practically speaking it's like—like—"

She couldn't find the words. Jameson said, to her surprise, "Like Newtonian physics and Inspace. Direction is a perceptual construct, but things still fall downward."

"Yes," she said, understanding him perfectly. "Yes, that's it."

"Suppose you were, as you put it, separated from the ship? What then?"

"I don't know. I don't think," she added, utterly forgetting propriety, "I would like it much."

Jameson blinked. Out of the corner of her eye Hanna saw Erik make a violent gesture, instantly controlled.

"Why not?" Jameson said.

Automatically, because it was her custom to let emotion speak for itself, she visualized herself alone in nothingness, knowing the thing that hid behind Nestor's warships was nearly upon her. The persons around her stirred uncomfortably, and someone made a sound of protest. But Jameson could only hear her words, so she said simply, "I think I would be scared."

He looked, for the first time, mildly surprised. He surprised her by saying, "How did you feel the first time you made telepathic contact with a F'thalian?"

"What? Why?"

"How did you feel?"

"Well. . . ." She tried to remember. The dizzying sweep of infinite circles was familiar to her now. She couldn't think of F'thalians without them. But at first it had been like falling, and at every attempt she flinched away until the Hierarchus showed her the circles intersected everywhere, and she would always fall to a momentary resting place.

She said at last, "It was strange. It frightened me."

"The novelty?" he suggested.

"Well—"

He made a gesture with one human hand that would have meant, if the Hierarchus made it, Similarity of the First Order. She stared at him, disconcerted. How did he know so much about it? Or about her trip to F'thal, for that matter?

She said, "All right. It could be the novelty."

She had forgotten Erik. He could not restrain himself any longer. He said suddenly, his voice furry, "Even if there's something to this, I don't know how practical it is to separate her from the *Endeavor*. She couldn't get very far in a reasonable time in the shuttles we carry. They're not Inspace transport."

Jameson made a barely perceptible gesture, and one of the men with him took up the discussion.

"You could Jump and leave *her*," the other said. "The shuttles are equipped as lifeboats and have Inspace communications capability, am I right?"

Erik said stubbornly, "It would take us away from ground zero for an indefinite length of time."

They went on talking. Hanna, finding herself extraneous, looked for a place to sit down. Her knees felt uncommonly weak. There was no vacant place near Tam, but she found an empty spot next to McCarthy and felt under the table's edge until she touched the button that made its associated chair unfold from the floor. McCarthy looked at her in astonishment, as if seeing her for the first time, but he did not speak to her.

She was shaken and apprehensive and she did not try to hide it. A true-human would have tried, but Hanna had not been among them long enough to adopt the habit, even if there had been any sense in it; and here, anyway, some of the surfaces were wearing so thin that her anxiety was not overly conspicuous. Erik was a stranger. He had a right not to take her seriously, she supposed, but she had thought that was because Marte Koster did not take her seriously. Surely if these men did, Erik would? But he did not, or adamantly refused to, and she watched something that she finally understood was a duel of words until Erik lost. When the man with Jameson was done—it was Kwomo Thermstrom, she discovered, and remembered his name from the *Endeavor* Project proposal—Erik had agreed to the experiment at some unclear point in the future. That was all. As if she had never been there they talked of other things, of staying and going and unmanned probes, and finally Hanna realized no one was going to talk to her again, and stopped listening.

She stayed until the end, but not with pleasure. Too many questions had come to her in the last half hour, and she kept thinking of more: of what it might mean to Iledra and to D'neera if she came back from the forthcoming vague mission with something to show for it, and what it might mean if she came back with nothing. She was used to acting on the basis of direct mind-to-mind communication, but could she have made a mistake? Here in this strange world of true-humans, might she have misidentified as alien a complex of her own past and fears?

Once she looked up and saw Jameson looking at her so closely that she stared back at him in shock. For an instant she felt naked—not as an object of sexual interest, but as if she were being stripped right down to the bone and implacably assessed.

It lasted a second or two, and then he looked at someone else. She might have imagined the whole thing. But she knew she had not; why should a commissioner of the Polity watch her that way? What possible importance could she have for him?

She could not think of any, but later, as she filed out with the others, she thought suddenly: Whatever it is I will not like. Whatever he's doing, I wish he would not.

Chapter 4

She would not even try to transmit the letter. It would not get past the censor. She went on with it anyway, speaking softly, watching words form and lines flow on a square of light in her darkened room.

"I don't understand what I feel, Lee. It's new. Is it fear? Today I told the commissioner F'thal frightened me once. That wasn't the same. It was strange and exciting. And I was so curious about them! I couldn't have been very afraid. And, oh, what people said to me after Nestor! How brave I must have been! Was I? I don't remember feeling like this. I don't understand this. I don't. I don't. Am I imagining it? I have to get off the stim boosters. . . ."

It was deliciously quiet in the tiny cabin. Hanna should have had the booster implant renewed some hours ago. She had not; she would not. It seemed to take a great deal of energy to move even a little. Her mouth tasted of metal.

"This might be the chance we talked about. I have to be good enough. Don't I? I never thought it would happen. But I thought, if it did, I'd show true-humans how to do it right. Do it right from the beginning. I'm not even curious about them, Lee. Why? How can I not be? Why am I afraid? I have to get off the boosters and think. We're not going anywhere. We're staying here a couple of weeks more. I'll have time to think. . . ."

The room's sparse furnishings seemed to move in the dark.

Hanna fell asleep with her head on the computer keyboard.

She spun through the thought of the Hierarchus, pursuing a meaning that just eluded her. It was essential that she find it, because behind her was something that pursued *her,* and what she sought was her defense against the seeker.

The terror was so familiar that it bored her.

"Hanna?" said a soft and urgent voice.

She swam toward the voice, up through dark waters. Pursued and pursuers receded.

"Hanna? Wake up. Wake up."

She straightened, surprised to find herself not in bed. The cold light of the text display hurt her eyes. Her back hurt. She was cold.

Tamara said, "What's wrong with you?"

"What?"

"You're shaking."

"Wake fast. Happens."

It came out in a mumble. Tam touched her shoulder anxiously.

"Did you hear the alert?"

"Yes. I did. What alert?"

"You and some of the others. Briefing Room Two. I've only got a minute, I have to get back."

"All right," Hanna said vaguely.

"Promise? You won't go back to sleep? Promise."

"Promise."

"I have to go. Hurry."

"Thank you," Hanna said. She heard the swish of the door as it closed.

She got up, feeling heavy and unwieldy as a statue come to life. It seemed that she could only think one thought at a time, very slowly. There was a weight of nothing tangible in the pit of her stomach. When she started for the door, she stumbled.

The walk took forever.

When she entered the briefing room all the heads turned toward her—again—as if the scene from a few hours ago were being repeated. Her stomach lurched and she stopped dead. But there were only three people there—Erik, Koster, and Hanna's chief from Navigation.

"You're late," Erik said, not quite in a snarl.

"I'm sorry...." She pushed a hand through her hair and looked at them blankly. It struck her that the discontinued stimulants were taking their revenge. The thought did not console her.

"Dismissed. Except you," Erik said, looking at Hanna. "Sit down."

She did. She was acutely aware of the hard seat of the chair. The pale blue of a wall was garish. The others' footsteps thudded loudly as they left. Koster gave her the strangest look—half smug, half resentful.

When the door shut Erik said, "Why didn't you come when you were called?"

"I didn't hear. I was sleeping," she said, longing for more sleep.

He looked as if he didn't believe her. He said, "I don't have time to go through the whole thing again. You know about Beta?"

She tried to remember something about a Beta, and shook her head.

"Signal Beta. An hour ago. My God," he said impatiently, "how could you miss it? Another alien transmission, an exact duplicate of the first one, except that the locus referents are different."

"What?" Hanna said, startled into wakefulness. Erik went on without slowing down.

"We're making the first Jump in that direction in four hours—sooner, if Navigation gets it worked out faster. You're staying behind. Shuttle Five's ready—should be ready by now. Get in it and take off. I want maximum distance between you and this ship when we Jump. I don't want you smeared all over the cosmos. Get moving."

"But—but—" A sense of time-run-out seized her. She could not remember why. She tried to pick out sensible questions from the mass of them that assailed her. "What about communications? I've never flown one of those shuttles—how can— When are you coming back for me? You're coming back, aren't you?"

"Of course we're coming back!" Everything she said irritated him. His anger had lost none of its edge. He said with plain restraint, "I don't have time for details. Communications has a station assigned to you. You can get all the information you need from them. You shouldn't have any trouble with the shuttle—if you're the hotshot pilot your dossier says you are."

She nodded. She wondered why she had never noticed that Erik's beautiful blue eyes were so small.

"But how long will I be out?" she said.

"I don't know. At least as long as it takes us to calculate the parameters for a second Jump. You wanted to do this, dammit, and now you're doing it, so get started!"

She got up cautiously, mindful of her leaden feet. "I didn't want to do it," she said. "Commissioner Jameson wanted me to do it. Why are you taking off after them? They won't be there either."

"Maybe they will. That'd be the end of your theory, wouldn't it?"

"What's wrong with my theory? A theory," she said lucidly, "is just a theory."

"We were doing fine without your theories," he said.

"I don't understand you," she said helplessly.

"I thought D'neerans were supposed to be the best at understanding everybody. That's what all your damn theories are about."

She looked at him in silence for a minute, her skin prickling. She understood one thing at least, finally and unhappily: that her quiet exclusion from *Endeavor*'s small society had lasted only as long as she made it possible for the others to ignore her, and Erik to enjoy her. Now that she had opened her mouth she might face—if Erik were a bellwether—open hostility.

She said, "Never mind. I don't think I want to understand you."

She was at the door when he said, sounding pleased, "You didn't have any warning this was coming, did you?"

"No." She turned in the open door and leaned against its frame.

"Why not?"

"I don't know. Maybe they didn't try to touch us that way this time. Maybe they did and I didn't recognize it. Maybe I'm wrong about the whole thing."

"Maybe you are," he said.

He wasn't going to say anything else, so she left.

Andrella Murphy's home stood on the opposite side of the river from Polity Administration, to the north and past a curve in the river so that the administration complex was not visible. What Murphy could see, on a summer night, was a basin of light. The river was thick with bridges here, and the computer-controlled ground traffic poured across them like streams of fireflies. Light lay heavy on the gentle slopes beyond the river. Murphy's house sprawled across a hillside, and the brow of the hill cut off a view upriver to the ancient monuments of what had been the seat of a mighty government before the stars changed the world.

Murphy had gone to some expense to make sure metropolitan noise did not reach the house. On her candlelit terrace the only sounds were of summer insects and the occasional night breeze. Outside the candlelight there was darkness, and then the precipice and the endless fall into light.

Most of Murphy's dinner guests had gone home. Her husband had swallowed a sober pill and gone to bed, and only three others were left. Muammed al-Nimeury of Co-op sat in a shadow and talked, ostensibly to Murphy; she rarely answered, however, because he was talking for the benefit of Henriette Guilbert. Henriette posed becomingly and did not answer at all. The story—no doubt true—was that Starr Jameson had warned her to look gorgeous and keep her mouth shut if she expected him to take her out in public. It was a fact (as Murphy had ascertained) that Henriette used intelligence boosters just to perform her duties for Admin's Central Records section. Whatever else she wanted out of life did not, presumably, require much intelligence. Murphy was not inclined to quarrel with her logic. Henriette was here with Jameson, after all, and having a remarkable effect on al-Nimeury. Murphy was willing to make allowances for Muammed. His wife was on Co-op, and Murphy supposed he was lonely.

Jameson had disappeared into the high-security communications module that was part of every commissioner's home. Murphy had not heard the call summoning him there. She was not concerned. If there were a Polity-wide emergency, she and al-Nimeury would have been wanted too. Most likely it had something to do with Heartworld's lively political infighting. But she wished Starr would finish and go home, and take Henriette with him; then Muammed would leave.

But when Jameson came back he dropped into his seat with every appearance of staying for a while. He looked very pleased with himself. Murphy sighed and said, "Well?"

"Henry," Jameson said.

"Yes?" said the woman, looking at him with great brown eyes.

"Go away. Go play with the Kits."

Henriette got up without resentment. An obliging puff of wind pressed her gauzy gown to her body, and al-Nimeury grunted in appreciation.

"Where are they?" she said.

"Locked in the garden, I believe. I hope."

"All right," Henriette said. "But aren't they asleep?"

"They're nocturnal. They haven't bred all the original Cat out of them yet."

"They're working on it," Murphy murmured.

"Abominations," Jameson said in disgust. He watched Henriette cast about and set off more or less in the right direction. When she was out of earshot he said, "*Endeavor*'s finally got a Beta."

al-Nimeury made a rumbling noise in the shadows. Murphy said, "What does it say?"

"Same thing as before, except for the locus description. That's different. It'll pull them off in a new direction. The question, of course, is what to do."

"What do you mean?" Murphy frowned at him. "Shouldn't they just go there?"

"Should they?"

"Are you asking for advice?"

al-Nimeury said, "Want mine?"

Jameson looked thoughtfully toward the shadows and said, "I don't know."

"Drop it," al-Nimeury advised.

Murphy giggled. Jameson said equably, "The *Endeavor* Project is a reality, Muammed."

"Worse luck," al-Nimeury said. "It's not too late to stop it, though."

"It is," Jameson said. "The question is not whether or not to turn back, but how best to proceed."

He was looking at Murphy again. She said, "Well, then, of course you want to go where they want you to go. To do anything else would be to turn your back on them and fly away."

"Unless," Jameson said, "they're playing a game whose results accrue to their benefit, giving us nothing in return. Shall we go on playing it, Andrella?"

"Not at midnight," Murphy said.

Jameson ignored the hint. He said, "If there should be no one at the new location, we'll have to rethink our response."

Murphy smiled. "You'd already decided to send them on," she said.

"This time . . . There is a new sensor in operation."

Murphy knew Jameson well enough to pick up the faint irony in his voice. She said resignedly, "Tell me about it."

"The telepath," he said. "The D'neeran child. She barged into the strategy meeting today. Fleming was wild. The *Endeavor* is leaving her behind, Andrella, behind and all alone. We might have an advantage in the game that Species X does not suspect. She seems to believe she has sensed something frightening about them. I don't know how much credence to give it. She said perhaps she can come up with more, if she is alone."

"You sound," Murphy said, "as if you're putting her out to be a sort of gauge of what there might be to fear."

"She could be making it all up, of course," he said calmly.

"Probably," al-Nimeury said. He got up and came into the dim light, a square and solid man compacted of darkness. "You know what I think about the whole damn thing," he said to Jameson.

"Yes," Jameson said. "It's new, so it's inadvisable."

"You don't know what the hell's out there. You've got two hundred human beings out there with their throats wide open to anything that wants to cut 'em. I liked Katherine's proposal better, but no, you had to have it go out unarmed. Bring 'em home, Starr. Before it's too late."

Jameson said, " 'Here be dragons.' "

"What?"

"Look at the old Earthly seafaring maps, Muammed. That's what they used to write in the blank spaces."

"As I recall," Murphy said, "there were some dragons."

"Starr?" Henriette said from the edge of the terrace. She cradled a tank-nurtured Kit in her arms. It was soft and round and playful and innocent, and it would never mature sexually or grow into a cat. It purred loudly. Henriette said, "Can I have some of these?"

"I'll get you as many as you want," Jameson said, "provided you promise never, never, never to bring one to my house. It's time to go, Henry."

"Past time," Murphy said.

But at the last minute she held Jameson back with a hand on his arm. His head was silhouetted against stars; she could barely see his face. "Is there really a danger?" she asked.

"You know the theory," he said. "Interstellar travel implies a level of technological achievement that makes it cheaper to manufacture wealth than to seek it through aggression. Likewise it implies a structure of rationality transcending aggression for ideological motives. Certainly F'thal has fit the theory perfectly."

"Then does it matter what the D'neeran girl thinks?"

He shrugged. "What do you think of Henriette?" he said.

"She's lovely. But—my dear Starr, what do you talk to her about?"

"Who talks? Now if you and I. . . ."

He did not finish the sentence but smiled at her, teasing. They had been friends for years.

"You know I wouldn't have you. Good night," she said.

She watched him leave with Henriette and went to bed, scooping up a comforting and undemanding Kit on the way.

The first thing Hanna discovered was not about aliens but about herself.

She missed *Endeavor*'s crew.

She was thousands of kilometers from the ship when it Jumped, and psychologically so separated from it that its vastly greater distance from her after the transit was of little importance. That was not a matter, as Jameson had put it, of proximity; it happened because she had begun detaching herself as soon as *Endeavor* released the shuttle she piloted. She had gone about *Endeavor* with a kind of low-grade awareness operating at all times, as naturally as sight and hearing, because that was the way she lived. But it could be shut off, as it was now. She would not use it again in any degree until she sought a specific entity.

The *Endeavor* made its Jump at oh-three-hundred Standard hours, which Hanna thought of vaguely as pre-dawn. By that time she had mastered the shuttle. It was a simple-minded machine, designed to ferry cargo or, as a lifeboat, provide life support and nothing more for twenty to fifty people for only a few days. It was bare of luxuries. It offered no entertainment. Its only sophisticated features were the anti-gravity plant which let it make planetary landings and provided Earth-normal gravity, and its Inspace communications facility.

Hanna found that Ludo Brown was assigned to monitor her. Just before the Jump she said, "Don't let the captain forget to set up relays if you go too far away."

Brown laughed at her. "He won't forget. If he does, Tamara won't."

"Are you going to come back here before the second Jump?"

"We don't know yet. It doesn't matter, does it? It wouldn't take long to get back."

Hanna knew a course could be retraced very quickly in deep space. *Endeavor,* having taken four months to come this far, could get home in a few days. Anyone from human space could reach them, now, as quickly—if there was anything worth coming out here for. But her new and unaccustomed isolation weighed on her heavily.

Brown checked with her again after the Jump, and then left her alone for an hour.

Without his voice there was no sound except the whisper of the shuttle's systems. There was nothing to look at but its no-nonsense gray fittings. The standardized color-coding of its displays shone without change when the lump of matter and energy that was *Endeavor* had vanished from its sensors.

Hanna sat in the pilot's module and looked about her nervously. There was no point in wasting time—indeed, the less she was out here the better she would like it.

She consulted the shuttle's handbook and discovered that she could not order it to turn off its lights; she had to douse them manually. She did so, and then had to turn them back on to find the switch for dimming the displays. She turned the lights off again.

She sat in the dark and looked at the stars and tried to relax.

She had been alone in deep space before. She had piloted a small freighter, by herself, all the way to Willow— partly because she wanted to see Willow and that was a cheap way to get there, and partly for the experience. The experience had been sheer joy. She had broken no new paths, but the currents of the space-time sea were deceptive, and navigating them had given her pleasure and excitement. Each Jump brought a new view of the universe. The solitude had been not fearful but wonderful. It made her think of her ancestors in humankind's dim morning, piloting organic cockleshells from continent to continent of the mother world in the days before it was mapped, navigating—as she did—by the stars. At times on that voyage she had felt her kinship with them so strongly that her individuality, her self, ceased to matter, and in her divided mind she saw herself only as human and undifferentiated from the species.

It was not a way of self-regarding that D'neera would ever foster. Her efforts to share it had been met with acceptance—but not understanding; and she had ceased to think of it. But she had not forgotten it.

Now she felt no pleasure. She was no far-flung outrider of a species of indomitable explorers, but a single scared being who wished only to retreat to the safety of the herd— for all that it was a herd of just such outriders.

She settled herself as comfortably as she could, and tried to clear her mind as Ling had taught her. This was the first step toward the *satya* trance of the Adept, wherein body and emotion alike disappeared and the universe took on new guises. But Hanna had not taken that path past its start.

Finally, tentatively, she let herself begin to drift through the field of consciousness that somehow was both inside and outside herself. It was closer kin to Inspace than realspace, its matrix less matter than life. Its essence was unknowable, and only its broadest contours had been sketched; but it was a medium real as air to Hanna and her kind, who used it without fear. Here in peace and solitude she might have touched Tam or Erik or even Iledra without effort, though they were caught in the flux and flow of other concerns and would not know her.

Hanna set the familiar aside, and quested for a shadow and an eye.

There was nothing. Nothing. Nothing.

A sound called her—real sound, made for the ears: Brown's voice.

"Mmff?" she said, emerging from shadow.

"*Endeavor* to Shuttle Five—"

"I'm here. Here," she said, forgetting the proper formula as she broke into the world of speech.

"How you doing?"

"All right. What time is it?"

"Oh-four-thirty. Why?"

"Nothing. That's all right."

She had turned out the lights an hour ago. She had not been asleep, only altogether focused on the ancient sense D'neera had brought to new flower. And telepathy, unconstrained by space, played tricks with time also.

"Anything to report?"

"Nothing."

"All right. I'm signing off for another hour."

"Ludo?"

"Yes?"

"If I don't answer right away, yell at me. I'm concentrating."

"Right."

Silence again.

She was reluctant to let herself go.

Why? It was utterly peaceful. She had sensed no threat. The shuttle's sensors showed nothing, absolutely nothing, near her.

She composed herself to try again. She was irritated with herself, and very tired. Perhaps she had been asleep after all; if she had not been, she would certainly fall asleep this time. But in the interval before sleep she would explore again, delicately, for the thing that might be nothing but the shadow of her own death-fear; and if that were all it had ever been, she would again find nothing.

There was nothing to report at five-thirty, at six-thirty, at seven-thirty.

"I have to get some sleep," she said then to Brown, meaning unbroken sleep.

It got her an interview with an exasperated Erik.

"You can't sleep," he said. "We'll be ready for another Jump by midday."

"How far away are they this time, anyway?" It had not occurred to her to ask before.

"No more than two or three light-weeks away. In clear open space. We can get there in a couple of days."

If, Hanna thought to herself, you drive Navigation like animals. And take unacceptable risks.

"I have to sleep, Erik. I was on boosters for days."

"Aren't you still?"

"I stopped them yesterday. I don't want to take them any more."

He started to swear at her, and stopped himself. The conversation was being recorded.

He said, "If you can't stay awake we might as well call it off. You're not getting anywhere."

There was no video transmission, but she imagined the look of satisfaction on his face. Her desire to rejoin *Endeavor* diminished.

"You could make the second Jump," she said. "How long would you have to be in place before the third?"

"The first approximation is five to seven hours. We're doing only essential observations. Are you suggesting that you stay where you are until then?"

"Why not?"

"We could use you in Navigation. And, uh, I know it must be very restful for you out there, but it's no light matter to maroon a crewman in unknown space."

Hanna smiled for the first time in days. It had not occurred to her to use the experiment to escape the rigors of Navigation. But now that Erik had brought it up, it sounded like a good idea.

"You want to give it enough time, don't you?" she said.

He was silent. He was imagining, she thought, what he would say if Jameson or Thermstrom suggested he had not been sufficiently conscientious.

"All right," he said finally. "But we're collecting you before the third Jump."

Hanna still was smiling when she went to sleep. It was very peaceful out here. There was more tranquility than she had known on *Endeavor* for a long time. Her fears were dissolving in it, and for a bonus she was getting, for a moment, a childish and satisfactory revenge.

She slept, and did not dream.

The change came even before the *Endeavor* made its second transit, but she did not recognize it at once.

She woke with so strong a sense of being watched that

before she was fully awake she was looking over her shoulder into darkness.

There can't be anybody there, she thought, but her fingers seeking the light controls trembled with a purely primeval fear of what lurked in the dark.

The lights came on and there was nothing. Gray metal stared back at her, unmoving.

She was ashamed of herself. But she left her seat and looked into the shuttle's bare compartments. She thought of getting into a spacesuit and checking the cargo bay meter by meter, or pressurizing it so it would be accessible to her as long as she was out here.

"There are limits," she said to herself out loud. Nonetheless she examined the bay with video monitors. And then, cursing herself, the exterior of the shuttle. She was, of course, alone.

The exploration had showed her where survival rations were stored. She gnawed a whole-meal pellet, and then another, with the lights on full. She wondered just what the side effects of quitting booster dope were, and whether she ought to be taking something to compensate for them.

Ludo Brown's voice said loudly, "You awake?"

"I'm awake," she said, swallowing crumbs.

"We're about to Jump again."

"What time is it?"

"Fourteen hundred hours. Don't you have a chronometer?"

"I guess so. Somewhere. Why are you still on duty?"

"We all are, dear. Anything happening with you?"

She was not going to say: Yes, I've got scared of the dark. "Nothing."

"You're more fortunate than the rest of us. It's a little trickier out here than we thought. Captain says to tell you you've got maybe twelve more hours. He says don't sleep anymore."

"Damn right I won't."

"What was that?"

"Never mind."

She was busy with Brown for a little while after the Jump, making sure her communication with *Endeavor* remained intact. Then the silence closed in again.

She was overfull, cramped, and restless. She prowled the

stark control module. The sense of not-aloneness still was with her. If it represented an alien touch, surely she would have dreamed; this must be a product of something else, most likely the treacherous stimdope. There was no point in seeking further for aliens, because there were no aliens there. And she did not want to find them anyway.

But what if they were there?

She dropped into the pilot's seat and stared uncertainly at the oblong patch of space the port showed her. She had an unaccustomed sense of duty shirked.

She could hear herself say to Iledra: I was frightened, and so I stopped trying.

She pictured Iledra explaining that to Jameson, without whom she would not have been on the *Endeavor*. Without whom, for that matter—

Whose decision had it been to set aside official policy and tell D'neera's magistrates where to find the Nestorian attackers? Who had ordered the Interworld Fleet to stand by?

The same man, possibly, who had given her this precious chance; probably against all advice.

"I've got to do it," she said, and made a face at no one.

She turned out the lights again, and closed her eyes.

The aftermath of stimdope vibrated in her veins, but now she was watchful and alert. This time there was no possibility of sleep. She thought of seeking the shadow again, and on an impulse rejected the idea and concentrated instead on her own wariness. If she was really being watched, there must be a watcher.

Slowly, slowly, silence deepened. Here was the kernel of her watchfulness. She closed round it coldly. And here was a thread which she followed out, out, timelessly into a deeper void.

Into the silence fell a single whisper:

Wait. Wait for Us . . .

Her concentration broke. She straightened, stiff and gasping. She was halfway across the module before she knew she was running away.

She turned and came back as fast, fumbled for the key that would call *Endeavor*, and stopped just before she touched it.

What the hell was she going to tell them, anyway? That

her palms were damp, her heart thudding—and that was all? That she had tasted strangeness, and learned nothing?

She wiped her hands on her coveralls and sat down again. Blindly, urgently, because she had to do it, she tried to recapture her sense of the touch.

Its shape was too foreign to remember.

It fit nothing in her experience; she had not assimilated it; but it had left a trace.

She found herself hunched over as if in pain. Yet no part of her hurt.

The stars were mist against the black of in-between. She remembered nothing of the touch except a pattern of darkness and light. She closed her eyes to see it better and it coalesced into a picture: dark islands that rose from eternal waters.

She was sure of it, and sure also that it had no referent in water and earth. It did not mean the beings were island-dwellers. It had to do with time; time and waiting.

It was not enough. Not nearly enough.

She had to do it right from the beginning.

She composed herself to try again. The air was chilly against her wet skin. She did not want to close her eyes and shut out the starlight. She did it anyway, and was immobilized. She thought in circles round the act of will she had to perform, and could not undertake it.

Yet after a long time—when her breathing had eased and the sweat dried on her skin and her heartbeat dropped to a normal pace—something she almost recognized stirred within her.

It was not curiosity, nor duty. It was darker than either, seductive, unknown. Half in trance she reached for it, and flinched away.

She could not examine it closely. But she let it draw her imperceptibly outward.

There were no whispers. There was only, for eternity, the dark.

A spark of light appeared. It was born of a single photon, and expanded.

It was an eye: the eye of a dream.

Her body vanished. She hung before the eye in a place without form. It *knew* her: personally, individually, malignantly.

She could escape to her body, to the shuttle, to *Endeavor*. With all her will she forced herself to stay an instant, and reflected in the eye she saw: serene hearthfires burning trapped living flesh, a glittering detection device become a flying forked spear, the mad wriggle of a severed serpent which was herself, lost barren unlighted worlds tumbling anchorless, the watery lunge of a streamlined shape with a thousand teeth—

Straight at her.

She was pawing at the communications key, limp and choking in the dark. She never knew what she said to Ludo Brown, nor how long it took them to come for her. Later she remembered that she had not taken her eyes off the mass sensor till blessed *Endeavor* appeared; and that they did not believe her when she said it had changed once before.

Chapter 5

"**T**ake a look at that," Erik said. He pushed a display module at Hanna.

Hanna looked. The central data column, stripped of accessory notations, showed average mass readings over a period of some hours. There was a bulge toward the end of it.

"Is that from the shuttle?" she asked.

"Uh-huh."

The bulge had to be *Endeavor*. She lifted her hands helplessly and said, "So I dreamed it."

He came around the table and stood behind her. He reached over her shoulder and made an adjustment, and the figures flickered and changed.

"This is the last ten minutes," he said.

Now there were two bulges, the first much smaller than the second.

Hanna shivered suddenly. "So there was somebody there."

"There was. And you missed a chance of contact by yelling for help."

He was profoundly disgusted. Hanna opened her mouth to answer, and shut it again. There was nothing she could say. It was possible that he was right.

Erik turned away and went back to his place. The table in Briefing Room Two was littered with coffee mugs and reference printouts. Everyone who had anything to do with direct contact procedures had been in here in the last few hours, questioning Hanna. She had not been able to satisfy any of them.

Hanna said suddenly, "When did you get this breakdown?"

Erik shrugged. "A long time ago. Half an hour after you came on board, maybe."

"You let me go on thinking I must have imagined that reading?"

"What difference did it make?"

"It makes a lot of difference to me! I wondered if, if I couldn't trust my own eyes, what else could I trust?"

"Not much," he said. "You didn't get one goddam useful fact. Just a bunch of space-happy hallucinations. They were coming to talk to you and you panicked."

"You don't know they were coming to talk to me. They disappeared—" She looked at the mass readings again, to be sure. "They disappeared before you came into realspace. There," she said, pointing.

"I'm going by what you said yourself. You thought they were coming to you."

"Yes," she said, remembering the lunge of the hungry fish-thing and her mad obsession with the sensors until *Endeavor* came.

"That's the only thing you said that made any sense."

He stared past her. His mouth was set, but he was no longer particularly angry. Hanna had felt his anger die through the hours of debriefing, and it was a relief to her, although she knew the reason. Erik was convinced that he had won whatever battle he thought he was fighting. He thought her too incompetent to threaten his version of the way things ought to be. She had proven herself a failure, and proven him right. Nothing about her could engage his emotions very strongly now.

That was not true of Marte Koster, who had gotten more furious as time went on. Hanna said, "Did you tell Marte about this?"

"Sure."

"No wonder she was so mad."

Erik said indifferently, "You might as well get some rest."

After a minute Hanna got up. Her muscles ached. She was in fact very tired. She also felt, in some way she could not define, injured.

She said, "What are you going to do now?"

"I'm not sure yet. Plant an unmanned beacon and go on to the new locality, probably. Depends on what they say Earthside."

Hanna looked down at her hands. "I could go out again," she said.

"No. Nobody's going to try that again. Don't ask me why. Not my decision."

She felt a surge of relief—and on its heels, taking her by surprise, disappointment.

She started to leave without saying anything, and then turned back and said, "When do you want me back in Navigation?"

"You won't have to worry about Navigation anymore."

She said uncertainly, "What does that mean?"

"You're going home. Very quietly. Just as soon as I can get transport out here for you."

"But—but what about my research?"

He finally looked at her. He said, "You're wasting your time anyway. Who's going to take you seriously after the junk you came up with out there?"

"It wasn't junk! I don't know what it meant, but it was meaningful!"

"There's enough computer power working on it to run half the Fleet. If it meant anything we'll find out. Go to bed."

"Whose decision was it to get rid of me? I want to talk to him."

"It's mine. Don't waste your time talking. Get out of here. That's an order."

She got out.

Jameson did not speak of Hanna's adventure to anyone outside the *Endeavor* Project until the day after it happened, the last thing he wanted being to suggest that he was alarmed. He had been in his office in the early dawn, staring at the analysis of the girl's report while the mists rose off the gray river and the red sun, despite the early hour, promised a day of sweltering heat. The commissioners of the Polity met each morning, and he did not mention the *Endeavor* at all until the end of the meeting. He showed the analysis to his colleagues and was pleased when they looked at the masses of question marks, logical branchings and variant interpretations, and shook their heads—all except Katherine Petrov. Petrov was a very old woman, so old that A.S. no longer could give her the appearance of youth; but she was a very alert old woman. She looked around with bright eyes and said that the whole scenario was terrifying.

"Not really, Kate," Jameson said.

"How can you say that! Spears and cut-up snakes and burnt sacrifices! Do you know what it reminds me of? An evil myth system, the old planting sacrifices—I don't suppose this girl's a virgin, is she?"

Peter Struzik spluttered. Struzik represented Earth along with Petrov, under the old rules that gave the mother world two seats on the commission; but he was its president and did not vote, and could afford to find humor in situations that drove the others to frenzy. Petrov looked at him suspiciously and said, "What's funny now?"

"She's D'neeran," Struzik said. "Know the D'neeran definition of a virgin?" He leaned forward, grinning. "A kid too young to know which sex it is. Then it decides it doesn't matter anyway and goes after anything that moves."

Petrov snorted, but only to hide a snicker. Jameson disregarded the exchange and said, "That's just what I mean, Kate. You looked at this data and immediately patterned it in human terms. Lady Hanna is human too. The familiar elements you see are part of her background as well as yours. She did her own patterning here."

"Perhaps," Andrella Murphy remarked, "Species X was the origin of the myths."

She smiled pleasantly at Jameson. Murphy when bored was inclined to flights of fancy and outrageous speculation. Jameson wished he were a telepath himself, so that he could object to her in silence that he did not want any such ideas put into the others' heads.

He said, "Am I meant to take that seriously, Andrella?"

"I suppose not," she admitted. "But D'neera was cut off from us for so long—"

"Never completely," Jameson said, and Petrov said, unexpectedly supporting him, "That wouldn't matter. The continuity of human culture is so strong, a few hundred years wouldn't matter. Not even a few thousand when you're talking about archetypes. The images that come down from before the dawn don't die. They're so embedded in all our cultures, they're nearly inborn."

Murphy looked rather sadly at the analysis and said, "So what looks like the source of a primal image . . ."

"Is only another image," Jameson said. "This is no literal rendering of the content of an alien mind. You're looking at Lady Hanna's creation."

"I wouldn't like to meet her on a dark night, then."

"Oh," Jameson said, "I don't suppose she's as bad as all that. It's not surprising the images she formed are frightening. She told me only hours before the contact that the quality of alienness, so to speak, frightens her. I think she would agree that she inevitably transformed the beings' thoughts in the act of perceiving them. It's impossible to disentangle a purely alien element from this combination."

al-Nimeury said, "What good is it, then?"

Jameson said regretfully, "Not much, I'm afraid. Not immediately. But it was communication, of a sort. It was governed by natural laws. After a few more such instances, perhaps we will begin to understand what those laws are, and form a theory that will make telepaths a useful addition to *Endeavor* in the future."

They were all beginning to look bored now. Struzik muttered, "This would make a pretty mess if the public got hold of it."

"Irrelevant, as long as Alpha and Beta remain secret."

al-Nimeury said suddenly, "I want to bring that up again. You came out to Co-op and talked the assemblymen into going along with this and nobody knows what's going on. Co-op's paying its share and they've got a right to know what happens—"

They all began talking at once, except for Murphy, who watched Jameson closely. Arthur Feng was not in the room but on Colony One. His head and shoulders seemed to hang in the air at the foot of the table; there was something wrong at his end, and through the apparition the wall of the room was visible. Jameson saw with satisfaction that something was wrong with the sound now too, and though the wraith's lips moved, nothing it said was audible.

Jameson let the others talk themselves into keeping the matter under seal. They subsided at last, more or less in agreement. Struzik said, "What if Beta comes to nothing and this is all the contact there is, Jamie? What will you do then?"

"I don't know," Jameson said. "Don't call me that, Peter. If Species X misses *Endeavor* again—and I think that may happen—I'll go out there to talk with Fleming and Koster."

Petrov said, "Why in heaven's name go all the way out there?"

"Review the troops, boost morale, that sort of thing."

Struzik said pettishly, "Couldn't you just do it by holo?"

"I'd be back in time for the budget hearings, Peter. Weren't you telling me only last week that personal contact is of utmost importance?"

"Is that new girl of yours going?"

"Maybe," he said with the trace of a smile.

"I thought so. You just want a few days off. I guarantee I'll make your life miserable. I'll call you a dozen times a day."

Jameson submitted to the teasing good-naturedly. He could afford to. He had set out to undercut the impact of Hanna ril-Koroth's report without entirely discounting her value, and succeeded. It was no small accomplishment in this group, and although they were predisposed to pay little attention to a D'neeran, he could not have done it so easily if Petrov had not, by chance, given him a custom-made opening.

At that, he did not think Andrella Murphy believed a word of it; she knew him too well.

Hanna made up her mind to risk smuggling out the data she wanted. She would record everything on a wafer the size of her thumbnail, and swallow it as she left; but so much of it was classified that she thought there was a good chance Erik would anticipate her, and she would be caught.

Therefore she worked frantically to salvage what she could from the wreck her venture on *Endeavor* had become. With no idea how long she would be on the ship, she plunged into its archives and worked with an energy that came not from stimulants but from desperation. She slept in snatches, fully clothed, and forgot to eat except when Tamara brought her food. The synthesis she had envisioned since one luminous moment when she fully understood the Hierarchus was tantalizingly close. An eyes-only report on F'thalian linguistics promised a foundation for describing a theory of separate but contiguous realities, and as she read it her notes on F'thalian thought, side-by-side with the Polity report, fell finally into place. The contradictions between true-human linguistic analysis and her perceptions were illusory; the two were complementary, paired but distinct outlines of the same structure, each lacking salient features. The reasons for omissions that had puzzled the analysts were clear, and so was the reason for F'thal's clear and baffling boredom with human beings. In the giddy swirl of F'thalian perception, interactions were substantial as material objects. Pan-F'thalian did not describe "things," only systems and an infinity of subsystems. F'thal had no word for "aliens" because humans were only a minor division of the great subsystems of life. There was nothing special about beings from other stars.

Hanna did not have to compare her memories of the Hierarchus with her experience on Shuttle Five to know that was not the attitude of Species X, though Tamara—her only contact with the life of *Endeavor* now—told her the aliens were invisible or absent from the second location they had selected. No dreams haunted Hanna. No one came near to ask what really had happened to her out there, and her report seemed to have sunk into silence and left no trace. But she thought of it anyway, the pain and the fear and the strangeness, whenever she lifted her tired eyes from her work or stretched out for a minimal nap; and she came to certain meager conclusions which she did not share with anyone—the persons around her having, it seemed, lost interest in anything she might tell them.

She worried a little about their insistence on ignorance, although in fact there was nothing she could add that would clarify her original impressions. She worried a little also when Tamara told her, some two weeks after the incident that Starr Jameson was expected a few days hence, and that Hanna, presumably, would return to human space when he did. Hanna said acidly that the return trip should be entertaining; but she remembered with discomfort her sense of being in the man's debt. It occurred to her that the last year of her life, viewed from a certain perspective, bore in abstract the imprint of his hand. It was an unpleasant thought, and she kept it at a distance as her concentration centered more and more strongly, to the exclusion of all else, on her work. Undistracted now that she had no other duties, she saw solutions to puzzles that had seemed insoluble. She left the thicket of references and drew more heavily on her own experience of F'thal and Girritt, her own observations of the Primitives. The underlying structure of her thought crystallized and she wrote rapidly and confidently, sure of her ground. No doubt no one would read what she wrote, but it was truth. She was constructing a monument whose existence was testimony to the validity of its thesis, for it was founded on empirical data—but the data did not exist in true-human reality. She felt, when she thought of the grand futility of her effort, the exaltation she had felt when the *Clara* began moving toward its end, and she gave herself over to it. She did not forget Jameson, but the apprehension retreated to one small corner of her mind where she looked at it from time to time in a detached sort of way. In the long run, she thought, it did not matter. In the long run nothing mattered except what she was doing.

No one bothered to tell her when Jameson arrived, or that he wished to see her. The door sounded several times before she heard it through a daze that was half obsession, half exhaustion, and then she thought it was Tam.

"C'mon in," she said automatically, and not until he came to her side did she look up and see who it was.

Unprepared for the apparition, she only stared and said, "Oh."

She had to look up a long way to see his face. She recognized him at once, but familiarity with his image had not prepared her for his height, nor for the really shocking sense that he was in charge here—that he would be in charge wherever he was. Her experience with true-human authority was limited to Erik, and what she sensed in Jameson was not the same thing at all; and it held her silent and round-eyed.

Jameson looked from her face to the passage she was working on. He said without formality or introduction, "I've seen some of what you're doing. Captain Fleming pulled it out of the main data bank. I'd like to see the rest."

Hanna moved finally—to look past him and see what entourage he had brought. The door to her room had shut and no one else was there. Questions chased one another through her head. She opened her mouth to ask them and found herself too tired. It didn't matter. She did not think she could refuse his request even if there were reason to refuse. Weariness and shock made her movements uncertain. She pawed through a litter of printouts for a display module, plugged it into her terminal, and cued it for a current draft. When she turned to hand it to him she caught him eyeing her with something that might have been surprise.

She said, "Yes?"

But he said only, "May I have the chair?"

"Oh. Yes. Of course."

She retreated to her bunk, which was as deep in annotated paper as the rest of the room. She had to move some of it before she could sit down, and under some of the scraps she found the remains of a sandwich. It occurred to her rather belatedly that Jameson probably was not used to such settings.

He spent a long time reading. Hanna set herself to watch him, but in the long unbroken silence she drifted irresistibly toward sleep. So much more work to do and she had to have some of those references, she could not emphatically criticize a structure of theory and double it in a new direction without references, lots of references, footnotes, oh Lord ... Annual Report 2832, The Committee on Alien Relations, Starr Jameson, Commissioner-Heartworld, Chairman. The Coordinating Commission had not had much power five hundred years ago. Now, in theory, three of the five voting members could override the unanimous will of all the populations of the Polity. For a while. Until they were pulled and more amenable replacements appointed. And how did it work anyway? Why did she not know more about history? But on D'neera you could study what you wanted and she had never cared about history or art either, only fighting and aliens. And maybe gardening, sometimes, but the millefleurs got into everything. . . .

Hanna yawned and fell sound asleep.

His voice woke her. It was a very deep voice, and she liked it. The inappropriate thought woke her further and she sat up straight, shaking her head. He was not talking to her. He was speaking to someone on the ship's intercom, asking for coffee and spirits.

He turned to look at her directly and Hanna stiffened, suddenly wide awake and unsure of herself. His eyes were cold, and she felt herself being measured as no one had measured her before, not even Iledra. Jameson was a presence, utterly sure of his power and his right to judge her, and her response to this new thing was blank astonishment.

He said without ceremony, "How did you know this?"

"Know what?" she said stupidly. She was staring at him again. His face was too interesting to be ugly, with strong bones and unexpected hollows. She liked that, too.

He leveled a long forefinger at the wallscreen, which still showed the passage she had been writing when he came in. It said:

"Most observers of Primitive B, citing winged-flight mass limitations as a curb on braincase development, have assumed this rudimentary culture will stagnate until environmental change forces it to evolutionary regression or extinction. However, the acknowledged complexity of B nestbuilding activity, until now wrongly attributed exclusively to instinct, illustrates the prevalence of logical operations in everyday life. For example, the pitch of the nests' woven-branch 'roofs' is determined not only by an explicit projection of expected severity of rainstorms in a given area, but also by individual preference for the fruit of certain vines which flourish best on more nearly vertical surfaces ..."

Hanna gathered her scattered thoughts and said, "I 'heard' them. I was there when the flock I was studying was settling in for a nesting season. 'I think I will make it higher and there will be more to eat.' "

Jameson blinked. "That's rudimentary agriculture." he said.

"I was coming to that."

They regarded each other in silence for a moment. Then he said, "So you were frightened after all."

"What?" She thought she had misheard him.

"You were frightened when you undertook the experiment you yourself suggested. Why?"

"Why?" She shifted uneasily. This was not a question that had occurred to her. She drew up her knees and curled her arms around them protectively. She said, "It was what you said, I suppose. That they were strange."

"Was it? Was that the only reason?"

"Why—I don't know. I don't know. You said that yourself."

"I wasn't there. You were."

It was hard to look away from his cold gaze. Erik had looked at her like this sometimes, and only irritated her. Now a mountain might have been addressing her, compelling her to answer.

She was not used to finding true-humans impressive. Jameson must have thought she was frightened, because he said with a hint of exasperation, "I'm not going to eat you, you know. Just answer my questions as accurately as you can."

"Yes," she said after a minute, but she saw there was no softening in his eyes. She looked at him very steadily, wondering what he was about.

He said, "I'm thoroughly familiar with your report. The imagery was all visual?"

"All. Yes."

"And frightening."

"Yes."

"It was anthropomorphic to an extreme degree. How much of it did you yourself create?"

Hanna had not asked herself that either. She pushed nervously at her hair and said, "I might have—I might have 'created,' as you call it, all of the images. But they were correlates of—of thoughts that weren't mine. That's how it works."

She could not keep away from his eyes very long. They were sometimes gray, sometimes green; she found them disconcerting.

He said, "Are you quite, quite sure of that?"

She was suddenly angry, for no reason. "Yes! Yes, I'm sure! I've had enough experience with F'thalians, with Girrians, to know that, that when something like that comes up it's a symbol for something that's really there!"

"And of what precisely are they symbols?"

She said unwillingly, "I pinned some of them down, as far as you can pin something like that down. They were impressions of—of a whole long stretch of time, and patience. And hunting."

"The spear?" he said quickly.

"Yes. But not hunting *with* it. It changed from something else, you know. It wasn't a real spear. It was all symbols I saw. It was—you read that I saw a snake?"

"I read that it was a living portion of a snake, and that you identified it with yourself."

"Yes. Well. It's not that they thought I was a snake, you

see. It was a perception of me as ... incomplete. Alive but divided."

"You did not say that in your report."

"I didn't understand it until later. That's all. Hunting and patience and that image of me. I haven't been able to think of anything else."

"I see," he said.

He leaned back in the chair and she jumped, the movement taking her by surprise. He looked past her, frowning a little. She felt herself, for the moment, dismissed.

It struck her that of all the strange events of her life, strange as any was to have this man sitting in her tiny cabin, discussing a first contact in her terms.

Her terms. It came to her forcibly that she was being taken seriously after all: somewhere. You could not be taken much more seriously than this. But somebody had not wanted her to know it; somebody had not even wanted Erik to know it.

Jameson said presently, still looking at something else, "You still think they are telepaths."

"Yes. Oh, yes."

"You must have been as strange to them as they were to you. Might that account for the rather ominous nature of the images?"

"I suppose it might — no. Wait."

She bowed her head and stared at the floor. Textured matting. Jameson's elegant boot. She did not want to remember. She shut her eyes and called to memory the fabric of an instant, warp and woof, presence and absence interwoven. Surely the aliens had felt her surprise and apprehension; but she had felt no such thing from them.

More. More. The absence of surprise had been so complete as to be a tangible thing; but so embedded was it in the shape of the gestalt that she had not even identified it, until now, as an entity.

"They knew me," she said softly. "Like F'thalians who've met us before. They knew me for a human being."

Jameson said flatly, "That's impossible," but Hanna was caught in recollection. She drifted among images, examining them one by one and all at once for a connection that was not a connection.

"Lost," she said dreamily. "Lost and divided. Lost planets, that was it. Lost worlds, found again —"

Jameson said very sharply, "What was that?"

"Hmm?" She looked up, open and unguarded and pleased with herself. But Jameson leaned forward intently. Hanna's pleasure passed into alarm.

Jameson said urgently, "Are you certain of that?"

"Yes. Yes! Divided—lost worlds—lost worlds? Where have I heard that before?"

She put her hands to her head, which had begun to ache.

"Legend," he said. He looked at her with open curiosity.

She could not keep up with him. She said, "What legend?"

"The legend of the Lost Worlds, from the time of the Explosion. You know the history of the Explosion?"

"I only know the name, and that it was the, the great period of colonization."

"Umm-hmm." His eyes were still on her, but he was seeing something else again, something far away and long ago.

"It began seven hundred years ago," he said, and she tilted her head, caught in the deep quiet voice. "No one knows how many hundreds of millions of human beings left the Earth and its moon in the space of some three hundred years, nor how many vessels carried them. The ships that went officially to Colony One are accounted for; but there were many that were not official, and some that were desperate, and surely many did not reach their destination. The East threw its poor and dissenting away in the wastes of Co-op, till Co-op broke free. Its records never were good . . . The private ventures were uncounted, ship after ship of men and women seeking better lives, freedom, riches, the fulfillment of dreams admirable or reprehensible. . . . It was the greatest fleet the human race has seen, and its full extent was never known. Some ships are known to have disappeared. How many others vanished? Often colonists were stripped of their goods and marooned—or simply killed. Some were found later, or their bones. Many were not . . . You should know this. Everyone should know it."

Hanna found herself breathless. For a moment she had stood high above a tapestry of history, watching the sweep and scope of it. She wrenched herself into the present, shocked and resentful of the power that could so easily impose its vision. And she did not like being told what she should know.

She said, struggling for objectivity, "It's only a possibility.

Though when you put it together with the—the quality of
the images—"

She stopped short, not liking the implications. Jameson's
face gave nothing away, but she knew he was thinking precisely the same thing.

In the sudden silence the door chattered at them. Hanna
went to it, unthinking. She could not focus on the meaning
of prior knowledge and the hunt. Her head was full of what
she did know of the Explosion: Constanza Bassanio shaven-
headed, pregnant and scarred, ransomed from death in a
Lunar stockade just before the last ship left for the green
promise of D'neera under Clara Mendoza's command.
"Dreams admirable or reprehensible"... the outcasts'
dream had only been to stay alive...

A serving robot drifted through the door and wavered
without orders to a landing at Jameson's feet. After a minute Hanna, compelled by courtesy, settled herself cross-
legged beside it. She said reluctantly, "Coffee?"

"The coffee's for you." He leaned over and picked up a
decanter and looked at the contents with distaste.

She thought of Heartworld and ancient wealth. She said,
"I guess they couldn't find any Arrenswood whiskey."

"I certainly hope not. Not paid for with public funds. I'll
have coffee after all, I think."

She went silently through the ritual of serving, obscurely
astonished at the scene. Was Jameson thinking of Species
X? His face told her nothing. She made no effort to probe
his thoughts or feelings—he might, she thought, recognize
the nearly palpable impact of telepathy for what it was—
but she was wide open for anything that might escape him.
Some true-humans, like Koster, were full-time explosions of
emotion, natural broadcasters who made the air around
them crackle.

But Jameson was as self-contained as any true-human
she had ever met. There were not even any physical cues to
help her guess what he was thinking. He did not fidget, he
did not engage in nervous mannerisms, and every movement was precisely controlled.

Hanna, to her surprise, began to relax. His stillness was
comforting, after the noisy activity of her own thoughts and
the tension that accompanied all her days here. Jameson

might have been alone, for all the attention he paid her now. But she could not doubt his intelligence or alertness; and she thought again of outriders and pioneers, and remembered a thing she had known but not examined—that Starr Jameson was the force behind the whole *Endeavor* Project, and the vessel and its crew and their work were the reflection of his will.

He said without prelude, very quietly, "You will not speak of this conversation to anyone. Not even Captain Fleming or Dr. Koster."

She said with casual curiosity, "Why not?"

"Because everything you have said is unsubstantiated."

She was startled. "I thought you believed me!"

"The question of belief does not arise." He looked at her with, she thought, a trace of something new in the sea-colored eyes. Speculation?

She shook her head. He said, "Is it so difficult to promise silence?"

"Yes," she said. "As a matter of fact, yes. You can't keep secrets very long on D'neera even if you want to. People guess. Bits of data creep into overt content. The harder you try to keep a secret the quicker you give it away. I can't help it. You seem to know more about telepathy than most people. I thought you would know that."

"I do," he said. "That is why you are not going home."

"I'm not?" Hanna said, and was unprepared for the wave of desolation that poured over her. She must have projected some of it because Jameson made a sharp, half-protesting gesture. Hanna scarcely noticed, absorbed in the surprising knowledge that for all her anxiety to finish her work, deep inside she had heard, all along, a glad song: "Home . . . soon!" In the maze of Standard dating she had not lost sight of her native seasons. First snowfall was due in Koroth. The D'neeran year was longer than Earth's, and the seasons of Koroth were long and distinct. Soon fantasies of ice would rise in the city: palaces, statues, crystal vegetation, slides and labyrinths elaborated as winter darkened. In sunlight it was a city of flashing mirrors. The fires of Sunreturn . . . she could be home for Sunreturn . . .

Jameson said something and she answered absently, "Yes?"

"I said: Have you thought of entering your work for a Goodhaven award?"

"Hmm?"

He said patiently, "The Goodhaven Academy's annual competition. You are familiar with it?"

"Yes. Of course." She came back reluctantly. "I've read a lot of Academy publications. They do good work, with F'thal at least. Not the kind of work I do."

"Then perhaps it's time you showed them something new."

"Me?" What he had said about the Academy's prestigious award began to sink in. She sat back on her heels and stared at him. She said, "Wait a minute. They wouldn't give it to a D'neeran. Especially not me! I'm saying D'neerans can do exopsychology better than anybody else. And it's true. I've found out things, just by being a telepath, nobody ever found out before. But they won't want to hear that, Commissioner!"

He said inexorably, "You are creating a completely original work of great potential value. You should be finished with it by the deadline for the next competition. Are you afraid to try?"

If he meant to sting her with insult, it did not work. She was too absorbed in the new idea to become angry. She had never thought of submitting her work to the Academy. The scholarship structure of true-human society was so far outside her frame of reference that she might as well have thought of competing in a F'thalian courtship drama.

But what it could mean to be a member of the Academy! Not for herself alone, but as a means of making it easier for other D'neerans than it had been for her to gain access to data and persons and places—

She felt Jameson watching her very closely. She looked up and opened her mouth to protest that it was impossible. But he said, "I don't dispose of the prize, but I do have friends in the Academy. Your work would have to stand on its own merits; but if there is a question of injustice, I think I can see to it the award is fairly given."

Some seconds passed while she turned his words over, wondering what they meant. She really did not know at once. It was hard to follow him in her weariness. He had said nothing expected or predictable since walking into her room. If he was trying to keep her unbalanced, she was easy prey. She knew little of true-human networks of influence and dimly, trying to understand, she opened herself a little, a little, a very little more, and added it to the slightest intrusiveness, the barest touch of query, just to see what he meant—

She gaped at him.

He had taken from her burst of homesickness a conviction that she wanted to leave the *Endeavor*.

He had offered her a bribe to stay.

He knew instantly what she had done. She saw it in his face in the moment of engagement, and sensed—not anger nor guilt nor apprehension, but an intense curiosity so at odds with the circumstance that she was unbalanced even more.

She got up slowly. She could not think of anything to say, and stared down at him. Light glinted off a scattering of silver in his hair. The gray-green eyes were remote. No curiosity showed in them, nor anything else.

He said, surprising her again, "Aren't you angry?"

"Angry?" She was only bewildered.

"That is supposed to be the appropriate reaction."

"Is it?" She shook her head in confusion. "I only want to know why. Why is it so important that I not talk of this?"

"You needn't be concerned about that," he said.

"But I am," she said stubbornly.

"It is important for you," he said. "Believe me, it is important for you."

A bare hint of threat hung between them. She might have heard it in his voice or sensed it elsewise. She said, thinking it through with great effort, "You mean because I won't get the prize if I break silence?"

"More than that."

It only confused her more. She shook her head again and said, "I don't know what you mean."

He folded his hands in his lap, an unexpectedly prim gesture. He said, "You're in an extremely ambivalent position, you know."

She looked at him helplessly. She did not have the slightest idea what he was talking about.

"You stand at a branching of the way for D'neera," he said, calmly as if he were commenting on the weather. "On the one hand this work of yours—what do you call it, by the way?"

"Uh—'Sentience,'" she said, startled into speech.

His face showed, for the first time, a flicker of amusement.

"A little arrogant, don't you think? Never mind. It is brilliant. It is a foundation, certainly, for arguments in favor of a position I have held for some time—not a popular position: that D'neera is the ideal interface between the human race and alien intelligences. The *Endeavor* is funded for a mission of three Standard years. I don't intend to see the project end in three years' time. It will go on, and on, and on—through our lifetimes and into the future. This vessel will be joined by sister ships. Within our lifetimes, if we are fortunate, we will see contact with a thing that logically must exist on some scale—a super-network of star-traveling species. We might then begin to call ourselves citizens of the universe . . . Have you ever thought of the part D'neera might play in such a renaissance? You might be our teachers, our translators, our first and most honored ambassadors. But it must begin now, my lady."

He paused, waiting perhaps for her to speak, but she could not utter a word.

He went on, "You are the beginning. An experiment; the first. Being first is a great responsibility, my lady. The arguments against your presence on this voyage were difficult to refute, and indeed you have fulfilled many persons' misgivings. I was told that D'neerans are erratic, promiscuous, unreliable and tinged with cowardice; over-emotional, stubborn, flouters of discipline and, of course, ridiculously communicative . . . You cannot babble of Lost Worlds to anyone who will listen."

Hanna bit at her fingers and stared at him as if her eyes alone would pierce his skull. Intangible walls of promise and threat closed on her. There was something he was not saying, and everything he did say obscured it. She had guessed something she was not supposed to know, that her silence was important enough to make him offer her a precious gift unasked, and still he skirted the real "why." Another answer hung round his head like smoke. She listened for echoes of the unspoken.

She said slowly, "If I don't tell anybody about this, you and I will be the only ones who know, won't we?"

His face was empty and detached as a mask. He said, "The Coordinating Commission must know, of course. And key persons in the *Endeavor* Project."

"But," she said, answering echoes, "the project personnel report to you, don't they? So they don't matter. You didn't even mention Alien Relations. They won't know unless you tell them. And the Commission—you can tell them what you think they ought to know. Any way you want to present it. You can shape how they think—"

She stopped, because he stood up. She had forgotten his height and she looked up, up, into eyes cold and dispassionate as the sea. She felt him put away the hope of deceiving her; he might have pushed away a useless object, but he said only, still calmly, "This is why you frighten us, my lady."

"Because you can't have secrets," she said breathlessly. "But you must have known!"

"In theory," he said thoughtfully. "In theory. I must say I was not prepared to test it myself . . . I offer you a straight-forward bargain, then. I am, as Lady Koroth knows, D'neera's only effective champion in true-human circles of power. This is not an easy thing to be, and I must have your cooperation. In this case I must have your silence. Without it—well. It is your world you risk. Not mine."

"But how can it be so important? Why? Why? Tell me that." Her voice was shaky. "Just tell me and—so I can decide! You would really turn against us? You would do that?"

He did not answer. Perhaps he would not do it. But he could; she felt the potential of his power, so intense and repugnant that she backed away from him involuntarily. She might have been running from rape, revolted. And then she knew that she had projected the sickening image, because she felt in the same instant his shocked disclaimer of any physical interest in her whatsoever.

She stood by her cluttered bunk, breathing hard. She had broken through his icy self-possession, anyway; they stared at each other in mutual outrage, and she knew he felt as violated as herself.

"You don't care," she said. "You don't care about D'neera at all! All that about a renaissance and what we can do—it's all for you, the project is all you! What are you doing? What are you using us for? What are you doing to me?"

She thought she heard him say: *After all, this is a terrible thing*—but he had not said it. He was angry enough now, furious with her. For a moment the sense of physical danger was so strong that she dared not disengage awareness out of fear for her very life.

The threat disappeared suddenly and completely. Hanna found herself in fighting stance, balanced and ready to move. She was ridiculous. She could not recover as quickly as he. Her muscles twitched. She thought: I went too far.

He stood before her silent and still. She felt the re-evaluation going on inside him, astonishing her again. She was dizzy. She did not know anyone, D'neeran or true-human, who could move on so rapidly and coldly after what had passed.

Presently he said, "Would any D'neeran have done what you just did?"

"No—" She shook her head. The slight movement rocked her. She was close to her limit from strain and exhaustion.

"No? It's you, then? I might have known . . ."

He pursued a tangential thought.

"What?" she said weakly, trying for the thousandth time to follow him with logic.

"Suicide maneuvers," he said as if she ought to have known. "You do believe in the direct approach, don't you?"

"Do I?" said poor Hanna. Her head thudded unmercifully.

"Umm-hmm . . ." His gaze turned inward. He said very softly, perhaps to himself, "What will you become when youth and luck and brilliance fail you?"

She almost knew what he meant. She did not want to know. She put up her hands and pushed it away. She said, "Just tell me why. Tell me why!"

He came back from wherever he had gone and regarded her, again, dispassionately. He said, "I will tell you this. The future should not be shaped by fear."

She was at such a peak of sensitivity that the tapestry-vision was tangible, obscuring him. Species X was a glowing point of change. Human destiny depended on a choice: advance or retreat.

She said shakily, "If, if they are too frightened of what I have found, they won't, they won't let *Endeavor* go on and there won't be any more *Endeavors*—"

The edges of her vision closed in, and she swayed. He stepped forward quickly and caught her arm. He looked down at her curiously and said, "That's it."

"But—but you could just have told me," she said.

After a minute, to her lasting amazement, he smiled. It was like a light breaking over his face.

"I never thought of that," he said.

Hanna did not hear him. Shadow lay on her sight and *Endeavor* writhed about her, insubstantial, thought not artifact. Dimly she saw it as seed for a new cycle of legend. The day of colonists lost and otherwise was over, having been but the foundation of a greater adventure. She looked at the hand that held her without seeing it, though it was a thing concrete and immovable among the shifting veils of time. Remembered islands soared above an alien sea. She muttered, "I understand now. I understand."

"I think you do. . . . Are you all right?"

"No," Hanna said honestly. She pulled her arm from his grasp and sat down with a thump. The *Endeavor* shivered and solidified. She looked up at Jameson resentfully. Meeting him, she thought, was like running head-on into a whirlwind. If you weren't careful it would take you just where it wanted, and you could not possibly ignore it.

He said, "You can do it, then? You will do it?"

"Stay quiet?" She hesitated. She did not know what she ought to do. Finally she said, cautiously, "For now. Because there's so little to go on. But not if I have—if I have what I think is proof they're hostile to all of us."

"I wouldn't ask that of you. You misunderstand—" Fluency failed him for the first time; she thought in surprise that she had touched him somehow. After a minute he said, "There is no going onward without danger. Not for an individual, and not for the human species. But I have responsibilities."

Hanna wished wearily that he thought plain speaking was one of them. Yet he spoke to her as to an equal.

She said, "You mean that I should trust you?"

He didn't say anything. She did not either. In the course of half an hour they had fallen into a strange and temporary intimacy; but she could not imagine trusting Jameson without direct access to his motives and intent.

He turned away without haste. He was going to leave without another word. She said impulsively, "Commissioner?"

"Hmm?" He looked around, almost smiling; he was very pleased about something.

"Do you trust me?"

"D'neeran sincerity is notorious," he said, amused.

"Well. Yes." Hanna pushed at her unkempt hair, tense and mistrustful. A hundred questions danced in her head. She picked one at random. "What if the aliens come back?"

"Do you think they are out here now?"

"No. No, I don't. But I don't think they're going to stop."

"No. We can't keep dancing to their measure, Lady Hanna."

"Meaning—?"

"The *Endeavor*'s voyage will proceed as originally planned. We will see how far the patience you detect extends."

The islands were momentous peaks; but the sea of time was infinite.

"A long way," she said.

"Then perhaps eventually we will have to do something else. Perhaps you will have to do something else."

"Me—?"

"You. You're a beginning, you know," he said, and was gone.

PART 2

Chapter 6

Hanna did not talk to Jameson again on that voyage, and the force of his presence and vision diminished.

Nothing happened to test her wobbly commitment. The *Endeavor* crept on, marking a trail through infinity, its progress even slower now because it paused before each Jump to announce a new destination.

No answer came. But the communications equipment sang again and again with the bugs now called, routinely, ambers. The working hypothesis was that they were overflow or feedback from Inspace communications between a ship outside sensor range and an unknown base that might be half the galaxy away; but their content was random, garbled, indecipherable.

There was a little space of hope when a series of robot probes were directed toward the star system that had served as a trigger, at least, for contact. The probes found a life-sustaining, pleasant planet, but it showed no sign of the work of hands or anything like them. Even Marte Koster finally gave up her dream of a super-civilization so energy-efficient as to be indetectable. There was no intelligent life here. Probably there never had been.

Hanna, immersed in "Sentience," ceased to think of Species X. It was background to a life settled into peace, even into contentment. She did her tasks in Navigation, and researched, and wrote, and watched "Sentience" grow under her hands. In her crystalline recollection of the aliens she knew, there was no space for those who insisted on remaining unknown. She felt sometimes a guilty relief at their silence. She did not know if her estimate of Jameson's responsibilities matched his own. If it did not, if events forced her to speak against his wish, he would—

She skipped away from the thought when it came, and also from the whisper that to know such a secret about such a man was power. But maybe not; who would believe her?

Endeavor went on its way, trailing a ghost.

She was slightly more respected after her lengthy interview with Jameson; not much more. Her mates regarded her as a sort of organic radio rig whose perceptions had been as valid, and as useless, as those of the ship's Inspace receptors. Hanna might quarrel with the generalization, but she could not correct it without breaking her promise to Jameson, and therefore let it pass. She never again had the conscious sense of an alien presence, and her nightmares did not return. Sometimes she thought on waking that she remembered dark and shapeless impressions, but they never came clear—not in her unassisted efforts to remember, and not with the help of Peng's skill in hypnosis nor even, with Hanna's reluctant consent, his pharmacopoeia, until she felt that she was becoming as saturated with brain-bending chemicals as the day's true-human fashion dictated.

The only result of these experiments was a greater liking between Hanna and Peng, and they became lovers for a while; until Hanna for no good reason grew bored, and drifted away.

She did not forget Jameson's prediction of what D'neera might become, and she finished "Sentience" with a daring and passionate plea that humankind make use of her people's abilities.

"Each sentient species," said the book which every day took on more life of its own, "exists perceptually, socially, and philosophically in a separate and entirely valid reality that in the last analysis is incomprehensible to us—unless we share their very thoughts. In our dealings with F'thal and Girritt and the two Primitive species, we have only made analogs of Outside realities from bits and patches of our own. The models we use therefore are riddled with error and at best incomplete. They have worked, so far. Yet tomorrow or the next day we might meet beings whose comprehension of us, or ours of them, is essential to amity—

or even to our survival, or theirs. Humanity would be wise to cultivate its telepathic cousins, who can reach into another being's heart, comprehend him from the inside, prevent dangerous errors of understanding and judgment, and ensure peace as we go on in search of the unimaginable — the same quest that shaped our ancestors, and has shaped us, and ultimately is the shape of humankind."

When she re-read the final phrases she recognized a voice that was not her own. She excised it from the text, but it was not so easy to get it out of her head.

When the work was done she applied for her release from the *Endeavor* Project, leaving to Iledra the task of submitting the book to true-human channels of distribution, and to the Goodhaven Academy. A flurry of messages passed between them. Iledra's were filled with uncharacteristic doubts; the refrain of Hanna's was an equally uncharacteristic "Be quiet and do as I say."

To Iledra's surprise, obstacles in important places evaporated. Hanna could not be surprised by anything of the sort — not since her discovery of an obscure sub-file during her research on Primitive A. It was entirely administrative and ought not to have been there, but there it was: documentation of her application for the visit, a handful of rejections bearing unknown names, and at the end a voice-recorded order to the functionary who had signed the final permit.

The order said: "Approve it." The speaker was listed by Admin's careful identicode system as SHJ.

Hanna wondered if she had been meant to find it.

Near the end of the Standard year she knew she would soon go home, because the *Endeavor* Project officially asked her for a recommendation for one or more D'neerans to succeed her.

She had few candidates to choose from. The D'neeran community of interest in exopsychology was small, and Hanna knew each member of it. She suggested Anja Daru of Sothred and Charl Zeig of Gnerin, and wrote to the two herself — and was informed by a Project Central missive that her correspondence could not be transmitted.

She understood why when she received yet another official communication; this one from Paul Rodrigues, whom she had heard of vaguely as some kind of confidential assistant to Starr Jameson. The recording showed a dark man impassive as Jameson himself. Rodrigues said, "It is requested that you do not communicate with your colleagues in any way before your departure from the project. Travel arrangements will ensure that you do not meet them aboard ship at the time of exchange. In the interest of maintaining—"

There was a pause. He was reading the last part from a note in his hand, and evidently had not looked at it before.

"In the interest of maintaining some pretense of scientific credibility, it is essential that Ms. Daru and Mr. Zeig should not be predisposed to duplicate your observations. This request is not subject to review."

"Both of them?" Hanna said in surprise to the oblivious Rodrigues. She stuck out her tongue at the image because she did not like Rodrigues's face, and played back the recording to appreciate the single sardonic sentence that had to be pure Jameson.

She complied with the order, however—if only because she could not think of a way to circumvent it.

Hanna left the *Endeavor* in January of ST 2836, having lived aboard the vessel a little more than ten months. Erik was guiltily relieved to see her go, and Tamara was regretful. Otherwise her departure drew little attention; she was only one of the first to leave in a cycle of personnel changes that would turn over a considerable portion of *Endeavor*'s crew in the second year of its voyage.

She came home to Koroth in mid-spring, ravenous for sweet open air and unpredictable winds. She went via a succession of spacecraft from the *Endeavor* to Earth orbit, from Earth orbit to D'neeran orbit, and from D'neeran orbit to Koroth's small spaceport. She walked from its tree-fenced expanse into Iledra's arms. It was morning, the starlight was golden, the very grasses rioted with blossoms, the trees were clouds of color, the windblown fountains were miracles, and her emotion collected a crowd. She came to the House in an aircar, like an invalid or an offworld dignitary, and some hours passed before she was composed enough for Iledra's remorseless debriefing.

All secrets were over now; but the passage of time and the aliens' silence had made them little, as (Hanna now guessed) Jameson had foreseen. The transmutation of human destiny had lost its impact in her thought, and in the bare outline of events that was all Hanna could provide, Iledra saw only opportunity. Bribery and threat at such a distance were harmless and abstract. Iledra was pleased that Jameson had reposed confidence in Hanna, and more pleased when Hanna made her understand the confidence had been forced, not given.

"You learned something of true-human diplomacy," Iledra said.

"Or expediency," Cosma suggested.

"Or corruption," Hanna muttered, thinking of Goodhaven. The three women, dining privately in Cosma's quarters, regarded one another's versions of the truth and found no common ground, though each was so fully aware of the others' perspectives that it was impossible to decide the validity of one over another.

The discordance did not trouble them, accustomed as they were to the imperatives of a telepathic society. D'neera was a collection of anarchistic splinters whose more-or-less cooperative functioning depended always on a breathless balance. The ship of state, as represented by the lords and ladies of D'neera, tended to lurch wildly, though the goals it eventually reached had so far proved satisfactory. The lords and ladies were in fact harassed administrators, charged with maintaining an open oligarchy and subject to removal if they took their anachronistic titles too seriously. Iledra had once referred to her title as "rather tatty," which Hanna thought an accurate assessment. When she remembered her long conversation with Jameson she had an uneasy feeling that he knew just how accurate it was; that his careful formality might have been a reproach or a joke or a calculated effort to keep her off balance; that with no such grand title he was far more powerful on his world and in a larger society than she was anywhere, and called her "my lady" to remind her of the fact.

But when she said so Iledra answered, "Never mind. If he keeps to his promise one of us will at last be recognized for what our special gift can do. And what can his hopes do for us but good? You made a success of the *Endeavor* after all, H'ana."

"Or he made it one for me ... Or made it appear so ..."

Hanna pushed uneasily at her hair. She was thoroughly disoriented. She could not see the season of *Endeavor* in perspective from this leaf-brushed balcony. A night breeze touched her face softly, smelling of flowers. The crystal jars of luminescence that lit their meal could not compete with the stars; when she lifted her head she saw them blazing past the fragrant leaves. Had she really been there in that starry abyss? Yet this commonplace dinner at home was unreal too.

The other women thought tranquilly of transitions and adjustments. Hanna said, "You are missing a point."

"You are," Iledra said, smiling. "But I have not told you about Alien Relations."

"What about them?"

"I did not try to tell you before you came because I did not think the censor would let it pass. A representative of the committee has asked me to study the possibility of D'neera's enhancing and expanding its formal programs of study in exopsychology. I have already approached the university at D'vornan—"

"He would do that," said Hanna, thinking of something else.

"I beg your pardon?"

... our teachers, our translators, our first and most honored ambassadors ...

"Nothing. Go on."

"There are difficulties, of course. The subject generally is not believed to warrant public support for full-time scholars. The Polity has offered some aid, but the university does not wish to accept assistance from true-humans. The first name mentioned was yours, of course—would you like to do that?"

"Me?" Hanna said, startled. "Teach? I don't think so."

"Good. We need you here. In any case, I hope the difficulty can be surmounted by inviting true-human instructors to D'neera, provided the course of study is integrated with the theories of 'Sentience,' and provided students manage field work with their own resources. They will have to make personal sacrifices to do so, but—that has always been our way. You did it."

"Yes," Hanna said, and sipped a delicate, tangy wine of southern Koroth. It was perhaps the wine that made her misgivings so disquieting, or perhaps she had suppressed them too long in the peaceful last months on *Endeavor.* "Sentience" had absorbed her utterly, and custom made the strange ordinary. Perhaps having stone underfoot made the difference now. Some of her reservations had to do with Jameson and the Polity and all it represented; but the rest were rooted in incomprehensible silence.

Cosma heard the echo of silence and said in confusion, "The aliens?"

"The aliens. Don't forget them ... We talk of scholars and studies and, oh, hypothetical beings in some other time and some other place, but there are *these* aliens, the ones I could never see clearly, and they slipped away because—because—I don't know why, and I should—"

Her hand jerked on the tabletop, the Heir's Ring flashing. Iledra and Cosma thought together and disapprovingly that so long a time among true-humans must surely be injurious. But Hanna looked at her own brown hand and thought of more than that, of what she supposed might be called sacrifice, though she had never thought of doing anything besides what had to be done and endured: exile among strangers, the obsession with "Sentience," haunted *Endeavor,* Shuttle Five, the nightmares; before that, war; and before that, a youth divided among this House that had claimed her early, and Defense, and the travel and sunlit studies that had brought her to—this table and this night. It was not so long a time, but so full that for a moment she stood outside herself, and regarded with astonishment what she had become. If she felt more weary than her years should make her, who could blame her?

"I'm glad to be home," she said. "I don't want to leave again, Lee."

"You will change your mind," Iledra said placidly. "There is no need for you to go anywhere just yet. But if your strange creatures who follow the *Endeavor* should call, I think you will not be able to resist."

"I suppose you're right ..." She thought of shadows and strange images. She said, "I should have been able to see them. I should have. I should have."

Patience, said Iledra's thought, but Hanna shook her head and did not answer. Slow-moving rivers and webbed tapestries had their place, no doubt. But she could not quite consign the X beings to a current or a thread, and be sure they would comfortably accept it; not yet.

The New City finally was building, and Hanna went out to it and took up old duties. Spring swelled toward summer. She heard nothing of interest from *Endeavor,* not a word, and one bright morning after a night of rain, without pausing to examine her motives, she called Jameson. He told her readily that the second leg of *Endeavor*'s journey was beginning uneventfully as the first had ended.

It was then mid-morning in eastern Koroth, but early evening in southeastern Namerica. Jameson was at home, and Hanna had no way of knowing how unusual it was for him to take a call such as hers at such an hour. She had not bothered with security, and Jameson talked to her informally, so that behind him she could see a well-furnished dining room showing the remnants of a meal. In the background a tall woman briefly appeared and disappeared; not without taking a good look at Hanna's face.

"If anything happens," Hanna said, "will you let me know? If there's a direct contact I'd like to be involved."

"You might have stayed, you know," he said.

"To what end?" she said, feeling cross. Jameson's face on a video screen did not have the subduing effect of his presence. She would not let him quell her into self-doubt.

"Why, to be on the spot when something happens, of course."

"But maybe nothing is going to happen unless you make it happen. You said something about—" She fumbled, trying to remember. "About not dancing to their tune, or something like that. Well, they're not dancing to yours, either. It seems to be a stalemate. They're still following, aren't they? You'd let me know if there were any change?"

He regarded her thoughtfully. She wondered in exasperation if he ever said anything or did anything spontaneously. Finally he said, "This conversation is not secure. You are no longer officially connected with the Project, and you are residing in a culture where secrecy is unknown. I'm limited in what I can say."

"Then there *has* been a change!"

"Nothing substantive," he said delicately.

Damn true-humans and their secrets. She said, "And how do I go about finding out what this non-substantive development is?"

"You don't," he said calmly. "Not without rejoining the Project. Which I may ask you to do. Your tolerance for the routine drudgery of exploration seems very low, however. When you had finished 'Sentience,' you wanted to leave the *Endeavor* at once."

Hanna decided she definitely did not like Jameson. Her hands, outside his range of vision, balled into fists. She said, "Do you know where I'm talking from?"

"No."

"Wait a minute." She pushed buttons, and panels slid open around her; a flood of noise poured in. She let him listen for a second before she shut it out again.

She said, "This is a construction site. There's a city going up here and I'm supposed to be in charge of it. Besides that I'm helping the university at D'vornan set up a program in alien studies. I've got responsibilities here. I'd rather be doing exopsychology than this, but I'd rather be doing this than creeping through space with nothing to think about but ambers."

"There is a little more to think about than that," he said maddeningly.

"But *what?*"

"We've changed the tune a little. We have had no success. There is a thing we might try . . ." His face became remote, with the trick he had of looking at something that was not there as if he saw it plain. She was on the verge of speaking again when he came back to her and said, "I would rather not try it. If I decide to do so, you will know about it, my lady."

Hanna's hair was full of dust. In the summer heat she wore only the tiniest of briefs and a bandeau to support her breasts, and beside her lay heavy gauntlets she had just taken off. "My lady" had never seemed less appropriate.

She opened her mouth to ask another question, and decided it was futile. Instead she said, "Just keep me informed, will you?"

"I will," Jameson said, and Hanna closed the call with mixed feelings. He had not forgotten the importance of Species X any more than she had, and the knowledge nour-

ished her in this self-absorbed world, where no one but
Hanna cared about such things. But Jameson's restraint in
the quiet elegance of his own milieu reminded her of how
she must appear to him: mud-caked and mostly naked, savage product of a backward world.

"Bastard," she muttered, knowing it sprang from her
own defensiveness; but she said it again for different reasons a little later, when she received his formal, written con-
gratulations on her acquisition of the 2836 Goodhaven
Award for her contribution to humanity's knowledge of
alien species—a message notable chiefly for preceding the
Academy's official notification by some hours.

Hanna had little use for remote supervision, and got mud-
dier as the days went on, and darker from the sun, and more
expert at soothing querulous engineers and sulky architects
and overly fastidious construction crews. The fact that many
of the New City personnel combined all three functions did
not make her task easier. In the old city by the slow Earthly
river, a hard winter began to give way to the thaw; it had
been going on for some time before Starr Jameson noticed
it, felt no pleasure in the prospect, and acknowledged with
a shrug the deeper winter within himself.

He had not forgotten Hanna, whom he thought of rather
grimly from time to time. He could hardly forget a person
who had gone straight through a lifetime's carefully developed skills in defense at their first and only meeting, and
taken a plain look at his heart. No less astounding was the
ease with which she had accepted what she saw there. He
wondered if she knew how rare she was. He did not think
so; but he could not decide if such simplicity was an advantage or a danger for his purposes.

Hanna also was remembered on the *Endeavor,* where
Anja Daru and Charl Zeig wished heartily that she were
there, either with them or instead of them. Something was
happening at last, and Anja and Charl did not like it.

"Locus referents. Finally," said Erik Fleming. He was a
little pale, but showed no other sign of tension.

The man who had replaced Tamara as communications
chief nodded. Translated to a visual display, the content of
Signal Gamma showed a pair of carefully described stars,
Endeavor's relative position and, overlapping it, a point

that pulsed with light. Ito Hirasawa had already ordered
preliminary calculations of a course for the indicated point
while the contact team was assembling.

"All right," Erik said to Hirasawa. "How long?"

"A day, maybe. One minim Jump and backtrack under
conventional power."

"Close. So damn close ..." He shook his head. "I never
thought it would work. Somebody at Central's got a brain.
But why did it work? When nothing else did?"

Marte Koster said, "It seems clear they're not interested
in making contact with this ship. As such."

"They lost interest in the drone, too. After a certain
point. But here's Gamma." Erik looked down the room at
Charl and Anja. They were much less trouble than Hanna
had been. They had formed their own community of two,
but they were polite and cooperative and deferred to
Koster, which Hanna had not done. It said something for
Hanna's impact, however, that they had been invited to this
meeting from the start.

He said, "You two notice anything?"

They looked at each other briefly. Charl said, "I don't
know."

"What do you mean by that?"

They looked at each other again. Charl said, "There was
something. About the time they approached the drone. But
I don't know what it was."

"Describe it," Erik said impatiently.

"I can't. It was just different."

"Different how?"

Outside Erik's perception Charl and Anja shared a conviction that might have translated to: I *knew* it would be this
way!

"I don't have anything to compare it to," Charl said.

"Well, was it friendly? Hostile? What?"

"I don't know. It was just there." He added hastily, seeing
Erik's mouth go tight, "I thought it was very strong. But I
don't know what that means, actually. Strong compared to
what? I don't know."

Erik stared at them hard and said, "Just let me know if
you get anything else."

"All right," they said with relief, but when Erik let the
contact team go they went back to Charl's room almost on

tiptoe, like guilty children, and Anja said, "I think we should ask for permission to talk to H'ana."

"Then he'll want to know why. And we'll have to tell him. He didn't understand what *I* was trying to tell him. What's he going to say if you tell him you had a bad dream?"

They fell from Standard into proximity D'neeran, an intimate shorthand that relied heavily on telepathic exchange as a supplement to the spoken word.

"Well, but H'ana dreamed too, uneasily. I heard him trace her dreaming—"

"But of what? The chance of connection is so vanished-remote—"

"Oh, why isn't there more in the log! Why didn't she speak fully! Might there have been more?"

"Why tamper? This must be new, and of little sense—"

Anja hugged herself for comfort, until Charl hugged her. She said, "Terrifying. That eye!"

"Anja, they can't mean us hurt. What cause have they to pain us? H'ana says aliens are crazy until you join them. If you read a hunting predator it terrifies too, until—"

"That's it," Anja said suddenly.

"What?"

She looked at him with wide eyes. She said, "When I learned loving animals I went to shadowed wilderness in Garfield Province, the Mason Range Preserve, do you know it? Where the long-clawed wicas are, where foresters place them if they wander deadly through the valleys. And I read a wica patient-stalking a sorrowful pollitt foraging for her young. That's what it was like, the dream-eye."

"Like a wica?"

"Yes—no. In a way."

"Show me."

"I can't. It was dream, I can't recapture it, I remember what I felt but it's distant and I can't project."

"Maybe you're right. Maybe we should call H'ana."

"No!" Anja said vigorously, reversing herself. "I won't have Marte Koster laughing-hateful, the way she is when she talks about H'ana so solemnly and respectfully and thinks we don't know it's deceit. What's she got to laugh about anyway? *She* never got a Goodhaven."

They told no one of Anja's dream and did not attempt to call Hanna, and the next day thought it would not matter;

Endeavor got to its destination in double-quick time, but nobody was there.

The formal presentation of the Goodhaven Award was made on a cool evening that smelled of mud and water and the secretive growths of spring. Jameson sat in the small audience, one of the few invited guests attending the ceremony in person rather than by remotes, and congratulated himself.

He had not doubted, from his first reading of "Sentience," that Hanna deserved the award. He had not doubted either that it would take every bit of his influence to procure it for her. Since the announcement of the prize he had made a point of personally complimenting each member of the awards committee on his or her integrity and resistance to popular pressure—and in a few cases refrained from mentioning other forms of pressure which had left the persons in question facing a choice between evils. His conscience, however, was clear. He had no scruples about coercing people to act honorably, nor much inclination to question his own tactics.

Now he studied Hanna as she gave a courteous, diplomatic speech Lady Koroth had written for her. He barely recognized her, which troubled him, and he tried to account for it. She was smaller than he remembered; perhaps that was because her personality, tonight, was muted by good manners. Her voice was different, too, low and a little husky. She was less thin than he recalled, more relaxed, and decidedly unshabby in formal black. Altogether she had little resemblance to the tense, ill-groomed woman he had met on *Endeavor*. She was in fact very pleasant to look at, a dark flower that seemed to rise gracefully from a fanciful backdrop of stars. Jameson was surprised, but he went on looking.

"In closing," Hanna said, and he snapped out of his bemusement. "I would like to say that 'Sentience' owes a great deal to Commissioner Starr Jameson, who gave me his support and encouragement—and, of course, his influence with the Academy."

Jameson felt the ground drop away under him. He was as angry as he had ever been in his life—and then knew no one but he had heard Hanna's last words, if they had been words. She gave him a smile that had a gleam of malice in it, and malice echoed in his head. Hanna remained the only source of his direct experience with telepathy, and he still could have done without it.

"When the final edition appears you'll see that the book—which has had no dedication until now—is dedicated to Commissioner Jameson. My very deepest thanks to all of you."

He stood with the others to applaud, and smiled at Hanna in a way she could not possibly interpret as gracious. He supposed the dedication of "Sentience," no less than that shocking stab in thought, was private revenge for his highhandedness. She would not let him forget the choices he had set before her on *Endeavor,* nor pretend she did not distrust them, and the dedication would be a subtle and permanent reminder of that ambiguous meeting. Her private grievances did not concern him, however. There would be public harmony; he was sure Lady Koroth, who had accompanied Hanna to Earth and stood composedly beside him, would see to that.

"My office," he murmured to Iledra as the applause began to die.

"Very well. As soon as I can detach H'ana."

"Did you have an opportunity before the presentation to speak to her of this meeting?"

"No," said Iledra, "but I will bring her."

He made a detour to the exit to avoid the Goodhaven Academy's ancient president, who was trying to catch his eye. His path gave him a momentary glimpse of Hanna; she was surrounded by a glittering restless crowd, Iledra bore down on her at speed, and Hanna alone was still, the focus of it all, the center of converging forces. An inexplicable surge of pity for her moved him. Her eyes fell on him and he wondered, meeting that cool blue gaze, dark as a summer sky at twilight, what reason there was for pity; he was in the process of making her career, and the future of her world.

When Jameson chose to make it so, his office in the vast Polity Administration complex, like his home, seemed to have been lifted from another century. Nothing was synthetic; the glow of fine wood was everywhere, and the banks of electronic equipment he used could be hidden when he wished. They were hidden tonight, and Hanna, for the moment ignored, stood aside and watched Iledra, a forester's child and an expert woodworker herself, admire the woods of Heartworld.

Her eyes moved to Jameson and lingered there. She had been intensely aware of his presence all evening. Now she watched him lift an exquisitely carved head for Iledra's inspection, and saw with sudden clarity the strength of his hands and the controlled delicacy of his touch. A long-absent warmth possessed her.

So that was it ... She smiled at herself, acknowledging without self-consciousness an element that might have been in play in their meeting months before, though she had not recognized it then. Like him or not, he was a most excellent male animal. Her body spoke earnestly, approving a likely hunter on an ageless, age-old level. She looked at his shoulders and his movements with simple pleasure.

He had watched her tonight too with discomfiting intentness, but not, she thought, with desire. She had felt something else and more disturbing in the instant of feedback when her barb sank into his brain. Behind his surprise and anger, which she expected, and the dreamlike complexities of any intelligent mind, was something she had not recognized. Shadow and strength, she thought, unable to put more precise words to it; some great defeat, and poised against it an inflexible assertion.

Defeat by what? Assertion of what? She shook her head in confusion. Jameson saw the movement and looked at her curiously. He left Iledra to examine his collection of F'thalian artifacts and crossed the room to Hanna.

"You gave a very good speech," he said.

"A very bland speech."

"Precisely."

She shook her head again, smiling now, and looked past him to the edge of the room, which merged unwalled with the moonlit river. She said, "I thought power would be guarded better."

"The Polity is an administrative apparatus. It has no power; only influence."

"And I am a two-headed hornmaster of F'thal," Hanna answered, and looked up just in time to see him smile. The warmth of it was glorious; it made him another man; and she was still staring at him when he turned to her, saw her interest, and—was himself again.

He said abruptly, "I think we have found a way to induce explicit contact."

Hanna forgot immediately about everything but Species X. Iledra turned and came toward them quickly. Hanna said, "What is it? Have you done it?"

"We have not done it yet. It is a last resort."

"A last—why? What do you mean?"

He looked at her very somberly. He said, "You were terrified after your single clear contact with Species X, were you not?"

"Yes. I was. So?"

"Look," he said.

He called up a projection of their sector of the Milky Way, *Endeavor*'s first voyage a thin green line threading among the stars, the present voyage—an extension of the first—in red. It hovered ghostly in the middle of the room. Hanna put her hand into it, watching the mist glow on her skin.

"*Endeavor*'s here?" she said.

"Approximately. You see it has not gone far past the point where you left it. That is because we have been—experimenting."

Hanna looked up quickly. "Changing the tune?" she asked.

"Yes. We tried inexplicable disappearances, without broadcasting prior information about where the *Endeavor* would go next. When the ship returned to its point of departure, Species X simply took up the chase again. We generated our own coordinates for rendezvous; they followed, and kept their distance. We tried varying the content of our base signal. There was no new response. Your compatriots on the *Endeavor* gave us nothing. Their perceptions were even more ambiguous than yours."

"What were they?"

"Nothing to the point, believe me. Not to any point. But we have done something, finally, that has made them begin transmitting location signals again. So far we have not responded. I think it is time to do so. On their terms, as nearly as we can guess what those terms are."

Hanna shoved her hands into the pockets of her short jacket and looked at him, wishing she dared try reading his thoughts. She felt Iledra's perception of her desire, and felt Lee's shock at the boldness and rudeness of the wish. But Iledra had not faced Jameson on the *Endeavor,* and won her way to a kernel of truth through layers of obscurity.

Hanna said, "I think you'd better begin at the beginning."

"Do you know what it is? I don't." The wintry amusement with which she was becoming familiar touched his face.

"I think," Hanna said cautiously, "you can dispense with philosophy."

"All right. I've told you about the experiments we tried—all but one. That one was more successful. You will remember that one thing, and one thing only, brought a reaction from the aliens while you were aboard *Endeavor.* That was your own approach to them, in isolation from the ship."

He paused, looking at her without expression. Hanna dug her hands in deeper. She thought she knew what was coming.

Jameson said, "I had them recreate that situation, in form though not in substance. The *Endeavor*'s engineering staff modified a shuttle for remote control. The *Endeavor* specified a location for rendezvous, took the shuttle there, and left it—just as you were left behind last year. A starship—to all appearances the same one that came to you—appeared at the proper location. It made a pass at the shuttle and disappeared. Shortly afterward the *Endeavor* began receiving locus references again. Now, it is clear, after so long a time, that the beings do not wish to contact the *Endeavor* itself. They were not interested in the unmanned vessel. I think they may wish to meet with a single representative of humankind, away from a vessel large enough, perhaps, to be threatening. I don't know if it matters who the representative is. But they—" He hesitated. "They know you, as it were."

Hanna had been very still. Now she moved suddenly, almost convulsively. She said, "I don't like it."

"Neither do I. I did not want to do this. I did not want to place any human being in so vulnerable a position. In a sense, of course, every person on the *Endeavor* is vulnerable. But I have not forgotten the intensity of your reaction to the earlier contact."

"Thank you very much," Hanna muttered.

"Hmm?"

"Nothing . . ."

She turned away from him and began to pace, flowing black trousers swirling about her legs. She said, "They veered off from your decoy. Why wouldn't they do it again?"

"They were telepaths. There is no doubt on that score; that is the one thing Zeig and Daru are sure of, without reference, incidentally, to your experience. I think they departed when they learned, telepathically, that the drone was not manned."

"Because it wasn't—" She froze where she stood. Iledra caught her thought and made a faint sound of protest and disbelief. Hanna turned slowly. She said to Jameson, "It wasn't the bait they wanted."

He looked at her without expression and said, "That is highly colored language."

"Is it? When I saw spears and carnivores?"

"Analogs," he said.

It was her own word. She could not repudiate it.

She moved restlessly to stare into the projection.

"What does Marte Koster think?"

"She does not know what to think," Jameson said, nearly at her ear. She had not heard him come near.

"Well, for once she and I agree on something."

She looked up at Jameson and said abruptly, "Send *Endeavor* on and ignore them."

"Why?"

"I can't give you a logical reason. They're manipulating us."

"I know."

"We shouldn't play the game without knowing the rules."

"We can't ignore them any longer."

"Why not?"

They spoke rapidly and quietly. They might have been entirely alone. Iledra moved closer.

"*Endeavor* has been in space more than a year. I need results."

"Don't do it. Don't hurry."

He said savagely, "I don't have forever."

Hanna jumped, shocked. His will transfixed her—the implacable will that had created the *Endeavor* Project from nothing. No half-formed fear would dilute it. He would go meet the beings himself, if no one else would go.

She said, bewildered, "Forever for what?"

He looked at her without comprehension. She had to know. She put out a hand and touched his arm with a hesitance foreign to any D'neeran, to whom touch came naturally as breath. But it seemed a great liberty to take with Jameson. He did not shake her off, however. She said, "What are we looking for?"

For a minute she thought he would not answer. Then he said, "We are children, my lady."

"Children?"

"All the time of humankind is a second, a tiny fraction of eternity," he said, so softly that she tilted her head, close as she was, to hear. "It is nothing, my lady. Each of us is caught in our little millisecond of life, and we think that millisecond is everything. But all human history is nothing."

He hesitated, looking into her eyes with the first trace of doubt she had ever seen in him. Something reassured him. She felt him relax, almost in relief. He said quietly, "The *Endeavor* Project is a turning toward a future unimaginable as the improbable past. I am speaking of the far future. Not next year, but millennia to come. We forget the vastness of the universe. We think, skipping among a handful of stars, we have mastered it. We are children, playing on the edge of infinity. . . . One day, my lady, we will meet the adults."

It seemed to her clear, pure truth. She said in wonder, "And they will teach us—?"

"The unknowable?" he said. It was a question.

She asked with simple curiosity, "Are you mad?"

"I don't think so," he said, as if he had thought of it before.

He had gone much farther than he intended. The moment of communication ended with a jolt in which Hanna felt his surprise at what he had said. He actually took a step backward.

He said abruptly, "I don't intend to order you into space on my authority alone. There will be some delay. But I think you can leave in a few days."

"But—"

Iledra overwhelmed her, thinking furious thoughts to an obstinate child. Jameson said, "You need not be entirely alone. You can take Zeig or Daru, or both of them. This time. Not the next time, perhaps—"

"Next time! I don't even want to go this time!"

"It is essential that a telepath greet them. You can make better guesses about them than any true-human."

"Of course," Iledra said, but Hanna could not let it pass.

"I don't know if I can!" She stopped in despair. Iledra's eyes were as cold as Jameson's. She went on stubbornly, "If they, if they didn't have a Change, if they evolved that way, they might be different, so different from us—We're still human. We're shaped by language. Telepathy's a function of the maturation of the nervous system. We learn to use it along with language. We've never got very far from the rest of you—whatever you might think," she added defiantly, but Jameson only nodded.

"The perfect interface," he said.

Soft-furred pollitts snugly burrowed, and downwind the eye of the hunter—

Iledra's hand closed on her arm.

Madness! Before the war you were not so. This fear lies in your own heart!

Hanna disengaged her arm easily; it was harder to free her thought. She said hopelessly, "We don't know enough about them," and saw Jameson's mouth set.

"You have the opportunity to learn more," he said.

"What they are doing does not make sense in any frame of reference we know."

"You," he said, and lifted a hand and leveled a long forefinger at her, arresting her. "You have just won an award for a work concerned largely with frames of reference—and with your own qualifications, as a D'neeran, to understand them. You have the opportunity to prove the assertions of 'Sentience'—that you can enter an alien's skin, obtain for us knowledge of his heart, and show him your own essence. Peace, you said, past any possibility of mistake, without conjecture, without deception, from the beginning. You have the opportunity to make a first contact. There has not been a first contact since Neil Girritt's two hundred and fifty years ago. No D'neeran has ever made such a contact. Shall I send Marte Koster instead?"

Iledra said empathically, "No!" The air pulsed with warning. Hanna needed no special sense to know what Iledra thought of: D'vornan's new course of study; a report, which Iledra would supervise personally, on the introduction of D'neerans into true-human mindhealing; a whole list of scarce-spoken hopes, a world's coming of age.

Hanna looked from Jameson to Iledra and turned away from them. She went back to the projection and stood beside it without looking at it. Hands in pockets, shoulders hunched, she felt Iledra's indignation that Hanna should even think of turning away from this opportunity. From Jameson she felt nothing, but exasperation showed in his face. He wanted her to see it, she thought. She had not missed his significant glance at the tiny jeweled symbol of the Goodhaven Academy sparkling on her shoulder. She was not through paying for it, nor for all those beginnings.

She took her hands from her pockets, and the Heir's Ring sparkled too. She tugged at it and pulled it off. She said to Iledra, "Have you forgotten the inscription inside?"

Iledra remembered. She looked at Hanna coldly. It was the first time Hanna had felt anything of the kind from Iledra.

Hanna said, "I'll tell you what it is. 'The first duty of the D'neeran citizen is to the integrity of the self; for the welfare of the state depends on the well-being of the individual.'"

Iledra did not answer in word or thought. Hanna said, "Take it. Cosma can wear it for me. Just in case."

She felt a question form at last, and shut it out. "Take it," she repeated, and Iledra took the ring as if she might not give it back.

On balance, Hanna thought, Iledra was right, or right enough to leave no real choice. If there were a first contact, it had better not be Marte Koster who made it; better H'ana ril-Koroth of D'neera; better another stone laid to found Jameson's seductive vision.

"All right," Hanna said. "I'll go."

Chapter 7

The space ship was called *XS-12*. "X" meant Extraterrestrial, "S" meant Scout; Hanna never found out what the Twelve was for.

It was as austere as Shuttle Five, and it was not big enough for three people.

When it had been in space six weeks Hanna looked out the ports in its nose and thought: It's just as well we hate each other. It gives us something to do.

("Why told you no one of your dreams?"

"Why left you no record of yours?"

"I did, they kept it from you—"

"As you knew they would. Placid you ate the argument—"

"It was sense!"

"Now you doubt, too late—bitch, witch!")

The transmissions *XS-12* sent into space could be traced by an audible signal. Often they played it for hours. It had been on for hours now, high-pitched and faint and pulsing. Hanna could not bear it.

She said suddenly, "I want it off."

Charl did not look up from the game he played crosslegged on the floor. Bright chips shifted position in the air.

"Leave it on," he said.

"It's been on for hours!"

"I'm used to it."

They spoke in careful Standard, having rubbed so closely together for so long that the emotional burden of telepathy also was unbearable. Hanna said, "It's my turn to have what I want. Silence!"

Charl hesitated, acknowledging fairness in spite of himself. Hanna's hand crept inevitably toward the keypad that would silence the noise. A memory of the *Clara Mendoza* stabbed her, and she felt sick. Charl looked at her quickly and said, "All right."

"Thanks."

In resounding silence she headed for the cramped cubicle where she slept and which—the operations manual said—was supposed to give her privacy. In the narrow passage she bumped into a sleepy and disheveled Anja. Hanna squeezed past her.

Hanna's bunk made her bed on *Endeavor* look sybaritic. It would improve Erik to sleep here for a while. The single thin blanket did not even pretend to be fabric. It kept a sleeper comfortable, but it did nothing for the need to snuggle into substantial warmth in the night. Not that *XS-12* was cold; it was always the same and just right. It did not have *Endeavor*'s subtle diurnal and seasonal cues, and its scant drift through realspace allowed no shift in the positions of the stars. The souls aboard her might have been in hell, a hell of isolation and sameness that drove them to tear at each other because there was no other outlet for a tension that rose and fell irregularly and permitted them no action.

(*"I thought," said Jameson's voice—it was only his voice, and the transmission was not as clear as it should be—"that what you report is impossible. That telepathic contact without affect is a contradiction in terms."*

"It is for us. I didn't believe Charl either, when he told me what he felt on Endeavor. *They're not us. They're different. I told you they could be different!"*

"They are interested in you, at least."

"Presumably. Who the hell knows?"

"And they've done nothing to harm you."

"But the dreams. I don't trust this change. Dammit, why didn't you let us talk before I came out here?"

"It wouldn't have mattered. They are analogs; for watchfulness and pursuit, perhaps."

"That's easy for you to say," Hanna said, but she liked hearing his voice. It was always calm and steady, and in each of their rare conversations it was a link to reason and the sanity of a busy larger world.

She said, "Jameson, I don't think I can take this much longer."

"Don't tell me that. The import of your presence surely—"

"Don't make a speech," she said quickly, and thought she heard the ghost of a chuckle.)

She was not scheduled to talk to Jameson for four days more. There would be nothing to occupy her thoughts and keep them from unanswerable questions except the laconic once-a-day contact with Project Central, and the prickly oft-broken truce with Anja and Charl, and the other thing. Which came when it would and was gone at once.

("To see what you are? To see that you are what you seem to be? I don't know. But you will stay there, harmless—"

"Helpless!"

"Until I tell you otherwise. You need no help.")

So telepathic contact without affect was possible. There were no dreams of eyes or stalking warships. There were no affective images crafted deep in human bones. The touches were an assertion of existence: nothing more. They came at irregular intervals, not in sleep but to the waking mind, and no sensor on *XS-12* had ever registered a manifestation of matter to go along with them.

Hanna's tiny compartment was not soundproofed. She lay uncomfortably on her back and listened to Anja and Charl. The voices were faint, and she cocked an ear to the dreary round of the same words, same questions, same uncertain answers all of them had been saying and hearing for six weeks. It was Anja and Charl this time, but it might have been all three of them, or she and Anja, or she and Charl.

Anja said in her soft furry voice, "They might be superbeings, waiting to see if we are worthy."

"Or not telepaths at all. Could they be non-telepaths?"

"Impossible."

"Something altogether different, I mean. Made for another sense which we perceive dimly with the only one we have that can perceive them at all."

"But why wait? Why not contact us?"

"Fear perhaps . . ."

Hanna shut out the voices as best she could. They receded to a murmur. They could say nothing new. They had been through this again and again and again. The words were wearily unchanging like everything aboard *XS-12*. Hanna longed for the D'neeran summer, or even the spring left behind on Earth.

Hanna had gone out to *Endeavor* in *XS-12,* which had not seemed crowded with only a Fleet pilot aboard. Marte Koster met her with a certain sulky respect. Erik, however, greeted her with more than courtesy. It seemed she was now a person of some importance, a protégée of Starr Jameson and a member of the Goodhaven Academy. Hanna felt only indifference. She would not forget Erik but mostly, she thought, the memory would remind her that true-humans were not very sensible about love. She had never figured out what sharing Erik's bed had to do with following his orders, although the connection had seemed plain to him.

She forgot about him as soon as *Endeavor* was gone, leaving *XS-12* behind with one tremendous jump. Fleming had played the locus-reference game with Species X right up to the rendezvous with *XS-12,* though more slowly and carefully toward the end. Hanna, busy comparing notes with Anja, had not cared about the details. When *Endeavor* was gone the D'neerans turned on their own transmission— here-we-ARE here-we-ARE here-we-ARE—and sat back to wait. And wait, and wait. And the first fragile touch of contact had come almost at once, and again and again—and nothing else had happened, except that the mission had disintegrated into a series of subtle territorial squabbles.

We are acting altogether too much like true-humans, Hanna thought crossly. They insist on having privacy for the oddest things—arguing, making love, having babies—but they expect three people to put up with each other and stay sane in a space maybe big enough for one-point-five. I will never understand them. If something doesn't happen soon I'll go mad!

In six weeks none of her reservations had left her, though all the logical benefits of "something" happening were fully present to her mind, and her curiosity about Species X finally was grown ravenous.

She turned wearily—and jumped, all her attention arrested by an impersonal impact like a stutter in her skull, an instant of total absorption that suspended all other thought. It lasted half a second, perhaps: then it was over.

They were used to it, she and the other two.

She got up and went back to the control room. Anja and Charl were both on the floor now. The glowing chips formed a rotating pyramid.

Hanna said, "I had it again. Did you?"

They shook their heads without looking up. Sometimes two or all three of them felt the same touch, sometimes only one. Why? They could not guess.

Hanna keyed a note of the incident into the scout's memory. On Earth they had tried to deduce a pattern from this record, but there was no pattern.

Then she turned to the others and saw that Anja was entranced. She stared straight ahead, motionless, eyes wide. Hanna had seen this look in the instant of contact, but this went on a second, three seconds, five—

She crossed silently to Charl and Anja and knelt on the floor. Charl, guiding a game piece with a fingertip, had seen nothing. Hanna hissed at him. He looked up and saw Anja.

"Anja! *Annie!*" He reached for her. Hanna caught at his arm.

"Don't. Shut up. Don't disturb her."

They waited. Hanna tried to glimpse Anja's awareness and found it closed. Yet there should have been a response to Hanna's touch, and there was none.

Anja sighed and shook herself and came back to them, and before anyone could speak the scout said: "Attention, please. I am receiving a radio transmission from an unidentified source analogous to communication identified as alien."

Before it was finished Hanna was at the compact control console, Anja and Charl scrambling behind her. Charl opened his mouth to give an order and Hanna said quickly, "No, wait. No radar. Nothing. Anja—"

Anja began, "Mental contact? If you two—"

"No! We've got to notify Central. Anja, what was—"

"Not Central! No. They don't want us to do that."

"What? Did they tell you that?"

"What?" Anja stared in confusion.

"Just then," Hanna said impatiently. "When you were—"

She stopped, because Anja was bewildered. She created a picture of Anja in trance and exhibited it.

"I don't remember that," Anja said.

"But you know they don't want us to call Central?"

The bewilderment deepened on Anja's face. "Something like that," she said.

"All right. We won't yet, then," Hanna said, and ignored an anxious sound from Charl.

There were two seats before the master controls. Hanna slipped into one of them and put her hands on the console as if to assure herself the scout would make no move of its own to change a precarious balance. She felt just as she had when Koster told her about Signal Alpha, so unprepared for this that she could not believe in what was happening. The aliens were unreal, a dream presence, hallucination. The message the computer showed her was the same old series of primes, so that it too had no more substance than a memory.

But it was a radio transmission; and creatures who moved among the stars used radio only across very short distances.

Charl half-thought, "H'ana, we must urgently act!"

She answered in the same way, "Patience . . ."

He looked longingly at the sensor panel. Most of the time they drifted blind, and silent except for their beacon. Charl thought of mass sensors.

Hanna said, "No. Nothing. Wait passive as water . . ."

(*"They have no prey that moves so,"* said an old echo in her thought.)

Which was bait and which was hunter?

Her hands itched to shape the event. There was something she could do. The computer could tell her the direction of the radio signal and turn passive receptors that way. She keyed the main video screen, a black polygon tall as herself.

"Uselessness," she said. "Too-far. Computer. Begin passive-visual scan. Target's a spacecraft. Search: hypothesized alien mass. Highest magnification and full enhancement—"

"Oh!" they cried together, and saw for the first time with human eyes a thing made by Species X.

"Done," said the scout, but no one heard it. The image fell off the sides of the screen. It flickered as the computer fine-tuned it.

Fuzzy, sharp-angled, brown in color-compensation:

"Close upon us, crush us, time run out to run—!"

"Anja, shut up!" Hanna said strongly. She shook with the panic-reaction.

"She wounds thee, true-human changeling," Charl crooned, holding Anja.

Hanna gave them a look of disgust. Roly had thought her too good at things of this sort too. But someone had better be good.

She said steadily, "Back off, computer. Scale it down. Are they using radar on us? Yes? Scale down another step. Another. All right."

It was not so threatening when it fit into the borders of the screen. Anja and Charl peered at it anxiously.

"So close," they whispered. "How close? Too close!"

Charl looked out the nose as if he expected to see the ship there.

"It's 'behind' us," Hanna said absently. "You won't see anything, Charl. There ought to be more detail. Why isn't there any detail?"

"They come upon us from behind, then, stalking!"

"I don't think it *has* any details."

"H'ana, please!"

"Hmm? They're not that close, Charl. Computer: What's the naked-eye view?"

A secondary monitor came to life. It showed only stars against black velvet. Anja sighed. Hanna felt Charl relax.

"You see," she said.

She strained her eyes and cajoled the computer, but nothing changed except the object's apparent size. She thought of *N.S. Havock,* spiked and bristling with destructors. Now a brown box approached her. It had never been intended for atmospheric flight. No openings showed, nor any instrumentation.

She said, "Everything must be embedded in the skin. Or in a molecular film on the surface."

The others only looked at her. They had not been much in space.

"Or. . ."

The angles seemed not quite right angles. The faceted sides bulged softly.

". . . it's disguised, covered . . . enclosed. . . ."

XS-12 seemed warmer. Light and life drifted, contained.

"This wait destroys me. I must know them!" Anja said suddenly.

Hysteria was far away, but too close for Hanna's liking. She said, "Use Standard, Anja. They spoke to you. Do you remember now?"

"No," Anja said obstinately.

"Cease tormenting her, not-one-of-us!" Charl said, not in Standard.

"You did not have to come," Hanna said, falling back.

But what were they saying that she had not said to the true-humans?

This might be a peak in the sea of time, but time stretched on. The box moved toward them, but slowly. Anja, calmer, detached herself from Charl. With the quick D'neeran forgetfulness of conflict she said, "H'ana?"

"Yes?"

"When are they going to do something that tells us something about them?"

"I don't know." Hanna sat back. Her shoulders ached. More time had passed than she had thought. She had been thinking the same question. She said, "I never thought I could see one of their spacecraft and not be able to guess something about them."

"They use right angles. The damn thing looks like a brick." Charl touched her shoulder. His anger was gone too.

"Not quite, but all I can think is they've deliberately designed something we can see without their giving anything away."

"The anthropomorphic fallacy," Anja said. "You've warned against that yourself."

"Yes, but if it's not that, you know what the only other thing is I can think? If this is just a typical spacecraft for them?"

"What?"

"They've all got galloping paranoia, and shut out *everything*."

"They're galloping closer," Anja said, and giggled. There was an edge to it, but not an edge of humor. She said, "In case you haven't noticed, it's partly off the screen again."

"Reduce magnification," Hanna said to the computer, and the box shrank with a jump.

Such optical tricks, Hanna thought, made the stately advance seem untrue. One could turn for ease to an illusion of distance.

They reduced magnification again and again. An hour passed, and a second hour. At intervals a data monitor showed them the radioed message was being repeated, but

its content did not change, Nothing happened, except that
the box came closer. Charl returned to his game. He moved
pieces aimlessly and looked at them less often than at the
image of X. Anja sat beside Hanna, curiosity submerging
her fear. And Hanna tried to touch the alien presence and
felt: nothing. So slowly, so painfully accumulated, the bits of
meaningless data. Did they know? Did they guess how little? Was it their intention? Surely.

Anja said into a long silence, "Collision course?"

"Maybe," Hanna said. She shook herself. "Ridiculous."

"But they must be awfully close."

"Yes. They must."

"Well?" Anja turned her head. Hanna felt Charl's attention too.

Do something something something something . . .

Their patience was giving way.

Slowly she reached out and silenced the unheard Inspace signal. Now it was inaudible to the aliens too.

"Wisdom?" Charl inquired, picking up Hanna's own
doubt.

"They know our knowing of their closeness. Logic inevitable. Radio is for naught but closeness. Realtime makes it
so."

"No purpose then in silence," Anja said.

They had fallen again into the use of more thought than
speech. In Anja's vision time separated into segments discrete as beads. To act would change everything; for two
civilizations. The moment of change was theirs to choose.
She whispered, "Now, H'ana?"

"But their wish—" Dilatory, unwilling, Hanna hung
back. "Silent and defenseless calls them—"

("*. . . their terms, as nearly as we can guess . . .*")

"*Our* terms," Anja said.

Hanna's hand moved, hesitating. Why not? Bomb them
with detectors, slice into the alien box for knowing's sake.
She could not quite touch the instruments to do it, nor order
it done with her voice. Anja and Charl looked at her strangely.

She took a deep breath and said, "Computer. Full scan."

Numbers flickered and changed on *XS-12*. There were
no strange shields, at least.

Charl said, "Fifty kilometers. Closing fast. I want a visual
on that. Yes. That hotspot must be the reactor core."

He talked softly with Anja. Hanna paid no attention. She was dizzy, as if she had taken a step and fallen off a mountain. The ranks of numbers drew her. Close and closer: an approaching veil. Finally to be withdrawn? She would see through the mist at last.

"It's not featureless," Anja said. "You can see seams. Look, H'ana."

Hanna looked blindly and then with attention. She said, "It doesn't have any ports. Don't they like to look at the stars?"

"*I* don't like to look at the stars, except from solid ground," Anja said.

"But beings who choose space, like space. I mean, individual humans and individual F'thalians who come out here, we like to see where we're at. We—"

"Oh, look! Look!"

Openings appeared on the box's leading edge, black and bottomless. Hanna blinked at a burst of retrofire.

The scout said, "Decelerating."

There was another, shorter burst. *XS-12* said without interest, "The object will be at rest relative to ground zero in thirty-four minutes sixteen-point-oh-oh-oh-four seconds."

Hanna looked at the box and thought she ought to be rejoicing. It was not a box. It was a space ship made by thinking creatures. She had trained for this for years.

She got up. Her stomach twisted but she said, "I'm going to suit up. This could be it."

Anja said nervously, "Shouldn't we try talking to them? From here?"

"You can try," Hanna said. "But *Endeavor*'s been trying for a year. To go out there alone—that's something new. . . ."

Her voice trailed away. She didn't want to do anything new. She saw in Anja's eyes the memory they shared of a dream. She said, "Nobody knows what they'll do. This is the only way to find out."

Anja said, "We're being foolish. There's nothing to be afraid of, is there?"

With one accord they looked at the naked-eye monitor. In the center starlight glinted briefly off something, still tiny, that had not been there before.

Charl muttered, "Paranoia. H'ana, we ought to make a preliminary report to Central. Now."

"We can't," Hanna said. She looked at Anja. "Not if they don't want us to. I was told—their terms. And it doesn't matter anyway. Central's a long way from here."

"Then let me record something for the black box," he said, surprising her. For Charl was not a spacefarer. It was not routine for him to store information against his death at first sight of the unknown.

But Hanna said, "Do that."

She left them to watch the growing image. Near the lock reserved for spacewalks she dressed for vacuum. Logic told her she should not need to do it. In spite of their caution, the X beings had been the aggressors so far. Logic suggested they would rather come here than have her, an alien, penetrate their flying box. Yet she was certain that she would have to go to them, and that there would be no communication until she did. She did not know where her certainty came from. Intuition? But she did not believe in intuition. It was only logic in less visible form, the product of a structure based on details unconsciously noted. She knew they waited for her, in silence.

Anja said suddenly, "H'ana, something's happening out there."

Hanna waited, helmet in hands.

Anja said hesitantly, "There's an opening now. A new one. They're not going to shoot at us, are they? Wait. It's lit up now. I can't see inside."

Hanna said, "Step up the magnification."

"All right. Yes. It's just a little bare room. An air lock, I guess."

"What's the light like? How's it compare to Solar illumination?"

She heard Anja put the question to the scout.

"It is within Sol-normal parameters," the computer said.

"You heard?"

"I heard."

"It's at the kilometer mark, almost. Barely moving."

"Have you tried calling them?"

"We're still trying. There hasn't been an answer."

"Maybe that's it," Hanna said.

"What is?"

"An open door. An invitation."

"Weird way to do it."

"Direct, anyway."

But Hanna went on waiting for what seemed a long time. She thought that even if someday she forgot whatever happened next, she would never forget this chamber with its comfortless benches and rows of tool lockers. It did not seem connected with anything else, not even in time. Her suit's EV environment was not activated and she was hot. The niche from which it had come had a shiny door. She saw her reflection in it, barely. Her hair was pulled back and tightly bound for weightlessness. The oval of her face was clear, and the wide, too-wide blue eyes. Other details faded in distortions.

She thought there were times when you couldn't think much about what you were going to do. You had to just go and do it.

Finally she put her helmet on and fastened its seals.

"I might as well go out," she said. Her voice sounded too loud in the helmet.

"All right." Anja sounded scared again.

"Maybe you'd better program a panic button. Just in case."

"A what?" Charl said.

"Just tell the computer. It'll tell you how to set it up. What you want is to get the hell out of here the instant anything goes wrong. If you lose contact with me, for example."

She went into the air lock, listening carefully as they talked to the scout. They were doing it right. Locked away from ship's atmosphere, she watched ship and suit pressure gauges and presently, when their original readings were reversed, gave the outer hatch an exit command. The stars wheeled and her stomach gave way for a giddy instant as she left artificial gravity. She tumbled in a bowl of distant, shining glory. For the first time in her life the pleasure of this experience was shadowed by dread dark as the hulking scout. She stopped the slow spin, locked in star patterns for an upright referent, and started the drive unit on her back.

The guidance controls were at her waist. She touched them and drifted round the scout. The alien vessel and the glow signaling the open hatch were clearly visible. She moved toward them slowly. She thought of the enormity of what she was doing, making history, and chose not to think about that. She thought of Starr Jameson and said in a whisper he could not hear: "If you were out here you'd think twice about a renaissance."

"What?" Charl said.

"Nothing."

When she had gone about halfway she stopped. She said, "If I wait here do you think they'll come out?"

"No," Charl said promptly.

Anja said at the same time, "Yes."

"Well, let's see."

After a minute Anja said, "How long will you wait?"

"Well—why not an hour? Why not, long as we've waited on them?"

But the bravado grated on her own ears. She was ashamed of it. She started to move her hand to go on, and saw a shadow against the alien light.

She let out breath in a long, deep sigh, believing, at last, in a concrete reality.

She said, "See that?"

"I see it." Charl's voice was tense.

"Well?"

"What?"

"Dammit, bring the picture up and tell me what it is! It's dark out here!"

"Oh. It's got four limbs. And a head. I think. H'ana, that's all I can tell. It's in a spacesuit."

"Can you see its face?"

"No, the face plate's opaque."

She hesitated. Move and counter-move. Stopping had brought a response. She would stay where she was.

It was moving faster than she had been. She put a hand to her belt and touched controls that would boost contrast on the scene before her. The alien changed from a featureless shadow to a figure in a spacesuit. The suit differed only in detail from her own; given a little time, she would be able to figure out what everything on it was supposed to do. It was pressurized, and she could not guess at the body beneath it.

It came closer, and its helmet was subtly different in shape from her own—higher, wider, but shallower front to back, as if its head were oblong. Like her own it did not have a full face plate. There was only a darker band about two-thirds of the way up, presumably for it to see through.

Closer: Protruding from its garment at one side was something that might be a tool, or a weapon.

And closer: She could not see through the visor. The gloved hands had each three fingers and an opposable thumb.

In the last seconds it grew bigger, bigger, bigger than any human she had seen, like a figure of nightmare that would never cease growing—but it did.

It reached out and a four-fingered hand, huge, closed on her wrist. She must have made some sound because Anja said sharply, "H'ana, are you all right?"

"Yes. Can you see?"

"We can see. Why'd it do that?"

She swung round in vacuum and tried to see what it used for eyes, but the visor was dark to her.

Charl said, "Did you know you're moving away?"

She had not noticed. She looked ahead. The alien ship grew as she watched.

"Pretty fast," she said uneasily.

"Try to pull away."

"No. I have to go along," she said, but her throat was tight.

Anja said, her voice too high, "Are you brave or just stupid?"

Hanna did not know the answer. She was close enough to see details of the compartment beyond the open hatch. But there were no details to see; as Anja had said, it was bare.

"I'm going to try contacting it telepathically," she said, and without waiting for an answer reached out in thought as she had been doing since childhood, prepared for the rich, living texture of an intelligent mind.

There was nothing. It was not a machine; it was living, all right; but she could tell nothing else about it. She sensed none of its emotions, intentions or attitudes, not even its awareness of her presence. The impersonal connections she had felt on *XS-12* were shadows of this strength. She had never touched such a barrier, not even among the most powerful Adepts she had known.

She tried giving it an explicit message. She could not think in words to it; pseudo-verbal communication was possible only when there was a shared language. But visual-emotional-conceptual content could be shared across species, and what she said to it in this way was: *I am friendly-curious though afraid oh so afraid and wish to know you in rich sharing. Will you oh please commune?*

It did not respond in any way. They were nearly at the open hatch.

"It won't answer," she said.

"I don't like it." Charl sounded anxious. "They're too damn mysterious."

Anja said, "You can't expect them to jump into our arms."

"We're jumping into theirs."

"H'ana is, anyway."

Hanna said, "Have you got that panic button set up?"

The air lock yawned in front of her. As if of its own will Hanna's free hand closed on the edge of the hatch. The being still held her right arm; her hesitation swung it around sharply. It caught at a handhold she could not see and edged into the cavity, and for a moment they hung facing each other.

Then it pulled her in, not with the gentle tug that would have been enough to break her light anchoring grip, but with a surge of effortless power that wrenched her shoulder and sent her crashing and rebounding from the opposite wall.

"H'ana?" said a voice in her ear.

She gasped, "Assume hostile—"

Gravity came on and she fell heavily on her behind with a jar she felt to the top of her skull.

There was an instant of tremendous noise in her helmet as everything on *XS-12* stopped working forever, and in her mind the silent screams of Charl and Anja as they died, and for an instant she was on the *Clara* again (shut them out, shut them *out!*), and made the screams stop and shrank into the silence. And looked up at the shape towering over her, too stupefied by that moment of death to understand, and thought without knowing why: I hope I die as quickly.

Chapter 8

She came back to consciousness all at once in a breathless rush. There should not have been any consciousness; she was supposed to be dead. She had charged the alien to make it fire its hand weapon, force it to kill her, because now there was no question of its hostility and she was afraid her mind would be open to it, all her knowledge of human science and defenses and government written out for it to see. The suicidal leap for its throat was the last thing she remembered, and she did not welcome this wakening.

Without opening her eyes or moving, she explored what her senses told her. She was spreadeagled on her back on a hard, smooth surface. Her wrists and ankles were tightly bound, and her clothing had been removed.

Sweat began to bead on her skin. This is impossible, she thought, and pushed against the bonds. They were metal; there was no play at all.

This cannot be happening to me. Can't be. Can't be.

She did not want to open her eyes. Through closed lids she saw bright light. It gave no heat and she was cold. Around her there was silence except for the subliminal hum of machines.

A voice of terrible power and clarity said to her thought: *Whowhat are you?*

She opened her eyes at last. She had never wanted less to do anything.

The alien stood near her, big as she remembered, half again her size. Its face was gray, and above that the skull was tufted with scales or coarse feathers. Two eyes were set very far apart in the flat face. Running nearly the length of the face and part-way to the top of the skull was a narrow strip of bony

plating set a little out from the face, and under that a wide
mouth that bulged outward, almost a muzzle. The skull was
higher than a human's, but more rounded than the shape of
the helmet had indicated. At the sides of the neck were organs
that looked like gill slits, but they were armored with bone. A
red tunic hid its upper body and arms. It also wore a garment
something like a kilt; she could not see its legs.

She only stared at it, paralyzed with disbelief and unsureness and the beginning of a fear she did not recognize.
Cold choices between life and death did not frighten her,
and what else had there been to fear?

It said again, meaning the personal "you": *Whatwho are
you?*

Her mind was blank in the face of the impossible. There
was no emotional content in the thought at all, only the
inquiry. D'neeran Adepts could do something like this, with
rigorous concentration and discipline, but it was only a
shadow of what this being did without effort. Yet there were
overtones also of hard certainties, of things it thought it
knew and echoes of other thoughts, and they were deadly.

It lifted a heavy four-fingered hand, and she saw that the
fingers ended in thick curving claws. It laid the tips of the
claws between her breasts and moved its hand, and there
was a stinging as her skin tore. She trembled, but the slight
pain roused her.

It said: *I am the Celebrant-Questioner and the triumph
that dissolves you. Show me truth!*

Shaken, struggling to comprehend through fear and
strangeness, she answered with an image: *I am Wildfire.*

Because that was how her own people sometimes
thought of her when they spoke directly to her mind.

A rivulet of blood trickled down her sweating skin. She
said to the being, without trying to hide her fear because
she could not: *What do you want with/from me?*

*I will know the heart of our danger: the place/strengths/
safeguards of the beasts: their tools of death, their watchfulness: fulfillment and prediction all at once: the use and proper
end of Wildfire. This is what I will have.*

Hanna moved convulsively against her bonds, knowing
at last and too late, an hour too late, a year too late, that this
was what she had ignored, this was what she had been
swayed from: the plain fact that the hunter's eye was no

analog, but literally real. The end of courage and birth of fear had their reasons. She had not trusted herself or dead Anja enough. The being's thought made it plain it was interested only in military intelligence and—a horror she did not yet understand and therefore, in extremity, dismissed. It did not care about culture or history, art or philosophy or any of the other things *Endeavor* had gone into space to exchange. It did not care about her luminous vision of all the rich varieties of life. Her own senses had warned her, and she had turned away from them. She had failed, spectacularly and dangerously.

She thought in despair: *I cannot in rightfulness tell you those things. Peace follows me. My people will not harm you.*

But the strength of her own conviction was lost in fear, and the being knew that in this moment she would, if she could, harm it or kill it or anything else to escape.

It said: *You are not-People: clever treecubs come of old to ground awash in blood. You will show me what I ask, for I will hurt and force you.*

It meant raw pain, so clearly her body twisted of its own accord in anticipation. It would come if she spoke or did not speak, inevitable, but still she could not accept that and thought in familiar terms of interrogations. She did not know what to do. No one had ever taught her what to do. Human questioning could not be resisted; there were drugs to free a prisoner's tongue; there was no need for systematic pain and no one had ever spoken of it to her, except in whispered tales of forgotten hell-holes.

She whispered, "I cannot tell you anything," and it took the negative from her terrified thought.

It said confidently: *You will.*

It also heard her incredulous question—why pain?—and answered: *Will strength and spirit must end thus ending birth of the beast.*

What it meant had nothing to do with questions. But when she tried to see the meaning, it added: *Thought is chaos, drugged thought worse, lest shaped by will. You will shape it as I ask until will fails.*

I will not.

You will.

She licked her dry lips and thought: *You will kill me. You know not my physical being.*

*We do know. We have met not-People, the treecubs, be-
fore. Not like you; not outward-bound in space; lost, their
ancestors abandoned. How did this happen?*

It showed her a handful of people, half-primitive, half-
sophisticated, settled in mist yet adrift as an uncaptured
moon. Distracted by wonder, she thought: *There is a story
that when my ancestors began to go into space, for a time
small groups went from star to star and of some all traces
were lost; yet some survived. I did not think it true.*

It is true.

It turned away and she tried to understand. A Lost
World was real. Myth was truth. Had been truth. She
thought: the humans they *knew.* They are all dead.

Accumulated shock made an abyss and for a little while
she fell through it. All the universe had changed in these
few moments and there would never be a foothold again.
She would not need footholds; the dead do not need them.
When this thought crystallized into certainty she saw The
Questioner had returned. It showed her and explained to
her a picture in its thoughts. It said: *Do you know this instrument?*

I know. I know in shame. I know.

She had not seen a neural stimulator that looked like
this before, a square of silvery fabric, but she knew its principle. Her experience of it had not been pain, and the being
added that knowledge to its store.

It looked away from her. It said: *My companion is the
Questioner's Assistant.*

Hanna turned her head and saw the other one coming
toward her with the shining cloth. It thought of triumphs
and transformations. The questions it would ask were secondary. Hanna did not understand and did not care. Her
mouth was dry. The neural stimulator could cause excruci-
ating pain, and although it did not damage tissue directly,
the indirect effects were frightful. Convulsions of agony, she
had heard, could tear muscles, break bones.

There would not be time to think about this or decide
what to do, if there was anything left to do. Endure, said the
deep voice of instinct. It was hard to hear past the clamor-
ing crowd of things she did not want to give up. Protect, it
said. Endure.

The Questioner said: *Show me the space of your Home.*

The image was strange and shadowed and wrapped in on itself, but Hanna understood. She said: *I will not tell you.*

The Questioner's Assistant stood over her for a long moment, perhaps reviewing its knowledge of human anatomy. Then it leaned over and carefully molded the gauze over her belly.

The Questioner thought to a hidden control, and she screamed.

Tonight Henriette had worn a pale golden gown that glowed where it touched her skin. It lay near her now on the thick soft carpet, still shining a little with its own light. Henriette, chin propped on hands, looked up at Jameson in a way he knew well.

"Now?" she said, and he smiled at her from his chair.

"In a little while," he said.

"It's almost four in the morning. I have to go home and start working in a few hours. You just mean you're still too high."

"Possibly. Possibly."

But it was only that he had no inclination to move for any reason. Moments when the universe was orderly and forgiving of pleasure were rare, and he was balanced now between pleasure past and pleasure future. Henriette, who was now future, would be present. Soon. Whenever he wished . . .

The Imagos in his blood was living up to its name. Nothing had disturbed his weekend on the waters of the rich and wind-chopped bay, and its blinding blue and gold still framed Henriette's long graceful body. When he closed his eyes the bowl of scarlet roses at his elbow drifted before him, and everything was heavy with their scent. In a few days he would go home to Heartworld, his first visit in several months. The great Siberian tigers flourished there under greenleaf skies, not knowing and not caring by how narrow a margin they had escaped extinction. He thought he saw Henriette's gown stir and become sunlight dappling pale fur. He felt the shaft of a spear in his hand, and forgot for a moment that he was no longer young enough or foolish enough to hunt tigers with the spear only.

He got up with a sigh and pulled Henriette to her feet and against him. Her hands moved on his back, and he felt a tremor begin in her thighs almost at once. It was one of the things he liked about Henriette.

In his ear Rodrigues's voice said clearly, "Priority one," and followed it up with a series of tones guaranteed to wake him if he were half-dead.

He cursed the transmitter implant violently. Henriette said, "Oh, no!"

"House! Tell Rodrigues to shut up!" The noise stopped. He said, "Be a good girl and get some clothes on, and bring me the Imagos antidote, would you?"

Tucked away behind an elegant bronzewood door was a private communications center. He disliked using it; it was a cold reminder that chaos was no respecter of his working hours. It would not open for anyone but him, and required palm, voice, and retinal identification. He gave it a slap, a curse, and a glare; there were certain liberties one could take with machines. Inside the lights were too bright, and a sharp reflection from somewhere shaped itself into a spearpoint before his eyes.

He said, "All right, Paul," and blinked to focus the other man's face.

Rodrigues said without preamble, "Anja Daru and Charl Zeig are dead. *XS-12* is out of contact." His face changed briefly to something else and back again. Jameson ignored it.

"What happened? Oh—"

Henriette was back. She injected the Imagos antidote with practiced fingers. She's used to this, he thought.

"Out," he said, and made sure the door locked behind her.

Rodrigues said, "Apparently Zeig and Daru died about two hours ago. I tried raising *XS-12* myself, no luck. I got General Steinmetz out of bed and he's got Fleet Communications trying."

"How did you find out about it?"

"Lady Koroth. D'neerans know when somebody they're close to dies, you know. She got a call from Daru's current, uh, spouse? He'd already been in touch with some of her other relations and they all thought she was gone. Lady Koroth then talked with Zeig's mother—same thing was going on in his circle. It took her a while to get to me. Central didn't know what to do and passed her on to Martinson first, and he put her through to me."

Jameson's head was clearing. He let the blue-and-gold go without regret. He said, "Has there been any alarm from *XS-12?*"

Rodrigues shook his head. "They checked in Sunday morning as usual—twenty-two hours ago now. Nothing to report. No contact since."

"Have you still got Lady Koroth holding?"

"Yes. I thought you'd want to talk to her."

"I do. Get back to Steinmetz and see if he's having any luck. If he's not, get on to the Commission. Let me talk to Lady Koroth."

It was midday at Koroth. Iledra, who must have been jolted hard by the news, appeared calm, but the younger woman at her shoulder looked anxious. Cosma ril-Koroth: Jameson remembered she was likely to be Iledra's heir if anything happened to Hanna.

He bit back the obvious question and said instead, "Rodrigues has filled me in. Did he tell you he's been trying to reach *XS-12?*"

"No, he didn't. We have not tried. It would go through Central, and be stopped. He has had no answer?"

"We're still working on it. Tell me what happened."

It was only a more detailed account of what Rodrigues had told him. She recited it with precision, filling in names, times, circumstances, but she moved restlessly as she did so and once Cosma touched her hand. When she finished he said finally, "You have no reason to think Lady Hanna also is dead?"

"None. I would know; so would her parents and cousins. I've spoken with them, too."

Jameson found it hard to picture Hanna with a family. She had grown up with her mother, he remembered, but likely had been close to her father; such relationships were common on D'neera. "Cousins" could be siblings or half-siblings or entirely unrelated people with whom one had intimate ties; D'neerans often did not distinguish among the categories.

He said, "Would you know if she were injured? Unable to respond to us, for example?"

"Probably not. It's nearly always clear and unmistakable when someone you love ceases to exist, no matter where they are. You seldom know of any trauma short of that, unless they're close at hand. It sometimes happens; not often."

"All right." The antidote had taken full effect now. He did not have to think about what to do next. "Unless we get some word from her in the next few minutes I'm going to get a search underway."

"There is already a D'neeran ship on the way. Estimated time of arrival is seventy-two hours."

Jameson blinked, taken by surprise. She was not supposed to know *XS-12*'s location. He remembered Hanna's insistence on finding it out. She must have passed it on before she left Earth, probably without even thinking of security. It could not be undone, however. He said, dismissing it, "We'll have something there sooner. Can you keep this quiet until we know more?"

"No."

There was no point in arguing about it. He could exert little influence on D'neeran public information policy. But it meant the news would be known on other human worlds in a few hours, and he would have to deal with that problem sooner than he would have liked.

He closed the call and paused, thinking. Hanna had not known, and Lady Koroth could not know, that *XS-12* had not been entirely unsupported. Sadam Aziz Khan in the Fleet warship *Mao Tse-Tung* was hours away. Clearly the communications blackout no longer was necessary. Better check with Steinmetz and get the *Mao* moving.

It was fruitless to consider what this disaster would mean to him personally. If *XS-12* had only blown up by itself it would not be so bad. If the aliens had something to do with it it would be the worst crisis for humanity since the plague years of the twenty-fourth century. And there would have to be a scapegoat, and he would be it. He would be lucky to end up an assistant to some village mayor in the wilderness; very lucky.

It was going to be a bad Monday.

The Questioner's Assistant shoved a nipple against her mouth, but it was still too short a time since the last red bout of pain, and the water dribbled unnoticed onto the tabletop, already slick with her body fluids. She could not scream any longer and her right arm, broken in some massive convulsion, hurt all the time now. Her body twitched and jerked uncontrollably even when they were not doing anything to her.

Her mind began to work a little again in a slow daze. She licked a drop of water from her lips with painful concentration. Her vision cleared for a moment and beyond the scarlet shape of The Questioner she saw others like him. They were not even trying to block out her pain; they were drawn to it, hungered for it, ate it, absorbed it. Always outside her own agony she felt their gluttonous satisfaction, and sometimes, dimly, savage flashes of joy and ancient victory.

When she could think — less often now — she knew it was impossible. Everyone knew it was impossible. She had accepted unquestioning the common wisdom that star-traveling aliens could not do things like this, that xenophobes do not take to the stars, that compassion and intelligence are inextricably linked. No telepath would know her suffering without sharing it, nor disbelieve her assurance of harmless intent. She had said so in "Sentience." She did not think she would live to write a retraction.

The Questioner saw her limbs quiet, and felt the fog clear from her thought. He said (she knew now it was "he"): *Where in misted stars do the unPeople lair?*

The thought was a glimpse of bloody fangs, and she shook her head weakly. A hank of sweat-soaked hair clung to her cheek.

We are not beasts, but People like yourselves.
With what arms would the not-People kill us?

It was utterly and absolutely impossible to avoid telling him something. Her perception of each question carried a partial answer within itself. The common barriers of her kind, which were all she knew, were nothing to The Questioner. She did not even have the privilege of thinking of the meaning of her death; there was nothing safe to think of for distraction.

Therefore she counted; did sums, remembered logarithms, cherished listings of the elements; that was all they would get, unless pain broke her. This death was slow and hard and worse than anything she had ever imagined, but she thought it could be endured. She was stubborn, adamant. Such qualities had given her trouble in life; they would serve her well in dying. The core of her was strong and inviolate. As long as it stayed so, she could keep silence. And no matter what they dripped into her veins to keep her alive, sometime she would die.

The Questioner said: *This tool has other uses.*

She knew that. She remembered them very well, from one riotous trip to Valentine that had left her shaken and unsure and forced to the conclusion that D'neeran sexual mores, notoriously flexible, had their own rigorous limits for her.

She thought the being was going to try bribing her with pleasure, since pain so far had failed. It made her angry; but that would not work, either.

When she understood its intent, however, she wanted to scream again, and could not.

The commissioners of the Polity rarely all met together in the flesh; for once all of them were here. Andrella Murphy had been a little distance from Earth when Rodrigues called her, going home to Willow, and was breathless from a last-minute rush to Admin. Not only the six of them knew what was going on. After Lady Koroth's announcement some hours before, everyone knew.

Struzik gave Murphy time to settle in a chair before he called the meeting to order. Murphy's single glance at Jameson was anxious; the others were nervous or resentful, angry or triumphant. He knew that all of them, even Murphy, had already taken steps to dissociate themselves as thoroughly as possible from the *Endeavor* Project. The groundwork would be laid—had been laid for months, no doubt—and all the subtle machinery would begin working as soon as they had a little more information. They would have it in a minute now, and he would be left to face the storm alone. He had never expected anything else, and had accepted the risk from the beginning.

"I think," Struzik said, "Starr has a new report for us."

From long habit Jameson spoke calmly, his face betraying nothing.

"I spoke a few minutes ago to Aziz Khan on the *Mao*," he said. "I'm sorry to say he had a worst-case confirmation. *XS-12* has been destroyed by enemy action."

He looked past them to the end of his career, and waited for the frozen silence to end.

al-Nimeury leaned forward and said, "What weapons?"

"Simple lasers, Aziz Khan said."

"Why? If these aliens have Inspace capability, why not anti-gravity derivatives?"

Jameson resisted an impulse to inquire how he was supposed to guess why aliens used one weapon and not another. He said, "Aggies are very destructive. It may be they wanted to preserve the vessel for study. Aziz Khan said there's very little debris, not nearly enough to account for *XS-12*'s full mass."

Murphy said, "Is there any trace of them?"

"No. You know how easy it is to disappear using Inspace. They know too, evidently."

Katherine Petrov had not been listening. She said, "They've taken it away, then?"

"It appears so."

"Then they've got everything . . ."

Her old hands hovered anxiously. Jameson said, "Maybe not, Kate. They might have made a mistake. Aziz Khan says the nature of the debris indicates central control took a direct hit. Main data storage almost certainly was destroyed, and the backup may have been damaged."

"Why?" said Murphy. "It doesn't make sense. Why waste the computer?"

"The theory is that their prime target was a human prisoner. It's likely that Lady Hanna, as the logical contact, was the first to come into their hands. It would not make sense to us, but when I notified Lady Koroth—" His eyes were on Murphy, but he found he was seeing Iledra's face, with its barely hidden pain. "Lady Koroth said if they are indeed telepaths they may find it easier and less time-consuming to interrogate a prisoner than to analyze human language and mathematics and hardware."

"You're sure Lady Hanna's alive, then?" Murphy looked worried but far from hysterical—and not nearly so thunderously angry as al-Nimeury.

"Quite sure."

Arthur Feng said, "How much does she know?"

"Too much," Jameson said wearily, thinking of that intent young face. "She has detailed knowledge of D'neeran defense capabilities. She's state-of-the-art where Polity defenses are concerned, although she's never been in a position to know the details."

Petrov said, "We'll have to assume she tells them. And that they're hostile."

Jameson said nothing. According to "Sentience," a defensive posture to a newly encountered intelligent species was inappropriate when a telepath made the contact. But according to "Sentience," not to mention humankind's cherished beliefs about intelligence, such a species would not, as its first act of contact, destroy a human space vessel.

Struzik murmured, "It'll have to be max security."

A storm of voices broke out. Jameson listened without comment. Probably it should be max security. He would speak with Damon Taylor, president of his own world's general council and the man responsible for Jameson's presence on the Commission, but he thought "maximum security" would be Taylor's first words. It was expensive, it was frightening, it interfered with commerce and lawful travel and it was of questionable value, given the nature of Inspace transit, but probably it should be max security. Until they found out what was going on. If they ever found out what was going on.

"But—" Feng's voice rose above the babble. "Three conventions next month in Foresight alone. Foresight alone! And anyway they don't have the computer data. And Lady Hanna might not tell them anything."

al-Nimeury growled, "I do *not* want to count on that."

There was an overtone in his voice Jameson recognized, something more than the bruise to pride the *Endeavor* Project had been. al-Nimeury simply disliked D'neera, and violently distrusted D'neerans. It was only an extreme form of a widespread prejudice; Coopers had made themselves into a human unity and combined a checkered assortment of settlers into a human whole against great odds. They were hard on outsiders.

Maximum security was the only realistic choice. It would take days to implement; there was no time to waste; even in this room, which was supposed to hold humanity's coolest heads, there was a shadow of fear. Jameson cast his vote without a word, knowing it might be his last.

When they got up to leave, Struzik nodded to Jameson, who recognized the signal to wait until the others were gone. But Struzik, who gently pried whenever he had the chance, only wanted to gossip, and Jameson was in no mood for gossip.

"You know everything I know," he said.

"I know. Still . . ." Struzik hesitated. "We've never had to do this before."

"No."

"Dust off the contingency plans . . . We never really expected hostile aliens."

"Somebody did," Jameson pointed out. "That's why the plans are there."

"But I never thought we'd have to use them."

Jameson shrugged. "You take your chances," he said.

"*Your* chance. Your idea."

Jameson waited, watching his oldest Earth-born friend. Struzik said, "How much did you know?"

"Nothing," Jameson said, understanding the question perfectly.

"Tell me the truth, Jamie. You thought she might have been right all along, didn't you? Being scared of them as she was?"

Jameson did not answer. Struzik said. "This puts you in a spot, doesn't it?"

"You might say that." Jameson had made mistakes before, but he could not recall another that had endangered the whole human species. In a day or so the pack would be in full cry. It would be folly to dispense with his experience in a time of crisis, but he did not know if Taylor would be able to avoid it.

Struzik began, "All the fuss about *Endeavor* in the first place—"

"Seems to have been justified."

Jameson started out the door. Behind him Struzik said, not without sympathy, "You really put your foot in it this time, Jamie."

"Don't call me that," Jameson said automatically, but his heart was not in it.

Hanna found humiliation could do things simple pain could not. The boundary in her mind between rape and the pleasures of love had been clear; that made it worse. Rape was a true-human crime which she had heard of but never met, and she had faced the possibility of the start of war with Nestor with a certain equanimity. If it happened she would endure it, and when there was a chance—even if years passed before the chance came—she would kill the man who did it. The principle was as clear to her as anything in her life, her mastery of this part of herself indisputable and a foundation of her existence. In this matter there were no gray areas.

What happened to her now was different, and beyond enduring. Bad enough, insane enough, to have the paths of pleasure charted by some monstrous being unmoved as the tool it used; but each time, at the end, to want what it promised! The instrument was forbidden everywhere except Valentine; her own experience had shown her why; it took away your humanity. The body had its own imperatives, and no matter how she set her will the moment would come when she gave in to them, and her will would be broken. And when she wept in shame and self-hatred the pain would come again, and it would be harder to resist that too.

Stop. Stop. Oh please, I beg, oh please.

I will not. Thus were beasts destroyed before you time-ago; in this and other ways: We learned.

Abject I crawl, I beg, implore, I will do anything save speak!

That too. How not? Ask when. There is no escape. Of all agonies that is the worst: no ending nor escape.

Pain merged with pleasure, she got them mixed up, the creature was as close as her self, the bond was irresistible. Yet she resisted.

Answer, if thou lovest me. A single flame. The heavens thus. Knowest thou this benchmark?

I know. . . .

And this? No? Then this?

No! I will not.

You will.

The universe contracted to Hanna and The Questioner. She resisted, surrendered, forgot she was human, remembered. The past died in the evil present. The little certainty that was left her blurred and dissolved; but The Questioner was certain. In an unguarded moment he let her see his sureness that he hammered at a fracture point, that she would split cleanly as a crystal, and he would not let her shatter into dust.

On Tuesday night Jameson went home and immediately broke an ampoule of a high-powered tranquilizing drug under his nose. After a minute he did it with another and the world slowed around him, and the muscles of his back and legs reluctantly, lingeringly relaxed.

He was leaning against the wall of his study, his breath clouding its shining surface, when the room said, "Ms. Guilbert is calling."

"Just give me audio in here . . . Henriette?"

"Hello. You told me to call you today."

"Did I?"

"Umm-hmm."

He shook his head, a gesture she could not see.

"I'm sorry, Henry. I haven't had any sleep for a couple of days and I don't know when I'll be able to get free."

"I thought that was probably—Starr?"

"Yes?"

"Can I ask you a question?"

He smiled in spite of his weariness. "You know the rules about answers."

"You'll either tell me the truth, not answer, or lie to me."

"That's right." He had laid the rule down solemnly early on, and Henriette rarely asked about the Commission.

"Are you worried?"

"No," he lied.

After a pause she said. "They're saying President Taylor is going to recall you."

"Who's saying that?" (Besides half the Heartworld council and sometimes Taylor too, he thought.)

"It's on all the newsbeams. They're saying—well. Somebody said you're a megalomaniac and you shoved the *Endeavor* Project through, knowing how dangerous it was."

She sounded uncertain. Very likely she believed it. Damned if he was going to defend himself to Henriette; she had never listened to a word of his public statements before she met him, and rarely did so now.

"Cut your losses, Henry."

"What?"

"Never mind. Henry, my appointment will not be revoked. A minority faction in the council will try to pass a resolution demanding my resignation. They won't have nearly enough votes. That'll be the end of it. It happens all the time, Henry, in one form or another."

"All right." She sounded dissatisfied. A village mayor's assistant would not suit her.

"I must go now. I'll call you as soon as I can."

He went to his bedroom, thinking the last thing he
wanted right now was Henriette beside him in the big bed.
No, not quite the last thing; he could do without partisan
politics just now too.

He barely had time to get his clothes off before the dope
put him to sleep.

> *Not crystal*
> *but steel.*
> *It is stronger*
> *than Lost Ones*
> *and beasts.*
> *There is more to protect.*
> *Much more. Worlds and*
> *weapons unsuspected*
> *it has shown us.*
> *Not enough! It*
> *cannot die*
> *will not die.*
> *Not yet.*

The promise and the threat were nothing to Hanna, nor
had she the clarity of mind to wonder what could follow.
She could not move. When she was sick from time to time
they turned her like a slab of meat so she would not choke
to death; she could not and would not have done it by
herself. Her mind also had retreated. For some time she
had not felt anything; blessedly detached, for a little while
she wandered the golden hills of her home. Once it was
night, the moonless star-clouded night of D'neera. It
seemed that at some time she had wanted to soar into the
bright cloud, borne by her own wonder and curiosity. That
could not be right. The stars were too terrible. Her mother
said, H'ana, when will you be home? Soon, darling, she
answered.

And where is this place? someone asked in her dream.

Here, you see, not far from the gentle sea.

And if I wish to go there from another star how may I
find it?

Dutifully she began to think of astrogation. And remembered in a surge of terror what asked the question.

They are stronger than
stronger than
We. Pierce its heart.
No! Lost We
lost the vessel
knew not Our aim
and Our goal and
destroyed it
unknowing; now
nothing
useless
metal
twisted
unspeaking.
Wildfire is all.

They did not bother to hide their thoughts. Hanna understood none of it. Their new agitation only threatened her precarious peace. An ocean's slow pulsebeat rocked her.

This was not the
purpose of the
purpose of the Rite.
Time is changed We
are changed. They too.
And they. The
old records the
Lost Ones the
Students knew the
key
which is death
which is madness
We will try.

A new and powerful voice said: *One star may be all that We need; its Home, whence it returns: first known, last to fade in the end-of-self. We will try.*
We will try.
They were specialists in their way. They knew what mutilation did to the human spirit and made a ruin of her breasts. They knew what disfigurement did to identity, and

destroyed her face. They knew what sudden blindness did to courage, and put out her eyes. They knew about humans and their children, and did things in her belly that made her pass out again, but not for long, because they never let her stay unconscious for long.

Wednesday night Jameson recalled the *Endeavor*. There was no choice. It was too vulnerable, too tempting a target, sailing space with its computers chuckling to themselves and blithely inviting the aliens to come say hello. So he was told, anyway, and reluctantly he believed this much at least: now was not the time to expound on the philosophical arguments in favor of alien contact.

Another name for the *Endeavor* Project was current in certain circles. It was "Jameson's Folly."

Erik Fleming asked to be reassigned to the hopeless search for *XS-12* and Hanna. Jameson had no direct authority in the matter, but he still bore his precarious title and his hint to Fleming's Fleet superiors would go a long way. He said he would see what he could do.

When he was done with Fleming he poured a drink and stood at the edge of his office for a while, looking out at the river as Hanna had done not long ago.

He did not think he would see her again, and in memory, memory of a time so separated from the desperate now that it might have been a distant past, she came before his eyes with her odd blend of adamant and innocent. He had thought: she needs only a little shaping to be a precious tool; a little patience with compromise, some skill in the way things work. Now he thought: she did not want to go. And did not even think about the courage that took her out there. And neither did I.

He had spent his life in public service. He was responsible for humanity first, then Heartworld. If he were to accept responsibility for every individual who came into his work the burden would crush him. He could not afford to forget the fact, and now he was reminded of the reasons he had learned it in the first place. He had begun to like Hanna ril-Koroth; and he had personally sent her to her death.

*   *   *

You know this configuration. I see that you do. And from here to your Home?

She was quite mad. When she thought of something they wanted they cut off another bit of her. That was her reward. Sometimes it was the other way around. It seemed proper and gratifying. When it was finished there would be nothing left of her. An orderly and needful procedure.

In a moment of vague anxiety she asked, it's all right, isn't it, Iledra? Yes, Iledra answered.

This being is your Leader? But there are others. What are you?

I am nothing. Nothing does not live, therefore I do not live, therefore kill me.

We will not. Show me the Homes again in your thought. Not that one. The others. The others!

I have no eyes, no hands, therefore no thought.

Have you learned any more?
No. No. No. Too late.
We must know.
Cannot know.
At the last....
Was it true? Its Home a mote
defenseless. The rest
beyond power. It is true. There is
more than We thought.
Then We must
We cannot
Yet I will.
Experiment only
new as the new-things
as Treecubs
as Renders
as old
but We are equipped and
supplied for the
bending the
shaping insertion
command
I will try.
We will try.

Iledra sat up in bed and called "H'ana?" but there was no answer. Dawn showed at her windows. It was night in Namerica, she could talk to Jameson if she wished, but what was there to tell him? Hanna was still alive. Iledra could not explain the shock that had waked her. She was not even sure it was real; perhaps she had been dreaming about Hanna, and only her own anxiety had roused her.

She lay down again and pulled the feather-stuffed quilt over her shoulders.

Four days later the mayday from *XS-12* reached the *Mao Tse-Tung* and the D'neeran light cruiser *Voltaire,* which haunted space where the scout had disappeared. It carried position referents which were arrogantly clear. The *Voltaire* had no chance in the race that followed. The *Mao* plunged through uncharted space much faster than was safe, and in a steaming empty place with an atmosphere that could just be breathed, Aziz Khan found the wreck *of XS-12,* the pieces of Charl Zeig and Anja Daru, and something he did not at once recognize as H'ana ril-Koroth, which still barely lived.

Chapter 9

It wasn't really dark. There were flashes of light, pinwheels, silent explosions of brightness, firework forms pursuing one another, a mad dance against the blackness.

Hanna watched them for a while. It did not seem to matter that she was blind.

Nothing hurt. She did not know why that was so important.

She felt nothing: nothing at all. If that was the alternative, fine.

Iledra said: *Beloved H'ana-daughter. Attend to me.*

Her mourning filled the darkness. Hanna felt tearful. Iledra was lost to her, it was only her own sad desire that spoke.

H'ana daughter, I am here.

Here? What is here?

The bright images gave way to a room where men and women clustered round a shrouded figure, half-machine, that lay unfeeling and unmoving.

That is you.

No. That is not me.

But it was not important.

"She is aware of me," said Iledra's voice through deep water.

"Ask her," said another voice she ought to know.

She felt Iledra's reluctance, but slowly an image formed, the details changing, shifting: a little space ship as Iledra imagined it, two persons whom she recognized.

"She does not want to think about it," Iledra said.

"She must. She will not for us. She must for you."

Think. Remember.

No. Oh, no.

But it was not so much a protest against thinking about what had happened, as against the thing itself. She was not sure what that was, but it was bad.

Think. It is important, H'ana-daughter.

The keystone so. Tomorrow rain. We rest by speaking pools, enclosed. . . .

Remember. It is important to me.

Her awareness leapt, and for an instant she knew she was alive.

Iledra?

I am here. Tell me.

"Tell her," said the voice she ought to know, "to think it to you in words. I want the clearest report possible."

"She's too weak. It will have to be images."

In the silence Hanna's mind murmured along pleasant, harmless paths.

"All right, then," the voice said presently. "Describe them as well as you can."

Show me the aliens. Show me what happened.

The urgency and sorrow seemed distant. It was, perhaps, safe to approach them; memory too, perhaps. She did so cautiously, for Iledra. Who would not push her to terror and then recoil from it as others (others?) had done. She fell through a kaleidoscope of the New City, Koroth, Earthly glitter, black space, and thought very clearly: *The signal.*

And then?

A picture: Anja and Charl at her shoulders, not knowing the last hours of their lives had come; the tension, apprehension, fumbling at a mystery.

And then? And then? And then?

It was not so hard to make the images, as long as she remembered it had all happened to somebody else. Not to her. Never to her.

A quick intake of breath, involuntary. "So they destroyed it without reason or warning."

Iledra's voice. "None."

The pain! I cannot, I cannot, no! No! No!

There were quick, half-sensed flurries of movement that she knew only through Iledra's perceptions.

"This is what happened each time—"

"All right. Yes. I can block it and go on."

"Not so much," said still another voice, a woman's voice.

Hanna's mind soared suddenly into the air above southern Koroth. Here was the little town where her mother taught the neighbors' children, and orange blossoms were heavy on the air. The summer sun late in the evening cast long shadows from every hillock, and the heat was thick as water. I can feel that, she thought, and reached for a shadow. She thought she knew how it would feel between her fingers.

She had no fingers.

The voice said close by, "What did you tell them?"

D'neera. D'neera. I told them only of D'neera. They asked where my People are.

"D'neera," said Iledra's voice, sounding sad. "Yes. The center of her universe is D'neera. She is not only human; she is D'neeran."

"Did she not tell them about the Polity?"

"Not much, I think. It is not clear. They guessed there was more. But it was too late then. Their only dangerous knowledge is of D'neera. I do not know how they made her tell them even that."

"You see what they did."

"It would be enough."

"For anyone."

"Yes."

The third, strange voice said, "Enough. Enough for today. No more."

"One moment." Something came near. Close to her ear the familiar voice said, "Hanna. I'm sorry."

Sorry? she wanted to say. But she could not speak, and the question still rang in her mind when they put her to sleep again.

"Horrible," said Iledra. She noticed, with detachment, that her hands were shaking.

"Horrible," Jameson agreed. He stood before her still holding the glass of wine she had refused. She had no comforting illusion that today's ordeal was over. She needed a clear head.

She breathed deeply, trying to compose herself. For a brief space, here in Jameson's private office, the world was quiet. The wall to the river was shut, although she could see through it. The water was gray and restless under black clouds, the horizon a sick glare of light. She saw lightning, but no thunder was audible here. In another room close by, Cosma was exchanging stares with Paul Rodrigues and with an assortment of military and intelligence men whose questions could not wait. Iledra did not know if they would permit her to leave Earth. She could not and would not promise to keep her new knowledge to herself; to do so would be a rejection of principle amounting to treason. And the true-humans would want to control what she had taken for them from Hanna. They would filter it, edit it, shape it and tell a hundred societies what was good for them to know. A D'neeran could not stand for it; but she did not see how they could keep her here without producing as much trouble as the truth would create.

Jameson moved away from her, looked at the glass in his hand as if he wondered where it had come from, and drank the wine himself. Iledra thought he would go to his desk, an enormous thing studded and surrounded with devices for spanning human space. The ambience the room had had on her last visit was lost in the glitter of tools for communication and information retrieval, and the array had the secondary function of subtly intimidating anyone who faced Jameson when he took his place at its center.

But he stopped short of it and looked aimlessly about the room, and Iledra's attention sharpened. She read signs that Jameson was very tired and had been taking stimulants for several days, but that should not produce this absence of mind.

He looked around, gauging her recovery from the hour just past. He said as if it were inconsequential, "Why did they send her back?"

"Why did—?"

"They send her back. You must have wondered."

Iledra said unwillingly, "Yes. But I have been too worried about her to give it thought."

"It was not altruism." He came back to stand before her, and she got up as if some subtle alarm had sounded. The conversational tone did not deceive her.

"You think it is important?"

"Obviously. They went to no little trouble to keep her

alive. She must have been near death when they stopped—
from shock, pain, loss of blood. They nursed her through the
shock, sealed her wounds, and provided her with a fair sub-
stitute for human plasma. Enough to keep her alive for a
day or two; enough to save her until Aziz Khan got to her.
Why?"

"She said nothing of it. I don't know." At the moment
Iledra did not care. "Can she be healed?"

"I think so. The medical people think so. They've seen
worse."

"Worse!"

He said dispassionately, "Accident victims. She was mutilated with surgical precision, and all her vital organs are
intact. Accidents are not so careful."

Iledra had never liked Jameson much. Now she loathed
him from the heart.

"I want to take her home."

"D'neera does not have the facilities to care for her."

"As soon as she is well enough."

"It will be months."

Iledra was a tall woman, and did not have to look up
very far to meet Jameson's eyes. She said flatly, "You would
not let her go anyway."

"The point's irrelevant. She must stay here for her own
sake."

"You would not have let me near her if you had not
needed me. If any of you had been able to communicate
with her without being unmanned by her fear, you would
not have let me see her. If the *Voltaire* had not been there
when the alarm came, would you have told me, even, that
you had found her? I think not."

She was right about all of it. He would not say so; but she
heard it anyway.

He said quietly, "It's pointless to exacerbate public fear.
It must be known of course that she has been found, but not
everyone needs to know exactly what was done to her. I do
not want to deal with a panic."

"I think you already have one," Iledra said. She had
come to Earth very speedily, but she was no pilot and had
spent her days and nights in gathering all the information
she could. She knew knots and eddies of the credulous already wanted to run—if only they knew where to run to.

Soldiers everywhere watched the void for traces of an invader, and an innocent merchantman approaching Colony One had been blown to bits. All the commissioners' seats were in jeopardy, along with the bodies that had appointed them. And someone, someone not unimportant, had suggested Jameson be tried for unspecified crimes against humanity.

But he said, "There is no panic yet. But it is not wise to provide fuel for one. There are disjunctions enough in every society, and more will come. You cannot be unaware of what is happening here. Security measures already are affecting our economies. Earth's old proposal for tightening inter-system controls is on the verge of approval. It will take lifetimes to complete, it will drain off more resources than we can afford and restrict our descendants' freedom of movement to an intolerable degree. I thought the idea was discredited years ago; yet the mood of Heartworld governments is such that if it comes to a vote I will have to acquiesce. Power is shifting on every human world, including yours. For you, if I read the currents correctly, it is taking the form of a return to isolationism. I do not like a new thing I hear from D'neera—that a movement is gaining strength to build up your own defenses, and dispense with Polity protection. What will your people do when they learn what we have just learned—that your world is the aliens' prime target?"

Iledra said softly, "Don't try that with me."

"I beg your pardon?" He looked genuinely surprised.

"Don't try to frighten me. You lie. The prime target is the Polity. D'neera is no threat to them. They are interested in D'neera only as a means of getting to you. H'ana did not tell them enough."

Irritation crossed his face; she thought she was not supposed to see it. He said, "When the attack comes their reasons will not matter. You couldn't fight off Nestor without the Fleet. You can't do without us now. I hope you can convince your fellow magistrates of that."

"I am not likely to have much success. The outcry against me has been great. You are right at least about shifting power. I may not be the Lady of Koroth much longer."

"And the call will come at any moment telling me I am no longer the commissioner for Heartworld. But we still have our responsibilities, Lady Koroth. Neither of us to

one world only; both of us to the human species. I will not
try to force you to keep silence about Hanna's condition
or anything else you have learned. But I will ask you to
use all the influence you have to ensure D'neera's cooperation. I will ask you to make D'neera see where its duty
lies."

"Duty!" she said, and turned away from him. She was on
the edge of tears, as she had been since her first sight of
Hanna; it had been a great shock, in spite of Jameson's
warning beforehand. She had made Hanna see where *her*
duty lay, and would regret that success forever.

There would be no attempt to detain her here, for she
had made her own prison. Her efforts to insinuate D'neera
into true-human society had ensnared her, and all ways out
were closed. It would not be her part now to shape a world's
course; the aliens glimpsed as forms of horror in Hanna's
tormented memory would shape them all. Jameson would
let her go free so that she could bend or frighten the Houses
to docility—meaning that she would smooth the way for a
Polity military presence that would come whether it was
wanted or not. Her part was to play the go-between; to discourage resistance and make palatable the truth that the
Polity would descend on D'neera not for D'neera's protection, but for its own.

She looked back at him and said, because she had no
choice and it did not matter what she said, "I will do what I
can."

He nodded slightly. It was not much of a tribute to what
she promised. He said, "There was no indication of their
motives in returning her?"

The repetition annoyed her. "None."

"Perhaps we will find out in time," he said too casually.

Iledra thought of the useless hulk that had been Hanna
and clasped her hands together. They would question
Hanna as remorselessly as the aliens had, and she could not
prevent it. She could not even say that they were wrong.
Where Hanna and the aliens were concerned, no information was trivial.

She said, "There is one thing."

"Yes?"

"Probably it does not matter—"

"What is it?"

She said slowly, "There seemed a difference in H'ana."

"What sort of difference?" His tone was unchanged; but she knew that every sense he possessed was concentrated on her answer.

"I don't—I hardly know. Images and, oh, turns of thought, the equivalent of phrasing, perhaps . . ."

She was unsure of what she was trying to describe, and the impact of her contact with Hanna was fading. She knew the contours and tastes of Hanna's personality as well as her own, or she would never have seen the subtle difference; and it might after all be only part of the memory of fear and pain, or the greater disjunction of trauma and drugs. The first would leave greater or lesser traces in Hanna, as tragedy always did, but much of it, and the immediate effects of her physical condition, would dissipate.

She looked up and saw that Jameson still waited for her to go on. She shook her head. "It's not important," she said.

"Are you sure?"

She hesitated, but the impression dimmed as she considered it. It had been difficult to induce and hold Hanna to concentration, and dream fragments had kept intruding.

"I'm sure," she said.

"All right. Are you ready to talk to the others?"

She looked once toward the river, as if she could escape to it, but rain obscured it now, silently. "Yes," she said.

They went to the door together. Just before they got there he said abruptly, "I was glad to hear about her eyes."

She trusted him too little to think he meant it, but she said, "I'll have them sent in a week or two. We were going to do away with the bank. None of our defense people have needed their spares for years."

"It was good news you have them. The plan was for a stock transplant."

"I know." Iledra's own eyes filled with tears. She said, "I would hate to think of H'ana with someone else's eyes. Her own are so lovely."

Jameson looked down at her and said to her surprise, "Yes. They were very lovely."

The door opened, and the questions began at once.

Chaos. Dream sweetly.
?
Not this Home. Circled
!
unfearing
not mine! not me!
we rest
oh help me oh help
unheard. Dream. Forget.

The next wakings were less painful, and even more
dreamlike. Some she would remember, some she would not.
Part of her mind began to store information. They were fixing her, re-growing much of her, patching together the rest.
Her own eyes, grown on D'neera and banked there when
she joined Defense, were available; that was good. Her flesh
responded eagerly to regeneration, the speed was something built in at the time of the Change; that was not so
good, not when there were so many different things to juggle. She could not move or feel anything. They explained to
her once that so many delicate processes were going on in
healing her that it was best she stay away, stay asleep, and
let them go about the business of repairing the envelope
that held Hanna ril-Koroth.

Presently they tried waking her to full self-awareness,
and in the first burst of memory she was frantic to flee, and
could not move nor even cry out. Her panic blasted a hundred people. They knocked her out to stop the nightmare-
silent screaming and, reluctantly, since Iledra had gone
home, asked D'neera to send a telepath to aid them.

Dale Tharan came without protest, approved by the Polity precisely because he was an outspoken advocate of giving it anything it wanted and taking in return all D'neera
could get. But he did not like Hanna, and when he had
eased her into reality as he was supposed to do, he told her
she had not done him or herself or D'neera any favor by
failing to hold out against the aliens. *And hideous now. A
limbless lump,* he added, but even Tharan was not proof
against Hanna's first clear sight, through his eyes, of what
the aliens had made of her. They made her sleep again, and
next time they woke her Tharan, with considerable dedica-

tion, painted her portrait as she had been and would be
again. It was not much to hold on to, but it was something.

Jameson had the interrogation sessions linked with his office. He listened while he went about his business, and when
he was with other people he had the transmission routed to
the implant in his ear, which was supposed to be used only
for matters of extreme urgency and when he had shut himself off from the world by every other means.

The data extracted from Hanna were, then, twice disembodied. She could hear, but she could not speak. The questions therefore were asked by the men whose business it
was to ask them, but the answers were filtered first through
Tharan, and then through the complex electronics that fed
Tharan's voice into Jameson's ear. What he heard might
have been messages shouted by Hanna across a river, the
meaning twisted, distorted, blown away by distance and the
wind. Those about him were often disconcerted. He wore a
wrist communicator, as was his habit, but ordinarily he was
courteous about its use. Now he would interrupt anyone or
anything to raise it to his lips and snarl, "Ask her—"

Ask her anything. How many? On their ship? On their
world? How many planets? What weaponry?—until they
had to give up questions, because Hanna would get confused, and think aliens not humans questioned her, and
send Tharan with a spinning head stumbling away, unmanned, as Iledra had said, by her fear.

What she said of the Lost World jolted Jameson. He had
not really believed in it until now, thinking it a bare possibility; but it was real; and the spectacle of a human population
tortured, manipulated, subjected to experiment and killed,
was appalling. Humans had almost stopped doing such
things to each other—a hopeful sign for the future, he had
always thought. Now there was the prospect of its starting
all over again with an aggressor to whom economic sanctions and human opinion meant exactly nothing.

He seized on what the sacrificed colonists could do for
him, however, without permitting himself compunctions
about using a ghoul's opportunity. The information came
early enough to save him for a time, because it was immediately clear that Species X had been searching for humanity for a long time. Jameson said publicly and privately to

anyone who would listen, playing the idea for all it was worth, that it was fortunate the first contacts had been with *Endeavor* and *XS-12* so that humankind had some warning. It was not enough to get back all the ground he had lost, but Heartworld did not replace him and he was still in control.

Except—control was an illusion. Maybe he had known it from the moment Rodrigues's voice called him from the illusions of his last hours with Henriette. If he had not known it he found out one night when he took an enormous dose of Imagos, hoping to lose grim reality in the blurred edges of beauty for a little while. But the coals in his fireplace were Hanna's charred eyesockets, bone showed through his own unsteady hand, and he could not get the antidote into his bloodstream fast enough for comfort. Nothing like it had ever happened to him before. He sat sweating in a room cool enough to need a fire and acknowledged something he had pretended not to know: the dreams that had given birth to *Endeavor* were finished. There would be no brave leap into the future; only torturous courses dictated by need. Past and future had come seeking *him*, and he was as helpless as Lady Koroth.

Another purpose?
Another. Old old. Incomplete. They did not finish.
Finish what?
I don't know. An ending. More than death. More than me. They stopped. And still another.
Purpose? What?
I don't know. I don't know!

"Tharan," said an audible voice. It must have said his name several times before it penetrated his dialogue with Hanna.

He got up, shaking off Hanna's frantic grab for contact. To stay sane himself he had to harden himself against her clutching terror. If she had been anyone else, if she had been here for any other reason, they would have let her sleep through the months of helplessness and enforced paralysis. They could not, and she sometimes skirted the raw edge of panic. Tharan kept trying to tell her she was safe now. She kept forgetting.

Stanislaw Morisz had called him. Morisz beckoned and

Tharan went out the door with him. There was nobody in the corridor. This was a very busy medical center, but they'd sealed off a whole floor for Hanna.

Morisz said, "I read yesterday's transcript. There was nothing. Nothing definite."

Tharan said patiently, "Telepathic communication is not a one-to-one correspondence with fact."

Morisz only looked at him. Tharan knew Morisz was impatient and beginning to get angry. Hanna should have been a mine of information and she was not, and the true-humans did not understand why. Tharan was not surprised. He had come to Earth prepared to explain the uses and limitations of telepathy. Now he settled himself against the wall in the corridor outside Hanna's room and began to lecture.

He said, "Every bit of information exchanged is surrounded by a network of associated concepts, memories, emotions. It can be very precise if you have a language in common, and fairly precise even without that if there's a shared cultural matrix. If you don't have either of those things, you have what H'ana was writing about in 'Sentience'—very broad, global concepts with a high degree of subjectivity. She's trying to put into words—or sometimes I am—things that were images, symbols, very fuzzy when you try to objectify them. To put it another way, she knows a great deal about the aliens, but it's not the kind of knowledge you want. You'll notice all they got out of her was hard-science information. Stellar configurations are a shared objective reference, so she could show them where D'neera is. But they were the ones doing the questioning, not her. And where the 'soft' side is concerned, how they think, how they live, that kind of thing—as I said, she has a lot of information, but there's no program to plug it into. So it doesn't make sense to her or to me and it's not going to make sense to you."

When he stopped he saw Morisz's mouth twitch. Morisz said, "There's some objective data, though. The Lost World, for instance."

"Sure—because there was something in her cultural matrix to connect it to. But it's very general. No detail."

Morisz pondered. He said, "I don't understand what she means. That they were doing something besides questioning her."

"I know. I don't either. Neither does she. It's very vague. Maybe religious but not really, she says, and then somehow divorced from its original context. They ripped her up for a reason, but she doesn't know what it was."

"You have to get more."

Morisz looked tired. Tharan said sympathetically, "Jameson on your back?"

Morisz did not answer. He didn't have to. Jameson kept turning up at odd moments, straight and stiff and staring at the remnants of Hanna with an inhuman lack of queasiness. The man had a strong stomach and maybe, Tharan thought, some things going on inside him a mindhealer could hardly resist. But he wanted Hanna sucked dry anyway.

After a minute Morisz said, "We're wasting time."

"Yes," Tharan said, and set about calming himself for the return to Hanna. What he was doing was hard. Everything he got for Morisz was filtered through layers of blind pure animal pain.

Tharan thought it was a good thing they had him. They'd have gotten nothing by themselves.

After a while it seemed to Jameson that he had been hearing Dale Tharan's voice all his life.

They found out what the aliens looked like and made pictures, and Hanna looked through Tharan's eyes and agreed (with what pain Tharan did not say) that the pictures were accurate. They found out what the outside of the alien spacecraft looked like, which told them nothing, and what an alien torture chamber looked like, which told them less. They found out you could make a neural stimulator from something that looked like living fabric and set about trying to do so, hoping if they succeeded they could work backward to some bit of knowledge about the aliens. They searched for records of the Lost World, but there were none; that was why it was lost. They tried to figure out how an alien stungun worked. They analyzed blood samples taken from Hanna on the *Mao,* and came up with something unexpected.

"Psychoactive drugs?" said Jameson, who saw every report anyone made on Hanna. His eyes hurt constantly and he seldom slept. The first narrow escape from being recalled to Heartworld might be over, but only his intimate knowledge of the situation here kept certain key councilmen in line.

"Yeah. Funny thing is, she doesn't remember any effects." Morisz's eyes were red too.

"Can you tell when she got them?"

"Late in the process. Very late."

"Before or after her memories gave out?"

"Impossible to say. The best guess is it was after she lost consciousness more or less permanently."

"There would have been no point at that stage."

"There's no point to any of it. Why do they think we're some kind of goddamn tigers? What could a bunch of ragged-ass colonists do to make them think that?"

"Whatever the reason, she ought to have been able to show them otherwise."

"What?"

" 'Sentience.' Section Six."

"Oh," said Morisz. "That."

And then?
The right response.
But then
Exactly the right response.
Then
One of us two of us three of us defenseless
Then
Vulnerable.
But later?
No later not ever.
There was later.
No later. No.

"What's that for?" Jameson said.

"What—oh. The screen. I don't know. We started using it at the beginning. I forget why." Morisz was so used to having a barrier before the module holding Hanna that he had stopped noticing it.

"Get rid of it."

"Right."

But when it was gone Morisz remembered why it had been there. This outer room was large enough to seem uncrowded in spite of its masses of equipment, for even minor regeneration was not a simple task, and Hanna was not a minor project. Now, however, it was crowded with people, and with the screen gone they had to look at Hanna. Eight weeks into the regeneration process she was, if anything, a more repulsive sight than she had been at the start. The medical people liked to see what was happening, though their eyes were not as good as their instrumentation, and sometimes they forgot to cover up the tangle of flesh and tubes and wires with decent sheeting. They had not forgotten this time, but the contours of the figure centered in its zero-g bubble were horribly suggestive. But at least, Morisz thought, she has a face again. The only recognizable thing about Hanna when he had first seen her had been the straight pretty nose. The aliens had not wanted to obstruct respiration.

The scene taking shape was Jameson's idea. He seemed not to believe Hanna had told Tharan everything, though the questioning went on for hours each day, and insisted on trying one more thing. Tharan, just outside the chamber where Hanna lay, was already in tenuous rapport with her; she was more heavily sedated than usual, and the effect showed in Tharan's face as a vague slackness. Neuro- and psychopharmacologists were in place, and a physiogeneralist stared over their shoulders at a mix-monitor panel. A Fleet liaison specialist and one of Morisz's assistants ignored each other from adjacent seats. There was nothing more to wait for. Morisz was about to witness—in a sense, even, to direct— something he had heard of but never seen: a mindhealer-Adept of D'neera undertaking a telepathic deep probe.

He said to Tharan, "You know what you're looking for."

"Something . . . hidden . . ." Tharan's voice trailed off. It would be difficult for him to maintain a double awareness— inward to Hanna, outward to the others—but it could be done. He would not attempt to speak to them unless he got what he was after.

"Anything new. Anything at all. You've been over most of it so often you should notice anything different. But don't waste time on the stuff we know. Get down to the end and concentrate on that."

Tharan did not answer. His eyes glazed as the contact deepened. Hanna, Morisz knew, had not wanted to do this,

but Tharan had appealed to her sense of duty—and, Morisz
suspected, her guilt.

He glanced over his shoulder. "Everybody ready?" he
asked, but not until he saw Jameson's bare nod did he say to
Tharan, "All right. Go ahead."

Minutes trickled by. Morisz watched Tharan, but he was
as motionless as Hanna. He would be living through her
experiences now, not just turning them into words for Intelligence, but guiding her attention to details unconsciously
noted. If he could he would damp the emotional strain,
holding her to detailed objectivity. Morisz had expected
signs of strain, but there were none. Time passed, men
shifted position and coughed, someone spoke. Morisz wondered why he had ever thought a deep mindprobe would be
a dramatic thing—

Blackblackblackno

"No!" Morisz whispered, and wiped sudden sweat from
his face. The sensation had been one of falling, as if he had
been on the edge of sleep and jerked back just in time from
an endless black pit, wide awake. He looked sidelong at
Jameson and saw a hand slowly withdrawn from an instinctive grab for support. He felt a flicker of satisfaction that
Jameson was not immune to *this* at least, and then was
ashamed.

He whispered to Jameson, "Tharan lost it."

"Mmm-hmm."

Morisz glanced uneasily at the pharmacologists. He had
been there for Hanna's first waking, and knew first-hand
what happened when a half-mad telepath lost control.
Tharan was supposed to be able to focus and channel her
awareness, centering it on himself and reinforcing the inhibitions against random projection that Hanna had internal-
ized in childhood and practiced all her life. If he failed, the
pharmacologists would take over. But even they were using
negative alerts, so a circuit would close and Hanna would
sleep if they made any move without warning. That first
time their colleagues had nearly killed her when all they
wanted to do was shut her up.

Tharan was quite still, his hand resting on the thin plastic
film that provided a visual cue for the force field containing
Hanna. Sometimes he went inside with her, but not today;

she could not be touched indiscriminately, and in the deep probe the urge to do so would be strong.

The tension had grown with that fragment of Hanna's memory, and Morisz muttered to distract himself, "He's getting attached to her in spite of himself, isn't he?"

"Yes." Jameson just breathed the word.

"Says she knows what a mess she made of it."

"Mmm-hmm."

Morisz was not an imaginative man, but he remembered Tharan's confidence and was chilled. What would it do to you, he wondered, to lie paralyzed and blind and anesthetized for weeks, remembering how you got that way, reflecting on your failure, living with the conviction of the man who was your only link to life that you had endangered everything you knew?

mistake mistake mistake stupid mess D'neerans look what how'd we get here goddamn

Words, even seemingly in Hanna's voice. Jameson turned his head and said, "She's getting that from one of us." There was ice in his voice.

"Not me," Morisz said a little nervously. He looked around and saw the Fleet major gone red-faced and too stiff, unused to his private thoughts becoming public property.

lovest me thy father mother brother lover here fullsharing lest cold night

Tharan shifted abruptly. Morisz was on his feet. No words that time, not until he created them, and not in Hanna's voice but silent strangeness, a jolt of madness.

Jameson said quietly, "Nothing new."

"What?"

"Think about Tharan's reports. That's what he's been describing all along."

"Oh . . ." Morisz sat down slowly. The men behind them whispered to each other. "She was identifying with them."

"Sometimes," Jameson said, but he was leaning forward now and watching the two D'neerans closely, as if he could force his way into Hanna's brain himself.

But Tharan, after a while, straightened and shook his head. "That's all," he said. The words were a little slurred.

Jameson continued to stare at him. Tharan put his head

in his hands. When he looked up his face was more alert; he had broken the rapport.

"There isn't any more," he said. "I told you there wasn't."

Jameson got up and went to stand beside him, looking through the transparency at Hanna. Morisz followed, uneasy. In the weeks since Hanna's return Jameson had become more reserved than ever. It had never been easy to guess what he was thinking; now it was impossible. He seemed to be turning to stone, perpetually preoccupied with something no one else perceived. But whatever it was focused the force of his personality instead of subduing it, so that when he spoke it was like a glimpse of flame, and Morisz sometimes thought that one day Jameson would explode.

Tharan stood up and Jameson said, "There is more."

"There isn't. It just ends."

"They hadn't finished with her. You know what was in her bloodstream: psychotropic drugs. You know what they would do. It must have been done *after* what you have shown us."

"It ends," Tharan repeated.

"Memory does not vanish. The organism records everything. On the cellular, the chemical, the molecular levels, if nowhere else. If you are as competent as you say, you could retrieve her primal memories of gestation. Why not this?"

"I can't retrieve something unless there was enough consciousness to organize the experience in the first place. There wasn't. They dissolved her ego."

"She perceived it as dissolution. That does not mean it was dissolved."

Tharan said blankly, "That's exactly what it means."

"I don't intend to argue semantics. Is there any possibility she is deliberately blocking you?"

"No," Tharan said positively.

"Could there be a block imposed by another?"

"No."

"How do you know?"

Tharan said angrily, "I'm a D'neeran, a telepath, an Adept, and a mindhealer. Don't try to tell me I don't know."

"You are either incompetent or a liar," Jameson said, and turned away and started for the door. The ghoulish little tableau was broken. Tharan took a fast step after Jameson.

Sweet winds, summerfruit, soft-plumed love eternal thy warm waters unbroken.

In a great rush of wellbeing Morisz saw a hand slip from its place. The circuit closed; he drifted for an instant toward sleep, and it was over. Hanna was entirely unconscious. Tharan stood still, looking toward her, and the others were between him and Jameson, babbling questions.

"Later," Jameson said. "Stan."

It was an order, and Morisz ducked between the others and followed Jameson into the corridor.

"What," he began, but Jameson shook his head, and they went through half the building, a long walk, in silence. Hospital personnel stared at them with covert or open curiosity, but Jameson paid no attention. Behind them trotted a man from Administration internal security. Two days ago someone had planted a homemade firebomb at Jameson's door; it was primitive but dangerous, and Jameson had reluctantly accepted this minimum of personal protection.

Outdoors the August sun burned hot. Jameson stopped on a deserted flight of stairs, waved the bodyguard away, and said, "They expect to permit her mobility in about three months."

"Yeah. She'll be able to talk then. Maybe we can get more."

"I doubt it. But from the moment she moves a finger I want her watched. With spyeyes. Without her knowledge. I want every room in this center in which she spends time wired for sight and sound, and I want you to form a team to study the record, every minute of every twenty-four hours of it, and report to me."

"Report what?" Morisz said in frustration.

"I don't know."

Morisz thought: He is going right over the edge. Right here. Right now.

"Starr..." It came out more plaintively than he intended. "It's a dead end. You can't get anything better than what Tharan did. Go right into her head and pull it out—what the hell can I do that's any better?"

"Then send the tapes to me and I'll study them myself."

Morisz could not refuse the direct request. There was his personal liking for Jameson, for one thing; for another, there were implications for the future. He did not want

Jameson telling anyone he was uncooperative in a matter of such weight, and certainly he could not defend himself by accusing a commissioner of unreasonable caution.

"I'll do it," he said. "But it's a dead end, all the same."

"Think so?" Jameson started down the staircase. The sunlight dimmed. The sullen air promised rain.

He said, "They don't leave dead ends. Every time it's looked that way they've set us up for something. Remember that, Stan. It's nearly the only thing we know about them."

"Yes," Morisz said, "but they've already set up D'neera. What else could they want?"

"Just watch her," Jameson said.

Chapter 10

The water was always warm and clear, and drew her irresistibly. She forgot sometimes to push against it, floating in a timeless sea, and the physical therapist who took her to the pool each day would call, "Hanna! Hanna! You've rested long enough." And she would make a dreamy effort, forgetting the purpose was to make her stronger, filled with wonder at the play of muscle and the sensations of water against her skin. It was strange to inhabit a body. She remembered inhabiting one familiarly, but she could not get used to it again. Parts of it surely were gone? Movement unbalanced her; food was distasteful and she spilled it; her face glimpsed in a mirror with clear blue eyes surprised her.

They had made her body whole by slight degrees, and would do the same with her mind. Living in the unworld of brain barred from body was painful, so she had been unconscious for five months, except for the sessions with Tharan. The exceptions might have been her undoing, for she opened her new eyes to memories of The Questioner, repeated daily and ingrained past forgetting, and very little else. Tharan had not been a reassuring companion. His head was filled with images of fleets on the move, chaos at home and his anxiety to return, mistrust of the men around him and violent dislike of Starr Jameson. That was Tharan's version of events, or all of it Hanna saw, anyway. Her final waking, therefore, was to unrelieved bleakness. To ease her transition to physical life she was given drugs that softened without changing the prospect. It was always at a distance from her, and so was grief—for herself, for D'neera, for Anja and Charl, for something else; but what? It was too distant to see. It was there in dreams she could not remember, a loss and an emptiness that would never be filled. Tharan was gone, and there was no one to uncover her dreams.

So faithfully had she been cared for that after a week she could walk. She could not walk very rapidly or very far, but she could walk. She came out of the hydrotherapy pavilion one day, moving hesitantly and wearily away from the water's support, and found Jameson waiting for her.

She thought he must have come to see someone else, but that made no sense. He was here for her, then. Barely clothed and wet through, she forgot the chill of dry air while she searched memory for the proper thing to say. Ordinary courtesies no longer came automatically, and never sounded right when she remembered them.

He said, "Hello, Hanna," providing the clue she needed.

"Hello," she said in relief, but fragments from Tharan came together without warning: the ruin of the *Endeavor* Project, the near-ruin of this man's career, the ragged end of his visions, devastation of his life, and had it not sprung from her? She had never given a thought to what he risked in trusting her. Now, when she saw the size of the gamble, it seemed to Hanna in her distress that he must have come here to accuse her. She might have panicked, except that he appeared utterly unchanged. As it was, she looked at him piteously.

He said, startled, "Are you all right?" and took her arm, which had seemed very far from his intention.

"All right," she said faintly.

"I can come back later, if you wish."

"No," said Hanna, so unused to having power to postpone the unpleasant that she did not really understand the option.

He went with her to her room, and she leaned on his arm most of the way. Seeing him had jolted her from her fog—and she wondered with new clarity how much of it was self-created, not chemically induced. But the question sank in her painful anxiety for his welfare, and she was not clear-headed enough to think such anxiety might be ludicrous while his strength literally held her up.

Her room was comfortingly dim. She sank onto the bed with a sigh, telling herself she must not fall asleep just yet. The light flared, and she blinked. She had forgotten that her preference for semi-darkness was not shared by everyone.

Jameson came to stand before her, tall and solid and wrapped in the old stillness. He watched her intently, not trying to disguise it. There were deeper lines than she remembered at the corners of the gray-green eyes, and his gaze was colder than she had ever seen it. She felt a twinge of unreasoned fear of something besides reproach.

She could not think of anything to say. After a while he said, "How are you feeling, Hanna?"

His eyes and tone were so at odds with the concern in the conventional question that she did not understand immediately, as if it were necessary to translate what he said from one language to another. "I'm—well. I'm feeling better. Time," she said, pushing at her hair. It was cropped close, a silken cap, and felt strange to her hand.

"Intelligence is rather anxious to get at you without the intermediary. Think you'll be strong enough to talk to them soon?"

"Soon. I think—soon." But Ward, her chief physician, spoke of that or something like it at least twice a day. He must know the answer. She hardly heard the next trivial questions, answering by rote. He had to have the answers already. He did not care what she said. He was not listening; only looking. He had come here only and specifically to look at her.

He took a step toward her and without warning, swept by fear, she shrank away from him, fighting an impulse to run. She could not run. She was too weak.

"Hanna?" he said, but she could not answer, huddled in on herself and shivering.

After a minute he sat down beside her. There was a tangled coverlet on the bed, and to her astonishment he picked it up and draped it about her shoulders. It was the first gesture of kindness she had known in many months; the men and women who cared for her were not unkind, but busy and impersonal. She began to cry, the acid tears tickling her nose incongruously, and to her further astonishment felt his hand on her back. The simple act of compassion overwhelmed her and she turned to him blindly, reaching out, expecting nothing. Very slowly, he put his arm around her.

"Forgive me," she whispered.

He shook his head, but the movement came from some sharp conflict within himself.

"Please," Hanna said urgently.

"There is nothing to forgive," he said as if against his will.

"What I did . . ." Tears blurred her eyes. The shameful memory smothered her.

"You did all you could . . ." He spoke slowly, reluctantly, but his arm tightened around her. She responded to it, not to his words, and laid her head on his shoulder without thinking, knowing he would not mind; he only thought he ought to mind it. He was a point of wholeness in a sadly tattered universe, and she clung to him, needing wholeness too desperately to care if he wished to be clung to or not.

He bent his head and she moved a little, holding her breath with a sense that time and space had slipped and left them, the two of them, miraculously alone and secret. He said close to her ear, very softly, "I wish it had not been you. But I'm glad it was you."

She said on a long breath, "Why . . ."

"You did not speak. It was not you. They destroyed you."

"Everyone blames me . . ."

"They are wrong. Who could have done better?"

"Anyone. You—"

"Not I." He touched her hair, a delicate gesture of comfort. "If anyone tells you he would have done better, he lies."

She turned her head a little, almost secretively, as if he would not notice that his lips now touched her cheek. Her skin seemed to have been dead, and suddenly was alive. She whispered, "But I told them—"

"Not enough. Not enough for their purposes . . ."

She was passionately grateful. He had strength enough for both of them. She was safe with him. *Safe:* from doubt, from guilt, from memory. She had never needed anyone before, nor anything so badly. She would tell him so.

Then he remembered something he had forgotten, and she felt it fall between them like a knife. He drew away from her with a movement so abrupt it was nearly violent. Time resumed. She actually cried out, bereft. The act was so deliberate and implacable that he might as well have gotten up and walked out, and she wept, uncomprehending.

He waited without moving or touching her until her sobs eased. Presently she straightened, sighing, and wiped at her wet cheeks. Jameson turned his head, but he did not speak at once and his face was unreadable. A last sob choked her. He said—it might have been another man talking— "Do you remember the probe Tharan did?"

She nodded, hardly hearing.

"What happened after he broke the rapport?"

"After?" Confused by his contradictions, still shaken to the bone, she tried to remember. It had been so long ago. It was mixed up with all the interrogations before it and after it, and besides she had been sedated, which was not customary. The healer was supposed to be strong enough to share your full awareness of whatever made you seek him out. But Tharan had not come to her as a healer, and nothing about that probe had been customary.

"I fell asleep," she said. "Or passed out. I don't remember which."

"I mean before that, but after Tharan broke the contact."

She shook her head. "I don't remember anything. Did something happen?"

He said after a moment's silence, looking directly into her eyes, "No. I thought perhaps something had occurred to you afterward. But if there was nothing . . ."

"No," she said uneasily.

He stood up, remote as ever, preparing to leave. She said quickly, "Commissioner?"

"Yes?"

There was a question she had asked no one because she was afraid of how they would look at her. But whatever he felt, it was not, at least, contempt.

"Why has there been no attack on D'neera?"

For an instant she saw exhaustion in his face, and pain so great it shocked her into silence. He said something she did not absorb; said good-bye, and she nodded numbly; left her staring after him. If she had ever thought him impenetrably armored, the minutes just past would have shattered that illusion. But this was different; she had with her question gone straight for a nerve, all unknowing, and seen something she was not supposed to see. Why, when it was a question everybody must be asking?

She could not think of a reason, but she stopped wondering about it because she was preoccupied with something else. She had finally remembered his reply, and also the inflection he gave it. It was a non-answer, but why had he said it that way? She could not get it out of her mind, and it worried her till other shadows hid it: "*You* ask me that?"

She saw Melanie Ward every day, and also Larssen, the physical therapist. When she asked them when she could leave they gave her no answer. She did not belong here. This was a Joachim Beyle Center, an acute care facility specializing in regenerative techniques. There were half a dozen of them on Earth, half the total in human space, and this one was within sight of the Polity administration complex. Hanna's small room had no window, but when she was strong enough she walked round and round the Beyle Center, scuffling through dry leaves over carved stone, and looking at Admin's distant spire with the stylized star at its tip. Somewhere in those buildings were Jameson's rooms, where she had been an honored guest. She wished he would come see her again, but he did not. She wished the medics would let her go, but they would not, though now she was as whole as she would ever be and needed only outpatient care. "Wait," they said, and tested her over and over, and days and then weeks went by.

"It is autumn here too," said Iledra. "We are together in that for once. Strange places you've been, H'ana-ril."

She paused, waiting. It was a minute before Hanna stirred. She was a faraway face to Iledra. Her eyes were dead. Iledra looked at her more closely. Fear seized her that Jameson had been wrong and Hanna would never be well again.

But the blue eyes shifted, came to focus, and were Hanna's: sad, but intelligent and alive.

She said, "Hello, Lee. This is a surprise."

It was the second time she had said it. Iledra said, "Are you all right, H'ana-ril?"

"Yes," Hanna said. Fleeting surprise touched her face. "I'm getting stronger," she said.

"Good. I expected to hear from you, and I did not, so . . ."

"Oh," Hanna said. Her eyes shone with quick tears. She turned her head away so Iledra could not see her face. She said, "I couldn't bring myself to— There was so much I didn't understand from Tharan, and I've read ... I've read about the, the, the ... tree ... tree—"

She stopped, fumbling. Iledra said, puzzled, "The what?"

Hanna now seemed utterly confused. Iledra watched her with amazement and alarm. Hanna said at last, triumphantly, *"Things."*

Iledra closed her eyes for a moment and thought: Her mind is broken. But Hanna went on sanely enough, "The soldiers of the Polity. Half the fleet's in the system, isn't it? They say there've been—disturbances—"

Tears glittered on her cheeks.

Iledra put down her mug of honeyed juice. It was the last of the season, and she would not take a meal outdoors again this year. The rainbow glimmer of fading falseoaks surrounded her, and fine nurturing dust powdered her hair and shoulders with a million subtle jewel-flashes; but the wind was rising, and one more stormy night would scatter the last of the tree-borne light. Had Hanna been thinking of falseoaks? But the connection was obscure.

Iledra said slowly, "There are disturbances everywhere. The Fleet strategy is to stop an invasion here, but it is not popular. I have secured the communication here. Are you secure?"

It did not occur to her that the question represented a marked change in her own attitudes. It did not occur to Hanna either, apparently. Hanna only shook her head and said with an effort at a smile, "None more secure. I tried to call Cassie and they wouldn't even let that go through."

"Indeed. I'll tell her I've spoken with you. I said there are disturbances everywhere. The governments of the Polity worlds bicker and shout. They think we have too many ships, men, guns, sentinels, and the Commission leaves them too little. You know the administrators of WestCon have fallen on Co-op? And the governors of Montana on Heartworld, though all Montanans are mad in any case. Even Lancaster's parliament has been overturned. I thought Lancaster forever asleep. I suppose you've heard of these things, but ..."

Her voice trailed away, because Hanna was not listening. Rather, she listened to something else. She turned her head and stared into a room so dark Iledra could see nothing in it. In reflected light from the video screen her eyes were a stranger's, and slitted.

"H'ana," Iledra said softly, but there was no response.

After a minute she went on. She spoke steadily and conversationally. Chill wind clutched her hair and trickled down her neck.

"You know all that, I'm sure. But probably you have not heard of Colony One's proposal to evacuate all D'neera and destroy the Houses and the cities, so if the aliens come there would be nothing, and the Fleet if it loses here could retreat to worlds the aliens cannot find. They might even have done it, H'ana—but they could not think how to resettle all of us."

"Yes," Hanna said. "That's right. All at once. I hadn't heard." She turned back to Iledra, looking only wistful. She said, "What did Jameson say?"

"Nothing," Iledra said. "Not a word. He knew it must come to nothing. And he is in no position to protect us."

"No," Hanna said. "I wish I could see him. But I haven't. Tell me more."

But her face was so sad that Iledra hesitated. She thought now that Hanna's deficiencies might be neither physical nor intellectual, that something else perhaps had broken, and she could say nothing that would not bring further pain. Hanna could not know all the tumult the forced marriage of true-humans and D'neerans had brought, because true-humans now controlled most of D'neera's channels of communication, and chose what to suppress. All the old prejudices had flared again, strong as in the years of isolation. Polity soldiers no longer were permitted to visit the surface of D'neera for rest and recreation; there had been rapes, batteries, thefts, finally a full-scale riot. Most Polity societies closed their doors to D'neerans for, they said, the outsiders' own protection. This meant D'neerans who wished to evacuate voluntarily—and there were many—could not do so. They stayed at home with everyone else, watching a hostile sky whose harborage of the true-human fleet seemed more threatening, for now at least, than hypothetical aliens of unknown power.

And it was Hanna's doing. And to know all that she had brought about would not help her.

Iledra said, "I will tell you more another time. Are you comfortable, H'ana?"

"Yes," Hanna said doubtfully.

"But unhappy . . ."

"I can't," said Hanna, lines creasing her forehead, "seem to think. They don't—want to talk to me. They're not allowed to, I think. The people here. I only ever see a few. And men from Intelligence. I go to, to where they tell me. The pool. The gymnasium. Nobody's there." Something like horror came into her eyes. She repeated, "Nobody's ever there. I can't, can't think to anybody. They don't like it. There's nobody to talk to. I'm living in a box. I'm not living—"

She stopped suddenly. Her eyes were dim again. Iledra waited. After a minute Hanna said clearly, "It's all right here. I'll come home when I can."

Iledra said, "Are you quite sure you're all right?"

"Yes. Yes."

"Not, perhaps, a little—confused?"

"Confused?" Hanna said. "Why, no." And now she only looked, in fact, tired.

Afterward Iledra called Jameson, but when she said she wanted to talk about Hanna, he would not speak with her.

She did feel odd. Fuzzy. Maybe even a little confused. She spent many hours in the pool, comforted by water. Melanie Ward talked of womb-returns and said she could not do it forever. But in the pool she could keep her eyes closed, and she did not like looking at things. Objects and bodies and faces had taken to having periods of unintelligibility, as if she had lost the patterns of what they were supposed to look like. Speech sometimes was mere noise, meaningless and almost painful. She was possessed by a lethargy of mind and body that seized her anywhere, at any time, so that she stopped what she was doing and neither moved nor thought until someone spoke to her or something else happened to rouse her. The commonplaces of technology were sporadically, unnervingly beyond her grasp; not that she did not understand principles, but that she could not remember which knob or lever or button did what, and she had to stop and think how her bath or the terminal in her room worked. She was glad her meals were brought to her so she did not have to cope with their preparation, though it meant always eating alone, when she bothered to eat.

She did not want to tell anyone about these things, but exhaustion drove her finally to tell Ward that sleep did not rest her. She woke in the mornings as tired as if she had not been to bed at all, and seemed always on the edge of remembering an evil dream. She thought it out with some difficulty, and decided the transition drugs must be responsible. But when she put the question to Ward, Ward said she was no longer being doped.

"But every day they give me—"

"Immune boosters, because your resistance is down. Nutrients, because"—a hint of reproach—"you don't eat properly."

"I don't understand," Hanna said. She made a vague pass at her hair, missing by some distance. "Can I have something, then? To help me with the dreams? To help me rest?"

"No," Ward said, and made an explanation to which Hanna did not attend. The truth was that she was afraid of sleep. She was afraid she would die in the night. There were mornings when her first thought on waking was that she *had* died, and somehow revived with the dawn. She felt as well an urgent need for sleep, no matter how much she got, and the conflict between fear and desire was painful. She did not want to tell Ward about it, because she also was afraid to confess that she was afraid. The Questioner had exposed too many unsuspected weaknesses. Hanna would not herself expose more.

"Tell me," Ward said invitingly, "about your dreams."

"I don't remember them," Hanna said truthfully.

After that the I&S men who came to her every day wanted to hear about her dreams too, but she could not satisfy them.

In December the first snows came.

Hanna got worse. She felt more and more as if she lived in a box that shut her off from the rest of the world. At first she thought the difficult, complete suppression of telepathy was the source of her isolation, but it did not explain everything. Her body, once strong and athletic, was unreliable. Her muscles twitched, she walked into walls, dropped things, fell sometimes. She had headaches and her eyes felt so tired she thought something was wrong with them, but Ward said otherwise. Ward did, however, tell the Intelligence agents to stop hounding her. They stopped; less for her health's sake, Hanna thought, than because there obviously was nothing more she could tell them.

The relief from that pressure did not halt the decline of her mind, however. She cast about in desperation for release, and a longing came upon her to go home. It seemed that if she were on D'neera she could be well; that the universe would look right, smell right, fit her comfortably. Even the passage through space drew her, even anything that was not here, where nothing but water was right.

Still they would not let her go, and they would not tell her why, and when she thought of tapping their minds to find out why, she was afraid. Because they seemed so strange to her: almost alien, in fact.

Early each morning Morisz went over the previous day's and night's reports on Hanna ril-Koroth. They were lavishly illustrated, because she was watched as closely as even Jameson could wish, though Morisz still thought it a waste of time and resources.

This morning, however, the report was accompanied by a nightside operative. Morisz canceled an appointment and had her brought in at once. She said, "This might not be important, but you did say to report anything unusual."

"I meant it. Let me see it."

He waited while she searched the night's record for what she wanted. His office looked inland from the river, and in the weak winter sun he picked out the bulk of the Beyle Center with its fringe of parkland and snow-dusted trees. What was Hanna up to now? Whatever it was, if Wills thought it important enough to show him, it had better be passed on to Jameson.

Wills said, watching the timeline, "Most of it was ordinary. She went to bed early, got up after a while, and started studying. A text on Terrestrial evolution this time. Toward morning she went back to bed, but this time she got up again, and she didn't seem to be in fugue. I think she'll say she remembers this if she's asked."

"I think she remembers all of it," he said.

"Well, it's just an opinion, but I don't think she knows

how much she's up. Otherwise why would she complain about being tired? Here it is."

They leaned forward simultaneously. The room from which the image came had been dark, but the picture was enhanced to full visibility. Hanna's room at the Beyle Center was, by the center's standards, highly decorated. The patterned walls with their ornaments of crystal and metal made it almost certain Hanna would not find the near-microscopic spyeyes by accident. The furnishings were spare, but Ward had had rich fabrics brought in, and pretty objects that when activated moved or spoke or projected rippling color. The object was to provide Hanna with plenty of positive sensory stimulation; but she seemed not to notice her surroundings, and did not play with the enchanting toys.

She was in bed, just beginning to stir, in the picture Morisz saw. She sat up, pushing away the sheets with a quick motion. She wore a white gown that fell from her throat to her feet and covered her arms as well. Until recently she had slept naked, but the habit had changed overnight and, it seemed, permanently. She stayed away from mirrors, too; Ward said she had contracted a revulsion to the sight of her own body; a reaction finally, she thought, to its mutilation.

Hanna swung her legs over the side of the bed and sat up straight. Her face was slack with weariness. She tilted her head as if listening for something. Her eyes moved, searching.

After a minute she got up. She moved to the middle of the room, so unsteadily Morisz thought she might fall. She looked around her and began to move again. She looked into the tiny bath cubicle, opened the door of the room and looked out into the hallway. She slid open the panel of the room's small storage module and pawed through her sparse collection of clothing. Morisz realized to his astonishment that she was trying to find something.

He said to Wills—in a whisper, as if Hanna could hear, although what he saw had happened hours ago— "I wonder if she's caught on to the spyeyes?"

"She's looking in the wrong places. She'd be looking in the room itself."

Presently Hanna gave up the search. She went back to

her bed and sat down slowly, dejection in the lines of her body. Still she looked about the room. It seemed to Morisz that she almost sniffed the air. She stopped that too and was still. Her lips parted and she said in a whisper, faint and sibilant but clear: "Come out! Come out where I can see you!"

And listened painfully for a reply. And heard none. And lay down again and began to weep, her face pressed into a pillow.

Wills froze the record and said, "That's all. She cried till she went back to sleep."

Morisz scowled at the sad little picture. He said, "What was she looking for, anyway? If not the spyeyes?"

"She's a telepath," Wills said. "She *says* she's not exercising the faculty, but I understand they can't always help it. If she senses she's being watched, she might be looking for something without knowing exactly what she's looking for."

"That's right," Morisz said, not happily. "So don't ask her about this incident. Next time she'd be looking for spyeyes, because she'd *know* she's being watched."

He told Wills to include the scene in Jameson's précis and got rid of her. He thought about calling Jameson, and decided against it. Starr was on his way to Heartworld, where Taylor had just succeeded—barely—in quashing a demand for hearings on Jameson's fitness for his position. "I seem to be making a career out of smoothing feathers," he had said to Morisz just before he left. It was something he would not have said a year before, but they were by way of becoming friends, and the strain of the last months was having an effect. The very term he had used was proof that Jameson, with his fine sense of discrimination for a phrase, was not himself; nothing native to Heartworld wore feathers.

Morisz decided this last bit of nonsense could wait until Jameson got back.

There seemed always to be someone looking over her shoulder. She heard sometimes a breath at her back, and turned to find no one. Some of her clumsiness came from starts at footsteps close behind her, but always when she looked there was nothing. They asked her occasionally what she did in the night. The question made no sense; she only slept; she sensed they did not believe her, but she never asked what they meant by the question. Because she was afraid—afraid of what she might hear, afraid she might be doing something dreadful in the dark, afraid The Questioner had kept some of her sanity and she would never get it back.

One day in desperation, thinking if she did not challenge her intellect she soon would have none left, she tried to catch up with developments in her field. The first extract the index showed her was a critique of "Sentience" that suggested all its conclusions—all her years of work—were suspect because her predictions about the uses of telepathy at first contact had been flatly wrong. It was cross-referenced to an item that informed her she had been, during the months of unconsciousness, stripped of her Goodhaven Award.

She stared at the text for some time, feeling nothing at all and wondering why there were tears in her eyes. No one had considered the matter important enough to tell her about it. She supposed it was not, then, important. The Academy's little ornament was somewhere in the wreckage of *XS-12,* or lost or destroyed or, fittingly, in alien hands.

"But it *was* important," she whispered despite the constriction in her throat; and she was reaching for the key that would erase the screen when Jameson's name caught her eye. His part in getting her the prize had been suspected.

Finally alert, filled with real anxiety, she searched for more information. There was no more; there had been only that one hint of it. But there was plenty of other information on the last six months of Jameson's life, and Hanna read into the night, fighting sleep.

Tharan had thought with some triumph of Jameson's crisis, but he had provided no details. Now Hanna learned that at one point only a single vote in Heartworld's general council had saved Damon Taylor from having to demand Jameson's resignation. Taylor insisted doggedly that Jameson was the best man to have in the commissioner's seat now, and as long as law permitted him to keep Jameson there he would do it. There had been talk of impeaching Taylor; it had come to nothing, but certainly he would be gone after general elections two years hence, along with a number of other councilmen.

The revelation that Species X had known what it was

looking for did not make Jameson better liked on his own world or any other. He had always been too liberal a commissioner for many Heartworlders' tastes, and controversial from his first day in that position. The *Endeavor* Project had not been popular at home; now the worst pessimists' fears were realized, and they did not let anyone forget it. There was another side to the early-warning argument Jameson and Taylor had used. It was this: the aliens might have searched for hundreds of years without success if it had not been for the *Endeavor*. On other worlds, and for the same reasons, Jameson was called everything from incompetent to insane. Muammed al-Nimeury criticized him publicly, and the other commissioners tolerated this breach of official etiquette. No one—not even Andrella Murphy, who was said to be his friend and possibly his lover—defended him.

There were images from an earlier life Hanna had not wondered about before: Jameson leaving a theater with an exquisite, dark-eyed woman on his arm; Murphy whispering in his ear at a hearing on interworld law, saying something that produced the kind of radiant, open smile Hanna had seen only twice; Jameson shaking hands with some Co-op dignitary at a glittering formal gathering, poised and inscrutable. His private life was very private indeed, but some of it had surfaced recently, not through the efforts of his friends. Hanna tried to tally the rumors of dissipation with the austerity of his usual manner and with her own glimpses past his self-control, but she could not make them fit together.

The present was easier to understand. Now he was always alone, except for a bodyguard or, sometimes, a grim-looking Rodrigues at his shoulder. She guessed his world was divided into two kinds of people—those who sought to bring him down, and those who were waiting to see if the others would succeed. What she did not understand was why he tolerated it; why he did not go home to comfortable obscurity; why he endured the weariness she had seen, when all his hopes must be ended and there was nothing left but duty.

But that is precisely what it is, she thought when she lay down at last. That is what I did: endured all I could, without hope, because it was my duty. He knew it. That was why he could forgive.

The thought comforted her, and she clung to it down the sickening slide into sleep.

But the dreams were worse that night, in the morning they were closer, and soon the days were nightmares too.

snow too deep and where the whitesky seeking prey? Lost, all lost and fallen. Death and loneness, waste of white.

"Hanna," Ward said, raising her voice.

Hanna lifted her head slowly. Ward's face *dark as deep-rock* was attentive.

"Hanna?"

"Sorry . . ." Hanna rubbed her face. Her hands had shrunk. The fine planes of her face felt deformed.

"Melanie," she said in panic.

"What is it?"

"Nothing." She licked her lips. They felt almost like her lips.

Ward stared at her, and finally dropped her eyes to the surface of her desk. The characters and diagrams on it changed as she keyed in, one at a time, the morning's test results. Hanna stood up and Ward said, "Where are you going?"

"Look out," Hanna mumbled.

"What?"

"To look out. The window."

"Oh," Ward said, and returned to her study.

Polished metal round the window showed Hanna her face. It looked wrong. She put a hand to her throat and stared blindly at snow, waiting for the fit to pass. This morning was the worst yet; but it had been getting worse for days. She was horribly afraid. She put her forehead against the warm transparent window, trying to remember if Ward had stopped recording before the onset of this last break in reality.

She jumped as Ward said, "You're all right. A couple of anomalies, nothing outside chance. I'll see you again tomorrow."

Hanna did not move. She said to the window, "Melanie, when can I go home?"

"Not just yet. You've been a very sick girl."

"You just said I'm all right. Why can't I go home, Melanie?"

There was a small sigh behind her. Ward said, "Hanna, you know you can't."

Hanna drew a fingertip across the window's surface. She said, "I'm a prisoner."

"You're not a prisoner. You go wherever you please here, you can go outside, you can go into the city if you want to."

"And risk being recognized and—never mind. That's not what I mean. I want to go *home*. To D'neera."

Ward said more gently than before, "Not just yet."

Hanna turned around. Surely Melanie would notice something was wrong with her face; but nobody ever did. So there was nothing wrong with it. So she was going mad.

"Melanie. I don't need you anymore. I need a mind-healer." It took some effort to keep her voice steady.

"Why," said Ward, looking up at her through dark lashes, "do you say that?"

Hanna did not answer. After a minute Ward said, "We could get Tharan back."

"No." Hanna's hands were quivering. She put them behind her back. "Melanie, what's your rank?"

"My—?"

"You're not on the staff here. Somebody told me. You're with Fleet."

"Yes. Well."

She looked disconcerted, almost guilty. Hanna did not know why it was supposed to be a secret and did not care. "Can you let me go?"

Ward shook her head.

"Who, then? Morisz?"

Ward hesitated, but decided, perhaps, she would save herself trouble by answering.

"I suppose he'd have to approve. But ultimately the decision would be Commissioner Jameson's, I think."

"Can you arrange for me to see him? I can't," said Hanna, desolate, "call him myself."

There was another hesitation. But Ward said at last, "I'll try. He's on Heartworld, though."

"When he gets back. As soon as he gets back."

"I'll try," Ward said.

On the way to her room Hanna had a moment of sheer terror when a spasm took her right arm and bent it at the elbow. She stumbled against the wall to stop it, to hide it. She got to the room, to the bed, and crouched on it for some time, biting at her hands.

She did not remember the beginning of her fear. Perhaps it had begun with The Questioner, who now visibly pursued her in her dreams. Sometimes in the morning she could not make herself look in a mirror, convinced she would see raw meat with bone showing through. Her body was more strange to her, not less. It made movements of its own accord, and caused her to stumble, shaking her with alarm out of all proportion to the event. She felt an urgent need to hide these incidents and did so, telling herself confusedly Melanie would never pronounce her well if she did not. There were times when she found herself in the pool when it seemed she had been in her room the moment before, or vice versa; times when she was staring at the face of someone who had not been there a second ago and who was waiting for her answer to some question. She did not tell Ward about any of these things, and she was afraid.

Fear had grown on her so gradually she was not aware of its progress, but now when she looked in mirrors she saw that her face, which had always reflected her thoughts because she had no talent for duplicity, had become a mask to hide the fear. Even that was a relief, though it was not always her own ruined face she was afraid of seeing. It was something else—someone else, she thought once—and she did not know what. But each day the fear was greater, and she moved in a haze where she examined each word and hid even her treacherous body's rebellion from unseen watchers.

And now this: reality distorted, familiar shapes shifted, images drifting through her tangled brain that came from nowhere she knew. Had the Questioner been less guarded than she thought? Had she absorbed memory, knowledge, an alien essence, despite his powers? She had told Intelligence otherwise, and they tested her when she said it and knew it was the truth. Truth at the time; perhaps not now; but what might surface now did not matter. She could not face questioning again. If her brain still held treasures of knowledge she would tell Iledra, and Iledra would tell

Morisz from the shelter of D'neera. If they suspected it now they would not let her go. And she had to go. Had to go.

At length she dragged herself off the bed and called Iledra. It took a long time for the call to go through. There was action at Morisz's offices, no doubt: flurries, discussions, but approval in the end, because Iledra answered. The quiet, familiar room behind her pulled at Hanna's heart.

Hanna passed a shaky hand across her mouth. "Lee," she said, knowing others listened, "I want to come home."

But Iledra said reluctantly that home might be no haven. Hanna made her say it plainly: many D'neerans blamed Hanna for their distress. Hanna had wondered uneasily about the possibility, but that did nothing to lessen the hurt of hearing it.

"How bad is it?" she said.

There had never been much room for evasion in their friendship. Iledra said, "H'ana, I do not know what place there is for you here."

"Well . . ." Hanna stirred anxiously. "Defense needs people, doesn't it? I'm trained."

"H'ana-ril, I think you had better consider resigning from Defense."

"Now? When there's going to be a war?"

"I do not think," the older woman said sadly, "you will be given any responsibility even if there is a war."

Hanna thought of everything she had learned and done for Defense, the years spent learning spacecraft, weapons principles, unarmed combat, the honor after Nestor, everything, all of it: all gone.

"What about D'vornan? The university?"

"The program has been closed," Iledra said, her face blank.

"Oh . . . But the House—there must be more work? And not enough people?"

Iledra looked away for a minute. Hanna said in dread, "Lee?"

When Iledra turned back there were tears in her eyes. She said, "Lord Gnerin has suggested to me that you resign from this House, and that I name Cosma my successor. There has been no formal motion . . . yet. If it comes to that they will all be against you."

Hanna looked at her hand, numb. The Heir's Ring had

come to Earth with Hanna's eyes. The frosty blue stone was not ostentatious; the Ladies of Koroth could be flamboyant enough when they chose, but they took their responsibilities seriously, and that was what the understated ring said. No one had ever given her a greater honor than Iledra had in selecting her to someday head Koroth. She did not think she would do it as well as Iledra, or Penelope before her, but she had always thought she would do her best.

She said, "What do you want me to do, Lee?"

"I will not—" Iledra stopped and drew a deep breath. "I will not attempt to dictate your course. They cannot force you to resign, or force me to repudiate you."

"But what do you *want?*"

"I want, I want things to be as they were before. And they can't be. They won't ever be. I will not alter my choice. I will not ask you to resign. But as matters stand now you would be entirely ineffective at Koroth."

Her face twisted, but Hanna could not spare a thought for her pain; her own was too great. She said stiffly, "I will send the ring back for Cosma."

"No. Bring it. Come home."

"But the House would not be home anymore."

"It will always be your home. It will be—it will be hard. But where else are you to go?"

"Nowhere," Hanna said. "I have nowhere to go, except to you."

After that conversation she understood at last the full extent of her loneliness. The haze of fear deepened, and she was unhappier than she had ever been in her life. In desperation she reached out to the only person here who had seemed really friendly to her, and invited her therapist to her bed.

Larssen was pleased; he had kept intimate watch on her body for weeks, after all. He was also kind and affectionate and not unskilled, but Hanna felt nothing. She hardly knew he touched her; all sensation seemed to leave her skin, it was like the hide of some alien animal, no part of her at all. Her thoughts blanked again, and she came back to awareness huddled in a cold ball on her bed, weeping bitterly.

"No use," she said from somewhere in space. "No use. Go away. Please."

Larssen was unoffended. He knew the details of what

had been done to her; he said it was only to be expected. He made sure she would be all right alone, accepted her apology, and left.

Hanna lay alone in the darkness with an emptiness in her and around her she had never known before. All the rich years had led to this, they were all poured out now, streaming away as such years did at the moment of death. Her work, her pride, her place in her world, even her physical being were come to nothing. She felt nothing but the pervasive fear. She had nothing left but Iledra. She was not sure that would be enough; she was not sure she could ever be filled again. But there was nothing else to try.

Starr Jameson would return to Earth in a few days. She would ask him if she could go home.

Chapter 11

"That's it," Jameson said.

The holograph image that seemed to stand in the center of his office moved slowly.

"See the hesitation? Now watch this."

The image kept moving. The figure tried another step, lurched awkwardly, and fell in slow motion. It was Hanna. Her face was curiously expressionless, even when one elbow hit the floor with a surely painful impact.

Stanislaw Morisz said doubtfully, "I see what you mean. It's not much to go on."

"Not by itself, no. But taken as part of a pattern, beginning with that set-up rescue . . ."

He waited while Morisz thought it over. His theory was far-fetched and he had broached it to few persons besides Morisz. He was not prepared to be laughed at unless it was necessary.

"All right," Morisz said finally. He leaned back in his chair. The winter day was nearly over, and behind him the river was black except for its edging of ice. "Maybe there's something to it after all. How'd you spot this?"

"I've been looking for . . . oddities. Anomalies in her behavior, besides the obvious ones. I checked this as a matter of course; it happened to pay off."

"My people should have caught it."

That was true, but Jameson said, "She's very good. It's hard to be sure even when you know what you're looking for. But I've watched hours of these things. Days. If you run an incident like this against a kinetic model, there's no doubt she's faking the falls to hide the other thing."

Hanna's insubstantial figure lay before them in a grotesque sprawl. Morisz stared at it, and Jameson, moved by some obscure impulse, touched a switch and said "Endit." The image vanished. Not that it matters, he thought. She hasn't had a moment's privacy in weeks, and after all this is only a picture.

"If she's supposed to do something—think she's supposed to do something? Sabotage? Spying? If you're right—" Morisz caught himself up short. He looked faintly embarrassed by his own half-belief. He said, "We'd better find out what it is, first. Conditioning, programming—we can do things like that too, you know. Shouldn't be hard to figure it out."

"She doesn't remember what they did."

Morisz answered with emphasis, "She *says* she doesn't remember."

"Tharan would have known."

"You weren't too sure about him yourself."

"I think he reported honestly what he saw. I think he did not see all there was. And of course there is still the possibility Ward suggested—that it's some sort of hysterical reaction, delayed shock or something of that nature, she's disguising for reasons of her own. Afraid to admit it to Ward for fear of losing even more autonomy—"

"Doesn't explain the nights."

"No. If I'm right she may know—as she says—only that she is tired in the mornings."

"But the rest of it . . ."

"She knows she is somehow out of control, of course, and she has spoken of it to no one. And I think Ward is wrong."

"Well, then?"

Jameson said, "There is only one expert on the aliens, on what happened to Hanna, and on Hanna's state of mind. I intend to ask her."

"Sure. And a lot of good that'll do if she doesn't remember, or she's hiding everything she can from us, or both."

"One can always ask. She's under a hell of a strain, Stan. She's frightened. It shows, when she thinks no one's watching. A direct confrontation might be enough to get a start, at least."

"So what happens if it doesn't produce anything?"

"I'll try to get her to agree to another deep probe. Maybe duplicate the drugs the aliens gave her—"

"You wouldn't let us do that before," Morisz said resentfully. "What happened to 'intolerable' and 'inhumane'?"

Jameson said, "They got lost somewhere between expediency and desperation," and Morisz eyed him doubtfully, not sure if he was joking or not.

"We should have done it a long time ago," Morisz said. "Six months since they dumped her in our laps. Six months lost, six months without a sign of them when we could have been getting somewhere."

"Not lost," Jameson said. "Perhaps if we'd done it at the beginning we'd never have seen what we're seeing now. I did not and do not think creating an artificial psychosis will accomplish anything except her further torment. I still hope it won't be necessary."

"And if it is, and she doesn't agree?"

"We do it anyway. We can take her into official custody as an intelligence source. You don't need to remind me how gently she's been treated so far. We do not have to keep doing that. There is no way for her to stop us from doing anything we want to do."

It took a greater effort than he expected to say that quite coldly, but Morisz noticed nothing and said only, "You're sure of this, aren't you?"

"I'm sure the implications are so important we have to assume I'm right."

Morisz was thinking ahead. He said, "If we have to go that far, how do we justify it to D'neera?"

"We won't have to. D'neera is united in nothing, and less than ever now. There will be no protest; except from Lady Koroth, of course, but she'll be alone. No one else on D'neera is likely to give a damn. Hanna is not exactly popular there."

"The old story." Morisz chuckled, but without humor. "After Nestor she couldn't do anything wrong. Now she can't do anything right. Yeah." He got up, stretching. He seemed a little larger than he had when he entered the room. There was a plain course before him, a thing to do. He said, "I'll get started on it right away."

"No," Jameson said. He sounded peculiar even to himself; Morisz glanced at him in surprise. He said, "I'd like to give it a try myself."

"You?" Morisz said, looking at him too closely. "What for?"

Jameson said slowly, "She knows me. Not well, perhaps,

but she respects me and I think trusts me as much as she trusts anyone here. She regards I&S as a threat. The analyses of the direct interrogation sessions made that plain. I should like to see how she responds."

"It's irregular," Morisz said disapprovingly. Jameson folded his hands and waited. Finally Morisz said, reluctantly but with no rank to pull, "It makes sense, though."

"Quite," Jameson said, and was shocked at his own relief. The reason he had given Morisz was sound enough, but he had not admitted even to himself, until now, the other reason: that his intervention might, just might, mean that Hanna could be spared some quantity of pain.

Morisz said, "When are you going to do it?"

"I don't know. Soon. Why?"

"I'll have to have somebody on the scene."

Jameson shook his head sharply but Morisz said, "He can stay out of sight. I don't—I beg your pardon, but you have to consider appearances. I don't mean to imply anything about anybody, but—we don't want anybody thinking this is some secret kind of—"

He was talking himself into a corner. Jameson almost smiled. He said, "You mean if Struzik or al-Nimeury were doing this without an I&S representative at hand, I'd bite your head off. I see. You're right, of course."

Morisz relaxed visibly. He said, "Anyway, it wouldn't hurt to have help there. If the worst-case scenario is true she might get violent."

This was a possibility that had not occurred to Jameson. Whatever his suspicions, he thought of Hanna now as so fragile that a look might break her. Yet the chance existed, and he had finally managed to get rid of his bodyguard, an appendage Heartworld considered a weakness—though the threat of assassination was real enough even now. The tradition of personal courage was strong in his culture, and he wondered what would be said about his accepting assistance with a woman still frail from illness. But Hanna was trained in personal combat and he was not, and he had not struck a man since early youth.

"All right," he said finally. "I might as well do it immediately. She's been asking to see me, in any case. I think I'll ask her to come to my house tonight. It might be as well to get her out of the medical atmosphere."

"Soft light and flowers," Morisz murmured.

"What?"

"I've seen the same reports you have. She's lonely. Vulnerable, maybe."

Jameson said frigidly, "That was not what I had in mind."

"Of course not." Morisz looked abashed. "Sorry. Larssen was after her again the other day, by the way."

"What do you mean?"

"Said he wanted to try again. I hear she was in tears by the time she got rid of him. I'm surprised she didn't just break his arm."

"She would have, at one time." Jameson had not seen the record of Hanna's earlier encounter with Larssen and had told Morisz to destroy it. He knew one or two of the Beyle Center's directors very well; now he made up his mind to see to it Larssen lost his job. Surprised by his own anger, he hardly noticed Morisz getting up until he looked up absently, hearing the man speak again.

"What did you say?"

"I said, I just can't believe it. It's fantastic."

"I know. That's what the others said. But you are becoming convinced, aren't you?"

"Let's say," Morisz said cautiously, "the evidence is suggestive. It would explain a lot. Are you just going to come out and ask her about it?"

"Why not? It would simplify things considerably if she admitted I could be right. And when she knows we've found out her evasions, what would she have to lose?"

"More than you think, maybe. The last man who sold Polity secrets—remember Harrison? He's still living on Nestor like a king."

"I don't think she's done that. Tharan would have picked it up."

"Not necessarily. It's no crazier than what you're suggesting. If that really was an artificial block Tharan ran into, who knows what they can do? Maybe they bought her and taught her to hide it. Maybe Koroth isn't enough for her. Maybe they promised her she'd be a queen. Keep it in mind. You can't leave out the possibility."

"No," Jameson said, but he did not mean what Morisz thought he meant. The slight, shivering woman who had shown him her agony at failing had not been bought by anyone; but he would not let Morisz see his certainty.

The evasion left him uneasy, and he was still uneasy when he left his office some time later. He had not spoken to Hanna, only left a message for her at the Beyle Center, but he did not doubt she would come. The interview would be recorded, and one of Morisz's men would be within earshot.

It was dark on the concourse before the administration complex, and a bitter wind was rising, laced with snow. Jameson suddenly remembered he had not arranged transport for Hanna. He had personally vetoed letting her have access to a credit network, which in effect made her a prisoner under the guise of making her a guest. That meant she would have to be on foot, and he thought of her walking five kilometers on legs that did not always obey her, and winced.

"This won't do," he said into the wind, but it was no use. It was too late. His detachment where Hanna was concerned was a poor illusion at best. He could not afford to hide the fact from himself; he doubted his success in hiding it from Morisz; and there was little hope of hiding it from Hanna, who from the beginning had ignored the face he presented to the world.

He had begun by pitying her, an easy thing to do. The wreck Aziz Khan found, considered as a human being, was pitiable enough. Considered as the author of "Sentience," the lively sharp-edged presence that once was Hanna, it had the impact of profound tragedy, a random discontinuity that mocked human effort to read meaning into the universe. Jameson knew very early that Hanna could be made whole physically. When he learned also that enough of her mind survived to answer questions, that should have been the end of it. It had not been the end; and in the months past, increasingly troubled, he had sought to find out why.

It had nothing to do with her beauty, as he half-suspected at first. It was true that as he watched the ruin of her face take its old shape under the physicians' hands, he understood at last why on each meeting he had the sense of seeing her for the first time. She was lovely, a fact he had ignored as best he could, and one which was the more piquant because she was entirely without artifice or seductiveness, unaware of her own impact and seeming not to care. But it was not that that affected him. Desirable women were everywhere, and all his adult life he had taken for granted the attraction his status and wealth exerted. He had been immunized to beauty more years past than he cared to remember.

Nor was it Hanna's personality that drew him, the antithesis of his own. Impolitic, honest, direct, she had ambushed him more than once into responses he did not want to make; it was a warning clear as a spoken word, and he had intended to heed it. He could have done so easily; could have put the attraction aside, ignored the flattery of her half-sensed interest, regarded her as valuable in her way, useful, nothing more—

Until now. Until her destruction; until it was likely (said Melanie Ward, citing the long-term effects of torture) she would not be the same woman again.

He had gone to the Beyle Center often when she could not see him, nor know in any way he was there. He felt no revulsion at her rebirth. Instead it seemed he watched a metamorphosis; that her steel-framed chrysalis was midwife to something new and, perhaps, rare. For what had she been before, after all? A girl becoming woman; a bright child who had never been hurt, defined and circumscribed by qualities he had named at their first meeting. What would she do, now that youth and luck and brilliance had failed her all at once? —Not through the slow pressures of time, the series of defeats that forced men and women into courses they did not choose, but with a single blow that tore her loose from every anchor she had known and left her harborless. It disturbed him that she had so accurately, in their brief meeting, perceived that he might allow her to turn to him, and her willingness to do so disturbed him even more. She had been kept deliberately—not maliciously, but coldly—from everything and everyone who could give her comfort; and in his occasional, erratic impulses to provide it, Jameson recognized the uncertainty of his own balance, which he had once thought so secure.

The cold truth was that he faced the ending of his own life, as he defined it and had chosen to live it. It was not only that there would be no more *Endeavors*. What was left was perilously fragile. His associates were slow to forgive mistakes, and his prestige had not recovered from the blow the aliens had dealt it. He had never walked such a tightrope. If he fell now there would be—nothing. Only the broad fields of Arrenswood, the life of a country gentleman in which he would dwindle and waste and grow old too soon. The miracles that gave men twice the lifespan they deserved were capricious, and unkind to him. There would not be time enough to wait for Heartworld to forget, not time enough to forge his career a second time. There would not even be another Henriette, because his pride, next time, would revolt. Hanna might recover from what had been done to her, in spite of Ward's opinion. Jameson might not.

For weeks now he had watched Hanna move against the backdrop of such thoughts. She did not know he watched her; she did not know he saw her uncertainty, and later her fear and despair. He knew her intimately, without her knowledge and against her will, and it seemed to him the aliens had created no crueler disjunctions than those that faced both of them now. For despite his intense familiarity with every terror that touched Hanna's face, she still held a final secret; and though his wish was to let her seek shelter, necessity demanded that he take from her the last hope of it.

It was a pleasant house, set among trees that were bare and frosted now; in summer it would be heavily shaded. It was faced with some wood Hanna did not recognize in the gathering darkness and looked old, old, like something from a more primitive culture than Earth's. Even through the leafless trees she could see no other buildings, privacy unheard-of in the heart of a Terrestrial city. She remembered the house belonged to Starr Jameson, not to Heartworld. He must have wanted this solitude very badly, she thought, to spend what it must have cost him when there were no guarantees he would last even this long on the Commission.

She went slowly up the long hill before the house, stumbling once. The spasms that racked her when she was alone had mercifully spared her during her long walk, but her coat was light and its thermal control had failed, and she was frozen and exhausted. He has to let me go, she thought. I can't take much more of this; it gets worse every day; but

D'neera was a blur in her mind and all that was clear was
the space she must traverse to get there, the freedom of the
void. That would be safe.

She touched the front door's beveled glass curiously, and
jumped when the house spoke to her. Mr. Jameson was not
yet home, it said. She was expected, however; would she
come in? She did so, grateful for the warmth, and followed
directions to a softly lighted room that was sleekly paneled
and breathed subtle woodsmells. The furniture was big and
comfortable and there was a working fireplace. A faint tang
of smoke hung in the air.

The house did not speak to her again. She took off her
coat and sat down uneasily; something shifted a little with
her presence and fell softly in the fireplace. The silence
was profound, and for all the need she felt to be alert it
seeped into her, and her mind drifted. This happened often now, and she floated on drowsy waves of images that
had to do with Earth or D'neera or places she had never
visited, half-formed glimpses of worlds she did not know.
An occasional gust of fear shook her, but most of the time
she was too tired to be afraid. If I do not get to a mindhealer soon there will be nothing left of me, she thought,
and terror woke her; the thought was too reminiscent of
The Questioner.

In that moment Jameson came in, and stopped abruptly
when he saw her, staring at her face.

"My dear girl," he said, "are you all right?"

"I was just dozing," she mumbled.

He said, "You told Ward you wanted to see the mindhealers."

She looked up quickly. "Yes," she said.

"Why? What's wrong?"

"Nothing," she said, lying hopelessly. "I just—it was the
trauma. That's all."

A long time went by. Finally he said, "No."

"No?" She turned back to him anxiously. "You won't let
me?"

"That's not what I mean." He paused then said, "Hanna,
you must tell me a little more. Just a little more."

His voice and eyes said: I am your friend. She believed
him. She longed to tell him. She whispered, dizzy with gratitude, "I'm going insane."

"Why do you think that?"

He spoke gently, leaning forward a little, and her lips parted but she could not speak. If she told him they would try to fix her here. And she had to leave. Had to.

She looked away, hardly breathing, knowing he waited for an answer. But she could not think what to say, and after a minute he said, "I know about some of it."

"You know?" said Hanna, but a voice said in her head in great alarm: *No. No. No.*

Jameson for a moment receded. He said, barely heard through a wall of mist, "Some of it."

She shook her head. "No. What?"

When had she become so inarticulate? Oh help me, she thought, but she could not say it. He went on quietly, "The muscle spasms. The movements you can't control and try to disguise with falls. The blackouts. The night-walking. The conversations you don't remember. What else?"

"How could you know!" she said incredulously. Her mind went blank. A single tremor shook her. She was an empty vessel filling slowly, inexorably, with fear.

When she could move again she looked down at her hands, afraid to meet his eyes.

"What else?" he said softly.

"It's been you. Watching me."

"Yes."

"Why?" she whispered.

He did not answer at once, but presently he leaned forward and took her hands. It seemed an invasion, and she shuddered.

He said gently, "Don't be afraid, Hanna. No one wants to hurt you. But there are answers we must have. Too much is unexplained. What did the aliens hope to accomplish by giving you back to us? What did they do to you with their drugs? When Tharan probed you he could not retrieve some memories that must be there—why? What does it have to do with what's happening to you now? Tell me what you think. Somewhere you must have the answers. You are the woman who wrote 'Sentience'—"

She shook her head violently. "A failure," she said.

"No. A brilliant work. In essence accurate, I think; flawed perhaps in detail, because you did not take into account some things that—well, that no one could imagine. Not a failure ... You are quite capable of reading the pattern, reading your own behavior. Do you read it as I do? Think."

She did not know what he was talking about. She said in confusion, "I can't—I can't—"

"Think, Hanna. Do it. This is your last chance."

"My last chance!"

She looked up at him in terror. His hands were warm and there was sympathy in his face, but what he said might have come from the man who had come to her on *Endeavor,* offering cold alternatives and enforcing them with threats. She tried to pull away but he held her hands tightly and she had no strength.

He said, "You cannot convince me nothing strange is going on. You cannot convince me you are not hiding something. At best, hiding; perhaps deliberately lying. And I am not alone in thinking so, Hanna. Stanislaw Morisz believes I am right. I have talked to General Steinmetz, I have talked to Peter Struzik, I have talked to Andrella Murphy. When I say this is your last chance, I mean it is your last chance to cooperate voluntarily. Trust me, Hanna. Tell me the truth and nothing will happen to you. I promise you will not be harmed."

She tried to think and could not, and felt nothing but unreasoning panic. She did not know where it came from. It seemed part of her mind was screaming before a long-expected danger, but she could not tell what it was.

He said, "The night-walking—"

She said through the panic, "What are you talking about!"

He said, "Do you really not know why you are never rested?"

"No. No. I don't know what you mean." It was hard to speak because, she thought dimly, she was going to faint. She spoke only because to speak, to comment on the unknown, was a human habit. Her thoughts were surface-level and sprang from no foundation of logic; under the superficial web there was blackness.

He said slowly, "You don't go very far. Only to the terminal in your room. And all night you study mathematics, history, military science, other things, astrogation—always, every night, astrogation. You have known for years the approximate route from D'neera to Earth, yet in the last weeks you have studied it carefully. Why have you done this, Hanna?"

"I don't know—I don't believe it—" She moved restlessly, helplessly. There was a great pressure behind her eyes and she thought vaguely of Ward, she ought to tell Melanie about that, maybe something had broken loose.

"I believe you, I think." He let go of her hands at last and looked at her strangely. He said, "You are exhibiting classic symptoms of a dual personality, you know."

She rubbed her hands over her face. She did not understand what he was saying. But something connected and she said, half a question, "The mindhealers?"

"No. I wish it were so simple. The evidence suggests you're under some kind of control, Hanna. From outside—"

"That is impossible," she said clearly, and then heard herself say, "I am not. That is not true."

He and the room seemed to have become very small, as if she were a great distance away. She saw that he shook his head.

"Who knows what's possible for the aliens? Powerful telepaths, evolved not engineered telepaths—you said once that you are too human to guess what that might mean. Until we know, we cannot let you go."

She stood up suddenly. It was not she who moved and she swayed, seeking balance in a moment of darkness. Her eyes cleared and she saw Jameson on his feet, his eyes wide with alarm. She stretched her hands out blindly.

"Help me," she said.

He said quickly, "Yes. All right."

"I remember," Hanna said, and watched her hands lift, and in a last wholly human moment wanted to tell him what she remembered: the drugs, the dissolution, the whisper in what was left of her mind, the overpowering presence of the creature who was their Leader, desperate, bending over her as if her ruined body would accommodate him.

I remember, she started to say again, but instead she backed away from him for more fighting room and Leader spoke, directly to Jameson's mind, and said: *I will kill you now.*

She sprang straight for his throat. The edge of her hand nearly broke his forearm, thrown up just in time to save his life. Her foot smashed into his groin and he went down in agony with a strangled animal sound. Through the roar in his ears he heard running feet, Visharta, Morisz's man, he would be too late, she was fast and skilled, one more blow—

There was no other blow. He managed to unfold himself. Visharta stood over Hanna, the snout of an armed laser handgun pointing at her head. She lay face down and limp, dead or unconscious. Visharta began to talk into a communicator on his wrist.

"Stop that," Jameson said. "Shut up. Not on an open channel."

"But Mr. Morisz—"

"I'll talk to him myself. Tell him to wait."

He eased painfully to a sitting position. It hurt to breathe too deeply and he was weak and nauseated. He said, "Is she dead?"

"Nossir. I didn't touch her. Found her like this."

Hanna suddenly rolled over in a single convulsive surge. Her eyes were open and unfocused. Visharta shifted his aim.

Jameson said, "Is that all you've got?"

"I've got a stungun, sir."

"Then get it out, for God's sake. She's no good dead."

Hanna's eyes focused on Jameson. Visharta said behind her, "Don't move." She swiveled to look at him and when she turned back to Jameson he saw she was breathing unevenly, gasping, eyes wide, an animal in the extremity of panic. She tried to say something and nothing came out. Her hands made erratic movements that went nowhere.

Flight reflex, Jameson thought dispassionately. Dangerous as hell.

He got slowly to his feet. The pain was bearable now and he could ignore it, with some effort.

"Back off," he said to Visharta.

"Nossir," the man said stolidly. "My orders were to protect you."

Jameson went slowly across the little space that separated him from Hanna and dropped to one knee in front of her. He was not interested in arguing with Visharta and would chance getting stunned. He looked into Hanna's terrified face and saw that it was, at least, her face. Perhaps he had only imagined that half-formed distortion.

He said, "Hanna?"

She still gulped for air in irregular sobs, but the convulsive efforts to move had settled into tremors. She nodded in jerks: Yes. I am Hanna.

"What is it?"

"One of, one of them." Her voice was thick. She took another breath. "Inside me. Alive."

"Impossible."

She shook her head and reached for him in the gesture she had not finished before. After a second, unwillingly, he put his hands on her shoulders and drew her closer to him.

"What does it want?" he said in her ear.

"It wants to go back," she whispered. "It came to find out what I didn't tell it. It knows now. It wants to go back."

"Back where?"

"I don't know. Where it came from."

"How did—never mind."

He patted her back absently, holding her close and looking past her at nothing. This was worse than even he had thought. She said, still against his shoulder, "It's gone now. Hiding. Inside me."

"But it can come out whenever it wants? Control you? Do what it wants?"

"No, not—" She lifted her head a little and let it fall back. Her breath was warm through his shirt and her voice was calmer. "Not whatever it wants. It wanted to kill you. I stopped it."

"But who's in control?" he said, and discovered with profound shock that he was rubbing the back of her neck. The skin was silken under his fingertips.

"I don't know. I don't know. I knew it wanted to kill you and I stopped it. I don't know how."

"Can you feel it inside you now?"

"Yes, like—" She fumbled for words. "Like carrying a stone around inside me."

"A physical entity?" he said, incredulous.

"No. No, I don't think so. It's been there all along. I didn't know what it was."

"Can you communicate with it? Try," he said, and deliberately held her more closely, reassurance against panic.

Another tremor went through her and she said, "It doesn't want to. I can't make it. It said so. It's afraid—"

She lifted her head and he saw the fear was gone from her face; there was only a look of wonder.

"It said so," she repeated. "It's gone again now."

He felt her curiosity, so strong it left no room for fear. She met his eyes, inviting him to share it. He could not afford the luxury. He said, "It only comes out when it wants to?"

"I guess—yes."

"You can't get at it unless it wants you to."

"No, I don't think so."

"Well," he said, "that settles that."

He touched her hair once, regretfully, and let her go and got up. She looked up, startled.

"What are you going to do?" she said.

"Call Morisz. Get the experts started on you."

"What do you mean? What are they going to do?"

"I don't know." All his aches had started up again. He said tiredly, "Maybe we can get to it if we duplicate the drugs. That must have had something to do with it."

"But—wait." She stood up too, a little unsteadily. Her eyes were anxious again. "What do you mean? What they gave me?"

"Yes. If—"

"Oh, no. Please. I remember. I remember what it was like."

"If it is the only way—"

"No!" She was frightened again. She came a step closer and looked up into his face. "They said that too," she said. "The only way. It's like dying. It's worse than dying. It was the worst, the worst of all. You can't. You can't do that to me."

He said with finality, "I'm sorry. I have twenty billion human beings to think of."

Her hands closed on his shirt. "No," she said. "No. Please." Horror blasted him, and a silent, powerful plea for help. She had trusted him, still trusted him, wanted to trust him. The flood of mental intimacy revolted him. He got hold of her hands and nodded to Visharta, and the contact ended, leaving him empty. Visharta drew her away.

Jameson said thickly, "Arrest her. The assassination attempt, for now. Maybe espionage, I don't know—"

"But I didn't! I didn't know!"

"It doesn't matter," he said, and turned his back on her outstretched hands and walked away. His footsteps were loud on the polished floors and he thought he heard her call to him. He did not look back.

He went on through the house to his private communications module and plowed through the identification routine, moving stiffly. He thought she still begged him, distantly; but it was only the aftershock of that assault on his emotions. He cursed all telepaths, Hanna above all.

Morisz was waiting for his call and said, "I'll send more men over."

Jameson thought of Hanna being taken away by a squad of armed men. He said, "That won't be necessary. The less disturbance, the better. Visharta can put her under light stun."

"I'll be waiting at the complex," Morisz said, and signed off.

Jameson leaned back wearily. The light in this little room was too bright, as always. He hurt in places where Hanna had not hit him, and he was more shaken than he had thought. He had done his duty—and he thought flatly that it might have been more difficult if he had not been fueled by fear and revulsion and pain.

It was time to put out of his mind forever the vision of Hanna as the fragile survivor of shipwreck, because she was not going to survive this one. The charges they would hold her on were a joke, but they would serve to keep her while they studied her, poked her, probed her, drugged her, took her apart to the bone to find the real prisoner, the alien spy.

She knew it, too. The look of betrayal on her face was clear in his memory. I have no choice, he thought, but the deep blue eyes accused him and he thought: Perhaps when this is over I should resign. I do not think I could do this again.

He would have to face her sooner or later. It might as well be now. I will tell Visharta to stun her, he thought, and went slowly back to the room where he had left them.

He had waited too long. The utter silence told him before

he stepped through the door that something was wrong, and as he did so he felt the cold draft from another door open somewhere to the winter.

Visharta lay on his back near the fireplace, alive but unconscious and looking peaceful as a baby. His weapons were gone, and so was Hanna.

Chapter 12

Murderer!
You too
I stopped you
too soon but you wanted
to kill—stop it! Stop!

Her skull seemed full of voices. They would shatter it. And all of them were right. She could not murder humans but she had to, if she had to, to escape.

Drifted snow sucked at her. She floundered, going no where, and sank to her knees. The pressure in her head was everywhere, it was going to burst. But she hadn't killed Visharta, though the thing inside her had urged it. Calculated tears, eyes swimming, body lax, a fake collapse, he had come to see if her heart still beat and then—

All hers. The plan and calculation were all hers. And the restraint, above all, at the end.

She was not going mad. She wasn't insane. Relief swept over her, all her own and so great she cried out aloud in gratitude. Alien-seeming reality, body, thoughts, dreams—they were all *his*. The presence that haunted her had been not the watchers but *him*. Now that she knew he was there he could be resisted. Her present danger seemed almost insignificant.

She stumbled to her feet with difficulty, possessed by an urge to run. Hers? Leader's? Both.

Leader gabbled in soundless terror. She tried to think where to run to.

Hopeless. Nowhere to go.

Another wave of panic nearly blacked her out. She swayed where she stood and screamed at him.

Stop it! Stop! I have to think!

The terror eased but she was shaking, gulping for air. It was easier to start these things than stop them and Leader, feeding on her terrors, feeding her his, for days, for weeks, was near breaking.

An oblong of light showed a hundred meters away: Jameson's front door opening. Trees and shrubs showed against reflected light with the vividness of hallucination, black and knife-edged. Her first flight had carried her halfway down the long hill before the house, and her footprints were clear in the dim snow-light shimmer. She cowered at the end of them.

"Hanna!" Jameson was silhouetted against the light, a target-practice cutout. Her hand tightened on the stungun.

"Hanna! Come back! You can't get away!"

Kill!

"Not him!" she said violently, but her hand jumped. The stungun dropped to the snow and she was holding the deadly laser. She cried out to Jameson: *Get back!*

His shocked comprehension mixed with Leader's rage.

Fire! What he will do to both of us!

I will not harm him! I will not!

The pressure suddenly was gone, given up, relinquished. He'd given her body back to her. She shivered on her side in the snow, half-buried. She struggled to her feet. Snow resisted her, heavy as sand. There was a hot trickle of blood down one ice-slashed leg. The door was closed and there was no sign of Jameson.

She was vulnerable, visible, her trail a pointing finger. Animal running. Easy to find. She would use the laser on herself before she let them have her and burn out her brain, she would burn it out herself, her own way, let them reconstruct her body but they could not reconstruct—

Snow stung her and glittered in the wind. The Questioner's Assistant came toward her with the shining veil, a palpable figure, companion forever. She cried out in horror and fell again.

Go on, or it goes on forever. You will live in dissolution every instant of your life—

Not that either. She would not give herself to the humans; but not to the aliens either.

She grasped the laser and tried to turn it on herself and—could not. It twisted in her alien hand.

She retched, racked with convulsions. A merciless eye impaled her and ice chips flayed her hands. She could not face the fear again, fear of helplessness and pain without end, not that, never again, and he controlled it, recreating it at will. If there were grounds she could fight him on, there were some where she could not. He would not die, and all the force of his refusal went into The Questioner's promise.

I run, then—

She could move. She gathered her battered body and ran. For what good it would do. Toward the house.

Not back!

He tried to turn her flight and she staggered.

It must be this way! Nothing behind but the river, and Enforcers—

She made him see her caught between the river and well-armed men, and he wrested the image from her. It took substance and the Enforcers were a ravening horde, more savage than sentient. The laser flared and cut them down, food and sustenance. Leader thought with satisfaction: *Succulent.*

The vision faded. She caught at a substantial wall to keep from falling, tasting foulness. This succubus that fed on pain was part of her, loathsome. She would never escape it.

Escape. Escape. Run!

No, she thought, grasping at slippery wood. They will follow.

In a disconnected moment of clarity she saw that she had stumbled to the back of the house and was leaning against a bay built into it. It had no windows and was surely a hangar for an air-land car. There were few private permits for flight over Terra's dense-packed cities, but Jameson would have one of them. Leader suddenly was silent.

Footprints. I could fly—for a while—till they find me.

It would open only to Jameson's personal code, perhaps only to his voice. Unless she cut her way in.

She fumbled for the laser. At maximum destruct it cut an entry in seconds. There should have been alarms. She heard none. Heartworld and its dangerous mores. Oh, stupid man, brave man, to go unprotected on Earth!

Leader agreed: *Stupid,* and she felt his contempt.

There was no time to explain what it meant; that life bounded by fear was no life. Instead she said: *Smart enough to spot you! If you want to escape, shut up!*

She used the laser on the aircar too, listening for the hum of aircars or groundcars, the efficient machinery of a city used to crime. Nothing. Metal smoked and glowed in the darkness and the car said querulously, "This unit has sustained considerable damage to—"

"Shut up. Shut up." She wrenched the wrecked door open, burning her hand, and slipped into the pilot's place. The stench of burning plastics faded and the smell of fine leather engulfed her. The enclosure was haven. She or Leader was sick with relief. She pawed at what she hoped was the right switch and all the displays came on. Her eyes flickered over them.

"Can you fly?" she asked the computer controls.

"Yes. Hours to maintenance—"

"Never mind. Open the door and give me manual control."

The exit door peeled open with maddening slowness and the car said "Ready," and she whipped it out so fast it complained again. The controls were standard, thank God. A meter off the ground she careened wildly to avoid a tree and the car said severely, "Is the operator qualified for this vehicle?"

"Yes, yes, yes!"

She went up in a hurry and her stomach lurched. She looked over her shoulder and saw the house fall away, a child's toy, impotent. The dark snow, the darker sky, were empty of pursuit. Ahead of her were low hills and then dense city lights. She made for the hills at top speed. They would be shelter, but not for long; her eyes caught a monitor that showed moving blips of Enforcement activity, heading this way. Trust Jameson to have this little feature. She muttered, "Thank you, Commissioner," and for a wild instant longed to go back. She meant more to him than danger, and what damage would this do him?

No. No. Do not think of that!

A shadow showed behind the protest. Reptilian beauty, unbreakable bond: she knew what it was and in a wild leap of hope reached for it savagely, it might be a weapon as powerful as The Questioner was for him.

But the agony of loss was her own. She was alien and human male and female all at once, Leader's bondmate, was that what she'd glimpsed? And, oh dear God, Jameson—

The car dipped. She broke free, gasping. Leader withdrew as violently as she, revolted. Human sex was a maze of dark tunnels that fed into each other endlessly. He wanted no part of it. He longed passionately for the simplicities of his Home.

Home, yes. Rounded towers in the dawn, the young splashing in pebbled pools, scarlet plumage warm at fullsun—this is not my home!

Leader said: *It is mine.*

The car hovered, bereft of guidance, and she passed her hands over her face, her human face. Home, safety, a refuge against the night; her own thought had sparked Leader's, was that how it worked? The arms of his bondmate were gentle. She left to wake the hearth before dawn. He was not whole without her. They were a single living animal, and neither would ever bond with another. They were that way because, because—

She reached for it, almost understanding the imprinted bond for life, so foreign to human instinct.

The sky lit up behind her. They were there, searching for her. She would go back. To Jameson, who could not hurt her—

Leader thought with contempt: *He will. You are not Us but separate. Duty compels him.*

The Questioner bent over her and the tattered mote of Hanna-then hung screaming in an abyss of nothing. Hanna-now whimpered, lost. The humans would make her endure that again, and forever.

Leader said: *Space. Safety. Freedom.*

She caught at it—some of it—space; time to think, time to fight, time to get herself back. Jameson would destroy her. A man with responsibilities.

She growled to the car, "Outport. Top speed," and sprawled with the burst of power, teetering in the broken doorway. The car tilted and spilled her safely to its other side. It began to remonstrate.

Her mind cleared. A public outport would do her no good at all.

Something she had read tugged at her memory. She cut

into the safety lecture. "Does Commissioner Jameson have private Inspace transport?"

"Yes. The *Heartworld II,* a Class D yacht, based at Nordholm Field—"

"Take me there," she said, shocked by sudden hope. "It's not a military port, is it?"

The car veered and nearly threw her out again. It said, sounding cross, "The field is maintained by the Nordholm Society as a service to its members."

Nordholm Society. The name meant nothing. Lights and water flashed beneath her. The car showed no Enforcers pursuing her. But by this time they would know the car was gone. It was now locked into local airspace control and could be located and stopped in minutes, maybe seconds. How far was there left to go?

The car decelerated gently, cruising in over a black ribbon of water to hover over metal shadows in the darkness. Above them on a hill there were lights. The reference connected. Nordholm Society: a private club; elegance and service for the rich and powerful. Tight security?

"Which is Commissioner Jameson's vessel? Put me down next to it."

"It is not his vessel. It is the property of Heartworld—"

Hurry!

"—and if we descend without the proper signal, Enforcement will be notified," the car said.

"Do you know the signal?"

"No. Air-surface vehicles are prohibited—"

"Land anyway. Down. Now!"

The alarm began before it reached the ground, a deafening burst of noise, and light flooded the field. What else would there be? She jumped the last meter to the ground, slipped on ice and nearly fell, wrenching her knee. The car shouted at her but she could not hear what it said over the clamor. The yacht towered over her, two hundred meters long and streamlined for atmosphere. The sun-and-crossed-spears of Heartworld gleamed on its bow. She scrambled along its side, slipping, until she faced the main hatch. She fired at it, hands numbing with cold as metal flared, waiting for the end, anything, sleepygas jets, supersonics to drill into her skull. There was nothing. Serves you arrogant bastards right, she said to all Heartworlders collectively and individually, and the hatch burst open and she sprang in. She touched a switch and the inner lock opened instantly, disarmed by the pressure outside. She heard an angry yell and turned, firing blindly at the voice; a man, private security probably, ducked, and the inner lock shut behind her. Its design was familiar. She knew how to disable it and used the laser to do so; they would have to burn it open, and private security forces could not carry lasers.

She shouted orders as she ran for the flight deck, still waiting for the end. But the ship responded as if it were keyed to her voice. Bulkheads opened for her, slid shut behind her; lights flashed around her; in her feet she felt the purr of a thinking machine coming to life. She could not stop now. Her own fear and Leader's propelled her, she had to get away, get to space, think or plunge into a star.

Leader said: *Why so easy? When the not-People steal?*

She understood.

Because on Heartworld you die for such theft.

Die? Die!!?

Adjustment. Brainsoup alterations. Death, more or less.

The flight deck was an elegant statement in black and white; this was a luxury machine. An enormous window in its nose showed more men running toward her, and then the white hull of an Enforcement vessel landing directly before her. She ignored it, her eyes on the master controls. Their simplicity stopped her; she was a defense pilot. Even if she knew what to do it would take too long to get power and they would shoot their way in. And it would be over. She sank into the pilot's seat, giddy with relief. She would let them stop her, Jameson deserved that—

Leader wailed without sound, and a communications signal spoke urgently.

"Shut up," she said automatically, and the beeping stopped but Leader did not.

Do something, do something, there, there!

The urgency was her own; she forgot about stopping. She touched something without knowing what it was and the yacht said crisply, "Conventional power at seventy-five percent and building. Takeoff checklist commencing."

"Seventy-five?"

Jameson must have to move quickly at times.

Her hand twitched on a lever, an unwilled weight. The

yacht said, "Inspace checklist commencing. Conventional power eighty percent and building."

"No!" she cried out loud.

Leader said: *Remember.*

Ship and Earth and she vanished and died; a split second later, wringing wet, she was staring at numbers, levers, winking panels, bright displays. The drug, she thought. The thing they thought of as human undeath. She could not bear it again. The humans did not even know how to make it, they would have to experiment. Endless dying without death, time stopped, all she was shredded and lost in the void. Jameson watching it all, cold sea-mist eyes in the cold howling winds.

"Conventional power ninety percent and building. Take-off checklist completed. All systems go. Is itemization required?"

Dust clogged her mouth. Leader said: *Tell it no.*

She said with difficulty, "No."

"Ninety-five percent."

The heart of a star, fiery ending—

"At power."

She said like a sleepwalker, "Commence countdown." Reflected warning lights blinked red on the Enforcement ship's hull. It stood sharply against floodlights, there was light everywhere, then it jumped as if kicked and spun away. Men would be running, getting clear. She hoped. She hoped no brave fool would charge into the wrecked airlock and try to cut his way in as she had.

"Minus five and counting."

The flight panel wavered, steadied, and suddenly was comprehensible. She reached for atmospheric guidance. *Heartworld II* would take off faster than it ever had before.

"Two . . . one . . . liftoff," it said, and shot up and out through an invisible ceiling just as the Enforcers decided to fire, and power flared under her and disabled God knew what.

She went straight up, ignoring atmospheric drag until the yacht screamed in protest: too much, too much! It was not made for takeoffs like this. Gravity compensation wavered and for a moment extra weight crushed her. The yacht skittered to one side, bucking and trying not to crash. A display

for local airspace said: RED ALERT. The city was paralyzed now, everything in the air dropping fast. Except this
vessel which was exempted anyway, and those of the Enforcers. She let the computer take over for a second, two
seconds, three: her path stabilized into a long glide oblique
through atmosphere. She changed the angle, more acute
now, and lights flashed but the stresses were tolerable. An
override circuit blinked in and a voice began talking about
its authority to order her to turn back. She located the
speaker, aimed the laser, and fired. The voice stopped.

"Go," she said to *Heartworld II,* which was already going
as fast as it could. It was a match for the Enforcers, who
would have only atmospheric capability. She could not remember what the law enforcement agencies of Earth had
to meet this contingency, a private Inspace vessel stolen and
on the run. Probably nothing. Probably this did not happen
very often, possibly never. She was doing the unthinkable,
but something would meet her from Fleet orbital stations
and treat her like an alien enemy. They would fire rather
than let her get away.

She said to *Heartworld II,* "I want to Jump the nanosec-
ond you can do it."

She did not know what Earth's limits were for Jumping.
Beyond Lunar orbit? The spacetime disruption of a Jump
was a disaster for anything nearby and the yacht would be
programmed for all the legal limits and inhibited from
Jumping inside them. She could not outrun Fleet vessels. If
the limit were not close she could not make it.

"Destination?" said *Heartworld II,* and she saw the sky
was black, the stars bright; already she was well out of atmosphere.

"What are you programmed for? And how many
Jumps?"

"Heartworld in thirty."

"Do Jump One and then program for a random Jump."

"Fifteen seconds to One. A random Jump is inadvisable.
The probability of failure is unacceptably high."

"Do it, God damn you! And show me Earth, naked eye."

It was more distant than she had thought. A spear of
pure blue stabbed her eyes from a sea in its bulge of light.

"Radar visual—"

Half a dozen vessels after her. She ought to be dead already. But automatic defenses were set for enemies coming in, not going out.

"Countdown, please."

"Seven . . . six . . ."

They were closing. There was nothing she could do. Private transport would not have weapons-evasion systems. And evasion would not help her; this was a race.

"Five . . . four . . . three . . ."

A backview monitor showed a flare of light. Someone had fired something.

"Two . . ."

If they killed her now at least she would not have to worry about what to do next.

"One . . ."

Leader said: *Thou art mine.*

"Transit," said *Heartworld II.*

The stars changed, and Leader was free.

It occurred to Jameson once that nature might have reversed herself and established permanent night, or that by some magic he had been transported to the endless ice and darkness of a polar winter. From his rooms at Polity Admin he saw floodlit river-ice melding into blackness and nothing else for longer, surely, than was possible in this zone of Earth. Nor was there order or normalcy inside the walls of Admin. There was one face or another or many at a time and he had to talk to all of them and they blurred together. There was the intricate dance of politics and defense and personalities and bureaucracies, an unceasing storm of words, the rigorous logic of attack and defense exercised by men who still were in irrational shock at the occult-seeming power of their enemy.

The Fleet, rather early in the night, had issued a directive that none of its personnel were to allow themselves to be taken alive by the aliens. Certain other things had been accomplished also, more to the immediate point. Fleet vessels were leaving D'neera and streaming back to the Polity worlds, for now an attack could come at any point. They left behind a contingent of some two hundred Polity troops who descended upon Koroth and quietly took over. No one was hurt, but the soldiers were armed and alert, and no one who was at the House left it, and no one came in. Their commander did not bother with diplomacy, and the word "occupation" was used freely. In the unlikely event that Hanna managed to come undetected to the city, she would not be able to shelter in her home. There was a scant possibility, Jameson thought, that she would go there, and the troops were ordered not to harm her if she did.

"Because," he said to Peter Struzik some hours after the occupation began, "if she goes home it will mean she has some measure of control. That is not where the alien wants to go. And, of course, if it's at all possible she must be taken alive."

Struzik appeared to be standing in Jameson's office, but he was in his own suite. It was only a few hundred meters away, but Struzik was lazy. There was a petulant look on his face. He said, however, "You've been right so far. I suppose you're right about that."

Jameson held his tongue. Not the least of his concerns this night had been making it clear to the Commission, to his own government, and to Fleet how right he had been; how wrong, by extension, others had been. He had gone after Morisz with a savagery that surprised even him. Somebody would have to pay for the events of this night, and Jameson did not intend for it to be himself. The unfortunate Morisz, responsible for Visharta's stupidity, was handy. A long and honorable career was about to end in disgrace. Jameson, without vindictiveness, motivated by pure self-preservation, would make sure of it.

Struzik said, "Anyway, it's done. One down."

He meant one point in the plan he and Jameson and the others had hammered out in the hours since Hanna's escape. So far they had met no serious opposition; not because any of them were loved, especially not now, but because they had a formidable weapon in reserve. They had not formally declared a state of emergency. If they did their power in the Polity worlds would be frightening. They would have the power in theory, at least; no past Commission had ever invoked emergency rights, and who knew what the reaction would be in practice? Not even Jameson wanted to find out—though it might be something to be one-sixth of a god.

His office was very quiet. There seemed to be a great

deal of noise in his head, however. Some of it was left over
from the frantic activity of the past hours, but some of it was
the echo of Hanna's pleas. He said, to shut it out, "Let's
have a quick review, Peter."

"All right," Struzik said discontentedly. He began ticking
items off on his fingers. "Defense. Saturation of the Polity.
Steinmetz is still working out the details. The non-Polity
worlds are getting the idea something's wrong. Nothing's
leaked from here or D'neera yet, as far as I know, but
they're starting to get worried. Their reps'll have to be
briefed pretty thoroughly and pretty soon. Search. Steinmetz wants a dozen vessels searching *Endeavor*'s route—"

"Nonsense." Jameson did not pound his desk. He would
save that for Steinmetz.

"If we don't search," Struzik said reasonably, "how are
we going to explain not trying?"

"We've got to give the appearance of trying, but I see no
reason to waste more than one or two ships on a hopeless
task. I dislike tying up even one."

Struzik had liked the idea of a search from the beginning. He said, "Well, it *is* a clear interface between us and
them."

"An interface many light-years long, where Hanna may
be lost effectively as a single drop of water in the sea. There
is an infinite volume of space in any direction from it, which
Species X may have explored though we have not."

"The rendezvous must be a pretty recognizable point—"

"There are thousands of easily recognizable points. Peter, it is a truism of space flight that an interstellar vessel is
simply invisible unless it wishes to be found. In effect, it's
just not there. And suppose there is no rendezvous? Suppose she goes straight to their homeworld? No, Peter. I'll
talk to Steinmetz."

Struzik gave up. "Public information. Are we ready?"

"Nowhere near it." Jameson looked away from Struzik.
A gray day at last grew over the gray ice. Plenty of expert
propagandists had been working hard all night, but he did
not think they would concoct anything that would soothe
the public. Hanna's possession and escape could not be
kept secret, not with D'neera involved. The prospect of warfare would be terrifying enough to a population largely free
of it for centuries. The revelation of what Species X could

do—what they had done with Hanna—would rouse the la-
tent xenophobia of a whole species. Plans for martial law
were being updated everywhere.

"Koroth," Struzik said, and Jameson looked back at him
quickly, waiting for news. But Struzik only said, "Still no
physical resistance. They're talking our people's ears off,
though. Lady Koroth's hopping mad."

"I can imagine."

"Why won't you talk to her?"

"I am the wrong person to talk to Lady Koroth."

"She thinks you're the right person. As you know," Struzik said pointedly, "she has talked to *me*. And to Andrella.
And to Muammed and Katherine. At length."

"Not Arthur?"

"Not Arthur. But she really, *really* wants to talk to you."

"I'm sure she does." On a panel out of Struzik's sight, a
light had been blinking all night. Lady Koroth was waiting.
If he pressed a key and said "Fourteen" she would be there.

"What else, Peter?"

"That's it, for now."

"All right. We meet in an hour. I'll talk to you then."

Struzik vanished. Jameson looked at the winking light.
Other, more productive lights were flashing too. He wondered what Lady Koroth had ever expected; wondered if
she had thought she could move D'neera into the tumultu-
ous mainstream of human history without paying for it. The
price, it was true, seemed high.

He also wondered what she wanted so badly to say to him.
He knew Andrella Murphy had told her of Hanna's escape;
did she want to speak to him of Koroth? Or of Hanna?

He discovered then that his reluctance to face her was
rooted in the latter possibility; and with the thought he
touched the key and said "Fourteen," and a video screen
came to life and floated into position before him.

He did not see Iledra at once. He saw a shadowed room,
a burst of light near the video pickup, more light farther
away, a window open to white daylight. It was late afternoon there; snowing, someone had said. The shadows were
a tunnel between the two lights and in it, suddenly, Iledra
appeared. She came closer quickly. The nearer light fell on
her face, and he saw it was cold as the snowlight.

She came as close as she possibly could, as if a handsbreadth mattered in the light-years between them. Her eyes were swollen, and her sleek fair hair was disarranged for the first time in Jameson's experience. He recognized instantly that Struzik was wrong, or the reports he quoted stale. There was more than anger here.

She said without preamble, voice hard, jaw hard, "I want you to tell me about H'ana."

For a moment he had felt kinship with her, which had something to do with Hanna, but it was gone. He said, "There is nothing to say you have not already heard. I know Tharan has told you of all the questions she answered, and those she did not answer. This is the final answer. This somehow was the reason for what was done to her, the one thing she could not remember. They made her over in their image."

"You saw her. You spoke to her. I do not believe she could be controlled as completely as I am told."

"Believe it," he said. "If you'd seen her face when she attacked me—"

"You don't know her." The woman actually clenched her teeth. "She is strong. Strong!"

He took a deep breath, for once disconcerted. He wondered fleetingly if Iledra had passed some endpoint of sanity. He said, "The alien persona, entity, whatever it is—it's very strong too."

Iledra seemed not to have heard. "Why did she run from you?"

"It was *not* she," he said emphatically. "It was the alien. I suppose its intention, when its work was done, was to get away from Earth as quickly as possible. Perhaps it was anxious to get to D'neera or just into space, where escape would be easier. But it found out I suspected its existence and knew I would not let it go. It had to escape then, or never."

She stared at him, the gray eyes so sharp he wondered if she heard him thinking. He said, watching her face, "Lady Koroth, you said I don't know her. I think now she is a stranger to you too. When you spoke to her last, was she herself? You know she was not. She was fighting something she did not understand. She did not know she was fighting; but she sensed she was losing."

Iledra looked at him with abhorrence. She said, "You are coming out of this very well."

"Yes?" he said, taken aback.

"I think in the end the consensus will be that you are brilliant. That no one took you seriously enough, and the only man who did gave you an incompetent for backup."

"Very true," said Jameson, who had spent a good portion of the past hours encouraging just that point of view.

"I think you are mad. Mad to keep power. I think you would do anything to get your way."

"You are entitled to your opinion," he said quietly.

She made a sound in her throat that was almost a growl. She said, "I once thought to find in you an ally. I have found instead a creature that cares for nothing except its own ends. I forgot the lessons of my ancestors, who came here renouncing your ways. We are not experienced with the hidden motive, we D'neerans. We do not always love one another, but each of us knows what another is about. I don't have the habit of disbelief. When you spoke of your hopes to me and to H'ana, I believed you. I gave her to you for your ill-fated Project with some thought of the unity of man. I was a fool to trust you or any true-human."

He should not be taking this from her or anyone, a personal attack that was at best a distorted reflection of reality. It was advisable to measure her enmity now, rather than wait for more drastic proof; but he had had enough. He was reaching for the key that would end it when she said, "You destroyed her. There is no difference between you and the aliens."

He should not answer at all. But he said as if compelled, "She made her own choices."

She said venomously, "Choices! Her choices have been those you gave her, or drove her to. Ruin and suffering and the waste of a life precious to me as my own—she was lost, and she wanted to come home. She only wanted to come home!"

He saw the anguish behind her fury, and understood. No one had to tell her some of Hanna's choices had been made by her Lady. He said, because it would be easier for Iledra if she could believe it, "She was not herself even when she told you that. The woman you knew as Hanna may no longer have a real existence."

"You can't mean that! When I am told she might have killed you, and refrained—"

"But she is gone," he said. "If she comes to you I will admit she has some measure of control, or if she returns here—"

"Returns! She would never go back to you. She was escaping from you!"

"The alien—"

"There is more to it than that," Iledra said. Her eyes glittered.

"No," he said, impassive from long habit.

"I think you are lying."

He said deliberately, "She struggled and lost. The path she made in the short time she was on foot looked as if she had been fighting a physical entity. I'm sorry. But those are the facts and you must accept them."

"I don't believe you. I saw her heart before she went away. It was turning toward you. She would have turned to you in her pain. What did you do?"

He cut her off, with finality. "Nothing."

"She was running from you. *She,* not the alien."

"No. Good-bye, Lady Koroth."

He closed the call without ceremony and was still for some time, staring into space. The guess was too close for his liking. Iledra could not know of his promise to Hanna that she would be safe, and her pleas when she knew he had lied. Iledra could not know he had taken Hanna in his arms and comforted her—and then put her away. Several people knew of that intimate little scene, to his profound discomfort, but none of them would have described it to Lady Koroth, not even Andrella.

And if someone did, what did it matter? His only mistake, he was told, lay in having been too kind. He should have had Visharta knock her out as she clung to him.

Oh, hell, he thought. If I had it to do over again that's the only thing I would change. Otherwise I'd do the same damn thing. There was nothing else to do.

He reached for the key that would call Rodrigues so he could get on with his job: Steinmetz next, another commission meeting, another attempt to get heedless F'thal to understand the danger. But he paused at a last thought of Hanna, words Iledra had used: the waste.

For an instant he saw clearly the woman Hanna had been becoming. Wonder had outweighed her fear, until she saw a new danger in him. She had had a chance to kill him after that, and warned him instead, with passionate concern. And then made a clean, straight escape, with that thing in her head and the hounds close behind her.

The waste, he thought. The waste.

After a while his hand descended, and Rodrigues said, "Yes, sir?"

"Steinmetz," he said, and leaned back to wait, thinking rigorously of organization.

Chapter 13

The planes of reality were all discrete, white emptiness cut by darkness, so sharp-edged Leader thought it would all fly apart at any moment. The split was intrinsic in the universe. He knew it, all the People knew it, and bridged it all-together. Now there was nothing to contain it but himself and this alien and memory unsupported by the binding We. Though empty, she functioned, an automaton operating by animal compulsion, automatic and implacable as the universe. She did not even see that reality was unstuck.

Her thoughts cut him, and he was entirely exposed to them now and sometimes, even, thought them. Revulsion and hatred washed over him; in denial of his existence she would drown him. Scalding blasts of negation threatened him. Hating in return was salvation: so the Student-Celebrants whispered long ago: *HATE AFFIRM. AFFIRM. AFFIRM.*

Stronger than captive or paradigm she had also her Home at her back close at hand and around her a Render's artifacts

they made none we stopped them in time

and now that her enemy was visible she faced him powerfully and he was alone, save for her. Save for her who

*would Us
kill, I would kill
the Students were
bloody were beastly were cruel were
right. You
kill. You kill!*

She made the random transit over the yacht's repeated warnings. The arcs of thought were not all hers. She followed them one by one. Danger danger danger too dangerous a game suicidal (but if it were not sometimes necessary all ships would prohibit it utterly. The instructor shook his solemn head. They should; there is no reason for it ever to be necessary. You ought to be with me now, Umberto.)

Artifact of beasts THAT IS NOT MY THOUGHT I WILL NOT THINK IT.

The random Jump would save her from pursuit; the computer that ordered it would itself need time to determine where it was. There is Sol. *Firsthome of water.* NOT MY THOUGHT.

In the strange starfield she tried to think, but the alien bubble burst in her head and she swam in its shards. *Heartworld II* trembled around her, its planes and angles quivered with immanence, poised, changing to something else. It too would shake apart and dissolve in non-being. There was no color in the universe. It was a white fog cut by shadows from dead space, being and unbeing clearly distinguished. She fell through its cracks to the Students' arms, experienced in pain and in murder . . .

clearly remembered dimly foreseen
and murder I will—!

She shook her head violently over and over until it ached. The pain made a handle and she hung on it. The disjunctions were Leader's reality, not hers. Or his perception of hers, shaped by living millennia; their weight crushed her. She ought to have a soul and she had nothing—

"Stop it!" she cried out loud, and buried her face in her hands. The skin of her face grew hot, grew coarse, and she moaned from her own deep fear.

Home, Nearhome, warm sea of thought gently turning
gentle sea indigo amethyst white spires of Home

"Home," she whispered, and slowly, painfully, straightened. Her thoughts cleared. She could go home. Iledra would protect her, help her dig out this monster and never, ever hurt her.

She said to *Heartworld II,* too quick for Leader, "Set course for D'neera."

"Working," it said, and all her muscles convulsed in his blast of fury.

*   *   *

He did not know how to speak. He was not made for it, and even using her he could not do it. Wildfire was constructed to find aural equivalents for thought and written symbol, and he was not. Nor was she exquisitely alive to currents in the atmospheric sea, so that even commanding her consciousness he was robbed of a potent sense and irreparably numbed. But he used parts of her well.

He held her paralyzed in horror and moved one hand to cancel the course she had just set. Fear and rage rained on him like blows. The hand jerked; toward her head; as if she could plunge it into her skull and tear him out in handfuls of dripping brainmatter. But he held steadfast to the hand. It was a soft and disgusting paw, nearly black against the white of this living, thinking room. Yet she was very light compared to many of the Treecubs, who ran a spectrum that confused him.

Their machines could be run without speech. He had learned how to do that in the long nights, driving her weary body so that in the end he knew more than she did, drawing fierce and invisible on her knowledge, for survival and escape depended on it. She understood the workings of this vessel only because he had showed her and forced her to see because she had not wanted to see and not wanted to know because: because of the other one. Whose eyes had picked him out.

Now the other hand, set to dancing over a keyboard whose logic was mathematical. He understood that, too.

Yes. More much more much closer his goal than he had hoped. Yes. Yes!

She said in despair, to no one but inevitably to Leader: *He was right.*
??
to keep me there. No choice
??
the future on his shoulders
I have too.

Heartworld II said, "The first portion of this course requires intensive calculation due exclusively to randomization. The remainder is known. The probability is ninety-five percent that no more than sixty transits will be required to reach subject terminus. The probability is 90.233 percent that the journey will require less than 144 hours."

* * *

Hanna stared at the course display. Its rainbow colors were incomprehensible, and then coalesced into something she could understand. It was almost a course for D'neera. Almost.

Points beyond.

He hid nothing. He could not. Numbers, only numbers. But their meaning to him and to her differed so that she could not grasp fact at once and worked it out painfully.

D'neera must be the rendezvous but it could not be but it had to be. Because the crew of the First (Sentinel) (Watchman) (Watchsetter) knew it and (from Hanna's own thought) could find their way there. Not there. Not quite there. To a star as such things went nearby. She knew D'neera's space intimately. Training cruises.

This was a triple, one a red giant that shone rust-bright over Koroth. They called it the Dragon's Eye.

A course once established in human space was logged centrally. The Polity ran the library and withheld some things, no doubt. D'neera participated in the give-and-take. The crisscross of safe courses in its little sphere of exploration was standard navigational programming, not much used but there it was. And there they waited, at the Dragon's Eye.

Luck, she said to him, *luck, you could not know the course would be here.*

Near is near enough, he said: *I am an Explorer: I would have found the way. This is a gift of time.*

She said: *I will not let you do this.*

You will.

His confidence was too much like that of The Questioner, who had been right after all. She shrank away from it, watching him use her hands. She was not connected with them. He was busy and occupied and she might have leapt upon him but did not, seizing instead on the moment to think. He was too busy to prevent her. She looked at the alien thoughts her brain somehow thought. But that could not be. He could not be a physical entity! He could not!

Watchsetter/Sentinel/Explorer at the Dragon's Eye. Red light—but no light penetrated. They were sealed in and would not/could not go out. She thought experimentally of old pleasures, whirling stars in free fall, the mind-wrenching glory of solitary consciousness lost in all of creation. Her body trembled. The ghost of The Questioner whispered in her brain.

Do not think of that!

Thou fearest the void?

Do not think of it!

There is much then thou fearest of space?

Much. Yet We came for thee. And dissolved thee.

She twisted away from the memory that was nearly upon her. She thought in despair: *You have won from the beginning.*

Since the dawn. I/We must. It is harder. You are stronger.

Stronger than?

Stronger than a furred and evil darkness. She did not understand. She did not feel strong. But it was true, because he could not deceive her.

He added: *A desperate chance.*

I?

You. Desperate. Theory. Process catalyst experiment who knew you would bend to Our use? You have. You are used.

A thousand memories rippled in his thought. They were his/not his; they were old. The living dead jostled her in them. What had they altered and dissolved? Before Hanna, before the colonists? Something not-People but other-than-beast.

She was close to it. He wavered and weakened *alone with a Render-thing!*

The memories invested her with strength beyond her own. She understood this suddenly and drew on all of it and unseated him with one great heave. Reality rocked and was hers again, her body was hers again, her mind was entirely clear. The hands Leader had used were hers, and she concentrated on remembering them earth-stained in a garden, caressing a lover, competent, dangerous: her hands, not scaled and clawed. She could speak.

"Are we still on course for D'neera?"

"No," said *Heartworld II.*

"Cancel the program. Calculate a course for D'neera— no—can—"

She was not speaking aloud any longer, and her hands were gray again.

So strong, too strong!

That was both of them, possessing one another's fear.

There was a resonance effect; it grew stronger with each loop, and each time it swung round and struck them they were weaker. He had not expected this. It had not been so with the Lost Ones. Who would think that one alone—?

He scrambled for balance and pounded her with memories of subjection and the alien limbs jerked. The stars twitched through her eyes and he thought they had Jumped. No. Not yet. But she had gotten the command out before he stopped her, and the course was direct for her Home. To make it work he had to reconstruct reality, rejecting hers, but that was her strength and his weakness. She could make a universe in solitude. He could not, nor could he master fear alone: not without the architect the People together were, not without the dampers, baffles, comfort of a billion living brains.

She thought triumphantly: *I can!*

And concentrated on the humming metal around her, building a universe on it and on its master, reconstructing reality from memory and a seed. The weight of millennia would not shape her. She herself was enough. She thought she could see Starr Jameson here, one eye on the readouts, the other on—what? Some theory of governance, perhaps, here in space, free for a little while from the clash of cultures, translating in the ambiguous pathways of thought (and his more ambiguous than most) abstract to concrete, principle to power. The largesse of solitude—

The first Explorer to go alone into space saw craft and cosmos dissolve, and opened a hatchway and stepped into unbeing. After that no one went alone. Solitude could not be borne. They had not known it. How should they have known it, never having felt it? Yet space was necessary. They had to go, to find what inhabited the stars, for fear that Renders did, having won the conflict otherwise. As indeed they had, it seemed, everywhere.

Now Leader impossibly lived with one. If it were really Leader he could not have endured it a single day. But he was not real. Not real, and not alone. He lived in close company with Wildfire, who was fascinated—

—and let *Heartworld II* slip away, forgetting to be afraid. What could he mean, real and not real? The People were just out of reach, but she saw what they made, a tangible network real as a magnetic field around their Home. A collective dream, impossible for one alone to maintain—

She understood too late that fear was as much defense as defeat. Leader was not afraid either now, and his strength was terrible. Something like the power of The Questioner seized her arm and she wiped out the program for D'neera and rose, trembling. They were not going anywhere now. The compulsion to reprogram was powerfully her own, and she resisted it. Leader was not in control, but neither was she. She stepped away from the console and her reluctant knees gave way and she fell against the equipment and then, squirming, to the floor. She did not feel her cuts reopening, but there was blood on the polished white floor. She lay with her face against its coldness and when she tried to get up could not. This time it was not Leader's doing, however. The weeks of exhaustion, the mad flight, the final struggle, were too much.

She begged *Let me rest* and images of peace descended: melodies of falling water, harmonies for the skin, she moved almost to meet it, almost felt the plangent drops.

Leader was arrested. This fragile flesh would serve neither of them much longer. Leader knew it, and did nothing to her now, and was gone: almost gone.

She rested and tried again, and this time pulled herself to her feet. She did not know how much time had passed, nor how long it had been since she ate or slept. Earth and D'neera were dim memories. The struggle within her filled time and space, and time was an all-consuming now.

She went painfully through the stalemated ship, a step at a time. The living quarters were luxurious and the food service area well equipped, but there was nothing to eat. She went on vaguely, feeling Leader at the back of her mind, waiting balefully for something but saying nothing.

Without conscious thought she found her way to the emergency stores. Nutrient tablets, which would keep her alive. Why? She swallowed two, compelled. She explored further, her knees shaking. Medical supplies. No stimulants. She would have to sleep, and was afraid to do it. That was what Leader was waiting for. Awake, she could keep some command of herself; asleep, her body would be Leader's to use as he pleased, voice and hands and all that was necessary to take her where she did not wish to go.

Another door opened and she looked at a room which burst upon her with the immediate and present sense of a human personality. In the deepest heart of space, centered in humankind's most sophisticated machine, he would have wood. It smiled warmly from walls and she tripped on the hand-pieced carpeting. The great bed drew her. The richly worked counterpane came from the looms of Arrenswood. It looked warm, though the colors danced before her eyes. She lifted it with a trembling hand and slid beneath it, leaving smears of blood. She apologized silently to Jameson and let her head fall with relief. Peace, stability: you could defeat him, but you could not break him.

Do not think of that! said Leader, and threatened her with a memory of The Questioner but it was weak and far away because Leader lived in this body too and its exhaustion was his too. *I cannot help it,* Hanna answered, human, female, and felt him drift away. She closed her eyes, comforted. Perhaps he would let her sleep for a while; this was his body too.

When Wildfire slept it was like being at Home, in some ways at least. The undercurrents of dream, the fragments of thought, were alien; but in a way it was a warm sea in which one knew one was not alone; not, in fact, one. The daemons that peopled her brain were a company, a shared reality her waking mind excised from existence, and he could almost forget it was her creation alone, and let himself almost believe it was woven of threads of We, changed but real.

The relief was so great that he wanted to dream with her, but there were other things to be done. He opened her eyes and heard her groan. He hoped she would dream of quiet things, pods and vessels, rooms and structures and houses, as she often did; but sometimes they were open to the wind, ragged, tottering, threatening to go dark and populated by monsters. And Leader was the monster.

Or was it Wildfire herself? Did she see herself as he saw her, as a Render, padding from forest to city? Although Renders were forever extinct; even if here there were worlds of them; even if—

* * *

She could smell the millefleurs, and they thought to her. Iledra did not; she only spoke. There was a split in her mind and one side spoke, but the other screamed without words. Here was Leader, an endless succession of Leaders blending into one another back, back to the beginning, outlines blurred and overlapping. She tried to fit into the spectrum and rebounded, reeling at Leader's revulsion. For an instant she saw herself through his eyes. She knew it was herself although her fangs dripped blood and she hissed, scarlet eyes speaking murder. The skies blurred in pain. Beast almost-other she writhed under knives. Their enemy was no-thing; they gathered it in, and harvested her. *YES. YES. YES.* Voluptuous agony; she was ash, assimilated.

He felt the pain of exhaustion in the alien limbs, and the dizziness was physiological. He stumbled against a wall and she nearly woke, but this time it was easy to make her tormented mind stay asleep, because she did not much want to wake up or even, perhaps, live.

The thought gave him pause; he let the fragile frame sag and thought about it. She was wired for self-destruction, in the months past he had seen it running like a silver thread through her thoughts, buried deep but shining sometimes clear and purposeful. She had come to them with it, bringing it like a gift and a readiness, a thing that must ease what they did. It was there long-before in the filament of consciousness the time they almost had her. And afterward: leaping gladly for Bladetree in order to die. And before: something to do with a human war, and were they all like this?

And now it was irreversible. For The Questioner knew intimately the original purpose of the rite, and taught it to her well, though present need called forth a different end.

She dreamed of Renders, and there was no one to soothe her. He was glad enough to stay out of this dream.

He had to feel his way through the vessel, putting one foot in front of another, steadying himself with her hands on the walls. Each touch sensed through alien cells was a shock. He had to let the body rest. But first there were tasks to perform, and he found the laser where she had dropped it and ejected it into space. She would try to damage herself, to die and escape that way, and he could not let her do it.

Then he set course again, and afterward let her head rest on the main control console, wishing he were still hidden from her. Everything had been easier when she did not know he was there, lurking behind her conscious thought, her fear masking his, acting when she slept, night after night matching her knowledge to written symbol . . . it was so much easier to hide. So much easier. And he might have done it longer and avoided this, except that in the end he could not hide his presence from one dangerous man.

Waking was difficult. It was the most difficult thing she had ever done in her life, because she was drowning. Her lungs were full of amniotic fluid and she fought to be born.

Leader was growing stronger.

I can't wake, I can't, I can't, and I will die.

A hand reached for her, a real hand, human, strong, and pulled her to the surface of consciousness. A shell cracked, and she was born. But when she looked for the hand it was gone. The controls of *Heartworld II* surrounded her, and no one was here except the two of her.

She tried to speak and felt Leader come alert, and ducked out of his awareness. She felt him searching for her, puzzled and alarmed.

She wondered: *How did I do that?*

It was midnight at the Center, and her fingers moved in the familiar sequence that would link her room to the library network. She struggled to interpret the Standard symbols she had been reading all her life. Sometimes they shivered into alien notation, and then she could understand. Her telepathic sense had never been this keen and she was on guard, and would not have heard the footstep but felt the intention. And turned off the display and slipped into bed, and someone came in.

Half her self disappeared. She almost felt a pop, and then forgot. She opened her eyes to a room no longer strange and reassured the attendant, and that was how it was done.

If he can go from hiding to control, can I?

She looked through his/her eyes and saw their course was toward a red point in nothingness where the alien ship waited, crewed by her torturers. And came out of hiding and took him by surprise, felt him unbalanced and falling, said "Cancel course!" before he could react, and felt his rage.

Her strength was terrible. He panted, or she did. They would careen back and forth forever, a pendulum till death overtook them, unless he could secure control. He needed a weapon; not one of matter, for this was his flesh too. But. But.

She moved. He went along, perforce. What weapon was safe to use? What had he used that she had not learned to take and use against him?

One thing. Only one thing.

She felt his intention and hunted for the laser. Maybe this time he could not turn her hand.

It came to her that she had done nothing with these aliens but try to die.

A forgotten reader lay in the lounge. It came to life when she picked it up. Philosophy: elegant abstractions danced before her eyes. She shook her head at them, feeling like a savage. In her universe abstraction had no meaning.

The ship is dying, she said. *Most of us are gone. We can let them take us prisoner. Or fly into final chaos, and take them with us.*

She could not find the laser. She supposed Leader had hidden it with her hands while she slept. There was nothing left to do but dive into a star. She should have gone for Sol at once, while Leader still was shaken. She would try it now. She turned back to the flight deck.

He was weary, weary as she. He had not believed the will to die could be so strong. The Questioner in truth bore a share of the blame. Bladetree, son of Celebrants a thousand generations old, had gotten his first name for a reason. Their voices were fainter to Leader. Bladetree lived *then* in the ancient rite. The aim of *now* was different.

But she feared The Questioner, lyrically though she had responded. The last weapon had worked well so far. He did not like using it, for the trauma made her briefly useless and was torment to him too, but it would stop her long enough.

The Questioner had conditioned her thoroughly. If he must, he would use her living memory again.

*   *   *

She opened her mouth to tell *Heartworld II* what to do and nothing happened. Leader, forewarned, prevented it.

She moved her hands with nightmare slowness, as if many gravities crushed her. But they moved toward an input terminal.

Damn you, thought Leader, and stopped, shocked. He had thought in words.

The universe narrowed to a keyboard. Her hand wavered; pain assaulted her, top of head to tip of toe. "The body," said a voice from the past, "forgets pain." She thought, *no it doesn't, you fool.* She did not remember falling, but she looked up from the floor to the terminal she could not reach.

She made another effort and The Questioner was there, and her vision halved as one eyesocket became charred bone. Pain consumed her intention, and she screamed. She tried to move and it happened again. Tried to move and it happened again.

Leader watched in a certain suspense as the small hand crowded with too many fingers jerked and fell back. Her heartbeat shook him and then she was gone and he lay panting on the floor. When he got up the limbs moved easily, though they hurt and were very tired. She was gone.

He set course once more, one last time. She was gone and it was easier to hold up the universe, now that he was not fighting hers. A little at a time, at least; these controls were all that mattered. He could do it in this body that was used to its brain's commands, used to living solitary. He could do it a little longer. If he were true-Leader he could not have done it at all. But he was Leader-in-her-thoughts, and drew on alien resources.

He thought: *She is the best they have. And she is not good enough.*

His/her body needed rest, and so did he. He gave himself a vivid suggestion and went to sleep.

The skin she thought flayed from her face was still there, and both her eyes.

Leader slept.

She said to Starr Jameson, "I am not strong enough."

He was standing in the corridor, looking at her with friendliness.

"Suicide maneuvers," he said. "What will you do when youth and luck and brilliance fail you?"

"Fail," Hanna said. "Again."

"You are on your feet and he sleeps."

"Only," she explained, "if I don't change course. Or try to kill myself. Or—" She considered. "Yes. Or if I try to communicate with anyone. Then he'll wake. And do that again."

"Well," Jameson said, "think of something else. Suicide maneuvers indeed! D'you think I'd be where I am today with those tactics?"

She said doubtfully, "What do you suggest?"

"Oh, something more oblique. Keep 'em guessing till the time comes, then go for the throat. That's called diplomacy. It's how you stay on top."

"Ah," Hanna said with satisfaction. "I see. But you hated doing it to me, didn't you?"

He said, "You're very pretty, but quite mad, you know."

"But you are a rock," she said, "and I have no place to stand."

He disappeared and she cried out, "Come back!"

But the misty walls sharpened and clarified and she was indisputably alone, and not even a footfall echoed in the corridor.

Leader half-woke at the echo of her soundless plea. It broke through the shadows that hid her, and the poignance of her loneliness made him think of Sunrise. He wished her heartily not to move; their muscles longed for rest. She subsided, falling into denser shadow. The intentions to which he had sensitized himself were absent; otherwise her thoughts were hidden with the trick she had learned from him; but they were on course and alive and would continue so. He was safe. He went back to sleep.

Ignored, forgotten, Hanna went to the yacht's galley, seeking her last hope. *Heartworld II* was big, far larger than a shuttle. One might sometimes use it to take colleagues in the exercise of power from place to place, and entertain them on the voyage. And feed them. And, if they were from certain cultures, give them meat. Which needed to be carved. In the ancient and most basic way: with a gleaming razor-edged knife.

She thrust the knife into her belt.

Leader would not let her die, but she was a Render. Renders killed.

Chapter 14

Darkness. Sough of breath, heartbeat's drumbeat. Paralysis. Like the months when—I can bear it . . . Where is she? Hiding not hiding how can she? Only We. They cannot but I am mad he is mad they are mad I am mad. In space a few are mad alone he is mad so he is doubly mad. And I prisoner passenger my body possessed by definition mad.

Do not notice the knife. I cannot find her. Eternities of love and bonds that do not break. I will believe that I will taste her, if not I then other-I the same but not I cannot bear. Such loss. All lost.

If he is mad he cannot be permitted but if I am mad I must not but I am mad and logic fails so

you do not
remember
the knife.

The first Watchsetter is alone in space. Its defenses are thick. Its deflectors overmatch all the creature Wildfire showed Us, all she knows. No stones will pierce this shield.

The First Watchsetter is alone and: *A different color from Our skins, she thought. What difference? What colors did she see that We do not?*

The First Watchsetter is alone and the gemstone light of a cooling sun illumes it the color of her blood. At Our backs, ice. A globe of rock and ice and frozen gas; no life here; no life, ever. Before Us the bloody giant dances, doubly escorted.

We have been here so long.
so long

so long
no Watchsetters before Us have been out so long, and
echoes of Home are faint and far and
probably unreal
the chronometer says nothing that means anything and realtime is etched in Our bones too long
too long
too long!
for five of the People five only.
I am Leader, he thinks. He must do this often, daily, ritu-
ally, all of Us must. For all of Us begin to forget, for five are
not enough.
Here, Leader. At Home, ah! At Home!
At Home he is Hearthkeeper's Fulfillment; as she is his.
Five is the least-shape. Five cohere; with difficulty.
We are exceptional
selected
trained
brutally
Explorers
Watchsetters
We
only five!
It would be better with twenty. With twenty it would be
better. But so few can survive sundering. So few are so exceptional. There are not enough for liberality. We cannot
spare three crews to augment one.

Thus will Renders rending space defeat Us in massed attack. Space is Home to them. They traverse it confidently, leaping through stars, unminding the void save in awe. Not horror.

Wildfire spins through stars, escaping.

Our craft is not the same physical entity as the First
Watchsetter. It is blind to the horrible void which We only
dare see through instruments, it is filled with memories, it is
propelled by the promise of Homecoming; it has these
things in common with the First Watchsetter, but also with
the others. It is First because its crew traces an unbroken
line to the First. The Apprentice of the first voyage of the
First Watchsetter rose to Leader of a later voyage, and the
Apprentice of that crew in time succeeded him, and so it
went in ever-endless cycle through the years.

And all of Us are here.

It is an honored calling, Leader thinks, *though in memory something else. Once*

> *We flew in joy*
> *in fascination*
> *not by need*
> *not in fear.*

In common memory the forays share in the pleasure of creation, darkness and abrasion making one current of a complexity whose rewards were/are worth seeking but

> *it is all darkness now.*

Here or there a world of beauty begs Us to stay. We cannot stay. We never stay. Wonders wait even in ice. They wait forever for Our return.

For this is the function of a Watchsetter and so has it been for a hand's-hundred years.

The Leader of the First Watchsetter Long-Ago remembering:

I was boy Apprentice lately tapped into the then/now of the First Watchsetter. Truly first for me; my first voyage. Left I Weaver at her loom. Left the mountain Nearhome, falling water. The Ordeal nearly broke me. Alone they said a little while. It seemed forever. Later the bond formed, one by one.

Then-Leader took Us dizzily through darkness. Mountain memories filled my eyes. Apprentice only, their good aid and hands. Knowing I will one day be Leader.

Weaving shuttle woven night. Ship the primal birth-sac. Air sweet-scented. Not mountain air. Long between stars. Not here: no globe cool enough. Not here: none warm enough. Here? No. None alive. They seek life, the Treecubs, leaf-lovers.

Barren rock. The universe is made of barren rock.

Always We were on the edge. Everywhere We went was new.

Rock.

We came on the edge to a brilliant star, beacon-lit. Its companion was shadow beside it. A shoal of planets, swarming. Some were near-stars, ripe with sullen heat. The rest were rock. Save for one, very-far-out, born by chance in the narrow rainbow strip where ice liquefies, gases volatize, the thick rich broth is jolted, transcends rock, and lives.

By chance.

Thick and rich and dark leaf-analogs coated rock. We went unwilling, questing, afraid. We breathed the air. The wealth of that air! The glory of its light! Objects peered from leaftops, bright-eyed. Treecubs, it may be. It may be that in some distant now they come to ground, grow savage, learn to leap into the dark.

The Treecubs were not here. Not yet.

We set the telltales carefully in caverns. The caverns shone with Our light like stars. I took their waters in my hand and tasted water pure as my Weaver's eyes. The telltales are skeins of energy, no more. Deep within this world is heat to feed them. We left them in darkness to wait. Sooner or later the Treecubs will come. Somewhere not-in-caverns they will call to their kind through Nospace. And the telltales will urgently fling forth warning; and dissolve.

We went to mountains, for my sake, which was Our sake. Air pure as my Weaver's hands.

It was not Home.

Afterward we set the relays, carefully. Which also will dissolve, once used, and used for nothing else. When they come here We will know.

It took a year to place the relays. I went Home then to Weaver. Not long. I left. Again. Again. At last I learned to be Leader, but Weaver died. Thereafter, soon, I too.

And this is what it means to be a Watchsetter. And this is why We honor Us.

This is not much of a brain, thought pseudo-Leader, and recognized the thin high note of hysteria. His. Not hers. But the sardonic despairing humor was not his.

She was, she must be, gone. He found no trace of her consciousness when he searched. She lived however in her cells and bones. The too-fragile hands were competent if he did not think about them. When he thought, they dropped things and trembled. When he was indecisive they flew to the soft heavy hair whose texture made his skin shiver. *Her* skin. The trim and rakish spacecraft was alive with noise. Her hearing was acute. The People barely heard at all. Sound cascaded on the alien ears. And was labeled, identified, and put away. Not by him. By, then, the residue of her that lived in flesh. It taught him when to eat. It taught him, shuddering with revulsion, how to care for the alien organism. Thin slick skin. It slept more than he.

He thought, washing it, I hid from this. From the intimate secret needs of her body I shielded myself, revolted.

He had succeeded in the first-aim, the People's need. But did he own her body, or did it own him?

Leader, pseudo-Leader, Leader-in-her-thoughts stood helpless in her body in the command chamber of an artifact of Renders. Black-and-white soothed his eyes. Dizzy rainbow colors elsewhere. The color perception was finer than his, widely ranging, delicately discriminating. They did not have true-sight at all, most of them. Only Wildfire and her kind.

An uproar of sound jolted through him. Only a chime, her body said placidly, undisturbed. The ship announced another Jump in tones he did not comprehend. It made the Jump. By itself. He saw no change; he had opaqued the port so he would not have to see the great emptiness. The ship had the name of a planet.

The government of reason and logic. The rational use of power. They do not favor eccentricity, but old money buys the right. Few in numbers, highly stable, formidably strong. The balance of real and ideal. Hidden warmth and loneliness—

He had the information. But all mixed up with it were her opinions, her prejudices, and also the drawing-near to one man of that place.

Too much like the People's bonding.

Too different and distorted.

Do not think of that.

Serene numbers announced to him the journey's end was near. He had done nothing but show the craft where to go. It bore him majestically across great depths. He was distant from the process. It was not like the First Watchsetter, demanding intimate involvement of brain and hands. Her body accepted it, unquestioning.

Was she still here in some way?

The unperceived does not exist, said an Explorer of long-ago.

You here! Leader said. The body shuddered with relief.

His living, long-dead mentor answered: *I am here.*

I thought you left behind with Us—

All of Us are here, Explorer said.

But there was a note of uncertainty.

Pseudo-Leader sat abruptly on the floor. The knees were weak.

Feel, he said. He meant the lightness, lack of weight, fragility; hair lightly brushing the slender neck; thin fabric over soft skin. The sensitive breast-pads, pointing forward, made him cautious. Naked feet; he couldn't bear her boots. He said, *You know well the invisible has real existence!*

A matter of instruments, said Explorer. His meaning was obscure.

The floor felt very cold to Leader's flesh. He said, *I cannot find the answer to my question.*

Explorer said: *Questions answer one another.*

That is no answer. Is she here?

I was present at such an answer, Explorer said.

Show me, Leader urged. Although he was not sure the question—is she here?—was the question he ought to ask.

Explorer said, *I wandered in the days before Watchsetters, the days of joy, though the question shadowed Us even then, having shadowed Us since eyes turned from forest to stars.*

The question was answered/not answered in a place of dull red rock. The star was red, like that We seek; the light was red; all things were red in the light. A planet's spectrum showed as We approached a Home like Ours. It was the first. Life was rare and precious in the slow early days; microscopic, mindless; lichens at best. Mosses answer no questions. Here was more.

We came to ground eagerly through ruddy cloud. Descended on savannah, crushing copper shrubs. The things that ran away were thin and black as wiry sticks. Six limbs they had and ran like rippling water with queer grace.

They were pitiless though terrified, bestial, disconnected, lacking true-sight, separate from Us and from each other. They were Render-things, though they had not a Render's spark or skill; not yet. Thus was the question answered.

And We said: now We know. Life bends elsewhere toward Renders not Us. But We said: now comes another question. Are there some who are Our equals in thought and in skill?

The answer came not in my time.

Leader said, *It shaped mine.*

The alien body twitched. He thought someone peered

over his shoulder. He thought miserably: *So was it with her when I hid. But is it the body remembering?*

You know not who you are, remarked Explorer.

I am Leader. Leader. Leader!

The instrument is the brain. Recall the purpose of the Rite, Explorer urged.

Leader struggled to fix his thought. For Explorer always since infancy had been his guide to objectivity and cold reason.

He said in obedience, *The objects of the Rite were two. First, dissolution; and second, identity with Us.*

It has not changed, Explorer said.

I never loved the agonies of the Rite, Leader confessed.

You did, Explorer said. He was afraid.

He was gone.

I did? Leader said. But no one answered.

Wetness blurred his Render's eyes.

Renders fought with tooth and claw, savage, wielding stones. Later they bound the stones to wood. They fought the water-People ages long, broke the living eggs, devoured the young. Different, separate, hardly seeming native to this world, though they were: the People tried to claim them.

Symbolic, remarked Explorer, and vanished again.

Leader thought in a kind of frenzy, *That is not a concept of Ours!*

He huddled on a square of polished black, half or less than half himself. If she were here, surely he could find her. Her brain the instrument was limited, however. It bound his powers and defined him. If she was here she suffered the same limitations; therefore she could not hide; therefore she must be dissolved as the Renders in the claiming of the Rite had been dissolved (but all of them had died), as the Lost Ones had been dissolved (but all of them had died).

They had not let her die. What happened when a Render survived the Rite? Was that the true question?

Heartworld II said, "ETA three hours," but Leader did not understand it.

Time is slipped, blended, schizophrenic. Hanna admires her former self. A lizard owns her pretty hands. She thinks few names for anything; exists in the infant's timeless wordless universe of light and dark. She has been his parasite forever. He is faulty and disorganized, wherein lies her hope, if hope it is. She does not think of hope. She thinks of blood, a deep contented song. Iledra would not know her for herself. She does not know herself. She is only *here*.

It is the end of the day's last sad watch. True-Leader rises. Ship's midnight is full around him. We think of the task We fulfill: always. We think of the avatar-of-Leader, distant. Triumphant?

The leads that enter Leader's brain differ little from those of the past. His thoughts are those of the First Watchsetter. He thinks of power and distance, orbit and momentum; the gravitational complex like heavy stones that can be grasped in the hand, smooth and round and water-worn. In their polish shine the eyes of Sunrise. In his braincase, in Our skulls, are sockets drilled and shaped ubiquitous as eyes. We are the First Watchsetter. The ship is We. It thinks Our thoughts. Unlike Treecubs enslaving metal. We knew long-before. That:

> *Renders*
> *their machines*
> *are separate*
> *primitive*
> *stones bound to wood*
> *inorganic*

as their homes as their hearths as their hearts—

It is time.

Thy task, says Leader to Steersman. Steersman sunk in recorded memories of Home and bondmate and sweet clean skies stands dutiful. We say to him: *We know the call.*

Thy task, Leader says, *thy watch.*

Steersman sorrowing says: *Grim task,* and the hearts of Our companions, some waking, some asleep, answer Us:

> *grimly answering*
> *need We are*
> *desperate, ends*
> *it now ends*
> *with new hope*
> *or despair—*

Hope withers, Leader thinks, looking round in dimness at the sturdy unfailing machines bright with winking lights.

(Unfailing ... but ... somewhere a failing craft drifts smoke-filled death-filled to deliberate oblivion. Bursts of dying hamper the tampering hands crazy-wiring wreckage into motion. Still she goes on. Not Ours! not Ours!)

Hope dies as days pass and We weaken long-absent from Home. The lattice of existence fades; its structure blurs. We move wraithlike through a ghostly ship, and the endless emptiness of outside weighs on Us through its walls.

> *Empty of hope*
> *in the new*
> *the untried*
> *Hope!*

he thinks, and seeks to turn the current of Our being. Leader truly, one of the great who appear in deep need; but it has been so long, so long, that even he can bend Us only to least-change, and Bladetree the Guard who was Questioner, answers: *The only hope,* and We are turned:

> *only hope*
> *it may be, though*
> *desperate, and*
> *brave, but*
> *is not desperation*
> *always hope?*

We acknowledge the truth of the equation, but Leader withdraws in sudden impatience. We let him go. For this too is the mark of the great, to retreat and consider and gather strength for Us all. And We have not strength to comfort one another's moods. And his sometimes might weaken not aid Us; for he is first-source of an experiment whose outcome will be hope, or not. It will work, or it will not.

And everything has been experiment since a long-placed telltale, a Watchsetter long-ago's shade, registered the Tree-cub transmission and stalking began. The less-than-People are coming, sailing toward Home, and their message comes before them, coruscating: *We are intelligent carbon-based oxygen-burning bipedal intelligent intelligent intelligent ...*

Steersman comes through the muraled corridors. We look at them through Steersman's eyes, and regard the

darkened command chamber along with Leader. The walls
once showed Us comforts of Our Nearhomes; but their
seeming life depends on shared belief; and now there is not
energy enough among Us to make them real, and they are
arbitrary and meaningless lines that sink and waver, and
darkness slowly overcomes them.

All is quiet, Leader says, and Steersman acknowledges,
entering: *All is quiet,* and We echo in Our thoughts,

> *quiet . . .*
> *quiet . . .*
> *quiet . . .*

Leader gives over to Steersman the traditional sidearm
of the one on watch, its weight cold and heavy in Our hands.
It is a relic of Renders, the transfer a custom spontaneously
risen at the start of Watchsetting. Not that the Treecubs are
prey to such weapons, with all their means of killing from
afar; but the ritual commands Us to vigilance.

Relieved of weight and duty, Leader paces through the
ship. We feel Ourselves together a pale shadow of Home in
boundlessness, dying caricature of a Nearhome. *We are doing well,* he thinks, *for so few so long in emptiness. But We
have been out too long, We starve for Home, We are stretched
thin and tenuous and Our functioning declines. How much
longer should We wait?*

He comes to the place of rushing water and strips off his
clothing, thinking sadly of the waters of his Nearhome and
Sunrise sporting there. Three other of Our living companions are bonded too, and find no comfort but in one another's pain. There is no comfort but memory. Only those
who endured before Us teach Us how to bear assault on the
unassailable, loss of that We cannot lose and live, disjunction that ends and reduces Us to ash.

For an instant he sees Sunrise in the stones that surround
him. We take alarm and warn him, as We always do. But not
immediately; We are not so quick as before; and will the day
come when We cannot? He will not look at the glimmering
stone. Blossoms and fireferns hang over him in damp thick
air, and he floats in warm stillness. We miss the pleasant
pooldarter, the little animal that lived in this place, but in a
mutual excess of revulsion We killed it and threw its body

into vacuum; its timorous isolated animal thoughts reminded Us too vividly of Wildfire, who—

Is not what We wanted. Is not what We expected. Does not yield as she ought to yield. Forces Us to final measures and a new one, thus herself designing fate. Is something new—

The worry of it weakens Us, then and now. Weakens Home too perhaps, but no, he struggles to discriminate in thought between We and We. Five here alone so long however wrong We seem now must have been right, the consensus of the People: right in stalking, enticements, patience to wait for a few alone, plans changed by the differences perceived but not understood in Wildfire and later two others. Why was there no memory of Wildfire's kind? So We could not watch as closely as We planned, because her kind perceives an eye. But We said take one and torment her and quickly she will show all We need for a crippling blow, their skills not Ours but We have had time to make them Ours and so We will save Ourselves.

But even faced with certainty, Wildfire does not believe it.

The final choice to which she forces Us is right, We say. Perhaps it were better to chance the one world, Wildfire's Home . . .

Folly, Leader thinks, repeating the arguments that swayed Us to consensus. Her homeworld is not what We seek. In the changing years the species is spread and increased. There is no longer one homeworld. Wildfire has hers; but there are those others shining half-sensed in her ill-shielded thought like the light of a mighty fire seen through water, blurred and trembling. All that power to fall upon Us . . . and she edged toward death, and what is to be done must be done before she thus escapes. And maybe she is dead anyway. Maybe the Treecubs cannot repair her, despite her faith.

Bladetree says implacably, *or they repaired her and the plan did not work,* and Flametender stabs Us with fear from his sleep: *and if it did not*
   work then. Steersman says,
   and Apprentice echoes: *what then?*
   Start again but
   they are gone there is

*only her Home which
is folly.* Leader says, and

Sudden shock takes Us, driving all else from Our thoughts:
He is coming! Now! At last! Steersman cries, We sway waking and sleeping in his alarm, and the patterned lights that warn him are bright in Our eyes as lightning striking long-expected

*here at last!
too late—
too soon . . .*

Excitement sweeps through Us in storm waves, gathering momentum and rebounding one to another and gaining strength. Fear and apprehension not joy nor sureness; it takes too long to damp it; five are not enough, We are gone too long. Our rigorous training cannot hold—yet it does. Leader splashes from the pool and across mossy rocks, trembling, and the sleepers wake, trembling.

Identify. Identify. Identify!

He sees through Steersman's eyes the keyboard We use, hands wavering in shock. He says: *We will have no intelligible answer. There is no translation program. We must wait for the arbitrary code.*

Steersman's embarrassment washes over Us.

I forgot . . .

Leader pulls on his scarlet uniform and runs through the First Watchsetter, shedding droplets of water. Bladetree comes eagerly, Flametender in alarm, Apprentice uncertainly. But Flametender thinks: *It worked!*

Relief is a long-unknown softness. Steersman says: *I was afraid. Wildfire was strong,* but Bladetree who was Questioner says: *Not at the end.*

And it is true that at the end she is not strong; seems, even, to understand something of the essence of harvest, and properly yields her pain; but still she denies Us. She is a shapeless lump of flesh, intelligence suspended, docile, surrendering to Our claim; but also mad, nearly mindless, leaving unanswered questions We did not ask soon enough. She evades us though captive and helpless, and in the long distracting ecstasy of her dying, slips away.

Therefore a semblance of Leader has gone with her, and now returns.

Touch me, begged pseudo-Leader, yearning for his People, and Hanna crouched in darkness and watched him, brooding.

He paid her no attention. For a while he had searched for her and then given up, wishing her silenced forever.

She was not silenced but hiding. She had had some practice in enduring isolated consciousness without mobility. Her long recovery on Earth had taught her something about it. Then she had clung to Dale Tharan's thoughts, inimical as they were, as to a lifeline. Now she was an observer of Leader-in-her-thoughts, though she hid from him.

Touch me, he begged, and they did, and Hanna flickered and was blinded by his/their burst of joy, and then went on detaching herself, observant and purposeful.

Home, Home, nearly Home and no longer alone—

Hanna was a mote, an atom, a spider death-still with its legs curled and balled, but they made a web of living threads intricately loomed and she sorted them out. The steersman, the apprentice, the flametender who was the engine master, the one who had been The Questioner. And Leader; but there were two Leaders. One of them was mad, a parody, a crippled thing. That was Leader-in-her-thoughts.

I am Home, Home, I have returned, he rejoiced, but the other said: *That is not I!* and all of them, true-Leader, pseudo-Leader, Hanna too, froze in consternation.

> *It was I*
> *it is We*
> *but not I*
> *it is thou!*
> *I am thou*
> *at least We—*

Ripples of confusion surged around her. There was a beacon now, however, and *Heartworld II* made for it. It was close, very close, and They were altogether present.

Hanna floated in her unworld and studied them. She heard their thoughts as speech, although they could not speak. The web was raveled and bedraggled with their discomfort. If she had been able to smile, she would have smiled. The germ of an idea, born from her struggle with Leader-in-her-thoughts and fed by his memories, was practicable. One's fear or distress affected them all. To control it they needed time, and this handful of long-sundered wanderers was susceptible to disruption and slow in control, like those who had found the colonists, the Lost Ones.

She knew how to do much that pseudo-Leader had done to her. She knew perhaps how to do more: she knew how to be alone: her human brain made it a condition of existence. And she had a Render's single-minded savagery, and bound to it true-sight and all that implied and more than that implied for she was something new and knew it, and they did not; and all their suspicion, being vague and tenuous, fell short of the truth.

It could work.

She darted through their communion like a hidden fish, listening.

> *I/not-I do you not see?*
> *it cannot be*
> *you but think it*
> *is that is*
> *madness*
> *danger*
> *chaos*
> *if madness I must*
> *die you must*
> *die I must*
> *die, but not*
> *into silence!*

Stark fear; not of death but something more; an obliteration. Hanna did not understand it, and ignored it. She was not part of the web. She could ignore it.

Die, she thought with satisfaction. Into silence or not, you will die; not I.

> *I cannot look on my own madness!*
> *But it is not ignoble its*
> *will is set to duty though*
> *it suffers; it has been*
> *long alone and*
> *in pain*

True-Leader said suddenly: *Where is Wildfire? Where is she?*

Hanna retreated in alarm into a deeper blankness. But Leader-in-her-thoughts said: *I do not know. She is gone into silence.*

There came a burst of triumph that battered them. Hanna watched with interest their reeling.

It was truth! cried an ancient Celebrant,

truth! echoed Bladetree

truth! all of them said and Hanna sickly, savagely, closed out the memory of the Rite, the Rite that had claimed her, or nearly.

In the triumph and the glory of victory spanning eons pseudo-Leader said: *Open the docking bay that I may enter.*

And true-Leader moiled the ebb and flow of radiance piercing it with fear: *That is I and not I!*

She is gone into
silence you
said so—
The Persona itself is changed!

She would have held her breath, if she controlled breath to hold, for she felt him near her.

They fell back, doubt swirling among them. But Steersman said: *Docking begins. I have opened the bay.*

Heartworld II, shining in red light, moved forward. They said:

We do not understand
why We fear why
it is thou
it is We
but not-thou?

On a level that was not hearing she heard them muttering, uneasy and straining. The Celebrant and Celebrants were gone. But they had really/not really been there and were there. True-Leader reached for her, stretching and pulling their strength to break free. Or break through.

But Leader-in-her-thoughts was Leader too, and they paused to hear him, and he said: *I do not think there is aught to fear, for We have claimed her.*

Only Bladetree stirred uneasily, remembering personal

hatred. Hanna felt his movements clearly as those of her own body as Leader-in-her-thoughts made it rise. He/she wore the knife. He did not know it. She hid it from him though it lay at his very hand, and laughter bubbled deep within all that was still Hanna. She thought with pure joy of what she was going to do to Bladetree, if she had half a chance.

Bladetree said, *You are strong,* and fear lurked in their thought.

Yes, Hanna thought, but only to herself. As you will see.

I am Leader. I am strong. I have been long alone, save for Wildfire.

Steersman said: *Docking is complete. I pressurize the bay.*

The space filled with air that she and they could breathe. Pseudo-Leader waited, barely restraining himself, eager to run to their arms. A secondary hatch opened at last (the primary having been destroyed; he had not forgotten that) and he leapt from it lightly in his new body. Hanna looked with savage alien eyes on the alien ship. Pseudo-Leader climbed stairs, with some unsureness; the risers were made for longer legs than Hanna's.

True-Leader said suddenly: *Save for Wildfire. She colors this change.*

Their attention shifted from pseudo-Leader. He passed through wavering passages whose bare-sketched living images leered distorted and the face of Sunrise transformed by stony fear made him stumble and—was forgotten. Did not exist. Had not happened.

He laughed. He did not know where the laughter came from.

True-Leader said: *In the work of the Students there was only negation of the Treecub, and identity. I do not understand this change.*

Pseudo-Leader walked on. Hanna waited in shock. He was too close to truth; what if they regained the balance of their unity, and pursued Leader's doubt with all its force?

But the command chamber of the First Watchsetter approached and surrounded her, and the moment of danger passed when they saw her, and forgot fear in common wonder.

Hanna watched it, and waited for her moment.

* * *

Deep in Our thought, Leader's thought, not-his thought, since Steersman's alarm, was this body. Surely We knew it would be she. Yet We are unprepared, for its thought is Ours. And its wholeness is wonder, because We remember a mutilated carcass, and memory sickens Us. Nothing could have made Us believe it would live a day past Our disposal of it; nothing but her conviction, until she passed beyond hope of life, that she could be repaired; and despite Our conviction We think now We had not believed.

Their skill in killing We believed, for that was Our long-present fear. But how can Renders be so skilled in healing? How can their biological science so far surpass Ours?

She looks as she looked when first she came into Blade-tree's hands, small and smooth and fragile and unharmed. But the destruction had been so great that now We think:

> *Keep them*
> *keep some*
> *to heal Us*
> *they can heal*
> *even death!*

It stands before Us and it is cruel as the junction of two universes. The color of its eyes is impossible. We did not see that before. How can such a small thing be so dangerous? But it bears a Render's spirit or would if it were not displaced by Ours:

We must know these things, it says,

these things! We answer in awe, and are distracted: drift helpless and suspended in a vision of knowledge and techniques past all Our experience. Machines move and hum, glistening; fluid bathes unfeeling limbs and the transparent air glows with energy; the Treecubs move around Us, shaping Us; cells dutifully reform remembered patterns: the tiny flame of life, almost extinguished, swells and grows steady.

And before it is time, before We are ready, he says/We say/it says from the alien flesh: *I will show you what We have learned.*

There is an edge of anxiety and uncertainty in the thought and We do not see its source. We mill restless and wary in the chamber, the heart of the First Watchsetter. It seems there are not five of Us but six of Us, seven of Us, not seven! The air is faintly acrid with Our odor. What does this mean? A life-support flaw?

A Student long-ago remembers and all of Us remember: *The disjunction of alien senses,* and We did not experience this before because then Wildfire's terror filled her and suppressed all else.

So this is right; but true-Leader says, *It is wrong.*

The alien that is We looks at Us with impossible eyes and says: *You will not have to bear me long. When this is done you must kill me. How can I look on Sunrise through these eyes?*

We tremble with many-edged grief for Hearthkeeper of Leader's Nearhome who is to true-Leader Sunrise, to pseudo-Leader Sunrise too, beautiful and unfailing as the dawn. His other self's loss is Leader's own. He is gone from Sunrise too long, and in this moment his longing is doubled, rebounding from pseudo-Leader and gaining strength each moment from each of Us:

Not sundered forever! he thinks despairing,

but the other weeps, *forever,*

and the chamber shatters and the air trembles and Sunrise appears but to each she is his own and longing overcomes Us; for Our bonding is endless and unchanging as the stars, and the unPeople's lack of it marks them beasts.

I did not mean to remember her!

Do not think of that!

We rock, are steadied, slowly make the vision fade. So slowly! Our weakness is greater, Our danger more each day. There can be no more storms of emotion. The bonds on which Our functioning depends cannot survive many more.

The alien body slumps in shared sorrow and apprehension. It says: *We must finish quickly.*

Clearly it is right; its very presence disrupts Us.

In Our acknowledgment of its reasoning it crosses to Steersman's place. He moves aside and awkwardly it takes his seat. Wrongness nibbles at the edges of the aftermath of grief, but We cannot bring Our selves near it. The alien looks at an input bank and its confusion tugs and jerks at Us, distracting. It says apologetically: *I cannot translate quickly from their terms. And this is not made for these hands.*

At last the stunted paws (pretty hands) ill-made and

fumbling move (in lost grace) and symbols stand before Our blurred eyes. We crowd together and all of Us long-ago crowd closer too, watching Our hope (or destruction) Our fear; it is clear fear was right. The locus references are clear, starbeacons ineradicable. There will be no escape for the Treecubs, who can no longer hide from a hidden enemy and must wait for Our blow to fall.

Here is one world, their birthplace, bursting with life. In alien memory it glitters with snow.

Here a second, long-settled and nearly as strong and its name is the graceful soft name of a tree.

What have We to do with sounding names?

Lights glow with acknowledgment from Home. The vigil there is ending, the data pouring into the Generals' hands—

The alien hands falter. Wrongness gathers in corners like smoke.

We have no such function—

We do but We do not. Something like it, since the Students' time; but not this; not quite. The new concept is pseudo-Leader's

contamination, Bladetree says, and all of Us fall back in alarm.

The alien says through Our great uneasiness: *I will show you how to translate the data in the human vessel—*

Human? What is Human?

—a clear course program for these worlds—

Its vision dazzles Us with wrongness—

—while We sought them their power increased. Five Homes rich and powerful are their heart and the heart of danger—

Five! We are frozen, the fear, the power, corruption, wrongness, aloneness resonating together. The fragile balance rocks. True-Leader struggles to anchor it: *Five but not that of the Wildfire-thing—*

And the alien says: *She might have been someone's Sunrise.*

Sunrise among Us again is created from his/its/Our longing and caught in tumbling currents of grief and fear the alien throws back its alien head as at a mortal blow

I did not think of her! It was not I!

Do not, do not!

When I am dead—

Stop, stop!
you must tell her I loved her even in this form—

The thought hurt them physically and sliced them in two. True-Leader, wrenched apart, existing twice, relinquished Sunrise to himself. He stumbled desperate toward the alien, reaching out, and the others reached for him, overcome with sorrow and altogether unbalanced with this last blow.

But pseudo-Leader's thought impossibly winked out, and the alien rose and reached for them too.

In that instant they understood the wrongness, the thing hovering behind this changed Leader, and the understanding was too late; the alien moved convulsively; something glittered in its hand; true-Leader's agony flared in his knowledge of certain death, and the knife ripped through flesh and membrane and all of them felt it, impaled and transfixed by horror. The alien was among them free and strong as rushing water, and Steersman stumbled toward the creature, fumbling at his belt, but he failed in the chaos of Leader's dying, and he also died. Then all of them were blinded, and it caught the weapon from Steersman as he fell, and killed Flametender and wounded Bladetree, and sprang for Bladetree with the knife while Apprentice sought to flee and could only crawl.

A weapon, Apprentice thought, *I must get a weapon lest it escape.*

But he could not, prisoned by the weakness of his kind and reeling in the dissolution of other minds dying without solace, the unbearable disruption of the last worst horror. And it took its time with Bladetree and Apprentice writhed with his agony, and Leader screamed both alive and dead and reality began to die about Apprentice. The corridors were a marsh in which he sank and drowned in hate. He clutched for support but there was none, the universe was ending, and he did not even know Hanna had come for him when she shot him in the back and he too died.

Chapter 15

A word drifted through the dark, half-transparent air, drawn out into many syllables and at first meaningless. Hanna saw clearly that it was a material and perhaps living thing.

It flared against the darkness; shortened, wavered, crystallized; settled into solid reality, and vanished.

Just before it disappeared it spoke. It said: "Blood."

When it was gone time was uniformly gray and blank. Not even memory marked it.

Presently she saw that time was the gray flooring of the corridor, centimeters from her eyes; saw blood on it; saw that some was subtly lighter than the rest, and remembered.

The lighter patch was *her* blood.

She lay unmoving and watched a pageant of fantastic deaths behind her eyes.

Thus have you wrought . . .

Dreary droning voice from nowhere. Her own thought.

Presently she considered turning her head. To do it, or not to do it, was a most profound question.

At last, because her right arm hurt horribly, she moved. Her cheek was sticky and stung as it pulled loose from the floor. Her flesh was insubstantial, but it responded to her will.

Only yours only yours only yours! cried the voice, and she shuddered and cringed from it.

Leader was dead. In her mind there was a whimpering where he had been. But he was dead. The whimpering did not stop.

Presently another word appeared. "Up," it said. She clung to it, used it for support, climbed it slowly, and was sitting. It disappeared.

Apprentice's torn corpse lay near her. There was a gaping hole in his back; Steersman had been carrying a projectile weapon. The custom was associated with a past shadowed by Renders, which responded unpredictably to any defense save having big holes blown in them.

"No. No," Hanna muttered. That bit of knowledge could not come from *anywhere*. They were all dead.

She stretched consciousness cautiously. The effort cost an almost physical pain. Nothing living met her. She reached inward and was empty, like this spacecraft, like the universe.

She preferred it to the frenzy of their dying, which had gone on for some time even when their bodies were certifiably dead and past reviving even with human techniques. It ought not to have been so much like the *Clara*. These things were not human. But the blackness was the same, and the wailing ghosts. She had thrown herself on the floor in shattering hysterics and clawed at her ears to shut them out. Her throat was raw from screaming. None of it did any good at all, and in the madness she had nearly died too.

Now it was finished, and to what end? Sunrise would wait forever, a whole Nearhome subject to her grief. That was all.

Hanna sat on the cold floor and looked inside her right forearm, which was on fire. It was clear true-Leader or Steersman had turned the knife back on her somehow, though she did not remember it. The wound was ugly, but it had missed the big veins and nearly stopped bleeding. Her whole arm hurt and was stiff, but she could use it.

Use it, she thought, for . . .

And quailed. She did not want to use it for anything. She wanted to lie down again and go to sleep, rejecting thought and purpose.

The whimpering went on and on and grew into a howl of pure and untainted despair. For a moment, in slow confusion, she looked at Apprentice's body; but he would never speak in thought again.

Leader still lived in her mind. He did not want her to stop. He did not want to die a second time.

Tears of weariness came to her eyes. Even dead he was not dead. There still was no escape.

She lifted a hand to her hair, but the pain in her arm was so great she let it drop.

Over the mourning came unbidden a memory of Leader's creation. He was a creature of drugs and suggestion, with true-Leader's power behind them, constructed in the chasms of an ego violently disorganized by pain.

So precariously founded he might, she thought, be vulnerable. Perhaps he could be destroyed. Perhaps the mind-healers could do it.

The thought compelled her to rise. She began to stumble through darkness, supporting herself against the wall with her uninjured arm.

and the oldest blackness and the falling years mourn us lost riches parts lost from the whole—

Be quiet, she said in despair, *oh, quiet!* and quiet descended.

She had no goal but clumsy motion. She was at one place or another with no recollection of getting there, as if movement required such effort there was nothing left for the perceiving of it. But presently she was in a docking bay, looking at *Heartworld II* through a fog of pain. The hatch from which Something had emerged was open. She went through it and in time found herself by a disordered bed. It was big enough for a big man, or one of the People. She was lost in it.

She fell on it. She felt the automatic pulse of thought from pseudo-Leader, she would sleep and he could regain control—and then her conviction and then his that he could not. He was herself.

She slipped into blackness, too tired to be grateful for the peace.

When she woke Leader was still there. If he had not been she might never have thought again, but as it was she said to him, *Go away, you are not real.*

I am, I am, I am, he wept, so clearly she heard the words.

Tears covered her face. Which was odd, she thought, because the People do not have tears.

She sat up. It was nearly as difficult as the first time. Weariness past enduring enwrapped her.

I am real, Leader insisted, and Hanna fell back again, helpless. Dark and warmth and wetness surrounded her. The medium she breathed was joy. She struggled to escape a clutching memory, not hers. "No," she said, but he would not be denied, and *Heartworld II* changed to:

A chamber hewn from rock richly carved in celebration. Lifetender's task was nearly done. She tapped an embrittled shell with a silver hammer, and tiny claws appeared at a crack, tiny fingers reached for the world. They fastened on the fingers of Leader and Sunrise, sealing a communion begun while the little one was an embryo. They bathed together in running water and all the community was a song around them. In other Nearhomes, and in other times, the same ritual simultaneously was being performed or had been performed or would be performed. He danced in the water, stretching his baby limbs *as swiftly as I,* said a long-dead swimmer, and now in this place he was Swift.

The vision faded. Hanna saw the rich woods of Heartworld again.

He is my son not yours, Leader said. *I am real. This happened to me!*

She turned slowly, unable to move quickly. Crumpled fabrics rubbed at her face and woke pain in her wounded arm. A trace of a familiar scent—imagined, perhaps—brought Jameson before her.

When she thought of him she got up slowly, swaying, feeling curiously light. She felt an edge of panic at the smallness of the room—no, at the absence of those other eyes, other dimensions, other perspectives which her two eyes alone could not see.

She thought of the hearthstone of Leader's Nearhome, a brilliant mosaic that made one pattern from many. She thought of the sculptures made to be seen by many eyes at once, at which Flametender had excelled.

"No," she said, pushing knowledge away, but it would not stay away. They were so vulnerable, so fragile for all their strength, subject to one another's pain so that a hurt to one robbed all of competence and a community's strength wasted exponentially. And through Leader she had come to see this weak place, and she had gone for it with all a Render's savagery.

I do not want to think like them! she thought, and thought: . . . *telepathic cousins, who can reach into another being's very thoughts, comprehend him from the inside, ensure peace as we go on.* . . .

She had written the words in another life, when she was herself and Leader, though she did not know it, stalked her.

Echoes of dashed hopes, confidence unfounded—what would Jameson say when she told him she had thought about nothing but killing? About what she had done to Bladetree?

That she had done all she could, perhaps. And then he would forgive her. Perhaps.

"Fraud, fraud, fraud!" someone said. It was her voice.

"But I had to. I had to," she said; and thought there were other things she had to do.

She moved slowly to the flight deck, seeing nothing, stumbling with exhaustion. Exhaustion would never leave her. She had to go on in spite of it. She had to get back to Jameson and tell him she had won.

But nothing lived on the First Watchsetter to signal the docking bay open. She could not leave it yet.

She shrank from facing the bloody work of her hands. But she must do it or never leave; and unwilling, unthinking, she stepped from *Heartworld II* into a ghost ship where nothing lived but herself. Nothing could; she had heard the end of their last fading thoughts.

The route to the First Watchsetter's command chamber was as familiar as if she had walked it a thousand times, though the stairways were hard to climb. The corridors were dim and their walls altogether blank. The murals were keyed to living brains, and had died with them. She felt that she had spent weeks, months, years maybe, in this ship. The command chamber would have been homelike as her rooms at Koroth, except for the evidence of carnage. A burst of grief, hers or Leader's, brought her to her knees among the crumpled bodies. She could not look at the tatters of Bladetree. True-Leader's face was twisted in death, and she knelt in his dried blood.

Fraud, fraud, Render!

"No," she said, "Oh, no. How can you call me that? After what you did to me?"

Renders, he said, *buried their dead. Not Ours.*

"I can't do anything! They're too big, they're too heavy, how could I move them?"

And what did it matter to the dead?

And truly death for Us, said Leader, *far from Home and transition and life in We, though you might for me—*

She did not know what he was trying to tell her. He

could not force it upon her. He was less strong than before. He had lived through his own death, but in the passage he had lost the greater part of substance. And what he tried to tell her was so strange there was no place for it in her reality.

She tried to get up, and her hand fell on something that yielded. It was Steersman. She rose then in one quick movement, driven by horror.

It was hard working in the dimness with the silent shapes around her. Leader tried to withhold his knowledge, but he could not, no more than she could reject it. There were more lights here than on a human ship, or there seemed to be more in the half-night the People preferred; all of it spun sometimes before Hanna's eyes, and once she thought it looked like nothing so much as a tinseled habitat seen from outside, a glittering explosion of life in the depths the People hated. She did what she had to do manually; her scalp itched; she was using backups, there was nothing wrong with the front-end system, she ought to plug the ship into her brain and *think* the First Watchsetter's instructions.

You do this very well, my friends dead at your feet, Leader said bitterly when she was done.

Her skin rippled. Almost she heard Roly long-before.

"I will pay for it," she said, not at once sure what she meant. But with the words a thing she had not thought of for two human years came with perfect clarity into focus.

Dorista had stopped her hand in time, but not her heart, which had gone on to touch the bit of metal that ended a universe, Hanna's universe. Some of her had stayed in the night, detached. Easy prey for the First Watchsetter, drawn to its dark promise . . . easy prey for Leader, who had only to expand a cleavage already there . . .

We do it better, he said.

She shivered, fighting the rush of her own memories which he pressed upon her.

Truly the body's death is ending for you, Leader said. *Not for Us.*

She had a hard brief vision of herself and her kind as a parody, an incomplete obscenity, as if an animal with thumbs grafted to clumsy paws were to think itself thereby human. She felt herself pulled and distracted at the sight, and then saw that his intention was to distract her. Something was happening, and he wished her attention withdrawn from it.

He could not do it. She had hidden a knife from him, and now he could hide nothing. New lights flashed on a communications panel, pulsing urgently. She read them without effort, but it was a moment before their import burst on her.

COME IN. COME IN. DO YOU READ? WHAT IS WRONG? DO YOU READ? WHAT IS WRONG? WE ARE COMING. WE COME.

She stared at the message, transfixed. It could not be true! But the denial was founded on what she wanted, not on what was, and she stumbled finally to the lights and peered at them, and then tapped a hesitant code on a panel shaped for other hands. A strip of paper, or something like it, unreeled from a slit. She tore it off and squinted in the shadow. The characters on it were sometimes intelligible, sometimes not. When they were intelligible they also said: *WE COME.*

They were coming because her/Leader's information had been fed Home as she gave it, by prearranged program, and the transmission had been interrupted without warning or explanation. There had been no answer to their increasingly urgent inquiries, so they were coming.

She remembered, then, and thought: No. Oh, no. An endless time spent watching Leader-in-her-thoughts and holding to her purpose, and all for nothing. They were coming, and they knew where Earth was, and Willow. True-Leader was dead, but he had beaten her. Tampering with them, unsettling them, unbalancing them, waiting for the moment to attack their disarray, she had hardly noticed what pseudo-Leader had told them. She had not seen its importance. They were coming, and it was all over. She might as well have told The Questioner.

She rubbed her face in confusion, bits of dried blood peeling off unnoticed, and looked at the mocking lights. She thought of using Leader's sidearm on herself, for what could she take home now except the acknowledgment of this second and greater failure? But pseudo-Leader stormed at her, *I will not die twice!*

She thought of waiting for them to come after all. Leader liked that. But there was still a great deal they would want to know, and she was not so lost as to tell them. There would be another Questioner to rend her.

"Not in my body you don't," said Leader, shocked.

It was her voice again. What, oh no, what was happening to her? She ought to be terrified—but she was past terror. Her capacity for fear was used up at last.

She would go. She could not stay. But she could not face Jameson, either; but she had to, to tell him Earth and Willow were uncovered.

Best to move the Watchsetter first, if she could, so the People could not find it and she could bring humans back to it. If she could do it. If one person could move it.

"No," said Leader, impatient with her stupidity. "One person alone in space cannot do anything. Why build spacecraft for the impossible?"

"All right," Hanna said.

She half-turned to flee, then turned back, weak with the importance of a new thought. The Watchsetter was a treasure for humans. She could not give it to them, but she could take with her the most important thing. It would skew the odds, at least. It might do more; might permit such destruction of the People's threat as to leave them harmless to humans forever. She might have failed utterly in what Jameson had expected of her in an innocent time longbefore; but she thought he would settle for victory.

She dropped into the watchman's place and entered a half-remembered code.

"No!" Leader howled. She saw her hands change to hairy paws, but Leader was weaker and her fingers barely faltered. She shook her head to keep coarse ghostly hair from her eyes.

"Render!" Leader hissed, but she went on. No madness or illusion could stop her now. She had strength still for one last hope. If the Watchsetter dissolved around her she would go on until her body failed.

More paper fell from the printer's slot. She did not try to decipher the heading in the bare illumination, but she knew she had made no mistake. She had in her human hands the clear route to Leader's Home, a mathematical map of safe channels through space that would permit humankind to go from this point to Home at wartime speed. If she got *Heartworld II* away the People would have no equivalent for human space. A location was one thing; the course program embedded in this substance was another.

She thrust the parchment into her shirt and went back to *Heartworld II* with memories of the People coming in waves, buffeting her. Voices shouted in her head. They were not all Leader's.

I was Student of animals only, Historian of Renders, prepared against the day. It came. They called Us, desperate Explorers having found Our dread. I went through space, a thing I had not dreamed. And hated it. The severing!

She veered from her course at the Student's power, fell against a wall and saw it flicker; a mural came briefly to life.

Found carnage in a star's light, Renders penned, Explorers dead or dissipated terrorized. The grasses were golden, like some of Home

A scarlet-suited Student reached from the wall. Hanna avoided his grasp; he disappeared.

Knew at once what they were what We feared had feared and fear: Renders without question, for they killed Us: Renders grown to master metal, worse: Renders of a distant star

She stumbled into a room she had not seen before. The chairs looked comfortable, though too large. The ceiling was hung with gems that would dance in moving air; but no air moved.

Prisoned them and questioned, but they knew naught. Called on a sky-born Render to crush Us, but it came not. Some said it was not. Hate scalded Us. We remembered Renders' hate. And its extinguishing.

The room shrank. There was no way out. "Let me out!" Hanna gasped, but the walls closed in remorselessly. The glittering stones were the People's eyes.

Remembered the Rite of Renders' days. We used it applied it to flatten to claim them, defuse and defang them. They crawled, begged, yielded, and died. One by one

Hanna chewed her fingers, crawling. Illusion! The door was where she had left it. She climbed to her feet and trudged toward it and through it, head down.

dissolved them and changed them and learned alteration the source and the secret and thou final fruit

The pseudo-familiar corridors dilated and expanded with her breath. She was a Student, and saw a helpless Tree-cub vanish in agony; was a colonist racked into insanity.

learned We the change that might aid times-to-come

She got through a last portal and *Heartworld II* was

there. All the beings stored in Leader flung history at her. Here were memories of a thousand Nearhomes still walled against long-extinct Renders, here was the Last Hunt which had spanned two hundred years, here were ancestral deaths remembered by survivors whose loss was more final than humans could know. More: burning brands defending misty seacaves, naked hunters hunted by the essence of evil, an archetype ages old that was a living presence still.

She walked into *Heartworld II* and to its flight deck, wobbling but upright, and still bombarded. Human fittings welcomed her. The computer's human-seeming speech soothed her.

"We are leaving," Hanna said to *Heartworld II*.

"Destination?" it inquired without anxiety.

"D'neera," she said, suddenly remembering it was a day or less away. "D'neera. Oh, dear God. D'neera."

Listen, Leader said.

"Shut up."

She let *Heartworld II* do most of the work—that was what it was made for and carried on with it a dialogue in which her part was more crystalline and uninflected than the yacht's. Leader brooded at the back of her thought, contemplating going as a prisoner to D'neera. He said, "You are now alien there as I."

"I am human," she said, opposing his doubt. To be human was to be Hanna, and she would not be Leader. Or the other thing, "which you are," Leader said. "No," Hanna said.

Nonetheless (the docking bay opened slowly on darkness, and *Heartworld II* meshed fields with the First Watchsetter, pushed against substance and non-substance, and lifted) it was true. The day when humans became Renders was not ended. The People had met therefore were meeting therefore would meet a handful of humans stranded on a hostile world, and had seen Renders and were seeing them and would see them. Hanna did not understand how this could be, but there was no question (*Heartworld II* floated gently into space, and frost glittered in pale starlight where it had been) that was what the People saw. No question they would see it again and forever "because you *are*" Leader said, complexes of Render instinct, and barren of the living omnipresent communication through time as well as space that made up this thing she must call the People, or their soul.

No Jump had ever been so welcome as the one that left the First Watchsetter behind.

Why were there no stimulants on this ship?

Clouds drifted erratically and at intervals into her vision. Her reading on Earth had hinted at glorious devastating drugs in high places. There was a guarded link to Jameson. Imagos, Fantasee, Reomla, Dite's Dream—why not the common ordinary boosters everyone used? Why couldn't he have left her some?

You will be Home soon, Leader said, *and will rest. Or not.*

Not I. Not you, while I am with you. They will not permit!

Hanna muttered through her weariness, "Iledra will."

He believed it. He shared her faith in Iledra; he could not do otherwise.

He said, *Close to Home closing destruction of mine—*

"Close," she agreed hazily; got up to keep herself awake; saw facing her a map of human space.

The map was an automatic display, an entertainment, a pretty pattern, a reduction of space to the dimensions of the mind. She wondered what it was doing here in a place that belonged to Jameson. He was not a man to diminish the reality of night and rock.

But other people came here too: Heartworld's councilmen, perhaps, or guests of its governments from other worlds. They would come to watch a pilot, maybe Jameson himself, manipulate the controls that flung them through space-time. Here it was, anyway. She regarded it with somber fascination. Schematic and out of scale it showed everything, a child's-eye view of the universe, where the stars humanity called its own twinkled merrily, connected by thin diamond-bright lines that showed common courses, relay networks—

She was near such a network. Within one? Yes!

(Kiri grinned at a face from Control, unflappable, unquenchable. "A tricky maneuver with minim data. Bassanio in command. Not bad!"

"I don't remember this group being reported ready to up-phase—"

"It was safe enough. Anyway I couldn't stop 'em."

The face said furiously, "Damn you, Kiri, one of these days you're going to lose a whole pod!"

Kiri, laughing, closed D'neera out. The training vessel
Star of Gnerin *was too filled with delight for gravity-chained
faces to distress it.*

*"We know better, don't we?" she said, smiling at Hanna.
"I wish there were no relays—they'd never know what we
do!" Hanna agreed, happy and triumphant. She was sixteen,
carefree, and immortal . . .)*

"D'neera," she said to *Heartworld II*. "Call D'neera, the
House of Koroth, I want to talk to Lady Koroth."

No! Leader said with violence. He needed time; D'neera
was too close.

Heartworld II made its busy calculations, located a target, and spoke. Its identicode preceded its message. This
was so routine that Hanna gave it no thought, nor the probability that through all of human space the code was flagged
and tagged—

"Stand by for holographic transmission," *Heartworld II*
said tranquilly.

—and diverted to—

A uniformed Fleet commander who stood before her
larger than life and with no warning, so that she jumped,
thinking in confusion that she had blacked out and they had
boarded and this was a flesh-and-blood giant and really
here.

He said politely, "I am asked by Lady Koroth to tell you
that she invites you to return home."

They stared at each other. It seemed a long time since
Hanna had looked on a human being. She found her voice
and said, "Where is Lady Koroth?"

He had to think about that a minute. She saw that he
looked weary. A patch on his shoulder said his name was
Tso.

He said, "She is nearby."

"I want to talk to her."

"That is impossible," he said, still courteously.

"Why is it impossible?" she said, already knowing the
reason as if the knowledge had leaped from the brain of the
invisible Lady Koroth to hers. There had been Fleet troops
in plenty on D'neera for months. The magistrates now were
only figureheads. Compromise was over. It was no longer
possible for Iledra to speak for herself. Hanna's dream of
going home had been folly from the start. And all Iledra's

other hopes. They would not even let her speak to Hanna. They must be afraid of what she would say. And what could that be but a warning to Hanna *not* to come?

Tso shifted tactics. "Nothing will happen to you," he said. "We are under the strictest orders, from the highest possible sources, not to hurt you."

Hanna said, "If Iledra tells me it's safe to come home I'll come. Not otherwise. I want to talk to Commissioner Jameson too."

"Of course," Tso said. "Immediately. It will take only a few minutes to patch through to Earth."

He turned away and issued orders to, from Hanna's vantage, a wall of *Heartworld II.* When he turned back Hanna had had a little time to think. Tso's official face was as blank as Jameson's at its best, but his eyes flickered. Hanna was thin and blood-stained and disheveled. Fleet would not be much impressed, nor whatever watcher of Morisz's they called in—and I&S certainly would be called in. What would they say to Jameson before she spoke to him, before he even saw her image for himself?

"I still want to talk to Iledra," she said, "or Cosma," but Tso did not answer. He said casually, "How long will it take for you to come here?"

"A long time," Hanna said as casually. She drifted without haste toward the communications panel of *Heartworld II,* skirting the insubstantial giant. The obliging yacht, without orders to the contrary, was projecting her semblance to D'neera. Somewhere—even, no doubt, in her House itself— her image walked ghostly through familiar space.

She cut off the communication with a movement of her hand. When she looked around, Tso was not there.

Leader had what he wanted, but she jerked at his wave of—pity? Pity! For her!

He said in what seemed a whisper, "Not to be able to go Home . . . !"

"You can't either . . ."

She fell wearily into the pilot's seat. Another Jump was imminent. She would not feel safe until it was over. They would pinpoint her location through the relays, and come here. She was not even sure *Heartworld II*'s course could not be remote-sabotaged. The dense-written course program for Leader's Home lay between her breasts, folded and crumpled. She could not go home; she must put the course into Jameson's hands. Why? She thought confusedly that it would be more sensible and safer to put it into Iledra's. But they guarded Iledra against her coming. To get to Iledra she would have to throw herself against a wall of them. They would take the precious thing from her and send it through safe channels to Jameson; and to the commanders and Intelligence and the rest of the commissioners. She would never see Jameson face to face again. If he permitted her to speak to him she would be a prisoner, powerless and subdued and far away from his presence. Half the security force of the Polity would be listening, and his public persona would concede what it must to all the other eyes and ears.

But Hanna had nothing to do with his public persona. She had never had much to do with it. Every contact she had had with him had come down quickly to essential truth. So she must get to him and see him alone, and tell her story to him and only to him; and maybe by then she would know what, after all, was essential truth.

Five days to Earth, said an ETA display. How long had she been gone? It might have been weeks or months, for all her prisoned time-sense could tell. In five days she would be able to think of being free from the People forever.

The chime she had been waiting for sounded. She was safe again, for a little while. She sighed and rose, thinking of the paper that would give humans mastery, and her duty to take it to them.

She looked out the port at the stars and the universe split at ill-made seams, and she fell through nothing, gasping, and then it was over. She had been looking through Leader's eyes; but he was not real.

He said insistently, "I am."

She looked again at the enormous port, the window on nothingness that frightened him so. Her eyes picked out a constellation that by chance resembled the Bowman, the tip of his shaft an ancient mariner's reference. But Bowman circled in Leader's sky, not hers.

She sat down, shaking. Her hands looked strange and were covered with dry blood. She was filled with longing to bathe in a golden pool where sapphire flowers mused and Swift played on sun-warmed stones, diving sleek into the shallows, rehearsing old courses of sea-born life.

She buried her face in her filthy hands. After all, it was only her own human wish to cleanse herself of blood; but it was transfigured.

"Yes," Leader whispered, and she felt something like a song begin. It was no music *she* had ever known; it was music by analogy only. And she did not know, huddled in this black-edged whiteness that was foreign to her in its very human-ness, why he sang.

He saw something she did not.

"Changeling," one of them said.

"Not me," Hanna said. She understood only dimly what it was she denied. She thought, desperately, not of D'neera but of Earth, birthplace of the species humankind. She concentrated desperately on Jameson, quintessentially male, reminding her that she was female; embodiment of human power, reminding her that she deserved a human fate. For all else seemed slipping away.

"We are both changed," said one of them.

She felt relief like soft rain to nourish her, but it was not her relief. Yet it was comforting. Leader-in-her-thoughts curled round her like smoke.

"Changeling, hybrid, two-in-one," he crooned with her voice.

Hanna got up again, and could not take a step. Leader did nothing to stop her; it was only that there was nowhere to go. This time it did not occur to her to say he was not real. She never thought of it again.

Instead she said, "I don't want that. I don't want it. I don't want it."

"No," Leader admitted, "but you begin to see."

"I see," said Hanna desperately, stubbornly, "that *you* are changed. *He* saw it." She meant true-Leader.

"And you," said Leader-in-her-thoughts.

"But I don't want to be changed!"

"But you are," he said. He seemed and sounded like a man come to safety through a tempest. Hanna felt his feelings clearly enough; but she did not know if they were hers also. They might be, if she let them. Because suddenly she had none of her own, none at all. Everything else seemed to have run out of her along with fear.

She took one aimless step and then some more. She faced a polished black panel and stopped because there was no particular reason to turn around and go in another direction. Her reflection was a dim shadow of herself, and she did not like looking at it. She called for darkness and slid into a heap at the panel's foot. All the lights went out, and all the black and white edges smoothed into grayness under starlight.

She said almost conversationally, "Look, I can't take any more. I just can't."

"There is not much more," Leader remarked.

"'Not much more.' What does that mean?"

"Why," Leader said, "I am prisoned in death. But if we come to my Home I will be freed."

She understood only in part. She shook her head. "They'd kill me when they were done," she said.

"But when you are finished with me in the presence of your People, they will obliterate me, who am already dead!"

"I'm sorry," Hanna said, meaning it, "but I won." She did not have to explain to him the significance of her mastery of this tired but functional human body.

"Fraud!" he said to her again, and lashed her this time with a memory of her own from an age ago on *Endeavor*, when she had in her arrogance criticized true-human limitations and proffered herself as the ultimate link to strange minds.

"You do not wish to learn anything," said Leader, a disappointed pedant.

"I am too tired to learn," Hanna said.

"It is easier to be a Render," Leader said bitterly.

She answered wearily, "What else can I do? If I choose your way I betray my own people and make my death certain."

"But you do not know what my way is," he said. "And even if it were only what you think, how is it worse than your way?"

The air before Hanna thickened and blurred, and in it she saw Sunrise burning, the silver groves of her Nearhome gone up in flames, Swift bewildered and deranged and his mother's death consuming him. "You rob him of my springtimes," Leader said. A child who was both Leader and Swift reached for the delicate, sweet-smelling tendrils of a young tree which blackened and melted along with the child, and with it melted also a million recollections and history known through living minds treasured since the first thought net formed in a primeval sea.

She wanted to tell Leader there was nothing she could do about it, but he was gone, hidden, sulking in a corner of her consciousness. The knowledge he had tried to thrust upon her lay between them, uncomprehended. Because she would not comprehend, or maybe could not; she was not structured to comprehend it. She spoke instead what seemed a truth she could understand: "It's got to be one or the other. The advantage depends on me, don't you see? They know where we are but not how to program all the way. Now I know where you are—"

She paused, dubious. We and they and you seemed remarkably interchangeable.

But Leader did not answer. He only sulked—and grieved.

Hanna stayed where she was for a long time. Most of the time her eyes were fixed remotely on space. Twice *Heartworld II* said a Jump was coming and ran aloud through chains of equations; twice a chime sounded, and what Hanna saw changed. Each change took precisely one chronon. Or perhaps it did not. She wanted to touch a human presence and reached out for Jameson, for Iledra, for anyone, and could not sense the existence of a single living entity. She was not an Adept, and she was very far from anything human. She was alone with Leader, and he had discovered something that might be her conscience, and jabbed at it unmercifully.

The fourth Jump showed her, very small and distant, a glowing nebula. Stars were being born in its heart. Life would come from them in their turn. By which time humans and the People too would have vanished, or gone on to "a future unimaginable as the improbable past . . ."

She heard Jameson's deep voice say the words. She almost saw the room beside the flowing river where he had spoken them. She moved finally. She was cold and cramped. She did not like the way her thoughts kept going back to him, and to her own blighted promise.

She got up and went cautiously through *Heartworld II* to the living quarters. Nothing looked quite right or entirely wrong. She took off her clothes and dropped them into a cleaning bin—she thought that was what it was; once she had known, but now she was not sure. Drawing a bath was less difficult, but when she slid into the water she cupped a little in her hands and touched her forehead to it. In memory, of course, of the First Home.

After that she bathed very quickly, and left the water as soon as she could. She was afraid that it would dissolve her.

She wandered naked through *Heartworld II* and thought about Leader. She had not thought about him before. You could not call it thought, that first battle for control. Nor had she thought about him during the days? weeks? as a passenger in her own body. Then she had only studied every detail of *his* thought as if he were under a microscope, so she could use it all for ambush. But Leader-in-her-thoughts, pseudo-Leader, changed Leader, had declined to die. He remained explorer, watchsetter, father, bondmate, an intelligent being steeped in a rich culture which resembled nothing humans had ever encountered before; a culture organically founded, more strangely structured than F'thal's, as limited as Girritt's but transcending its limitations.

On the flight deck she leaned across the unused pilot's console, looked again at the bright nebula, heard a chime, and was suspended in a dense field of stars. The starclouds shone for her, great drifts flung across the velvet of night, the jewels of creation promising gifts of life. A memory stirred: the old pull of curiosity beyond bearing, the seductive whisper born of desire saying she could deal with whatever she encountered.

With my body a weapon and fire in my hand and the great fleet pouring death from alien skies . . .

She saw herself and Leader, People and Renders, humans and bestial aliens, locked in a dance of hate.

She thought of the very first steps, which had determined the form of the dance.

She had thought, when she wrote "Sentience," that the meaning of her life was the pursuit of understanding.

She had pursued nothing. She had only fallen into the pattern of the dance, not acting but reacting, seeking escape, even into death.

Leader whispered, "Full sentience is the power to choose the harder path."

She turned her head sharply, as if he stood beside her.

"What can you know of it," she said, "when you see us as nothing but beasts?"

"I know what I have learned from you," he said. He meant "Sentience," as if he had read it, and she saw, shocked, that he had. He had read it within her; read it in her cells and brain and the perspectives she brought to all that he saw through her eyes, whether she was consciously aware of them or not; and he accused her now of denying all she was.

"But I didn't know about you then," she said. "I didn't know it could mean this!"

"But what if—?" he said, and he meant: What if someone stepped outside the dance? What if there were a hybrid, changeling, two-in-one, someone who could think simultaneously in two realities and show each to the other without the fear that was the heart of the dance?

If one could do it without being insane to the eyes of both, or be reassuringly the same and yet different. If one could do it. If she could do it. She and Leader—

"Yes," he said; for it was his thought she thought.

"But how?"

"I don't know," he admitted.

She sought within his reality for a key. His memories lay complete behind her thought, a secret known to no other human being. His knowledge was hers to use as she chose, freely. Death and transition and life-in-We—

"Saved safely in thee—"

But transmuted—

She said, "I think I know." She put a hand against the thick transparent barrier that kept out the cold of space. The hand trembled.

He said after a little while, "Have you the courage?"

"I don't know. Oh, I don't know!"

He said slowly, "You must know more."

"More," she said, seeing what he meant and dreading it.

"You must *be* more."

She rubbed her bare skin, shivering, clinging to her humanity.

"I will be utterly mad," she said.

"No more than I," he answered ruefully. That was true already, in any case. Neither ruefulness nor any other form of humor was part of the People.

"All right," Hanna said, and bowed her head. Choosing. But no gratification accompanied the choice; she was compelled rather by the shadow of what she had been—which would mean nothing and be nothing if she did not make this choice. And she only knew that she had chosen when:

Smoke rose beyond marsh grasses that obscured her view. Something screamed barely audible in agony; barely audible though its throat was bursting because another battle was joined; on one side the cloud of which the thing was both part and (to the People) whole; and locked with it, wrestling with it and seeking to consume it, the People, savage and new, near foundering.

The grasses rippled past her, traveling. Or she moved, though without body or volition. She was coming near the Celebrant, on whom their power was focused. She could not see him past the ragged band that circled fire and stone and sacrifice.

"Not sacrifice." Leader stood beside her in the wholeness of his prime, uniformed. Scarlet blinded her in the sunlight of the People's beginnings.

"Then what?"

Through the kin-group, through the fiery circle to the stone where lay the Render, screams diminished in extremity to choking sounds. She saw herself. Her flesh convulsed. She cried out in anguish and:

". . . not sacrifice," Leader was saying. "That is a human concept. This is other."

She lifted her head from the floor of *Heartworld II*.

"I cannot," she said. "It's *him*," meaning Bladetree.

"It is all of Us," Leader said. "We are not human."

She lay on ice. Her skin shrank from it.

"I will try," she said, though it was impossible, and at once the common memory seized her again, vivid as if this ancient day from the morning of the world were yesterday.

She stood beside a fair deep pool, freshwater, tree-shrouded. The sea was far away, though ever-present in the soul; the People had spread far in great migrations. They had well-made weapons of stone and wore glossy furs. Before her stretched on massive stone was a Render. Its fangs gleamed; but its eyes were intelligent, its thought aware and utterly filled with hate.

It was less alien to her than were the People.

Celebrant lifted the stone knife and Hanna's hand rose
with it. A ring of fire surrounded them. She would use fire
too.

"No," she said. "No!"

*Taken one by one and costly beyond measure for they kill
Us easily and overpower Us. Leaving no-time for transition.
Quicker increase, many mates. Meat-eaters even as We and
We are their prey. We are no match. Therefore We must be-
lieve and shape . . .*

The thing thrashed, crying out, lost. Hanna saw herself.
The knife slipped from her hands.

*Honor thee who taketh pain transmute to joy create their
end. Lest coming-time sees Renders only weaponed, powerful, dominant, Our vanishing all the ages of Our selves*

The mountain stream spoke icily. Fire and stone. Fishers
and farmers gathered for the Rite. Precious stones gleamed
on her breast. She wielded knife and fire with scaly hands.
The implacable bestial will flared, faded, and was malleable.

*This is true. Is real. We change the real, make truth. They
dwindle, yet We kill few. Yet they dwindle, unsubstantiated by
past years past lives directed by a Rite that*

Sea wind blew strongly on her sea-colored skin, and tore
at her rich garments. A city gleamed beyond the dunes. The
creature's pain was ecstasy.

Vanish and dissolve! she cried, all cried, and it was nothing, strength and self obliterated and with it all its kind. Reduced to protoplasm, mind gone, will gone, it was ripe for
harvesting. They took it in, its nothingness.

*So are they nothing, harmless, impotent, and blown and
tattered on the wind and threat no more, and We have made
them so*

Once more for an instant she was Hanna. She lay in
darkness in *Heartworld II* and a human mind sought to understand, and could not, because: under the knife and her
hard bloody hands a sentient species expired, driven to
death by the People's will. And nothing else.

Chapter 16

Dreamdust is a transparent powder with potent effects on the human nervous system. It produces, inevitably, sleep, but it is taken because it guarantees pleasant dreams, shaped by the dreamer's desires and providing whatever gratification he does not get in waking life. It is a product of Co-op, where the first, mostly unwilling settlers used it and thus, according to one view, survived the years of privation with some sanity intact; or, according to another view, failed to achieve any lasting thing until it was outlawed. Now it is used for the alleviation of chronic nightmares, and in expert hands for the guidance of dreams to modify personality without brainsoup intervention. But it also is used—not legally, since it is addictive—for its own sake. Most users dream of the erotic, and after many nights with ideal mates no longer form real relationships. But some use the powder to evoke tranquility, though that too is dangerous unless they are sufficiently strong-willed to refrain from comparing night to day.

Starr Jameson, lately not much interested in eroticism, spent his nights dreaming of sun-warmed seas or, sometimes, Arrenswood; of broad empty sweeps of water or forest or grain, warmed by the light of unspecified suns. In these dreams he did not have the insistent transmitter implanted in his ear, and was relieved of responsibility and twenty years younger; all of which only made each day's waking reality a more potent shock.

The part of his mind that guided dreams was puzzled, then apprehensive, then alarmed when it got out of control. The sweep of radiant water faded, its coolness vanished from his skin, and he was in the dark. Hanna ril-Koroth was back, a nightmare shape crouched on his bed with a hand twined hard in his hair. Something icy nicked at his throat. She said, *Wake up. Now! And don't move, or you die.*

The not-quite-words were frantic. He mumbled, "Not me, Hanna," and started to move, and nearly lost a handful of hair.

She said out loud, "Damn you, I'm real. You're not dreaming. Wake up!"

He thought she was Iledra's pale hand reaching for him, vengeful, and then that she might be real after all; but it was hard to tell with the Dreamdust coursing through him. He opened his eyes and saw a blacker figure melding with the darkness.

He said with difficulty, "Turn on the lights."

She gave the command and in the burst of light moved convulsively, shoving a knee hard into his stomach. It hurt. He lay very still. She was real, all right, and so was the knife against his neck. He blinked until her face came into focus against black draperies, pale and familiar; but she was changed and haggard.

She said, "I've g-got something you want. We, I, want something. From you."

He stared into her eyes and their blue mixed with his dreams and he fell into a summer evening's sky, a new dream stirring. Knife, fist, and knee evaporated. He lifted a heavy, tentative hand that brushed her hip.

"Stop it!" Her voice was high-pitched and impatient. Her face blurred, but not before he saw it was a stranger's. She said in a stranger's voice, "What's, what the hell's wrong with you?"

"Dreamdust?" he said, but it did not come out right and she said, "What?"

He said more clearly, "Dreamdust."

She said, "Oh, hell." The hand in his hair relaxed and she drew back. The knife left his throat, but it trailed across his chest and the point stopped between two lower ribs. If she drove it in it would not kill him at once, but he could be entirely disabled.

He had to get the fog out of his brain, which told him even now, earnestly, that he was alone with a woman who had a knife, and grievances, and maybe an alien army at her back. He wanted the Dreamdust antidote. He made her understand, and felt a suspicious probe for the truth of what he said. In his helplessness it was a violation.

"Get it," she said, but she kept the knife where it was while he reached for the panel that hid the antidote. Dream-dust is physically disabling, and his hand wavered. Ordinary people could burn out all the brain cells they wished without having to worry about instant recovery. Jameson kept antidotes for everything at hand, because he did not have that common luxury. He resented it.

He had trouble with the phial and after a minute, word-lessly, she took it from him, letting go of the knife to do so. It lay close by his hand, but he was so foggy he had no chance of making a grab for it without risking death, and both of them knew it. She opened the phial and held it out to him. The bitter liquid trickled down his throat, and he saw her take up the knife again before he put his head back and waited for his thoughts to clear. He closed his eyes and felt her weight shift. Her hands, knife and all, rested intimately on his knee.

Presently he said, "I hoped you would come back."

"What?"

"The house let you in, didn't it?"

She was silent for a moment. Then she said hesitantly, as if precision were costly, "I thought, I thought you'd forgotten to, to tell it not to. After I was here before. I didn't, I didn't know how I, I was going to get in. But it knew me and it . . ."

Her voice trailed away. In the dark behind his eyelids he pictured her creeping through the silent house, fumbling through unknown rooms in search of him, waiting each second for discovery.

"I didn't forget. I wanted to make it easy. You might have come for shelter when I wasn't here," he said, and felt her reach for the truth again. This was why D'neerans did not lie; there was no point to it. But he was telling the truth.

He opened his eyes and saw her clearly for the first time. She looked terrible as his dream had made her: thin, hollow-eyed, the pale brown skin bloodless and sallow, her body stiff with tension. Her clothes were torn and hung on her loosely.

She said, "Was there, was, was there an alarm?"

"What kind of alarm?"

"To Morisz. Or somebody. Because you have to listen to me."

"There was no alarm from here," he said. "I don't know what you might have done getting this far," and irritably, at another stab in thought, "I wish you would stop doing that. Do you think I would lie to you?"

Yes! said her thought resoundingly.

"All right. All right. May I get dressed?"

She hesitated a moment and said, "All right. But move very slowly."

He pushed away the coverlet and saw her eyes widen, taking in the heavy muscles of his chest and arms. She backed away from him. The knife fell to her knees and she was holding some kind of archaic gun. She said, "I don't forget you hunt tigers. This would stop one. I got it from the, the, the aliens."

He barely kept still. "From—you have been with them?"

She nodded. He looked at the chunk of metal she held. Her thumb hovered near a stud whose function was unclear, but the hole in the end was pointed toward him.

"I believe you," he said, and eased out of bed very slowly indeed.

He slept nude, but it did not occur to him to be self-conscious. He dressed slowly, giving himself time to think. Leaving himself open to Hanna's return had been a hopeless gesture. It was inconceivable that she should get this far, even supposing she wanted to come to him. And she ought to have been headed for D'neera, if anywhere in human space. "Rational but uncooperative," Tso had said. Lady Koroth, witnessing that interview but kept from interfering, had been less temperate; she had used words like "hunted" and "driven." They might both be right, Jameson thought, watching Hanna as closely as she watched him. Her sleeves were rolled up and an angry red wound showed on one forearm. Tso had reported it, with a note: Combat, query? The fast-healing D'neeran flesh had closed over it already, but scantily and unevenly, and the skin around it was dark and unhealthy. She held the heavy alien weapon awkwardly, using both hands; but the muzzle did not waver.

When he was finished he said in a carefully even tone, "Why don't you put that down, Hanna? You know I was half-expecting you and you know there has been no alarm. I'm willing to talk to you, but that thing makes me nervous. What does it do, anyway?"

She looked at him with round eyes and said, "Are you— are you going to call for, for help? Don't lie," she added.

He did not think she would like the truth, and answered reluctantly, "I won't tell anyone yet that you're here. Sooner or later I will have to. Not immediately."

After a minute she nodded. She looked down at the weapon and turned and pointed it at a shrouded window. Her fingers moved and there was a loud click. Nothing else happened.

She said in mild surprise, "Oh. Must be out of power or something."

She let it fall on the bed and with it, as if it were an after-thought, the knife.

"I didn't want to hurt you anyway," she said.

Tension Jameson had not been aware of left him. He went to her and picked up both weapons and took them to a far corner of the room, where he locked them in a cabinet that until now had held nothing more dangerous than a lady's forgotten jewels. Hanna did not object. When he came back and stood before her, she looked at him quite trust-fully, almost smiling, as if she were glad to see him. He did not smile back. He said, "You know what I want from you. Tell me what you want from me."

"What," she said rather vaguely, and just as he began to speak again, "do you want from me?"

He said, puzzled by the disjointure of her speech, "I want full cooperation. I can promise you nothing, except that you will not be pilloried unnecessarily."

"It's all right." The smile disappeared, and she was sol-emn. "I won't fight anymore. I won't run again. Just listen to me before you talk to anybody else. That's all I ask."

"I will do that."

"Really?"

"Really."

Her face lit up with gratitude. He was not above encour-aging it, and he sat down beside her and took her hand. But relief, in truth, made him weak. She had seen the aliens and been in a fight, but she had escaped, with God knew what knowledge of them.

"How did you get away?" he said.

She was very still for a minute. Then slowly, slowly, she reached into her shirt. She pulled out a long tangled strip of a paper-like substance, edged with incomprehensible script. She held it close to her breast, looking at nothing.

"What is that?" he said, but she did not move or answer and was still as death, so that he looked at her carefully, trying to gauge her sanity and stability. He saw the marks of privation, exhaustion, and the poorly healing injury that must keep her in constant pain. But he did not see fear or madness or any sign of alien control.

"Hanna," he said softly, and touched her face. She shuddered and moved.

"It's the course program for their home," she said.

He stared at her, disbelieving, and reached for it. She twitched it away uncertainly.

"But you have to listen to me," she said.

"I'm listening. How did you get it?"

"I don't want to talk about it," she said clearly.

He said carefully. "I wish you did not have to talk about it. But you must. And you must give me that program. You understand why, don't you?"

"Yes, but—oh, he doesn't want me to! He can't bear it!"

Jameson made a patient, noncommittal noise. He did not have the slightest idea what she was talking about.

"Will they see the ship? And come for me?" She looked up with sudden anxiety, and he was uneasy. She had displayed half a dozen moods in ten minutes. He had always thought her volatile, but now she seemed a feather on the wind, immediately responsive to whatever was going on inside her.

"Where is the ship?" he said.

"In the hills." She nodded vaguely in the wrong direction.

"If they find it I won't let them take you away until you've said what you have to say. How did you get past orbital surveillance?"

She said with perfect clarity, "Hung around until I found something coming down that had about my mass. Fell in behind it and faked a duplicate of its ID. Followed it down and then split off when I thought it was safe. I was hoping they'd think I was a freak echo. I guess they did."

Heartworld II was not too large for Airspace Control to treat as just another traffic blip. If it had gotten so low without being identified, it was unlikely that anyone suspected Hanna was there. The technique was clever and daring, and he was impressed. He made a mental note to make certain no one else got away with it.

She did not elaborate, but turned to him and laid a hand on his shoulder and smiled, and then looked at the hand as if confused. She seemed lost inside herself, and after a little while he said, using the D'neeran form of her name, "H'ana? What is wrong?"

She looked up, blinked, and was there again. She said, "It would take—" She started counting on her fingers. She got up to four and started over again. She said, "It would take five days to retrace my route and eight more to . . . to . . . to Home."

"Home? D'neera?"

"Home," she said impatiently. "That's what they call it. I mean, they don't call it anything, but that's how they think of it. Not their, their, towns? Not that. Groupings. More personal homes. Hearths. They change. There's no spoken language at all. No fixed names for things or people. Except writing of course and that's numbers. It's just what they agree on at any given time. But Home is always Home. And they are—*now* there should be some of them—I can't tell you about that." She gave him a sideways glance, almost sly. "We'd kill each other. They know where you are, I mean where Earth is. And Willow. I couldn't prevent them from finding out—"

"Hanna!" His hand closed painfully on her arm. "What did you tell them?"

"I didn't. I didn't tell them anything. Oh, stop!" she cried in distress. "You said you'd listen!"

"There is no time to listen if you told them that!"

"But there is. Please! They had time to chart the way to D'neera before, but it's no different than that was. It will take them months to work out the course here!"

"Are you telling me the truth?"

I am telling you the truth, she thought painfully. He could not disbelieve her. He let go of her slowly. The fear and anger she had roused would take longer to subside. The marks of his fingers showed on her arm, but she did not try to rub them away. He eyed the paper she still held out of his reach and said, "You'd better begin at the beginning."

"There isn't one," she said. "It's a closed system."

He had the vivid impression that a tired child was speaking from a dream, and wondered if he would be able to get any sense out of her at all.

But she said, "Wait. I'll try. Listen. I'm not myself. Not anymore." She looked at him intently to see if he understood, but he did not.

"I wanted to understand them. The People. Do I sound insane? I am thinking now in some ways like one of them. And they are very different from us. But I think I understand. I think maybe, maybe there is a way to make them understand. I think maybe I can stop it."

"Are you sure?" he said, too roughly because the sudden hope was painful.

"I can't be sure," she said, almost whispering. "It's only a chance. They might kill me. Or question me again. If I can break the loop—I don't know if I can. I am human and alien and cannot be either. I must stay detached, outside the dance. Let me try."

She laid her good hand against his cheek. Her face was luminous, and his skin prickled at an eerie thought that much of what had been Hanna was burned away, leaving a wraith that might, if she were right, prove stronger than armies. It came to him then with a certainty whose source he did not know that the Hanna he had known was gone.

Hanna said, "I'm still here. For a while."

Don't read my mind, he wanted to say, and shook his head instead. He said gently, "You must tell me more."

"It will take a long time."

"You'll have time. As much as you need."

He took her to the room she had left many days before, put her in a deep chair, and gave her a drink loaded with nutrients. When he lit the fire she leaned toward the first flames as if their warmth drew her, and a little, a very little, of the tension went out of her face. The silence of deep night was close around them, and they might have been the only two people on Earth.

Then he sat down near her and said, "Tell me, Hanna," and she told him.

                    *   *   *

It was not yet morning when she finished, but his muscles ached from long stillness when he moved. He felt then a curious detachment, as if a potent drug still worked in his blood and customary realities were in abeyance, and he was a spectator at events that took no notice of him save to demand his acknowledgment. Hanna seemed sometimes an essence of otherness, a creature come from new dimensions, as if the impossibilities of Inspace had come to life. An alien being spoke with her lips, paradoxical: grieved or aggressive, fearful or stately by turns. "I cannot explain!" it cried, or Hanna cried, at times; and then they would bear him, willing or not, to other times on another world, and it seemed a massive alien held out its hands to his fire.

But sometimes it was only Hanna, though (he thought again) not the Hanna humans had known. He kept to himself a new conviction, born of the story she told and the ways she used to tell it, that neither he nor Hanna nor any D'neeran had properly estimated the power of telepathy—nor the cost to one who used it to its fullest. For even when Hanna spoke in her own voice she was new—or damaged. There was little straight-line logic to what she said, and he stopped her again and again, mystified by statements from a separate universe of discourse, making her show him the foundations of a reality more strange than any she had guessed at in writing "Sentience." And always she did as he asked her, painfully sometimes when memory shook her, but dutifully and doggedly, until he began to feel he was kin to The Questioner and Lady Koroth was right after all, and all his dreams had come to in the end was the torment of a woman who would not fight him.

Because he did not think there was any defiance left in Hanna. She had given him her weapons, and in the spaces between her words he heard her clear intention not to take them up again. With every separate sentence she put herself more firmly in his hands, offering herself for his use this last time. Her trust was terrible; and yet he saw, as he had seen from the day he betrayed it, that it was not new. It had always been there, from their first meeting: her conviction that he would choose rightly for the future, a faith as strong as his in his own vision. Perhaps she was not even conscious of it. It seemed part of an implicit, unspoken communication that had gone on under the surface of their words and actions each time they met.

He wished he could uncover and deal with that alone. He was tired, and he wished he did not have to listen so hard to what she was saying. He had had enough of strain and threats and sleeplessness, of aliens and work. He had spent half a lifetime gaining the responsibility of choosing for mankind, and now he wished he did not have it. The face of mankind was not as close as Hanna's face, and all that she said and showed him led in one direction only: to sending her away again. Yet that was what she wished him to do, and the bitterest ending of all was that, though she did not know it, he might no longer have the power to do it.

Silence lay between them when she was done; he broke it at last, inadequately. "I never dreamed of anything like that."

"Nor did I. But that was the point of 'Sentience,' was it not? That each species shapes its own reality ... but I didn't mean it quite so literally. And is shaped by it, you know. Is shaped by it ..."

She seemed to drift away. Jameson stood up, a little stiffly, and went at last to get a drink for himself.

"Run through the reaction model again," he said. "Simple fear! I don't believe it!"

"The dynamics aren't simple."

"Quite obviously. Tell me again. I want to make sure I understand."

"All right." Toward the end she had been talking more easily, as if human speech came more readily with practice. Now she said quite normally, "It starts with what the People are, full telepaths. I don't know just where in their evolution the ability showed up. It seems there are other animals on their homeworld with a form of it, even plants somehow, but in the People it reached a peak of mutual consciousness that's nearly a group mind, and shaped them and their history and their culture all together. And the past is alive. Very seldom does anyone just die, just end, as we do. That's the worst thing that can happen to them ..."

Her voice faltered, and he saw grief in her face. She said, "It happened to the ones I killed. Because of me. They were so far from Home, it happened so fast, there was no chance for the living to absorb them."

"I don't know what that means," he said.

"Why," she said, as if it were very simple, "the experience of generations is transmitted directly, not in words or pictures, but what it was to *live* it. They *are* those who came before."

"But they have individual identities as well—"

"Clearly, yet they can't exist apart from one another. Space travel is painful for them. Dangerous. They're a space-time collectivity, and individual identity depends on it. And its most important manifestation, where we're concerned, is that life for them is Us or not-Us. No exceptions. No borderlines. There are the People, and there is everything else. And everything else is harmless, or prey, or predator, and because they are so self-identified, they lack the ability to identify with anything else. They make analogs from their own reality to ours, just as we do with other things, but they are even more limited than we are in the sources they have to choose from."

She looked at him uncertainly, and he said with some relief, "I think I do understand that. It's a blind spot, like Girritt's limitations in technology."

"Yes. And what makes it worse, what makes it more dangerous for us, is that the deaths of not-Us beings are gratifying to them. It had to be that way, you see. Because you cannot subsist without killing other life forms. They even sense something—I'm not sure what—from plants. And you can't eat something if you experience its death as your own, can you? I think they have entirely different receptors for each other and for not-Us beings, and the perception of the death of prey or predator is something we don't have any words for at all. I could call it a kind of pleasure, but that's not fair. It makes them sound like sadists, and they're not, not really. You like the taste of meat, don't you? But you don't think that makes you a killer because the meat has to be slaughtered. Well, they don't kill or torment for pleasure; it's a by-product, so to speak. But it's there, and at the same time, among themselves, they've had no experience of war or conflict, nor compromise nor accommodation either. Because to kill another is to kill oneself. And everything else—"

She hesitated, and he said, "Is harmless or predator or prey. Yes? And which are we?"

"Predators," she said promptly. "And that's where the next element comes into play. There are dangerous animals on their homeworld. They are not specifically dangerous now, of course, because for many centuries the People have had a weapons technology that deals with them easily. But the most dangerous of all for many ages, the archetype of the beast, a sort of primate as it happened, was very close kin to us. Not literally, of course, but in the structure of its instinct and behavior it was much more like us than we are like the People. It was non-telepathic, and growing sentient. And it was—it was them or the People. There was only one that was going to be the dominant species, and take the niche humans got here. And so they—they—" She stumbled. "*Made* them die. With ritual death as the focus. They made the ... the disappearing, the dissolution they wanted, real."

Jameson did not understand this any better than he had the first time she said it. He let it go by. He said, "But they were wiped out long ago."

"Yes, oh, yes. But they still live in the ancestral memory which is this generation's memory. And the People have not left their evolutionary response to danger behind any more than we have. You know what that response is more intimately than most of us, I think. You don't hunt tigers with disruptors; you use a spear. And I saw you have scars?"

Her easy tone caught him off guard. Tiger-traces were a mark of honor, women of his own culture found them exciting, others sometimes were revolted and could not understand why he kept them; but to Hanna they were just there. He pulled himself back to the matter at hand and nodded. "I was lucky. I made a mistake once, long ago, and lived to remember it."

"Were you thinking of trying to reason with the tiger at the time?"

"What do you think? Of course not. There are only two things to do with tigers—stay out of their way, or kill them."

"Well," said Hanna, looking at him with some distaste, and he lifted a placating hand.

"No, don't," he said. "I'm quite fond of tigers, actually. You'd be surprised how much I know about them. But we are talking about instinct, are we not? And instinct has no middle ground."

"Yes," said Hanna, "and that is where the circle closes,

and the model is what happened to the human colony they found, and not only what happened to the colony but what happened to the People because of it. Just as things happened to them because of those others. Although they don't know that, I think. *He* doesn't think so."

Jameson waited, but Hanna, eyes unfocused, was silent; inwardly arguing a point, perhaps. He said encouragingly, "But they couldn't make the colonists just disappear."

"Oh," she said from her dream, "it took centuries with the others. And the People had the upper hand technologically, of course. But not at first. And that was how they got it. Or at least they believe that's how they got it. By willing it."

"But it is objectively true?"

"Starr," she said with finality, "it is objectively true for them."

She had never used his first name before. It startled him. He said unwillingly, "Then I suppose it doesn't make any difference," and gave it up.

He stood near her and stared into the fire. Soon he would have to decide what to do about this, the parts he understood and the parts he did not understand. If his decision, any longer, would prevail. His judgment still would make a difference, he thought, but it did not carry the weight it used to have. Hanna did not know that.

She said suddenly, "It's quiet here." He looked around and saw that she had leaned back into her chair, eyes closed. She seemed to have drifted into sudden sleep. He had put her in that seat, which he did not use himself, deliberately. Its comfort came from more than seductive fabrics and soft cushions; it also emitted a subtle mélange of subliminal commands to relax and feel safe. He found it useful for semiofficial guests, especially adversaries. He had not used it the night of Hanna's escape because there was a witness then. Now he looked at her curled and softened in it, trusting, vulnerable, and thought: *I wish I had not done this. I wish her safety were real . . .*

She was so weary, and her bone-deep tiredness woke echoes in him. Better for both of them if he were to put off decision and take her gently to his bed, warm her in the cold dawn, watch over her and give her a space of peace. It was not sensible to think of her as fragile: not with the knife so near that bed, not with her tale of blood. But she declined to be sensible about him; she insisted on speaking to parts of him he had successfully forgotten, almost; he supposed it gave him the same right.

She lifted her head and smiled at him as if in answer. He sighed and sat down on the arm of her chair. He said, "You haven't told me everything."

She looked disappointed, then guarded. It was characteristically human, but it was not Hanna. "No?" she said.

"No. You haven't told me just how you propose to—to stop the dance, I think you said."

"I can't explain it," Hanna said. She looked away from him.

"That is not easy to believe. After all you've managed to explain tonight."

"I mean I won't. You won't understand."

"If you won't tell me," he began, and stopped. He could not threaten her or press her one more time. He could not.

But he had to.

He said, "If you won't tell me I can't let you do it."

She stared into a corner. The room's one clear concession to the present gleamed there, a pattern of abstractions that appeared and disappeared because in certain aspects it was not real, and was created anew on each appearance. He did not know if she saw it or not. She said, "If it doesn't work, things won't be worse than they are. I've already told them everything important that I can."

"So you think you might fail. They might try to get more from you. The same way they did before? You would risk that?"

"I don't know what they would do. I told you."

"I wish you would tell me what you think you can do."

After a minute she said, "Even if it does work, I don't know what's going to happen to me."

He looked down at the top of her dark head and saw that a twist of wire salvaged from *Heartworld II* held back her hair. It seemed infinitely pathetic. He reached for it, and Hanna sat very still while he unwound it. Her hair drifted across her shoulders. He brushed it aside and thought of kissing the nape of her neck.

He thought: If I coax her she will tell me. I could use the affection I have not earned.

No. No.

Hanna said suddenly, "It's the hybridization. I'm *him*. You've talked to him. He is the . . . the . . . the key. To change them."

"All right. But how?"

"I'm already one of them. The perspective is unique, something they've never had or even imagined. But I really can't explain any better than that. You will just have to trust me," she said with finality, and looked up at last into his eyes.

"I suppose I must," he said. But even as he said it he thought: She is lying. And then: But Hanna does not lie. She does not know how to lie. It is the truth.

And then he could not put off decision any longer, because the implant in his ear erupted at such volume he clapped a hand to his head, cursing.

"Come in," said someone, not Rodrigues. "Jameson, are you there? Come in immediately."

Hanna looked at him as if he were a madman. He roared an order to his house that shut off the transmission in mid-word. "And find out who the hell that is and put them through in here," he said, because he did not want to bother with the security module.

"What is it?" Hanna said.

"I think," he began, but Stanislaw Morisz's voice filled the room.

"Jameson, are you there?"

"I'm here. What the hell's going on?"

"Are you all right? *Heartworld II*'s down near your location—"

"I know. I know. Lady Hanna is here. It's all right, Stan. Everything's under control."

Morisz said too casually, "Mind if I come see for myself?"

"No. Come on, if you have to make sure. How many people know about this, Stan?"

"Uh, a civil patrol that spotted it and went in for a closer look. Enforcement personnel. How long's she been there?"

"Not long." Jameson glanced at Hanna. She looked frightened. He said, "This is most-stringent-restricted, Stan. As of now. Get Enforcement out of it."

There was a silence before Morisz said, "Who have you notified?"

"Nobody, yet."

"There are regulations. Enforcement is already in."

"You can hold them." If you will, he added, but not out loud. "What about I&S?"

"Some of my people are alerted. Naturally."

"Some of your people? What have you got, a task force around the house?"

"I can't discuss that. Under these conditions."

"Then come see me," Jameson said, and waited for an answer. There was none.

Hanna said, "What does this mean?"

"It means we're running out of time," Jameson said. He leaned back, a hand on Hanna's shoulder. He thought of the ripple the news must make as it spread in erratic circles; the play of action and reaction, responsibilities real and fancied, the stir among those for whom Hanna's coming—or capture—might be turned into advantage. Morisz could control it for a while—if he would. Once Jameson could have counted on him to do it. Not now.

Hanna said, "Why not?"

"Are you reading my mind all the time?" He looked at her curiously.

"Not all the time. A lot. I have to," she said apologetically. "You don't say what you think. Why won't he help you?"

Jameson said slowly, "I did something that—in the end made no difference anyway. Sentiment for Stanislaw's resignation was rather strong after you . . . left us. He wouldn't resign, but he is . . . temporarily acting in a subordinate capacity. Pending outcome of an investigation into the qualifications of operatives who joined I&S during his tenure as director. He is back where he was thirty years ago—regional duty officer on the nightside."

Hanna regarded him with utter lack of comprehension. She said, "Are they going to come get me?"

"I don't know. I hope not. But the truth is—" He thought of softening it; but Hanna would know if he tried. He said, "The truth is you are wanted more intensely than any fugitive within my memory. From Enforcement's vantage alone you have broken so many laws that local and Fleet jurisdictions might argue for years over who will try you first. And I&S wants you, and I want you, and all the commissioners.

Morisz is a conscientious man. Under the best of circumstances he would not keep silent very long. And these are not the best. Don't say anything when he comes, Hanna. Don't mention that course program. You'd better give it to me."

She had put it back into her shirt when they came into the room. Now she gave it to him, still warm from its place against her skin. Her face was grave, but there was no hesitation; perhaps she saw the nightmare vision he had formed of Morisz taking her away over Jameson's protests. He took it, hurrying, to the security module no one but he could enter. When he came back to Hanna she was on the hearthrug, hugging her knees. Soothing the doubting alien? He said, "You have not told me exactly what you want from me."

"I only need one thing," she said without looking around.

Jameson's ears were pricked for the sound of Morisz's arrival. He said, "What's that?"

"Authority to act on behalf of the Polity."

He stood behind her and looked down with bleak amusement. "You came to me for that?"

She glanced up uncertainly, not understanding. She said, "I must be certain any promises I make them will be carried out. If I had gone there on my own, you see, they would have known. They would have known I spoke for no one but myself and they would not have understood or accepted it. I must have your word."

"Mine alone would not do in any case. You need formal authorization."

"Can you get it for me?" She looked anxious now; sensing, at last, that something was wrong.

He said, "I don't suppose you connected with a newsbeam on your way back."

"I had other things to think about," she said stiffly.

"I'm sure you did. If you had you might have heard—"

"Mr. Morisz is here," said the house, and Jameson said, "Let him in."

Now there was no time left at all. He had not exaggerated the passion with which so many people, so many agencies, wanted Hanna. If he waited for a meeting of the full Commission there would be nothing but trouble. The formal motion of which he had spoken would never be approved if the commissioners consulted their home worlds. al-Nimeury would be hopeless in any case, and the paranoid Petrov too. Endless time would be wasted in objections and obstacles, and Jameson's own time was almost gone. He would have to get the Commission to move while he could, and to move on its own, as it could but rarely did; and how would it move? Feng, who was not a decisive man, might easily be swayed to side with Petrov and al-Nimeury. The longer it went on the more people would insist on having a hand in it. He could not keep Hanna to himself legally or for long.

He said to the house, "Get me through to Andrella Murphy. Commission emergency, priority one override. As soon as I'm done with the call, do the same with Arthur Feng— hello, Stan. Satisfied I'm alive and well?"

Morisz looked at them doubtfully from the doorway. "I'd feel better if I could see her hands," he said.

Hanna turned and lifted them silently, palms up. The wound on her arm had begun to ooze blood.

Jameson said, "Stanislaw, it is essential to keep this quiet. Commissioners Murphy and Feng will be here within the hour—"

Andrella Murphy's voice said sleepily, "Starr? What's wrong?"

"Wait a minute, Andrella. Stan, keep your men where they're at. Don't let anybody in here except Murphy and Feng, don't let anybody get near *Heartworld II,* and don't report to anybody, anywhere, without checking with me."

Morisz said, "I can't do that without proper authorization." His hostility was so palpable that Hanna would not have to be a telepath to feel it. She sat upright, astonishment on her face.

Jameson said coldly, "I am your authority. I am still a member of the Coordinating Commission. This is a commission emergency. My word is enough. Do as I told you. That is an order."

Morisz's eyes glittered. For a moment Jameson thought he would refuse. Then he said, "Yes. Sir," and turned and left.

Hanna said, "What's happened to him? What haven't you told me?"

"Starr?" Murphy said. "Who's that? What is it?"

"Andrella, I need you at my home at once. Don't waste time talking. Just come."

"Starr, it's five o'clock in the morning!"

"I know," he said, although he had not known. "Just do it, Andrella. I don't have time to argue."

"All right," she said crossly, and was gone.

Hanna scrambled to her feet, her eyes wide and doubting. She said, "What is it? Tell me!"

He said evenly, "Your escape was too much for my council. I have perhaps a few hours left on the commission. There has been some disagreement about my successor, but it is nearly over. Murphy and Petrov and the rest will not have to deal with me in future. What I think no longer matters much to anyone. But I think you must go, and go quickly. If I am to get you what you need, there is only one thing left to try."

He stopped at the rush of sorrow he felt in her. She said, "I'm sorry. I'm so sorry. It's because of me, isn't it?"

Perhaps he ought to be angry with her. She was, in fact, the cause of it all. But for too many days he had seen only triumph, open or suppressed, on the faces around him. He bore it, he hoped, gracefully. But he was not proof against the understanding he felt in Hanna of what it meant to him.

He took her hands and said, "I'm not finished yet."

"What are you going to do?"

"Something marginally legal. If that."

She said with grave approval, "That's all right, then," and let her hands rest in his with simple trust as Feng's voice sounded in the room and Jameson began to talk very urgently.

Chapter 17

Not even Arthur Feng's best friends counted intelligence among his virtues. His appointment to the Coordinating Commission was a compromise, a least-repugnant choice made to satisfy half a dozen Colony One political factions. Jameson had for two years made a conscious effort to avoid treating Feng with the tolerance he usually reserved for rather stupid dogs. Now he looked round his study, transformed to an emergency conference room, and thought perhaps he would have to think of something else after all. Feng still was trying to cope with the idea that Hanna ril-Koroth had returned to Earth of her own accord, and that the aliens she spoke of might be something more than a vast deadly mystery.

"But what do they call themselves?" said Feng, returning to the beginning yet again. "They have to call themselves something. We can't call them People. It's too confusing. We're people."

Hanna said, "But they don't call themselves anything. Words are phonetic. They don't use words."

"But they have to have a name."

Murphy said, "All right. All right, we'll name them." She was looking not at Feng but at Jameson, reading his worry from long practice. "Girritt was named after Captain Neil Girritt. Let's call them after Lady Hanna."

"No," Hanna said. "Please. Not after me. If you must give them a human name, call them after Charl Zeig and Anja Daru, who died contacting them. Call it Zeig-Daru, and talk of Zeigans."

"Zeigans," said Feng, trying it out. "But they didn't really discover it."

Jameson closed his eyes for a moment. "Suppose we use it as an interim term in an emergency situation," he suggested. "A code name for unknown hostiles, applicable in situations calling for intelligence analysis."

The doubletalk satisfied Feng, but he had more ground to test, his bureaucratic instincts in full cry.

"What section are we convening under?" he said. "Appointment of an envoy? Can't you do that, as head of your committee?"

There were no commission by-laws specifically applicable to this situation, but that would be the wrong thing to tell Feng. Jameson said, "I can't act alone in this prior to the establishment of friendly relations. We are talking about a peace mission. Majority approval is required."

"This is a majority. But look here," Feng said warningly. "It's not the full commission."

"You noticed," Murphy murmured, and Jameson gave her a cold look.

"I don't think I can go along with this. Can I?" Feng said.

Jameson said warmly, "Of course you can."

"Let me think," Feng said, and Jameson thought there was some sort of contradiction in terms there.

It was nearly dawn, and the drip-drip of prematurely melting snow fell into the sudden silence. Hanna had left this temperate coast in the deep grip of winter and returned with the promise of an early spring. Jameson wished he could think it was an omen, but he was not a man to count on omens. And hope lay now in speed, and Feng had decided not to be rushed.

Hanna sat cross-legged before the fire, and Jameson was beginning to worry about her too. Her hair was loose about her shoulders, an unkempt tangle. Her face was drawn with fatigue, and he saw now that in the last few minutes she had torn off the end of one sleeve and was trying one-handed to wrap it around the gash in her arm. Murphy looked at her curiously. Andrella remembers her from the time of Goodhaven, he thought: poised, graceful, even elegant in her way. Now all her grace is gone, and she is a bleeding scarecrow. But Murphy herself looked entirely normal, fresh and decisive as if she were listening to an unusually interesting bit of testimony at some routine hearing.

Jameson stirred, composing himself to go on patiently

and soothingly with Feng, but he was interrupted. His house now was tied to Morisz's communications system, and Morisz said into the room, "Commissioner Jameson? I think you'd better come out."

The voice was expressionless. It was more alarming than agitation could have been. Jameson said, "What is it?"

"Some visitors would like to see you."

"Who are they?"

Morisz said stubbornly, "I'd rather not say."

Hanna lifted her tired face and said, "They're important."

"Who?" Jameson said, just as Feng said, "How do you know that?"

Hanna did not answer. Jameson got up and went out with a sense of foreboding.

The light from the door was dim on the faces of al-Nimeury and Petrov and Struzik. Morisz stood nearby. He looked satisfied and unpleasant.

al-Nimeury said at once, "What are you trying to pull?"

Jameson shrugged, looking past him at the others. Petrov, like al-Nimeury, looked furious; Struzik had the face of a man in shock.

al-Nimeury said, "What the hell are you having a secret meeting for?"

"Lady Hanna came back in the night," Jameson said. "She brought valuable intelligence."

"I know," al-Nimeury said. "Morisz told us."

Petrov said, "Weren't we going to hear about it?"

"Eventually." Jameson knew when there was an end to the usefulness of evasion. There would be no quick secret mandate for Hanna, thanks to Morisz; he would have to salvage what he could from the wreckage of his plan. He said, "Come on in. You too, Stan. You'd better hear this."

He turned and went into the house and they followed him, talking loudly. He ignored them.

Murphy was kneeling by Hanna when they came in. She looked up and said calmly, "Hello. Starr, have you looked at this?"

"No. Why?"

"There's something wrong. Lady Hanna says she had medical supplies and used them. It shouldn't be infected."

"Compatible biology, then?"

"In some way."

Jameson frowned at Hanna, who looked back at him without expression. Something new to worry about now, and no way to tell how dangerous it was because no one had had an alien corpse to dissect, or visited the world in question, or even had the artificial environment of a captured spaceship to study. Environmental traces in Hanna's own body on her first return had been inconclusive. She was, however, alive after two contacts. That was encouraging, but the still-open wound could mean she was slowly being eaten alive by something nasty that might or might not remain confined to her. And there was no time to study her. She had already violated biosphere protective regulations by returning here, and ought to be quarantined. The fact clearly had occurred to Murphy. Jameson wished he could tell her privately not to mention it in front of Feng— and then saw her turn suddenly to Hanna, puzzled, and knew Hanna had told her.

He said, "Sit down, all of you. If you please."

"I want an explanation," al-Nimeury said.

"You're going to get one."

Only al-Nimeury remained standing, his eyes on Hanna. They had not met before, but there was no need for introductions. Hanna regarded him bleakly from her seat before the dying fire.

"A D'neeran," al-Nimeury said with contempt in his voice. "So much damage. One D'neeran!"

Hanna got up slowly. What he thought, what he meant, reverberated behind the scarcely heard words. Trouble. Difference. Separation. Arrogance. A whole history. But al-Nimeury could not know she was his sister; he had not seen the void that lay between human beings and the others. The strangeness. And he was strange to her as she to him. Her body felt curiously light. Sleeplessness, disorientation, and her own urgent purpose kept the room at one remove from her. Her careful schooling in the uses of telepathy was confused by the functioning of Leader-in-her-thoughts, still here, still alive, crouching waiting watching while she tried to do what he and she together would do later somewhere else. Alliances. She and Leader. She and Jameson. She and al-Nimeury? She hardly saw the commissioners of the Polity. They were presences nearly without flesh, and only two of them counted. One was Jameson: steady, fearless, committed. And reckless, a thing she had thought never to find in him; but he had not much left to lose. The other was al-Nimeury, and his dislike, even disgust, was the strongest force in the room. It woke chords of hostility in her, the ancient emotional response to threat that fueled war within humanity and might now reach outside it if she could not, as she had said to Jameson, put an end to the dance. And she would have to end it here first to reach the People. On the edge of thought she heard or felt Jameson thinking, trying to find a way around his colleagues. Already he was separate from them. Already they saw him stripped of the power his office gave him. But there was a power in him that depended on no office, and she felt it with gratitude. Because there was no way around these others. The only way was through them.

She went to al-Nimeury, feeling that she floated. She stumbled and Jameson moved toward her, but she got balance back and took the last step. al-Nimeury was a short man, and stocky; her eyes were nearly level with his. They were deep brown, nearly black, and she might have thought there was fire in them, except the fire was behind them in the accumulated prejudice of generations.

She said, very softly, "I have to go back."

He took a step backward and opened his mouth. He was going to say: I won't listen. She held his eyes and it was not her eyes or her words that kept him silent so much as Jameson like a flame at her back. She drew on his strength as on a tangible current.

"Do you want war?" she said. "They're so delicate. So cruel. You could win it. They know nothing of war. They tried to keep up with human warfare, as the colonists of the Lost World knew it. But that was long ago, and the colonists had forgotten—"

"Wait," somebody said. The word slipped by her, but she felt Morisz's urgency and answered the question before he asked it.

"I don't know when it was." She still looked into al-Nimeury's eyes. "They have a stable written history, but I know nothing of it. I know only the common memory, which shapes time according to the importance of events. The great human exodus began seven hundred years ago and more, and lasted three centuries. Only in the first century and a half were fragments of humanity lost. Count back and you'll know what they thought our capability is, as the colonists' descendants remembered it. And then they got me and found that we'd learned—so much more. How to kill. How to destroy. They can't match you. You could destroy them—"

Leader seemed to explode in her head, in her whole body. The humans babbled at her but words melted into Leader's silent shocking clamor. *It is true it is true you must see it is true!* she cried to him. She felt hands on her shoulders, Jameson's hands. They drew her back to the light. She trembled violently. Leader read her conviction and her purpose and she said to him, *Trust me. Trust me!* He answered mournfully, *I must. You have the way Home.*

She could lift her head. She did, and saw they watched her warily but, except for Jameson, without understanding what had happened. The living presence of Leader was a thing she dared let no one else recognize. Jameson said quietly, "She is very tired. She has been with them and returned with news of . . . a willingness to open discussions."

She twisted under his hands at the lie, but they were suddenly attentive; skeptical, yet open to hope. al-Nimeury's eyes were on her and she said, "You could have them in thirteen days. I can show you how to reach their homeworld in thirteen days. They know where you are but that's all. They haven't got the program to get here. They will need weeks to reach you at least. You fear them for nothing, and all because they fear you."

al-Nimeury looked away from her, uneasy. She felt his uncertainty growing; he had not expected any of this. He said to Jameson, "Is that true? Why didn't you say so?"

Jameson said, evading it, "Listen to her."

Hanna said, as much to Leader as anyone, "They know nothing of wars. They have never had one. They know only the slaughter of dangerous beasts, and you are not beasts. Not unless you choose to be."

"Are you sure? Is this something you've guessed?"

It was Morisz's question, but she watched al-Nimeury, who was unwilling to meet her eyes. She said, "I know."

Morisz said, "What exactly have they got?"

"It doesn't matter."

"Doesn't matter—" Petrov sprang to her feet in vigorous denial. "Doesn't matter!"

"Doesn't matter," Hanna said. She glanced at Petrov and thought: She could be trouble. She is afraid. Earth-island and outside the blackness—

Hanna moved a little, so that she faced al-Nimeury and he could not ignore her.

"I want to go to them," she said. "I want to be appointed your envoy. They don't understand they can't win."

"You want to tell them they can't?" He was doubtful, suspicious.

"It won't matter to them. If you send anybody but me they'll attack anyway, because they won't understand anybody but me. They might do it even if I'm the one who goes, but nobody else has a chance of convincing them—not that war is futile, but that it's unnecessary."

al-Nimeury said to Jameson, "I thought you said—" but Petrov said violently, "Nonsense! She's lying. She came back to do something else for them, she came back to keep us from fighting. Starr, why did you not immediately call for help? She's still under control. Anyone can see it!"

"Do you really think so?" Hanna said. She swayed, sickened and dizzy from the power of Petrov's fear. Jameson put his arm around her quickly. He said to Petrov, "Hanna killed five of them to get away and bring us the way to their home."

"So she says!"

"I did," Hanna said faintly, and used everything she had learned from D'neera and from the People to take Petrov there. She leaned against Jameson and showed Petrov the chaos, the soundless screams and the thick blood and reality ending, and Leader-in-her-thoughts lived his death again, and Petrov recoiled in horror, and Hanna let her go.

Petrov sat down abruptly. Her face was haunted, her eyes inward. She did not try to speak.

The others had glimpsed some of it too. Jameson said close to Hanna's ear, "A demonstration of the usefulness of D'neerans, or at least of Hanna. After that, can you doubt her ability to communicate with the aliens?"

Someone moved restlessly. al-Nimeury said not to Hanna but to Jameson, "I don't care. Even if it's all true I want to send humans. Not her. The aliens are telepaths themselves, we don't need D'neera."

Hanna said flatly, "You can't shut us out any longer. You cripple yourselves with fear of us. *He* knows." She meant Jameson. "You think I will reach into your mind and know its secret places. All your shames, the dark hidden things you won't acknowledge even to yourselves . . . what can you do with these beings, who can do that more surely than I can? You know they took me and tortured me—"

The Questioner came alive for an instant, and her voice caught. The effort of projecting to Petrov had drained her more than she thought. She turned her head and for a moment put her cheek against Jameson's shoulder, fixing herself in present reality, and went on.

"They took fear from my heart and used it. I showed them my own fracture points. Pain and mutilation, humiliation, all it took to make me a blind, screaming animal. I told them all unwilling how to destroy me and end my spirit. And they learned from the colonists too. Whom they slaughtered. Everything I most feared, the greatest terrors humans have, they learned from humans. Will you go to them yourself? But I have learned from them. I have some things no one else has. And you would send someone else, defenseless, to treat with them?"

She knew al-Nimeury acknowledged the logic; but disbelief fought logic.

Morisz muttered, "If we can beat them so easily, why is there a chance they'll fight? You can just tell them what will happen. Won't they give up? What will happen?"

"Genocide," Hanna said.

There was a murmur of disbelief from Struzik.

"They would not give up," Hanna said. "You would have to kill them. You would not kill all of them, but you would destroy them. All their culture. Every fragile thing they have built through the millennia. They are more vulnerable than you are, than we are. They may be a dead end like Girritt—or evolving toward something neither we nor they can guess. Perhaps they will become a group mind, a step maybe—" she glanced up at Jameson—"toward becoming adults. Now they are a fabric, and too great a rent will destroy them. They must be sheltered—"

"Sheltered!" al-Nimeury said, and she felt his outrage. When she thought of The Questioner it was incongruous even to her, but she knew it was true.

She began, "A moral choice—" and the word made them look at her with distaste. Morisz said skeptically, "Don't they know they're weak? You still haven't told us—why do they hate us? Why would they fight?"

"The colony," Hanna said. She let the words drop among them, and quite suddenly felt that she had reached the end of her strength.

She sagged against Jameson, indifferent to their eyes, and said nothing more. After a minute he said gently, "Explain. Explain to them as you did to me."

"I can't," Hanna said, and roused herself enough to turn to him. She wanted it to be over, she wanted him to hold her, she wanted to go to sleep in his arms in peace and safety, and what she wanted was clear to him. He was alarmed, but he held her, and she was happy. She did not, at this moment, care about the conflict she felt in him. Slowly he was coming to his senses. He would come to them in the end. This would do for now.

"Hanna," he said, and pushed the moment aside with an almost physical effort.

I want you to stop doing that, she thought, but not so that he could hear her, and looked up obediently.

"Show them," he said.

"Show them what?"

"What happened when they met the colonists. What they saw in us. You showed me a little. I don't think you knew you were doing it. It wasn't all in words."

She thought back slowly. Trying to concentrate on a single memory from the past hours, days, months, was a matter of slow drunken circling, an absent-minded bird looking for a landing place, distracted by currents that had nothing to do with its goal. She found it at last, and shook her head.

"I can't," she said. "I'm too tired."

"You can."

"It's not the same as with one person. It's harder. I'm not an Adept."

"I think you're something more than an Adept now. Something different. You can do it. Show them," he said, and she resented his certainty.

She bowed her head and said against his heart, "How often have you made me do things I did not want to do?"

"I have never 'made' you do anything," he said, and then

could not hide the thought that if she pulled this off perhaps he would survive after all, and *Endeavor* would go out again.

You only want to use us for your dream, she said, or remembered saying, or he remembered it, and when she looked up he would not meet her eyes for the first time in all their acquaintance. But she stood groggily with her arms around him and knew she was going to do it anyway.

Behind her she heard Murphy speak anxiously. The words meant nothing, but she understood the vector of communication between Murphy and Jameson.

She has reached her limit, let her rest.

There is no time for rest, we must resolve this now.

It is not so urgent.

It is. If we do not immediately present a solid front to our governments and the military, I do not think we will ever do it. And if she is wrong about the timing, it could begin tomorrow, or today. We do not know their capabilities in unknown space.

But if she is right we have the firepower.

To attack. But we do not know what there is to defend against. I do not think she knows, except in the most general terms. And how many lives does that mean?

Yes. I see. I see.

They stood on a broad river plain and looked at the sky. The plain was fertile, washed annually by spring floods that left rich deposits of soil. They were not ill-fed. They had that much to thank the river for.

The thing in the sky had been there a day now, and sometimes seemed to move nearer. It was no longer a dot visible only to the sharpest-eyed of the young, but clearly an oval.

(Murphy moved uneasily. Is this apprehension what they felt, she wondered, or is it Lady Hanna's, knowing what happened? Or my own, guessing what is to come?)

The radio worked well enough, and was all they had. Some of its parts were pirated from the useless Inspace communications equipment that still bore Eden Unlimited's logotype. This third generation joked about the name; the company that had found this world, and dropped their grandparents here with (they discovered too late) second-

hand, shoddy equipment, had passed into their jerry-rigged
culture as Flybynight Inc.

This would not be Flybynight coming back. It had to be
from Earth, or maybe Colony One or maybe another colony, maybe there were hundreds of colonies now. But if the
radio worked, why did it not answer them?

(Hanna sat on the floor, so limp in Jameson's arms he
knew she would topple if he let her go. He knew where he
was, sheltered in his own invaded home, but the river was
there too, and he was highly critical. Stupid to build there.
No wonder they lost their computer. As sensible to build on
a volcano's slope as on a flood plain.)

They swarmed from the stilted wooden houses, calling
back and forth through the thick bright air. My God, it's
coming closer. Oh, Jesus. Tell your mother, tell her to stay
inside, no, come out, oh, Jesus.

Do you read, said the radio, come in Overhill, do you
read. The UFO's descending, we'll keep in touch. Have you
heard from N'Gomba's group, are they sending anybody,
what, wait a minute, it's landing, I never heard of anything
like, they must have changed the design.

(The air was hazy and Struzik blinked into the sunlight,
trying to see. Featureless metal; it must be damned claustrophobic inside. No markings, nothing like that in the Polity,
then or now or ever.)

They gave it plenty of room to land. As soon as it was
down they started running toward it, laughing and crying.
Sometimes they had been sure they were forgotten and
now it was all right. They wouldn't leave, it was a good place
to live, unless some of the youngsters, well kids are like that,
even some of the adults, but it didn't matter, it was all right,
they could get machines, a grant, a doctor, news, they could
make a world, it was all right now.

There were two hundred of them here and when they
were all quite close they waited for the crew to come out,
but nothing happened. Nobody came out for a long time.

(al-Nimeury wiped sweat from his face. Is it really taking
this long, he thought, or is she making it seem that way? The
gray hull shimmered in the sunlight and through it he saw,
very far away, the D'neeran woman. Jameson held her tightly
and his eyes were closed, his face pressed against her hair.
My God, al-Nimeury thought, he's in love with her, how

extraordinary; but something began to open on the hull, and he waited to see what would come out.)

There was a hole of black nothingness in the sunlight and something huge and gray showed in the opening. The first ripple of fear struck it and was flung back redoubled. They thought it threatened them, not knowing they were the threat, and some screamed and ran, and others surged forward. Round and round went the loop accelerating in an instant of thought, a paradigm of cornered fang and claw. The People saw Renders, the first weapon was fired and it was confusion, warfare, death and dying, red blood in the hot hazy morning and happening so fast they had only time to hate and did not even know why they died, D'neera's time was just beginning and they knew nothing of telepathy and each felt the things' terror as his own, the instant response of murder to danger, savage animals spilling from the grayness, savage animals twisting on the grass, and the pleasure of their dying *proved* it—

(STOP, STOP—)

"Stop!" cried Katherine Petrov, weeping and gasping, rocking back and forth.

The vision shivered and was gone. al-Nimeury made an inarticulate noise, and into the frozen silence came other sounds: a sigh from Murphy, Petrov's sobs. Feng stared into space, ignoring Petrov moaning at his side. Morisz started to curse and changed his mind.

Jameson eased Hanna's head into his lap. He thought she was unconscious, but her eyelids fluttered and for a moment she looked at him. Then her eyes closed and she lay still.

He waited for the others to say something. Morisz said at last, "That's—that's what's going to happen every time we make contact?"

Jameson looked down at Hanna and saw that she could not or would not answer.

"Presumably," he said. "That's how they see us, you know. All of them, in a great collectivity. They've been searching for us as a deadly danger ever since that day."

"Then how in hell are we ever going to get anywhere with them?"

Jameson said, "Either Hanna will, or maybe nobody ever will."

Murphy's head was buried in her hands. She said indistinctly, "How is she going to do that?"

Jameson started to stroke Hanna's hair, hesitated, and went on with it. The hell with it, he thought; I've gone too far already.

He said, "She was in intimate contact with one of them for some time. You all understand, I think, that she was under the control of a non-human personality. I have learned tonight that it was not altogether non-human. It was partially created from elements of Hanna's own personality; it was not entirely imposed from outside. She succeeded in integrating it, in making herself a kind of hybrid. She hopes she will be able to forestall the instant-feedback effect."

al-Nimeury said, "What about—how did she get them to agree to negotiation anyway?"

Jameson said, treading a narrow divide between fact and fiction, "She has one important contact."

"I don't see why they won't just kill her on sight."

"They didn't the first time. They didn't kill all of the colonists immediately. They kept some alive long enough to interrogate and experiment with them. They found nothing but the hatred and fear they expected, of course, under the circumstances, and the same has been true for Hanna. If she can control her own reaction, perhaps . . ." He left the thought unfinished.

Murphy said in an odd voice, "Perhaps?"

He said bluntly, "The only risk is hers."

Murphy stared at him, upright and indignant. "You'd send her to them again? After what they did before?"

Jameson shrugged. It cost him more than he would have cared to admit to her.

Petrov was recovering. She said querulously, "We'd better send the whole damned Fleet with her."

"No," Hanna said unexpectedly. "Nobody."

She tried to sit up and Jameson helped her. She held his hand and said without looking at any of them, "I've got to make them restructure reality. Not frighten them. All I need to do is convince a few we're not what they think, really convince them, and it'll spread through the whole population. They must have gone a lot faster than we did. No war, that kind of communication—it took us longer every time we did it."

Struzik said, "Did what?"

"Changed the shape of the universe. Like knowing Earth goes around the sun, like accepting evolution or the size of the Milky Way or meeting F'thal. It changes everything for a whole species."

Murphy said in astonishment, "*That's* what you're going to try to do?"

"Well," said Hanna, "what else is there to do? Except kill them?"

She listened to the voices drifting around her as if they were a kind of music, sense forgotten. The room was very bright now. They were arguing about her nebulous contact, about studying and waiting and the gathering of intelligence, about weaponry human and alien, about what Co-op would say and what Fleet would want, about the course to Home and—with Jameson picking a most delicate course—about Leader's impact on her.

They would go on arguing for a long time (humans talk so, she thought) and then they would let her do it. Jameson still was not sure of them, but he could not feel what she felt: the bare tilt of a balance to one side, the change in al-Nimeury's reality, at least, that would make the difference.

She struggled to her feet and found herself looking into Jameson's face. She said: *I'm going to sleep now.*

"Don't do that," he said, not meaning, don't sleep.

She could argue with his constraints later, if there was a later. She found her way back to his bedroom and opened it to the sunlight which had bred her ancestors and his, and fell into his bed and into sleep.

Chapter 18

Hanna slept so soundly she did not even wake when Melanie Ward came in with her flickering instruments and began the series of feather-touches that would tell her if Hanna was fit to go on or not. Hanna woke at last not because of pain but because of its cessation. The varying ache in her right arm, which had become part of the landscape of her body, was gone. She dreamed that she was well and whole and when she woke and turned her eyes to where the pain had been she thought for a moment it was true; she had never gotten in the way of the knife, the fight had never happened. But Leader-in-her-thoughts whispered to her and she saw in harsh noon light that the wound was only hidden under a neat strip of false human hide. Then she saw Ward, and behind her Jameson silhouetted against the light. They were talking as if Hanna were still asleep.

Jameson was saying, "But there is nothing immediately life-threatening?"

"Not immediately." Ward spoke with the irritation of a physician who already knows her advice will be ignored.

"Well, then . . ."

"I won't be responsible for the consequences. And I won't be responsible for starting the sequence of stimulants."

"You will. Or must I have your commanding officer give you a direct order?"

They converged on Hanna, tall shadows, and she shrank away in irrational alarm. There was the slight pressure of an injection in her uninjured arm. After a moment her head cleared with a rush that threatened to suck her into the sky, she was sitting up and looking wide-eyed at Jameson, and Ward was gone. The immense relief of new energy seemed to touch every cell of her body.

She sighed with pleasure. She had forgotten what it was to feel well.

Jameson said, "The vote was four to one."

She had been admiring the new steadiness of her hands. She looked up, distracted.

"Who didn't—?"

"Petrov. Who still can see that you are stopped, if you don't leave at once."

"At once—" She stood up obediently. Artificial strength steadied her legs, and she nodded in satisfaction. She had never liked using stimulants, even when the need was urgent. Why? They were a fine thing.

She took a step, her head swimming, and he stopped her.

"Not this instant," he said. "*Heartworld II*'s not ready. And there are things you should hear."

"All right." The first burst of well-being was settling down, curling into the corners of her body. Her vision was sharper than usual. She saw that Jameson looked tired and careworn, and said, "You ought to've had Melanie give you some of that stuff."

"I'll be taking enough of it, I assure you. So will you. Ward advised against a direct booster implant, and you will have to be very careful about giving yourself injections at frequent intervals. You'll have no time to sleep. How do you feel? Can you attend to what I say?"

Leader-in-her-thoughts was singing some melody wrested from Hanna's memory. She made him shut up.

"I'm listening," she said.

Jameson was detached as she had ever seen him, and she stood with tilted head, entirely alert, and listened to a dry sequence of orders. The People's course program could not be used until it was translated into human mathematics. Hanna would work with Fleet to do that while she still traveled through human space. When she was finished the Fleet escort would leave her, but she would not be able to rest. She would program a powered projectile to return to human space. Into it she would dictate every scrap of information she had gotten from Leader-in-her-thoughts about the People's military capability, technology, biosphere, biology,

history and cultural patterns. She would describe in detail
their remarkable development of telepathy, especially their
use of it to control machines, which had only a coincidental
resemblance to human direct-control techniques, D'neeran
or otherwise. She would continue reporting until the last
possible moment, and send the projectile back just before
she contacted the People.

She thought there were other things she had better be
doing as contact approached, but she did not say so.

When Jameson was done giving orders he waited for
her to comment on them. But she had lost interest in orders several minutes before. She had heard none of the
latter instructions; she was caught up in the open strain in
his voice, and sensed a new fragility in the surface he presented.

She would do him no favor by breaking it. But she could
not help saying, "Are you going to be all right?"

His face changed in the instant before he turned away
from her. It must have been a very long time since anyone
had asked him such a question. She moved toward him too
quickly and was light-headed again. The space around her
was luminous and his shoulder when she touched it was the
form and substance of warmth.

She whispered, "S-starr?"

He made the very slightest of movements, a fractional
lessening of tension. He said, "You haven't got it right.
You're not supposed to hiss." His head was bowed and she
could not see his face, but there was something new in his
voice.

She rubbed his arm gently, at a loss for words, and moved
a little dizzily to face him. She leaned against him without
looking up, and he made a sound of exasperation or defeat
or desire and abruptly pulled her to him without restraint.
They kissed with concentrated, mutual greed. Hanna had
not even thought of lovemaking in so long that the violence
of her physical reaction took her by surprise. But she did
not think of it then; she did not think at all.

He raised his head after—it seemed—a very short time.
She murmured a protest and leaned on him in earnest now
because her knees were weak.

He said reluctantly, "They're waiting."

"In a minute . . ."

She meant she could not face anyone else without time to pull herself together. She was sure she did not say all that, but he said, "Me too," and moved away a little. Inside her, newly roused, Leader mourned again for Sunrise. *Shut up shut up shut up,* she said, but it was too late. Jameson kept slipping with her over a border into a lovely unknown land, but she could not get him to stay there.

She said, "Ah, you have such discipline."

"Not enough." He folded his arms—possibly to prevent himself from reaching out to her again—and looked at her with bright eyes. The odd, irregular face was younger and no longer tired. The consciousness that half a dozen people expected them to appear annoyed her.

She said anxiously, "If I come back will you remember this?"

"I will."

"Promise me."

"I promise," he said without hesitation.

"Oh, good. Oh, I'm glad. What ever happened to that girl in Central Records?"

He said in some alarm, "How did you know about her?"

"I snooped. While I was here before. Where is she?"

He shrugged. "Back in Central Records, I suppose."

"And always will be?"

He looked at her carefully and said, "Unless she learns to distinguish between a setback and the end of a man's career, yes."

"Why," said Hanna, "do you have such a wall around yourself? What are you hiding from?"

They faced each other in the center of the room, and she saw the habitual shutter begin to drop over his face. He shook his head. "No questions, Hanna. Not now."

"I might not have another chance. Even if I come back. If you're gone."

He said heavily, "Does it really matter now?"

She sighed and said, "No. I suppose it doesn't. And if we knew each other better we might not get along at all."

"I wonder. I wonder about that sometimes."

He took her arm again before she could answer, and this time, knowing she would get no more from him now, she went out with him obediently.

*   *   *

Today air traffic froze by order of high authority. The river became a ribbon. The city shrank to invisibility and disappeared as Hanna rose into cloud and then the clouds were under her too, dazzling.

Entering black space meant re-entering a personal reality from which she had briefly escaped, and it was more real than the one that had Jameson in it. If it were not for the Fleet vessel that trailed her, she would have thought her little time on Earth a dream. As a sleeper, waking, remembers sharp singular images shorn of context, Hanna remembered details: the color of al-Nimeury's eyes, the texture of Jameson's hair, the curve of Murphy's back as she knelt touching Hanna's arm. And as if she were waking from a dream, Hanna (as she spoke with Fleet and *Heartworld II,* slaved ship's systems to *Willowmeade*'s, prepared to analyze the precious course program) felt sorrow not sensibly connected to events, as sorrow ought to be, but the shadow of the sorrow of a dream, truncated and distant from consciousness.

They might have let her speak to Iledra, but she had not asked. She might have spoken to Jameson frankly of love, but she had not.

She was going back into the night, which was real, and on to a deeper night. Only this commanded her attention.

Heartworld II was half real, half not. Faces looked at her from every wall, voices echoed in chambers whose silence only she had broken for what seemed all her life.

She was busy at every moment. Leader would not be a translator. He did not have to be. She knew the People's notation as if she had learned it in infancy. She was no mathematician, but she did not have to be. The Fleet vessel threw mathematicians at her, summoned hastily to this flight not in body but through the skein of relays that filtered into every part of human space.

Hanna did not know any of them. Their faces ran together.

She did not sleep, ever. She did not need Leader, but he talked to her anyway. He meditated in a corner of her mind, content:

I will not die but live. Strangely. In thought and bone of generations past and those to come. Not memory, but real. No longer bearing precious burdens in my own true body;

*no life that you understand; not to act, but to advise. To love
those past and those to come. And pass into history more
than Self. Sacrifice less great than you think and payment
and exchange for final value. Logical progression, natural
act, next and last phase of life, and that for which I was most
joyfully destined all my time.*

Only those who die without this truly die.

Now Alta was nearer than Earth, but neither was near.
The alien program cracked and broke. The mathematicians
leapt upon the prize, the programmers and engineers went
without sleep. The commander of the *Willowmeade,* a courteous man, thanked Hanna. She stared at his face, distracted, thinking him Erik.

It was not Erik. He talked like Erik. But, "We have met
before," she said.

"Briefly," he said, smiling. "Rescue mission to the *Clara
Mendoza.* I always wondered, did you scrap her?"

"We buried her," Hanna said. "With her crew."

"Funny thing to do," he said.

Yes, Leader agreed. Then he thought of the First Watchsetter and was not sure.

The commander—Tirel, she remembered suddenly—
said, "We won't be with you much longer. I understand
you've got plenty of power and fresh stores. Anything you
need before we withdraw?"

She shook her head. She needed nothing more. She had
had a great deal. She had been—

*Lucky. Lucky to have had D'neera. The Mason Range
Falls crash a kilometer down jutting rock and rainbows leap
in sunlight mellow as Earth's, and clean. At B'ha the sea
rocks gently only with the sweet star's motion. There is no
moon. On no human world do stars shine more clearly. On
no human world is freedom so friendly. I was shaped by no
mold. Made myself. And chose my own loyalties.*

Lucky. I have been so lucky, so fortunate, so happy!

Tears must have glittered in her eyes, because Tirel said,
"What's wrong?"

"I was just remembering . . ."

Willowmeade's next Jump would take it back into human space. Hanna's would start her on the path the People
had charted.

Tirel knew the purpose of her mission, but neither he

nor anyone except Leader knew what she expected at the
end. He looked at her curiously and said, "Sure there's
nothing you need?"

"No, thank you," Hanna said.

"Good luck," he said.

A little later, when *Willowmeade* was a light-year gone,
Hanna wept. All the human faces had vanished, all the human voices. But the reason she mourned had to do with his
last words to her; they seemed the sum and essence of what
being human was, and her tears were not for herself.

Time ran on, shrinking. She had no time to watch it run.
She had too much to do. Why? Why tatter her voice with
talking, reciting facts, surmise, portraits of the People? Why
work so for Fleet with its guns, or for Jameson who sent her
again into night?

It is for the future, Leader answered, comforting her.

She was not comforted.

She went on with it, though. The stimulants drummed in
her and distanced her from all save the tasks before her.
The hard part was remembering human speech; and sorting
out the knowledge Leader had given her in the days when
she came scarcely human toward Earth. Singular concepts
triggered hallucinatory visions that touched all her senses
and forced her to think with precision of how she could
describe them. Strange flowers filled the decks of *Heartworld II,* predatory fleshy living things whose massed
shapes pleased the People. When she bathed, the water
seemed a running stream, and the walls that surrounded her
shifted to angles their designers had never intended.
Leader, caught in the interstices of her self so that though
he was a functioning unwelcome intruder it seemed he
ought to have been there always, said of every moment: it
should be *thus.*

It seemed to her she was more alien than human.

The theories of "Sentience" were nonsense. This was
what she had meant, but she had not known it before. "Sentience" was a failure because neither she nor anyone else
had fully understood what she was talking about.

Leader thought quietly in corners:

*I too was most fortunate. Saw Sunrise, Hearthkeeper's child,
one rainy dawn in early youth and I too was a child, younger
even than most at bonding and all of Us in your thinking chil-*

dren. The bond cannot be otherwise. There is no place for jealousy for doubt for dolor unknown to Us but known to me since known to you. There was no ceremony, nor need for one. Came I to her Nearhome. We grew and flowered together until time came. Sealed the bond in a space of time apart. Those who passed the Bower knew and took joy and strength from creation of love which was shaped from our bodies and selves. The future born anew with each bond.

She did not wish my leaving yet they called me: Explorers, Watchsetters: from the first waking, ever: she knew. Yet she is my rest and true Home and ever was. And ever is.

Hanna listened to Leader within her, and to the voices within him. They passed a halfway point in space, passed it again in time. Time was material. And shrinking.

She turned with more than human patience to the task of disentangling the People's written language, a tricky blend of mathematics and pictographs with all its own structural complexities. She analyzed flawlessly, drug-driven, the relationship of its precise, concrete symbolic structure to the ambiguity of the People's living mind/s. Behind her acute attention drifted shadows of lost futures, dreamlike. Might have built a city, guided Koroth, loved, learned to laugh . . .

Might have grown wise . . .

Living is, said Leader, *and will be. Different. Yet real.*

"For you. Not for me."

How do you know?

"I do not know. I hope. I do not want your future. I want only mine, and will not have it. There will be naught but the dispersion. And the ruined self and I think the body's death. And then nothing."

Not nothing. He wanted to ease her grief. *Even among Us it is said one can live for the Good. And die for it.*

"That is no comfort. I choose this, but I do not know why. I do not want it. But I choose it."

You will be remembered. The work of your hands and thought and self will live. You will live. Not as We do; as humans do.

"That is no comfort!"

When the last Jump was near, it was Leader who remembered to send back the return projectile, and to program it with messages for Iledra and Cosma and her parents and cousins.

She left no farewell for Jameson.

At the very last she programmed *Heartworld II* to begin broadcasting a plea for tolerance that would, she hoped, induce the People to consider some course besides blasting her to atoms at once.

She knew (from Leader-in-her-thoughts) that security around Home was as tight as anything humans had ever produced in their most paranoid moments, and he could make a fair guess at their reaction to what they had found on the First Watchsetter.

They will not make for your Home, I think; for the others; the fleet flies toward them.

"Not much of a fleet, is it?"

Not much. Not like yours, for which we/they wait in readiness; they will think you the flagship. And fire.

"Will what I write now stop them?"

???

"Well?"

Hope!

The People's defenses, like humanity's long ready but unused, were not automatic. They had to be ordered into action. But even if they did not fire on her single small vessel immediately, what would they do when they sensed *her?* The crew of the *First Watchsetter,* she knew now, had brought every conceivable discipline and defense to stalking the *Endeavor* and examining the precious prisoner. They had shut themselves away from her. But *she* could not use the barrier, the wall, the absence of a connecting medium she had found when (who? Bladetree, Leader answered) came to meet her. With an effort that drained them the crew had, while they questioned her, operated in the Hunter's mode, subsuming the killing reflex into the purposefulness of stalking, though their prey was information. But that was an artificial state, an unnatural event, which drained and dismayed even the remarkable individuals who created it. What would happen when Hanna touched the edge of a whole population's awareness? It depended on her, and on Leader, of course. She could see no recourse except to distance herself from her own fear; with Leader's help—if he could help. She did not know if she could do it or how she would do it. Therefore she prepared *Heartworld II* to plead for her, to get her time, and at the final Jump was glad of it, because the first thing she saw was a Render.

It seemed painted, two-dimensional, though the texture of its shaggy brown fur was reproduced in detail. Its eyes were filled with red light. It floated in semi-darkness, bright against the shadows. She saw it clearly from the corner of one eye, but when she turned to look at it directly it was gone and the shadows fell again.

Hanna thought automatically: That's silly. What would a painted Render be doing here?

She was much closer to Home than she had expected to come with the last Jump, and the curve of it nearly filled the pilot's port with the fertile marbling of a terrestrial world.

Heartworld II's song went on, the binary version of Hanna's version of the People's binary version of their version of symbolic communication. It said: (This individual) is harmless flesh and blood, unclawed, not predator, not prey, not harmless, a quantity N. (This individual) stands outside reality strange as the nospace of Inspace, stands outside logic strange as We and I, stands—

It is a Lifetender with blood on its breath, someone remarked skeptically, and a Render sat in the empty and redundant co-pilot's seat, and the air crackled around it, and Hanna leapt to her feet and was alone again.

Heartworld II went on talking:

—with you in the unnamed haze, this time they see without fear, We have—they have no need to kill, inertia is reversed and—

It was a hand's width from her face, fur blurring into grayish scales, fangs glittering at her throat. She started to scream and strangled the sound and did not move. It disappeared. She shook with reaction and her legs were weak and the hammering of her heart frightened her.

—one being in this unit, harmless flesh and blood, unarmed, unclawed, requesting permission to land—

Does it lie? said a Render on the edge of sight, and another said: *Beasts lie.*

Then they said: *What is lie?*

Hanna stumbled back to her seat. Eyes closed, hands

over her ears, she waited for the Renders to go away. They did not.

> *The value of*
> *what We lost when*
> *and one being*
> *but blow it away*
> *and lose the*
> *Let it land*

"I have," said *Heartworld II,* "a landing beacon."

Hanna opened her eyes and peered through more Renders. "Land," she muttered.

Heartworld II whistled quietly. "Awaiting orders," it said.

"Go on down," she said more clearly. "Land."

The fall was slow, the Renders whispered at her back and somewhere, everywhere, the equivalent of fingers rested on the equivalent of triggers. She had no illusion about what would happen if she tried to deviate from the course they set her, or why she was still alive. They wanted *Heartworld II,* the prize *XS-12* should have been to them if they had not clumsily destroyed most of its value to them. They wanted the data this ship carried. They must not be allowed to get it. Surely someone, Jameson, Petrov, somebody had thought of this?

She asked *Heartworld II* about it and got no answer. There were more devious ways to ask and she did so and found her suspicions were correct. While she slept *Heartworld II* had been programmed not to self-erase but to self-destruct if alien hands touched it.

So I get off and try to make peace and they come here and it blows them up, she thought. Me too, if I'm still aboard.

The Renders went on talking among themselves, paying no attention to her. Imaginary Renders. She wiped sweat off her face and listened intently to their talk of defense.

But Renders were dust and did not speak.

She was listening to the People. The Renders were her own creation, an objective referent for her fear, which she dared not direct toward the People themselves. Perhaps Leader-in-her-thoughts, who must share her fear but could not fear his own kind, helped her create them, had helped her find this brief precarious solution. They winked in and out as her eyes moved, but their numbers seemed to be growing.

She had stopped watching the monitors. She looked out the port and saw a civilized world. There was less green than she had expected, more brown and blue, and now she was close enough to see clusters of light past the terminator.

The Renders fell silent. A claw brushed her cheek and with an effort she remained still, biting at her fingers. She reminded herself they were an illusion, one possibility of many and that the most destructive. There were alternatives. There had to be alternatives. She was here to create them.

She said to *Heartworld II,* "I want to meet with one individual. Tell the Defenders—"

She stopped short. Was that the right word? *Yes,* whispered a Render, and the mutter began again. The southern hemisphere, the Nearhome of the Defenders, that was where she was going. Thousands of them there.

She started again, "One individual. The, the Hearth-keeper of the Nearhome of, of—" She stumbled and finished the thought: "Of the Leader of the First Watchsetter."

Heartworld II chuckled doubtfully and began the translation.

She knew then that Leader had been thinking of Sunrise all along; and he came suddenly to life and cried out with longing.

Heartworld II settled slowly to a city. It was white in the midday light, though other colors showed here and there. Its rooftops were landscaped and decorated and made into space for living or beauty to be seen from above, a convention inconsistently followed on human worlds but perhaps universal here. It was not large, but she had seen smaller towns clustered round it during her controlled fall.

Thousands of them here, she thought, and felt the Renders crowding round her, and licked her dry lips again and again. She was afraid, and her fear created the beasts. The cabin was hot, surely with their body heat. Yet it was the animal in the People she must fear, and the animal in herself, and the Renders could not harm her though they kept the truth before her eyes.

"They will bring you the individual you request," said *Heartworld II.*

So near, whispered Leader-in-her-thoughts, and Hanna shivered. Sunrise was indeed near. Among the Nearhomes scattered round Defense were two or three occupied mostly by Watchsetters, and one of them was Leader's.

Heartworld II drifted gently downward, under the rounded towers of the tallest buildings. In them, unlike the People's spacecraft, there were windows, transparent openings in immaculate walls; but she could not see anything through them. The Renders surrounded her, muttering. Beyond them on the edge of perception she seemed to hear a grim vibration of floodwater or landslide, a threat inescapable as an incoming tide complex and unpredictable under dancing moons. The Renders held it back. Behind their red eyes were hundreds, thousands, millions of eyes watching her. She hid behind draperies of coarse fur and hoped the Renders would not go away.

Heartworld II touched down at last. Automatically she checked monitors, rounding out the view the port gave her. This was clearly a landing field, though no other vessels showed around her. Its floor was brilliant white, and she saw that only *Heartworld II*'s compensation for light kept it from hurting her eyes. The nearest structure was a kilometer away; the work of the Defenders was carried on deep underground. Nothing moved, except once when a blood-red flash drew her eyes to something like a bird that vanished almost at once.

Heartworld II said, "You are to leave this vessel and walk to the building you see before you."

"All right," Hanna said. She was busy for a few minutes, modifying *Heartworld II*'s destruct program slightly. She said, "What is *Heartworld I,* anyway?"

"Heartworld I," said its sister, "is reserved for the president of the General Council."

"And the commissioner from Heartworld gets Two?"

"That is correct."

"Well, good-bye," she said.

"Good-bye," it answered without surprise.

She went out, accompanied by a rapidly multiplying retinue of Renders. Those nearest her had solidified, and jostled her now. Their odor was delicate and sweet—no. That was the warm lambent air. She scarcely saw her goal through the crowd, though the Renders thinned in substance at a distance so that even in their infinite numbers those on the horizon were only shapes of air, hollow spots in the atmosphere, which she could barely see by squinting because she had forgotten to protect her eyes and the light was indeed too bright. But all her memories of Home and the First Watchsetter were of spaces filled with dimness, and she did not understand this light.

Her footsteps made dull sounds on the shining ground, but the Renders made no sound at all. The structure ahead of her grew slowly. It was not large. She knew it was made for observation and maintenance, that was all. It was expendable.

She had miscalculated how long it would take her to reach the building, and before she got there *Heartworld II* blew itself up with a roar and a hot blast of wind that knocked her flat. Debris rained on her unshielded back and the arms clasped over her head. Before the roar was finished she looked up and saw that the Renders had gone, and one of the People said to her, invisible: *Why did you do that?*

His voice was clear over the roar that was also the relentless waiting flood. She answered: *I did it to protect both of us.*

He seized and examined the thought and she cried out aloud, remembering The Questioner; though to Bladetree she had said little so clearly, having been consciously obscure or blurred by madness.

The presence vanished, but it was not replaced by silence. The sound of the explosion must have ended, but still she heard it, a thunder of countless voices. The ground seemed to tremble and she dug her hands into it: earth now, not the flat whiteness. Bluish stalks came loose in her fingers, studded with tiny blue pinpoints of flowers. She cowered before an impending avalanche, but nothing happened, it was only their immanence she felt, the giant awareness of her presence.

She turned her head, licking dust from her lips. She had not given any thought ahead of time to how she would handle the minutes just past, because she had had no idea where to begin. The right response, by luck perhaps, had come from some deep unconscious well, and she had managed to distance herself from the People, transforming them into dangers she could understand. But the innumerable Renders, the tide, the landslide, the avalanche, all were ultimately irresistible and this was not good enough. She would have to succeed quickly in what she had come here for, or she would go under.

She remembered a moment from the struggle with Leader-in-her-thoughts and forced her attention to physical reality. The earth was warm, something had burnt through her clothing and there was patch of fire on one leg, there was dirt under her fingernails and the tiny blue flowers gave the air its odor. The People's sun shone on her indifferently.

She carefully relaxed all her muscles and lifted her head—and saw Sunrise standing over her.

Chapter 19

Leader-in-her-thoughts cried *Lovely how lovely my love how long absent o stay with me!* and . . .

Hanna choked, her face in the dirt again because she wished to reach for Sunrise and draw back all at once and was helpless and . . .

In the stunning surge of longing and desire Sunrise took her shoulders and turned her without effort. The pressure of the thousand million voices was gone. Sunrise regarded her with eyes hidden behind the membrane that kept out the sun and said very intimately: *Thou art not truly my strength.*

Sunrise's headfeathers were intricately groomed and her face was decorated with stylized flowers. A flame-shape, symbol of her office, hung from a chain round her neck.

Hanna shook her head numbly, over and over. She spoke, and so did Leader.

I live. I live and love thee and—

I killed him. I killed him as he cried out for thee and for the little one who swims so swiftly—

I live—

He is dead, I his murderer—

Sunrise's face was a nightmare mask, vaguely reptilian, so cruel as to acknowledge no conscience Hanna could recognize; but it wore the hearthkeeper's dignity.

The great rending paws moved over her with a sadist's anticipation. And wavered and were tender hands with elegantly pointed nails, fingertips softly ridged, palms soothing and cool.

Thou art injured, my love?

Thine enemy. Thine enemy!

I cannot see my enemy. . . .

And through Sunrise's eyes Hanna saw herself, not alien animal altogether, but shadowed by Leader's form, visible to eyes not her own. Her own hand, its knuckles scaled, reached for Sunrise.

The crystalline air reflected a thousand faces, which trembled and shattered with a long tinkling sigh. Her hand fell short, her arm was not long enough, her face was wet and The Questioner lifted her to her feet and she nearly fell and Sunrise held her up. She clung to the great arms and tried to hide from the shards of voices that pierced her eyes whispering

New, something new, this is new, o news . . .

Something new, murmured the earth, and an arched dome of muted blue closed them in and fell to indigo and blackness, and when light came again she was walking.

She did not know why they were walking. She wished they were not, for she was tired. From the air she had seen elegant lines of roads for surface transport, arranged it seemed not for speed or convenience but for the patterns they made. But they walked, Sunrise shortening her stride awkwardly to Hanna's. Columns rose by the roadside at intervals, higher than Hanna's head, black, and heavily carved. It was high summer, and fruit hung swollen from the trees. *Drop,* whispered the trees. *Fall away, I shall cast you to the wind and increase.* Hanna dissolved into the landscape, bit into a red-gold globe and licked the juices from her hand. Very far away a voice screamed that this was dangerous. Never never *never* eat unknown vegetation or breathe unknown air or touch unknown herbs, lesson number one in the age of space. But this was not unknown. It tasted purple.

Here is something new, said Sunrise among stalks of grain-to-be, who wore their spent flowers proudly. Their roots drew on earthblood and sang. A swelling grainbud trembled at her brown fingertip and shrank toward Sunrise in fear. Under their feet a million invisible lives took up its cry and something, nothing, snake or scarab, centipede or dream, skimmed the uneasy earth and was silenced.

The grasses froze, the frame cracked and Hanna stepped outside, saw it whole and enclosed, the blue dome the sentient grain Sunrise all one. Fragile in the surface of her

throat's tender skin was a recorder, tiny, a dot just big
enough to see, in case they found her body someday. She
started to speak to it and was inside again and time flowed,
unstopped.

Tell me of thy death.
I died unchoosing—
No, my love!
none to comfort me last-kindness absent—
of all deaths the worst—
they died at my side and I saw myself die. . . .
This alien—
Hanna leapt at the touch like a startled bird.
did not know. They all die alone and forever.
Animals, said Sunrise, and Hanna shuddered at the
hands on her throat, the great thumbs gouged its hollow
and she choked.
No. I live in it, and fade . . .
They are soulless—
Only new.
Here is something new, said the sky, but Hanna did not
hear it, absorbed in a streamlet's speaking waters. She lay
on her stomach and her head fell gently toward the water,
nodding, looking for the faces. A silver streak whisked by
her eyes, warning: *I am not good to eat, no no not I not for
you,* and her belly hurt. Her head drooped lower. Pink and
turquoise showed in shadows under stones. Her hand crept
into the water and the colors vanished with a muted scream.
Under the rocks—
No. Thou art careless as Swift.
Sunrise tugged at her hand. Something under the rock
would strike, whether she would be good to eat or not.

Here was no one, except the two of them, but the air was
full of voices. Faces showed in the clouds. Hanna sat in dust
and listened to the flowers, which dreamt of dying at summer's end. Her blood stirred with their satisfaction. The
communion of Leader and Sunrise went on without her.
Vessel, seedpod, something new, a chariot for Leader and
nothing more, she dreamed with the flowers of insignifi-
cance and thought of winter's stillness and waiting seeds.
Her ring cast blue dazzles into her eyes. She pulled it off,
lifted it, licked it, dropped it, forgot it. The tiny characters
engraved inside said, *The first duty of the D'neeran citizen is*

to the integrity of the self, stopped speaking, flickered, and
went out.

Kill it, they said. *Now, instantly.*

The rest of them were Sunrise. Who said: *It is my love.
Was and was not; is and is not. But is. He died but did not and
dying yet not dead comes to Us for easeful proper death. He
also she is of Us/not of Us. We cannot deny the kindness she
refused him.*

They said (though only of Leader) *That is true.*

Alone as Hanna was, helpless as she was, still they feared
her. She lived only because of Sunrise; because of Leader-
in-her-thoughts, whom Sunrise would not harm; because
the communion of bondmates was a whole within the
whole, and the greater whole stretched to accommodate it.

Hanna or her avatar stood at the gates of her Nearhome.
The gates rose into a sky grown pale in the late afternoon,
traced with magical symbols in lapis and silver. The People
had outgrown magic, and the designs were merely traditional, but in this world of softened edges the meaning of
spear and dagger had not changed.

It was harder and harder to be Hanna. They were surging
seawaves; she a soft bubble of foam.

The gates will not hold against death from the skies, someone said, and the human fleet rained death. Death also fell on
Willow, on D'neera, on Earth, their peoples vanished. Cold
and shining, past present and future, the handful of gray-brown
boxes worked its way through the void, slow but unerring.

The voyage was happening now; in space and in the
mind/s of the People. Hanna struggled with the vision, overwhelmed. Spearpoints danced with symbols of another
world, a glowing sun, great cats yawning and thinking
bloody thoughts of hunger and changing to Renders, and a
murmur of astonishment surrounded her. She saw no one
except Sunrise.

The gates were open, but seemed closed. They would not
let her in, tiger, Render, alien form.

Held they, said a Hunter, *against Renders past.*

Yes, Hanna said, *but We did not.*

There was a great stillness of incomprehension. *No,* said
Leader, but less strongly than he had argued by a fireside
otherwhere.

Behold, Hanna said to the ghostly gates, and fell into
memory; searched the persons she had been; watched (adamant now, alien and unmoved) a Render die. Pain destroyed
it and the People ate its death, absorbing it

like air
like food
like flesh
thus must it be, they said strongly, but:

The Celebrant wore only a loincloth, which shimmered
golden in the fading sun. Behind him in an age-long-past
boiled a sea of dark blue cloud, and the wind blew hard. He
said: *Felt Renders' power and channeled it to memory unending. Each time at unity was I new and all of Us and stronger. That was my being and purpose and that I fulfilled.
Strong grew my Nearhome and fearless*

She sat on stone and its heat scorched the burned place
on her thigh. Quartz sparkled in the spaces between stone.
She summoned an early Explorer, one of the first of the age
of space. He wore a uniform something like Leader's. Metal
gleamed around him and he mastered it. *Saw We in my time
the field of all-life and We its fulfillment and shaper. Saw We
were not separate but part of Our world and it part of Us and
knew Ourselves separate from beasts yet not. But then there
were no Renders. We did not think of that. Naught vanishes,
but is changed. But We did not think of Renders.*

Leader, wavering, drew on memory and Hanna. Renders
died and died again. The years were the whirl of a kaleidoscope. In centuries of Rites the Renders died, and their passionate savagery passed again and again into the People.

"Thus is it," Hanna lectured them, "in all and each part
of Our lives."

She was, oddly, speaking. The wind took her words and
measured them and turned them about for meaning, and
absorbed them.

"Look," Hanna said, urging.

Through her eyes looked Sunrise and Leader and a vast
omnipresence. They saw:

The lapis which was stone and art all at once, and
thought, and the shaping of hands, and before that the eons
of creation, and all the years to come. So the artist's hands
and his brain shaped the stone, and the stone and its color
and texture shaped also his brain and the brains of all who

saw it, and those in turn shaped others, and each was changed and returned refreshed and new to create what was real in the viewing and be created by it. Thus it was with sky and water, earth and stars, and always with each other, through the ages. And with Renders. For each that died, each principal in the Rite, dissolved indeed; but not into nothingness.

"Not here," Hanna said. "Not here, at least."

It seemed they listened, silent, holding breath.

"You made them part of you," Hanna said. "That was the purpose of the Rite. I know. He told me so. But did you not see that you were thereby changed?"

No, said the thickening air.

But Sunrise said: *It is We who speak. Taste truth.*

No, said the wind.

Truth was kernel and seed, though. It was hard. It would not go away. They could not make it not be. It was, and grew.

She tried to tell the recorder: Yes I was right I hear feel smell *see* truth acknowledged, one and one and ten and exponentially a shift a change I was right!

But her tongue was too thick.

(In deepest space and the wells of time a particle of dust pulls gently on another and it comes. To them, drawn, another. And another. Ruled by final forces galaxies form—)

You are right, whispered Leader-in-her-thoughts. Hanna did not hear him. She was in this moment at home, and the season was turning. The falseoaks at their peak shone even in the night, the shining dust fell on her upturned face from the shining sky.

Sunrise took her arm softly, softly, as if touching a lover grown frail and strange. Carefully Hanna stepped to the gates.

She thought the gates said that she was dangerous. She could not be dangerous. She lifted a hand to her head and felt feathery, delicate scales. The sunlight was warm as water, and she swam in it. Beyond the gate a maze of passages began, and hidden among them was Swift.

Leader said: *This creature is I, and not dangerous. I am the Leader of the First Watchsetter, and I tell you so.*

There was an authority in Leader-in-her-thoughts that Hanna had not heard before. He drew strength from Sunrise, from the People, from the persons of his Nearhome, and was completed by them, unmistakably himself. His assurance checked their doubt. An infinity of circles swept away and faded out of Hanna's perception, conflict resolving in harmony. And dizzily she saw that this would not have been possible if she had not in the first place accepted Leader's right to exist; because then he would not have accepted it, nor would those who watched him now—the knowledge was plucked from her thoughts and reverberated and faded outward through the dimming circles.

The wind said: *Enter.*

It was dark. Time played tricks. She had walked for hours through the People's debate, dreaming and bemused. She had been part of it, irresistibly, and now was not. The indefinable roar that had filled her was gone. She was apart in a circle of light, and there was a great silence.

She shook her head, hard, suddenly wakened to herself. She felt something in her hands and looked down to see that she held a stone knife. Its slender hilt was delicate as her hands, gold-chased, gem-encrusted. The jewels were bluish-green. They matched a leaf that bent low, shyly tapped her arm, and whispered welcome.

She jumped at the touch, and saw that Sunrise sat beside her on a stone bench. Copper-colored metal lay polished at her feet and stretched into the nearer darkness. Beyond that gray shapes of growing things rose, against a wall, and the wall against a cloud-torn night sky. She was inside—just inside—the Nearhome of the Defenders.

"Why?" She was hoarse. She cleared her throat and said to Sunrise, "Why can't I hear them anymore?"

We are apart, you and I . . . I wished to know with whom I walked. I think I cannot know. You are he, yet not. Nor are you altogether other. New, I said. New indeed . . .

The surface of the bench somehow had been softened, though it looked and felt like stone. It was finely carved, and all its design (she knew, though human eyes alone would find no sense there) was the story of a far-famed Hunt. There were rituals for the completion of such works. There were rituals for everything. Ritual imbued all of life, a complex outer structure for the incomprehensibly complex inner structure of the People.

It pleased Hanna that she had thought of that. It meant she was still human, and still Hanna.

They had no ritual for anything like her. Except one, which she had endured.

She said kindly to Sunrise, taking up the debate anew, "You knew not how Renders changed you. How could you? Knowledge is the opening of doors in what is known, through which one walks to new dimensions. And you are enclosed."

Sunrise said, seeming very human: *We liked it that way. Yet time brings new truths; or reversal of the old. It has been long since there was a new truth. And did We then perceive it truly?*

Hanna rested comfortably in the silence, almost at home. She said, "What are they thinking of? Will they call back the ships?"

I do not know. If the threat is not real? But the threat is real.

"Only if it is made real. Willed real. Don't you see? You do see!" She meant all of them. "I know you do!"

Perceive the past, Sunrise said, and Hanna knew that the doubt she felt in Sunrise was an echo and reflection of a debate that still went on. And she perceived indeed the past and the weight of it, obstacle and illumination at once.

You ask a new thing, Sunrise said.

"It is new for the others as well," Hanna said, thinking of her last hours with humans, who had not understood that the balance of weapons would not sway the People, who had leapt at an idea of negotiation when nothing that could be done with the People resembled human notions of compromise even slightly.

She had not been honest with them, not even with Jameson, from whom she had learned the art of withholding full truth. They would not understand (she and Leader agreed) the strange new thing to be done. But the People understood it, and therefore the debate continued.

It is pity, Sunrise said, *that you-other must die too.*

Hanna thought of what was left of her future, and shivered.

"I must complete his death," she said.

No. The fullness of his life.

Nonetheless there was grief in Sunrise, deep and poignant. He would not come to her again in the union of their bodies, or dart through the waters in play with Swift. She would not look on his face again. She would have no other bondmate, and soon her own life must fail.

Why? —a human question. A scientist's question. Sunrise was a fertile female; why must she waste and die when her love's end came?

Hanna saw the answer suddenly, unexpectedly. In the single organism that was the People, there was no room for internal competition for mates. The bond was permanent, imprinted, and exclusive. When it ended the reproductive function did too. There could be no instability in family structure, no intra-group source of stress. In murdering Leader, Hanna had condemned Sunrise as well.

She said in anguish, "I am sorry. So sorry, so sorry!"

Sunrise said nothing. Instead she took the dagger from Hanna, and drew a fingertip across the blade. The ages had dulled it. A thousand Celebrants touched it with her. It was a relic of times past, and Hanna did not know why a species on the edge of extinction would stop to contemplate truth, knowing they shaped it. She did not know how Sunrise kept her waked from the People's dream, nor why they were to her a dream, so that the passing hours were a series of fragments with blankness in between.

"I do not understand," said Hanna, and halted. She lifted a hand to her throat. The tiny recorder Ward had put in place still was there. She would go on speaking, while she could speak and think. Someone would hear this someday by the river. If not Jameson, someone else. It would not tell him much.

Sometimes you can't think very much about what you have to do. All you can do is to do it.

"Why, yes," Hanna said, wondering. "How did you know?"

So my love said to me of his travels.

Sunrise smiled. It was little enough like a human smile, but Leader had seen it before, and Hanna's human body warmed with delight.

Sunrise said, *You do not understand why We learned not these things from the Lost Ones.*

"Yes," Hanna said, thinking of their terrible end. She ought not think of it; she must maintain this precious equilibrium.

Sunrise said, *They were different; or We did not know them. We knew Renders only, and Renders they became, and resonated with the Render in Ourselves. I think that is true.*

"But surely you knew there was a difference!"

There was none. Or else We would not see . . . For We did not know, having never seen. We see in the part of you that is she an infinite variety. The Lost Ones knew it not . . .

Hanna pressed cold hands to her hot cheeks. "They must have. They must have known F'thal, surely, even then."

They did not, Sunrise said.

Hanna shook her head, but she could not protest again; she could only accept. In the People's reality the colonists had known only—certain things.

They did not die as We would have them die, Sunrise said. *So we tampered with the brain itself, as with yours. And thus, if they would not be Renders, we made them Renders . . .*

Hanna turned her head sharply at a whisper in the darkness. But there had been no audible sound. The great voice was beginning again, and whispered, though conditionally, though tentatively: *Yes. Yes. Yes.*

Leader said, *It is time.*

Time, Sunrise said; *time,* said the leaves.

"Time . . . ? Oh, no . . ."

Hanna began to shiver. She said thickly, having scarcely had the courage to think of the question before, "Must I die in th-the pain? Again?"

Not, Leader said, *in my body.*

Sunrise stood and walked into the darkness. Light glimmered at her feet. When that faded too Hanna knew she was sinking back into the dream.

The passages were too dark for human eyes, and Sunrise guided her. Around her were walls of silence, the telepathic barrier with which Bladetree had met her when he took her from *XS-12*. It seemed tangible, so that she shrank away from physical walls with the sense that she would run into them. She stopped sometimes in the complexities of darkness, thinking Sunrise had gone on through solid substance, but always Sunrise turned and held out her hand and Hanna followed, trusting her. The barrier began to shiver; through it she heard whispers and sometimes identified those who made them, though in doubt and confusion. For their con-

ceptual names were those of their tasks, or descriptive, or
spoke of one person's relationship to one or more other
People, and everyone had many such names, and everyone
but Hanna always knew who was meant. She was herself an
alien-too-small-Render-thing and many other things, none
pleasant; but also she was form-of-Leader.

She knew dimly that she walked, but her consciousness
was erratic and it seemed she was in one place or another
without volition or movement. The empty rooms she
crossed with Sunrise were bare of ornament, the rich imagery of many thoughts sufficing to fill them.

Not bare, said the People in surprise. *Do you not see
beauty?* A wall of fine mosaic came to vivid life, and she
admired it. Here was a column of pale light; but its final
form depended on its union with other columns in other
rooms. For a moment she saw the work whole. "Beautiful,"
she whispered.

Someone said, *That is no Render,* and others answered,
Yet it is. Yet he is. Yet We are.

Here were more walls that danced with symbols waiting
for a thought to rearrange them. All history was here.
Hanna asked a question without knowing what she asked,
and Sunrise paused and the symbols changed. Sunrise said:
*In the long days when my love was gone, in the days when
my duties permitted, in the nights when my Child slept, I
studied these matters.*

A web of lines enclosed a globe of stars. Here was the
People's sun, here the sun of the less-than-People, here the
travels of generations. Hanna reached out to point, and did
not have to. Sunrise knew the place she meant, and knew
her question.

*No others. Only the Lost Ones, the less-than-People; only
your own kind.*

"But why? Why go that way?"

Why not? It chanced to lie in Our path.

"If you had gone another way it might have been—"

Leader-in-her-thoughts took it up: *The slippery-thinkers
or the uncarpenters, the tree-dwellers or the not-yets or others
still unmet—*

And all of them shouted at her: *Are they all like you?*

"No. No. Yes." Hanna looked up at Sunrise's flat face
with the noselike projection she knew, had known for some

time, was a bony plate to protect the organ of telepathy, distinct and localized as Hanna's own eyes.

"They are all like me. They are all like you, too. They fear death and protect life, as I do, as you do. It is the first lesson life teaches any world, the first lesson life learns. It is life."

You teach Us, yet you know not soul, they sighed, and the deep vibration began again, a cavern of winds at her feet.

Hanna said with downcast eyes, "I cannot know its meaning."

We are soul, they said.

"But there is something else," she said, and Leader said, *That is true.*

What else? they said, and Hanna almost knew.

When Hanna looked at still another room Sunrise had vanished. Hanna was not in the room of records anymore; this was a dark and pleasant place with soft lights that flickered, light enough for the People's unveiled eyes, but she could not tell why the light was not steady. *Many lights are not,* they said. *It is pleasing this way.* She took an experimental step, and then another. The floor wavered before her eyes, from one substance and one level to another, and she knew she was seeing many floors through many eyes, and had not their perceptual adjuncts to tell her which she stood on. The walls had a calm and warming polish, though their color changed or seemed to, and sometimes she saw stone. She called on Leader, but he could not help her. *Your body,* he said, *is not mine. You must sort the flux yourself.*

Many hours had gone by since the last stimulant injection. She had not expected ever to need another one. There were weights on her feet, her chest and head hurt and the darkness was caught in her eyes. She stumbled on softness and the carpet made a hollow for her body and a cushion for her head. This was a room for children, scattered with bright toys, some of which a human child would take up at once. The room was empty because the alien-Render-thing had come. She crossed the rug and it flattened obediently. A couch offered to enfold her. She did not have to climb up on it—she dropped onto it—it was made for persons even smaller than she. She did not lie down. If she did she would go to sleep, and there was not much waking left.

She sensed Swift before she saw him, sleepy and compliant in Sunrise's arms. He rubbed at his eyes and Hanna felt the down of his child's plumage against Sunrise's cheek. Her body trembled with Leader's eagerness. Swift was big as a human six-year-old, but he did not seem heavy when Sunrise put him in her arms. She was abruptly isolated, watching tears stream down her own cheeks, and saw herself with amazement. That body, her body, was shaken with emotion. Bowed with fatigue and Swift's weight, it caressed the child and Sunrise and dimly, as if through a pane of solid substance, Hanna felt the joy of their reunion, and all their Nearhome rejoicing in it.

But dimly, dimly. And then not at all.

She was apart from them. There was no room for her. She had no power at all—Leader had it all—she would never have any again. To her eyes—but they were not her eyes—Swift seemed to grow larger. He filled the field of vision, he was the largest thing in the universe, he was its center, he *was* the universe. Green gentle eyes looked into hers, and he laughed soundlessly with pure infant mirth. His father held him like a treasure of innocence, unscathed.

Time to come. Time to come in my arms. Now truly it is my time!

I am not ready, Hanna cried, *I have no child!*—for she saw in Swift the something else she had almost known before.

But no one heard her. No one.

Fear clawed at her and would have clutched her throat, but it was not her throat anymore. There was a panic urge to try to seize control again.

She mastered it.

No. Let it be! I came here for this. . . .

She tried to say to Leader: *I knew it would be hard. I do not know if I have the strength.*

But he was still absorbed in Swift, and did not hear her.

Time is, said the voice of a wind astray in starlight; *time* echoed the sky, white again (night was gone); *time* whispered a tunnel of arching blue leaves whose thin flexible branches bent low to caress the heads of those who passed; *time* sang a moat of rushing water; *time* murmured flickering flame; *time time time* said the voices of a world, until:

Time evaporates. Past is ended and present ending, and only the future exists as Hanna hurries on from moment to moment. But she sees where Leader bears her: through passages of leaf and bough to a silver spire from whose peak a flame beckons like hope, and up, and up, and up, until she has ascended to the radiant sky.

Thus rejoice We that We share not the fate of all life else. . . .

They do not speak to Hanna anymore nor even, now, to Leader. The great thought has no subject nor any object. It is thought thinking itself.

(Do not think of what you have to do, thinks something-of-Hanna caught in a crevice of stone.)

What will last-kindness do to this alien form?

(What will it do to me!!!)

We do not know.

(I recline—)

Terror is a palpable thing. It is no stranger; it has an old companion's face; but now she is utterly contained with it. It does not touch her body. No heart beats faster, no breath is shorter, no muscle is weak with it. *He* is not afraid. She sees through eyes that were hers, and feels terror that is only hers. She wishes to report, report, report; to objectify; to become the observant scientist postponing the future moment by moment by reporting, reporting, reporting as if there were a future, as if it matters her voice will live on in the object in her throat. But she cannot speak.

(Think it then. Think my death. So that at the end it will pass into this great plurality and be remembered and someday somehow be returned—but how transmuted?—to those who ought to hear it. Survive. In some form, survive!

I lie, no, recline, not on the altar I feared—there never were altars, they needed no gods, there were laboratory tables not altars—at ease—*his* ease. Bondmate clasps my hand. She does not fear the alien flesh. The Child clings to me, now puzzled and lamenting. Knows his father. How can he among so many? How can he in such strange form?)

The sun rises, warming the vivid height. Such places do We choose when there is choice. This is the time We choose, when choice is given: the rising of the sun.

(The drink is cool and has no taste to my alien mouth—)

The cup of last-kindness thy father's own skull, carven, gemlike, polished. Last-kindness, like water, is tasteless. This path We choose (no others so choose) for saving, for peace and full joining. Drink! Like water is formless is shapeless: life gives it form: ever filling, ever bursting forth. Life shapes itself. You have shaped your time, your self, your Home and Us for the good or the ill of your days and those to come. Water purifies flesh. Flesh dissolves in sweet water. Now join the eternal completing!

The purpose, We affirm, for this is needful, and

The purpose, he affirms, and knows Us, each of the persons of his Nearhome and beyond them the persons of all others past and present, and in others at this very dawn those who like him wait for the sun to give up completed lives:

The purpose, he says, and Bondmate bows her head grieving and assenting:

The purpose, he says, and the Child is still, hands on his father's alien heart:

The purpose, he tells Us, *is life and the absence of death; life unending in the soul, life renewed in the Child.*

It is the true and proper answer and he fully freely gives it. And We ask: *What have you learned?*

He says: *I have learned that my love's eyes are green.*

Green. A word. A thing a color We cannot see.

It is all of me which comes to you, he says. *That We know and that We do not know, save I; new lives, new deaths; the balance of a stranger's form, and worse: a stranger's death.*

We do not want this thing. To change Us?

Renders changed Us. It is no Render completes Us now, but one of Us.

We doubt. His limbs are weak, the alien strength is waning.

He says: *Think with pity (though We could not pity Renders) on their end. These are not beasts and yet they die: finally, irrevocably, beyond recourse. The sorrow! A race of sorrow, a species that knows its fate: they invent immortality, and invent belief in it: it bends and twists and warps them even the best. They are what We might have been; pity them!*

And this is what he has learned. And so We also learn. For this is how We learn.

The limbs come near to weightlessness in the morning light. They are no longer his nor anyone's. In each moment he is nearer. He looks back/We look back at the silent strange form, a rag of a thing, small and harmless. He is almost visible; We are always almost visible at this ending, almost on the edge of sight a puff of smoke, almost in clear dawn light. It is so always, and this is the same. One of Us. And each of Us always is different from all, and so with each death and new life We are changed, and changed all the more by the Great.

Therefore begins the final scrutiny and shaping, judgment and acknowledgment at once, and We pare to a structure of light his life and honor it: fear met with courage, suffering with duty fulfilled to final measure in the company and sharing of a beast.

Not beast, he says. *Returned she to grieve with Bondmate and Child. Beasts do not do that. Forswore she attack. Beasts do not do that. She is Ours. We are she.*

And the lives intertwined are a skein of light, he stretches thinning toward Bondmate once more, and is attenuated, and settles without fear or grief into each cell of each one of Us.

And the alien form is a wisp of darkness in the light of a sun no longer strange, and

It is done.

She dreams of water. Mist, really. The cool spray of falling water bathes her face. *Her* face. She lifts to it a hand that has a cobweb's weight and strength. *Her* hand. Strange thought.

Why strange?

Her eyes open, with effort. See the scaled gentle face, familiar as her own. She smiles, and whispers a question.

Sunrise cannot answer. She does not know why the human body lives. But she tends to it carefully as she tends Swift, and the food she puts into its mouth comes warmed and softened from her own. And is gratefully accepted.

The ships have been called back. They are not necessary.

The security module was not in Jameson's house anymore. The place where it had been was a cavity, the walls scarred and strange from amputation. He felt as if a part of his body had been removed. The transmitter was gone from his ear and it seemed he would never again know what was going on anywhere.

He slept drugged to the top of his skull and severed from

the world and they almost had to break his house down before it sounded an alarm of intruders and he finally woke, sick with dread. The antidote to oblivion didn't really take effect until he was on his way to Admin in al-Nimeury's aircar. He had fallen on the way out his own front door, and he did not remember anything al-Nimeury had told him. He was too proud to ask for a repetition. He watched the night go by and waited for al-Nimeury to say something else. When it came it was a string of curses, but absentminded, as if al-Nimeury had been through it all before.

Jameson tried his dignity and found it, with relief, returning.

"Calm yourself," he said.

"You sonofabitch, you never answered me. Did you tell her not to talk to anybody but you?"

Jameson said vaguely, "You never know."

"I'm not sure she's all there anymore. Maybe Katherine was right—no. No, I take that back. I was there, she wasn't faking. But she sure as hell sounds strange."

Jameson knew who he meant then. al-Nimeury said, "Here, are you going to be sick?"

"No. Sorry."

"What the hell then?"

"Never mind. Shut up."

The aircar swooped down to a wet rooftop and al-Nimeury said, "We're here. Come on."

They ran through the labyrinth of Admin to al-Nimeury's rooms. Pain shot through Jameson's head at every step. al-Nimeury kept talking. "She's patched in through *Willowmeade*. How did she know Tirel was out there? Did you tell her? Or did she get it out of your head?"

"I don't know."

"Little bitch," al-Nimeury said inconsequentially, and a guard fell back and they were in his chambers. Morisz's replacement was there, and a dozen men from Fleet, and Murphy, who must have been roused from sleep too but was sleekly groomed as always. Her eyes were wider than usual, though.

Murphy said, "I thought she might talk to me, but she won't."

"Right. Well, he's here now. There's no video," al-Nimeury said to Jameson. "She can hear you."

Jameson said cautiously, "Hanna?"

The faintest of sighs filled the room. There was nothing else. After a minute Jameson looked uncertainly at the others. Murphy muttered, as if Hanna could not hear her, "She's very strange. Talk to her."

He said to thin air, feeling like a fool, "Hanna, are you all right?"

A voice said slowly, "Ye-es. Yes. All—right."

He sank into a chair, beginning to forget the others, all his attention concentrated on a faint sound from infinity. It might have been the voice of a ghost. But even if they had not already checked the identity with every means at their command—and they must have done that at once—he would have known the voice was Hanna's.

He said, trying to sound ordinary, "What happened?"

"It's all right," Hanna said.

"What's all right? Where are you?"

"Here," Hanna said.

"Are you on the aliens' home world?"

There was a long silence. "Yes," said Hanna.

"Have you come to an understanding with them?"

This time the silence was very long. Hanna said finally, "What?"

Oh dear God, Jameson thought, they have destroyed her mind. Desolation swept over him. He said very slowly and carefully, "Hanna, can you understand me?"

He waited. Nothing. His shoulders ached with tension; surely he listened for a voice from the dead. He had had time to think in the last terrible days, much too much time to think, while all he valued most was taken from him and he could not know if the great price had purchased anything. He had not been able to make Hanna's weary face disappear, except when he eradicated it in sleep. Now it seemed he might have bought something after all—and now the sound of Hanna's voice was more important to him personally than anything it might say. It was not a thought that fit in with anything in his life, anywhere. He thrust it aside.

"Hanna?"

She said suddenly, "Yes. Wait."

But he was nearly ready in his anxiety to speak again when she said, "Very difficult. This. Talking."

"All right. All right. What's wrong with you?"

"The interface," she said. "Wait!"

He was not even sure the command was addressed to him, but he waited. Presently she began to speak, slowly and awkwardly.

"It's all right. They won't attack. I'll come back. You shouldn't have sent the ship. To follow me."

"How did you know about *Willowmeade*?"

"I guessed. I know *you*," Hanna said. She said this strongly and without hesitation, and sounded irritated. He breathed again, weak with relief. It was Hanna, all right, and whatever had happened to her, she was herself.

"You're positive they won't attack?"

"Positive. They were going to. They aborted. It's all right. If you don't do anything stupid."

"What do you mean?"

Speaking more easily now, she said, "Don't frighten them. Pull *Willowmeade* back."

"Are they demanding that?"

"*I* am. Demanding it. I promised them."

He glanced at al-Nimeury, but it was Murphy who said, "Yes. Yes, we'll do it."

"You have to. They'll know. Look," Hanna said, "it's started. Now it's up to you."

Not me, he thought. Not any longer.

Someone else had come into the room. He knew who it was without looking around: the new commissioner from Heartworld.

He said, "You have to come back. We have to talk to you."

"I know. I'll come. Not yet."

"Why?"

"I have to, to, see some people. The others from—the ones who belonged with the people I killed. And find—I lost my ring."

He hesitated, and decided not to pursue it. He said, "I'd rather you came back right now."

"I can't. I have to show them—Starr?"

"Yes?"

"I didn't do much. He did it."

"What are you talking about?"

"The alien. Made the interface. In me. He was—he is one

of their great ones. They know that. I miss him. I like his, his, wife," she added with apparent irrelevance.

Jameson, at a loss, said, "That's nice."

"They might not have any more—" There was a long pause. Then she said, "Watchsetters. They might have communicators instead. She'd be good at it."

"I'm sure she would. When can you come home?"

"But this—oh. Does Iledra want to know?"

"I mean here," he said to his own surprise.

"Oh. I don't—a few days. I was wrong."

She seemed to think he would know exactly what she meant. He said, "What were you wrong about?"

"I didn't go far enough."

"No?"

"No. It's not enough to . . . to . . . to think with them. To know what's real. You have to live with them too. And then—"

There was another long silence. The space and time between them disappeared and he could almost see her face, alight with wonder. He thought she reached out to touch him, and shook his head to make the vision disappear.

"Then?" he said. "What then, Hanna?"

"Why, then you have to die with them," she said.

Chapter 20

The room Tirel gave her on *Willowmeade* was small and cramped. There was a guard at the door. Tirel said she was an honored guest and the guard was there to keep curious crewmen from disturbing her. He lied. She was guarded because no one knew what to make of her yet; because suspicion lingered, and Tirel wanted no alien monster stalking his ship. If sometimes Hanna felt like a guest, it was because of the very crewmen who were kept away from her. Her room filled up quickly with their gifts: fresh flowers grown in cubicles cramped as hers; tapestries as carefully woven as the coverlet incinerated with *Heartworld II;* strange and beautiful animals carved by clever hands; presents of food from the galley; cherished garments from the women. The room took on the look of D'neera, crowded with beauties stacked and tumbling over one another. It was only later that Hanna wondered why the phenomenon had happened, and found that as the full story of her contacts with the People spread through *Willowmeade,* with it spread a wish not so much to honor as to comfort her.

She hardly left the room, because she was weary and sad and unwell and it was difficult to get used to human beings again. Still, she resented Tirol's strictures. She had been the prisoner of someone or other for a long time now—or maybe sometimes she had really been a guest—but she wished they would stop calling it one thing when it was the other.

A true-human mindhealer came to see her, and asked questions she would not answer, and proposed a moderate intake of drugs (a suggestion she rejected with some violence), and said that she ought to have the most normal regimen of living possible.'

He must have forgotten to tell anyone else. Her other visitors were not normal, they did not pay social calls; they asked questions about the People. They thought she must have all the answers and she did not. A lifetime of study would not be enough to get them all. She could not even answer simple questions with the expected yes or no. To do so was to disregard a world of connotations, implications, and interconnections, and a simple answer, being incomplete, was false. Her ambiguous answers satisfied no one, but they were all she had.

She talked to Jameson sometimes. The transmissions were clear; behind lurking *Willowmeade,* as Hanna moved toward the People's Home, other ships of Fleet had worked feverishly to set human relays in place. Whatever came next, the line was in place for communication with the People, and *Willowmeade* now followed it home. It was a remarkable achievement, Jameson told Hanna complacently, but she was not interested, and barely nodded in acknowledgment.

Their conversations sometimes were private, but Jameson was cool and impersonal. The caution with which she was treated must have had his approval, and she asked him finally, bitterly, what she had to do to prove herself to him, and, indeed, what exactly she was supposed to prove. He was jolted for the first time from his abstraction. He said, "You must understand, Hanna, we still don't know how human you are."

"But he's gone. *Gone.*"

"His memories are there, are they not? His knowledge?"

"Yes, but *he* isn't. I 'heard' him sometimes before I came away . . ." She fumbled, searching for words to explain. "He's still *there,* in them. But it's a change. By the time I left he was already almost archetypal, like the others—the ones who'd been in him. They lose some individuality . . . She'll die soon, his spouse. Not right away; in a year or so. Just slowly, gradually fade. I think I might too."

He gave her a very measured look. "I don't think so," he said. "Not if you're a human being. And you weren't united with him very long. I think you're just grieving, Hanna. Because you've lost him . . . Did you love him?"

"I don't know. I don't think it matters. He was *me.* And I thought if I lived through it, somehow he'd still be there."

Jameson's explanation was insulting—who should know how human she was, if not Hanna herself?—but it explained the medtechs who swarmed about her. They examined her as soon as she came aboard *Willowmeade;* decontaminated her, corrected some nutritional imbalances, pounced on her still-bleeding arm with delight; and analyzed her skin, her hair, her nails, and every conceivable body fluid, along with the air that had been in her lungs when she arrived. After a day or two they came back and began scanning every cell of her brain. They talked enthusiastically of dendrites and axons while the traces of light that defined Hanna formed ambiguous amoebic shapes on portable video screens, and the mainframe computer in medical mode emitted strange gobbles and pings as comment on what Hanna had become.

They were on to something. They would not tell her what, so she read their thoughts, and was frightened. Perhaps Jameson was right after all; there were subtle physical changes in her brain. Interpreting them was difficult, but something, plainly, had happened to her.

"Give us just a little slice of cortical tissue," they coaxed her. "Quick, simple, safe, painless—"

"No!" she said. She had been tampered with enough. Her head ached at the very thought. "Enough is enough!" she cried in despair, and Jameson unexpectedly supported her.

"Should I thank you?" she asked him.

"No. Why? What you are now works. Just the way it is."

"Then you'd want to be able to replicate it. Replicate me."

"It will be a long time before we can do that. I dislike using the word 'impossible,' but it just might be applicable."

He was using holographic transmission, exceedingly rare for him; he said it was too difficult to remember that you were talking to an illusion. And indeed he appeared so substantial, seated at ease in Hanna's cabin, that she yearned to put out her hands to touch him, and restrained herself with difficulty. She brought her mind back to what he had said and asked, "Why?"

He shifted a little in his unreal chair, and Hanna, recognizing the signs, prepared to be lectured.

"The theory postulates two elements that are too difficult to deal with," he said. "One is the shaping of consciousness the aliens did when you were their prisoner. The other is the massive regeneration you went through on Earth. The changes probably were in place before you left, and were overlooked because no one recognized their significance. We might be able to modify the regenerative effect in a healthy subject. But the first part of the business ... certainly we wouldn't reproduce it, even if we could. And we'll need the aliens to find an alternative means of producing the same effect. No, you're a synergistic product. Getting the same result, with due attention to the safety of the subjects, will take years. You've made it possible to proceed with contact along more conventional lines. I don't see why anyone should be permitted to dig around in your head."

Hanna thought rather doubtfully that it sounded like rationalization for a decision made on emotional grounds, but probably not; probably he meant just what he said.

She spent two weeks on *Willowmeade,* and through all of it, when she was not being questioned or examined, she grieved. Whether her brain's changes had anything to do with it or not, she was still more than half alien. Now she felt herself to be much as the persons of the First Watchsetter had seen her—a part of an organism severed from the whole, and bereft. Before Leader's final transition she had not looked beyond it, thinking there would be nothing, or still-Leader; if she had looked beyond it she could not have predicted this loneliness. She refused to talk to Iledra. She did not know if she wanted ever to go home. She had said farewell to D'neera, deeply and it seemed irrevocably. She could not easily undo the parting; and there was a question she sometimes contemplated, without daring yet to test it: whether or not she might have become so different that she belonged nowhere.

Presently *Willowmeade* came to Earth, and she was invited aboard a shuttle for the trip to the surface. The two men with her might have been an honor guard, or merely guards. They were not sure themselves—as Hanna discovered by shamelessly examining their thoughts. She had not asked anyone on *Willowmeade* what was going to happen to her next. Jameson had talked of "developing and implementing a plan of systematic contact with the Zeigans" —

but she did not know how much choice she had about participating, what role was designed for her and how much pressure would be applied if she declined it, or what the official attitude might be concerning her humanity or lack of it.

The shuttle dropped to an Admin landing pad, and Hanna's guards took her through a section of the maze she had never seen before. The place was nearly empty; it was a down-day, and she moved through the hushed corridors feeling like a ghost.

A door opened, and Jameson came out of it. The guards disappeared.

Hanna looked at him in silence, and saw that he regarded her speculatively. She shrank in on herself; felt herself grow smaller, tighter, harder. It had occurred to her that when she saw him she might throw herself into his arms. But not when he looked at her like this.

"Come in," he said suddenly, and she walked past him cautiously, stiff-legged, into a strange room from which she could see the river shining far below. It was very quiet. It was almost always very quiet wherever Jameson was, as if silence were something he created as an extension of himself. Hanna caught her breath; it was nearly irresistible.

She did not want to look at Jameson. She looked instead at an object in the room: the head of an alien animal, carved in wood. A memory came from months before of Jameson lifting it with careful hands to show it to Iledra. But this was not where she had seen it.

She said, "Where am I?"

"My offices," said the quiet voice behind her.

"No, it's not!"

He said carelessly, "New job, new rooms. They needed someone to head up the contact project. They're thinking about sending *Endeavor* out again, too. Gives me a chance to stay on Earth. Heartworld has a new commissioner; have you forgotten? He likes my old quarters very well."

His voice was entirely controlled. If she looked at him his face would be tranquil too. So she listened with the other, inward hearing, more sensitive and finely honed than it had ever been before her sojourn with the People, and felt his pain. Her head drooped.

He said, sounding merely curious, "Why are you angry?"

"I hardly know where to begin!"

It was not what she had meant to say; it came from Leader's empty place. She twisted her hands together nervously and said, "Why did you send *Willowmeade* to follow me? After the promise you made that I'd be alone?"

"It was necessary. It could have gone either way. By your own account the beginning was shaky—"

"You endangered everything I was trying to do!"

"Did we? *You* believed we would put nothing in position for an attack. It was worth the gamble that they therefore would believe it too—and not look too hard. If you failed, we had an alternative. It was necessary," he repeated.

"It wasn't." Hanna took a deep breath. Leader was gone, but she would speak for him. She said, "It was stupid and dangerous, and you cannot, you can *not*, behave with these beings the way you behave with each other. They're different. They play by different rules. You can threaten them without meaning to. If you behave like the beasts they remember you'll undo everything I've done. They know I'm an aberration. They could reject me as quickly as they took me in, if you can't give up something of yourselves the way they did, the way I did. If you can't understand that, then it was all for nothing!"

"Good," he said approvingly.

Astonished, she turned to him at last. He was smiling.

"Good?"

"That's exactly what we must learn from you, and through you."

She looked at him suspiciously, but he was serious. For once he was telling the whole truth. But if he thought it would soothe her, he was mistaken.

She said, "You mean you want to use me some more."

He said thoughtfully, "You can put it that way if you want to."

"Can't you go on without me? What do you want from me now?"

Jameson said slowly, "I want your recommendations on how best to establish regular communication with the aliens, with the exchange of knowledge to promote mutual understanding as your highest priority. I want you to organize a detailed plan of contact. I want you to go back there, if need be; with companions, if that is best. If so, I want you to train the others. I do not think you should be questioned any longer. Our questions come from a human perspective entirely. I want to know what you will say when you are allowed to speak spontaneously, with due reference to 'Sentience.' I want you to be the guide for a future spent sharing the universe with these beings . . . That will do for a start."

She felt sick. She said, "I don't want to do anything."

He looked at her for a long moment and then said, "All right."

She eyed him with disbelief. He added, "Trying to force you is futile. There is no weapon to use against you. I cannot threaten you, even with confinement. You're too important. You don't know anything about the kind of personal power that has its source in the way others perceive you, but you have it now, whether or not you know how to use it. I can't touch you. Not now. No one can. And if you don't care about power or riches, and I don't think you do, I have nothing to bribe you with . . . What do you want? What is the dearest wish of your heart?"

She was taut as she listened, but it was all true. She felt— the lifting of a great weight? No, not its vanishing, it was too soon for that, but the first intimation that a burden she had long carried might, in time, be put down.

There was only one thing she wanted. She said simply, "Rest."

He nodded. "You can leave for D'neera today, if you like."

She shook her head abruptly. She was not ready to go home to D'neera. It was not time. She did not know why.

"No? Well, then, there are quarters for you if you want them; near here, near my home. You can be the guest of the Polity for as long as—"

"Not that!"

"What?" Her vehemence startled him.

"I don't much like the way the Polity treats its guests," she said, but she said it forlornly. Her vision was blurred. That happened often of late, but she could not remember the last time she had wept.

After a minute he said slowly, "You could come stay with me."

He spoke with an edge of reluctance, as if he were not sure what he was offering or if he should offer it at all. But

the fireside and the warmth and the quiet of his home, the
sense of enduring, solid-founded peace, were fully present
to her mind.

"Yes, please," she said.

She slept; slept for three weeks; slept through the nights and
half the days, waking to eat when Jameson insisted, waking
sometimes to slip from his house by night or by day to walk
a little in an endless spring rain. Her eyes were swollen with
sleep, and she was slack as a broken bowstring. Jameson
gave the house orders, and it guarded her. People came to
it, but it would not let them in and sent them away. People
called, but it let no one speak to her; and she slept. Her
dreams were strange and restless and sometimes terrifying.
She woke from a nightmare one evening and in a sort of
daze made her way to Jameson's study, where he sat reading
before a fire. He must have spoken to her, but she never
remembered what he said. There was space for her beside
him and she crept into it, easing her head onto his shoulder
and pressing so close that she might have been trying to
erase herself as a separate presence from the universe. He
looked down at her for a long time, and finally laid down
the reader he held and very gently put his arms around her.
Hanna began to cry. She cried for a long time and he held
her through it, until she was done and exhausted with weeping and lay down with her head in his lap and slept again.
When she woke near morning he had not moved; he was
sleeping too, and still held her hand.

A day or two later Peter Struzik said, "I don't care how you
do it. Beat her, dope her, make love to her, tell her she can
name her price—just get her going so we can get somewhere."

Jameson said nothing. They had just disconnected from
an all-project conference that was another installment of
the ongoing quarrel the whole endeavor had become. Hanna's reports from *Heartworld II* were rich in detail—too
rich; there were no guidelines for interpreting them. If
Hanna had died with Leader-in-her-thoughts, they would
have made a hero of her and gratefully accepted the finite
body of knowledge and speculation left to them. Since she
had made the mistake of staying alive and only declining to

cooperate, resentment had turned to suspicion. How much of what she said was true? Had she been mistaken in some places? Had she even lied? It was evolutionary nonsense for a child-bearing female to die soon after her spouse. It was ridiculous to suppose that objective reality could be altered by the consciousness of a species, that flora were in any way conscious, that a world's direction could turn on the shaping of a single mind. Why had Hanna's answers on *Willowmeade* been so unsatisfactory? If she had once translated the People's written language, as she claimed, why would she not do it again? Did she wish it to remain a mystery? Perhaps if they could read it, they would learn things that contradicted her testimony. Perhaps she knew it.

Struzik walked up and down Jameson's new office with small fussy steps. When he went out of this room he would walk through the project's main workspace, where the air was that of a battlefield. Most of Jameson's former staff still worked for the commissioner's office, assisting in the transition; but some, like Rodrigues, were here. They were not expert in the matter at hand, and personal loyalty prevented them from complaining of the project's direction or lack of it, except perhaps among themselves. But there was a larger group of specialists recruited just for this undertaking, and they were frustrated and angry, they could not get at Hanna, and they had begun to talk of her absence as deliberate sabotage performed, for inscrutable but probably political reasons, by Jameson. The two groups did not mix well.

Struzik looked down forty stories at the river, an ice-blue ribbon today. He said, "You could get her to stop sulking."

"She is not sulking," Jameson said mildly.

"Well, what do you call it? Sleeping her life away when we need her."

"Peter. It has been almost a year since she went into space with the other two to meet the Zeigans. Do you need to be reminded why we named them that? She was present at the deaths of her friends, she was taken apart in body and spirit and intellect, she was rushed through regeneration and was conscious far too often while it was going on, she was kept a prisoner here and treated—not badly, but not particularly well; and all that was the easy part."

"I know, I know, I know. But she could be made useful anyway."

Struzik peered over his shoulder to see what Jameson made of the suggestion. Jameson knew exactly what he meant. He said, "She's had enough of chemical tampering. It's not a thing that has ever been accepted on D'neera in any case. She doesn't like it and she's not used to it."

"Living with you must be an education for her, then."

There was no response, and after a minute Struzik went on, "She wouldn't have to know about it, you know. She'd just feel better. Calm. Cooperative. Happy. If—"

"No."

"Maybe somebody else could make her see reason, anyway. If you won't. If you'd let one of us talk to her—"

"No."

"No?" Struzik swung around and said experimentally, "Look, you could be removed from the project. Not that I, that we want to do that. It's hard watching an old friend go under. We all got here more or less the same way. What happened to you—it could have been me or Kate or any of us. The point is, you're answerable to us. It's going to be our hides if you don't produce. Do I have to spell out what it means to you? Your own council dumped you and we grabbed you. For this. If you last a month and that's the end, with all the talk, what are you going to do then? I hear people say already you've been overrated all along, and that's when they're being nice. Now, think about it, Jamie. I know you can do it. It's her or you. You just decide."

He stared at Jameson. There was no reaction for a long moment, and then Jameson's right hand moved in a rude gesture. That was all.

The mists were thinning. She slept well for several nights running, and the half-heard echoes of Leader that made her anxiously turn her head, as if to hear better, were muted and vanishing. She communicated a little with Iledra, but not by holo or video or even voice; she wrote, as she had from *Endeavor;* it was easier that way to be cautious, to be sure of saying neither too much nor too little, to hide behind the shield of distance and make noncommittal answers to Iledra's fulminations on the Polity, whose occupation of D'neera was finished but far from forgotten.

"Don't you," Iledra asked again and again, "want to come home?"

"Not yet," Hanna answered each time.

She had no energy for going home. She felt she was at home, maybe as much at home as she would ever feel again, anywhere. Jameson's house emphatically was not D'neeran; it was uncluttered and largely unadorned; but it was luxurious for all its look of austerity, and suited Hanna better than the gaudier conventions of D'neera.

She absorbed the spaciousness and quiet gratefully. She liked the quiet especially, because there was no peace inside her. Leader's voice was fading, but others took its place. In one way or another they were all her own, but often enough the notes her spirit played were taken from elsewhere, from others. It amused her to put names to them.

You shirk your duty. You have come through fire and agony and now at the flowering and fruit you turn aside. Why then did you do it? What good will it be? What benefit?

Was that Iledra? Jameson?

See them, all the differences. Those in the higher classes have two mutually functioning brains. They move whitely, gracefully. Swaying they mean—what do you think they mean? How do you think they think with two brains?

A teacher long-ago? Or H'ana Bassanio long-ago, a small girl contemplating pictures from F'thal?

Thus the turn and the shimmer that is faster than the eye or comprehension and we catch the facets sparkling and dance in our turn live die and know all or naught—

The Hierarchus, surely; yet it sounded like Leader.

Worth it all. Not much in this life worth it all. Transforming transcendent the will straight and sure worth the gift. Choose, and do not hesitate.

That was her own voice, and the cruelest of all. But she had learned some things since the black day of the *Clara*. She had thought that day a hard one. Now she knew it had not been hard at all.

She crept from the voices to Jameson, because there was nowhere else to go. Rock. *The universe is made of rock.* Here was rock, grim and immovable. She spent the evenings sleeping with her head on his knee, a most satisfactory resting place. He always held a reader propped on his other knee; he held it with his left hand, and his right lay on her waist. It did not wander, except sometimes, with restraint, to smooth her hair.

She is a sick child and so I will treat her, said his thought, stubbornly, and he declined to remember the kiss, far from a child's, that she had given him. But she was not a child and she was not, she discovered, the thing Bladetree had left for Fleet to find. Her face was unflawed, her breasts round and whole, her skin soft to the touch, the arc of her hips an invitation whether she wished to be inviting or not. And Jameson was not altogether rock, because she learned these things through his senses. And finally learned more; not willingly.

There was no fire tonight. The east-looking doors stood open to a mild wet evening, and when the last gray faded from the horizon the clouded sky was altogether black. A fragrant breeze whispered through the room, fretful, impatient. A new and unsatisfactory report on linguistic programming—the last perhaps that would be made to Jameson—still showed on the reader's face when he put it down. The movement woke Hanna from her half-sleep, but Jameson did not get up, so she only sighed and turned to settle her cheek more firmly on his thigh. The room was cool and she shivered a little, but she had no desire to move from Jameson's presence to somewhere warmer. Her arm hurt, no nearer healing than before; and the voices were very bad tonight.

I do not hide from you my grief and fate my love gone my end approaching my child left to kin's care and comfort; I/We in him yet not the same and grief to all though not what you know in like case; yet mourning I think is for all the same and universal, so it seems; though We are ignorant still; you, I, all of Us.

The room was very dark; the reader, half-hidden from Hanna's sight, a vivid spot of light.

Grief, that is all; defeat and bitterness. In Peter's place I would do the same. He knows the cost to me. I think he even cares, a little. In his place I would do the same.

Hanna's muscles tightened. She put her hand suddenly on Jameson's knee. She would not have spoken, but he said, drawn from his abstraction, "Hanna?" He meant: Is something wrong?

"Nothing," she murmured.

"All right . . ."

But her eyes were wide open in the dark. Since coming to Jameson she had made no effort to tap into his thought. His kindness and the care he took of her were all she wanted and all she cared about. The conversation of confusion inside her had kept her from looking for more. She thought of it, when she thought of it, as a sign that she was more true-human now than otherwise—

They don't have to care for anyone, child; for anyone but themselves. We haven't got that luxury. True-humans, they call themselves. The authentic thing. What does that mean, "human?" What do you think it means?

Strange, this . . .

Oh don't, Hanna said silently to herself, and almost sat up, almost spoke, to make him stop thinking. Or she could stop listening, break the contact inadvertently formed in her drowsiness, go quietly to the garden or her room; he did not know she heard him and wished her, undoubtedly, to remain ignorant of his thought.

A voice from the past said severely: *You turned away when you should have stayed. We are all of us entitled to our pain. You cannot deny another's truth. That's selfish. Don't do it again.*

Hanna stayed where she was, and listened. Jameson thought in words, and though bitterness attended it, his thought was clear and precise as his speech, stripped and pitiless.

. . . to feel that one cannot, and know one must and will. Hanna I suppose knows it well. But I had forgotten; so long has it been since the reek of tiger breath and pain forgotten too; the weight and the spear out of reach and the long knife slipping from my hand. When I was well, I had to hunt again. Had to. A Jameson of Arrenswood, of Starrbright. I could not but I did. No one knew I was afraid. They watched me close and hard. They saw no fear. No sign of breaking . . .

Hanna closed her eyes and saw color. Green: deep shadowed forest paths. Russet, aquamarine: grain against an alien summer sky.

. . . and I will not break now, though I never loved it there. The girls' bright eyes see only Starrbright. Their mothers are worse. Arrenswood affairs; a council seat someday if I live

*this down long enough. The years run short and I die day by
day into night. At the Capitol a tiger is caged. . . .*

The dark closed in and split into bars. Shafts of sunlight
between them warmed shabby fur. Hanna let another
nightmare seize her, Jameson's nightmare; he lived it, waking. His hand stirred restlessly on her flesh, but he did not
know what he touched.

*Perhaps I have had enough, enough for any man. I
thought always that I would know when it was time to give
up the future and its shaping. Is this it? My heart says no. But
I always knew need when I saw it, and I see nothing else,
nothing left to command but myself. Well, then, I will. Turn
away, let it go, diminish and meet the final test and prove I am
master of myself; that at least. Hard to turn away from the
turning, though. The furlcrum shifts, the balance changes and
history with it. Immortality, of a sort. Should it be? Never
mind; it will be. The question is only how—*

In the depths of nightmare Hanna made a pitiful protesting sound. "Hanna?" he said in sudden alarm. She struggled
to sit up and did it though she seemed weighted down with
rock. A ghostly procession wound through the dark, humans and F'thalians seeking in the People some kind of
survival. Nightmares of negotiation—

The lights came on. "You can't do that!" she said. She
saw that Jameson looked at her with deep concern; he must
think her mad and stumbling in painful memory.

"You can't!"

"Can't do what?"

The room was full of loud voices. There were only hers
and his.

"What can you be thinking of? You have no right!"

He said with sudden comprehension. "You've been reading my mind."

"Yes. Yes. Who is doing this? Why are you doing it?"

"I do nothing. It will be out of my hands very soon."

"But you're planning—"

"No. Hush. Wait. There are no plans. Hush . . ."

He reached for her but she moved away, avoiding his
hands. She said, "Immortality. What do you mean? It can't
be that. I must have got it wrong."

"I don't think so. The potential for survival as some kind
of entity in the Zeigan mass mind is . . ." He did not finish

the sentence. He got up, not suddenly, but with one of the movements that always startled her when he ended a long stillness, and she saw him with new eyes. He was not part of the comforting background now, but singular and alive. It struck her for the first time how worn he looked; not by comparison with the recent past, but gauged against the icy and self-contained presence he had been when she met him on the *Endeavor*. He looked absently around the familiar room, as if he had not seen it before. He said, "Everything will be new, soon."

Everywhere We went was new.

"No," Hanna said to the trace of an old Apprentice, or perhaps it was Apprentice who spoke. Jameson thought she said it to him. He said, "It can't be helped. I don't know if what is coming is 'good' or 'bad' or even if those judgments are applicable. I don't think they are. What's going to happen — just is. Is exploration good or bad? It doesn't matter. It just is, inevitable. So is this. There'll be no hope of stopping it — even if stopping it might be good. All that will be left, all that is ever left, will be to minimize some evils that may come. There are some dreadful possibilities for exploitation, violence, enslavement, among ourselves or in conflict with them . . . There are no plans, Hanna. None that I know of; though I might not know, now."

She said hopefully, "Has anyone but you even thought of it?"

"Oh, surely. Surely. I must," he said, thinking aloud now, "get Peter to institute a study of the questions. Secretly, of course. It can't be done too soon and they will put it off if they can."

They would rather put it off for a century or two, Iledra said. But she had been talking about something else. Or maybe not. *To have a telepath at a first contact — they must see what it could mean!* And this was what it meant.

Hanna ran. Pure instinct. She fled through the wide inviting doors, stumbled on a dark terrace, crushed barely nascent growth underfoot (there was no complaint; flowers here did not complain).

And stopped. There was nowhere to go this time.

Jameson came after her, picking his way more carefully. She gave him her arm and let him take her back to the house. They were silent. He was neither surprised nor distressed by her abortive flight. She thought he had expected it. Predictable.

He brought her, predictably, a tiny glass filled with brilliant red liquid. The chemical man; though his head had been clear these last weeks. She glanced up at him suspiciously—she was not entirely unaware of certain suggestions he had rejected on her behalf—but he said, "It's only Valentine brandy, Hanna," and she drank it. It was bitter.

He said, just as if there had been no interruption, "Individual survival has always been humankind's first dream. You accepted as self-evident—it has always been so accepted—that awareness of one's own inevitable death is an early mark of sentience. Did it never cross your mind on Zeig-Daru that in doing what you did you had found a kind of endless life for yourself?"

The questions would not go away. *Questions answer one another,* said an Explorer long-ago. Hanna said doggedly, "It did not. Anyway that wasn't me. It was *him,* just changed. I don't think I *want* to live forever."

"You'll change your mind when the end is closer." There was a sharp secret amusement in him that made her stare at him.

She said, abandoning right and wrong, "They'll never agree to it."

"Will they not? They're extraordinarily malleable. And maybe," he said very gently, "that is their function. You find the prospect unimaginable. But consider yourself: a new thing in the life of the human species. Unimaginable, until you were real. Did you know there was a time, before your people left Earth, before the oppression began, when telepaths were called new-humans? Then the rest of us became true-humans—a term coined in hostility toward what your ancestors were. Because they had been unimaginable, and were new, and perhaps better. You have indicated that the Zeigans regard themselves as instruments of life. In the strict sense all of us are—and this, perhaps, is one more step in its progress. Life experiments, you know. The Zeigans so far have been successful. Perhaps success for them means absorbing us, and the F'thalians, and others we will come to know together. Can you say this is untrue? When we don't even know—as you know better than anyone—what is real?"

His voice enchanted her. It had always enchanted her, resting her with its sureness, creating a spell in which she saw the universe he knew—or made. His eyes were distant, set on visions. But she saw with her fresh shock-born sight that they were the eyes of a very weary man.

She took a deep breath and stood up. The spell was broken.

"What you are thinking of is not real," she said.

He answered without resentment, "How do you know?"

She did not know. There was only her own inner insistence that what he proposed somehow was not right, and against it his certainty that it was.

She said, "I don't want to believe that it can happen. You do. But I think in the end that what the People want to believe is what will be."

"That," he said, and after a pause: "That. I had forgotten that."

He bowed his head and she saw the direction of his thought. She said sadly, "Must it be war between us, then, to shape their reality?"

"What?" He looked up, scarcely seeing her. An odd expression touched his face. He said, "It won't be. We're both out of it."

"But I could—" Hanna said, and then the word struck her, and the pacing aging tiger and the prison of the fields and the dwindling days racing into night.

"Both?" she said. It was only a breath.

He looked as if she had caught him in the act of performing some unspeakable crime. She said, "What have you done? What are you going to do?"

"That's entirely my affair," he said, in an instant cold as stone.

He meant to stop her. But she said. "You're leaving the project. It's over for you. Everything's over. But *why*?"

"I'm in need of a rest too," he said, lying without a sign of guilt. "I should like to go home for a time."

"That is not true."

He said with a sigh, "I wish one could lie to you successfully. I ought to have learned better by now. Leave it, Hanna. Just leave it. The project is a shocking failure, and the responsibility is mine. That's true enough."

"But not the whole truth?"

"It's all the truth that matters," he said impatiently. "The failure is complete, and all mine. You'll drop it, if you have any kindness."

She said, remembering more, "I could ask Peter."

"You don't," he said, and the world split for her; he appeared angry but the appearance was a trick, a diversion, a ploy to cow her into silence, and underneath that was real anger, entirely controlled, but he adamantly would *not* let her know all the truth. "You don't," he said, "know when to give up, do you? But you never did. The subject is closed. Good night, Hanna."

He turned and started away, escaping. His footsteps echoed on hardwood, a nightmare of abandonment from the past. Hanna said, perhaps aloud, perhaps not: "Not this time." She slipped in front of him and blocked his way. She said, "Tell me. Tell me the rest of it or I will take it from your mind. I will tear it out by the roots." *Bluff.* "You owe me. I've died for you, yes, you! how many times? You owe me the truth. You owe me a little of your precious self! You can give it to me or I will take it."

How admirable the uses of deception! He believed her, and she had learned the trick from him.

If he thought there was only one thing to do he would do it, however distasteful. He told her about Struzik, the threats, the ultimatum, the coming end. She stood before him, small and immovable, and listened. He could not bring himself to say: I did this, I gave it all up, for your peace. But it was manifest in everything he said.

Yet still in the short recital there were things he did not say. He had been this way at their first meeting, layered, giving up what he must in order to hide another thing and yet another. She had been his match even then. She was stronger now, and bolder. When he was finished she put out her hands and touched him. His heart beat under her right hand. He made a sharp movement as if to turn away, but he did not. His eyes rested on her face curiously now, and with, she thought, a kind of fatalism. She thought he knew what was coming.

She said softly, "More. The rest."

There is no more.

She heard the words form, but he did not say them. He was caught in suspense and watched himself through a stranger's eyes. It had been hard for him always to resist her touch. This time he could not. Something hurt, wavered, and broke. It was so nearly audible that she started and stepped closer protectively.

All over. It will not matter to anyone. Why not?

He said without any expression at all, "Are you familiar with the term 'profound geriatric failure'?"

"Yes . . ." She looked up into his face without comprehension, distracted by the irrelevance.

"What do you think it is?"

She said, puzzled, "The standard techniques of cellular and hormonal regeneration and toxin removal don't work and they have to use a modified procedure. Everyone knows that."

"No. That's the popular understanding of the term. The medical definition is quite different."

She had gotten very good at disentangling Jameson's substance from his style, and she remembered that he was never irrelevant. She stood very still, except that her hands moved a little, not to caress him but to touch while she could the solid warm flesh, strong and unchanging. She did not want the moment to end. She did not want to go on to the next one. Jameson's face was a mask and she knew past any doubt that she was going to hear something she did not want to hear. But she said, compelled, "What is the medical definition?"

He did not answer at once. He drew her back into the room and to a seat before the cold fireplace. He sat close beside her. Even now, she thought, it was for her comfort, not his.

He said, "It is the rare inadequacy of *all* anti-senescence techniques. Occasionally a victim who continues standard treatment will begin to respond normally. More often, at some unpredictable point, treatment accelerates aging without warning or recourse. The failure is so rapid and overwhelming that no treatment is of any use. The victim dies, of old age or something else, within a year of the last treatment, regardless of his chronological age."

I cannot bear this, Hanna thought.

To feel that one cannot, and know one must and will . . .

Jameson said softly, "The Heartworld political arena is an exciting milieu," and Hanna listened through a blur of

pain. "I was involved in it from the time I could talk—
earlier perhaps. My grandfather might have been commissioner at one time, but Progressive fortunes were low in
those years. My father for many years headed the Provin-
cial Court. He's dead now; he was one hundred and forty
when I was born. My sister married a man of another province and perpetually runs for a council seat. Someday she'll
win, I suppose ... I was very happy. Full of plans, full of
ideas, eager for power and it came year by year, always
growing ... There was so much I wanted to do. A world was
not enough. I thought two centuries would be too short. I
wanted to get to the top early. Later I wanted to do so even
more badly, though for other reasons. But even at the start
I thought of little else."

His voice was very quiet, but he spoke without hesitation. His skin was faintly golden in the soft light and etched
with fine lines Hanna had hardly noticed before. She
thought: *You can't do this. I love you.*

"Nothing," he said, "is constant except change. I came to
want another thing. My family helped found Heartworld
seven hundred years ago. Starrbright has descended in the
direct male line ever since that time, and I could take you
today to Southwest Namerica and show you where my ancestors lived before the Explosion. Starr is a family name; it
has been borne by many men through the centuries, and
some women. I wanted to continue the line. It was time. In
my twenties I thought an entire world of attractive women
had been created just for me; at thirty I looked for a wife. I
wanted a great deal. Beauty, intelligence, breeding, education, character—I don't remember all the list. I have not
thought about it for years. No one suited me, but there was
plenty of time. I thought it was time to prepare for the long
fine future. You haven't started anti-senescence treatments
yet, have you?"

"No," she said, startled into speech. "In a few years, I
guess. There's—" She nearly choked on the next words, but
said them anyway: "No hurry."

"I got around to it at thirty-two, in Standard years. You'll
find that before the initial treatment they do the most extraordinary battery of tests. Before they let you go they tell
you to come back in thirty days and again in six months for
more tests. The six-month visit helps them determine what

modifications need to be made in future treatment. Most people think the thirty-day visit is required for the same reason, but it is not. It's because the infinitesimal fraction of the population for whom the procedure fails react predictably—with a massive immunological failure that will kill if it is not caught at once. I didn't even last the thirty days. I was extremely ill before the time was up. I had never been ill before. I was appalled, even before I knew what had happened. I suppose I thought I was immune to death . . . Afterward I changed my plans."

She waited for him to go on, but he did not. He had said what was necessary. He would not embellish it. Presently she said unevenly, knowing the answer, "You have kept trying?"

"Yes. Each time it does not kill me I gain a little time. There has always been talk about the obscene length of some of my vacations. It takes time to treat widespread carcinoma."

There was not a trace of self-pity in the way he said it. He presented it as a matter of fact, dispassionately. Hanna lifted her hands to her face. They were icy. Everything she knew about him and everything she had not understood was in place now. The mosaic was complete. *There was so much I wanted to do.* So little time for intellect and ambition to mark the passing years, leave an imprint or a legacy. The gamble! Time after time—! For an instant she saw his world as, perhaps, he saw it—a shadowy place of uncertain values, where he stood over an abyss and made what he could from whatever was at hand, building for eternity in spite of time.

She said—with difficulty, because her throat was tight— "I've never heard a word about this. It must be almost unknown."

"It is. It's limited to a handful of medical personnel on Heartworld and at the Beyle Center here, and a very few other persons. My sister . . . I suppose Morisz knows. He knows everything about everybody. The last time I spoke of it was five years ago to Andrella Murphy."

He leaned back, exhausted. She could not guess what these few minutes had cost him.

And all the past weeks? What of them?

The enormity of his sacrifice gained on her comprehension, but only slowly; it was too large to see all at once. All debts were cleared forever. He could owe her nothing more. He had paid back everything at once, magnificently, with everything he had and everything he wanted; with all of himself.

She found her voice somewhere. There was one question more that must be asked.

"Why . . . ?"

"Why what?" He looked at her finally. He was exhausted beyond fear or need of defense.

"Why did you—do what you did for me?"

He said, "I don't know why."

"You never do anything without a reason!"

He said with the ghost of a smile, "No doubt there is one."

"You must . . . you must have said something to yourself." She touched him at last. He took her hand; automatically, it seemed. She said, "You must have told yourself something. What did you say? When you decided?"

"Just that—I couldn't." He was mystified by it still. "I couldn't press you, persuade you, work on your sense of duty, seize on your—your frightening generosity—let the others try to do it, coerce you into service—or 'adjust' you, as Peter suggested—I couldn't. You'd earned freedom many times over. I couldn't do anything to keep it from you. I just could not."

Why? But she did not say it again. He really did not know. Something dormant and forgotten had been forced to new life by circumstance, or by Hanna herself. He had said: No more. I will not buy power with her pain. I will not.

She got up and drifted away from him, thinking she ought to speak and unable to say a word. What was there to say? She could not talk of gratitude. He did not want her gratitude. He would not like it. The wind from the garden whispered round her head. She felt curiously light: light and free.

Freedom. It had an odd taste. Her life was her own. He would let no one else shape it. He stood between her and all the massed moral force of the Polity, unbending.

"What will they do without us?" she said.

"Damned if I know . . ."

"Try to live forever?"

"Yes. Oh, yes."

"Was that why you—?"

She looked around hesitantly. He was standing now, wrapped in all his old dignity in spite of weariness.

"That is not for me," he said. "It could never be for me."

Truth. Whole truth.

She wandered uncertainly toward the outer door and looked into the dark. "Will they think of the evils that may come?"

"Some. Not much. The reward is potent."

The future on his shoulders—

I have too . . .

"You know," she said slowly, "I thought that you would be in charge. That everything was safe. Even if we didn't agree on what should come you would listen. Even tonight. You would judge. You wouldn't decide lightly. I could leave it to you."

He said, "They're not evil. They'll manage without me . . . I must learn to believe that."

"But will they think of the People?" she said. "Someone must."

Free, oh, free! To go home and build a city, arbitrate the Riverine dispute which surely went on still, prod a university to action, play sweet starlit games with laughing boys . . .

He said at her back, certain as ever: "There is nothing you could do. Even if you were willing to participate, what could you do against all the rest?"

She saw D'neera suddenly and clearly, as if all her life there had been compressed to crystal and brought to this room for her pleasure. Flowers, laughter, light, beloved sea, star-powdered nights; but it did not need her—it receded as she watched—the laughter faded.

She said, "I could do more than you think." It was true. She did not know all her own potential yet, but it was true. "I'm unique. We haven't talked about it much, but you know it. Unless you create another like me—years away, you said—there will be no one who can do what I could do. And I could—be their guard and sentinel. They shouldn't be our servants. Or maybe we would become theirs, and maybe that would be wrong too. Or maybe not. But they must see all of it, all the possibilities. That they must shape themselves as they want. And we must see it too. And if I were to—when you told me all the things you wanted me to do, that first day—if I were to—"

She turned and saw that he seemed to have stopped breathing. There was no color in his face. She went on with difficulty, "If I were to do all that, it would be ... you were giving me more than tasks to do, weren't you? You were asking me to ... when you said I would be the guide—you meant, did you know it? that all the project would be in, in my image, our future with them—and yours, if we worked together—"

The words came very hard. She was so tired of decision and labor, someone, someone, must instruct the People not to permit themselves to be bent to human self-serving, there was no one else but it was so hard to give herself freely, even for this. She wanted Jameson to say something, but he did not. He was utterly still, remote as the People's star. Her hands crept together and her fingers sought the Heir's Ring of Koroth, but it was not there. She had searched, but never found it. It was lost in the dust of Home.

"And you could—you would—if I came to the project, the way you wanted—then you could be there too, and—would it have to be war between us?"

He shook his head abruptly, and suddenly sat down. He put a hand over his eyes. She looked down at him with compassion and a profound regret. She was giving back the gift, and it was a terrible gift to make to one so proud. She thought: Perhaps I have just lost whatever chance there was for love in his strange code. But no one else will ever see again what I see now. But I wish it could be the other way.

"I will do it," she said. The voice sounded strange in her ears, as if it were someone else's. But at last she knew it, clearly, for her own.

THE MASTER OF CHAOS

This book is for Maurine K. Kelly.

Chapter 1

Rubee of Ell of the world Uskos said to Hanna ril-Koroth of D'neera, "You are the possessor of a wonderful house. It is fair as the Wonderful House of Piore."

Rubee lied, with utmost courtesy. Hanna accepted the courtesy and disregarded the lie.

"It is your house as well," she answered with equal politeness, and lay back on a pale blue couch that glimmered cool pastel in the dusk, like everything in her house at twilight; wonderful to her, at least, as the Wonderful House of Piore could ever have been to him. Or to her? Or it? Uskosians all were called "he," because they had to be called something. But no human word was really right.

Rubee and his selfing Awnlee wandered about and touched things in the growing gloom. Their fingers at full extension resembled thin tentacles; flexed, they were like roots. An Uskosian had not truly seen a thing until he had touched it, and here on the world D'neera, where nothing that could be embellished was left plain, the lively fingers of Rubee and Awnlee were busy.

There was not much to touch in this house, however. Though it was the home of a D'neeran, the place was austere, the character of its rooms a matter of color and form. The sunward wall of Hanna's sitting room was transparent; the house was built into a hillside, so that this upper level looked down on a lawn and water garden (the pool frozen now), and past that a line of trees, and beyond that a distant fringe of light marking the edge of the city D'vornan. That was decoration enough for Hanna, and the view was fresh after her long absence.

Hanna had been gone from home for six Standard months.

Since the Uskosian envoys' announcement of their presence
in human space, she had spent all her time on the powerful
Polity worlds, Earth mostly, studying Rubee and Awnlee—
and often feeling more like a tour guide than a scholar.
Neighbors had tended her home, made sure the servomechanisms kept working, cleared away the debris of autumn
storms. She thought, smiling, that when she came home for
good, she would owe a great arrears of community service.

But that would not be for a long time. There was yet a
longer journey to make first.

Rubee formulated a question. Hanna was a telepath, but
she knew Rubee so well that she saw it coming with her
eyes. The alien said, "You live in this house alone?"

"When I can. When I can live on my homeworld at all, I
mean; when I am not on other worlds doing its business. I
lived here alone for some months before you came. Before
that I lived in City Koroth, in the House of its governing
women, which we visited yesterday. I lived there with many
others. I came here to D'vornan to teach at the University,
which we visit tomorrow. I like it better here."

"But I thought," Rubee said, "D'neera is a—" *(something,*
said the translator tucked into Hanna's ear) "—society, because it is a society of telepaths."

"Think that again," Hanna said wearily, and dipped into
Rubee's thought, unclipped the memory bank at her waist,
and gave the translator a new word.

Communal.

She said, "On the whole D'neerans live communally. I
am an exception. Exceptions are freely tolerated."

"Ah," said Rubee, understanding, or thinking that he understood, and Hanna watched Rubee and Awnlee and wondered how long it would be before she saw her home again.

She was so glad to be there that for all her liking for
these strange guests, and in spite of the importance of her
work with them, she dreaded going away with them again.
She was only at home because the envoys were making
courtesy visits everywhere, and Hanna's own planet was a
stop on the itinerary the Polity's officials had made up for
them. The portion of her duty that would start in a few
months more—to accompany the envoys when they returned to Uskos—meant it would be at least two Standard
years before she saw her home again.

The six months she had been gone were already too long. *No one else can befriend and guide these beings as well as you can,* Polity Alien Relations and Contact had said to her when the Uskosians arrived; *no one has your experience, there is no one like you.* The director of Contact had given her other reasons for accepting the task, not including personal ones. If he had included personal reasons she would have listened, even though that was another story, an old love story, a finished one; for Hanna it was not as finished as it ought to be, and perhaps memories had helped make her decision. Yet in the end it was no one's good reasons, no flattery, no sense of duty that had captured her. It was curiosity. She was heir to the governing House of Province Koroth and would one day be its Magistrate, but first she was an exopsychologist. She knew the aliens of F'thal and Girritt, she had walked among the Primitives, and she was humankind's authority on the People of Zeig-Daru, but she could not resist a new thing.

Awnlee was too young to be anything but honest. He said, "This home cannot really be like the Wonderful House of Piore."

Rubee turned and looked at his selfing. The Uskosian face was rigid except for the ciliated mouth, the eye-spots were shifting patches of gray sparked with iridescence, and the gaze was a new experience for humans. Body language said everything the face did not, and Hanna saw (from the position of the whiplike fingers, the carriage of the lumpy body, even the angle of the stubby feet) that Awnlee meant to return to the plane of realistic assessment.

Rubee conceded, "It is not. But it has its own beauty."

"It belongs to you as well as me," Hanna said correctly. Then—because she was working, because she was always working—she said, "What was the Wonderful House of Piore?"

"Do you wish a formal presentation?" Rubee asked.

"Informal," Hanna said promptly, because she was less interested in ritual presentation of the elaborate myths of Uskos—though that was an important art form—than in their function in everyday life.

"In a year," Rubee said, and his unmelodic voice was richer, deeper, "Piore sought to build a house. 'I will shelter me from the elements,' Piore said, and he builded a

house of importance, and admired it, and widely admired
it was. The earth quaked, and it foundered. Piore stood in
the ruins lamenting, and the Master of Chaos came to him
and signified amusement. 'Why do you signify amusement?' said Piore, and the Master of Chaos answered,
'High was your house and imposing; yet the foundation
was not strong.'

"And Piore said, 'I will build me a house of great
strength,' and he did. Yes, strong it was, well-founded and
impenetrable, so that all his selfings came there saying,
'Now we shall be safe.' And safe they were and earthquake
did not move it. Yet it was forbidding, and save for Piore's
selfings no one came to it, and Piore was lonely; and the
Master of Chaos came to him and signified amusement.
And Piore said, 'Why do you signify amusement?' 'I signify
amusement,' said the Master of Chaos, 'because you have
forgotten the Tale of Taree.'"

(The— *Oh, God,* Hanna thought. *Myths within myths
within myths!*)

"Then Piore remembered the Tale of Taree, and he
pulled down the house and rebuilded it, and now it was
both strong and fair; but Piore was jealous of it, and let no
one in, and sent away his selfings. But Authority came and
said, 'It is not permitted to make such a thing just here,' and
tore it down. Piore stood in the ruins lamenting, and the
Master of Chaos came and signified amusement. Piore said,
'Why do you signify amusement?' 'I signify amusement,'
said the Master of Chaos, 'because you can't win.' 'I know
that,' said Piore, 'as who does not?'

"The Master of Chaos disappeared, and Piore builded
again. He chose a place by a beautiful river, but consulted
Authority first. He made a fine foundation and the beauty
of his home was remarkable, and it endured through quake
and windstorm, and all came there and were happy.

"Yet finally Piore died; and the Master of Chaos came,
and signified amusement. So it is until this minute!"

Rubee made a quick motion of the feet that meant he
was finished. Hanna mentally assigned the tale to the category she had begun to think of as "the dark stories" and did
not ask for interpretation. She was not in a mood to hear
how Chaos always got the last word. She only said politely,
"Thank you for your fine telling."

"It is now ours," Rubee said graciously.

"Yes. Well." Hanna pulled herself to her feet. "Now there are friends I promised to call. Later we will feed, and later sleep. We have a busy morrow."

"I wish," Awnlee said wistfully, "we had not to address your colleagues. I am weary of speeches."

"Me too . . ." Hanna reached for a light and was shocked when her fingers did not at once remember where the control was. Then they did, and the room was bright. For a second the outer wall reflected all of them, before the house damped the image to transparency: the aliens with their changing hands, bundled against the cool air, so like in appearance that one might have been a reflection of the other, except that age had altered one; and the slight human being, dark and blue-eyed, looking about as if she were the stranger here.

"I would like to see the waterfall you love so much, and the sea you love to walk beside. And your sib-selfings, no, your 'family,'" Awnlee said with increasing enthusiasm. "And, oh, the beasts on whose backs you learned to ride nearby, which are beautiful through your eyes. Must we have speeches?"

Hanna was very fond of Awnlee. She looked at him with affection and said, "My dear friend, I'm afraid we must. The university program here is me, or I am it, at least sometimes I think so. Anyway it's here and important because of me. They would never forgive me if we didn't go."

"But I will show you all of my world when we go there!"

"Well, I will show you as much of this one as I can. But I think it cannot be as beautiful to you as your own."

"Perhaps," Rubee said. "But remember the Journey of Nlatee," he added, and looked at her sharply.

Hanna knew that one, and signified amusement properly.

The order had all the frills and flourishes at the beginning that the administrators of the Interworld Polity could wish. Underneath the frills there was a line specifying that the order had been issued by the Director of the Department of Alien Relations and Contact. The document looked official, but it was only a draft. It said: "The following personnel will report on the schedule shown to Level 14,

Conference Room A." That was innocuous; it gave nothing away. The schedule that followed was a long one. It stretched over three weeks, and assigned dates and times for one hundred and fifty names.

Commissioner Edward Vickery scrolled through the list. His mouth was screwed up with distaste. He said, "You can't do this, Starr."

"Why not?" said the Contact director, who had written the order.

"Probes of this many people? With no legitimate reason? They've all got clearance for the Uskosian project, they've all been investigated—you have to have evidence to justify a probe, Starr. *Each* probe, on an individual basis. And what have you got for justification?—one unconfirmed rumor. No. I don't know why you even brought me this."

The Contact director said, "Your authority might carry sufficient weight. And think of the consequences if the rumor, as you call it, is true."

"It isn't. It can't be."

"What if it is?"

Vickery looked up from the moving script, exasperated. He preferred to be tactful with Starr Jameson, but it was not easy. Vickery was Heartworld's representative to the Coordinating Commission of the Interworld Polity. Seven years ago the man on the other side of his desk had held that high positon, and left it, if not quite in disgrace, at least under duress, to accept the directorship of the then-new Contact department. The Commissioner from Heartworld also was chairman of the Commission's Committee on Alien Relations, so Vickery had inherited that from Jameson, too, and with it hegemony over Contact and Jameson himself. Jameson had never said to Vickery: *I ought to be still in your place.* But maybe he thought it.

Vickery said, "When I say you can't do this, I mean literally that you can't get away with it. Mass probes are a rights violation on the face of it, not to mention a gross breach of protocol. There would be an appeal to the Commission and you wouldn't have a hope. Don't try it."

Jameson did not answer at once. He was a master of the uses of silence; Vickery knew that, and resolved not to speak first. The list of times and names finished its passage and went dark. It was summer in southeastern Namerica on

Earth, and the morning sun shone placidly on the river that ran by Vickery's office; this room also had once been Jameson's. The water came to the very edge of the room, its whisper the only sound.

Jameson said finally, "There is something you should see. Tap into my office files."

"I don't have much time, Starr."

"It isn't long." Jameson began to recite a string of codes. *Humor him,* Vickery thought, and entered the sequence in his desktop. "Holo," Jameson added. Vickery made an adjustment and there were flickers of darkness in the center of the room: moving shadows of roughly human shape. Jameson swiveled to watch them.

Vickery said, "What's wrong? I can't make it out."

"The figure on the left is an Intelligence and Security undercover operative on Valentine. The one on the right is an informant. The visual and vocal patterns have been scrambled to protect their identities. Listen."

"—satisfactory?" the shadow on the left said. The voice was metallic.

"All right. I guess. Not exactly getting rich."

"Come up with something good."

"That was good, wasn't it? The . . . connection?"

Vickery said, "What?"

"A name," Jameson said. "Censored."

The agent said, "We had it from another source. Give me something new."

"All right, here's something, you'll like this. Somebody knows where the bird will fly."

The agent said after a minute, "Well?"

"Well, what?"

"What's that mean?"

"The *Bird. Far-Flying Bird,* the aliens' ship. Somebody's interested in how it gets home. It's carrying value, isn't it? I think: hijack."

"You're spaced."

"All I know is what I hear."

"You must've heard wrong. Can't intercept a ship in Inspace flight, not even in the realspace interludes. Too many variables. Ship's computers can't predict on the mark where a Jump brings it out. Much less an outsider. Takes time to home in, gives a target time to get away."

"What I hear. Anyway it's been done. Man right here on Valentine did it."

"That was different," said the agent. "That was a trick. Nobody's going to fall for that again."

"So you won't pay me?"

"No bonus. Not for that. Get me more."

Jameson's deep voice cut into the conversation. "The rest is just haggling. Turn it off."

Vickery touched a switch and the figures were gone. Jameson said, "Suppose it is true. Suppose the Uskosian vessel's course program for the return flight has been, or can be, tapped in detail, so that interception is possible. Would you care to explain to the Uskosians how their envoys died on the way home?"

Vickery said, "What if somebody just wants to get to Uskos before a diplomatic party does? One of the non-Polity worlds. An alien alliance is the kind of thing they'd think of on Nestor."

Jameson said, "The risk is negligible. Uskos is a sophisticated society. The difficulties for Nestor would be insurmountable, with or without the presence of the envoys and Hanna ril-Koroth. I am concerned with the cargo, the gift, the treasure the *Bird* will carry. It is enormously valuable. The rumor that has come to the attention of I&S came from criminal circles. I think the issue is the material value of the *Bird's* cargo. I&S even has a likely name—the name of the man the informant referred to. Do you want to know what it is?"

A red light began to blink on Vickery's desk. He was overdue for an appointment. "Later, Starr."

"Do you remember the piracy of the *Pavonis Queen* twenty Standard years ago?"

Vickery shook his head impatiently. Jameson said, "It carried a fortune in negotiable currencies of all sorts under the terms of the Colonial Credit Standardization Agreement of ST 2822. Its course was known, or was supposed to have been known, only to a few of the highest-ranking officials of the Polity. Nonetheless the *Queen* was intercepted, and all the monies stolen. The perpetrators were never formally identified. The man believed to be responsible was never charged. I&S has mentioned him in connection with the supposed accessibility of the *Bird's* course."

"I have to go."

"His name is Michael Kristofik. He lives on Valentine, and he has been a very rich man since the *Pavonis Queen* incident. The *Bird*'s cargo would appeal to him."

"Is I&S in favor of this mass probe?"

"Of course."

"They would be. But I tell you anyway—you can't do it. Think of something else. Alter the program."

"The Uskosians will not alter it."

"Have you asked them?"

"I have not. But I have read all Hanna's reports. I do not think they will alter it."

"Ask them!"

"Naturally," Jameson said. He got up without warning and went to the door. When he got to it he turned around and said, "All the same, they won't."

Vickery supposed Jameson was right. Usually, infuriatingly, he was.

Coming down through the great sky the planet looked like any other world where humans could breathe the air. It might have been Valentine, it might have been Earth—but Michael Kristofik, looking out the nose of the sporting yacht *Golden Girl*, automatically corrected the thought. He didn't go to Earth any more. He could never go there again.

The name of this world was Carrollis, and it was not safe for offworlders. That was not because of natural hazards, but because of the colonists. The name of the planet's only town was Town. Carrollis produced furs, brilliant blue, poisonous green, flaming gold; the fauna were colorful there. The skins of hard-hunted amphibians, splotched with color, dazzling, decorated the richest women in human space.

There was no government. Governments meant taxes, and the colonists did not tolerate taxes.

If you went to Town on the night of Market Day you went armed, and everybody went; tonight Michael Kristofik did, too. He did not worry about danger. He was tall and broad-shouldered and visibly armed, and he was not alone. He went through Town asking questions with two people at his back. The fair young man with the uncertain face might not be much protection, but the woman was something else. Like Michael she carried a stunner, but her hand kept going to the butt and she caressed it sensuously. There was a glitter in her eyes that made men look away.

Michael was looking for a man called Prissy. He wasn't hard to find.

Prissy ran the only sensory all-around in Town. On Market Day the shows were continuous and Prissy packed them in, the hunters and the trappers and the offworld buyers, so the whole-sense bubble a man occupied might overlap his neighbor's and the edges of the scene and the sound were blurred, the smells and the tastes and the pressures on the skin got mixed up. The shows in the morning were not so bad, sex and skin in tired old patterns, old as video. They got rougher as the day went on. By nightfall on Market Day every trader and trapper in Town was spaced and flying, there were no more restraints, and some of them liked to watch recorded death.

Prissy took hard money or barter for payment, either way. He kept the skins locked away in the most sophisticated vault Polity technology could provide. He liked to count the cash, though, especially on Market Day, when it poured in. He counted it in a locked room behind the all-around, where a window that from the other side looked like a wall let him monitor the sensory generators running the show.

On the night of this Market Day he counted his money while the show went on. He did not look at the video monitor, but he heard the sounds: screeches and moans and sometimes a shout, rattles, screams. It was a new show. Not all the performers in it had survived it, neither the women nor the men, and they had died in peculiar ways. While the taped agonies played out, Prissy counted his money and a girl sat at his side and watched. She was a child on the edge of adolescence, very fair and pretty. Her face was bruised and she was sulking. Her name was Lise.

Something hit the door from outside and then it fell in without much noise, not enough for the crowd behind the other wall to notice. Prissy had a disruptor in his hand before it finished falling, but there were three of them running in, two men and a woman, and he didn't decide fast enough who to aim for first. He fell over his money, stunned. The girl was out a second later.

They laid Prissy out like a dead man. The fair man unstrapped a case from his waist and took out instruments. He began to feed a yellow liquid through a tube into Prissy's right arm. The woman glanced at a monitor, where numbers were superimposed on the action. She looked at the convulsed bodies without expression and focused on the numbers. "Twenty minutes," she said, and set herself to face the broken doorway, stunner at full power. Dark hair licked with bronze, taut body cased in black: her face might have been carved in stone.

Michael Kristofik looked down at the pair on the floor and waited. He also wore black. Theo the medic had known him six years, but looked up now and was struck as if by a stranger's face, the tension and the concentration. Theo thought: *Portrait of a Man Waiting*.

Theo said, "He ought to be ready, Mike," and backed away in a crouch. Michael knelt and took hold of Prissy's flabby chin and turned it. The woman moved a little, still watching the door, to shield Michael's back.

The eyes of the unconscious man opened, focused on nothing. Michael said, "Prissy. That's what they call you, isn't it? Prissy?"

"Yeah . . ." Barely a word.

"You had a meeting," Michael said, "two weeks ago, here, with a man who called himself Chrome. Remember?"

"Remember," Prissy said obligingly, slurring it.

"Where was he going from here?"

"Val'ntime."

"Valentine?"

"What I said."

"Christ . . ."

The woman with the stunner made a hissing sound. Michael looked up and met Theo's eyes. He made a wry face. "Might as well have stayed home," he said.

"Shit."

"Prissy. This Chrome. What's he calling himself on Valentine?"

"Maz'well."

"Mazwell?"

"Max. Well."

"What Maxwell? Where?"

"Shor'ground."

"Shoreground. Maxwell of Shoreground. They're having a festival in Shoreground. It's packed. How long was he going to be there?"

Prissy heaved. It was a whole-body shrug.

"You have any way to get in touch with him?"

"Gran' Square Inn. Just ask. Maxwell."

"What about after that? What if he's left the inn?"

"Won't. Be there a while."

"How long is a while?"

"Just said a while."

Theo said, "We have to get back to Valentine."

"Yeah. Now. Six days home, Christ! Our timing's bad. He's up to something and on the move. If we lose him now, we start all over. All right. Knock him out."

They grouped at the door a little later. The sounds still went on from the all-around. The screams were steady now, and terrible, and the crowd roared.

"Mike . . ." The woman touched his sleeve. She pointed at the girl whose bruised face in sleep was that of an angelic child. The woman said, "You hear in there? Around here today, I heard this Prissy'll do a new show, the fatal kind, like that. She's in it. Doesn't know it. Kill her slow, she doesn't know."

Michael's arm twitched. His face, alive and expressive the moment before, went dead. He said, "Where'd he get her?"

"Don't know. Some mother some father some poor sick colony place sold her. Thought, better life for her, maybe. Innocent, maybe. Maybe not so innocent. Maybe they knew."

Michael went to the girl and picked her up. He slung her over his shoulder without difficulty. He touched one thin arm; there was an old scar on the back of it. He said, "Come on, Theo. He's yours, Shen. I don't care what you do."

Theo said in a strangled voice, "What's wrong with you?"

"Look," Michael Kristofik said. He jerked his head at the monitor but did not look at it himself. Theo did. He turned away quickly; a second later, as if squeezed by a violent hand, he vomited.

"Somebody else just pick up what he leaves," Shen said.

"I know. I hate this place."

Theo whispered, "He wouldn't have remembered a thing."

"I know."

Michael and Theo slipped out. Shen followed a minute later, flexing her fingers. She said, "Anyway this Prissy might have warned *him*. Nobody's looking at us. Gotta keep it that way."

They melted into the night, the girl still unconscious and so light she was little burden.

Now they were on Willow. The five worlds of the Interworld Polity had among them most of humanity's people and nearly all its wealth. Willow was the only one Hanna found tolerable.

Earth, oldest and first, was too crowded. Flying above its knots of light at night she longed for darkness, caught in the cities' ceaseless noise she wanted silence, met at every turn by servos she was conscious as nowhere else of the power in her own slim strong body, the talents of her hands. The planet also was too ancient, groaning with the weight of its past. Hanna was a child of the colonies, none of whose histories went back more than seven hundred years. (Yet she thought of seven hundred years because that was how long it was in Standard years, and Standard was synonymous with Earthly.) Earth furthermore was the seat of Polity Administration, and Hanna's whole experience of humankind's first home was colored by her work for and with and sometimes against that triumph of committees and bureaucracy. Earth was where she had learned to navigate the currents of power, more dangerous and deceptive than the tides between the stars.

On Co-op the air changed erratically and sometimes was hard to breathe. Some years the wind scraped the best lands clean of growth. Coopers taught their children early how to shoot; they had good reasons; a boy of eight had once saved Hanna's life there, shooting by reflex before she turned and saw the toothed shape behind her. Coopers did not like D'neerans. Their ancestors had not wanted to go to Co-op in the first place. The Founders of D'neera also had been outcast from Earth, but more justly, Coopers thought. It is one thing to engineer a populace to telepathy, another to live with the results. Why had true-humans gotten Co-op, and the telepaths lush D'neera? It was not fair. It ought to have been the other way around.

Hanna didn't like Coopers any better than they liked her.

Toward Colony One she was indifferent. It sought to be another Earth and disregarded what Earth should have taught it. There were towns without beauty, one much like another, forests falling, air dark with grit, machines carving the land, a maddening buzz of change. Colony One, Hanna thought, lacked character.

Heartworld had character, but she did not like what it had. That was Starr Jameson's home, and while she lived with him—though she had lived with him only on Earth— she had learned all she needed to know about Heartworld's character.

("I could not take you home with me. Not permanently. As a visitor, of course—"

"As mistress you mean, then. Never the partner of your life."

"Impossible for many reasons. We should not even talk of this."

"I know there are other reasons. But this is the only one to cause me bitterness. I am not good enough for the aristocracy. That is what you mean."

"You are good enough for anyone. But appearances."

"Are more important than the love I bear for you."

"Yes. You cannot reproach me with dishonesty, at least. Yes.")

So when she went to Heartworld (because she had to go; as unofficial ambassador to true-humans she went everywhere), she stayed in the cities and never saw the lands where a family estate might take up an appreciable part of a continent, and Starrbright not the least; never saw the silent wilderness or the harvests that fed much of the human race. And he was right, of course. H'ana ril-Koroth of D'neera was an important person everywhere—except on Heartworld. They made her feel it, too, and they did not even mean to.

Willow, though: all its meanings to Hanna were good. She was in love with the sky-capped trees that gave the world its name. They did not grow in a wide range, so that many citizens of Willow had never seen them close up, but they grew where the first settlers had proclaimed a capital city. The sinuous branches came to the ground in cascades of delicate green, and to stand within the hollow space they made when the sun shone was to feel that you rested inside the peace of a single leaf, so sweet a green was the light.

Unlike Heartworld or Earth or Colony One or Co-op, Willow had a single government and one capital, the city of Ducelle. It was named after one of the explorers who had come upon this jewel in the night of space, and its buildings were fair and commodious. Many were built of a pink-tinged stone quarried nearby, and the rosy facades were impudent against the willows' green.

Hanna had spent some weeks in one of them, before she was famous. She remembered Ducelle's good wines and its strong young men with pleasure. When she went to Willow she did not feel thirty-one and official. On Willow, sometimes, she could forget what she had gone through to get that way.

Now that Hanna was famous, when she came to Willow she lived comfortably in private homes. She and Rubee and Awnlee were lodged in the home of Willow's Commissioner, bright-eyed Andrella Murphy.

On the party's last night in Ducelle, which was not supposed to be its last night, Hanna and Rubee and Awnlee dined in Murphy's home. There were no visitors, Murphy's husband had gone out, the meal was informal, and Rubee and Awnlee were relaxed. They had taken many meals among humans now, but they had not learned to like being stared at while they ate. Hanna was too used to the pair and their foods and their habits to stare, and Murphy was too polite. The four shared the evening companionably, Awnlee doing most of the talking and bubbling about the willows, which were so famous that many persons had forgotten they were named after an Earthly tree instead of the other way around. The wines of the region were as good as Hanna remembered. She became a little light-headed. She wished to learn to speak and understand the major language of Uskos without a translator and so she had switched it off; but she was not yet proficient in the tongue, and resorted automatically to telepathic receptivity, so that Awnlee's excitement, imperfectly understood, entered her blood with the wine and aroused her.

She stopped listening to Awnlee and drifted with the

lavender evening and the blushing stone, thinking of Uskos.
Hers would be the first human eyes to see it, as they had
been the first to see Zeig-Daru. This time the privilege
would cost much less. Rubee's folk were not like the People
of Zeig-Daru. Probably nothing was, anywhere. The People
were almost a good enough reason to give up space. But
this time there would be no horror to face. "I promise you,"
Starr Jameson had said when he first told her of the envoys,
"that this time there is no threat, no hostility; you will be
guarded and protected until you are satisfied; if you find the
slightest cause to fear them, you can stop at once. No pain
this time. No torture or danger or fear."

Only excitement. Only the work she loved best. And the
long voyage, longer than any human had yet taken, to a
civilization that next to those of Zeig-Daru and F'thal
seemed blessedly comprehensible.

Into Hanna's reflections, and the gentle lights that twinkled in her head and kissed every part of the room, there
came from somewhere in the business part of Murphy's
home an aide. He bent low and spoke in Murphy's ear. She
excused herself and left with a look of surprise. Awnlee
rambled on: "—and the horses possessed by D'neera, but
they came from Earth, you said. But we saw none there.
You ride as one with them, but I fell off. Did it take you long
to own that skill—?" He did not wait for an answer, but
went on. He liked humans' wine, if not their food; his ready
speech was stimulated.

Murphy returned. She sat down and said to Hanna, "I
have just talked with Starr. I have news for you."

Everything seemed agreeable to Hanna. She anticipated
no anxiety. "What news?" she said.

"Your visit is to be curtailed. You are to return to Earth,
all of you."

"Why?"

"I don't know. He wouldn't say. He said he will speak of
it when he sees you."

"Should I call him?"

"No, no, it won't do any good. He means: when he sees
you. Not before."

"Is something wrong?"

After rather a long pause Murphy said, "Perhaps."

Hanna looked at her silently in the candlelight. It was

clear that Murphy had some knowledge connected with this matter, yet had not expected the call. She felt Murphy waiting suspiciously, waiting for Hanna to search out the current of thought withheld. Ordinary humans, true-humans, non-telepathic, thought such currents were crystal to D'neerans, and easily accessible. In the usual way of things, though, they were murky as the mudpits of Nestor. It took effort to bring them to light.

Hanna let it go. *How like Starr to summon us so; a trip of days through space without explanation, and worry at the end.*

She smiled at Murphy, poise unflawed. And changed the subject.

Rubee and Awnlee had understood the words they heard, but the nuances of human communication were beyond the translator. They could not hear what happened between the words. Hanna talked of something else, and that was enough for them. The night passed quietly to its end. Next day they were traveling again.

Her mouth was soft and delicious. Oh, blessed desire. He did not wake all at once. Body first: *yes yes yes.* Skin painfully smooth, hair drifting on his hot cheeks like cool tangled cloud. Mind was slower. There was no one here to do this, no one who should be doing this. Trapped between alarm and lust he called for light. Lise smiled down at him. The smile faded when she saw his face.

"There she is . . ." Shen stood in the doorway. She leaned against it with folded arms. "Interrupting?"

"No. Not. Take her," he said with regret, "out of here."

His bed was on a platform, not very high. The wall at his head was cut away to show the stars. He turned and they spun; he buried his head in thick cushions.

"C'mon," Shen said from close by. "He doesn't want you that way."

Michael muttered, "Don't bet on it."

A hand slipped under the single cover and trailed down his back. His skin quivered and the fine hairs stood up. Lise said to Shen, an edge in her soft voice, "Are you his woman?"

"I'm nobody's woman. Come on. Mike? Some help."

He came out of the cushions long enough to say, "Go with her, Lise. That's not what I brought you along for."

"You like boys?" she said dubiously.

"Not especially. Tomorrow I'll try to explain. Again. Go on, now."

She let Shen take her away. When they were gone Michael got a time readout. Still early, Shen's watch, but he wanted no more sleep. He got up and discovered that the burst of longing so painfully ended had left him feeling physically sick. Self-congratulation on morality was no consolation. He had gotten little Lise mixed up with the women who came to him in dreams, perfect, elusive. While he dressed the room sang to him sorrowfully.

> *Dear, when I from thee am gone*
> *Gone are all my joys at once.*
> *I loved thee, and thee alone;*
> *In whole love I joyed once . . .*

The sweet harmonies belonged to an age a millennium gone. A lute kept them company. Michael sang along with the voices, fluent in the archaic language. His voice was an excellent baritone, not untrained but unself-conscious. He stopped singing when Shen came back.

"Put her to bed," Shen said. "Maybe stay there this time. Thought you told her yesterday."

"I did. And the day before that and the day before that. I thought she understood."

"Doesn't understand much. Thought about what she'll do?"

"Not much. I don't have any idea what to do with her, to tell you the truth."

Shen waved at the bed. "All she knows. Since eight, nine, maybe sooner."

"Don't tell me about it. I'll get sick. How old do you think she is now?"

"Eleven Standard, maybe? Tried talking to her. School, home, like that. Blank. Like I said—all she knows."

"So we keep her a few years and when she's old enough she can be a Registered Friend. If that's what she wants. We couldn't leave her there."

Shen did not answer. Perhaps she was thinking they

might very well have left her there. Michael said finally, "All right. What?"

Shen said, "Bad time, Mike. No room for a kid."

"Wasn't room for you, Shen Lo-Yang."

The green eyes snapped. "Not fair."

"You talk fair to me? Never mind fair. Listen, when we get home I'll talk to Flora. She'll come up with something."

"She want a baby girl? Dump her back in your lap. Be gone a long time, Mike. If we catch up this time."

It was a long speech for Shen. When Michael did not answer she added, "Long time maybe before a start. 'Maxwell of Shoreground.' Say he's not at the inn. Then?"

"Find a lead and keep moving."

"He started 'bout when we did. Moving. Running?"

"No. Not away from something, anyway, certainly not from us. He doesn't even know we're after him. Look at the pattern of his contacts. On Nestor he bought a corvette. With its teeth pulled; but there was the arms operation at home, the one I thought shut down a year ago. He made that buy. Look at what he bought. Heavy stuff. He's arming that 'vette for big game. Then Carrollis—that Prissy brokered more than blood. He's moving in on something."

She sat down on the edge of his bed and said unhappily, "New. Don't like new."

"Not so new. He's had armed craft before. And used the arms," Michael said, and there was another wrench in his stomach.

"Not here." Her eyes slanted up and she waited for the effect.

But the answer was calm. "Not here. Nobody knows him here—at least, the Polity doesn't, not Fleet, not I&S. He can go anywhere. Nobody looks twice. He wants to keep it that way. Why guns? What's he going after? So maybe he's getting ready to head out."

"Better catch up quick."

"Right."

"'Cause if he goes we lose him. Couple years at least."

"Yeah."

"Got this kid."

"I know. It's a day yet to Valentine. We'll think of something."

"Strays," Shen said on her way out.

"What?"

"You got another stray."

Michael smiled. When Shen was gone he stopped smiling, not because of anything she had said but because the aftermath of desire had left him hollow. *The trouble with a dream.* He sat down and thought about it carefully. The trouble with a dream was that it had everything you wanted, promise and fulfillment at the same time. When you were awake there was the promise, or you thought it was there; then fulfillment was elusive. Not the women's fault. They thought you promised something, too. *Do you know what you want? What is the promise you think you hear?*

The *Far-Flying Bird* orbited Luna. Hanna had been aboard her many times, but she never approached the *Bird* without feeling the pleasure first sight had given her.

An Interworld Fleet harbor jockey took her from Earth to the *Bird,* so she had nothing to do but watch the glorious silver sight come closer. The *Bird* was long and slender and carried what appeared to be folded-back wings like those of a diving water bird. The "wings" harbored the *Bird*'s mechanical and Inspace-analog systems, and they had an arrogant curve to them, a daring arch that challenged space. They were in no sense functional wings. The *Bird* had never entered atmosphere, and her designers might have housed her guts in a thousand different ways. But the Uskosians, so far as Hanna had been able to ascertain, made nothing without making it beautiful; not consciously or deliberately, but carelessly, easily, without thinking much about it.

Presently the shuttle she rode docked at the junction of wing and body. When she stepped off the shuttle, she walked into a world where it was a little hot and she weighed just a little more than on worlds the human race had claimed. The walls were curved and colored so that the self-contained environment of the *Bird* offered an infinite selection of vistas. That was intentional. Rubee and Awnlee had been in space for three Standard years.

Starr Jameson waited for her by appointment in a room designed (she had been told) to lift the spirits. It was an eruption of color and had many odd angles she liked. She heard voices far away, filtering through the air with a distant sound, as if they came from another star. They were human voices piped through the *Far-Flying Bird*'s internal communications system.

"What is that?" she said. "What are they saying?"

"It's a check of the navigational computer seals," Jameson said.

She frowned at him. "Why?"

"It's a long story," he said.

She tried to pick out a comfortable-looking seat, but none looked better than another. The *Bird* was supposed to get some human-contoured furnishings before it departed with Hanna on board. She gave up and fitted herself as well as she could into a boxlike affair that had bumps in the wrong places. Jameson was standing. Hanna said, "Does Rubee know about this?"

"Not yet ..." He looked around and chose a seat for himself, easing into it gingerly. The apprehension that had grown on Hanna all the way from Willow bit at her.

"Something has gone wrong," she said, and it was not a question but the words for what she felt in him.

"Maybe."

"What is it?" But he did not answer at once, and she said, "We came very quickly, and disrupted the official schedule dreadfully. Rubee and Awnlee don't like to do anything quickly—at least, Rubee doesn't. While we were coming here, they learned from my thought that I was worried. They're puzzled and unhappy and I couldn't explain. Because I didn't even know what I have to worry about."

"You will be able to explain when we have finished talking. I think you will like it even less than they will."

He told her in a few words what he had told Edward Vickery. She listened in bewilderment to the strange story: an informant, some suspicions, a name. "It is clear," Jameson said at the end of his recital, "that if the *Bird*'s course program has been or will be pirated, someone within the project, someone who has been bribed, must be responsible. I tried to obtain authorization for probing all project personnel; of course I could not get it, but I thought that if I followed that with a request for probes of half a dozen key persons, the lesser demand might be met. It was not. There are political complications ... So we must think of another way to protect the *Bird*. Changing the program is a logical solution. Rubee and Awnlee are highly skilled in trailblazing, in navigating unknown space. You are trained in the equivalent human techniques. It seems to me that the three of you could develop an alternate if less direct course. I want you to explain the situation to Rubee and Awnlee, and persuade them to do this."

Hanna looked at him in silence. What he said meant— and he knew it—the difference between a journey of weeks and one of years. Each Jump of an interstellar voyage required days of calculation, sometimes weeks—if it were the first-ever leap between one point and another. Charting a new course was a different matter from following, in reverse, an established path. And Rubee was determined to come home on a date already fixed in his mind.

"They will not change it," Hanna said.

"Oh, but they must," he said.

"They know the difficulties of making contact in deep space, when one vessel does not want to make it, as well as you and I do. It's a hard thing to take seriously."

"I have a feeling about it," Jameson said, and Hanna blinked. She had never heard him say anything of the kind before.

"That's my specialty," she said. "Premonitions, hunches— what's got into you?"

He took the question literally. "I don't know," he said.

"Well—start from the beginning. What's the beginning?"

He leaned back in the awkward chair cautiously, folding his hands and looking past Hanna as if he picked a pattern from obscure details and saw it clearly regardless of where his eyes rested. The ability was part of his genius. He also was exceedingly clever in the manipulation of human beings, and his will was potent. He did not respond to the antisenescence procedures in universal use, and age had come upon him prematurely. The dark hair had grayed since Hanna's first meeting with him, and a network of lines encroached on the hooded gray-green eyes; but they emphasized the strength locked in the bones of his face. The big body was strong and desirable as ever, the presence as self-contained. Even now a well-remembered movement could take Hanna by surprise, so that she would look at the powerful hands, their touch once intimately familiar, and feel her knees weaken. She had seen him so often as he was now that her heart tore a little though five years had passed since the day he told her they were not suitable for one another.

She gave no sign of the movement in her chest. She had learned from him how to conceal what she felt. She had learned a great deal from him.

"An Intelligence and Security undercover agent on Valentine was the beginning," he said. "This man or woman—I don't know which, I don't have a name, I don't want one—has an informant— You've been to Valentine. How much do you know about it?"

"What everybody knows. You can get anything you want there. About all you can't do is kill somebody, because that discourages the vacationers."

"True, as far as it goes. But the salient point is that Valentine is concerned only with wealth. If you wish to transfer cash or credit to Valentine, no one will ask how you got it. If you get an illegal fortune elsewhere and can get it away, you can safely take it to Valentine. Occasionally—rarely—the authorities of Valentine will turn over an individual to the law enforcement agencies of another world; almost always a person known to be violent, with no appreciable wealth. But in general it is a safe place for men and women who would not be tolerated in a decent society. Consequently all the law enforcement agencies of the Polity are interested in Valentine, and so is I&S, which shares information with the domestic agencies. This is no secret, although you might not have known it."

"I didn't . . ." She had been very young when she visited Valentine. Every amusement known to humankind was there, wholesome or not. Not all her pleasures had been those "tolerated in a decent society."

"That's where the informant comes in. He, or she, told the agent, for a price, that—I quote—'somebody knows where the *Bird* will fly.' This seemed to be the extent of the informant's knowledge. He confirmed—I say 'he' for convenience—that he was indeed talking about the Uskosian vessel, and specifically about its detailed course program. So," Jameson said, coming back abruptly to the present, "the course must be changed."

"Couldn't he find out more?"

"Could not or would not. He was encouraged to do so.

He has not been heard of since, although he was promised a rich reward. Or perhaps he tried, and asked too many questions. More murder is done on Valentine than comes to light."

"You said I&S suspects someone—what about him?"

"Michael Kristofik? He disappeared from Valentine three weeks ago; another cause for concern. And he is protected, Hanna. He is very wealthy, and has become respected on Valentine, as such things go. He has been politely, adamantly sheltered. He is quite safe on Valentine—though he has not dared to set foot on a Polity world for fifteen years—not since his connection with the *Pavonis Queen* affair was discovered."

"What was that?—I never heard of it."

"It began the same way," he said. "With a pirated program . . ."

He was silent for a moment. She saw him gather and pattern the threads of the story. Then he said, "The course was taken by a man named Ivo Tonson. He was a high official of the Polity, a member of the Exchange Committee. He had arranged all the details of the *Queen*'s mission. That was to pick up from many worlds an enormous quantity of currencies of all sorts given up by governments, banking organizations, merchants based everywhere, in trade for equal value in the credit networks of the Polity. Nothing wrong with the money, though. No, it was spendable. No doubt some of it circulates still . . . I must talk with the inspection team."

There was a reader near his hand. He picked it up and scrolled through the index. When he had found what he wanted he held it out to her. She got up, moving carefully because she was suddenly aware of the extra weight the *Bird* seemed to have piled on her shoulders. When she took the reader it was unexpectedly heavy, too, and she nearly dropped it.

"What is this?" she said.

"An eyewitness account of what happened. It is the report of the chief of security on the *Pavonis Queen*."

"He survived it, then?"

"She did. All of them did, except one of the attackers. Study it carefully."

He got up, too. She did not look up at him; she looked at

the reader in her hand. She said, "What am I supposed to learn from it?"

"Whatever you can," he said.

The first page the reader showed was an unintelligible mix of file codes. When Hanna tried to go on to the next, nothing happened; then the reader began talking. A woman's voice came out of it, cold, methodical, untouched by the twenty years that had passed since the statement was recorded. Hanna put the reader on a chair and settled on the floor in front of it. The voice said:

"My name is Honoria Hood. I have the rank of commander in the Interworld Fleet, and I am a specialist in the transport of sensitive materials. On ST July 21, 2822, I was assigned chief of the Interworld Fleet security team ordered to accompany the merchant *Pavonis Queen,* a civilian vessel which was under contract to the Coordinating Commission of the Interworld Polity for a one-time mission involving the transfer of negotiable currency.

"The mission schedule called for the *Pavonis Queen* to leave the Terrestrial stellar system on September 20, 2822, and to return to her point of departure on or about January 27, 2823. All security arrangements were approved and in place before the *Pavonis Queen* departed Earth. The vessel carried a civilian crew of twenty-six and a security force of ten. The *Pavonis Queen* was unarmed, but warships of the Interworld Fleet were to meet her at each berth and remain in sentry position for the duration of each stop on the itinerary. Precautionary measures were concentrated at all times on the *Pavonis Queen's* ports of call.

"The itinerary of the *Queen* included Nestor, Lancaster, and D'neera, along with twelve lesser settlements. The last port before the *Pavonis Queen* returned to Earth was Alta. We left Alta on January 4, slightly ahead of schedule. The final leg of the journey was Common Route Gamma between Alta and Earth. This route uses one hundred twenty Jumps, and for a ship of the *Pavonis Queen*'s class the usual time in transit is five-point-five to six-point-five days.

"The *Pavonis Queen* completed Jump Number Fifty-five at oh-two-hundred hours on January 6. At approximately oh-three-hundred hours I was awakened by First Officer Philip Seal, who told me that upon completing Jump Number Fifty-five the *Pavonis Queen* had picked up a mayday from a vessel identifying itself as the freighter *Pastorale* out of Colony One. I met on the bridge with Mr. Seal and Captain Karsh. At that time we were in position near Relay Number 18.09.232, through which the mayday was being transmitted. The *Pastorale*'s reported position was also in the vicinity of the relay. According to the mayday, a reactor malfunction had rendered the *Pastorale* unfit for habitation, and the crew had abandoned ship in lifeboats. Of the crew of fifteen, five men were said to be suffering acute radiation poisoning, and rescue was urgently needed.

"After discussions with Captain Karsh and Mr. Seal, I approved their request to proceed to the aid of the *Pastorale*. I made the decision at oh-four-thirty hours after discussions with Colony One, Intelligence and Security, and my Fleet superiors. My opinion of the authenticity of the mayday and the minimal security risk involved was based on the following facts as they were reported to me. One, the owners of the *Pastorale* had reported her out of contact twenty-two hours previously. Two, search efforts already were underway—not at Jump Number Fifty-five, however, but at Jump Number Sixty-one, her last reported position. Three, the *Pavonis Queen* was three hours away from the point of contact, whereas all other vessels were no less than ten hours away. Four, the reported condition of the ill crewmen made early rendezvous essential. These are the reasons I agreed to Captain Karsh's request to undertake the rescue, with the approval of my superiors.

"We made audio contact with the *Pastorale* at once. A transcript of Captain Karsh's and Mr. Seal's communications with the presumed captain of the *Pastorale* is available. They were marked by the highest degree of tension on the part of the presumed Captain Weng. We were told that the sickest of the crewmen was aboard Captain Weng's lifeboat, and background sounds bore this out. Crewman Durand was said to be—well, never mind. They had invented a history for this imaginary man. It's still hard to believe there isn't a Crewman Durand with a sick mother and a very young wife. It was impossible not to be concerned about him. This was meant to keep our attention engaged, and it worked.

"Visual contact with the supposed *Pastorale* followed at

oh-eight-hundred hours. It was definitely radioactive. There were three lifeboats, each said to have one or more toxic patients aboard, and Captain Karsh ordered all three to be onloaded at once. The men in them did not come out immediately, even when the docking bay was fully pressurized and all the *Pavonis Queen*'s people were waiting, with the medics at the front. I believe they had a scanner and were studying the dispersal of the persons aboard the *Pavonis Queen*. Everyone was in the docking area except myself, Captain Karsh, and Communications Officer Alves on the bridge; two persons in the engineering section; and two members of the security team, who were standing their regular watch at the internal entry to the cargo hold. Three members of the security team were on standby in the docking bay staging area, with a clear view of the bay itself. The others were inside with the *Pavonis Queen*'s crew, having reported to offer assistance.

"After approximately two minutes, the men inside the supposed lifeboats attacked without warning. A large quantity of sleepygas was released from all three vessels. None of the persons in the docking bay escaped; all were unconscious in less than half a minute. Simultaneously with the release of the gas, the personnel in the vessel nearest the hull fired on the inner pressure seal of the *Pavonis Queen*'s docking bay, damaging but not disabling it. The attackers threatened to vaporize the inner and outer seals, which would have resulted in the deaths of all the sleepygas victims, if the guards in the staging area did not lay down their arms. I ordered them to comply. Immediately upon entering the bay, they also were overcome by gas. At that time the attackers finally emerged from the lifeboats. There were four of them; I do not know if others remained inside the vessels. They were dressed in utility spacesuits, so no physical description of them is available, and by sight they were indistinguishable. There were now only seven able-bodied persons free to defend the cargo—myself, Captain Karsh, Mr. Alves, the guards by the cargo hold, and two members of the engineering staff. I advised the civilians to remain where they were, although I am told that Captain Karsh later disregarded my order and was stunned for his trouble. Note that the attackers did not at any time use lethal weapons, only sleepygas and, later, stunners.

"I left Captain Karsh to call for assistance and ran to the docking bay after obtaining a gas filter and a handheld colloidal disruptor. I could not enter the bay because Captain Karsh had sealed off the area to trap the attackers in the bay. However, the main cargo hold on the *Pavonis Queen* backs onto the docking bay. For this mission the connecting entryway had been sealed with a security wall. But the attackers removed a heavy-duty laser cannon from one of the lifeboats and brought it to bear on the interface between the bay and the cargo hold.

"I therefore proceeded through the interior of the ship to the alternate entrance to the cargo hold. I had the combinations for the locking mechanisms of all three of the intervening doors, but the sequence was so long, and included so many halts for identification, that several minutes were required to effect an entrance. We found that the attackers had entered the hold and were using the *Pavonis Queen*'s own equipment to move the cargo. My personnel were armed with disruptors, and all of us began firing as soon as the last door was opened. One of the attackers fell at once. I believe a clean hit was scored in the chest and that he was killed immediately.

"We continued to direct heavy fire at the attackers. At one point more sleepygas was dispersed, but Mulready and Serlio also had filters, and none of us were affected. The attackers were unable to proceed with the transfer of cargo to the lifeboats as long as they were under fire, and it was my intention to harass them until, one, all were dead or disabled, or, two, help arrived. However, they took cover behind the largest of the cargo pallets. These were antigravity pallets, and the one they chose was solidly packed to a height of four meters and was opaque to the disruptor beams. They activated the pallet and began to move it into position in front of the entryway, making it necessary for us to enter the hold to avoid being trapped outside. We therefore came into the hold, at which time Ms. Serlio was stunned. Mr. Mulready and I reached the barrier. I waved him to the left of the pallet, intending to rush the attackers from the right myself. That is the last thing I remember. Mr. Mulready told me later that just as I fell he was conscious of a movement overhead, and was then stunned also. I believe one of the attackers had scaled the barrier from the other side, and fired on us from above.

"I was unconscious for six hours. When I awoke, the *Joyeuse* out of Willow was on the scene, and I was in its sickbay. The cargo of the *Pavonis Queen* was gone."

The voice ended, impersonal and didactic as it had been at the start. The reader did not make another sound. Hanna's cheek was pressed against the smooth covering of the chair, and her eyes were closed. At the beginning and the end the voice had belonged to the quintessential bureaucrat, but in between there had been pictures in its hesitations, its stilted formality and the lapses from that, its confidence in the recitation of numbers and dates, the omissions on less sure ground. Everything had been so neat out there. Everything had been planned. Even the urgency of an emergency in space could be handled, there were procedures; then the unexpected entered, the men and women falling in heaps, a man dead with his heart turned to jelly . . .

Jameson said close by, startling her, "What do you think of it?"

"I'm sorry for Honoria Hood . . ."

"Oh, it didn't ruin her. It was a long time between promotions, but she's still with Fleet. What else?"

Hanna opened her eyes finally, and straightened. "How could they do it?" she said. "How could anybody know ahead of time that the real *Pastorale* would be out of contact?"

He smiled at her. It was a particular smile which she recognized; it meant she had said something naive.

"They arranged it," he said.

"Arranged it?"

"The *Pastorale*'s communications system was sabotaged. The damage was repairable, but it took a day or two. The man responsible had been hired to do only that, he knew nothing of the plot, and he was not punished very severely."

"All right. Still. The *Pavonis Queen* was ahead of schedule, isn't that what Hood said? The timing—"

"It was not as close as you think," he said. "Remember the accomplice at Admin; he knew the *Queen*'s precise location at all times."

"Who was he? What happened to him?"

"I told you: Ivo Tonson. He left Earth and vanished a few hours before the robbery. One supposes he went to a new identity and a comfortable life."

Hanna tried to fit it together. The more she thought about it the more improbable it seemed. The restrictions, the safeguards, the controls, the agencies, the Interworld Fleet, the hounds of I&S—! In the last few years she had become well acquainted with them. She herself was ordered and official, pigeonholed and tamed. Someone had looked on all the regulations as simple problems to be solved, one by one. She could not imagine it.

She said, "They must have known every detail of the mission."

"They got the information from Tonson, undoubtedly."

"What happened to the one Hood killed?"

"The body was taken away, along with the lifeboats, the money, and the *Pastorale* replica, the decoy—which must have been safe in essential areas."

"And all those people in the docking bay—"

"They had Alves and the two engineers move them all to safety before they cut their way out of the bay and escaped."

"They thought of everything."

"Everything."

"Then how did I&S hear of that one? Kristofik?"

"The name was brought to their attention by a man whose grievance—there must have been a grievance—is unknown. The information produced by the initial investigation was promising. Kristofik's activities at the time of the incident bore out the theory of his involvement. But when the investigators sought to question the informer further, he had disappeared. No trace of him was found. Probably he was dead."

"And you think that now the same people, or Kristofik at least . . ."

Her voice trailed off. It seemed impossible to bridge the space of twenty years; when the *Pavonis Queen* was attacked, she had been a child, running barefoot in the bright morning of Province Koroth.

Jameson said, "That's what the I&S computers think. They were asked to generate a list of known felons who might be capable of planning and carrying out a theft on the scale this would be. There were four possibilities. One is in prison on Nestor; one was Adjusted, and is now tending cattle on Lancaster; one is dead, ID certain. The fourth is Kristofik."

"Who is he?"

For answer Jameson took the reader from its place. The long fingers moved delicately, searching the index. She could not ask a question the file could not answer. It was all there, neatly cataloged. She wondered if the robbers had been patient with files, kept them tidy, known where to look for everything. When Jameson handed the reader over, a face showed on its screen. He watched Hanna's eyes and saw the pupils of her eyes dilate. He said, amused, "A typical woman's reaction, I'm told."

"What?" She did not know what he meant at first; then she did, but she did not take her eyes from the image. The man was beautiful—there was no other word for it. There was just enough sharpness in the lines of brow and jaw, nose and cheekbones, to save them from effeminacy. She said doubtfully, "Is that his real face? Or did he have it constructed?"

"From all accounts it is his own. No one really knows."

"Why not? Valentine has good records."

"He has not always lived on Valentine. He turned up on Alta as a child of twelve or thirteen. The monks of St. Kristofik have a school for homeless children there, and they took him in. That's where he got the name he uses. Before Alta there is nothing. Certainly his face was not changed afterward. But his origin is unknown."

"Unusual. But possible. So many little settlements, half-forgotten, or more than half . . ."

She bent over the reader, studying Michael Kristofik's eyes. They were amber-brown in color, long-lashed, oddly flecked with gold. He looked out of the picture with half a smile, as if someone had just said something pleasing.

She said, "He doesn't look dangerous."

"It's true no one was hurt on the *Pavonis Queen*. But there were incidents of violence on Alta and Valentine both before and after that, and later everywhere. And don't forget the man who accused him. Do you think he disappeared naturally just then, by coincidence? Kristofik was dangerous. He is still dangerous."

Hanna turned off the image and got up. The faraway voices sang around her and she felt misplaced in time.

"I will try to persuade Rubee to change the plan," she said.

"You don't have much hope," he said.

"No."

When Rubee and Awnlee left the *Far-Flying Bird* for good to sojourn among humans, it had been necessary for the three of them—the aliens and Hanna—to establish semipermanent lodgings near Admin. Starr Jameson had offered his own home for their use. Hanna refused it. She had lived in that house, and had not entered it since the day she left without farewell; she would not enter it now. She was obliged to explain her refusal to Rubee and Awnlee. At that time—when human beings were new to them—they knew in an abstract way that humans came in two sexes. The principle was not new, it was commonplace on life-bearing planets, but Uskos had not met it in a sentient species. Linguistic analysis then had laid in only a foundation for the translator, and much of Hanna's communication with Rubee and Awnlee was telepathic. Her explanation therefore was three parts emotion, and it shocked them. It was their first glimpse of the complications human sexual arrangements made. They got them mixed up for a while with the permanent bonding of the People of Zeig-Daru, of which Hanna had recently informed them.

"Does obtaining such loss mean that like those beings you will die?" they said.

"Humans don't die when they lose a love," Hanna said. "It only makes them want to."

Such discrimination was beyond Rubee and Awnlee at the time, but they were pleased to acquiesce in whatever Hanna might suggest. Therefore when they were on Earth they rattled around in a pile of a house that occasionally slipped its moorings and floated above the hills and meadows around it, high enough for the inhabitants to see Admin and its city sixty kilometers to the east. When the house had taken flight four or five times, Hanna found that it did not do so of its own accord; Awnlee had found the key to the place's programming, and had something to do with the phenomenon.

Even at rest the house made them giddy. It was fili-agreed, frescoed, fretted, and gilded. The ceilings crawled with molding, the exterior with mosaic and bas-relief. The first time Hanna stood in a jet of perfumed air after bathing, she saw that even the airstream nozzles were engraved with detailed scenes so tiny that they were almost indecipher-able; she deciphered them, and discovered their theme was scatological. Rubee, at about the same time, tried to revise gravity in the area of his bed, and spent a night on the ceil-ing. He could not get down until Hanna and Awnlee missed him in the morning and went in search of him. The house or the estate or both for some reason were called Puddin'. Hanna could not remember the names of the people who owned it, nor where they had gone while they left their property at the disposal of aliens.

Here Hanna told Rubee and Awnlee what she had heard about the *Far-Flying Bird*. They sat in a grove of maples whose shade at noon did little to cut the muggy heat. Rubee and Awnlee were thoroughly comfortable; Hanna, wearing nothing, tolerated the heat. D'neerans as a rule were not particular about clothes, and with only the indifferent aliens for company, it did not matter if she were clothed or not.

They took the news well. Uskosians understood crime. They were even pleased, Hanna thought, that the gifts to be made to them by the peoples of human worlds should be great enough to inspire it.

But they would do nothing to avert it.

"Tell me why," Hanna said. She lay on her back, arms clasped behind her head; wiggled a toe, closed one eye, and took aim at the toe with the other. The heat soaked into her bones. Should she, before going to Uskos, have her long hair cut and its growth inhibited? She would spend much of her time in hot climates, so it would be wise, but she did not want to.

Such a question seemed ordinary. Nor did it seem odd to lie under a tree with beings from another star, talking of a crime to which all three of them might fall victim. She had done stranger things.

"To alter the course is to alter the design and end of our voyage," Rubee said. "I have fixed the day of return."

"Yes, I know, but why?"

"Why not?" said Awnlee, and shook all over, fingers flexing rapidly. This was laughter. He had once heard Hanna respond thus to an absurd question, and lost no chance of using the phrase.

"We are expected on the fourteenth day of Strrrl," Rubee said. "That is the appointed time."

"Yes, I know that, Rubee, but I do not understand. I am sorry. We have had fixed dates for our travels together here and changed them. We ought to be on Co-op now, in fact. The changes have annoyed you because they are a nuisance, just as they have annoyed me, for the same reason. But if we are on Earth instead of Co-op on the eighteenth day of an Earthly August, how is that different from being in space instead of at home, on the fourteenth day of—what you said?"

"Details change," Rubee said gravely. "Grand designs must not, except by the hand of the Master."

She thought she felt her ears prick, a physical movement. She said casually, "You mean the Master is the only permissible agent of change in a grand design?"

"Not at all. Yet if the design is beneficent, who would wish to change it? And this that we wish to recreate is a design of peace and amity between peoples divided by distance."

"But what if the Master does intervene?"

"Then it is a new design, and the meaning may remain obscure forever."

Hanna concentrated on her toe. They were within a step of granting the Master of Chaos the status of a physical agent, it seemed; she had formerly gotten no hint that he might be so regarded.

"By whom are designs made?" she said.

"By persons."

"And persons can alter them?"

"They may; but each alteration may be a place for the Master to enter, and the persons who make them his tools. Therefore, in such a case as ours, the old," said Rubee simply, "is better than the new."

"So this journey of yours . . ." She looked up into the shadows of leaves. "You set out to seek—something. Intelligent life, anyway. Not specifically us. You didn't know we were here. You didn't know you would find us. Or if you would find intelligent life at all. And yet you mean this is not something new, but something old?"

"Very old."

"It was once new, wasn't it?"

"In part. But only in part."

"What is it, then? What is the old thing?"

"It is best illustrated," said Rubee, "by The Travels of Erell."

"Will you tell me of the Travels of Erell?"

"Gladly. Do you wish a formal presentation?"

Hanna almost said no, but hesitated. The Travels of Erell might illuminate an attitude that to humans seemed entirely irrational. She did not want to summarize a summary to Jameson in a matter so important, nor make him further summarize it for Vickery.

"I would like that," she said.

"We are honored."

"I think I would like for Starr to see it, too. If he can come tonight, would you do it then? Is that too soon?"

The restless cilia around Rubee's mouth moved in a way that meant he agreed with grace and pleasure.

"Then it will be his, too," Rubee said.

There was no taboo against watching preparations. The aliens prepared in Rubee's room, and Hanna stood by with Starr Jameson and watched them get ready.

First each put on a garment of white cloth, plain but fine in texture, so soft that it fell about his chunky body in a hundred delicate folds. Round the neck went another piece of cloth, this woven in a seamless circle and falling in equal lengths over chest and back. A pattern was woven into it: an endless spiral.

The outer gown was brilliant in color and made of such heavy stuff that it kept its shape by itself. It was floor-length and hooded, and covered everything except the face and the elusive fingers. Rubee wore a blue so bright it was shocking to human eyes; Awnlee wore scarlet. They also had masks colored like their gowns. These were simply constructed of some artificial substance, and were pierced so that the eyespots and tendriled mouths were visible.

They were not doing the thing the way it ought to be done. At home the vast costumeries held accessories for every conceivable performance. "The Travels of Erell" rightly called for more than two hundred participants, each with his own individually painted mask, special jewelry, and symbolic garments. Rubee and Awnlee had apologized before for the poverty of their resources; they apologized again now.

"Thank you, the loss is unimportant in your company," Hanna answered properly in their tongue.

Jameson was using a translator; he did not know a word of Ellsian, the principal language of Uskos. He said, "You're picking it up very well."

"It's not difficult. The grammatical structure isn't nearly as mad as Pan-F'thalian."

"Does knowing the language help? We saw that recording of a 'formal' together, you remember, shortly after they came. I got nothing out of it."

She thought for a minute, remembering "The Journey of Nlatee." She and Jameson had gone to the *Far-Flying Bird* to see what Rubee had to show them, hardly anyone knowing about it; information about the aliens was jealously guarded then. Jameson had managed to look as if he were not hot. Hanna's hair was damp. The translator did its best, an adequate job in fact, since the tales used a simple, straightforward vocabulary while the drama was acted out. Jameson watched the play courteously but without much comprehension; so did Hanna, until—guessing already the importance of the tales—she began "listening" to the Uskosians' emotional reactions to the show.

She said slowly, "I can understand it as they do—sometimes. It's not only because of the language, though. It takes practice, saturation. Even with the translator you might not understand this very well, and it's only a sort of outline anyway. Rubee is going to be both narrator and principal actor for this, and Awnlee will be all the others . . . Narration doesn't seem to be really important in a true formal presentation, but it will be almost all you have."

"But you don't rely entirely on narration."

"Oh, no." She glanced up at him. The comment was not idle; he was getting to something. He was right. Since that first recorded presentation, Rubee and Awnlee had allowed her to enter their minds while they performed, as thoroughly as her considerable ability allowed. Her perception was multifaceted and enriched in ways words could scarcely explain, and sometimes in her reports she did not even try, and made audacious statements of fact and prayed no one would ask for an explanation.

"Could you share it with me?" he asked, and she started.

She looked at Rubee and Awnlee for want of somewhere to fix her eyes; they were making final adjustments to each other's gowns with darting fingers. She said, "I thought you didn't like it when I thought to you."

"It's tolerable, within reason," he said. "And knowledge is my job, too."

"Then I must do some preparation, too," Hanna said, and walked out on all of them.

She went to the terrace where the little party would assemble. Lights were sunk into the stone, making sharp constellations in near-night. The sky was blue-black and stars were coming out, and the evening air smelled of grass and earth. There was a balustrade set at intervals with glass-clear flowers from Co-op. She leaned over it, seeking the scented breeze. She was angry. Jameson asked for an intimacy denied her when it might have counted. Her abilities were cheap now, they might have been tools wielded by a computer. The computer had a name and reputation: Lady Hanna ril-Koroth of D'neera, the human race's leading authority on aliens. She knew her official biography by heart, having heard herself introduced to too many expectant audiences.

"... member of the Goodhaven Academy for the Study of Alien Species since the remarkable age of twenty-five ..." *Twenty-one,* god damn it, screw Standard chronology, what's wrong with D'neera's years?

"Consultant to Polity Alien Relations and Contact, chief architect of the Zeigan Contact Project, she also organized the nucleus of D'neera's program in alien studies at the University of D'vornan ..." It's called The University, idiot; just happens to be at D'vornan.

"... and many other honors."

And. And. And.

(And when they get to me after the speech, late at night when they've had a few drinks, they want to know what the People *did* to me ...)

That's your job, woman. "Alien relations."

Her hands were too tight on the railing. She relaxed them, with an effort.

True-humans never liked it when she touched their thoughts. It taught them more about her than they wanted to know, and exposed them uncomfortably to her. Jameson was no different from the others. But she had learned a thing or two since their time together.

She went to the shelter of the wall of the house, sat cross-legged on the stone, and cleared her mind.

Four years ago she had thrown herself into the study of D'neera's Adept disciplines with a passion whose source was not precisely as disinterested as its teachers advised. She had said: *I must master my body so pain cannot master me; for now that I know my own weakness I live in fear.* The teachers had not sent her away. Motives more reprehensible than fear had led some of them on the same quest, but the studies themselves had a way of shaping the student. Her progress had been rapid, and now she had some skill in the art of consciousness clarified and disciplined to pure purpose.

She had also learned not to regret her ignorance at the time of her first contact with the People of Zeig-Daru. If she had known more, even if they had done the same terrible things to her, she would not have felt any of it. But history would have been different.

Presently the soft summer air and the dark and the stars drew far away. Her body lost its weight and vanished.

Jameson came outdoors to something that seemed a statue, so still was Hanna. If he watched her closely, he saw at long intervals an eyeblink or a slow breath. Otherwise she did not move until he sat down nearby and spoke her name. She turned her head without haste. Her face was remote: alien as Rubee's. He waited warily for the first stab at his consciousness, the sense of an intrusive presence in one's own inviolable mind. What came was barely perceptible, a cold thread like nothing he had felt before, devoid of personality as the eyes that a little while ago had been Hanna's.

He was relieved.

The aliens came in their rich vestments like gliding stones, figures of geometry with substance and bulk. The lights at their feet cast shadows behind them which bent over the balustrade and flowed into the night. Shadow seemed to thicken round them and slowly, like the swirl of black cloud in black sky, the darkness shaped other forms. Their masks were of all colors. Jameson did not see them with his eyes. He saw Rubee's knowledge and memory: what ought to be. So now he had two kinds of sight, one of them directed by that force he could not identify with Hanna; also he heard the rasp of Rubee's voice, and laid over it, impersonal, mechanical, the Standard translation.

"And this is the story of the Travels of Erell," Rubee said; and at a distance a gong sounded, or seemed to.

"In a year on the second day of Urrt, Erell set forth. At his side was his selfing Awtell, and they sailed a fair ship; for Erell was of Ell by the ocean."

The night wind blew from an Uskosian sea. At parting the people played the Path of Stoell; no, the shadows played the people's play; no, it was only Awnlee playing a multitude of players.

Awnlee sang in a voice like rough metal and was the wind that bore the ship away.

"They crossed the eyeless ocean steering by the moons. There were storms and the Master appeared in the towering waves but neither sank nor aided them. They sailed on without hesitation until they came to an empty land. They rested and went on."

Rubee faced the terrible waves and Awnlee, compressing fifty roles in one, was the sea. The storm keened with a furious voice. No one ever played the Master's part; but in the patterns of the movements of the play, a space was left for him. Then they were still, resting, though sea and wind murmured on. In rest the cowled shapes bent toward one another with great dignity, selfing sheltered by sire.

"Days passed and the moons dipped and danced. A great bird of a kind unknown appeared and sought to seize Awtell, but Erell drove it away. Then he knew this voyage was not discouraged."

Awnlee danced like the icy moons, and his fingers wove strange figures about one another. He and Rubee clashed with formal violence: Erell and the bird.

"On they went and came to empty lands and the seas were long. They they came to the land of Sa. And they could not understand those of Sa, but then they learned. And they feasted and were welcome."

Some distant part of Jameson's consciousness told him

he was in trance; but all the rest of it saw the emptiness of the water and land, and later the welcoming.

"At length they departed; and when they left the land of Sa they bore rich gifts, and with them traveled Porsa of Sa. They knew fair winds as they went; and on the fourteenth day of Strrrl they came again to Ell. And when they told those of Ell what they had learned there was rejoicing, and welcoming and feasting of Porsa of Sa, and in after years many went from each land to the other, and Awtell was a leader of all. So did the beings of sundered lands come first to know one another in the ages of the world. And the bond of the lands of Ell and Sa to this minute is not torn by war nor broken by any thing.

"Precious is this minute!"

Rubee and Awnlee withdrew. The shadows went with them. Some time passed, but Jameson did not know how much; time might have stopped until suddenly the presence he had forgotten withdrew from his thought, and he came awake. When he looked at Hanna, she also had returned to normal consciousness, though a trace of remoteness lingered in her eyes. She got up slowly, as if it took a minute to get used to her body again.

She said, "Do you understand now?"

He shook his head. "I thought I did while it was going on," he said.

"Yes, that's right. I can't keep it up all the time either."

"I guess you have to be a little inhuman," he said, meaning no insult.

"That's right," Hanna said impassively.

"It's got some kind of symbolic meaning, then? This schedule they're tied to?"

"Symbols come in differing degrees of abstraction," Hanna said. Her voice was cool, pitched in the lecturer's mode. "They stand for living forces that shape the way we think and live. Humans often dissociate visible symbol from its sources. Your sun and crossed spears, the seal of your world—your people think what they feel for it is pride. What it is, is the comfort of the tribe. The Uskosians are fully conscious of all that underlies their symbols—but those foundations are just as powerful for them as ours are for us."

He said frankly, "I can accept what you say as an intellectual proposition, and I take it on faith that you're right. But I will not be able to convince Vickery and the others that Rubee will not change his mind if only the situation is explained to him clearly enough and logically enough."

"Well, I promise you that I will keep explaining it, clearly and logically. But what is the logic of the gifts we take to Uskos?—jewels, art, a treasure to tempt a thief. What is the logic of that?"

"Everyone knows that," he said.

"Yes," Hanna said, "and everyone on Uskos will understand Rubee's logic."

"Then we'll have to think of something else," he said.

It was hot in Shoreground that year. Outside the central dome the air had a rank ocean smell, and the wind blowing inland carried sand and grit that clung to damp skin and stuck in eyes and hair.

Inside the dome it was different.

Inside the dome at midnight the streets were cool and full of light. Michael Kristofik walked through them invisible, hidden in patterns of shadow that tricked an observer's eye. There were other figures like him in the streets, anonymous clouds that looked half-real, trans-dimensional. Many who came to the dome did not wish to be recognized there, and there were vendors to supply the generators that broke up the light around them.

Shoreground-under-glass was called Carnivaltown. Michael stood at the center of the cauldron and looked up. At intervals shapes lit up the sky: flowers, beasts, abstractions, some of which were salacious. The names of establishments flashed in the air, and images of their attractions. Near the top of the dome, perched precariously on the curved surface, habitats clung to the inner skin, their windows dots from the ground. The masters of Carnivaltown ran the dome from there. Michael had been there often, the last time not long ago: a rich man among his peers, looking down on the lights, removed from the activity below.

This was the third consecutive night he had spent walking the streets of Carnivaltown. Before that, he had not come to them for a long time.

He turned through an entrance wreathed with arabesques. Synthetic happiness jolted him. It ended when he stepped into the room beyond, leaving a residue of good feeling. A woman with polished silver skin greeted him. The happi-bar lobby was nearly dark and she glittered, a creature of quicksilver eyes, the top of her head a gleaming bald dome. She wore only a golden anklet, but she looked too made of metal to be tempting. She was used to apparitions like Michael. He was used to apparitions like her.

She took him to the kind of cubicle he wanted: a watcher's station, half of one wall a telescreen. From here a customer could overlook the private ecstasies in all the cubicles of the other kind, occupied by people who liked to be watched. The watchers paid heavily, but the others paid just as much, and complained about it; did they not provide the entertainment?

Another silver woman brought the dram of Fantasee Michael ordered. He left it untouched and used the telescreen methodically, ignoring what he saw except to search for a face. This was the third night he had looked for it, and he was prepared to keep going a long time. But in the happi-bar he found it almost at once: the face of a boy perhaps twenty years old with black eyes, fresh white skin, mouth curved in a professional smile. He was alone. Waiting.

Michael looked at the young face for a long time.

Good thing to do when you've been earning well and don't feel like working hard. Display in a voyeur's haven, the quiet kind, like this. Relax, have a drink, let the peepers peep, let them make the moves. Just make sure they know what you are so there won't be an argument later.

Tricks of the trade. Who had told him about that one?

You couldn't miss Gian Filarete's trade. The medallion round his neck showed, prominently, the clasped-hands symbol of the Registered Friend.

Michael touched the Talk switch and then the credit plate. Making contact cost extra. He left with Gian a little later.

He took the boy home with him, an hour from Shoreground by groundcar. The car could have found the way, but Michael piloted it to cover a rare, bad case of nerves. He put away the distortion device when they got in the car and when he looked into Gian's speculative eyes, he could almost hear the boy thinking. *Good-looking. I like that. Strong, though. Mean? Or the soppy kind? All night. Weird?* There was music in the car, but it was not helpful.

> *As the spur is to the jade,*
> *As the scabbard for the blade,*
> *As for digging is the spade,*
> *As for liquor is the can,*
> *Man is for the woman made*
> *and woman for the man . . .*

The song was in a dialect fourteen hundred years old, and the voices wove a dance around one another. Gian did not like it. He was not impressed with the car, either, which was not new. Michael's stock did not go up until he offered wine and Gian saw the goblets. Gian held his carefully, stroked the crystal, became friendly. He got even more friendly when he saw where Michael lived.

They ate on a terrace overlooking a night-black lawn, and past that the heavy shapes of full-foliaged trees. The lighter darkness farther out was the sky. Beyond the trees a cliff dropped away to the sea. There was just enough light at table to show the food they ate and, dimly, their faces. Theo served the meal, and Gian took him to be a personal servant. The boy ate well, drank sparingly, and tried too hard to charm. His head was full of possibilities: standing appointments, bonuses, gifts, the mansion behind them. He had come to Valentine from Co-op less than a year before. Michael knew that, but he did not know why Gian had come. He would not have the stability that came with belonging to one of the old Valentine families for whom prostitution was an honorable business; he was not attached to a combine like Flora's, where he might have learned to move in the best society anywhere in human space. He was only pretty and cunning and young, and the shell that had begun to grow around him sooner or later would be impenetrable.

When they finished eating, he followed Michael indoors without suspicion. By day, big as it was, the house was bright and airy. Tonight the darkness weighed on it. Few interior lights were on, and they went through the shadows to a central room with no openings except the door through which they entered. A single light floated unsupported near a chair. There was a table nearby with an odd assortment of objects on it, part of the casual litter that accompanied Michael wherever he went. The weightless globe made one sharp-edged pool of light, and shrank the universe to the man and boy within it. Gian sat in the chair and looked up at Michael expectantly. Michael stood half in shadow and studied the boy.

If there were problems, Theo would come with his kit of chemicals. But simple bribery would be better.

Michael said, "All I want from you is information."

The practiced smile stayed in place for a minute, lost its gloss all of a sudden when the words penetrated. For Gian the expected stood on its head. Michael's manner was subtly changed. There was no threat in it, but there was sureness. The common meaning of what had gone before vanished; none of it was what Gian had thought it was.

"There was a man at the Grand Square Inn last week. Red hair. Blue eyes, very light. About my height, heavier build. I don't know what name he used with you. Whatever it was wasn't his real name."

Gian's smile disappeared altogether. He was a long way from Carnivaltown, and this had not happened to him before. He looked around once, quickly. Michael had chosen this spot by instinct, and chosen well; Gian could not remember where the entrance lay, and the little space of light trapped him.

He said, "I don't know what you mean."

"Sure you do. You're thinking of the Guild rule, right? Don't jaw the customers. Not to each other."

"I'm registered," Gian said. "I don't want whines."

"Save the ethics for the slops. In the Guild it goes, 'unless the price is right.'"

He had the inflection right. Gian looked at him in surprise. Michael said, "Don't get righteous. I was in the Guild five years."

"You?"

Gian looked around again, this time speculatively, as if he saw through the dark. He had seen enough to know how Michael lived. He said, "Five years for this?"

Michael grinned in spite of himself. "I didn't get it that way. I was good. But not that good."

The boy's face was transparent; Michael watched him reevaluate the situation. Haggling over an indiscretion that could get your registration canceled was one thing. Professional gossip was something else.

Gian said, "What's it worth?"

"You tell me."

"I can't till I know what you want."

"He left Valentine the day after you had him. Private ship, private business, no flight plan. I want to know if he said anything, did anything, if you noticed anything, that'd tell me where he was going next."

"Why?" The boy was curious; almost impudent, now.

"He owes me money," Michael lied.

"How much?"

"None of yours. You're not in for shares. Give me a flat."

"I'll think about it," said the boy. "Throw me in?"

"In already, infant. Can't hook me thisway."

The patois came easily. Gian was visibly relaxing. He said, "How'd you target me?"

"Security. A favor."

Gian nodded. Shoreground security officers were almost incorruptible—because very little was considered corrupt. The woman who had found Gian was near retiring. Not much provision was made for security personnel after they retired. As a rule not much was necessary; with a little initiative, an enterprising officer could provide well for the future. Gian understood, and took it as a matter of course.

Michael came all the way into the circle of light. He picked up an object from the table and held it out. Slender vase with graceful lines, a little darker than turquoise; it looked like glass, but it was not. The material was thin, and opaline sparks danced in its fragile skin. There was considerable value in the medium, but Michael held it so that Gian saw the bottom and the finely etched mark that referred to an embedded electronic pattern worth a great deal more.

Gian looked at it appreciatively. "One of a kind. You got more?"

"Sure. Some better than others. But ones, yes."

"I got a couple."

"What you got?"

"Sisty Whitemore from Earth, you heard of her? She does ones for walls. Programs a robo, that's what you get, the robo does it all. Got a big bonus once, flashed it all on that. You got a Whitemore?"

"Downstairs. Show you later."

"The robo self-destructs."

"Yeah. You have to jet it out fast."

Gian took the vase and held it lovingly. A work like this, like Sisty Whitemore's multidimensional walls, like anybody's work of art, could be reproduced down to the last molecule. Most were. Those that were not, that were certified as one-of-a-kinds, were prized.

"You want it?" Michael said.

"Sure. Sure I do."

"You know how to get it."

Gian made up his mind. "He was going by the name of Pallin."

"Just that night. Just with you."

"So it doesn't mate. All right. Didn't say much. Just told me what he wanted. You know how some are? Better than the talky kind, though. But no repeat for this one. Too rough. Don't mind if I flap him. He made a call."

"Who to?"

"Don't know. Didn't hear a name, couldn't see the face. He thought I was asleep. I didn't hear much," Gian said apologetically.

"Anything about where he's headed?"

"Yeah. He said—" Gian thought about it, caressing the blue vase. "He said, 'When we get to the Rose we'll start the countdown.'"

"The what?"

"The Rose. Like the flower."

"Sure?"

"As tomorrow."

"What else?"

"That's all."

Gian got anxious. It wasn't much. He held the vase harder, wondering if Michael would take it away from him. But Michael was only thoughtful. "Have to do," he said.

He showed Gian around and called an autocab for him. At the last a streak of conscience pricked Gian. He said, "I could stay. You paid for the night."

"Never mind. Go on back. Take that pretty home."

"You don't like boys?"

"Not especially."

"Is it good being rich?"

"Very good."

"I guess you get anything you want." Gian said with greed. *Nothing like,* Michael thought, but he did not say so to Gian.

I&S patiently turned over pebbles. All the project personnel had been investigated before; now they were screened again. Toward the end Vickery said to Jameson. "It's just what you'd expect if there was nothing to it. We're talking about an impossibility to begin with, you know."

Gil Figueiredo, who had been in charge of security for the aliens since Rubee's first incomprehensible call touched the edge of human space, sat in front of Vickery's desk. Jameson stood at the outer edge of the room and looked at the river going on its peaceful way. Vickery's office was on the lowest level of the fifty-story administration complex. The other forty-nine were heavy as a mountain overhead. You could walk through their passages for days and never find the place where you had started.

"We're missing something." Jameson said. "Is there, anywhere, another source for the program?"

"No," Vickery and Figueiredo said together.

"There's the *Bird* herself. She's been studied."

"Only the Inspace engineering," Figueiredo said.

"Could anyone have gotten into the navigation computers that way, without breaking the seals?"

"No," Figueiredo said positively.

Jameson stared across the water, where trees dreamed in the summer heat. The nights had gotten cooler, and the mass of green was softened by hints of gold. He said, "What I'd really like to do is get Kristofik under probe."

Vickery said, "You've got him on the brain," but Figueiredo laughed out loud and said, "That's been the dearest wish of some people at I&S for fifteen years."

Jameson's tenure on the Coordinating Commission had given him a certain disregard for the law. He said, "There ought to be a way to do it."

"Oh, it could be *done*. He doesn't bother with personal security on Valentine. But we've never tried it because even if we probed him there, we couldn't get him back to the Polity without creating a hell of an incident. If we couldn't transport him for trial, there's no point starting it. You remember his name didn't surface for something like five years after the *Pavonis Queen* robbery, when he was already established on Valentine. There were talks then, and Valentine shut us down. And that was fifteen years ago. He's an important citizen now."

"He is also back on Valentine where he belongs," Jameson said. "Perhaps we've gone wrong there instead. Perhaps he's not the man we should be looking at."

Figueiredo said impatiently, "You saw the reports on the other names. He's the only one left."

"It's too neat."

"All we have to deal with is known factors. That's what the known factors give us."

Jameson almost heard Hanna's laughter. Figueiredo could not know what it was like to specialize in the unknown. Figueiredo added, "Don't forget the *Golden Girl*. It fits."

"What is that?" Vickery said a little wearily.

"Kristofik bought a yacht a few months ago. Dru class, beautiful thing. Six staterooms, two lounges, gymnasium, staff quarters. He refitted it and named it the *Golden Girl*. The color's not really gold, though—more like brass."

"Appropriate," Jameson murmured, but Figueiredo went on, "He provisioned it for a long, long voyage. He hasn't taken one yet. But there are indications he's planning to leave Valentine again and be away some time. He's turned over his business interests almost entirely to his head manager, Kareem Mar-Kize, for one thing."

"The *Golden Girl* is not armed," Jameson said quietly, but Vickery was more interested now.

"Is he in financial trouble?"

"No. And that's where it doesn't fit," Figueiredo admitted. "He just keeps getting richer. He might be crazy enough to want the cargo for himself, though. From what we know of him, he'd appreciate it."

Vickery's interest waned. He shook his head. "Chances are he's just like everybody else in human space. One, all he knows about the *Bird*'s course is what direction she's going and what star she's headed for. And two, he doesn't care."

"Maybe," Figueiredo said. "All the same, if Director Jameson could get them to agree to an armed escort, it would solve everything."

Jameson said, "I will push Hanna as hard as I can. She will, in turn, push Rubee and Awnlee as far as possible. I doubt very greatly that she could under any conceivable circumstance get that result."

Vickery said, "She's under your direct supervision."

"The aliens are not."

Figueiredo said, "There's another option. If we didn't send any gifts, there wouldn't be a target."

Jameson said, "If the gifts go, Hanna goes. It's a package. And the Commssion strongly favors her preceding a diplomatic party by some months, since that's what Rubee wants."

"Very advantageous for her. Her professional reputation, I mean. The gifts—is that how she persuaded them to take her along?"

Jameson turned around at last. His eyes were so cold that Figueiredo shut up abruptly. He said, "Perhaps it's time I&S officers charged with protecting aliens spent some time at D'vornan under Hanna's tutelage. The arrangement was Rubee's suggestion. It has to do with the Travels of Erell. If you don't know what that means, you had better find out. Check out the navigational systems once more, if you please. I will see to it that Hanna knows as much as possible about this man Kristofik. She may have to negotiate with him."

Figueiredo was not happy, but he nodded.

Now there were no more places to go. The aliens and Hanna stayed on Earth. For their protection—and to their bewilderment—they were placed under the surveillance of bugs, spyeyes, airspace monitors; the aliens could ignore them and forget that they were there, but Hanna could not. She thought of them as everything that was worst about Earth, about Polity Admin for that matter. They gave you no privacy, if they thought they had a good reason to take it away. What if she needed real aloneness? What if she were to take a lover?—an academic question, because she had

had no lover since Jameson. She had discovered in herself, with him, an unsuspected capacity for exclusive love. Passion had no power to touch her now, and after five years celibacy had become a habit, so that she had nothing to be private about. There was a principle involved, though, and she had good-byes to say. She would have liked having privacy for that.

"I found I liked teaching better than running things, but you will listen to one more suggestion, won't you? Institute the program in F'thalian mathematical thought, and get Tai-Tai Ling out from Earth to teach it. You will? Good, oh, good. And, oh, if you should hear from my mother, tell her I tried to find her . . ."

Communications that ducked through Inspace—that disappeared at one point in realspace and appeared in another—never reappeared at all if they were sent too far, and over long distances had to be transmitted from one automatic relay to another, just as a spacecraft could not go from star to star with a single Jump and so made each journey piecemeal. Rubee and Awnlee had left no relays behind them. They had not been able to speak to Uskos for nearly four years. As the day for departure came close, Hanna thought of her own voyage on the exploratory vessel *Endeavor,* the one that had led to contact with Zeig-Daru. She had never examined her dependence on the relays that marked *Endeavor*'s path. The controllers of *Endeavor*'s voyage—among them Jameson, a commissioner then—had always know what was going on. *Endeavor* had always been able to shout for help. Its crewmen had remained in contact with their homeworlds, though the contacts had been censored. It had not occurred to Hanna that space exploration could proceed in any other way.

The gulf Rubee and Awnlee had crossed—silent, beyond help, incredibly vast—was a gulf indeed. The way they had done it marked them alien more clearly than anything else Hanna had learned about them. They did not even know how courageous they were. They did not think about it. They followed in the footsteps of Erell, and Erell had not said, "Good-bye until I think of calling home." He had only said: "Good-bye."

"I noticed the stoneveins were fading in the snow. They need to be cut back. You will? Oh, thank you, thank you. You

can keep the fish. And, oh, if my mother comes by, give her my love . . . Good-bye, good-bye, good-bye . . ."

Jameson wanted her to come to his office. He wanted her to study a file which could not be transmitted out of Admin. She did not want to spend any more time in offices. Her days in human space were going away quickly. She would be isolated for the last seven of them, having her immunities (as she thought of it) fine-tuned. She had paid no more attention than she had to the army of biotechs who at the start had tampered first with her, then with Rubee and Awnlee, then with all of them, then with the *Bird* itself; now they were going to do it all over again, in reverse. So she would spend a week in a sealed environment and go straight from that to the *Bird,* and she did not want to waste time at Admin.

"I will have plenty of time to study whatever you want when I can't go anywhere," she told Jameson.

"You have to see it *here,*" he said stubbornly.

"Nothing I have to do with now is *that* highly classified."

"When it comes from I&S it is."

"You weren't always so careful about regulations!"

"I wasn't always accountable to Vickery," he said.

Hanna had had an inadvertent hand in Jameson's fall from power. She took his last remark as a reproach, though perhaps it was not meant to be one.

"Dear Samuel, I didn't know you felt that way for me. You didn't when I left, did you? It's just missing me? I'm sorry, I'm sorry, I never thought of you that way. Don't wait for me. Go on to someone else. But please say you'll still be my friend. Good-bye, good-bye."

"How can you negotiate with a man you know nothing about?" Jameson asked another day.

"The same way," Hanna nearly snarled—she had been saying good-byes all the morning—"I negotiated with the People on Zeig-Daru. And with Rubee and Awnlee. Do you think I can't assess a human being?"

"It's never been your strong point in the past!" Jameson's temper was frayed, too.

"From what I remember about the *Pavonis Queen,* there won't be *time* to negotiate. You can't negotiate when you're full of sleepygas!"

"He has left Valentine again. His offices there say he may

be away some time. He filed no flight plan; Valentine does not require the filing of flight plans by private pilots. You have never met anyone like him before."

"There are not that many varieties of true-humans."

"He was a Registered Friend at seventeen. He must have known every worst thing there is to know about men, yes, both men and women, before he was twenty-one. He put much of his earnings into education, and saved the rest: an aberration in a Friend. He also cultivated extralegal contacts from the day he came to Valentine. When he met Tonson—who made several trips to Valentine in those years, and was Kristofik's client—he was ready. I&S believes he had been searching for such an opportunity from the start. You need to know about him, Hanna."

"I do not." She smiled; not a pretty smile; savage. "I'd like to meet him, though. He'd be a refreshing change, don't you think? I have some calls to make. If I come see you it will be from curiosity."

Jameson's smile was not pleasant either. "I don't care about your motives. Just do it."

"I hope that when relations are established and I can come home, I can come back to the House and do my work for Koroth. I have worked so much for the Polity that I have been useless at home. If I cannot end it, perhaps I should leave the House altogether. If you find out where my mother is, would you please tell her I love her? And say good-bye. Good-bye. Good-bye."

◆

Something tickled the far reaches of Michael's memory from time to time. *The Rose.* He could almost remember something it meant. When he repeated the phrase it had an edge to it, as if there were connotations buried in his mind that distorted the common flower name.

He might have started a search program for The Rose as soon as Gian left, but the general access information networks would have a billion references to roses. He did not even know what category to start with.

In the night he woke to a thought that stopped his breath: might The Rose be one of the things he could not remember, the whole reason for the search for the many-named man?

But then he started breathing again. He was certain that wherever he had heard of The Rose, it had been recently; part of his adulthood, at least.

The next day he searched a few classes at random. Planets?—he had never heard of one so named, but it might be a variant or the local name for a world known officially as something else. It might be a star or a satellite or an asteroid. But it was not, or so the networks told him.

"Spaceships?" said Theo, and got a quick response, and tied up data retrieval the rest of the day tracking down forty-two vessels named *Rose,* none of which were likely to have anything to do with the man Michael wanted.

"People," Shen suggested the morning after that.

"Bars," said Theo wistfully.

"I don't think we're getting anywhere," Michael said.

He got them back to work, with some difficulty—it was this week's day for an army of housekeepers and grounds-keepers to descend on the estate and impose order on it— and tried to work himself. He had investments to look after. It was hard to keep his mind on them, though, and anyway he was not necessary to their success.

"In fact," said the man who managed most of them, "I was looking forward to that long trip you were talking about."

Michael smiled at the dark face on the telescreen. "I just couldn't stay away, Kareem. I'll leave again; any day now."

"The sooner the better!"

Shen was nearby, taking a break from haranguing gardeners. When Kareem Mar-Kize's face disappeared, she said, "Not so."

"What's not so?"

"Better. Not so." She glided closer, stood over him, leaned over and poked a rigid finger into his belly. The flesh did not yield, but she said, "Soft."

"I am not."

"Lived good too long. Baby girls, stray cats—"

"Like you."

"Like me. Listen, that Gian, say he knew more. Call that an answer? You want answers? Ways to get 'em. One way or another."

"I know Valentine. I know how he thinks. Go away and let *me* think."

The thing he was trying to remember twitched at intervals through the day. Theo and Shen stayed away. The animals of the house came one by one to doze in the warm
afternoon. None were native to Valentine; humanity's
bonds with its pets stretched back beyond recorded history,
and humans had not been on Valentine long enough to
breed anything native into something that could be loved.
But dogs lay at Michael's feet, cats stalked through the
shade, a kitten slept on his knee; presently a F'thalian tourmaline, an exotic abandoned by some human visitor to Valentine, inched up his arm and perched on his shoulder.
Later Lise, too, came to the open-air study where he
watched the sun and shadows. She stayed some distance
from him, curled in a chair with a reader in her lap that
showed pictures of pretty clothes. She did not say a word
and it was impossible to guess what she thought. He supposed she was occupied with new plans for ravaging his
credit, to which he had given her access; the string of deliv-
eries, having driven Shen nearly mad, had tapered off, but
probably not for long. Lise had not wanted to live with
Flora, she refused with lamentations to be parted from Michael, and was on her way to becoming a permanent member of the household.

The sun finished its morning arc and the shadows grew
long. The blossoms of the trees Gian had seen only in darkness blazed brighter in the slanting light. They were hardly
more colorful than the flowers mounded at their feet:
D'neeran millefleurs, difficult to grow most places, but here
showing their native bent for taking over everything around
them. They were so much a fixture that most days Michael
scarcely saw them. But it was the millefleurs—little known
outside their home, obscure symbols of a place off traveled
paths—that gave him the idea.

In the evening he went back to the computer and specified a search. He wrote: "Subject—human settlements, associated features, geographical or social, Standard or
colloquial terminology. Exclude Earth. Exclude all cities
above population 100,000. Exclude all official place names.
Mark: Rose. Search."

He left the program running and went for a walk outdoors. He had bought the house and grounds two Standard
years before from the heirs of a gambling magnate who had

finally died in spite of all that artificial organs could do. There was no satisfactory replacement for the whole of a deteriorating brain. The place was not a home, but it was the closest he had ever had to one. When he was tired of walking, he sat on a wooden bench and listened to the sea. He was high above it, but it was audible from here, a steady thump-and-rumble, the pulsebeat of a planet.

After a while Shen came to find him, unerring in the dark. She carried a light and a long printout. She sat beside him and gave the things to him without comment. He looked at the printout and saw that the computer had finished its search.

"The Rose: Colloq. Mt. Greene, near Thule, Montana, Heartworld.

"The Rose: ST. Biennial underwater race limited to modified human organisms. Town of Eiger, Nestor.

"The Rose(s): Colloq. Metatree forest near Hai, Co-op."

There were more entries like that. He scanned them impatiently. Near the bottom of the list he saw: The Rose: ST (1) Stone venerated by The People of the Rose, Riordan's Revenge. (2) The People of the Rose."

Shen saw his attention. "That it?"

"I don't know. I've been there. A long time ago, ten years maybe. I forgot about the 'Riordan' part, I only heard it called Revenge. Come on, let's look it up."

They went back to the house and got what they wanted immediately. Riordan's Revenge was obscure, but properly cataloged. Michael read:

"Riordan's Revenge is one of thirty planets visited and reported as habitable by Miles Riordan in the years 2463 through 2481, only two of which—Riordan's Revenge and Isle—are actually classifiable as such.

" 'Revenge' is little known and is seldom visited except by representatives of the Colonial Oversight and Protection Service once each Standard year, and by merchantmen on no fixed schedule. Though terrestrial in composition and atmosphere, the planet is locked in an ice age which may be permanent. (See Subfile 1.) Revenge is considered marginally habitable, under the guidelines of the Colonial Oversight and Protection Service, only in the following regions: (a) The so-called Long Archipelago, approximately 8N-12S, 60E-75E; (b) the southernmost portion of the planet's largest continent, the habitable portion lying 6N-4S, 94W-113W. Even in these areas the growing season is short, and the population of Riordan's Revenge relies exclusively on accelerated-growth crop strains for agricultural sustenance."

There was more, but Michael quit reading. His memory had gotten the jog it needed. The City of the Rose was not a city but a scanty town, ugly under a cold sun. Stone ranging rust to scarlet in brutal outcroppings of rock; rose-shapes everywhere and a temple whose interior no unbeliever could see; pathological rejection of outsiders, so that Revenge did not have Inspace communications, not even a single transmitter; veiled women he had hardly glimpsed, because they feared defilement if an infidel's gaze fell on them—

A man could hide on Revenge.

"Mike?" said Theo, reading over Shen's shoulder.

"Yeah?"

"Why would he go there?"

"Stay out of sight. Stay hidden. Maintain a base? Where'd he dock that 'vette he got? Where'd he go to install the guns? You want to be hidden for something like that. Cheaper to do it in atmosphere."

He spoke with authority; from experience.

"Think this might be it?" Shen said.

"Worth a try, maybe. It's his kind of place." His breath caught. Shen looked at him narrowly. "God, yes, it's his kind of place," Michael said with feeling. "Isolated, primitive, helpless—that's why I went there. But it wasn't the place."

Theo had punched up a subfile. He said practically, "It's a long way out. That Riordan, he must have been right out on the edge when exploration slowed down. That was just before it did, wasn't it?"

"It was at the very end of the Explosion," Michael said. He did not have to search his memory for details of the great age of exploration; he had made himself an expert on the topic. "I know about Miles Riordan. He was one of the reasons they put the freelancers out of business. Then the big colonies started breaking away, Heartworld first and then Willow and Co-op, and nobody had time for exploring."

Shen folded her arms and stared at him without expression. She said, "Catch up this time, maybe. Lousy place. No people. No people, no cover. You get spotted first. GeeGee's got no guns. Shields'll stop a meteorite. No more. Stupid."

"Yes," he said.

"Crazy man."

"I want him alive. I want his records intact. The guns come later."

Shen said to Theo, "Crazy man wins all the arguments. You noticed? Start packing."

Michael nodded. They would be in space by morning.

There was a full moon the night before Hanna entered quarantine, the night she finally went to see Jameson. She rode under it in an Admin aircar, and the moon-frosted land below slipped past like water. The aircar made no sound. It homed in on Admin and guided itself. Hanna, with nothing to do but be carried through the silver night, thought she stood still over the turning Earth. She thought perversely that she could change course, fly away at random, look down on the busy towns and quiet countryside contemplative and unseen. Why not?—all her good-byes were said. Admin could not possess her much longer; her ties with Earth, with all of human space, attenuated. It was the same for Rubee and Awnlee. Of late they seemed more alien, not less; as if the days running past already brought them nearer to their home, and they could begin to take off a conforming skin they had worn politely through the months with humankind. The vast gulf waited for all of them.

The guards at Admin's rooftop hardly bothered to check Hanna's identity. *Not bad for a spacer from D'neera.* The tubes that wound through Admin shot her down, south, east, and spat her out at Jameson's door. *With luck I will not come here again,* she thought, saw in his puzzled face that some of the thought had escaped her, and to forestall a question said good evening hurriedly.

"What is it you want me to see?" she asked.

"Oh—" Her abruptness startled him. He drew her into Contact's deserted rooms and said, "It is an historical piece. In a manner of speaking."

"It is about this man? This ghost who haunts I&S?"

"Yes, of course. Also this is farewell, or nearly," he added, and when they came to his inner chamber she was prepared to accept with courtesy a glass of wine, a stirrup cup—courteously, because Rubee and Awnlee had taught her more about manners than all her life before.

"You can regard the file as the evening's entertainment," he said.

He had forgotten or chose to ignore the past days' strain. Hanna was glad to let it pass. She settled onto a couch that tested the contours of her body, shuddered and reshaped itself to her measure. Jameson sat beside her and the couch shuddered again. *Universal minor earthquakes,* she thought.

"Is it a pageant?" she said. "Like Rubee's tales?"

"How odd that you should say that." He smiled; the parting near at hand might be a relief to him, too. "I haven't been immersed in the tales as you have," he said, "but I must confess I find myself at times reinterpreting events as an Uskosian might, or as I imagine he might. What you'll see is interesting enough without adding an alien perspective, however. It's neither text nor pageant; it's a holo recording of an interview between an I&S investigator and the former head of the Abbey of St. Kristofik on Alta. The abbot is dead now; the monks believe an extended lifespan pleases the Deity less than a natural one. I'm told that shortly after he died an anonymous donor made a generous gift to the school in his memory. The source was Valentine; you can make what you want of that. The interview took place fifteen years ago, five years after the *Pavonis Queen* incident. It concerns events that happened even earlier, between the time Kristofik appeared on Alta and the time he left—ran away, the abbot said, to Valentine."

Hanna started to say: *It seems irrelevant.* But Jameson spoke an order and the room went dark, and before she could say anything there was a new burst of light, the light of a holographic projection that took up most of the room. In its center, stone-still but three-dimensional, stood two men. One, cloaked and booted in black, had the look of assured competence that marked the men and women of Admin. The morning light left no shadows on his ebony skin. Surely he looked just the same today, performed the duties of the present with confidence. Fog lay on the fields behind him, as on a damp morning in autumn. Also he stood on

gray-white stone, so that Hanna's eye fell automatically on
his darkness and solidity, drawn to the only thing of substance in that land of mist.

The other man was old and pale. His cropped hair was
snowy, and the top of his head was bald. He wore a long
white robe loosely belted with rope. He was frail beside the
investigator, an aged wraith, part mist, part old white stone.
More than age twisted his face, but Hanna did not know
what it was until the figures moved; then she saw that it was
sorrow.

"I am still trying to assimilate what you have told me . . .
Accept it? No, not yet. I cannot accept it yet. I must forgive,
but my charity falls short. In time. Time and prayer . . ."

The investigator listened, but the old man spoke to himself. They walked together on stone pathways, past twisted
trees or treelike shrubs, stone walls, stone statues, white and
ghostly.

The old man said, "To think the boy I knew could do that
deed! And then you say he turned to evil long before!"

The other man said quietly, "There is evidence to support the theory that he was involved in the matter I spoke
of. There is no doubt about the rest of it."

"Oh dear, oh dear, how distressing this is! Please forgive
me. You have questions, don't you? I'm not helping much."

"I'm sorry to have such news to bring. Believe me, I am
sorry. You were fond of him?"

"Yes. Yes, I was. It was a blow when he ran away. I always
hoped to hear of him someday. To have news at last, and
such news!"

There was a stone bench by the path. The old man sat
down on it, gathering his robe with a wrinkled hand. His
face was unabashedly grieved. "Oh," he said, "his immortal
soul! How I pity him!"

"I'm very sorry." The investigator remained standing.

"Yes, yes, I know. Pray for him. I will, all of us will. That's
all that's left to do. We failed, you know, failed at everything
else we should have done. That's plain enough!"

The I&S man waited a moment. Then he said, "You understand that I must get as much information about him as
I can. I hoped you could tell me how he came here, what he
was like, what he thought about, why he left."

"Oh dear, oh dear. What he thought about? Who knows?

Things I never guessed. There must have been things I never saw. His confessor, maybe—but that is out of the question," he said, the old voice suddenly stone, and he looked at the investigator with eyes of iron.

"Of course," said the I&S man mildly. "I don't think we need to worry about that. Just tell me where he came from."

"I don't know where he came from." The old man stirred; there was a new glint in his eye. "Do you want to hear a mystery?" he said.

"By all means."

"Well, then, I will tell you a mystery. You can confirm it with the secular authorities. I won't say you can find out more about it; you won't find out any more. Eleven years ago—pardon, me, fifteen in Standard time—I came out of the rear gate one morning—have you seen all our grounds? No? The rear gate opens on an alley behind the sheds where we keep our tools. Sometimes we put food scraps in the alley. It doesn't happen often. We waste very little here. That morning Brother Cook burnt the bread. Some of it was past saving, and so it was put out for the dogs. Later I went out, I forget why I went, I forgot it then and never could remember. I found him in the alley. He was too busy eating to hear me. He was so starved there was no room in his belly for caution; there was only the hunger. When I spoke to him, he would have run away, but he would not leave the bread. I think he would have killed me if I had tried to take it from him. A wild animal. Nothing but bones, and at the time when a boy can hardly keep up with his bones, they grow so fast. His eyes were yellow, a strange sick color. Later it went away. Do you know how I finally got him to trust me? With food. Like an animal. And so we took him in."

"Was he from Alta?"

"Oh, no. I don't know where he came from, but it wasn't anywhere on Alta. Listen to this. He did not understand Standard speech, and we could make nothing of what he said. We recorded it and sent it, oh, everywhere. To Earth; even to Earth. The report would be still in his file. It said the language he spoke came from Earth, originally, I mean. As long ago as the twenty-fourth century, they said, his people must have been isolated; just before Standard was mandated, or maybe just after, so they hadn't got into the habit of using it. I don't remember what language it was. He learned Standard fast. He always learned fast."

"So he came from a colony? Which one?"

"That's the mystery, you see. I said there was a mystery. No one knows. The dialect didn't match anything."

"Who did this report?"

"Oh, famous people. Experts." The old man looked up, bright-eyed. "You know, during the Explosion, in the early days, the colonists went out so fast, *so* many from all parts of Earth, the records broke down. Ships vanished, too. Hundreds of them. Hundreds of thousands of people, I think it was millions, they fell into space and disappeared. I think about that sometimes. I thought about it when he was here. You've heard of the Lost Worlds?"

"Yes," said the other man, "but I don't believe in them. I'd like to see that report, if I may."

"Of course you can. But you'll find it says just what I've said."

"All right. How did he get to Alta from wherever it was?"

"I don't know. We guessed. A month before I found him a merchant put in at the port here. There were others, merchants and freighters come here all the time, but the others had nothing to hide. They were tracked and questioned. They'd never seen him. One of them couldn't be tracked. The port here isn't as careful as the ones in the Polity. That's what I'm told; I wouldn't know. When they looked into it they said the registration was false. There was no ship with that number and name."

"He could have told you something, surely. When he learned Standard."

"Could have, but didn't." The old man's grief had eased as he told the story. It caught up with him now. He bowed his head and took hold of the coarse rope that gathered his robe. There were knots in it; he fingered them as if for comfort. The investigator waited patiently. Presently the abbot began to speak, slowly.

"We asked him. He said he didn't know. I think he told the truth. That was at the beginning. When he said it, his eyes had that lost look, the look you see on children's faces when they've lost everything, parents, homes, and don't know why, don't understand why they've been hurt. We had

sixty boys here then, homeless children from everywhere.
It's near eighty now. Their faces run together now that I'm
old. But he stands out. He was a beautiful child when we got
some meat on him. He had beautiful hands, too, except, you
know, they'd been broken. Broken on purpose, the doctors
said, and set too late and badly. They weren't good for much.
So I took him to Willow myself to have them fixed. There
were signs of—of other kinds of violence. I don't need to
tell you about that. It's in his file."

The I&S man hesitated, let it pass. "All right. He was
injured, starving, came out of nowhere, as far as he and you
knew. What about later? There should have been evidence
of his origin."

"He said he didn't remember anything. He always said
that." The old man lifted his head. His face was dreamy with
remembering. The investigator let him run on unchecked.
"He meant he didn't want to talk about it. At first we told
him if he helped us find the place, maybe he could go home.
I think he didn't want to. I think it was the worst thing we
could have ever said. 'I remember nothing,' he said; he was
frightened, and he stuck to that always, though I taxed him
with lying, scolded him, taught him the evil of falsehood as
well as I could. Yet for the most part he was a good boy. He
was lively and intelligent, a leader. The boys of his time
looked up to him. Did his lessons, did his chores, worked
hard, played hard, the way a boy should. I don't know what
he said to God. He went through the forms. I don't know
what they meant to him, I don't know what the memories
meant that he wouldn't tell us. I used to worry about it. It
was deceptive because he seemed—"

The old man stopped suddenly. A minute went by. The
investigator stirred and seemed about to speak. But the
other man went on, slowly now. "When he had been here
awhile, he seemed so open. Sunny. When I think of him, I
see him smiling. It makes me forget—it made me forget.
The first year wasn't smooth. He fought with other boys,
bigger boys. When he did, he was like an animal again, the
wild animal I saw at the start. We told him finally we
couldn't keep him if he kept doing that. After that he mastered it, we thought, the demon in him—"

The pause was longer this time. At last the investigator
said neutrally, "Perhaps he did."

"Oh, I know, you don't believe in demons, do you?" There was irony in the old eyes now. "They come in many forms, you know. They gnaw at human weakness. They fatten on pain. Our exorcisms are sophisticated, these days. We tried. We tried all that love could do. We tried to help him trust us. But he never talked about where he came from, never told us what he'd been through, not even a hint. Brother Healer tried every trick he knew, too. Said he knew pain when he saw it, said it wasn't good to let it fester in a child, said it could make monsters. But he never got anywhere."

The old man fell silent, eyes on the stone at his feet. After a while the investigator said, "Did he say anything to you when he left?"

"Nothing. One morning he wasn't here."

"Had he given you reason to think he might go?"

"No. I don't know why he did it. I must not have known him at all. I must have been blind." The old man had been staring at the paving stones. He lifted his head and looked outward, straight at Hanna. "The seeds must have grown all the time he was here. I never saw it. I know *how* he left. A freighter from Willow signed him on. He was not well educated, not by your standards, but he was strong and quick to learn. We learned the freighter took him to Valentine. I was afraid when I heard that, but I thought . . . He had a strong will. He wasn't docile; when I say a boy is good, I don't mean that. I prayed. I did not think he would be bent to vice against his will."

"I've heard nothing to indicate it was against his will."

"No. No, of course it wasn't. Corruption doesn't work that way. The sinner collaborates with the sin. He knew about Valentine. He knew enough to choose. We don't try to keep the children from the knowledge of evil. They need to know the enemy to guard against him. We teach them to shun the tempter. Sometimes we fail."

The old man looked as if he might weep. The investigator said, "I won't trouble you any more now, sir. Except that I'd like to get a record of his file, especially the linguistic report."

"Certainly. Certainly."

The old man got to his feet. He was even paler now, the color of the stone, and bent.

"Where did you get his name?" the investigator asked. "Did you name him Michael?"

"We did. What he said when we asked him his name sounded something like that."

They walked in silence; thinned to mist; disappeared.

Hanna found she had been holding her breath. She said, as if she had been listening to a good story ended too soon, "Isn't there more?"

"Hmm?" Jameson looked at her curiously when normal light returned. The light was warm, but not bright; after the pearly radiance of a fog-washed morning on Alta, it was stuffy and confining.

"Nothing . . ." She held herself still. The gaze she turned on Jameson was cool. She said, "Why have you shown me this?"

"It's interesting, don't you think?"

"You did not have me watch it for its intrinsic interest."

"Granted." He got up and moved across the room. She regarded the broad back coldly, knowing that in the silence he examined a range of words and picked among them. At last he said, "If the worst should happen you will need to know how to deal with him. I believe the key to this man lies in his earliest days. Which are dark. Dark to him because they are shadowed by hunger and violence; dark to everyone else because they are hidden."

"Perhaps I can take a thorn from his paw and make him my friend," Hanna said a little wearily.

He swung around and gave her a look that was not as friendly as before. "A classical reference? From you?"

"Me? The over-specialized H'ana? No, don't worry, I won't disillusion you. I only know about it because there is a similar tale among the Uskosians, and someone told me about the parallel. Starr, you take this man too seriously— all because the I&S computers bumped out his name."

"I take their judgment seriously enough to be glad the person going with Rubee is capable of quick defensive action."

She said immediately, "No. I'm done with that."

"I hope so," he said, and now he was deliberately mild. "I know how you feel about it; about, especially, the Zeigans you killed. I understand your reluctance to consider doing anything of the kind again. Yet the fact remains that you were trained for war, and you fought in an interhuman war; and later, in a desperate situation with the People of Zeig-Daru, you were capable of doing what you had to do. I hope you are never again put to that test. But consider, Hanna, what this man is. Consider: after the monks had saved him and sheltered him for years, he left them without a word and went straight to a life they despised. Then there was the leap to piracy and, most likely, murder. Will you smile at him and wait for him to kiss your hand?"

Hanna's mouth twisted. Put that way it was horrible. She said, "There was a Lost World. Nobody knew about it fifteen years ago. But the Zeigans destroyed it long before our time, before his time. He couldn't have come from there."

"If he got to Alta from a Lost World, it couldn't be considered lost," Jameson said sensibly. "There are enough backward pocket settlements even within the Polity to keep a linguist occupied for eternity. I don't put much stock in the abbot's speculations. I should think their healer was right, though, when he spoke of monsters being made."

"I would be interested in seeing his psyche profile," Hanna said, and then, because he gave her an odd look, "What's wrong with that?"

"I don't have it," Jameson said.

She might have let it go, except that she sensed a rare uncertainty in him. "Did you try to get it?" she said.

"Yes. Figueiredo said it was not to be disseminated outside I&S. He said it was anomalous and contradictory. He ascribed this," Jameson said—with a straight face, but Hanna saw the amusement behind it—"to the fact that an I&S operative who got close to him, and ought to have been a definitive source of information, was female."

"Oh, nonsense!"

"I think so, too. Still, for whatever reason, there is no consistent and therefore no valid profile."

"Well, if you start with the presumption that your subject is a monster, and then he doesn't act like one, I suppose you have trouble putting the pieces together."

Hanna gave up. She wanted to go home, or to what passed for it here. This would be her last night planet-bound for some weeks; the quarantine facility orbited Luna. After that her course would take her outward; past Heartworld, which she had visited, and Carrollis, which she had never seen; past a settlement named Revenge, which she had never even heard of until the *Bird*'s course became important; and after that on and out and out. She said before she left, though: "All this is a waste of time, isn't it? There's no sign of tampering with the program; not if you've told me everything."

"I've told you everything. I'm uneasy, all the same."

She gave the last words little thought when he said them. She did not mean to think about Michael Kristofik any more at all. But she yielded to her wish to ride the wind in the Earthly night, high above silver and black; and as she sailed through the moonlight the reason came to her for Kristofik's irrational effect on I&S and Admin, Jameson and Figueiredo and all of them. They were the keepers of order and rules, and the stranger from nowhere cared nothing for any of it, and ignored both rules and keepers; successfully, too.

During the week she spent in the isolation chamber, they took so much blood from her that she became weak. Each time they took some they came back and fed her more chemicals, poisonous brews, some of which contained living creatures. The ones put straight into her veins did not make up for loss of blood. They said she would make more quickly. They had to get it right, though it would be impossible for her to walk among human beings until she came home and the work was undone. They were stripping her of her immunity to certain dangerous organisms at large in human society, because in some way she did not understand it was incompatible with immunity to common Uskosian equivalents. Rubee and Awnlee, separated from her for now, endured the process in reverse.

Hanna did what was asked of her, and otherwise withdrew from human intercourse. She had planned the withdrawal, not consciously, for a long time; she understood that almost as soon as she entered quarantine. The isolation chamber was built into a habitat in orbit around Luna. The accommodations were spare but comfortable, and though she could not touch another human being (except those swathed in protective garments), she could talk freely with anyone she knew at any distance. She might have said her good-byes then. But she had planned, not consciously, to get that done beforehand. She was finished because she had sensed a subtle internal warning that she would need this space of time in between Earth and embarkation, though she hardly knew for what.

The reason unfolded as the quiet days passed. When first she stepped into her chamber she sighed and felt relief; thereafter all her thoughts turned away from Earth. She did not so much think as feel; feel Earth drop away from far under her feet, not physically, not yet, but in importance; feel Rubee and Awnlee as lodestones close by; feel her thought change as her body changed to something that could no longer stay whole among humans.

In a year Nlatee said to his sire, "With fire we might warm ourselves in winter, and the path to the land of the mountains of fire is not long."

The path was discouraged by the Master of Chaos, however, and Nlatee's sire and all his sire's selfings and all the people sought to dissuade him. They said, "Who knows what will happen to us if you take that path?"

Nlatee on a night therefore broke open the winter stores and took what he needed, and he set out alone on the path to the land of the mountains of fire.

On a day of his journey the Master of Chaos came to him and said, "I see that you travel, Nlatee. Where are you going?"

Nlatee, because the Master had discouraged this path, answered, "I am going to the great river yonder, to steal fish from the persons who live there."

"That is forbidden by treaty, Nlatee."

"Then I will take care they do not catch me."

The Master signified amusement, and disappeared.

Nlatee thought it would be best for the Master to see him no more; yet how could he not be seen? Who knows what the Master sees?

While Nlatee pondered this he saw a beast. He killed it and skinned it and while he ate its meat he said to himself, "This path is not discouraged to beasts. If I were a beast, the Master would not notice me."

And so he put the skin of the beast on his shoulders and its horn on his head, and went on his way clothed in the hide of the beast.

Nlatee went on his way and the land was warm though it was winter, because he came near to the mountains of fire and they warmed all the land about them, so that green things flourished forever. He came to the mountains of fire and there he kindled a flame, and he returned with it to his land.

When his sire and all his sire's selfings and all the people saw that he had tricked the Master of Chaos and that no evil had come to them as a result, they took the fire and warmed themselves, and would have made Nlatee head huntsman. But Nlatee refused.

"I am going back to the land of the mountains of fire, and there I will bring forth my selfings and rear them," he said.

"But why?" said all the people.

"It's warmer there," said Nlatee, "and if the fire goes out you can rekindle it easily. I don't like it here any more."

So Nlatee returned to the land of the mountains of fire where all was green forever, and in later years his descendants warred with the descendants of his sire's other selfings and with the descendants of all the people, and the descendants of Nlatee won because if their fires went out they could easily be rekindled.

And the Master of Chaos came, and signified amusement.

From her position deep in the interior of the habitat, Hanna could not see Luna or Earth or any stars; yet paradoxically, though she was confined and enclosed, her awareness of infinity outside grew and grew. She did not need to look out to see stars. They were there when she closed her eyes, rank on rank of them, blazing in spinning islands. Always deep space had drawn her, from the first; always her desire had led her there; she had commanded her first Jump at fifteen. *I am an exopsychologist. That is what I do.* Being an exopsychologist was a fine excuse for straying on the edges of space. Was that the real reason for the paths she had chosen? The knowledge of her connection to the great void expanded daily, hourly it seemed. The universe was in motion, it vibrated, it shouted with joy, thunderous. She stood stock-still in a bare sealed room and listened to it. She was an arrow in the instant before release. She heard a great heart beating, and she would fly to it as to a homecoming.

On the very last day before launch, Starr Jameson came

to see her. It was day where he had come from; in Hanna's chamber, attuned to the rhythms of the *Far-Flying Bird*, it was night. A transparent barrier separated them, and there was dusk on her side of it. Rubee and Awnlee slept; Hanna heard them sleeping. She stood at the barrier and watched Jameson pretend to find her normal. It was hot inside the chamber, as it would be on the *Far-Flying Bird*. Hanna's concessions to Earthly convention were sloughing off one by one; she wore nothing but scraps of fabric molded round her breasts and hips, and her body distracted him. It was something to get a physical reaction from a man futilely desired for so long.

He talked dispassionately enough. He told her about all the precautions Contact and I&S had taken. It did not matter now that there would be no armed escort for the *Bird*. The course program was secure; it was more secure than any other knowledge in human space. All the anxiety had been over a rumor, a wisp, a nothing. He had come to reassure her so she would not be afraid.

That was considerate of him. Hanna listened, and thought that here was someone else who had taken blood from her. The fullness of the freely, generously given self was a memory; her love had gone wrong somehow; it had become thin and acid and if she let it would only leach the life out of her. After tonight she could put it far behind her. She was eager to be gone.

At the very last he said, "I will not see you again until you return. Rubee rejected the idea of a formal leavetaking."

"I know. He wanted to be alone with Awnlee. They have spent much time in meditation."

"So I hear. An attitude of prayer, I'm told."

"Oh, no, it's not that."

"No? I'm afraid I've never gotten it straight about the Master of Chaos. None of us have yet."

"I wrote a paper about it."

"But no one understood it."

"I'll try again when I get back, or while I'm gone. But you must have understood that they don't worship the Master. They recognize his hand, they beseech him, they curse him—but they do not worship him."

"That seems very wise of them," he said.

Because he could not touch her to say good-bye, he put his hands against the barrier. She set her own, much smaller, against them. It seemed that a trick of dimension had set him far away. Before he went away finally, he turned to look at her once more. He hesitated. She saw herself just for a moment as he saw her: beautiful, unique, a creature who moved freely through strangeness and somehow always came back to being Hanna. He had known her for a long time, he had watched the shaping of her, and he was so used to her that the fresh perception of the moment surprised him profoundly. It seemed to her that he might come back.

Hanna turned away. She melted into the darkness of her chamber and did not sleep, and waited for the hour when she could come to the *Far-Flying Bird*.

"There's the bastard," Shen said after the last Jump. It brought them out close to Revenge, compensating for the season so that they were at the right place in the planet's orbit and even looking at its dayside. It was still a million klicks away, and they boosted magnification for a better view. Cloud and ice made it nearly all white; it reflected back the light of the determined star and never got warmer, it was ice and ice and ice. A surge in the sun's radiation might make it productive, that or terraforming. But nobody needed it badly enough to bother with terraforming. It was left to the People of the Rose.

"Got something on infrared," Shen said. "Just vulcanization, though."

Michael said, "*GeeGee*. Is it day or night at the settlement?"

"Night," said his ship laconically.

"Check again when it comes around," Shen said. She got up and stretched. *GeeGee* would handle the final approach. Michael stayed where he was, looking out at the sterile brilliance of Revenge. Presently he began to sing. It was a measured dirge.

There were three ravens sat on a tree,
Downe a down, hay downe a down;
And they were black as they might be,
With a downe.

One of them said to his mate,
When shall we our breakfast take?
With a downe, derrie derrie down . . .

Shen made a rude noise and disappeared. Michael sang
on.

Down in yonder green field,
Downe a down, hay downe a down,
Lies a slain knight under his shield
With a downe . . .

Lise unpeeled herself from the wall of *GeeGee*'s control
center. She was pink and gold, the walls and carpeting were
the color of a ripe apricot, the light was faintly golden and
suited Lise well. She belonged here; Michael and Shen, grim
and dark, did not. No wonder he had thought of ravens. She
came lightly to the seat Shen had left and dropped into it.
She said, "Why doesn't Shen like the song? I like it."

"It's a sad song."

He leaned back and put an arm around her thin shoulders. She had gotten it into her head that he preferred
grown-up women, and accepted him happily as a kind of
older brother; though, "I will be grown up someday," she
had said.

"What are ravens?"

"Big black birds."

"Like swans?"

"No, and what you're thinking of aren't really swans.
They just call them that on Carrollis. Ravens aren't that
big."

"What did they have for breakfast?"

He turned his head and looked at the fresh, pretty face,
into the bright blue eyes. He said gently, "They didn't have
breakfast that morning."

"It isn't good to be hungry," she said seriously.

"I know."

They sat in companionable silence for a time. *GeeGee*'s
motion was not perceptible, but Revenge was a little larger.
Presently Lise said, "Why didn't Shen want me to come?
This is fun."

"She didn't want you to come because it might be dangerous. She's right, too. If we hadn't left so fast, if I'd been able to think of anything to do with you, you wouldn't be here. I'm telling you right now that you're not getting off this ship until I tell you you can. Do you hear me?"

She looked rebellious, but she nodded. She said with a startling switch to adulthood, "What's all this about?"

"None of your business, little puss."

"I will find out," she said placidly.

"I bet you will." He grinned, but quit at a vision of Lise in the hands of the man he hunted. She nestled in the crook of his arm, excited by her new status as a traveler. Once upon a time he had taken responsibility for Theo, and once again for Shen. A lump of defeat that could not be called a man. A madwoman who had tried to kill him for a handful of cash. This was different. But probably he would not be on Revenge anyway, Chrome-Maxwell-Pallin-Anyname.

Must have had a thousand names in thirty years. B they called him thirty years ago, just B. Saw him once in Shoreground later. Putting together the stake then. Looking for the chance. Knew it was Tonson, didn't know how. Thought about that, nothing else, wasn't room for more. Coming out of Flora's. Mind's not on your work, she said. Lady had complaints, Mike. Said you were bored. Sorry, won't happen again, pretty boring lady you know what I mean. Walked out and there he was. Looked at me straight. Knew me. Smiled I knew that goddamned smile take it off with his face with a blade if I see it again. Went round the corner, I got there he was gone. Almost had him in my hands and he was gone.

"Mike? That hurts." He looked down at Lise and saw pain in her eyes. His fingers clutched her shoulder too hard. He let go quickly.

"Sorry, puss. Didn't mean to do that."

She said, dismissing it, "Can I watch the landing?"

"Sure you can."

"When?"

"Later. When it's day there."

She smiled, the ache in her shoulder forgotten. They watched Revenge come closer.

Michael knew what to expect of Revenge. Theo had not been there before; he began making noises of displeasure as soon as the *Golden Girl* came to a landing outside the

city of The Rose. It was early in autumn, but the red rock
jutted in patches from a layer of ice; there were clouds over
the city and it brooded bitterly under the gray ceiling. The
city was scattered over the rocks instead of the snow-
covered fields close by, as if the settlers had chosen to make
things difficult for themselves. There were some seven hundred buildings, all low and making no use of the ubiquitous
rock; they were premanufactured structures of varying ages
and designs, some welded together, badly married. At the
end of the descent they had seen people moving in the city,
and the *Golden Girl* must have been seen also; in a place
like this the ship could only be an object of wonder; yet they
landed only half a kilometer from the nearest modules, and
nothing moved outside them.

Michael said, "Come on, Theo. Let's go see if we can find
somebody to talk to."

"Looks nasty. *I* should go," Shen said.

"They're harmless—at least they always have been. I've
never done anything to get them mad. I wouldn't take a
woman with me, though, not and expect any cooperation."

"Me," Lise said softly. She tugged at Michael's arm.

"Not you. Especially not you."

He detached himself and went with Theo to find winter
gear, warmcoats, heated boots. When they left the *Golden
Girl,* they still had not seen a single inhabitant. The walk was
short but not easy. The *Golden Girl's* landing site was the
only flat place among the rocks; a hundred meters from the
ship they had to begin climbing over them or skirting them.
There was ice underfoot, and stones that turned treacherously. When they passed the first buildings, there were people at last: half a dozen small boys, bundled in black. One
held a ball, another a tapering metal rod. Perhaps they had
been playing with the objects. Now they stood and stared.

Michael said, "Hello. We come from the Polity. I want to
speak to an elder."

Theo muttered, "Polity?"

"I don't know if they've heard of Valentine. They know
about the Polity."

For a minute there was no reaction at all from the boys.
Then one moved; he took off at a dead run into the town.

"Is that an answer?" Theo said.

"I don't know. Maybe. We'll wait."

They waited a long time. The children did not go back to
their game. They stayed where they were and stared. Michael felt a prickly wrongness and tracked it down. He got
on well with children and knew their ways; he and Theo
could not have come in such a way to another such isolated
place without being surrounded by children and besieged
with questions when the first shyness wore off. But not here.

The boy who had run away did not come back. An adult
came finally, moving without haste through a stony channel
that could not be called a street. A cap covered his ears and
clung to his skull. He was heavily bearded and dressed, like
the children, in a loose black tunic and trousers. There was
no warmcoat, though, nor any real protection against the
cold. The season would not be cold for him.

He said a word and the children moved away, walking
quickly but not running. One disappeared into a house
nearby. The others straggled on and vanished among the
rocks and structures beyond. The word had been unintelligible; even Standard was changing here, where contact with
the linguistic mainstream was so rare.

The man said nothing else. He did not look as if he were
going to. Michael had prepared a speech; he made it. He
regretted intruding on the peace of the People of the Rose.
He would disturb them for no more than a few minutes'
time. He wished to join his friend, a red-haired man who
might have come here in recent months. The world was
large. Might the People of the Rose have word of him?
Might they know where he had gone?

The silence when he finished was so long that he wondered if the man had understood him, or, understanding
him, would not answer. *Answers one way or another.* He
glanced at Theo. It might be necessary to come back, and
bring with them Theo's answer kit. And indeed, when the
elder had stood for a time in silence, he turned around and
walked away.

Theo stared after him. "Hard to carry on a conversation
with, isn't he?"

"They weren't this bad when I was here before."

Michael started after the elder, Theo following. When
they had gone a few paces the elder turned. "Begone!" he
said.

"I would like to do that," Michael said. "I intend to. Will

you at least tell me if my friend has been here? I only want," he added truthfully, "to take him away."

He had worn no gloves and his hands were cold. He folded them under his arms and waited some more. The elder said finally, "If you do that, the Lord will bless you."

Michael's heart jumped so far he thought the jolt must show in his face. He heard Theo draw a breath. He said carefully, "He will go as soon as I find him, and so will I. Are there others with him? They won't stay after he goes. And I'll tell the Oversight Service you want them gone."

The elder thought it over and said, "I am Elder Rann. Come with me."

They followed him through icy pathways to a building perhaps a little larger than most. Inside there was a bare hall, unheated, with doors on either side. The elder opened one of them. Past it there was a flurry, but when Michael and Theo went in no one was there. A woman of the house, Michael guessed, had slipped away. Inside the room were a table and six hard chairs. There were no ornaments, and no other furniture except a case set against one wall. This held two roses carved in stone, a third of some softer substance, and six books.

"Wait here," Rann said, and left them.

The room was stuffy, and no sound came into it. "What's he gone for?" Theo said.

"Man-eating dogs," Michael said solemnly.

"They have those?"

"No. Of course not. They don't have any animals. It's against their beliefs."

He looked closely at the roses. He had taken the central one to be made of fabric, but now he saw that it was molded from a plastic with the texture of flesh. The lines of the petals were obscenely suggestive. He lifted an eyebrow and took down one of the books, listening for the elder's return. The book was covered in fine linen and had been bound by hand. The pages were handwritten. He opened it and read:

"The one-hundred-twenty-sixth subclass of the sixty-seventh class of knowledge is this. The land which is given by the LORD is HIS and HE gives a small part of it to man. It is the will of the LORD that man encroach not on the land under HIS sway.

"The one-hundred-twenty-seventh subclass of the

sixty-seventh class of knowledge is this. The hand of man is heavy on the land, but less heavy than the hand of the LORD."

He heard a sound outside the room and shelved the book quickly. The elder came in carrying a long scroll. He put it down on the table and unrolled it: an exquisite hand-drawn map. Michael bent over it and saw that it showed the city. Every shabby building was on it, with a name or a function written neatly from corner to corner, and the gradations of rock were indicated in shades of rose and red.

"You landed here," Rann said, pointing. "We are now here. They are *here.*" He set a blunt fingertip on a rectangle larger than the rest. It was at the side of the city opposite *GeeGee*'s landing site.

Michael said incredulously, "They're in the city?"

"They are not here now. They have gone."

Gone. He was paralyzed. One faint lead after another, traces, guesses—where the hell could the trail lead from here? Theo glanced at him anxiously. But Rann said, "They will return. They said they will return. They said if we touch their possessions we will die. We do not want them. I have seen them. There are tawdry, frivolous things and offensive machines. When the Fleet ship comes, it will drive them away. But the ship will not come for one hundred days, and the Lord has sent you to expunge them from his land."

Michael breathed again. "I will certainly do my best," he said.

The warehouse was booby-trapped, but at a primitive level that suited B's assessment of the People of the Rose. The safeguards gave Michael and Theo no trouble. Inside was a great empty space, but also, stacked against one wall, a mound of crates. They broke into some of them and found that the "tawdry, frivolous things" were treasures. There was a silver tree that swayed and sang. A portrait of a lady came to life in pearly-rose flesh. When Michael reached out to touch her he felt softness, but saw without surprise that his hand came out her back. A plain black cube when touched produced a symphony of color and sound accompanied within a small radius by gravitational variations that made them dizzy. Near to it a crystalline complex of shapes winked in and out of real existence. There were many more beautiful things. Nearly all were marked "ones"; the creators of some were known throughout human space.

Against silver-gray walls the wonders stood and moved and sang. He looked at them with wide eyes. Kia's hand pulled him on, but he hung back, staring. It was the first time he had seen beauty like this, and he had no word for it.

"Mike? Mike!"

"Yeah." A thick sound. His eyes cleared. He was back in the warehouse on Revenge, and Theo stood among the crates, apprehensive. He was pale, and he looked at Michael with something like fear. Michael took a deep breath. The blood-deep rage retreated to the place where it lived, mocking him; frightening him, this time. It had stayed where it was supposed to be for years. Yet in a few hours it had shown itself twice, leaving the bruise on Lise's shoulder, the look on Theo's face. A name hung in his mind: *Kia.* There was nothing else with it. Whatever it meant was gone back deep inside him with the fury.

Theo said slowly, "If he's stored all this here, if it's got to be gone before Oversight comes in a hundred days, do you think . . ."

They looked at each other. Michael finished it. "That he'll be back soon?"

"We could be close, Mike."

"Could be. Could be."

He had the priceless ability to think of one thing at a time. He put everything out of his mind except the coming days.

"We got some luck," he said. "Now we wait."

Chapter 2

The setting forth of the *Far-Flying Bird* was a stately processional. Cheers accompanied it, wrenching Rubee, Awnlee, and Hanna from their seductive detachment. It seemed there were human beings on every bit of rock or ice in the stellar system of Sol, and all of them had something to say. "I did not know there were so *many* of you!" said Rubee, but he had known the number, twenty billion, from the start, and knew that eight billion occupied the home system.

"Talking germs," Hanna said. It was not her habit to disparage humankind, not even the nontelepathic majority D'neerans called collectively "true-humans"; but she had hoped they were done with this.

She was the more derisive because the bombardment of talk was not necessary. The *Bird* might have Jumped from Lunar orbit directly into deep space, there was no need for this sequence of in-system Jumps, it had been planned for political reasons. Rubee and Awnlee were not to escape without a formal leavetaking after all; only instead of getting a single banquet of platitudes, they were getting it piecemeal.

They were also widely seen. The Polity could not pass up the opportunities for propaganda provided by this quick peace with friendly aliens. Hanna thought the citizens of the Polity worlds must have seen enough of Rubee's and Awnlee's mild lumpy faces, but somebody, somewhere, did not think enough was enough. There were many requests for visual transmissions from the *Bird*. When Hanna played back edited versions culled from assorted newsbeams, she found the public eye was directed rather too much to herself. Someone discovered where she had gotten the opal that gleamed provocatively between her breasts, which Starr Jameson had given her long before. The old gossip about the two of them revived and was flung about human space all over again, titillating God knew whom. Were true-human lives so dreary that the long-dead affair of an aging man and a demolished woman could be some kind of entertainment? She listened with her lip curled, but she took off the opal.

She did not take off the other thing she wore close round her throat, a worked silver strand that was not a present to Hanna from anyone, but one of the gifts from humankind to the peoples of Uskos. The others were stored in the *Bird*'s cargo hold. They were precious works made by human hands and brains, and they were (thought Hanna, who had seen them on one ceremonial occasion) very beautiful. The Uskosians would like them. She liked better the filigree chain that for all its look of delicacy could be used; a thing of practical import she could cup in her palm. It held secrets to be read with the proper tools. It was a key to the Outside, and it traveled to Uskos warmed by her skin, stirred by the surge of her blood.

"I *could* remove it, if I wished, if I tried, if I knew the proper codes," Awnlee said, his fingers impossibly thin, prying gently at the chain. He teased her to remove it, she could do that, the invisible clasp was keyed to her voice; she laughed and refused, teasing him. The scanners sent the picture to every part of human space.

It seemed to her obscurely that something would change when Sol's system was left behind, but the border was passed, and it was not enough. Voices still fell into the *Bird* like music, men's voices or women's, in Standard speech accented more or less strangely. The accents all together sketched the settlements of man, and all of them were official. Hanna thought: *That is noise.* To escape it she prowled the ship. When the optics were finally blanked, she reclaimed her opal. The hot air of the *Bird* comforted her skin.

Another Jump, another and another: for all the distance the *Bird* ate so quickly, the pace seemed slow to Hanna. Yet once it had been slower, because new. Someone had come this way a first time, without foreknowledge; before Willow

Terry A. Adams

was found; before the Founders of D'neera, fleeing genocide, escaped to a new world; before the ragged bands settled Nestor and Lancaster and created from the dirt and
rock of one world a sickness, of the other a pastoral dream.

That was history. Hanna did not care much about history.
Starr Jameson had tried without success to teach her its importance, "because if you do not understand it," he had said,
"you will be its blind tool."

She was then working on Zeig-Daru, coming home to
him and Earth at the intervals she herself had prescribed as
mandatory for any D'neeran whose work meant being lost
in the People. To communicate with the People meant, by
definition, giving up the separateness of the self. Hanna said
to him: "Contemplation is the luxury of the detached." She
could not be detached and do what she did so successfully
that when Rubee and Awnlee came, he begged her to do it
again: saturate herself in an alien culture until she was more
alien than human.

Now detachment was her only wish, though she did not
understand why. She only knew that the increasing distance
between herself and humankind was not enough. And so
she waited restless and impatient and trapped by the murmur of human voices in a space that seemed not empty, but
crawling with life.

On one day of the voyage through this busy waste, Rubee
called her to the central command module from which he
directed the *Bird*'s Jumps. This was a circular platform in the
center of the circular bridge, bordered by a skeletal structure made of thin columns of light. The light was composed
of mathematical symbols that changed rapidly when the
Bird was in Inspace mode, and Rubee monitored them by
eye all at once. When Hanna passed through it to Rubee,
the hair on her arms and the back of her neck stood up. In
the center of the module a column of golden metal rose
from the floor to the height of Rubee's waist. Its top had
only two features: a ring of flame-green jewels surrounding
a well of darkness, and below that a small indentation.

Hanna asked, "Do you wish me to see a thing, Rubee?"
She was fluent in Ellsian now, and no longer used a translator.

"I do," he said, "and I will have pleasure in your perceiving it. I wished to do this sooner. But I have not because it is a thing among we three only, you and Awnlee and myself, and we have not been truly alone. The surveillance skills of your people are admirable."

Hanna laughed out loud. "You are courteous to speak so, Rubee. I do not know if 'admirable' is the word I would use. But now that we are alone, I will serve you in any way that I can, and it will be an honor to do so."

"Indeed, part of my intention is to ask you to give a service to me," he said, "and if you will undertake it, the honor will be mine. Yet also I have in mind a token of friendship between our peoples, but even more a token of the bond among we travelers, and especially the amity between you and my selfing. When I brought him forth on a winter day, I did not know that he would befriend a creature of another star! Therefore in a year I will make the story of the Friendship of Awnlee, and so it will be remembered forever like the friendship of Porsa and Awtell. But this story is not ended yet, and it will not end in my time, for I am no longer young, Awnlee coming to me late. And the service I ask is this: that if it is your fate also to survive Awnlee, you will finish the tale for my people. I would charge you with this; for our friendship is such that if you will, you stand to me as a selfing, and Awnlee's close kin. Will you accept this charge from me?"

"With gratitude, Rubee," she answered, but she was startled. Uskosians did not take kinship lightly nor speak of it casually; on the contrary. She said uncertainly, "Have I heard more than you have said?"

"You have not," Rubee said. His fingers rippled with pleasure. "I used those words with deliberation: 'You stand to me as a selfing.' They are the words of formal adoption in the second degree. Though you may reject my choosing, if you wish," he added.

"No! I am more honored than I can say. Yet I did not expect this, sire."

"No one will expect it because it is new," he said with some complacency. "I do not know what my people will think. You will be a citizen of Ell now, though an alien, and it will be interesting to hear what will be said. Perhaps they will say: if Rubee wished to adopt a selfing, could he not have chosen a person of our world? It is known among my friends and farther kin that I will bring forth no more self-ings, to my sorrow, and that I have long wished that Awnlee might not be without close kin. It is an old loneliness for him, and for myself as well; and who better to assuage it than one who shares with us what no one else of any race will share? By that I mean the circumstances of our meeting, which had great significance for those of both our worlds, and this our journeying together. And perhaps in time you will think of this, and have less loneliness, too; you, the ever-homeless traveler."

Hanna stared at him. *The ever-homeless traveler*—she wanted to say, *Rubee, isn't that going a little far?* She had a home, D'neera was her home, she had a house upon it near a lake in a cold climate—

A house cared for by others, a house in which she could not remember where the light switches were.

Her hand went slowly to the opal at her throat. The occasion surely called for an exchange of gifts, as most Uskosian occasions did. But she had never been fond of having many personal possessions, and in the last years she had left behind those she had one by one, so that all she had of her own on the *Far-Flying Bird* was the jewel Jameson had given her.

She said, "Sire, I give you all my gratitude, and I would gift you with treasure; but this is all I have. And it signifies a bond that was broken."

"Then we will defer gifting," he said. "I will own with pleasure whatever you choose to give when the time is convenient; but indeed, I cannot give you now what I wish to give, because it cannot yet be spared."

He bent and touched the green jewels on the column between them. "Look!" he said.

She came around the column to stand beside him. He touched the darkness centered in the stones and she saw that its surface was not, as she had supposed, a miniature screen for electronic display, but a transparent covering over blackness. She leaned closer, and looked into an infinite depth clouded by silver webs whose threads appeared and disappeared at random and directed the eye to—where?—she could not tell, and she could not take her eyes from them. They were beautiful, and cold.

"What is it?" she whispered.

"It is the visible aspect of a confluence of dimensions. There are eleven at least; no doubt there are more."

The remote lights absorbed her. "I do not understand ..."

"It is a portion of what you call Inspace," Rubee said.

"Of Inspace...?" Hanna looked up, with some difficulty; the depth attracted her powerfully. She said, "How can this be?"

He was proud, and pleased by her wonder. He said, "I have learned that the making-visible of the confluence of dimensions is not a skill that humans have. We possessed it nearly from the time we learned to distort the dimensions and so cheat the limits of lightspeed. In the designing of the *Far-Flying Bird* it was deemed suitable to place here what you see; but when we have come to my home, I wish it to be yours."

Hanna said, "Sire, my people have never made a thing like this. We use Inspace, but we have never made any of it visible. The value of this gift is precious beyond words to say, either in your language or in mine. I cannot think of anything I might give you that is not small in comparison."

"Yet its true significance lies in more than its intrinsic value," Rubee said, "and I will show you that it is already yours."

He touched the phenomenon, the ends of his fingers thin as blades. He slipped them under the green jewels and pulled; the stones proved to be fastened to a thin cylinder that came up smoothly from the column. He gave it to Hanna. It was no longer than her hand and felt weightless. It was finely engraved with glittering spirals, and when she looked at it closely she saw that script was woven through the spirals, some of it Standard, some Ellsian. The Standard words said, with many formal flourishes, that Rubee and Awnlee of Ell, on a day aboard the *Far-Flying Bird,* had set into the molecules of this metal a program that marked in the symbols of two planets completion of the course from Uskos to Earth, the homeworld of their honored friend. If they had not assigned Hanna quite the correct birthplace, that did not matter; they regarded Earth as the home-world of all humans, and they were, Hanna supposed, essentially right. She said, "My dear friend, when did you make this?"

"We did not 'make' it," he said. "It has been a part of this ship from the beginning of our journey, and we had only to refine the programming contained in the surface when your Fleet gave us the end of our course. As to the embellishments, and addition of your name, I began them, in our script, soon after you joined us on this ship. Awnlee, when he had learned your script and mathematics, did the remainder; also he entered the course in a form a human ship can read, for your sake, when one day you wish to come to our home, which is yours. The gift you yourself bring to Uskos, the course which is contained in the fillet you wear, proves that the ways of thought of our peoples are not so different. Yet this is not a gift of state, but for your possession only. It is yours although you cannot possess it wholly yet; we stand over the main course computer at this moment, and this is what it reads. But at our journey's end it will be altogether yours, and it will be a memento forever of our travels together, and of our trust which is that of sire and selfing."

Hanna turned the precious thing slowly in her hands. She could not find words adequate to thank him, and so she touched his thought: *There is nothing like this in the universe. It is unique. It is both yours and mine. I shall have no other comparable gift, ever. And I will remember you forever.*

They moved rapidly through the remainder of human space. They followed the route Fleet had given Rubee when he came, a clear, well-charted path, though first Hanna had been rushed to meet him so that a telepath could examine his thought for hostility or hidden motives. After that the Fleet vessels surrounding the *Bird* had become in fact what they pretended to be at first: the escort of an honored guest.

Hanna resumed her restless tours of the *Bird* and counted the Jumps and the good-byes, checking them off against an invisible list in her mind. When no more were left, it would mean escape. Among columns of crystal and silver in the *Bird*'s engineering section she asked: *Escape from what?* And answered the questions in the banner-bright lounge where Jameson had met her some weeks before: *From Starr. From humankind and its rules and demands.*

She did not know why this was so. Perhaps she only needed a vacation. Perhaps she ought to have gone to Valentine. With Rubee and Awnlee in tow?—the thought of the stately Rubee astray on Valentine made her laugh. But laughter left her quickly. The *Bird* seemed hotter in the "nights," and she slept badly. The list of Jumps and farewells dwindled each hour.

On the last day there was a final farewell from Lancaster. After that the messages stopped, except the routine transmissions from Fleet stations monitoring the *Bird*'s progress. They had come to the edge of the greater gulf, past which all was unknown, except for the thin thread of their course and Uskos' small sphere of space at the end.

Here they paused for final systems checks. The light of the command module faded; the free-standing columns of numbers dimmed. Rubee and the *Bird* and the voices of Fleet technicians talked together, examining life support, servomechanisms, data banks, plasma engines, navigation, course computation, quantum-dimensional mechanics; they went over all of it again and again.

While that went on, Hanna paced, unable either to be still or to leave the bridge. Apart from the central module, the bridge was not exotic to human eyes. The predominant color was a soothing cream. The interior semicircle was thick with displays and work terminals all along the wall; the exterior curve was transparent, so that those on the bridge always could see, in a sense, where they were going. Hanna passed back and forth behind the padded benches that rimmed this section of the circle, and kept looking out, looking Outside. The *Bird* pointed in the direction of its next Jump. Already far behind it lay a relay whose number no one used any longer. In conversations with Fleet it was Omega, the last, the end; Uskosian tongues turned the word into Oneba. The vagaries of space-time made it safe for the first Jump past Omega to be long: four light-weeks, a liberal beginning for their journey. If its liberality could be taken as an omen it could mean, in Uskosian terms, that the journey was not discouraged.

But it would be a Jump into silence. From the next position an Inspace communication would stretch beyond its limit and never reach Omega. Radio or microwave or laser communications would get there—but not until four weeks after they were transmitted. Hanna felt that she looked toward a final, outer limit, into a place where the ubiquitous voices of humankind did not go. Somewhere ahead was an invisible but real barrier. Perhaps she was not the first to pass it here. Perhaps long ago in the great exodus from Earth, some ill-prepared colonists had gone this way. But if so, no one had ever heard of them again. They had vanished into the great silence.

She shivered at the thought in spite of the warmth of the *Bird,* and rubbed her bare arms. There was a movement at her side; Awnlee joined her just as the hum of the *Bird's* Inspace mode began. The air sang with it, the floor, the walls. Through the clear sound a last human voice rang through the *Bird:* "Logoff from Omega complete. Fair winds attend you!"—and then it was gone.

Her heart lifted. She took a deep breath and came closer to Rubee. The light about him was brilliant; through it she saw dimly that his hand hovered above the golden column. When he touched it, the Jump would come. He seemed to have grown larger, though that was a trick of her eyes and mind, for he was the same stumpy personage she had known all the time, not much taller than herself. But now he was where he belonged. He did not need to be careful and diplomatic; without any diminishing of his native courtesy, he had become the pure traveler, the master of starflight, himself, the essential Rubee. Hanna knew that look. She had seen it in certain human beings, and in the Explorers of Zeig-Daru. The wind was up, and Erell trimmed the sails.

At the proper time by his reckoning, and not a moment sooner, Rubee said to the *Far-Flying Bird* in his own language: "Prepare to ride the gales of the stars!"

To ride the gales of the stars . . . Humans did not talk to their spacecraft that way. Rubee at the center of a cylinder of pulsing light, standing, was not ugly or misshapen; he was magnificent. Hanna stood also, as if at attention. Awnlee beside her wrapped his fingers around hers, all the way around. Hanna said directly to his mind: *We have this in common: I, you, all intelligence; naught else in the universe feels and does this.* The *Bird's* common sound, a low sweet humming, grew louder, higher, louder. The ship under Hanna's feet gathered herself; poised on the edge of space and time; lifted her wings; in a chronon was somewhere else. Hanna turned to the transparency and looked in all senses Outside. The configuration of space had changed; the stars had shifted. All the worlds she knew were at her back. Awnlee chattered as the *Bird*'s song faded sweetly. "Five of your weeks, a short time, till the fourteenth day of Strrrl. Think of what I will show you! There are forests like scarlet plumes under skies as blue as yours. There are ruminants big as your house. There are sparkling wines colored like the grain, and pink insects sweet to eat. There are—"

"Awnlee, come here," Rubee said in a voice so ordinary that Awnlee suddenly silent was at his side before Hanna registered the movement. Then came a knowledge of something she had not felt before in Rubee: not fear, but a kind of deep concern.

She followed Awnlee to the central mandala. It no longer glowed; that should not be. The omnipresent humming dropped to silence. The *Bird* should not be so quiet, not in Inspace mode. Rubee was intent, Awnlee apprehensive, and Hanna saw that they were concentrated on the ghostly columns of numbers which were all that remained of the brilliant light.

All of them showed, uniformly, the Uskosian symbol for zero.

Rubee and Awnlee forsook the central mandala for the work stations that lined the bridge. Hanna did not speak. It was not easy to refrain, but she could not interrupt their urgent absorption. She only said once, "Is there a way in which I might be of service?"

But Rubee said, "No. We are grateful, but you have not the necessary skill with our vessel."

Therefore she listened with all her senses. With her mind she perceived that Rubee was worried and surprised; in Awnlee there was a chill of fear, and he kept reassuring himself in terms that in words would translate to: *It is not so bad, we will be safe will be safe will be safe!* With her ears she heard them talk of technical matters that baffled her. Their hands flew over glowing banks of keypads which responded with unintelligible schematics and columns of numbers. The *Bird* talked back to them, sounding anxious; or was that Hanna's imagination? She stood at Awnlee's back and watched what he did until she could endure it no longer. She must ask what had happened. Before she could do it he said, not to her but to Rubee, "That is the thing, then. It is a simple electrical malfunction. Simple, yet extensive; it is the power infrastructure for the distortion of dimension. I have not heard of such a thing before, neither in the prototypes nor the test voyages. I do not know how it could be."

He looked at a many-colored pattern that looked like (and, Hanna now realized, was) a wiring diagram. Large portions of it blinked on and off. Two meters away Rubee sighed, watching an identical image.

"There will be no quick journeys without repair," he said, "and repair means retracing our course. We will not come home on the fourteenth day of Strrrl; not this year."

Awnlee was still tense, but he said with the appearance of cheer, "If we must have this trouble, it is good that we have it at once. The conventional engines are unaffected. We are near Oneba, some thirty light-days; a long journey, yet not impossible nor more than inconvenient."

"That is true. Yet it will be best to remain here and signal distress, for the searchers will come quickly when our call comes to Oneba. That will use only thirty true days, and in one day more someone will come. And what are thirty-one days?—a grain of sand."

Hanna absorbed it slowly. They meant that the Inspace system was out. The *Bird* could not Jump. Without the Inspace option, the *Bird* was months away from Omega. They were, it appeared, marooned, for at least a month. Then she thought, surprising herself: What of it? Here was light, warmth, air, food, companionship. The *Bird* had not suffered a disaster. It was only a routine breakdown in space; it only meant delay. *It means rest,* she thought, and said half-consciously but aloud, in Ellsian, "There will be nothing we can do. There will be nothing we must do."

But Rubee had made a negative with his hands. "It is true that we have no present danger," he said. "Yet I am troubled because of the error that has occurred, and I wish to study it further. Also I wish to investigate the systems that continue to function. The failure of dimensional manipulation has bereft us of much power. If the old-style engines should fail also, only emergency generators will be left to retain life support—and I do not like having only one system as our defense against death in space."

Hanna knew well the perpetual caution of starship cap-tains, whatever their species or form. She said, "That is proper. Yet how could two such errors occur, Rubee?"

"How could one occur? Yet there is not one, but two; there are two already. There is the error that effected the malfunction. Therefore I must deduce that there is an error also in a diagnostic program, or else we would have been forewarned. What else might there be? What else might fail? We will work until we find out."

He said this with finality, and he did not intend to wait; at once, Hanna and Awnlee following, he rose and took his way to the "wing" that housed the *Bird*'s Inspace systems, which Rubee and Awnlee accurately called the distorters of dimension. Hanna had spent little time in this part of the *Bird*. It was a world of soaring silver spaces, arched and dizzily high. It was impressive, but it was not designed for comfort.

Hanna was not comfortable, and there was nothing she could do to help the Uskosians, except to stay out of their way. She did that for a long time, watching the units of time the aliens called hours go by on the strange chronometers. She was left to her own thoughts, which were not comfortable either. At about the time help could arrive, she had expected to be making a ceremonial, mythic landing on Uskos. She had expected a period of such intense work that it might produce the most brilliant results of her life. All her expectations had led to this, a profound anticlimax, and she was—not distressed. It even seemed that she might be treacherously relieved.

"There are erasures I do not understand," Awnlee said suddenly and very loudly. His voice echoed in the curved spaces, solitary in the great expanse.

"But what is the cause?" Rubee said.

"I do not yet know. They have not the appearance of randomness."

Hanna listened absently. A smile twitched at her lips. She was unquestionably released from the expected, at least for a little while. No human voice could follow her here for a month. She formed phrases and turned them over in her mind, trying them out: *I'm very sorry, Starr.* But they did not have the ring of truth.

Rubee, peering over Awnlee's shoulder at a console a few meters away, straightened with a gesture of disappointment.

"It is garbled beyond retrieval," he said.

"It is not," Awnlee said. "I will need some days, but I will reconstruct it. I will start at once."

Rubee said, "Do not begin now. Night has come. No reason has occurred to hurry us. I wish to observe what you do, but I do not wish to do it tonight."

The tendrils around his mouth drooped. Hanna remembered what he had said of his age. She said, "Indeed, Awnlee, it is time to rest."

"Then I will wait," Awnlee said, though it was plain that he longed to begin, and Hanna left him to talk to Rubee and take "one look more" at the mystery.

Hanna slept uneasily in the hot night. She dreamed too much, and woke often. The dreams were all a confused medley of the past. Here was the governing House of Province Koroth, vast and cool. "Do this," said the Lady of Koroth, "do that, you must, it must be done." The pale face altered; Hanna looked into her own blue eyes. She would be the Lady of Koroth one day, a magistrate of D'neera, lawmaker, law-abider. The People of Zeig-Daru thought to her, fondly accepting. Their great hands held instruments of torture. Hanna woke sweating; turned, and slept again. She rested comfortably in Starr Jameson's arms. She was loved. "Not yet," he said. "There is something you must do first." He turned into the Master of Chaos and then into Rubee, who lectured under a tree.

"Details change," Rubee said. "Grand designs must not, except by the hand of the Master. The honor is greater that way. By honor I mean sureness and security. Nonetheless persons make designs, and the Master enters in their alteration."

Rubee's face changed in its turn; first to something cruel with many pointed teeth; then to a human face that looked at Hanna with a pleasant smile and gold-flecked eyes. It said in a stranger's voice, "No one can hear you out here."

"No, no!" Hanna cried, trying to scream. Her own muffled shout woke her up. She sat up in the dark and pushed at her hair. It was wet with perspiration.

She turned on a light and looked about with an eerie sense that all that surrounded her was unreal; that she still dreamed. The room had been made over for her in blue and lavender, as comfortable and human as her own fading home. The air circulated with a faint whisper. Except for that there was silence, and Rubee and Awnlee slept deeply nearby.

She lay back uneasily. The face with the gold-flecked eyes was still nearly visible. An old sensation gnawed her, as if she whispered to herself, "You have overlooked something!" But it was associated only with danger and fear; and what was there to fear?

But she had thought that, too—sometimes, before.

She made a face and thought: Be paranoid, then; think of the worst; think back, seeking anomaly; think.

There are erasures I do not understand. They have not the appearance of randomness—

She felt vulnerable and exposed. She got up and put on some of the skimpy clothing she had brought with her. The tight singlet and shorts clung to her; her skin was clammy.

Think.

The programmed distortion occurred, the *Bird* had told Awnlee. And then the Inspace failure. *No one can hear you out here.*

She paced the room. Her bare feet trod the resilient floor without disturbing the silence of the *Bird.*

Suppose there was no random error. Suppose what appeared to be error was the result of a skillfully implanted series of commands.

The course program had never been touched. For that it need not have been touched. There were people who had studied the *Bird*'s Inspace engineering systems. Hanna did not remember Jameson saying anything about those persons being investigated beyond the common bounds of security clearance. It was just possible, therefore, that the engineering failure had been planned. And the route from Earth to Omega was available to anyone who wanted it. It was standardized, part of the common programming of Inspace navigation. Given such detailed knowledge of the *Bird*'s course so far, and knowledge of its general direction beyond, which had never been a secret, anyone might have extrapolated the *Bird*'s approximate location after the first Jump past Omega. After that first Jump the possibilities for error would grow exponentially, but the finish of the first must be within a reasonably confined radius. The calculation could not be precise, however, without possession of the course program; and without precision, even if someone were searching within that radius, there would be a margin of safety for the *Bird*. But Hanna could not estimate its extent.

Should she go to Rubee now and wake him from sleep? She leaned against a lavender wall and pressed her cheek against it. It was the wildest speculation, but she thought of how it could be done. Someone who was not afraid to go out past Omega could do it, exploring in weeks of small patient steps the logical path outward, until the data were complete and the leap as safe as any inside human space. Given the necessary skill, it needed only time. And Awnlee and Rubee had been in human space nearly a Standard year; had someone come this way while they went with Hanna round the worlds?

She closed her eyes and shut out the lavender light. Reached out, out, past Rubee and Awnlee, beyond the sleeping *Bird* and farther still, in all directions and no direction. In the isolation of the *Bird* she might, with all her skill and all her mind concentrated, touch a familiar presence though it be light years away. There ought to be nothing else for her to touch. There should be no stranger near at hand.

There was something. She brushed against it and jerked away, chilled. It was in space and thought of the *Far-Flying Bird*. It thought of the treasure in the *Bird*'s guts.

"God damn it," she said softly, scarcely able to believe in what she had felt. But it was there. It was close by, and purposeful.

She did not know exactly where it was. Telepathy could not tell her that.

She went to Rubee's room and pounded on his door. He answered at once. He wore a sleeping robe that brushed the floor and he adjusted it punctiliously as the door opened. Hanna felt his surprise. She said, "I am sorry to wake you, Rubee. But I must, and *now*."

"Enter. Enter—"

She was already in the room, talking as quickly as the need to think in Ellsian allowed. He did not understand her at first, so that she had to back up and repeat her knowledge and surmises; when he grasped them his eyespots worked and shone.

She finished, "All that would be necessary, would be a command for the system to fail upon completion of the first Jump after Omega. I think that was done. Our position is exactly what they would wish. No signal from us can reach Omega for one Standard month. We cannot Jump to get away. These humans can be sure that we will transmit a distress signal that includes our exact location, which is all that they need. Perhaps they even believe it will be directional toward Omega, and will confine their search accordingly. I think we had better not do that, Rubee. I think we had better not send a signal at all, and begin the long journey to Omega as soon as the old-style engines are at power—and not in a direct line, either."

Rubee said, "I will activate the engines and set course at once. But I wish one of us had thought of this more quickly. The signal was initiated some time ago. I saw no reason not to do that."

"Directional?" She watched the margin of safety shrink.

"Yes. How long will it take a human spacecraft to find us if all that you say is correct?"

"Hours."

"Hours have gone by already."

"Then we had better think of evasion instead of escape," she said. "They may be nearly here."

He went quickly to the bridge and she followed him. He did not speak again, but manipulated a work station without explanation. She understood that he ordered the *Bird* to extend its scanning range. The display at this station was blank and black at first. Then it showed one thing: the arrowhead-shape of an atmosphere-efficient spacecraft. Rubee's fingers stretched to pointed threads and touched tiny keypads in a blur of speed. Numbers appeared beside the image.

"What does that mean?" Hanna said.

He said, "They are moving in from the direction of Oneba, and they come with great speed. They have scanned the *Bird* as we slept. This vessel could not match the speed of that one even at full power; not in a hunt; it was not made for chase or pursuit. There is no hope of escape."

He turned away from the terminal and started out. Hanna called after him, "Where do you go?"

He answered without stopping, "I go to wake Awnlee.

They will arrive in one of our hours; less than one of yours. We are caught completely."

Awnlee, so calm until now, lost his composure and his courage all at once. "This was not supposed to happen!" he said over and over, and all efforts to soothe him were ineffectual. Hanna wished to learn what she could of the distant presence that was perceptible in this waste of isolation, but she felt only Awnlee's agitation. Rubee took him away again so that she would not see his pitiful terror. It made no difference. To close him out she had to shut down telepathy altogether, as a true-human might close his eyes, and then she was insensible also to the presences she wanted to touch.

Shutting consciousness to all of them had one advantage: she was able to think of their situation coldly and without distraction. It came more easily than she expected, as easily as even Jameson might have wished. Alone on the *Bird's* bridge, she thought about that. She felt no fear or uncertainty. That was new. In D'neera's brief war with Nestor, and even more in her first agonizing contacts with the People of Zeig-Daru, she had lived on the edge of madness. This was different. It was as if the years of order and protocol had not passed; as if, in her official life of courtesy, she had grown more callous to danger. Yet she had not faced danger for a long time, so that what she felt could not have come from habituation. She traced it, and saw that its source was anger. This event was too much. She had gone obediently where she was sent, produced what was wanted, done as she was told by D'neera, by the Polity, by all the human voices, for a long time, all her life. Now she must stop and surrender to—well, to the Master of Chaos, if it came to that; Rubee surely discerned that unpredictable hand. After all she had done it was going too far, after all she had done for Polity; could they get nothing right? But she knew she was unfair, that at least Jameson had tried to ward off what was coming, and that it was her own skepticism, conspiring with the aliens' stubbornness, that had brought her to this position of helplessness.

Then she thought with more logic of other things. And the first thing logic told her was that they could not escape or get help.

The next thing was a question. How far should they go in defending the cargo of the *Bird*?

She did not have to think about that much to come to a decision. The robbers could have it. *Here, take it, is there anything else you would like?* Precious it might be, irreplaceable even, but it was dust next to the lives of Rubee and Awnlee. And Hanna did not want to die either, not defending a crateful of baubles.

The last thing was whether their lives were in jeopardy in any case, and whether anything could be done about it. She was no longer critical of Jameson's urgency in educating her about Michael Kristofik. She wished she had paid more attention. Twenty years ago on the *Pavonis Queen* no one had been harmed. With luck it would be sleepygas again. But men change in twenty years. Probably Kristofik did not know that he was already suspected, in advance, of something he had not yet done. He might think that eradicating the *Bird* and her passengers would be the safest measure; that the *Bird* would be presumed lost in space on a course that was nearly untried. It seemed to Hanna that murder was the logical step for a man capable of taking it.

Was he, then, capable of taking it?

She sat on the bench that girdled the *Bird*'s bridge with her chin on one hand, and retrieved certain statements from memory. Honoria Hood, twenty years ago: "At no time were lethal weapons used . . ." Jameson, drawing on sources that went back that far and farther: "There were incidents on Alta and Valentine and later everywhere. He was dangerous. He is still dangerous." Her own voice, casual, dismissing the threat: "I suppose if you assume your subject is a monster, and then he doesn't act like one . . ." But here was Jameson again: "He must have known every worst thing there was to know about men . . . don't forget the man he's believed to have killed . . ."

It was so sparse, there ought to have been more, but she had not wanted to listen. And now she must estimate the extent of her danger, and she did not know enough to do it.

A communications module that ought to have stayed silent for weeks made a sound. Hanna scrambled for it. "Acknowledged," she said tightly.

A man's voice said, "This is the trader *Avalon* out of

Lancaster. We've picked up a mayday from your location. You in trouble?"

You could say that.

Hanna said, "We're the *Far-Flying Bird* out of Terra on special mission for the Polity. What's a Lancaster trader doing out here?"

"Just looking around."

The voice was thin and toneless. It disturbed her. She said, "Nobody comes out here. You're well out of Omega's range. I don't know if coincidence goes that far."

"You want help or don't you?" said the voice.

Rubee came in. His comprehension of Standard was limited. He said, "What have they said?"

"They play a game."

"Do you play?"

"I will. To discover what we may expect."

The light voice outside said, "Talk Standard."

Hanna said, "We don't want help. We'll handle it."

"Not good enough," said the voice.

Only three words. The hair stood up on Hanna's arms, she had heard nothing like them before, nothing like the irony and finality in the slow light voice. If this was Michael Kristofik, Jameson's assessment had fallen short of the dreadful truth. Her hand shaped itself for a weapon, though she had not held one in years.

She said coldly, "Let's work with the truth. I know what you want."

It must have startled him. There was a pause before the voice said, "Yes?" so softly it was nearly a whisper. There was a suggestion of hollowness, of echoes in empty spaces, a trick of acoustics.

"Is it whom we feared?" Rubee said.

"Who else could it be?"

"Tell this person to take the cargo and leave."

Hanna thought of her own estimate of the reasonable thing to do. She had qualified it before: murder was the logical step for a man capable of taking it. The reservation no longer counted. The man who owned this voice was capable of it.

The voice said, "I don't want to hear any more of that alien noise. I said: Standard."

"All right. I'll talk Standard." Some of her fury might

have gotten into her voice. She hoped it had. "Listen to this. The Interworld Fleet and Intelligence and Security expected trouble. You got by them, I don't know how. But this isn't going as smooth as you think. They've got an idea who to look for. The Uskosian envoys don't want trouble. They want you to take what you came for and get out. So do I. You come right aboard and get it. We'll stay out of the way. But believe me, you don't know what trouble is. Trouble is what you get from Fleet and I&S if you touch an alien envoy. I'm not talking smuggling, Earthside Enforcement, port patrols, that kind of garbage. I'm talking top-level Polity Admin. If you're smart, you'll make sure nobody gets hurt. How does that sound?"

The voice said, "That's fine. Glad you take it like that. Just remember what you said about wanting trouble. The kind you get if you ask for it, is a battery of Fleet surplus wide aperture laser cannon. Give us an airlock and stay where you are. We're coming in."

The approach took an hour. The *Bird* waited dead and silent. Awnlee appeared on the bridge, apologetic and calmer. He said he did not know what had happened to him. He sat between his sire and Hanna and held Hanna's hand.

"I thought I was brave as Bistee!" he lamented.

"I don't think it was an unnatural reaction," Hanna said.

"But you and my sire did not act so!"

"We are older," said Rubee.

"Yes," Hanna said, "and I don't know about Rubee, but the last time I was in such a position, I was jelly. And I may yet forget myself before we are done."

"I wish I were like Sirsa of Sa," Awnlee said with a return of his natural enthusiasm.

Hanna opened her mouth to ask what had happened to Sirsa of Sa, or who Bistee had been, for that matter, and shut it again. This was no time for legend.

She said to Rubee, "We must think of defending ourselves."

"Do you think we will have need?"

"I think it is very possible."

"We came with weapons; a small number only; meant for defense against beasts if we met such danger. You saw the weapons destroyed, all of them." Rubee hesitated. "Did you know then why I did it?" he asked.

"I did. I gave you then my gratitude, even before I gave you my love."

Awnlee said, "It was a token of good will when 'Anarilporot joined us."

"It was another thing also," she said, watching Rubee over Awnlee's head.

"You had great fear," Rubee said. "I then knew nothing of your kind of speech, thought to thought. There was no other common language and when words came to you I did not know what they meant. But there were pictures. You stood here, where we are now, and remembered another meeting. I could not endure your memories. And so I put our weapons into space. I knew, because of you, that we would not need them."

"It was a token of good will indeed, and has been so ever since. But now we may need weapons, Rubee."

"Is there not an accommodation?" said Awnlee.

"I would not give my trust to these men," she said. "I do not wish you to have alarm, Awnlee, but I think we had better think of the worst case. We have tools. Perhaps we could use them. Even something to throw would be better than nothing; better still would be tools that could harm from a distance."

"There is nothing," Rubee said. "There are objects we might modify, given time. But there is no time."

The air lock was open. The *Bird* would announce at any moment that it had been entered. Hanna's mind was busy with possibilities that she rejected as quickly as they came—close the lock, seal the inner one, trap them inside it—but the cannon that could punch holes in the *Bird* as easily as a fist smashing through paper rendered all her ideas useless.

Awnlee's grip on Hanna's hand felt strange. She looked down and saw his fingers change. He said, "Tell me of this accommodation."

Hanna could not answer. She had not laid out all her conclusions even for Rubee. But Rubee said, "I think 'Anarilporot and I are of one mind. I think our danger is great." He touched his selling gently. "We are in a tale, Awnlee. We thought it another telling of the Tale of Erell. That was what we wished and planned. But the Master has come to us. The danger was there always. It is present always, and especially in a great undertaking such as ours. And now we are in a new tale, a dark one."

"They have entered," Awnlee said. He moved closer to Rubee, looking at a schematic that showed new points of light where none had been. "There are four. I wonder if that is all?"

Hanna watched the blips of light. When the lock finished its cycle, they moved out and turned for the bridge. She said, "There are probably others on the *Avalon*, if that is its name. But now that these are aboard, they are not likely to use the cannon. As long as they are here, our only danger is from whatever weapons they carry with them."

"Perhaps we should attack at once," Rubee said. "Yet there are four of them and three of us, and we have no weapons."

He was icy: a good being to have by you in a fight. Hanna said, "Yes. We must wait and find out their intent. It would be foolish to provoke them if there is a chance they will not harm us. If there is no chance—then an attack may give us only a small one, but it will be the only chance."

The blips were almost at the bridge. Awnlee quivered. Hanna put her arms around him suddenly and said, "Do not be afraid, my friend."

"I wish you could give me some of your courage!"

"All that I have is yours," she answered, which was an expression of deep love at any time. She felt Awnlee formulate a response, *And all that is mine I give to you,* but there was no time to say it; four spacesuited figures came onto the bridge, two by two, and quickly.

They held stunguns, which gave her a moment's hope. Then she saw that each also had in his belt a disrupter or a laser pistol. So they were prepared to wound and kill. That was not good. Worse was the transparency of the faceplates of their suits. They did not care who saw their faces. They were not worried about being identified.

Hanna said to Rubee and Awnlee, silently: *They mean to kill us. We will have to fight.* Rubee made no sign, but Awnlee started and looked at her, and one of the men stepped forward.

"D'neeran," he said, and she almost shrank away; this was the man with the voice. But the face was not the one she had expected to see.

He said, "We don't like D'neerans. We don't like what they do with their heads. You have anything to say, say it out loud. Or else you're dead. Understand?" He looked at Rubee. "You. How's your cargo secured? Open it up."

Hanna said, "He doesn't understand Standard very well."

"I will translate," Awnlee said in a steadier voice than Hanna expected to hear from him, and he did so.

Hanna listened to their conversation and assessed them. The man I&S had expected to be here was not here, but he might have remained on the *Avalon*. There was the man with the voice, red-haired and fair-skinned; there was a tow-headed giant; there was a thin brown-black man whose fingers were nervous on his weapon; and—hanging back a little—there was a smaller man with a straggling mustache and eyes that looked anywhere except at her and the Uskosians. The red-haired man talked with authority and clearly was the leader. I&S might have been wrong. They might have wasted all their worry on Michael Kristofik, and while they researched and watched him, this other man with the empty eyes might have crept in undiscovered. Which did not change the basic situation, and Hanna wished I&S had been right. She would rather face the man who had taken the *Pavonis Queen* with sleepygas and stunguns, rejecting a massacre.

Rubee went to a work station and began the procedures for releasing the cargo hold locks. His back was to all of them. Hanna said to him: *Rubee, if they are divided, if some go to the hold and others stay here, it may be our best chance.* His hand moved in a way that meant assent. It would be meaningless to the intruders.

She said to the red-haired man, "What is your name?"

"Castillo," he answered, his eyes on Rubee. Hanna's skin prickled. It was a lie. But there were overtones she was not used to finding in the perception of a simple lie; a glimpse of a depth not uninhabited, into which she would not care to descend. It went with the voice.

She said casually, distractingly, "You've done this very well. I&S was looking in the wrong places, and at the wrong man, too, I think. You can laugh about that when this is done. But there is one thing you might have forgotten that might increase your profits. I meant what I said about trouble from the top. We're worth much more to you alive than dead, especially the aliens. You could name your price for their safety and the Polity would pay instantly. Have you thought of that?"

He said without looking away from Rubee, "Hanna ril-Koroth bargains for her life."

"That's right. Half of what you've heard about me—you've obviously heard of me—isn't true. I don't want to be hurt and I don't want my friends hurt."

Rubee stepped back from his station. Awnlee said, "It is done. The hold is open."

The red-haired man put away his stungun and drew the disruptor. He did it casually and with no trace of emotion at all, so that Hanna had no warning, she did not even know the moment had come until he lifted the disruptor and fired it at Rubee. The beloved ugly body jerked and fell. It happened in only a second, which for Hanna was an eternity of paralysis. The muzzle turned toward Awnlee and she threw herself at it, but she was too far from Castillo to reach him and he fired at once. She heard a single sound from Awnlee, higher-pitched than anything she had ever imagined coming from an Uskosian throat. It was not as clean a shot, and Awnlee's shock hit her like a wavefront, and then so did something else. Not a disruptor beam, though she thought it was at first. In a heap at Castillo's feet, still trying to think in the moment of terrible grief, she felt Awnlee die crying for his sire, felt the weakness and tingling that meant light stun, and tried to get up again. Something else hit her, in the side of the head: a boot. Her vision swam.

Awnlee, Awnlee! she called hopelessly, knowing there would never be an answer.

The voice said, "She's dangerous. I told you to knock her out."

The last thing she saw was the thin man standing on the command platform, bending over the golden column, attracted by the jewels. A heavier blast from a stungun hit her, and all of them went away.

She thought of the ship ever after as the *Avalon,* and of the events that occurred there as things that happened on the *Avalon,* though that was not its name any more than the red-haired man's name was Castillo. In memory, later, the ship and the man would be unreal. That was because during her time on the *Avalon*, Hanna held on only to the edge of the real.

She had been stunned so heavily that it was many hours before she woke. When she did, at first, she was aware only of bodily misery. All her muscles were cramped from the stun effect and hours of not moving. She was cold, frozen. Her head was a weight of pain, and trying to move made it worse; the throbbing started where she had been kicked and radiated outward to fill her skull. She was also desperately thirsty.

When she had identified these things, she remembered the rest: Rubee and Awnlee. She called to them from her misery, without hope, and though thinking minds surrounded her, the dear shapes of Rubee and Awnlee were not there. She had known they would not be.

Finally she moved. She was not a stranger to suffering. She did not welcome it, but she knew what could be endured: more than she had once thought possible. She also knew the value of hope. And so she moved.

Very slowly she got up, holding on to a wall because her knees kept giving way. The room where she was had one dim light overhead. It was not large, and all the surfaces were bare metal, but there were outlines on the metal showing where fixtures had been stripped away. There were two doors. She tried them both, feeling her way from one to the other along the wall. The first was locked. The second opened into a claustrophobically small bathroom with no other exit. So probably at some time this had been some kind of crewmen's quarters.

She splashed cold water on her face and drank from her cupped hands with gratitude, though when she bent over she thought her head would tear apart. Still, she could think more clearly.

About Rubee and Awnlee?—no. She would think about them later. Instead she must think of questions. Why was she still alive? Where was the *Avalon* taking her, and why? She could not answer the questions. Her head was only clear enough for sorrow, not for reason. Now if ever was the time to put to use the disciplines of the D'neeran Adept. But entering trance would not be easy. Once pain had begun, attenuating concentration, it was harder.

She went back to the icy cubicle that had once been someone's room and eased cross-legged to the floor. Tremors ran through her from the cold. She closed her eyes and prepared to control breath and blood. But then the door opened and she knew the room had been watched, they had seen her wake, and she would not get her chance, not yet.

She opened her eyes and looked up at Castillo. The blond giant was behind him, and the thin man from the boarding party. All three had stunguns pointed at her. It was flattering—and devastating to any hope of escape.

Castillo squatted in front of her. There was an empty smile on his lips. The pale blue eyes were empty, too. He said, "You said I&S knows about this operation. Tell me about it."

She thought it might be a good idea not to tell him. She thought that if he had kept her alive in order to ask her that question, it would be advantageous to put off answering as long as possible. She said as much.

He said, "You're going to stay alive for a while anyway. If Fleet's tracking us, you'll come in handy. I don't want to play games with the Polity, but D'neera might pay well for you—without getting the Polity involved."

He did not go on, but in the minds of the other men she saw that there would be another, sexual use for her. Because she was there and helpless, had been thrown into their path like a bonus and there would be no retaliation because no one would ever know; that was all.

She was sick, and knew it showed in her face. She knew also that Castillo lied casually, indifferently, about D'neera. She would never see it again.

"Now tell us about I&S," he said.

"No," she said, as an experiment, to see what kinds of threats he would make so she could learn more about him.

He did not waste time with threats. He stood up and stepped back. The blond man jerked her to her feet and held her upright while the other man, the thin man, beat her. He enjoyed it; after a while his eyes glazed, and he panted. Castillo watched, the smile unchanged on his lips. She threw at him once a desperate silent plea for mercy, a cry of stark pain. He still smiled and she did not do it again, she would not beg again, never in what was left of her life. But she had not known that unaided hands could bring the unendurable so near. Her flesh broke under the fists, her body felt as if it disintegrated. "Yes, yes!" she cried long before it was over, but the only thing that happened then was that Castillo said, "Don't break her jaw." So when the giant dropped her on the floor she could have talked, if she had had breath to talk with; but then there was another boot that smashed into her right side so hard that she heard a crack, felt the balanced structure of bone shift, and passed out again in agony.

The little man with the mustache was a medic of some kind. When he brought her back to consciousness she answered questions in a wilderness of pain, unable to think clearly enough to lie. Castillo held out the promise of painblocks as a reward. She was lucid enough to know he lied, that they were still afraid of her and would do nothing to make her competent. Strangers had joined the group, the room was full of silent men. They would not make it better, but they could make it worse. She did not want that to happen. And it did not matter if they knew the truth. I&S had been wrong, they would look for the wrong man, Castillo had done what he set out to do and it made no difference if he knew it.

When she said Michael Kristoflk's name, Castillo laughed aloud. "Him! We're clear," he said. So he knew Michael Kristofik. There was a connection after all. That made no difference either.

Then Castillo got up and went out. The little medic disappeared, too; the others stayed. Her clothes came apart under more hands, her legs were forced apart and agony ran right up into her chest and choked her. The pain in her side stopped everything, rage, disgust at this casual rape: "Nothing personal," she thought one said, and the pain in her side held her down so she could not even move to kick him. It could not get worse but did so in improbable peaks, until it was finally, surely unendurable and she escaped into darkness again. She was unconscious when the last one left.

"Be quiet, don't say anything, don't move—!"

She turned her head at the whisper. Her head seemed to be full of something thick, so that she could not hear or think very well. She was not cold any longer; she burned. There was a dull ache in her side.

"Be quiet, be still, I can't stay long . . ."

It was hard to focus her eyes. The face of the little medic danced and divided and came back to being one face. She said something in a drowsy mumble.

He said, "That's all I can do. I'll come back if I can. If I can!"

He edged away from her. She tried to call after him, but her tongue was as thick as everything else in her head. She could still think to him. *Wait, wait!* she cried, and he did, compelled by something in the thought, maybe despair.

He said, "I gave you enough for a few hours. I can't do anything about the fever. I don't know what it is. In a few hours we'll be on Revenge."

She listened with more than her sluggish ears. Revenge? The end: a place to die. That was where it would happen.

Why there . . . ?

Telepathy made him nervous. He twitched. "He kept you in case of trouble. If they came after us somehow. We won't be there long."

Why did you . . . ?

He jittered, moving toward the door. "I don't know. I was a physician once. I learned some things too well to forget. Like relieving pain. You hurt. You're going to die, I know that, it could be easier. I don't know if I can come back again. Don't tell him I did this. Please!"

Him . . . ? She formed a picture of the red-haired man. The medic shuddered and was gone.

Heat not cold, fever not pain. On the whole a better set of problems. What fever? Could be anything. Reconstructed my blood, who knows what's got in?

The pain was easy to manage now, though she staggered when she got up because her head floated. She tried moving as if in free fall, but that didn't work. She kept lurching against walls no matter what she tried. She gathered up the rags of her clothing and made knots in them and put on the result. A glint caught her eye in the dim light: a gold chain, broken on the floor. The opal was gone. The other chain was still around her neck, unbreakable. They had tried to break it; the skin under it was tender.

She drank water, a lot of water; the thirst was worse than before. Then she sat down on the floor again. The heat and the fever were nothing. The pain was in abeyance, and that was all that mattered; she could anesthetize herself before whatever the medic had given her dissipated.

And then? They would think her helpless. She would not be helpless. At the first sign of a chance she would act. As she had not acted on the *Far-Flying Bird.* They had waited, she and Rubee and Awnlee, civilized, rational, for an optimal opportunity. And so Rubee and Awnlee had died. It was necessary to forget about the civilized. There was no place for it out here.

She put herself into trance easily. The fever helped.

"Getting bored," Shen's voice said from Michael's left wrist. "Every hour, every half hour, kid says—" her voice rose to a whine, " *'Can I go out?'* Theo's gonna start doping pretty soon. How much longer?"

"You ask me that every hour, every half hour. *'How much longer, Mike?'* "

He tried to imitate the whine, with fair success. Shen snorted. He added, "Long as it takes. Stay there. I could need you fast."

"Know that."

"All right. Check in again—when you're bored."

Shen signed off, grumbling. He leaned back against a rusty rock, bundled against the cold of an autumn night outside the City of the Rose, and stared into the darkness.

He was bored, too, and perpetually cold. A week ago he had had all the warehoused beauties put aboard *GeeGee*— from motives of pure malice. *Hope I see his face when he finds out it's gone. GeeGee* lay behind another pile of rocks at the horizon, far enough away, he devoutly hoped, to be missed unless B made a detailed scan of the region before coming in to land. Michael meanwhile lived in the rocks outside the warehouse like a rat, never really warm, as close as he could get to B's customary landing site. Michael gambled B would use it again. His plan was simple: to stun everybody in sight as soon as B appeared, get him onto *GeeGee,* and run like hell. Subtlety was not the way to deal with B.

He scanned the sky once more with goggles adjusted for infrared. Nothing. The sky had been empty all week. The planet's single dim pocket-size moon was below the horizon. The sky was clear and stars spilled across it like sand.

He pulled up an all-season tarp to cover his mouth and got ready for another uncomfortable night. He did not sleep well with rock for bed and pillow. For the sixth night running he slipped into the same interminable half-dream that was also half-waking, so that he could think *oh no not again;* slipped back through the chain of years on Valentine, back to Alta, inexorably back. It was like watching history run in reverse. He had to go through the part with B at the center all over again: the empty smile, the soul-killing, inescapable demands. Back: the night spared him none of it: flames and death and the agony of his shattered hands. *You'll carry no more messages, boy.* Then memory ended and he stood on the edge of a void. Maybe there had been happiness there, but he did not know; would never know, without B.

The transmitter on his wrist burped and pricked the skin, hard. It was the signal he waited for.

He kicked away the tarp and grabbed the goggles. He had been sweating, and the icy air bit his face. *I'm ready to sell out the whole operation for a hot bath,* he thought, but he watched the spot of heat come in from high in the south. One fast coded answer to Shen and then silence, prearranged. He pulled the stunner, tested its weight in his gloved right hand, and crouched behind the rock, waiting.

It had grown easier, with the years, to become a machine. That was one of the pitfalls on the path of the Adept, the teachers said. It was easier not to feel, not to cry, not to rage. It was easier to turn aside from rejoicing. The disciplines were seductive to certain spirits, and Hanna might be one of them. It came too easily to her. She was very good.

Burning with fever and caged in ice she felt nothing. She held her broken bones upright and monitored the pain as if she watched a visible gauge. The pain was separate from her. No time passed. It was always the present moment. The sick life of the *Avalon* was visible to her as if she watched a play, though she did not use her eyes. Castillo was an empty black hole in which the commonest thoughts turned into things that crawled, more alien and more terrifying than any animal or sentient being she had known. She acknowledged the fact and filed it away without emotion. Gaaf the

medic twitched inside all the time. He thought of Hanna
with misery. The big blond man, Wales, wondered why he
had wanted to take her, ugly from the beating as she was; he
must have been too long in space. The one called Suarez
thought with ordinary pleasure of someday going home,
and what he had done to Hanna was a footnote to memory.
Juel who had beaten her slept heavily. He always did after
something like that. The release would relax him for days.
She had no names for the other two. One was impatient:
*Get the rest of it and get Outside, get paid, head for Valentine,
spend it all. God, how I want to get drunk.* The other thought:
*That might have been too much. But they were only aliens.
And a D'neeran. So what?*

No time passed for Hanna, but she watched time shrink
in their perception as they came close to their destination.
Revenge. The Rose. There was a great stir of landfall and
night. They stopped thinking of her. But soon they would
come to kill her, said the voice of pure reason. The landing
pods screamed through the hull, and she saw or imagined
there was dust blowing, rocks flying. The ship was down.
The scream fell to an at-ready hum. Men went out.

She monitored, distantly, consternation and rage. Something was gone. That did not matter. What mattered was
that someone thought of her. There was a use for her, a last
use before she died. They would take her into the open.
That was good.

When Juel came for her, she walked passively through
the *Avalon* with the muzzle of a disruptor jammed into her
back. He would have to be induced to move the muzzle. But
it stayed against her skin and stayed there when they
stopped. They had come to a lock in the side of the *Avalon*,
open to the night. A short ramp led to the ground.

She looked straight ahead into the night. There were
presences.

Castillo: "Look at this. Look at her. This is what your
wives and daughters will look like when we get done."

From the ground, a shadow just starting to be afraid. "I
tell you the truth. We did not touch the things. There are
others on this world. I do not know what they did with your
goods. I do not know!"

In the darkness at her left, another presence, silent, invisible to eyes. Watching with animal alertness.

Slowly she turned her head and looked into the dark at the tail of the ship. She said clearly, "Who is that?"

The muzzle of the disruptor shifted away from her. Remotely, in no-time, she twisted and turned. Her left hand hard as a steel blade caught Juel on the side of the neck; her right had the disruptor and fired and he fell. In no-time she turned it on Castillo—and jerked at a jolt of stun from the shadows at her back. She staggered down the ramp. In trance she could even fight stun, a little, for a while. The Castillo-target was gone. Running feet came toward her from somewhere and she swung the disruptor toward them, but it weighed more now than herself. Another wave of stun: the end. She did not get off another shot.

The ice of Revenge was in his veins, holding back the fury. He kicked the dead man aside, useless meat, whatever he knew was locked in the dead brain forever. The woman was another matter. He thumbed the emergency summons for *GeeGee* and pulled the woman away from the storm of coming liftoff, counting on darkness and luck and surprise. He threw her down behind rock and ducked just before light split the darkness where his head had been. The light quested, found its range, and began to melt away the rock. He measured the distance to the next one. Might make it. The high-pitched howl of *GeeGee* moving fast in atmosphere filled the night. The killing light blinked out; the ship without a name took off with a roar.

He forgot it instantly. His blood had turned to liquid fire. He knelt by the woman and got his hand on a light; it shook. His ears rang and he instructed himself: *I must not kill her. I must not.* The light swung wildly and settled on her face. Crouching in the darkness, watching the shadowplay at the lighted lock, he had thought her skin strangely mottled. The mottling was as fine a selection of bruises as he had ever seen. Somebody didn't like her much.

Shen was out of *GeeGee* before the ship was fully down, running and yelling. "Goddammit, answer! You all right?"

"Yeah." He touched the battered face with itching fingers. He said, "He got away because of her."

Shen stopped at his side and said with interest, "What is it?"

"I don't know, but I hope it can talk."

The body stirred a little; eyes gleamed through swollen slits.

"You can talk, can't you, yes you can," he said.

"Later," said Shen, but he did not hear her. The fury came out of its cavern and he lifted a hand high, all his strength gathered to strike. Another movement caught his eye and he stopped because it might mean threat. Lise stood on the edge of the light and they stared at each other. Her chin lifted and she took one small, perceptible step backward. Away from him.

He let his hand fall, got control of his voice, and said, "What the hell are you doing here?"

She said nothing. She kept looking at him with bright blue eyes, betrayed. Then she melted into the darkness, back toward the *Golden Girl.*

Michael did not move. Shen knelt beside him and waited, silent and stony. The noise in his ears died away with the rage. He was sick and exhausted and his head throbbed.

Shen said finally, "Cold out here. Turning blue." She pointed at the body on the ground.

"Yeah. We have to go. He thinks *GeeGee*'s armed, I guess. If he comes back shooting, we're in trouble."

He felt a violent aversion to picking up the stranger. When he did, it was worse; she was too light, too limp, too helpless. When he reached the *Golden Girl,* it was a relief to hand her over to Theo.

It was night on *GeeGee,* adjusted to the cycle of the City of the Rose. The gentle light in Central Control was made for amusing conversations, leisurely journeys in luxury. He appreciated it. He never stopped appreciating it. Lise was tucked into her place against the wall. He tried to talk to her, *I would never hit you, I would never do that to you,* but he got only silence in return. Lise had learned early what kinds of evidence to trust.

First things first. He took *GeeGee* into space and made the first Jump on a common route chosen at random so that for all practical purposes they were unfindable. When that was done, Shen said economically, "Well?"

"Wait a minute . . ." He leaned back, soaking up warmth, sorting out what had happened, getting used to the idea that there were no more reasons to hurry.

"There was a lot going on out there," he said. "They landed without spotting me. A couple of them came out. They were starboard-on to me and they opened up portside. The ship was between me and the warehouse and I couldn't see what was happening. I worked my way around behind the rocks. Took the last hundred meters without cover. Good thing they came in at night. There was a lot of coming and going. They'd found out about the warehouse. One of them took off into town and came back with one of the elders, Rann, I think. Poor old Rann. What happened to him, anyway? Think he's all right?"

"See his body?"

"Good point. I was at the tail and coming up along the side by then. B was talking to Rann, accusing him of taking the stuff. Then they brought that woman out. Who the hell is she, anyway? I got in range and I was ready and she told them I was there. I swear I hadn't made a sound. She was standing in the light and it was pitch dark where I was."

He hesitated, replaying the blur of violence. He said slowly, "There was another one holding a disruptor on her. She got it away from him and killed him. I was starting to fire at B. But she was going to kill him. So I stunned her first. It was *that* close." He held up two fingers close together. "And while I was doing that, B jumped back in the ship. And then she almost got me before I stunned her again. Shen, there's something wrong with the power pack in that gun. I shouldn't have had to hit her twice."

Shen said, "Recruit her."

"One of his monsters? You don't know what you're talking about."

Shen shrugged. Michael got up and said, "I'm going to go see if Theo's got her up to talking."

"Need help?"

"Maybe later. Somebody'd better stay here for a while."

He had not told Theo where to take the woman. There was a medlab on *GeeGee,* as sophisticated as everything else on this ship. He went there first; when he opened the door the equipment hummed at him, but no one was there. He went to the two unoccupied staterooms, to Theo's room, and to the smaller quarters over the engineering section before he decided that he should have asked *GeeGee* in the first place where Theo had gone. Now there were not many places left, and he went to his own cabin with some indignation.

He went in and said bitterly, "What's she doing here? Bleeding on my bed."

"It was the first one I got to," Theo said simply. He stood by the bed and peered at a reader in his hand, scowling. A scanner pointed at the woman's right side, looking more deadly than helpful. A tube in her left arm snaked across the bed and out of sight. Half a dozen metal cases of varying sizes littered the bed, some talking quietly to themselves. Theo had cut away what passed for the woman's clothes. The bruises ran into one another, except in one place. Michael said, "Nice of them to leave her jaw alone," and the body twitched for the first time, startling him. He said, "Can she talk yet?"

"No."

"How long?"

Theo looked up and shook his head. His eyes were watchful. Michael cocked his head and said, "You can't talk either?"

Theo said in an odd voice, "Maybe in a few days."

"You can do better than that."

Theo braced himself. "Her temperature's forty-two-point-four. That's critical. She's got broken bones. She's dehydrated and I don't know how long it's been since she had any nourishment. She might be dying."

"There's heavy life support in the lab."

"I don't know how to use it. I never got that far with the courses. You know that."

"Then I want you to wake her up now. I can't talk to her if she's dead."

"If I juice her nervous system now, she could be dead in an hour."

The reader trembled in Theo's hand. Michael said experimentally, "I'm going to talk to her. That's what I want. Wake her up and the hell with it."

"No," said Theo. It was barely audible.

After a while Michael sat down on the bed and rummaged in one of the metal cases. He found a pouch and opened it and took out the saturated pad inside. He began swabbing the woman's bruised face. "I liked you better when you were a worm," he said.

Theo took a deep breath. He started talking, not quite in a normal voice. "She's got Dawkins' fever. I don't know how she could, but she does. She's got two broken ribs. I'll have to go in. I'll need your help. Shen's, too, probably."

"Blood all over my bed."

"There won't be much blood. That's the other thing, her blood. I can't make any sense out of it. I'll have to take some to the lab where there's more to work with. Somebody has to stay with her."

"All right. I will."

Theo was silent for so long that Michael finally looked up. He said, "What's wrong with that?"

"It's just—look at her. Think she got that way falling downstairs?"

"I won't hurt her," Michael said, shocked.

Theo said, "You haven't been yourself lately."

"So tell me something new—" He waited a minute to make sure his voice would be steady. "Consider me under orders. Just tell me what to do."

Theo looked into his eyes and relaxed. He said, "Keep doing what you're doing. Stay away from the right side. I don't want accelerated healing there till I've done the bones. Don't worry if she wakes up. There's no pain in the side, I took care of that, and what you're doing will block out the rest." He started out with a vial of something red in his hand. At the door he said over his shoulder, as an afterthought, "I think she might have been raped, too."

When Theo was gone the room was quiet, except for the boxes talking to each other. Michael touched the woman's side; the flesh had a spongy feel. How could he ever have thought of beating her? She wouldn't be the first terrorized innocent to escape from B.

The full impact of the possibility hit him; he dropped the swab and was still. When some time had passed, quite a lot of time, he felt heat under his hand. He looked at it and saw that it was cupped about the woman's cheek. Her skin was on fire.

He found a fresh swab and went on with the job very gently. When he touched her thighs, her eyes opened and she made the first sound of protest he had heard.

"It's all right," he said. "I'm just trying to help you. That's the only reason I'd touch you."

Her eyes focused on his face. He did not know if she had understood. He leaned closer to her and said softly, "Don't worry. We don't do things like that here. It's different here."

She understood that time. She looked at him with intelligence; he might have said with recognition, if that were possible. Her lips parted and she said something he would not have heard if he had not been so close. It was: *"Not much improvement."*

He drew back and stared at her with astonishment, and then with appreciation. He said, "Look, I've got enough consciences hanging around here. I don't need another one."

He thought she said something else, but her lips did not move and he did not know what the word was. He almost thought she had thrown a giant question mark into the air. That was impossible, too.

"What was that?" he said, but her eyes were closed again, and he did not think she heard him any more.

B returns to Revenge with caution. Sweeps land and sky for a trace of technology beyond that used by the People of the Rose. The other ship has gone. They hunt down Elder Rann again; the city prays and quakes. Rann cannot talk fast enough. "A golden ship, a man with a companion, he called himself your friend—"

B has a visual on the marauder. Enhanced, it shows name and registration clear on the bow. The Golden Girl *out of Valentine. Who is her master?*

Theo said, "You have to clean up."

"Huh?"

"Nobody comes in my surgery that dirty."

"You never had a surgery."

"I do now."

The picture of what was happening on Revenge faded. It was accurate; Michael was as sure of that as if he were there.

He said, "She's dirtier than I am."

"Shen's going to clean her up."

"My bathroom looks like a biosyn supply house. Thanks to you."

"Use mine."

Theo was implacable. Michael looked at him quizzically. He said, "Sure you're up to this?"

"It's not that hard." To Michael's surprise Theo blushed. He said, "I was pretty good, you know. Before I got thrown out. I can handle this. But we ought to be heading home. She's really sick."

"Before we go home I want to see what she says."

"If she lives long enough to say anything, you mean. Look, I can only do so much. We need to head for Valentine and we need to get Rescue out for rendezvous. 'Cause I told you, I can't use the heavy stuff. And she might need to be on it real soon. If her heart stops."

Michael looked at the face of the unconscious woman. It was less swollen, but she had not stirred again. He thought of her single-handed ruin of the plan that had almost succeeded. There was nothing to do but accept it. They could not go back to Revenge; B had heavy arms and was warned. He would watch the empty sky. There had been no time to think about the size of the disaster, the waste of two years' work, the hunt that should have ended on Revenge. So close. So goddamn close to the secret, the path that led back to the start.

"We have to do it all over again," Michael said. But Theo did not know what he was talking about, so he said, "God knows where he'll turn up next. Maybe he'll go on Outside. It might be years before we pick up a trail—before I do. You're out if you want to be."

Theo shook his head. "No."

"Think about it."

"I already know. I've been with you six years. Where would I go? I'll never do what I wanted to do, I doped it away. No med faculty in space'll let me back in. What would Shen do? Go back to Nestor? You're stuck with us. Mike, it's not as bad as you think. We can get something out of this woman. We have to keep her alive. Let me contact Rescue. Please. You said you were under orders."

He was right. He was also anxious about Michael. Michael's face was treacherously transparent; he was desolate

and it showed. There were limits to what he wanted even
Theo to see. He could not smile, not yet, but he rearranged
his face somehow and Theo was relieved. He would have to
fight the rest of it out later, when he was by himself.

He went to Control and called Rescue. He told a voice from
Valentine there was a sick and injured woman, unidentified,
aboard. Would Rescue pick her up? The voice balked. *Gee-
Gee* was outside their customary range. They were short-
handed. Michael went on talking. He quoted regulations
(making some up) and precedent. He appealed to humanity. Shen listened with a sneer and Lise, her interest caught,
forgot to be afraid and came close and took his hand. Finally he did what he ought to have done at once. He reminded the voice who he was and mentioned a Valentine
Ecomanager whom he knew personally. When it was over,
he had what he wanted and Shen was as close to smiling as
she ever got. "All right, all right," he said. "I forgot the
Kristofik theory of social structure."

"What's that?" Lise said.

"Money always wins."

"Ah," she said, enlightened.

He gathered clean clothes and went to Theo's room,
walking the corridor as if the stone of Revenge had gotten
into his feet. The game he had played for the last two years
was over. As soon as B knew who was after him, it would be
a new game: not a private hunt but a private war. It would
start soon. It might have started already.

*The People of the Rose have no use for Inspace communica-
tion, but the relays come near Revenge, as on all norm-
pattern routes in human space. The Interworld Fleet has
sown relays like seed for centuries. B puts a query to a
common-access information network. The request has low
priority and traffic on the relays is heavy. Access is skewed by
the demands of Fleet, which often commandeers great
chunks of the system's capacity for an hour or a day. B waits.*

Hot water did not relax him; it only reminded him of his
weariness, and of too many nights of half-sleeping on rock.

Had it all, Kristofik. All that money. Couldn't you just enjoy it?

The answer comes, the name. Maybe it means something; maybe not. The man with a thousand names puts little stock in them. He gets a picture, too. He knows the face. Twenty years ago: a boy on a street in Shoreground. Thirty years ago: a terrified child.

Then it is war. And B's first object is the elimination of Michael Kristofik.

Dressing in Theo's darkened room he jumped at a movement on the edge of sight and spun to face it. His savage reflection looked back from a mirror. His hands were clenched. "Quick with our fists today, aren't we?" he said to the mirror, but there was no humor in the face that looked back at him. And after all, he thought irrelevantly, the woman was probably property of the pack that ran with B this year, willing enough to watch a night of flame.

He saw inside his eyes another fist from long ago.

Never again. Not any man.

"Shut up," he said to the voices inside his skull, wondered why he had ever started the hunt; but he knew the answer to that; only he had not known how hard it would be.

When he knows it was me, he'll wish he'd killed me years ago in Shoreground. Seeing me there must have been a shock; but he thought I couldn't be a threat. Just another kid fallen into Valentine. And lost. Like the troubadour's song— "*Since the soul in me is dead, better save the skin*"*—knew what that meant first time I heard it—*

Hanna thought it might be time to come out of trance.

The cool voice of reason said it was time. The disjunction of consciousness should not be maintained past necessity. It drained the body, especially when it was held, as she held it, against the body's sickness and wounding. Necessity, said reason, was gone. This was medical treatment she was getting, no worse; unorthodox, perhaps, but competent. If she stayed in trance, she might find a way to overpower the men

and women who held her, and then?—without them she
would die.

Reason also warned her of the consequences of letting
go. Everything was there, waiting its time—pain and fear,
grief overdue and thus strengthened, some particularly re-
volting memories from the *Avalon,* and the knowledge that
she was lost outside—no longer human space, perhaps, but
certainly human law. Not even reason could assess her exact position; she had missed some important facts. The stun
effect had made her memory patchy, like her consciousness
as she fought it. She had escaped the *Avalon,* but she did
not know what she had come to. She remembered an up-
raised fist and brutal rage, somehow averted. She remembered indifference to her death, provided she remained
alive long enough to be useful. It was all connected to the
face she recognized and the gold-flecked eyes; that made
sense; but she also remembered pity and a soothing touch,
and it was all the same man, and that did not make sense at
all.

While she thought about this, she was touched again. She
gave herself up to the hands with indifference. She knew
without opening her eyes whose hands they were; they belonged to the woman and the girl. They washed her carefully and renewed the healing salve. The woman did not like
it. *Babysitter, medaide, nurse: didn't sign on for this: he'll
want me to cook for them next!* The girl might have been
caressing a doll endowed with imaginary life, healing its
hurts and her own with narcissistic devotion. *Poor baby,
poor darling, I'll make it better, oh help me, oh hold me!*

Hanna opened her eyes to see what they would say when
they knew she was conscious.

The woman called Shen did not say anything. She
thought: *What a constitution. We could use her.*

Hanna turned her eyes on the girl named Lise. She could
not see Lise very clearly. Lise did not know that, and it
made no difference anyway. She responded with the ego-
centricity of her age. She leaned over Hanna, a sudden jerk.
She said, "He didn't mean it."

"What the hell?" Shen said.

Lise said in an urgent whisper, "He wouldn't have hit
you. He wouldn't. He doesn't do that. He won't hurt you."

It was overpowering love, it was worship that excused

and did away all faults. Hanna thought that the child deceived herself. But Lise said, "It's hard for him. I don't know what it is, he won't tell me anything, anything at *all*. But he won't hit you. He won't."

She touched Hanna's shoulder lightly, mindful of the bruises.

Hanna acknowledged without emotion that all of them were careful with her, even Shen. Reason said they would care for her; that it was time to submit to the body's claims and let herself be healed.

Since reason anchored the trance, and the balance of reason urged leaving it, she did so.

The first thing she thought as her mode of thinking shifted was that the concept of the Master of Chaos was more clear to her than it had been before.

The next thing was that she wished she were safe within the strictures of Polity Admin.

The last was a question even reason had not raised. She knew the Polity well, and especially how Jameson thought. Admin had the course to Uskos. Fleet might have tracked the course of the *Far-Flying Bird* as a precaution, a day or two behind, listening for messages of distress. If they had done that (a thing that would suit Jameson), they would know something had happened. The context of her situation would be changed, and she would not be as alone as she felt; the power of five planets waited to help her, if only she stayed alive long enough.

It was her last conscious thought. Exhaustion waited outside the trance, and took over.

GeeGee sang:

> *The hounds they lie down at his feet,*
> *So well they can their master keep;*
> *His hawks they fly so eagerly*
> *No fowl dares come him nigh . . .*

"I don't think that's exactly what I want to hear," Theo said. His face was shiny, but his eyes were intent, and the fingers that manipulated the instruments were steady. The living bone quivered, an artist's medium.

"I thought it would help you with your incising," Michael said gravely.

"Incising? There's no such word."

"Sure there is."

"How do you know?"

"I'm educated, remember?"

Down there comes a fallow doe
As great with young as she might go.
She lifted up his bloody head
And kissed the wounds that were so red ...

Theo said, "I haven't done anything like this in years. Shut it off, all right?"

"Remind me not to let you touch me, if I get hurt."

"Dammit, Mike—"

"Yessir. *GeeGee,* the music is not appreciated. Turn it off."

The sweet voice stopped in mid-song. All of them were in Michael's room, leaving *GeeGee* to tend to herself. The room was brilliantly lighted, especially the bed where the injured woman lay in a cone of blinding light. Movement had a sharp edge in the light, and some of the sharpness was tension, but imperceptibly it drained away. That was because Michael so far had not slipped, to all appearances was himself, and the others were reassured.

A splintered end of bone shifted a millimeter and a metal box said suddenly, "Optimum match."

"Not quite as good as the other one," Theo said. "Still. She can be grateful. It should have punctured the lung." He used a spindle-shape the size of his thumb to fuse the fixative saturating the bone. The metal box chirped and displayed patterns of relative binding strength. Theo touched up his handiwork and the chirps steadied to a hum. Theo said with satisfaction, "That's good. Sealed tight. It waited too long. This must have happened two days ago."

Lise, watching avidly, said, "Ow."

"Mike?" said Shen. She was at the woman's feet, watchful. Theo had not wanted to burden the weak body further with a general anesthetic; he had stationed Shen and Michael so that they could restrain sudden movement if the unconscious woman stirred. It had not been necessary. Michael still held her right hand, stretched above her head and out of Theo's way, but his grip was light. Her left hand lay on her breast, puffy in spite of quick care; that came from the blow to the man with the disruptor. How had she managed to do it, painful as it must have been to move?

Shen said, uncannily echoing the thought, "Two days like that, she did what you told me? Couldn't."

"You wouldn't think so."

"What did she do?" said Theo, who had not heard the story; and when Michael told him he would not believe it. He said, "She couldn't even have walked without screaming."

"She did. I saw it. She might have been doped. It would've had to be a hell of a brew."

"She wasn't doped. She had a broad-spectrum anesthetic at some point, but that was a long time ago. There was just a trace left when I looked at her blood, not enough to make any difference. There was a high concentration of endorphins— still. She couldn't have," Theo said, firmly rejecting fact.

He put away the spindle and selected a slim object with a bulge at one end. He drew it carefully along the edges of the incision. It made no sound, but the layers of fat and muscle quivered. Michael looked away, queasy. There was no difference in kind between what had happened to the woman already, the beating and the rape, and this even more intimate invasion of the flesh. *What nonsense,* he thought, and heard faint clicks; he looked again and saw Theo with a handful of clamps. "That's a good job, if I say so myself. Ready to close," Theo said in a strong, efficient voice that was an echo from some past time.

Michael said, "You said you couldn't make any sense out of her blood."

"I finally did. In some ways. You know what I can't understand? Dawkins' fever. Nobody gets that."

"I've never heard of it."

"You're immunized against it, though. Everybody is. It came out of Colony One at the beginning of the Explosion. You've heard of the Plague Years, I know; well, that was Dawkins' fever. Ever since then you can't even get a vital signs readout without having your immunity tested. It's still around, but you don't find it very often. It would be just possible for her to get it if she'd always been in some iso-

lated place and never had any medical care. But she's had
the best—there's evidence of a massive regeneration effort
in adulthood—and she's been around. Has she ever been
around!"

The edges of the incision melted together under Theo's
hands. When he was done, there was only a red line cutting
across the inflamed skin. He ran a finger over it with a
craftsman's approval and said, "Rescue can worry about
scarring. That's good, though. You can let go now."

Michael held on to the right hand anyway. It had escaped
the general destruction and was smooth to the touch, but it
radiated heat. He said, "What did you do? The same kind of
profile you did on my blood a couple of years ago?"

"Yes, and she's been everywhere. All the Polity worlds.
Valentine. And the Outside worlds, too, which is very rare—
Girritt, F'thal, even Zeig-Daru. And there were some other
things the tracking program couldn't match up."

"Maybe there's something wrong with it. That doesn't
sound right about Zeig-Daru. Nobody's been there except
a few D'neerans."

"Well, the base pattern is D'neeran."

"It's *what?*"

"D'neeran." Theo, puttering among metal boxes, stopped
and looked at him curiously. "What's wrong with that?"

"Well—it's just that getting anywhere near B would
have to make a telepath sick."

He was shocked and it must show; Shen was too still,
Theo looked too uncertain. He pulled himself together and
said calmly, "If she's D'neeran, she wasn't with him by
choice. She might not have much to tell us. Are you sure?"

"That's what it said," Theo said stubbornly. "And if she's
not D'neeran, why would she go to D'neera? Nobody goes
there either."

"I did once," Michael said reminiscently. "I was spaced. I
thought I was going to D'ning on Co-op, from a town an
hour away. I couldn't figure out why passage cost so much
and why it took so long."

Theo looked at him suspiciously, but the story was true.
It had happened in the years just after the *Pavonis Queen*,
when he had spent money wildly and the drugs and the
women were interchangeable, the craving for something
unidentified insatiable, the fights a constant in every space-

port bar. Twice he had nearly killed men with his fists, and later bought them off. And lately it seemed he had not changed so much since then as he had thought. *Not much improvement,* she had said.

Theo cleared away equipment. He left a monitor bracelet on the woman's wrist. He studied the readout module at her shoulder, frowning.

"She's no worse," he said. "You said three days to rendezvous, if we start now? I hope she holds out."

Shen said, "Mike, they called back just before I came down. Want to talk to you."

"Why?"

"Want to know what happened."

"They don't have to know."

"Told 'em you'd call."

"Forget it."

She shrugged. Theo said, "Mike, I said let go of her hand. You'll confuse the monitor."

Michael released the hand with a twinge of reluctance. "Think she'll make it?" he said.

Theo said, "Somebody help me take this stuff back to the lab."

Michael watched him gather up instruments and load them onto Shen and Lise like pack animals. He did not repeat the question.

When the others went out, he stayed where he was. The woman on the bed looked more like a human being now that some of the bruises were clearing, and he was uncomfortable. After a minute he realized that her nudity disturbed him, and drew a sheet over the limp figure. It was not possible for her to be an object of desire, and he had known more than his portion of naked flesh; it was her helplessness that troubled him.

He thought of Theo's judgment of her origin. D'neerans were no more faultless than other human beings and had some faults of their very own, but they were too sensitive to psychic pain to live willingly with evil. This woman could not be one of B's pack. Instead she had had the bad luck to become his prey. And she did not think Michael was much better.

He thought: *Live. So I can tell you that wasn't me you saw. He just drops in sometimes. Please live.*

                                *   *   *

The dark lifted a little from time to time. When it did, she
thought she was in a nightmare. Past, present, and future
bounced around inside her skull in urgent jolts—

*Contact the Polity Admin Starr Starr Starr! They must not
find out who I am—hide from them!*

Michael slumped with his head on one hand, half-asleep.
The room was dark except for a pool of light around the
bed. The iris that opened on space was shut to the shifts that
came with each Jump. The edges of the room melted into
the dark, and Lise slept in shadow on a padded couch, her
fragile legs in an awkward sprawl. Theo sat near the bed;
he did not sleep. He got up often and looked at the patient,
the monitor readouts, the tubes that fed into her arm all the
help that was left to give. Shen had shrugged and left them
to their vigil. There was no sound except for the whisper of
GeeGee at night, and the sick woman's difficult breath.

*I must do it, I must. But in nightmare one cannot move,
the body has no strength, I cannot breathe, I feel nothing . . .
nothing . . .*

Michael brooded on the face that healed before his eyes.
The lesser bruises were gone, the others disappearing. It
was like watching a blurred image come into focus; as if it
were not her face that changed, but his eyes that cleared. In
the slow hours he saw the clear arch of the brow emerge,
the mouth soften to delicate curves. A silver chain that
could not be removed glistened against skin turning to pale
brown satin. Once, her eyes opened. When he leaned over,
he saw that it was reflex and she was aware of nothing near
her; he saw also that her eyes were the deepest blue he had
ever seen. They closed and he drew away, troubled. She had
begun to look familiar, but he did not know her.

*—oh no I have failed all alone with the dead I feel NOTH-
ING—!*

Six years of Hanna's life vanished. She fell into the past.
The People of Zeig-Daru tore her apart, humans regener-
ated her, and she woke, a disembodied consciousness in
null-space, sightless, paralyzed, disconnected from muscle
and nerve—

Lise stirred and moaned. The sides of *GeeGee* rushed in
and sucked out with a roar. The air went with them. Michael

woke to the dark, paralyzed. He could not lift a hand, could not breathe, there were weights on his chest. *"GeeGee!"* He was choking. "Life support! Air!"

"All systems A-OK," *GeeGee* said, "don't you like the atmosphere mix?"

He flailed at stifling darkness and then it was gone. His heart pounded and he breathed in gasps. He felt something he had not known in years: panic. He was incredulous. Lise lifted herself with a struggle, dazed. Theo said, "What was—?"

"I don't know—" His heartbeat eased. Nothing was changed. He must have slept and dreamed something terrible—but Lise and Theo had felt it, too—

D'neerans learn before they are six to suppress unwilled projection of thought. In extremity inhibition gives way.

Oh God they are big so much bigger than I cruel and ruthless oh agony no—! No!

The room filled up with ghastly shadows. Michael got a good look at them, impossibly there, bestial figures of malignant intelligence. Lise flew across the room and into his arms with a terrified cry—right through the shadows.

"Theo!" He shouted into a well. "Something on Revenge, what did we pick up!"

Shen tumbled into the room. She held a knife and yelled, "Where are they, where!" *Oh help help help me!* Hanna screamed, but silently, dreadfully, and Lise shrieked an echo in Michael's ear.

The monstrous shadows touched the sky. The sick woman writhed in a pile of sheets and tubes, center of a storm. Michael fell on her. "Stop it," he said, "stop, stop!" He took her face in his hands, took her shoulders and shook her. Her eyelids flickered. He saw her face and nothing else, shadow was everywhere. "Wake up! Stop it!"

She shrank away from his hands and lifted her own and struck at him. He felt the effort as if it were his. He thought she clawed his eyes, chopped his neck—but that was only her intent; she had not touched him. A strong woman with a newborn's strength.

The light came back.

Lise cried in great gusts, howling. Michael held her tightly with one arm and kept the other hand on the stranger's shoulder. Over Lise's head he saw Theo and Shen shaken, staring, waiting for him to say it was all right.

"All right. It's all right," he said, and disentangled himself from Lise. He did not want to loosen his hold on the woman. He brushed a lock of tangled hair from her face and she made a pitiful sound, still lost in a private horror. But it was private again.

"It's her. Telepathy." His fingers were tight on her shoulder, but he made his voice light. "Wonderful thing, telepathy. What do the books say about this, Theo?"

"Huh?"

"Go check the lab library. Or call Rescue. Find out what this is about." He let go of the woman cautiously. Lise crowded against him and he held her and stroked her hair; she snuffled against his chest. "Theo, it could start up again, go find out what to do!"

Theo, an automaton, looked first at the tubes and readouts. "But the fever's down," he mumbled, and stumbled out.

Michael looked at Shen and said, "Put the knife away." She growled and shoved it into her belt. She took Theo's place and stared at the patient balefully.

"What the hell?" she said.

"I told you. Telepathy. I thought for a minute we'd all been doped or something, got some kind of mind-bending bug on Revenge—but all that came from her."

"Those things? In here?"

"Not real. Illusions. Some kind of shared hallucination that started with her."

Lise said with a last sob, "What were they?"

"I don't know. Something she made up. Or maybe saw . . ."

It was past. He began to relax. He sat on the bed and watched the woman's face. Lise wound herself into a ball, her head on Michael's knee; she looked at the telepath fearfully. Michael thought about the shadows. What kind of mind could think them up? But they had had the detailed immediacy of experience: the gray skin, scarlet garments, paws with long curving claws.

He said restlessly, "I've seen those things before. Not them, but pictures of them."

It was just out of reach, as if someone had just told him the answer and he had already forgotten. He went on thinking out loud: "Nothing looks quite like that except—well, Zeigans do a little; they might be exaggerated Zeigans.

They might be, she's been to Zeig-Daru, Theo said. And she might think of them like that. The first person to make contact, a D'neeran woman, had what you might call a bad experience—"

After a minute of dead silence Shen said, "So?"

He got up, dumping Lise out of his lap. She retreated quickly from the bed. There was a library terminal in the room and the library was well stocked. He sat down at the terminal with some reluctance. He kept wanting to look back at the unconscious woman, as if it were dangerous to turn his back on her.

The guess had to be wrong. There had to be some reason for her look of familiarity besides his reading about Zeig-Daru.

But the search took no time at all. When he asked the library about Zeig-Daru, the first answer was a woman's name. There was a portrait with it. He looked toward the bed once, quickly, without needing to; now he knew why it seemed he had seen her before. He had seen pictures of that face over and over in the months just past, because of the envoys from Uskos.

After a while he got up and went back to the bed. He looked down at Hanna ril-Koroth and said tiredly, "This is very bad."

Shen lifted an eyebrow. Lise was frightened; she did not understand, but his tone warned her something was wrong.

"This is an important person," he said. "I knew a lot about her once, at the time of the Zeigan contact. Which she made. Among other things she's Contact's darling and a commissioner's lady. Former commissioner's. I don't know what the hell we're going to do with her. I thought she belonged with B, thought she was nobody, nobody cared what happened to her, we could question her and hand her over to Rescue and that'd be the end of it—but we're going to be looked at like I haven't been looked at in fifteen years. Like I never wanted to be looked at again. There's no way to keep this quiet."

Theo came in, steadier. He said, "There's not much we can do if it happens again. One of us can try to keep her attention and focus the projection, so we don't all lose our minds. In D'neeran medical centers they keep mindhealers on staff for that."

Shen said, "You got it wrong."

"What?" Theo said, but she was talking to Michael.

"Wrong? How?"

"About quiet." The knife was in Shen's hand. She touched the blade. "Cancel Rescue. All they know is the bitch died. We jettison the body. She never had a name."

Michael said, "Theo, what did you do? Contact Rescue?"

"No, it was in the library. I'll do that, though. I'd better do that."

"No. Don't."

"No?"

"No." He looked at Shen. "If she dies, all right. No name. Some stranger from anyplace but D'neera. But we don't do anything to hurry it along."

Shen hissed. "Gonna run *Gee* with those things around?"

"I'll try what Theo said. Try to keep her attention on me, keep her mind focused."

"Dangerous! What if she lives?"

I don't know, he started to say, but there was no time. The figure on the bed moved with a moan. Lise whimpered. Nightmare moved in.

Hanna crept through a maze of stone. The People of Zeig-Daru were at her heels; she kicked at a flat-muzzled face. "I am a friend!" she cried. They answered: *Thou hast killed he with whom thou wert bonded, that is one; his spouse, the lady of the dawn, that is two; the persons of his crew, that is four others; the spouses of three of these, altogether nine; likewise he who took thee to selfing and thy close kin Awnlee. That is eleven; oh thou human who communicates with We who differ from humankind!*

She called for Jameson, for her mother, for the Lady of Koroth. *Starr, Cassie, Iledra, help me!* she cried, and beat with her fists against stone. The air was hot and close and stifled her. There was no end to the rocky passages.

"We could go somewhere nicer," someone said cautiously.

The stone diminished; the People receded; there was a blur of light. She was just as hot and the breath on her cheek was scalding. She pushed it away impatiently.

"Think of something nice," the voice pleaded.

"But what?" she said, or thought she said; she could not have named the language.

The voice said hopefully, "Springtime? Flowers. Raindrops."

She thought a burst of millefleurs and smiled at their color. Trees she had never seen before arched over them: alien vegetation. She was confused. The stone half-materialized again. She said, "Whose spring? D'neera's, Earth's? Zeig-Daru's or F'thal's? What planet, what place on it, what latitude, where?"

"Pick one."

Her hands were gritty with dirt; they held a plant with naked mud-caked roots. She set it carefully into the hole she had dug. Its tight-coiled buds were shaded with pink. The slanting springtime afternoon light bathed her house in gold. She patted dirt gently around the plant, anticipating its blooms with pleasure.

"That's better," the voice said in relief. There was a body to go with it now, rangy and well-knit. The face was pleasant, though it was sometimes a man's and sometimes a boy's. The eyes had vivid flecks of gold.

"I have tangentially conjoined you in past!" she said in F'thalian, and knew that he understood it to mean *Why, I know you!* and knew therefore that she had not said it at all, but thought it.

"So I see," he answered. "But how?"

"They thought you would attack the *Bird*," she said, the "they" encompassing I&S, Fleet, Contact, Jameson, Figueiredo, and Rubee and Awnlee.

His shock nearly bowled her over; she clung to the dream, she did not want to fall back into the wilderness of accusing stone.

"Why?" said the voice. "Tell me why they thought that!"

Her house slipped away, though she held on as hard as she could; flat on her back she looked up at a blur of a face. She said weakly, "The computers said so."

"Computers," said the voice. "Oh my God, their damned computers!"

She could not find her home again. She had escaped the stone, however. She wandered in the summer of another Home, the People's Home. The lady of the dawn, Hearth-

keeper of a Nearhome, dead these five years, walked with
her. *Thou killest my spouse and my self,* Sunrise said, *and
whom else? Not the beings of F'thal; but you did not make
that contact; it predated you. Fortunate F'thal!*

*I did what I had to do. Thou wouldst have killed me. He
whom we both loved would have done so.*

*And thy sire and sib-selfing? There also thou didst what
must be done, heedless of precautions wise men urged.*

*Rubee's wishes were fulfilled. I did what he would have
me do.*

Sunrise laughed. That was an anomaly, the People did
not laugh. Therefore Sunrise was not really here and it had
to be the fever. And it was, she had been dreaming, she was
awake now and trapped in a cube of metal on the *Avalon,*
in great pain; she waited in rage and disgust for her clothes
to be torn away. The hands had not yet touched her flesh,
but she felt them crawl on her body anyway. And screamed,
outraged.

"No, please," implored the voice. It was shaky. One
chaste kiss touched her cheek. She held hard to a hand.

*It doesn't matter you know I can endure it what I have to
do have to do have to do—*

"Oh, think of something else!" he begged. There were
tears on her cheeks; not her tears. A child sobbed at her
side. They were in a spacecraft without a name, which both
was and was not the *Avalon.* She turned to the boy although
it took all her strength, and put her arms around him.

"It was over long ago," she said grieving.

"I thought so, too. But it wasn't. In a way it only started
later."

The amber eyes widened. Tears were caught in the long
lashes. "You're not supposed to know about that!" he said,
more surprised than angry, but she shrank away, he had
grown up suddenly and smelled of jungle.

He vanished in a lingering fashion. A blurred outline remained which was somehow palpable to the touch, so that
she could hold on to the disappearing arm. There were
other voices. She could not understand them, but she heard
them:

"You all right?" Shen said through her teeth.

"I think so—"

He tried to move his arm, but Hanna held it fiercely. He moved enough to give his cramped muscles some relief; yet surely he could not have been long in that shadow world. He mumbled, "She's too strong for me."

"Then stop it," Shen said, bending close. "Stop it now!"

He had forgotten why he had begun this. The abyss of dream was close, easy to slip into again, and tempting—and suicidal. Some part of him knew that it could strip him of secrets without meaning to, without even wanting to. It was the danger he had avoided for a lifetime. Why, then, was it so seductive?

Brother Martin, all white stone and smoldering eyes: "There is a joy in degradation. The freedom from all rules. Cry to Heaven: I do not care! Let go. Wash away ..."

Theo and Shen talked. There were echoes; he heard with two sets of ears. The words had meaning for him, but not for the other personality of which he was so powerfully aware. She seized from him whole and unbroken the meaning she could not sort out for herself.

Shen raged; that was some of the meaning. Theo said, "I don't think there'll be long-term effects. I think it's harmless."

"Mike? Mike?" whispered Lise. The sound was close. He opened his eyes to a dazzle of light and felt his solid body with surprise. He had thought himself immaterial. Lise hung over him. Her anxiety and fear were blows, channeled by the sick woman.

"Don't be afraid," he said.

"But I am!" she wailed. "Why don't you just let her die?"

"It's all right, little puss—"

Not for her. Silly. Can't you see she's afraid for you? Aren't you afraid of anything? Weren't you afraid on the Queen?

"No," he said. They stood in the docking bay of the *Pavonis Queen.* It was empty and its angles and substance were unreal. Hanna understood that where they were was in fact an engineer's diagram. Every symbol was reproduced on the intangible surfaces. He had a laser pistol in his hand and held it competently, thoughtfully.

"But where did you get the plans?" she said.

"You know how I got them."

"Why weren't you afraid?"

"What was there to be afraid of?"

"Well—being caught. Of course. Prison or Adjustment. Even death?"

"The Polity never executes anybody."

"Prison, then?"

"I would have chosen Adjustment. They let you do that."

"But why? That's death, too."

"Sure it is. It was worth the risk, that's all."

"How could it possibly be?"

"Freedom is worth any risk."

"In theory, yes—" The snow fell outside her house. A fire sang on the hearth. She served tea: a polite accompaniment to polite conversation. He was urbane and relaxed. Too relaxed; his eyes were too knowing; they had seen too much of the other side of civilization.

"The best you can do," he said, "is choose your own parameters—choose, that is, which game you'll play. What I had in mind required money. I got it, too. Got my choice."

The glass wall dissolved; snow blew in with a howl. Hanna, teeth chattering, served tea.

"You sit here in this storm and tell me that?" she said.

"I didn't plan the storm," he said.

The wind cut through her with knives. Hanna stood in a drift of snow. Beyond the long black line of false-oaks, in the direction of D'vornan, the sky was red. She turned to see him bent in agony, cradling his wrecked hands close to his body. "You see it never stopped," he said. His voice shook with the pain. The glimmering snow parted and a crevice gaped black at their feet, bottomless. She fell to her knees in the snow, weeping; took the twisted hands and kissed them.

"You don't have to do that," he said.

"I want to. Nobody else ever did it, did they."

The crevice pulled at them. He knelt before her and they pressed close together, turning their faces from the abyss as if, unseen, it would go away. It did not; it moved under them and they fell gasping, clinging together, through its deeps. They landed not ungently in a blood-red sky filled with shooting stars and long measured howls. Hanna cried out in a nightmare that was not, this time, her own. Black ruins stood stark against a wall of flame. A face leered from the fire: the man she knew as Castillo.

She cried, "What's burning?"

"Everything. My mother. Oh, my poor mother!" He wept again.

"I can't bear this. We have to stop," she said.

"Yes," he said, but the tears ran down his cheeks all the same, and she understood that this landscape that was new to her was one he visited only in dreams and never willingly. But he had lived in it. And suffered in it.

"Where are we?"

"I don't know!"

He vanished and the light went with him. "Michael!" she called. "Michael, I'm lost!" And he came to her at once, but now they were in a forest of scarlet plumes which beat together with a sound like rattling bones.

She held to him and said, "The Master's here."

"He always is," said the man at her side.

"You know about the Master?"

"I didn't know that's what he was called."

"I'm tired of him. I don't want it any more."

"There's a choice?"

"I'm *tired*. I didn't want to kill again, I didn't want to fight, I didn't want to hurt and grieve. I'm tired of pain, I had enough!"

"I know," he said. "Me, too. Could we help each other?"

They were on another spaceship: "Welcome to *GeeGee*," he said, she was in his arms and they lay close together; had she taken a lover after all?

"I didn't want that either!" It came out in a strangled cry, but they were still in a place where speech blurred into thought, and he understood.

"You choose what you can and the rest is just there," he said.

He seemed to know where they were. Hanna did not; she tried to go home and was on the *Bird* with Awnlee dead at her feet.

"I will not do this any more!" she said, and he put his arm around her shoulders. He was concentrated and alert.

"I've been lost a lot," he said.

"That's good," she said, because it was preposterously reassuring.

"Why don't we just go home?"

"I don't know where it is," she said painfully.

"I don't either. We'll find it, though. Let's go see my friends first."

"But where are they?"

"Here. They always are," he said, confident. The *Bird* got lighter and lighter, dissolved, and resolved into:

Ordinary light, most extraordinary of all things. Blurred faces floated in it. She turned her head and looked into the amber eyes. They were wary and exhausted. "Hello," he said, and she felt a great astonishment in him.

She whispered, "Can you control that woman who wanted to kill me? And her apprentice. The little girl."

"Sometimes."

"Try."

He said something to the faces and they retreated. Hanna sank toward sleep. Before she got there she felt him twine around her comfortably, possessively. It felt good.

We have to sleep, she said.

"Can I dream my own dreams this time?"

It struck her that he was true-human and had no right to accept so equably what had happened. But she answered, *Yes, I think so, good night.*

"Good night," he said. He put his cheek against her hair and fell asleep.

◇

Watson Sellers was an experienced officer of the Fleet. This was not the first derelict he had boarded, spanning the space between ships in free fall, suited against zero and vacuum; behind him the bulk of a Fleet vessel—*Comet*, this time—and his team strung out in a wavering line; before him a dark hulk whose luck had all been bad.

The *Far-Flying Bird* was not dark, though, and not silent. Uskosians built windows into their spacecraft with abandon; the *Bird* looked from close up all light. And it broadcast a continuous mayday, not the sedate rote of a human spacecraft in trouble, but a frantic shout. A ship this noisy and this bright should not be derelict. It should answer *Comet*'s call. It did not even drift or spin; it stood to unmoving, nose lifted toward home as if it smelled the way.

An air lock was open. Sellers already knew that; everyone on *Comet* knew it. The noise and the light and the lock made them think of old spacemen's tales that had once been seafarers' tales of undamaged vessels found with lights burning, meals cooking, gliding calmly before the wind with no one aboard and nothing to say where everybody had gone.

Sellers had not been on the *Bird* before. He was a man of some aesthetic sense, and when the boarding team broke through he walked through the *Bird* stunned by the sweeping lines that made small spaces look large and large ones vast, and by the palettes of color. Then they came to the bridge and found rags and swollen fleshy bags: Rubee and Awnlee. The *Comet*'s skipper heard Sellers grunt inside his helmet and said, "Well?"

"We've found them, ma'am."

"And?"

"They're dead. That's the aliens; Lady Hanna's not here."

"Keep looking. How did they die?"

"There are no visible wounds. We need a medical team here."

He heard her give the order. Then she said, "Getting word to Omega is first priority. Find out as much as you can as quickly as you can, and find Lady Hanna. I shall wait only for a preliminary report before Jumping to Omega. You'll remain there in charge of the investigation until relieved. Understood?"

"Yes, ma'am," Sellers said. He split up the party to search for Hanna and set off in the direction he had asigned himself. In his helmet he heard the controlled bustle of the *Comet*'s bridge. The skipper speculated with her officers on disease; Sellers knew that she was wrong. There was the open air lock, and the aliens had the look of beings who die suddenly and in pain. He listened, unconsciously at first, for sounds besides those transmitted from *Comet*. Then he found himself trying to adjust the audio pickup of his suit and knew what he was doing. The pickups were working fine. There was nothing for them to hear. When the sounds of the *Comet* were gone, complete silence would descend. Sellers thought for the first time in twenty years that he was a long way from home.

Michael drifted in and out of sleep. He had been very tired
even before Hanna's hallucinations began, and those had
gone on for a long time. In his dreams scenes from Hanna's
life and his tumbled together. He thought at first that he
saw pictures from his own imagination, made-up events
from a life inferred from the dream-truths she had shown
him. Later he knew they were real. He had not been to Koroth, but if he were set down in its House, he would know
where each corridor led, he would know the women's faces,
fair or aged with ironic eyes: *The child has left us.* White
whispers of F'thal in crazy-angled chambers: *Poorly the
creature gyres!* Polished echoes in emptiness, a deep voice
colder than any unhuman's: *Do not ask if I love. What's all
must be enough.*

Someone dreamed: *I am lost.* He did not know who
dreamed it.

Theo shook him from time to time, talked quietly and
went away, full of worry. He ought to tell Theo there was
nothing wrong with him, he only needed sleep, there would
be time enough for waking. And meanwhile the woman in
his arms was a firm anchor to reality, a sensuous burden that
differed from the others he had known in feeling just right,
tailored to his comfort. Or had they all felt that way in the
deep contentment of half-sleep? — perhaps they had. But he
could not remember any of them. There was only the tent
of warmth he and Hanna made together, a cathedral-space
of sufficiency.

But there was the other part of her and what she represented: the implacable hand of the Polity.

The last thought woke him fully. He let go of her, startled.

Don't leave me, please don't leave, she dreamed, and her
longing overwhelmed him. The longing was for somebody
else, but that did not matter. *I am empty, fill me,* she
dreamed, a powerful erotic plea; he kissed her throat and
touched her, unresisting, unresisted; he nuzzled and nestled
into the hollows of breast and flank. His cheeks burned and
her skin burned his urgent hands. "Oh, yes!" he whispered,
but her memories rose between them. Powerless, hurting,
revolted, she felt other hands, and *No!* she said, and "No!"
she moaned aloud, so that he separated from her and left
her, aching with desire.

He turned his face away and waited until the faint sounds of disturbance ceased and she was quiet. When he looked at her again, she was profoundly asleep.

Jameson found out about the *Far-Flying Bird* from Gil Figueiredo. He got the news late at night, in the dark, and once or twice during the recital he thought he heard echoes of Hanna in the stillness of the house she had loved. Figueiredo's face glared from the white light of a video screen, and he was furious, apportioning blame, assigning some to the commissioners of the Polity for permitting the *Bird* to depart unescorted, some to the Uskosians for their folly. Jameson, it appeared, was exempted. His anxiety was well documented, and the efforts he had made to communicate it to others. But he was appalled when Figueiredo said, "We should have probed Lady Hanna. She's gone. The treasure's gone. She had access to the course. There's an implication of complicity."

Jameson said bluntly, "You're mad."

"I'm objective. I don't think you're objective about her."

Jameson did not argue. He regretted those two spontaneous words; there was no chance of Figueiredo's accusation being taken seriously, and when he found that out he would drop the idea.

Later, in the morning, he tried to reach Edward Vickery, but Vickery had no time for him yet. It was not like the old days when he could reach whomever he wanted whenever he wanted, whether it was convenient for them or not. Now he only learned what was going on at the pleasure of others, no one rushed to tell him anything, no one asked him what to do. He told them all what to do anyway, transmitting urgent memoranda that dealt with approaching Uskos. "Send a mission at once," he wrote. "There should be no delay in carrying news of an event which the Uskosians will understand as an irruption of Chaos. They will look favorably on an attempt to appproximate, insofar as the event permits, the legend-determined landing date set by Rubee and Awnlee."

But Vickery finally called him and said there would be no mission until Michael Kristofik had been caught, so that human justice could be displayed to Uskos.

It did not occur even to Jameson that someone besides Kristofik might have been responsible for the rape of the *Bird*. The only objection he made was: "What if you don't catch him?"

"We will. He doesn't know we came up with his name before it happened," Vickery said with satisfaction, "and he doesn't suspect anything, because he arranged rendezvous with a Rescue craft out of Valentine."

"I beg your pardon?"

"Evidently there was a casualty. He contacted Rescue a day ago with some story about picking up a sick woman somewhere—he wouldn't say where—and we'll have I&S and Fleet personnel aboard the pod when it makes contact."

"A sick woman?" Jameson said with interest.

"The *Bird* is not a safe environment for human beings. One of his crew probably caught something."

"It's not that dangerous." Jameson wondered how much of the material on Uskosian-human biological analogs Vickery had read.

"There were injuries, too. There might have been a fight. *Comet*'s gone back to get a report from the team on the *Bird*. We'll know more about it soon."

"The aliens and Hanna were unarmed."

"It doesn't have to have been a firefight," Vickery said impatiently. "Lady Hanna knows unarmed combat, doesn't she? We'll find out when we get him."

"Valentine has agreed to switching the Rescue craft's crew?"

"Oh, yes. There were token objections. But this is not an internal human affair. This concerns relations with a sovereign nonhuman species. We made it plain we had to have compliance. We mentioned travel sanctions, and that was that."

Jameson murmured, "I should think so." Valentine's one-trade economy would fail overnight without the Polity's millions of visitors to its pleasure domes.

After that, acknowledging reality, he stopped urging an immediate expedition to Uskos. He had time to think about Hanna. Michael Kristofik would hardly show himself so quickly if he had not gotten rid of her. Yet it was odd that no one from D'neera had contacted him, Hanna's frantic mother perhaps, nudged by a daughter's ghostly awareness of impending death, or by the disappearance from the universe of the entity that was Hanna. D'neerans were strange about things like that; they always knew. But it might be that Hanna, in her long absence from home and her increasing detachment from the persons there and elsewhere, had come to maintain such a tenuous place in the hearts of her friends that when she left them altogether, they had not know it.

As for himself: should he not feel something more than concern about relations with Uskos?

Then he realized that he did not believe in Hanna's death, regardless of probability. She was clever and aggressive, he had made her learn a little about Michael Kristofik, and she was amazingly good at staying alive. She did not have as many scruples as a peaceful D'neeran ought to have. The Hanna who had said in the safety of Admin that she did not want to fight again was one person. Hanna alone, out on the edge of law and life, was someone else, as she had proved in the past—though she might not wish to admit it.

He might have loved her better if civilization had sunk deeper than her soft skin. But then she would not have been Hanna.

GeeGee sang in an archaic tongue with glee, but not much sense:

> *The bay horse is in the pasture, hurrah!*
> *With two unshod feet, with two unshod feet.*
> *She goes at a sweet ambling gait.*
> *The bay horse is in the pasture, hurrah!*

Michael sat at Hanna's bedside, an invalid himself. The bay horse had a blaze down her nose; on cool days she was frisky, snorted at pockets for sugar, danced when you got on her back, not enough to throw you off, just enough to tease you so that you laughed, and so did she; when she was really in a snit she swerved to trot under low branches, tried to scrape you off and made you duck and yell. He knew the feel of the saddle under his thighs, the reins in his fingers, the partnership of human and beast.

He had never ridden a horse in his life. He had never even seen one that was close enough to touch.

Theo pottered among the tubes and metal boxes. The light was dim now because Michael, waking, had tried weakly to shield his eyes, which were filmed and unfocused; he might have been drunk. Hanna's temperature was in a safe zone, but Theo worried over the incision, which had suffered in the tumult of her first panic. At intervals he asked Michael questions. "What's the name of this ship? What's your name? What's my name? Where do we live?" The answers were accurate, but they came slowly.

"I'm not crazy," Michael said.

"Of course not."

"I just feel a little funny."

"Sure."

"It's like double vision."

"Really?"

"Or like—like being expanded."

"Expanded," Theo repeated with a glint in his eye.

He waited for more, but Michael shut up. He slouched by Hanna and stared at her. He knew more than how to ride a horse. He knew what it was like to communicate telepathically with an alien intelligence; he knew what F'thalians and Zeigans and Uskosians were like in ways his reading had never told him. He had a name for the hand that had striven with his for control of his life: the Master of Chaos. He knew what hid behind the library's portrait of Hanna. He knew what he looked like to her: half threat, half comforting guide.

There was a sound like the ocean in his ears.

Shen came to him and said, "She's better. Gonna live. Cancel Rescue?"

He looked at her helplessly. Somewhere in his slow brain he remembered learning something that made canceling Rescue a good idea. He could not remember what it was, though, and he said, "No."

"She doesn't need 'em."

"Does she?" he asked Theo.

"Need Rescue? Maybe not. I'd feel better if somebody else looked at her, though, and she's so weak she could get worse again, or get sick with something else. Anyway, you said yourself we can't keep this quiet. She's got to be identified sooner or later."

"Later!" Shen said.

"How long to rendezvous?" Michael said. He was dizzy.

"Two days now," Theo said, "You slept a long time."

Sleep still sounded good. "Stay on course," he said.

Shen said, "Wish she'd died."

"I don't."

He eyed the space beside Hanna with longing. Lise said from the corner, "Wish she'd died."

Emma Maurello was an assistant to Valentine's chief liaison official in Admin's External Trade Affairs Department. That department was a cell of a larger congeries that dealt with nuances of trade within and outside of the Polity. Somewhere there must be a clear organizational chart, but in two Standard years Emma had not found out to whom, in the long run, External Affairs answered. In any event Emma's offices ordinarily did not care. It was enough, said the transplanted citizens of Valentine in Liaison, to go along at a quiet clip, maintaining routine without expediting it unnecessarily. The work was easy, the surroundings comfortable, there was more talk of leisure than of work, and Emma lived a quiet life which had nothing disturbing in it.

Today was different. Today was an uproar. And Emma, when she had found out what it was about, got away. She slipped away from the towers of Admin, not without frequent glances over her shoulder; she skulked (or felt that she did) through the walkways, the parklands, the structures that housed services for Admin, to a public message center looming against the hazy autumn sky. Here she took a cubicle, placed a call to Valentine, and watched the charges mount against her credit. Private interstellar calls were expensive and Emma was not rich. There went a dress she coveted; there went all her luxuries for a week, and for another week—

She took her eyes from the racing figures. It was a hot morning, though in the fall of the year. The message center's environmental system was poorly programmed and the cubicle was hot, too, so that her hair stuck to the back of her neck. She looked anxiously behind her again, because she was doing (or supposed she was doing) an illegal thing for the first time in her life.

In Shoreground it was (she remembered too late) the middle of the night. When Kareem Mar-Kize answered, there was no video and she knew from the sound of his voice that she had gotten him out of bed. He sounded as if she had better have a damn good reason for this.

"It's about Mike," she said, and in the silence she heard the unspoken answer: *Reason enough.* Because her voice must give it away, and her face, which Mar-Kize could see though she could not see his.

She plunged into her story with no other preamble. Halfway through it he activated video and she saw the bronze face, the intelligent black eyes robbed of sleep. He asked questions. She answered them as best she could for her nervousness. She was not used to listening for footsteps behind, or waiting to be caught in an illegal act.

At the end he said, "Why are you telling me this?"

"Because I know Mike—"

She felt herself blush. Mar-Kize had been at Mike's house that night, must have seen some of the evening's long flirtation. Mike was not easy to get: as if she had ever thought in those terms before! As if she would! Finally the others left. She went with Mike into the garden, helped him extinguish the glittering starpoints of light in the big old trees, and he kissed her just as she began to think she would have to start it herself. They stayed outdoors. The sea pounded distantly, the wind sighed through the long night hours, the thick moss was soft on her bare skin. Near dawn she said, "I must go." "Dear Emma, stay and rest. You've had no sleep." But she went, not wanting to face the midday light later, the disinterested courtesy of the persons of his house, the amicable acceptance of the animals (who had come to the trees from time to time to see how they got on)—

"—very good of you," Mar-Kize was saying.

"I can't believe he'd do what they say. Can you?"

"Good God, no. Does anyone know you've called me?"

"What? Oh. I don't think so, I'm at a public call center, I don't think I was followed or—they don't tap these places, do they?"

"Not routinely. Do they know you know Mike?"

"Everybody knows Mike. Don't they?"

"Seems like it. All right. Thank you. I'll try to get a message to him."

"Can you? Do you think you can? The I&S people, I heard they said they've got the ship's access codes tagged, so if the relays pick up any transmission for Mike it can be stopped. Can you do it anyway?"

"I'll try," Mar-Kize said neutrally, but Emma did not know how much hope he had.

The call was over. Emma sat in the heat, afraid to find out what it had cost her but not regretting it. It was the right thing. Even if the affair had been brief, even if Mike had not been her lover for long; because better than that, he was her friend.

A hand fell on her shoulder, and when she looked up she was more afraid than she had known she could be. The man behind her wore the uniform of Admin Security. Behind him was a woman, not uniformed but with the look of I&S; and behind the woman was a robot with a Domestic Enforcement patch where its head should be. It was the end of Emma's future. *Maybe Mike will give me a job.*

She went with them without protesting. She thought that if she were docile, what happened to her could not be as bad as anything that would happen if she fought.

She was wrong.

Kareem Mar-Kize placed Emma when the call was finished, not before. He had met her at one of the parties Mike occasionally gave for a handful of old friends and new acquaintances. Maurello was one of the recent acquaintances. She had had a hard time keeping her eyes off Mike; that was not unusual, though hers was a worse case than most. What was unusual was Mike's response. It was (Kareem had decided then) sweet innocence that did the trick. Mike was adept at dodging the predators, the sophisticates with hungry eyes, but Emma had made him helpless for a while.

Kareem's wife, who had waked near the end of the conversation, said, "What's wrong?"

"Mike's in a little trouble."

"Trouble? What kind?" She sat up in bed suddenly. "It's not that old thing, is it?"

"It's related. Never mind. Go back to sleep."

"I won't be able to now. Where is he?"

"Somewhere in space in that flashy toy spaceship. I've got to get in touch with him—and the Polity's fixed it so I can't."

He told her everything Maurello had told him, on the principle that two heads were better than one. He was right; she said immediately, "Some of those luxury craft scan all the newsbeams and flag the crew if there's something interesting. Does *GeeGee* do that?"

"Of course. That's common for a ship that class. Why?"

"Well, will what the Polity's doing prevent Mike from getting information that way?"

"Shouldn't, but I don't see—Wait a minute. One of the things she scans for is his name. He set her up that way. I told him it was paranoia. He said he was being realistic. This is top secret, though. It's not out on the 'beams."

"Not yet," said his wife, "and wouldn't any 'beam service just love to get it first?"

He gave her a hearty kiss and made a call. It only took one.

Shen shook Michael awake. He came up out of a deep sleep, without dreams this time; it was a black cave, and it sucked at him. The tension in Shen's hard right hand was a warning. He turned to Hanna in anxious reflex. The room was dark, but there was a soft glow near the bed. It showed Hanna's face and he saw that she slept in peace, her breath coming easily.

"Gotta hear something," Shen said. Her mouth was tight. He got out of bed reluctantly and found that his knees shook. So Theo had been wrong and what he had done with Hanna had hurt him somehow after all, at the least had drained him.

Someone had relieved him of his shirt and boots. He found them in the dark, fumbling, and put them on while Shen waited impatiently. Lise and Theo had disappeared.

"What time is it?" he said.

"Fourteen hundred hours. *GeeGee*'s back on Standard time. Another day to Rescue. Rescue!" she said bitterly.

"What's wrong?"

"Come on."

He followed her to Control. The brighter light outside his room hurt his eyes and the climb up the spiral stairs seemed long; his strength was not at norm. Lise was in Control, her nose almost touching a display surface as she scowled at the words there. She could read, but not well. Shen flipped a switch and a perfectly modulated voice (robo, he thought automatically) said, "Rigorous identification procedures are in effect for incoming traffic to Nestor and Lancaster as well as Valentine. Private vessels approaching Polity ports should be prepared for security checks and possible boarding."

Shen stopped it and said, "Newsbeams." He didn't know what it meant; he didn't want to have anything to do with it. He looked at Shen, baffled. She touched another key and he saw a face that made him blink; it was gaudily painted and the eyes glowed with artificial light. It was human, though. He had seen it on the 'beams before, slashing at more or less deserving targets. It said, "My contacts inside I&S admit Kristofik is the man who robbed a Polity vessel in deep space of a fortune in '23. They don't say why he's been allowed to spend it unmolested all these years. They say there was advance warning of danger to the *Far-Flying Bird*. They don't say why Kristofik wasn't detained before the *Bird* started her flight."

Shen shut that off, too. "More?" she said. Michael shook his head, a reflex action; he was dazed. What he had heard percolated and sank in slowly. So they'd found out what had happened to the *Far-Flying Bird* and—

His head was stuffed with dust. He needed to think clearly and could not.

He said, "They thought I was going to do it ahead of time. They don't know about *him*."

Shen said incredulously, "You knew? About this?"

"No. Yes. I mean, I should have realized what it meant."

Shen stared at him; so did Lise. He could not be making sense. Shen said to Lise, "Go wake Theo up."

"No. Wait—" A connection made itself without his volition. He picked words carefully. "They knew somebody was after the aliens, I don't know how. They'd made up their minds if anything happened it was going to be me, and they don't know anything about B. So now they're after us. How long to Rescue?"

"A day. Told you. *Was* a day. Changed course soon's I heard this. Good thing I didn't kill her."

"Huh?"

"Witness. Tell 'em we didn't do it."

"Yeah. All the same. They'll want to know what we know about B, why we were after him, how we knew he was on Revenge, lots of questions. Questions I don't want to answer. Don't want to get near it, Shen. Too good an excuse to shove me under probe."

His mind was working better. Shen relaxed. She said reflectively, "Can't go home. Or anywhere."

"Right. Until she's in condition to talk."

"Take real good care of her," Shen said warmly, and the turnabout should have been funny. It was not. With Hanna dead the only way to prove his innocence would be to go under probe. If they got him under probe, they would not be content with his ignorance of the present crime; they would go on to the *Pavonis Queen* and that would be the end. Without Hanna there would be no escape. Not even Valentine would shelter him from this; surely Rescue had cooperated in a trap. So all his life had hung on the thread of Hanna's, and in saving her he might have saved himself; though he had done it for no charitable motive and almost in spite of himself, because of Lise and Theo. Left to himself he might have killed her, he would have killed her in a frenzy of rage or obsession—Hanna who was part of him now.

Shen misinterpreted the look on his face. She said, "Big trouble."

"Not so big," he said, although it was; but also there it was, and there was no point thinking about the size of it. He looked for ways out. Best would be a way that did not mean running, a way to sidestep I&S. He said, "I want her to talk to the Polity as soon as she can. We stay lost until then. See if she can keep them off our backs. If she will. Maybe she'll do it. She's not interested in us. She never used to care about anything but her work, although— But maybe she'll want to get back to Contact and the hell with I&S."

He saw that Shen was astonished by the implied knowledge of Hanna, and became tongue-tied. Shen said, "Maybe. *Can* she do it?"

"I don't know," he said after too long a pause. "It's worth

trying. She's got influence. The council of magistrates on D'neera gives her anything she asks for. In the Polity there's the Contact director. Jameson. He knows all the commissioners. Some of them are holdovers from when he was on the Commission. He knows everybody in I&S, too. And he owes her. God, does he owe her! But he won't care about that."

Michael sat down suddenly and put his head in his hands. He wondered if Hanna knew as much about him as he knew about her.

She had forgotten. She woke without strength, still fevered, and alone. She was not altogether awake. With enormous effort she propped herself on her right elbow, swaying. There was something on her left wrist and she lifted her hand, which seemed heavier than rock, and looked at it intently. It was close to her face, brown and out of focus; it seemed to have floated there. She examined it as well as she could for the blurring. A medical monitor bracelet gleamed at her, silvery. She reached suddenly for the chain at her throat, lost her balance, and fell back.

The bracelet had done its job and signaled someone. She was lifted and there was a steady arm behind her back. A hand held a cup to her lips. She swallowed clear water, the sweetest draught she had ever drunk. Her mouth was sand-dry and she sucked at the water greedily. Pieces of the world came back one by one. She looked into Michael Kristofik's unmistakable eyes. She remembered doing it before—but the memory slipped away. *I will help you,* she thought. Or was it, *Help me!*

He moved so that her head, which she was not strong enough to hold up, lay against his shoulder. Fogged with fever, unsure where she left off and he began, she felt his pleasure in holding her. She thought that was odd. And sorted through the broken pieces of the recent past that came back a little at a time. And remembered.

"God. Oh, God."

"What? What is it?"

Awnlee. Rubee. I must contact—

She made pictures of Awnlee and Rubee dead and alone in the *Bird,* and the hive of Admin waiting for her call. He said, "They've found the ship. They know."

There were tears in her eyes. She had not cried for a long time and the wetness was strange and awkward. She cried for Awnlee, her friend, and Rubee, who had extended kinship to her. It seemed the event had happened a moment ago. She knew it had not, time had passed, and there were things she must do, if only she could stop crying. But she could not, it was beyond her strength, and she was angry. Michael held her and made sounds of consolation. She remembered that he was connected with Castillo. She tried to push him away; she hated him. She made him feel it, and knew it wounded him.

He said in distress, "Oh, no, I had nothing to do with it, I only came later and found you," and it was the truth, but how could it be? He knew Castillo. He had known the monster for lifetimes, the beast of flame.

Don't touch me, don't touch me! she cried, and heard him swear. He let her down gently and leaned over her, painfully anxious. It added to her confusion; he treated her as an intimate might.

Short as the episode had been, she was exhausted. She could not lift a hand again, not even to wipe the tears from her face. He did it, uncannily responsive; then he kissed her eyes, each in turn. She was paralyzed with rage; she threw it at his head like a weapon. It hurt him. She did not know why. How could he do that to a stranger and then be surprised by her fury?

She could not sustain anger; she drifted away. She wondered if she would ever again in her life be strong enough and well enough to do anything besides sleep.

Michael stayed beside her until he knew she had gone back into the dark. It only took a minute. He thought that he would keep away from her. Perhaps when she was stronger and rational, he could explain. Perhaps by then he would be himself again.

When it was "night" he slept in the lounge. He dreamed of Claire, Claire of the moonlit hair and milky skin, Claire who had agreed to marry him. Then he dreamed a dream that was an accurate memory, except that he was in a dark, threatening emptiness instead of the comfortable dome-mounted flat he had occupied ten years ago.

"I disobeyed a direct order," Kareem said. "You can do what you think best about that."

He looked so peculiar that Michael was alarmed. "It's that serious? I'm poor, or something?"

"You told me not to run confirmation on Claire's background. Because if she found out someday, she'd be hurt."

A light answer died on Michael's tongue; he looked at Kareem's face and could not say a word. Kareem said, "I did it anyway. You have to know. She's an I&S agent."

When Michael could speak again he said, "She can't be."

"She's not even real. They made her up, she turned herself into what they thought you'd want. I'm sorry, Mike. I'm so sorry."

He woke sweating. No one else was in the lounge. The video screen was in the middle of a biography of Hanna. He did not look at it. He knew enough about Hanna. No wonder he had dreamed of Claire; he had thought that he knew her well.

Early each "morning" Shen, faithfully grumbling but faithfully, went to bathe Hanna. This morning while she was gone, Lise brought Michael and Theo coffee in the lounge. The video screen yammered on. Starr Jameson answered questions about Uskos. Michael watched him with unfriendly eyes. The man had not wanted Hanna. Only an idiot would not want Hanna. Therefore Jameson was an idiot. Simple logic.

GeeGee finished with Jameson, searched, and landed in the middle of a statement by a woman of D'neera. She spoke with a faint accent, as if, among themselves, D'neerans shifted Standard pronunciation to suit their own ideas of correctness. Michael had heard no such accent in Hanna's speech, but she had spent much time on Earth. The eyes of the image were eerily like Hanna's, widely spaced and the same deep shade of blue. D'neera's founding population had been small; those splendid eyes might be common there. H'ana's intimates, the woman said, were convinced she was alive. She was held hostage, no doubt. D'neera had complete faith in the Polity's ability to rescue H'ana from her captors.

"That's us," Lise said, excited.

"So it is," Michael said.

Theo said, "Maybe we should go ahead and contact I&S. Tell them what happened."

"I want her to tell them. Think she could do it today?"

"No. Maybe tomorrow, but I'm not even sure about that."

"She's not out of danger yet, is she?"

"Not weak as she is. Don't push her."

"Can he kiss her?" Lise asked.

Theo blushed. He mumbled, "That was just because of what they were doing with their heads."

"Not that time. Later."

"Later?" Theo said. He looked at Michael suspiciously.

"Where were you?" Michael said to Lise.

"In the door. You didn't see me. She didn't like it."

"No," he admitted.

"You shouldn't do it again. She's too sick. Theo said so."

"I suppose you're right," he said.

GeeGee kept music going behind the anonymous noises of the 'beams. A choir of male voices chanted in unison in a long-dead language. The solemn songs had echoes behind them, as if the singers stood in a cavernous space and drew deeply on the hollow past. *Nostra corda fove laetitia prabe praesidia,* they sang: Warm our hearts with happiness, offer us thy protection!

The structure of Michael's life in these last years had been carefully planned. He had worked hard to make it as it was: peace, freedom, security, beauty. It had not been enough, but he had valued it.

It disintegrated and dissolved.

Kareem Mar-Kize, having proved uncooperative, was restricted politely to his home. Michael did not try to call him. It could not help; it could only harm.

Emma Maurello, apprehended for unspecified reasons, had disappeared into I&S custody—into, no doubt, the half-world of the probe. It would take from her the details of their sweet shared nights and they would never be hers or his again.

The banking officials of Kingstown, where most Shore-ground money went, froze all of Michael's holdings. It was possible that they would be irrevocably seized with an eye toward reparations. His credit was rescinded so that even if he were fool enough to land somewhere and try to use it, he would be a pauper.

I&S personnel from offworld overran his home. If he closed his eyes he could see it as clearly as if he were there: cats glared from trees and stairways, dogs whined outside closed doors, the F'thalian tourmaline balled up under his bed and hid and starved.

Fast little Fleet scouts fanned out through human space to every habitat, mining station, or satellite that supported a human settlement. Revenge would be on the list. The People of the Rose would show an incredulous I&S that Michael had been on Revenge during the taking of the *Far-Flying Bird*. The hunt would be widened to include B, but it would not slacken for Michael. B would know that, too; know, when he heard this, that his time was gone. Then he would flee forever. The secret would go with him, while everything that might have been left to Michael here vanished, too.

He heard again and again about the *Pavonis Queen*. If five years' grace between the event and his linkage with it had not saved him from the scrutiny of I&S, at least it had kept him from the attention of the public. Now the crime was resurrected and greeted with a clamor. It would not be forgotten again.

The Fleet scouts got to Carrollis and someone added up the facts of Prissy's murder, the brass-colored ship, and the dark man from offworld who had been in Town on that day and no other. They talked about the fate of the child Prissy had owned. She had not been on Valentine long and her presence in Michael's household had gone nearly unnoticed, so that now she was said to have disappeared. There were speculations on Michael's reasons for taking her away from Carrollis. He did not recognize himself in them.

After that he thought: *I had some good years. I knew it could end.*

He looked up and saw that Theo watched him. He tried to make his face indifferent, but Theo said, "For a while there I thought you didn't know what it all meant."

Michael was silent. Presently Theo went out.

Nostrorum scelerum tolle maliciam — lift the weight of our transgression —

He wondered if, even after he was cleared of the present crime, I&S would take him from home one dark night and he would wake up in a cell on Earth and find out he had confessed to every unlawful act he had ever done, and everything he had ever tried to hide.

Probably.

The monks of a world far away from Alta, treasuring the ancient music, sang on.

Miserere nobis: Have mercy on us!

Chapter 3

It took Hanna a week to wake up fully. At first she understood only the music that surrounded her, which was not like any music she had heard before. The instruments were strange to her, and the oddly syncopated rhythms, and when there were voices the languages as well. On some level she knew they were very old. They reached into history, and even those presented in Standard breathed no modern spirit in their phrasing. *Sweet Robin, lend to my thy bow,* a man's voice sang; *I must a-hunting with my lady go . . . With my sweet lady go . . .* That time there was no accompaniment; the song was not recorded, and the singer was nearby. Hanna rested in the music, at peace.

Later her eyes cleared and she saw the room she was in. It was colored in tones of earth and sun, and there were spaces filled with a patchwork of furnishings, paintings, fabrics, and oddments sifted by a curious, acquisitive hand. For sky there was a polished ceiling etched with bronze traceries of leaves like the shadowed roof of a forest. The little world breathed a personality: sunny and clever and brash.

And later still the anonymous hands that cared for her had faces with them, and the faces had names: Theo and Shen. The blue-eyed half-crazy girl, Lise. And finally Michael, *the one with the eyes,* Hanna thought, the man who was supposed to be dangerous. He wasn't dangerous now; he sat by her bed with lines of strain around those eyes, and the lines disappeared when the others were around, and she felt the effort it took to make them vanish and the reason behind it: the love. *Everything's fine,* he told them with his smiles. And therefore, for them, it was.

By the time Hanna began to think again, she had forgotten that she was supposed to be afraid.

"You're not a monster," she whispered when the slow swell of thought finally crested in speech, and the man by her bed started, worry thick in his eyes, heavy on his mouth.

"You're not going to hurt me," Hanna said.

"Of course not," he said. He looked at her with diffidence. His mind was on what had happened to her on the Avalon—not so much the beating as the rape. She was too weak to explain that where she came from the two were considered much the same. It was not as large a thing as he thought. Killing Castillo's men would satisfy her.

For economy's sake she held to the important fact. "You almost did hurt me," she said.

"Yes, well," he said. His eyes pleaded with her. Gold filled her vision; her small stock of strength was exhausted. "That was a mistake," he said. Hanna went back to sleep, unafraid.

Lise said, chattering: "You look pretty in that." She meant the gown Hanna wore, a fragile white shift that slipped softly across her skin. "It's mine, that's why it's too small for you. But even Shen said you're pretty. Only she doesn't say much. It's because her tongue was cut out."

"What?" Hanna said.

"Theo told me. Her tongue was cut out and when Mike found her he made her go to the Polity. He made Theo go with her because he couldn't go. And she got a new tongue. But she still didn't say anything for a long time."

"Naturally," Hanna said.

"How long have I been here?" she asked later, when she felt strong.

Michael counted on his fingers, childlike. "Eight days," he said.

She was sitting up, propped up by pillows. She had decided it was time to ask questions. It had become apparent that Michael knew exactly who she was and what had happened to her. Therefore he must know that the Polity would be searching for her desperately; but he had not mentioned it.

"You haven't said anything about getting me home," she said.

"There's a little problem," he said, looking hunted; she had never seen so expressive a face.

"What problem?"

"Your friends in I&S think I'm responsible for what happened."

"I can tell them otherwise. That isn't a problem."

"It won't be enough," he said. "They'll want me all the same—to find out about *him*. If they do—thirty seconds under probe and I'm finished."

"Because of *him*?" she said, and answered herself: "No. Because of the *Pavonis Queen*. But what good does keeping me do?"

"Maybe you could persuade them not to probe me," he said, looking away, not liking to ask. "And maybe"—this came harder still—"if that doesn't work, you could be used. As a hostage. If it comes to that."

"Used," she said, tasting the word. It had a familiar feel. "I don't want to be a hostage. I just want to get back."

But that was a lie. She didn't want to get back to anything yet. The rest and the music were good. They were better than anything waiting for her in the Polity.

"At least I can tell them the truth," she said.

Night: the eighth night? The ninth? She woke often, thinking of what she would say when the time came to speak. Her thinking kept sliding away from the point she wanted it to have. Her memory of the union into which she had drawn Michael was dim, but there was a bond she wished was not there. And he had a swimmer's body, broad-shouldered and sleek; his skin was the color of burnt sugar, his hands beautiful, the curve of his mouth a pleasure to her eye. *Oh, stop it!* she said, ordering herself, denying the bond and an astonishing physical pull. *Remember the point!* The point was that he had not asked much of her. Only to use her influence. She had enough, had some with people who had more. He had only asked her to help him survive.

And if he gave something in return? Told them what he knew about B? But she knew already that he would not tell it all. He would answer only to a point. A point of his choosing; not too far back. Would he go far enough? No.

She turned in bed, sighing. He would not tell them enough. Castillo would escape. Saving Michael Kristofik

somehow meant saving Castillo, too. And that meant her
duty was clear.

In the morning Michael came for her. Shen had brought
clothes and Hanna dressed and tried her legs, but they were
unreliable. She had to lean on Michael's arm, and when
they came to the spiral stair that connected *GeeGee's* two
levels—a pretty, impractical conceit far beyond Hanna's
strength—he carried her. He carried her into Control and
said, "What are you going to say to them?"

"I don't know," she said.

A little later she was telling her story to Gil Figueiredo.
Figueiredo admitted (angrily, defensively) that one of the
team that had studied the *Bird's* engineering was missing.
Michael stood nearby, but far to one side and out of
Figueiredo's line of sight. Control was nearly dark, and
Hanna saw him as a shadow on the edge of vision. His head
was bowed and he looked at his folded arms.

"He told you his name was Castillo?"

"Yes. That's not right, but I don't know what it is. Michael Kristofik," she said, "knows more about him."

"How much does Kristofik know?" Figueiredo said.

"Everything about him, I should think. It goes all the
way back to—"

Michael moved as she started the sentence. She struck at
his left hand and hit it as hard as she could. The effort made
her dizzy; his right hand found its object, and Figueiredo's
face was gone. *GeeGee* floated unconnected to anything.

He was rocked, tottering closer to death or Adjustment.
"Why the hell'd you do that?" he said.

"It's your fight. Not mine."

He did not take her back to his own room. He took her
to another, smaller chamber that blazed with reflected light.
There were many mirrors. There was no feel of habitation.
There was a bed, though; he put her down on it. It pulled at
her like sand.

He said, "It seemed like a good idea to get this room
ready, so we did. The only thing you've got for communication is intercom. The only thing it talks to is this." A wafer
of metal appeared in his hand, disappeared into a pocket.
"*GeeGee* won't respond to you. The lock's voice-controlled
and you'd need a laser to cut a way out. If you want some-

thing we'll get it for you. There's a gymnasium on the upper level and you can use it when you're stronger, but I'll be there, too."

"I did what I had to do," she said.

"I thought you might."

"What I said didn't have anything to do with you anyway."

"It did and you knew it. I asked you to help me keep out of the probe."

"You go back a long way, you and that man."

She felt a flash of pain. It showed on his face, too, so naked that it was indecent. But he said nothing. He left her there alone, to think about what she had refused to do.

The voices drifted windy and murmurous; through air, space, night, invisible; swirled into currents, spilled into windrifts; were patience, dedication, efficiency. The dark between the stars hummed with them. They made up a single thing, a thing in itself, a web or a net vibrating in the night.

One voice was light and toneless, except where the edges were rough. That was Figueiredo's.

A. woman's, soft, with a smile in it: the psyche expert from Admin, the negotiator.

Furred and slipping toward the guttural: Denkovitz, head of I&S.

Even, staccato, edging toward high harmonics: Edward Vickery.

A voice that was a deep bass bell: Starr Jameson.

Others. A woman's voice like the clear note of a violin. A man whose speech was a breathy sigh.

The voices cut in and out in a dance between Earth and points outward, points of light in the dark.

"What will he do now?"

"Bargain."

"With what?"

"Her life."

"He is innocent."

"Only of this."

"And maybe not this."

"Conspiracies . . ."

"Plans gone wrong . . ."

"A struggle for mastery within . . ."

"He planned it and meant no loss of life, perhaps."

"And lost control."

"Even if innocent—"

"They are connected."

"Clear on the evidence."

"So Hanna said."

"But how connected?"

"We'll learn how."

"He has no power."

"Nowhere to flee."

"No escape this time."

"Valentine will comply."

"And her life?"

"We'll trade. After that—"

Michael sat in the lounge, which was lit up brightly, as if to shut out the spread of night and the Jumping stars. It was still littered with hand-held readers, music cubes, clothing and blankets, though it was no longer necessary for Michael to live in it.

He held a reader that showed the first page of a stores inventory. He held it for some time without scrolling onward. Lise perched on the edge of a chair nearby, as if she had drawn an invisible line between *too close I'll annoy him* and *too far he's too far away.* Presently Theo came in, looking about casually but not at Michael or Lise, as if they were not really there, as if no subtle pull had called him there where Michael was. A little while later Shen, abandoning Control, came in, too; she glared at Michael *(What are you doing here?)* and sat down.

They turned to Michael in silence and made a circle, shutting out everything else with their backs.

GeeGee sang with great unhappiness:

Now, oh now, I needs must part;
Love lies not where hope is gone!
Now at last despair doth prove
Love divided lovest none.
Sad despair doth—

"*GeeGee,* shut up," Michael said.

He looked at the others one by one. "There's one thing left," he said. "We've got a hostage; we'll use her. I don't expect it to work. If it doesn't, it's not the end. Remember that, all of you. I want you to remember it. If we have to, we'll head for D'neera. They've no great love for the Polity there and they'll settle for getting Hanna back. I'll get rid of her and leave the rest of you there. No—" The movement caught his eye. "Don't say it, Theo. I'm not taking flak from any of you. That's the way I want it. You can do more for me that way. When you get off D'neera they'll probe you, but they'll let you go. Theo's clear with Co-op. They won't send Shen back to Nestor, they never make anybody go back there, and it won't matter what happened on Carrollis. The less attention Carrollis gets from I&S the better they like it. When you get to Valentine, you can start helping me. Work with Kareem. He'll know what to do."

He heard himself with satisfaction; his voice had less expression than *GeeGee*'s. They looked at him warily. Theo said, "What do you do in the meantime?"

"I go back to space and wait. *GeeGee*'s powered and provisioned for years."

"Years!" Shen repeated, incredulous.

"If necessary."

Lise's face crumpled, but Theo and Shen looked at each other with grudging accord.

It was working. What he said made a kind of sense. They saw the picture he wanted them to see: *GeeGee* glittering here and there in human space, disappearing and reappearing, outwaiting I&S.

But it was not a real hope. No one ever outwaited I&S. Instead he would take *GeeGee* out, out, on a hopeless quest that would end only with the end of his life, or of his sanity. But he would not take anyone with him.

He left them to look at the illusion with hope, and went to call I&S again—without Hanna, this time.

Figueiredo's voice said: "We have contact. Make it quick."

"Make him wait," said the expert's smile.

"Is Hanna with him?"

"I think not."

"Dead perhaps?"

"I think not."

"Why did she. . . ?" The violin.

A sigh. "A warning of some kind."

"Suicidal," Denkovitz growled.

"An old pattern." The deep bass, rarely heard.

"Not quite," said the expert, light and sweet. "That is, yes and no."

The voices hushed to respectful silence. The expert went on.

"She was shattered once. I think not whole since. There are ways to give warning. Ways and ways. This might have been one. So public? So direct? Inviting attack? Consider what happened. Besides the deaths. The trauma. Her instinct is: become rigid. Cling to what's known. Those near breaking make shows of strength. She is not well. Perhaps not quite sane."

"No good, then." Disapproving. Vickery's voice.

"Those who do what she does must somehow be split," said the bass.

"This is different," said the smile. "There's nothing solid, she stands on air and swings at nothing; it's been long since there were foundations, else she would not have risked what she risked. It may mean her time with us is past."

After a long silence the bass said, "And next?"

"I do not know," the expert said.

"How do we find out?"

"Watch," she said.

Hanna was dozing when Michael came to her again. She had not been able to turn off the light because *GeeGee* would not answer or obey her, and it was a vicious glare even to his eyes. He noticed the cold for the first time also, and spoke to his ship. The light dimmed and a current of warm air brushed his face. Hanna did not stir. He sat at her feet, which were bare; he took them in his hands to warm them and she came awake all of a sudden, kicking at him by reflex, savagely.

"Sorry. Sorry!"

She had been on her stomach. Now she was upright. She put a hand to her chest, where her heart pounded too hard.

Michael raised both hands in the ancient peacemaking gesture.

She waited to see what he wanted.

"Don't kick," he said cautiously. He touched her feet again and she jerked and said, "What are you doing?"

"I didn't mean to freeze you to death."

His hands fell easily into a pattern of massage. He knew what he was doing and the blood moved into her icy toes. He talked quietly, eyes on his task.

"We've Jumped. Several times, in fact. I'm talking to someone on Earth. Not the man you had before. They say there might be a compromise, but they want to see you first. So they'll know you're all right. You'll have to come up. I hope you'll keep your mouth shut. If you don't, there's not much I can do about it. But if you think about it, you'll see that the sooner we get it over with, the sooner you can leave . . ."

He went on talking, but Hanna ceased to listen. Something was happening in the soles of her feet. The warmth went straight up her legs and into her belly like current carried on a pair of wires.

She thought: *This man was a Registered Friend. He has forgotten nothing.* She had entirely forgotten it, however. Until now. He did not look up. If he met her eyes while his hands were busy in this way, it would be a challenge. Somewhere in the training (and how was he trained? What else had he learned?), he had been taught when to challenge and when to submit, or appear to submit.

She drew her knees up suddenly, pulling her feet away from him. He looked up. His eyes were innocent; he had only wanted her to be warm. But something else came into them now.

He said, "Just once I'd like to meet a woman who didn't know. I might as well have stayed in the trade."

"It must be a great burden for you," Hanna said politely. "The curiosity. The expectations. You must have to say no all the time. What a pity."

The corners of his mouth twitched. She was right, and he nearly laughed. He stopped it, but his eyes danced; somewhere there was a well of merriment hard to suppress.

"Come talk to I&S," he said.

The spiral stair was not long, but Hanna's knees felt the

552 Terry A. Adams

climb halfway up. In Control she sank into a seat with relief. In front of her she saw, first, a chronometer engaged in some kind of count. It was counting up. Then she saw the face of the I&S negotiator, the dark brown face of a woman with a mild, almost sweet expression. The brown eyes were lustrous and made her look very young. Her hair was styled in yielding curves and there was a frill of lace at her throat.

Michael said, "Hanna, this is Colonel Stiva Waller. As you can see, Colonel, Hanna is alive and well. Shall we get on with it?"

"And how are you being treated?" Waller said, ignoring Michael.

"All right," Hanna answered uncertainly, and looked at the gentle face with wonder; then she understood. How like I&S; how like the Polity! This would not be a straightforward negotiation if they could help it. They would tip the balance in any way they could, they would use a pretty woman whose smile and soft voice might disarm Michael and confuse him; might, even, suggest this affair was a peccadillo that did not threaten him and need not be taken too seriously. Did they hope he would flirt with her? Or be distracted by a subliminal mother-image?

"Would you like to tell me what you've been doing?" Stiva Waller asked sweetly.

"Doing. . . ?"

"Are you well? How have you been treated since we saw you last? Some hours ago?"

"I've been sleeping—" Hanna's voice wavered. She pulled her scattered thoughts together and said, "I was very sick, you know. I've been cared for well."

"It must be nice to know you're in good hands," Stiva Waller said.

Hanna did not say anything. She felt Michael behind her, unmoving. Waller said, "And have Shen Lo-Yang and Theodore Jadinow helped in your care?"

Hanna did not understand the reason for the question. She said, "Theo saved my life."

Michael put his hands on Hanna's shoulders and said, "All right. Tell her, Waller. You're dying to."

Hanna screwed her head around to look up at Michael. He watched Waller's face and for once she could not read his expression. Disgust? Contempt? His fingers moved a little. It felt like a caress, and she was still; but the invisible watchers on Waller's side would see those graceful hands near her throat.

"Shen Lo-Yang," Waller said, "was an executioner in the service of General Greenway on Nestor for many years. She loved her work. So much that when she fell from favor—the punishment, I believe, was mutilation—she turned to robbery with murder to support herself. Theo Jadinow enjoyed a lucrative and illegal medical practice—gypsy practices, they're called—on Co-op's frontiers. He was motivated by the need to procure large sums to pay for his use of—well, of nearly any drug you care to name. He does not seem to have killed anyone, at least not personally, and he was not remanded for Adjustment. His medical training beforehand was minimal. Yet you feel safe?"

"Quite," Hanna said.

"I see. That being the case, Mr. Kristofik, we can talk about terms."

"Mine are easy," Michael said.

"Let's hear them."

"Safe passage to Valentine. A personal guarantee from Ecomanager Mejian that when I go back there I won't be handed over to I&S. Restoration of my property. I want you to quit harassing my friends and I want you to let go anybody you've got in custody because of me. In exchange I'll give you Hanna—and everything I've collected on the man she told you about. The places he's been and the names he's used and his contacts for the last two years."

"That will do for a start," Waller said.

"It'll do for a finish, too."

He did not say anything else. The tips of his fingers shifted and rested softly on either side of Hanna's jaw, on the pulsepoints under her ears. It was a blatant bluff and she was astonished—first, that he thought he could make anyone believe he would harm her, with that transparent face; and secondly, that she had not denounced the fraud at once.

Before she could make up her mind to do it Waller said, "We'll discuss it. I'll contact you later."

"No." He glanced at the chronometer. The call to Earth had given away *GeeGee*'s position, and he would not linger. "We're moving on. I'll contact you."

That was the end. As Waller's image disappeared, Hanna turned and saw Michael's face as she had not seen it before: stone. Perhaps they would believe him after all.

He changed; he looked only tired. He dropped into a seat beside Hanna, forgetting for a moment that she was there. She put out her hand and touched him of her own accord for the first time. The golden eyes turned to her face and she saw that this desperate bargain was not what he wanted to do; he was not doing anything he wanted to do. She took her hand away, surprised at what she had done.

"I have to lock you up again," he said.

"All right, if that's what you want. But—" She hesitated. "It's hard for me to believe all the things I heard about you."

"They're probably true," he said.

He got up and took her back to the mirrored room. It was dim and warm now, and she fell asleep quickly. She was not present two hours later when he settled the details of the trade with Waller.

The voices considered details.

"If it fails—"

"It won't fail."

"If it does—"

"Then what would he do?"

"He has nowhere to go."

"D'neera," said the bass.

"D'neera?"

"D'neera's mad enough," someone sighed.

"Not that mad!"

"If she is," said the bass. "And she is."

They were quiet.

The expert said, "You watched. You know her well."

"I did. He touched her. You saw it."

"Yes."

"That was threat, was it not?"

"It was."

"Was not. She was not afraid. More important: she was not angered."

"How do you know?"

"She would not hide it if she were. When she lived here,"

said the bass, as if it talked of a long-ago time, "she met eager men excited by her beauty, or by the ease with which, it's said, D'neerans contract affairs, or by, perhaps, her belonging to me and the challenge that meant in the games of men. I've seen her touched against her will—more ambiguously than this. The look in her eyes freezes blood. What happened, she says— the beating, the rape, most especially the rape—well. I wouldn't like to be one of those men, if she meets them again. Wouldn't touch her myself, old friends that we are, without care. But *he*—what did you see in her face?"

"Surprise," someone said. "Only that."

"Only that. She did not dislike it."

"I thought so," the expert said.

"Thought what?"

"She's unstable. Old wounds reopened."

"And so?" someone said.

"D'neera," they breathed.

"D'neera might shelter him. At her request."

"Not for long. There's no life for him there."

"When it's done—"

"When it's done, then what?"

"Their cobweb plan is done. Hers, the aliens'. When it's done we'll do it—"

"Correctly," said the bass, weary now. "By rule. A mission staffed with those she's trained. Not her."

"No?"

"No. When we get her back, she can help us—if she will. But I do not think I will trust her. I think," he said, "her loyalties are suspect. Does she know it herself?—perhaps not."

The rendezvous was fixed for six days hence, even though they were near Earth at the start, at the heart of the network of common routes humanity had developed in the course of seven centuries. The intercom in Hanna's room, as Michael had promised, worked—after a fashion; when she used it to ask if anyone was there it did not answer, but soon afterward Theo appeared to make sure she was all right. She did not need to use it again. Theo came at regular intervals, solicitous of her health. But the solicitude was mingled with resentment, as if Hanna alone were responsible for what was happening to Michael and his household.

When Theo was not there, and Hanna had done all the sleeping she could, there was nothing to do except listen to silence. In the silence she "heard" fragments of thought. From Theo: *I can do without the money and all. But how can I do without him ?*

From Lise: *He is so sad. He doesn't want me to see.*

From Shen: *I will kill for him if it helps. Or die for him. But I will not say so to anyone though they take my tongue again.*

But Michael only thought: *Why in hell'd this happen? Bad timing. Pure dumb luck.*

One day she asked Theo, "Why do you love Michael so much?"

He was reading what her blood had to say; he looked up and looked at her as if she were a nonperson with no right to ask such a thing.

Hanna said, "I'm trying to understand. Why won't you tell me? Is it something to be ashamed of?"

In fact he looked ashamed. He muttered, "Only for me."

She waited. It was plain that he ached to tell someone. And she had asked.

At last he said, "You heard what they've been saying on the 'beams? About me?"

"No."

"You didn't hear anything?"

"I can't make anything in here work. I haven't heard anything at all."

"Oh." He was still trying to make up his mind; he fidgeted. He looked at her slantwise and said, "I used to use a lot of dope, you know."

"I didn't know," she said, not quite truthfully, remembering what Stiva Waller had said.

"Well, I did." His skin was very fair, almost transparent. The blood climbed behind it in a violent blush. "I got into some trouble trying to support it. They're saying, they say, Mike's mixed up in the traffic. Or was back then. He never was, though. You'd think as hard as they've tried to find out things about him they'd have gotten the truth about that."

"How did you meet him, then?"

He stared at her for a while. Finally he said, "Like I told you, I got in some trouble. When they let me go, I couldn't—there wasn't anything for me to do. I'd been studying medicine on Co-op but I couldn't—well, I'd been thrown out. And deported to Valentine. They're not that particular on Valentine. And I was, as soon as I got there I started doping hard again. I didn't have much money and it ran out. I was in Port of Shoreground, that's where it's easiest to get the stuff, you understand? And Mike—"

He stopped, looking at her uncertainly. Something about her attention reassured him. He went on: "I was sitting on a curb in the port. In the rain for God's sake. Wondering if I was strong enough to pick up a few hours' day labor. If anybody'd hire me even for that. I'd slept on the street the night before, a lot of nights actually. Some people came by, they were eating something from one of the market stalls, one of them didn't like it and he threw it down in the street, some kind of meat roll. Half eaten. I hadn't had a meal in a couple of days. I couldn't wait till they were out of sight, I jumped on it. There was this dog heading for it, you see. They saw me and they started laughing. I was sitting there eating it and thinking about the ocean. I can't swim. I wouldn't have had to go out very far. Somebody sat down next to me, I looked over and it was Mike, he'd seen the whole thing. He said, 'You want a job?' I went with him. At first I thought he wanted the obvious thing, and I would've gone along with it, I guess, but it wasn't that. Then I couldn't figure out what he did want. He never said. He never has said. It's been six years and he never said why he did it."

He added after a moment, "He took the dog along, too."

"'There was only the hunger,'" Hanna murmured.

"Huh?"

"Something someone said. Nothing . . ." She looked at him thoughtfully. "You never thought of leaving him later?"

"There wasn't any reason. At first it was just because I had it good. Later he picked up Shen on Nestor and—" He blushed again. "I didn't trust her, actually. I thought she'd cut his throat some time if I wasn't around. After that I just sort of never thought about leaving."

"Why did he take Shen on, anyway?"

"Don't ask me. Never made any sense, far as I could see."

"Did you ever ask him?"

"Sure. Never got an answer, though. But we're not the only ones, me and Shen. Mostly they take him for what they can get and move on. Steal him blind sometimes. He's thrown a couple out. It never stops him, though. Once I told him he was crazy and he reminded me what he'd done for me. It's the only time he ever brought it up, he just wanted to shut me up. So I quit asking questions. You're a telepath, maybe you can figure it out. I can't."

Hanna was not done with surprises. Perhaps as a result of her attention to Theo, Shen came to her some hours later. "Want a drink?" said Shen, slouched in Hanna's door.

"Why not?" Hanna said.

"C'mon, then."

That was how Hanna got to Shen's room, which looked like military quarters. Worse; it was entirely bare, as if, when Michael refitted the *Golden Girl*, Shen had said: "Strip a spot for me."

Shen produced brandy and told Hanna, in blunt language, what Michael had saved Lise from. This appeared to be the reason for the invitation, and after that there was not much to talk about. Hanna asked certain questions, but with the greatest caution. She did not want Shen to feel cornered. Shen would be dangerous that way. Hanna knew it; she was impressed.

All the same, with care, she got some information about Shen herself, though most of it was only a terser version of Stiva Waller's accusations. When Hanna spoke of Shen's fall from the Nestorian hierarchy, she thought she had gone too far. She was alarmed at the look in Shen's eyes. Shen was hard as primal rock, she had the balance that comes from knowing how to fight, and she was healthier than Hanna, who still was disgustingly weak.

The shotglass in Shen's hand was full of brandy. She drained it without taking her eyes off Hanna; then she refilled it and handed it over. It seemed Hanna was safe after all. She drank, refraining from making a face. She had an anthropologist's approach to dreadful tastes.

"So they didn't treat you so good," she said after that— and reflected that the brandy, her third, was having an effect; she was beginning to talk like Shen.

"Not good," Shen said.

"Cut out your tongue."

"Yeah." Shen's eyes glittered.

"And then?"

"Can't talk, can't do much."

"Robbery with violence." Hanna added hastily, "That's what the Polity said."

"True. Bastards," Shen said obscurely.

"So how'd you get here?"

There were indefinable ripples in the sullen face. "Picked the wrong one," Shen said. "Picked Mike."

"Wrong how?"

"Bastard looked easy. Big, yeah. But rich. Soft. Careless," Shen said with disapproval.

"And?"

"Wasn't easy. Ended up, he hauled me off over his shoulder. Had a nice place. I stayed. Went back to Valentine with him. That's all."

"All," Hanna repeated rather helplessly. "Why'd he take you away?"

"Dunno."

"You don't know? After all this time?"

"Never asked," Shen said.

She drank more brandy, filled the tiny glass, and gave it to Hanna. Who drank, afraid to refuse.

Michael had locked himself in his room. He saw the others occasionally, fleetingly. He knew that Hanna was free. *Of course she is. They would like her. I could love her.*

He was studying charts. One wall of his room could be turned into a bank of video screens, and he filled it with representations of Outside. There was a lot of it. In seven hundred years the human species had barely stuck a toe in this sea. There was the Polity, there were the other scattered worlds that would support terrestrial life, there was a lot of rock and gas, and then there was—everything else. Which was everything there was.

The charts in which he was interested had two things in common. They showed areas that were largely obscured by interstellar dust, and, because of the dust, they were guesses. He was going to pick one.

About the middle of the last night he dragged himself out of the dust and relieved Shen in Control. There was solitude enough there after Shen left; only Lise had been waiting for him to appear, and now went to sleep curled in a seat nearby.

Between Jumps he made a handfall of calls. All of them went through without interruption, but somewhere, surely, they were monitored. There was no overt evidence of a trap. Stiva Waller's promises were being fulfilled. Michael was a rich man again, and Kareem Mar-Kize was free. Kareem talked with enthusiasm of Michael's coming home. But he said, "Why do they have to link up with you in space? Why not here?"

"Guess," Michael said.

His last call was to Earth. He got a lot of people out of bed while he tracked down Emma Maurello. He found her at a medical center near Admin and the caretakers there got her out of bed, too; it seemed that notoriety gave Michael a certain importance. Emma was a tear-stained wraith. She was not recovering as she ought from the I&S probe. She would not meet his eyes and when he spoke to her with tenderness, she wept. She said something he could not disentangle from the sobs. "What was that?" he said. "What is it, dear Emma?"

"I hate you. I hate you," she said.

After that he sat for a long time with his face in his hands. *Dear Emma, good-bye.* The sound of Lise's breathing disturbed him. He had wanted to be to her, at the least, what the monks of St. Kristofik had been to him; he had meant to watch her grow up. *Good-bye, little puss.*

A few hours later, after all the waiting, it was time.

Hanna sat in the lounge where Theo had put her and looked out at the stars. If she were to go closer to the transparency and look toward her left, toward *GeeGee*'s nose, she might see the ship of the Polity that had come to rescue her. She sat on the edge of a divan with her fingers gripping it as if she might fall off. She had no possessions to take with her; she owned none. There was only the silver chain at her throat. She knew nothing of the procedure for transferring her to the Polity vessel. Now she wondered about it, and when Theo put his head into the lounge, to make sure she was still there, she asked him.

He said, staying where he was, "Somebody's boarding with a suit for you. We don't have any to spare."

"They can't dock a shuttle—?"

"No, of course not. We're not big enough to take one in. Why? Can't you use a maneuvers pack?"

"Yes, of course. I just thought—wouldn't it be easier to dock *GeeGee* in the other craft? Or is it too small, too?"

"It's big," Theo said. "But that would be stupid. Once they had us in there we might not get out. No, this way we keep some distance between us and them, see?"

"I see. Will I see Michael before I go?"

"You wouldn't if it was up to me," Theo said honestly.

"No?" She looked at him as closely as she could from where she sat; he still had only one foot inside the lounge, as if he were impatient to get away from her.

"It's really not my fault," she said.

"No, I guess not, but the result's the same."

"He has some kind of plan, hasn't he? If it goes wrong?"

"If he did, would I tell you?" Theo gave her an incredulous look and withdrew.

She waited, thinking of nothing except anxiety. It ought to be only for her own safe return to civilization, but it was not. Presently Shen came and led her to Control, and there was Michael. He was not quite calm, but Hanna saw that what he felt at this moment was not unpleasurable. There was excitement in him, a bright edge of daring. He was going to see what he could get away with.

She began to understand more about the *Pavonis Queen* affair.

The Polity ship lay not far from *GeeGee*'s nose, outlined in light. No one in Control was doing anything, but one display module showed the two ships and, between them, a pinpoint of light that moved. Hanna shivered. It did not take much effort to find out why. The last time she had watched a blip of light approach, Awnlee had been huddled at her side.

She moved at the thought, and Michael glanced at her for the first time. She said awkwardly, "I guess it's time to say good-bye."

He said, "Think so? We'll see. He's supposed to be unarmed—" Michael pointed at the dot of light—"but we've got no way to tell. *GeeGee* doesn't have detection sensors for things like that. They said we had to be all together up here. I don't like that."

"Couldn't you refuse?"

"Sure. Then they would have had to think of something else. I hope this is as obvious as it looks."

GeeGee said suddenly, "He's approaching the lock. He says the agreement was, you all have to be visible to the craft standing by. Except the one who comes to get him."

"All right. Link us up. Go, Theo. Fetch."

Theo left them. *GeeGee* said they could be seen by the Polity vessel's crew, but the transmission was one way; there were no voices or faces from the other ship. They waited in silence, Hanna and Michael and Shen.

Hanna opened her mouth to say: Where is Lise?

Then she shut it without speaking.

Theo came into Control with a spacesuited man behind him. A patch on the shoulder of the suit showed a name: Mencken. Mencken had removed his helmet and it hung loosely from his hands. He looked at the others clustered at the farthest point of Control and said, "How are you, Lady Hanna?"

"I'm fine, thank you."

"Everybody's here? Good," he said, and dropped the helmet. There was a stungun in his hand. He said, "Come over here with me, Lady Hanna."

But she stood beside Michael and said, "I hoped you were acting in good faith."

"Necessity, ma'am. Please come over here."

And still she would not have moved, if Michael had not given her a push. She went then to stand beside Mencken. She looked at Michael anxiously. If he was going to do anything, he had better not wait much longer.

"That's right," Mencken said. He lifted one wrist to his mouth and said, "All right, Commander. You can send the others over now."

Hanna thought she had made a grave mistake. She thought she had overestimated Michael's intelligence. Nonetheless she turned in a single swift movement, kicking. The point of her toe caught Mencken's hand and the stungun went flying.

At the same moment he grunted and went down like a rock. Lise stood behind him, another stunner held in both her hands, her eyes wide with responsibility.

*   *   *

They moved fast after that.

"If you shoot," Michael pointed out to the faceless commander from the Polity, "your own man goes up in atoms. Not to mention Hanna. And you want me alive, too, right? So don't shoot. And you'd better put some distance behind us because we're going to Jump. Now."

"What about Mr. Mencken?" said a cold voice.

"I'll think about it. That's nice EVA stuff he's got. Did he even bring gear for Hanna? I guess he did, that's where he hid the gun, wasn't it? Maybe we'll dump him at a relay someplace."

The voice said, "Where'd the kid come from?"

"She's been here all along. What did you think I did? Carved her up and ate her? Get moving. For your own good."

"Lady Hanna?"

Hanna did not answer. *GeeGee* broke the audio link; the two ships moved apart. They were alone again, except for the unconscious Mencken sprawled in the door.

"They're clear enough," Shen said. "Now, *Gee*." She touched a switch and the field of stars changed and the Polity ship was not there any more.

Michael stood looking at Hanna as if he had never seen her before. She said, "I don't know why I did that."

"Fair play," he suggested. He said it as if the idea were funny. "All you had to do was nothing."

"You didn't tell me that. You didn't trust me."

"True," he said. "But there was something else, too. If you were caught the way he was, they couldn't say you had anything to do with it."

"Now's a little late to be telling me that," she said.

Hiero-volan Mencken of I&S was shut into a small cabin over engineering. There were three such rooms there, former servants' quarters, bare and isolated. He made a lot of noise at first. Presently he was quiet, but no one on *GeeGee* forgot he was there. His anger was spread from end to end of the *Golden Girl*, a subliminal thunder that underlay all their hours. When it was time to take him food, Michael and Shen went to him together, armed and implacable.

Hanna, unable to account for herself, turned to other

things. She wanted no part of keeping Mencken locked up
and she wanted no part of whatever plans the others might
make. To keep from thinking, she found her way to the gymnasium on *GeeGee*'s upper level. It was dark there, not because it was supposed to be, but because Hanna turned off
most of the lights as if to hide from herself her own lingering
weakness. There she stretched, pulled, bent, reached, until
her muscles ached and trembled and she was covered with
sweat. The small chamber was deep inside the *Golden Girl,*
entirely enclosed, and the only stars Hanna saw were those
exertion floated in her field of vision. The only other things
to see were padded walls hung with mechanical devices that
looked like weapons, or like instruments of torture. She had
always been bursting with health, taut and fit as a sleek
young animal, except when the People of Zeig-Daru had
taken her apart. She had not liked weakness then and she
did not like it now, and struggled with it bitterly. The work
kept her from listening to immaterial echoes of Mencken's
fury, but it could not stop her from thinking altogether. This
still was not her fight, or her flight. She was not needed; Michael and Lise would have managed quite well without her.

She caught herself thinking, was enraged, and punished
her unfaithful body. She could not let it continue to be
weak.

She did not give up until she hurt everywhere, every
muscle throbbed; there was also a pain low in her abdomen
that made her straighten, panting, at a new thought. The
medic at Halber in Province Koroth, where she had gone
briefly on assignment for her House. When had the trip
been? Exactly when?

*(". . . and so after regeneration, nothing was done about
fertility control. It was not necessary. I had only one lover
afterward, and he was sterile by choice. Not that I did not
want—but he did not—"*

"I understand. And now you wish—?"

"Yes. Please."

"You're celibate, I hear. Then why—?"

"Why not?"

*"I don't recommend implants unless there is need. I have,
oh, a prejudice against tampering unneeded."*

"But the bother. And the aches. Every thirty-five days!"

"You don't need an implant to control that; only as a guard against conception."

"But I want it! I'll go elsewhere."

"No, I'll do it. For how long? Three years or five?"

"Twenty?"

"At your age? That I won't do."

"All right, then. Five years.")

Five years Standard, or D'neeran? If D'neeran, she was safe, she could not have gotten a child by rape. If Standard—well, if Standard, she should be safe, too, though the margin was terribly narrow.

Safe or not, she stood with her back to the door and rubbed her belly cautiously. She had stripped to briefs and tied a scarf tightly around her breasts, but otherwise she was naked, and the skin she touched was hot and slick with sweat. When she looked down, the scar of Theo's surgery stood out like a red beacon.

The lights came up, startling her. "Are you all right?" Michael said.

She turned quickly, thinking that she was safe nowhere. The people of the *Golden Girl* appeared and disappeared at random like particles subject to continuous creation and demolition, as if they had some basic right to materialize in her life.

"I'm fine. Why?"

"Oh, nothing. I just—"

His eyes were peculiar. *I just saw you touch yourself like a woman suspecting new life,* said his thought.

"You ought to have a pool," Hanna said at random.

"Huh." He was distracted; his eyes danced. "I went to Earth on a Dru once, years ago when I was a Friend. It had a pool. Halfway between Valentine and Earth something went wrong with the grav stabilizers. One minute we were three times our weight and the next it was free fall. There was water everywhere pretty soon—except in the pool. Ever thought you'd drown in your own bed?"

She saw his memory of the sodden luxury craft and the bedraggled passengers, nearly laughed, then bit it off. She stood stiffly, a sullen droop to her shoulders. So he could surprise her into laughter; it was good to know. She could guard against it.

He watched the smile fade from her eyes. "I want you to tell me about D'neera," he said.

"Why?" she said.

"I want to dump you. Also him from I&S. Also my friends. I go alone the rest of the way."

"What way is that?"

"I've got friends on Valentine; maybe they can get something done if I hide long enough."

He might as well have put out a sign that said "evasion," though he had lied to Stiva Waller with flair and precision. But the first part had been true. He meant to go alone from here.

"Why D'neera?" Hanna said, but guessed the answer. "A more humane place for your friends to be caught?"

"I hope so. Will it be?"

"It should be. Especially if I'm there."

"Then tell me this," he said. "Suppose we turn up at the closest possible Jump terminus to D'neera. Shen estimates — if I push *GeeGee* to the limit and slow down for nothing — *GeeGee* can land, offload passengers, and get back to Jump-legal space in thirty minutes. What I want to know is what's going to stop me."

"D'neerans aren't." The sweat had dried; she was getting cold in the blazing light. "What do D'neerans care about you? There's nothing to stop you."

"You're wrong," he said. "You gave your sympathies away, back there. I always meant to go on to D'neera if they tried something like they tried, but it wouldn't have been an obvious move before. After what they saw you do, it is. There'll be a welcoming committee from the Polity waiting for me."

She said after a long pause, "I've got no way of knowing the exact situation. I could call D'neera. Find out."

"Then they'd know for sure we're coming. The only chance is speed. And no warning."

"Yes. Of course."

"Can you even make a guess at what they'll do?"

"Speed," she said half to herself. "Maneuverability; that's what you've got. No guns. They must know it. Wait." She thought about D'neera's defenses. They were taken seriously since Nestor's short, vicious attempt at conquest several years before. "You'll have to identify yourself. You can put it off for a little while. Not long, or they'll shoot; D'neerans will, I mean. Then if the Polity's there, their people will know who you are, too. They'll let you go down, but they'll have you targeted by the time you hit the ground. Have you thought about where you'll land?"

"Koroth, that's all. Your own House is least likely to risk you, right? You tell me where to touch down. *GeeGee* can do the rest."

"There's prairie west of—no, don't try the prairie. City Koroth's got an outport. Land there; there won't be any shooting. Too many people around. They'll get you going back out. If I were a Polity commander, I'd have a lot of small, fast gunboats there. With atmospheric capability, as many as I could get the magistrates to agree to. They'll be faster than *GeeGee*. And I would—I don't know. Try talking you down, I guess. If it didn't work—it won't work, will it?" She saw the answer in his face and said, "Then I'd start shooting. Sharpshooting. Not to destroy *GeeGee;* just to disable her so you'll have to land. But if that doesn't work either—well, then they might shoot to kill."

After a minute he said, "I'll try it. Just make sure your own folk know who I am. I don't want them thinking I'm a Nestorian kamikaze who's forgotten the war only lasted a day."

He turned away. After a moment Hanna went after him. She was very cold now. He glanced around and waited for her; she came up beside him and looked up with troubled eyes. It was too easy to see him riding *GeeGee* down the sky in a burst of flame, plunging toward Hanna's native soil.

"Mike. . . ?" The friendly diminutive came by itself. She had not wanted to use his name.

"Yes?" he said.

"Do you have to do it that way? Are you sure you can't go back to Valentine?"

"Oh, yes. We hooked into a relay a little while ago. I tried a transmission to Valentine. It didn't get through; I got a Fleet officer instead. That's all I get to talk to from now on, Fleet and I&S." There were shadows under his eyes, but he was tranquil. "A Jump later I scanned the 'beams. Valentine's officially turned over ownership of *GeeGee* to I&S as reparations for the *Pavonis Queen*. I&S got an order waiving trial; did you know they can do that? *GeeGee*'s stolen property now. Valentine's cut me loose, Hanna. And believe me, when Valentine's bankers don't back you, you're done."

She said, "Let me try talking to Starr."

"Who?" He was blank; she nearly laughed again, but it would have been bitter. "Oh," he said. "Would it help now?"

"I could try. Even," she said, looking away, "if it's a little late."

And she was still a person of some importance, because the censors permitted her to do it. There was a delay that seemed endless, and she shivered in Control. Michael disappeared briefly and came back with a blanket which he draped over her shoulders. "I wonder just how close the nearest Fleet ship is," he said, watching the chronometer. *GeeGee*'s mass detectors were at full power, and she was ready to Jump the instant they registered anything larger than a hydrogen atom. "Traps," Michael said succinctly. Hanna waited, listening to unknown voices murmur through the great distances. She thought of the *Pavonis Queen,* and of the outrageously simple approach to the trap Michael had just escaped.

"Have you always seen traps everywhere you looked?" she said.

"I always looked for them," he said, "but I only saw them when they were there." He paused, and when he spoke again his voice was grim. "There were one or two I didn't see."

She would have asked what he meant, but the light-raddled screen in front of her cleared, and there was Jameson. Her heart rose up all in one piece. There was stability, there was everything she had craved; it was in the irony in the gray-green eyes, in the imperturbable mouth.

"Well?" she said.

He looked past her, looking for Michael, but Michael had faded into the shadows. "Yes?" Jameson said.

"What about that bargain?"

"It didn't work very well, did it?" he said. Hanna studied him carefully. This was not a private conversation; many ears would hear what they said.

"Why don't you just take him on his terms?" she said. "There's information you could use. Take the bargain or you get nothing."

"Stop saying 'you,' " he told her. "Don't use that word. I have very little to do with this."

"Why are you talking to me, then?"

"You asked," he said; she saw amusement.

"Well, say what they told you to say," she said. It went home, but he recovered.

"Enough is enough," he said. "You're valuable. So is Mr. Mencken; possibly more so. A mistake was made. Mr. Figueiredo is willing to start over again. Give him the information that was promised, and Mr. Kristofik can go free. He has only to return Mr. Mencken. As for you: your position seems ambiguous. You can do as you please."

She was watching him intently. The amusement had not gone away.

"We'll think about it," she said, and broke the connection. She did not hear Michael come up behind her, but as she stared at the blank screen, he spoke almost in her ear. She did not take in what he said.

"Starr was lying," she said. "He was saying what he was told to say, and it was a lie. And he knew I would know it."

"You don't mean they'd try the same trick again!"

"Probably not the same. Not exactly the same. Maybe this time they would do just what they undertook to do, and then when you got home to Valentine and walked into your house, they would be waiting for you. They'd do something like that, this time."

"You said he knew you would see through the lie," Michael said. "Why would he be so careless?"

"He's not careless about anything." She stood up, letting the blanket fall from her shoulders, feeling the bite of cold air. "He wants to see what I will do," she said. "He's curious. He wants to see what will happen now."

She went out then, back to her room, where she could try in solitude to set her thoughts in order. They resisted. All she could think was that the rules for domestic order that she had accepted as necessity on civilized worlds had turned into a cold machine. They were meant to protect people like her. They were meant to protect her from people like Michael. Maybe that was right. She supposed it was.

The journey to D'neera night have been made in three days. Michael extended it to ten for misdirection's sake, to weary the watchers' eyes on D'neera and make them wait and wait. *GeeGee* had not gone in a straight line to anywhere since leaving Revenge. She went in no straight line now; she zigzagged across human space in a butterfly dance. All the space outside looked the same: black with sparks and the swathe of the Milky Way.

Late on the first night Hanna came to Michael's room, and to his bed. Throughout the rest of the flight she kept coming back. Sometimes he looked at her eyes and thought they saw too much—inevitably she saw the charts that haunted him—but she did not ask questions. They did not say much to each other at all. But when she was with him she made these last days a time of pleasure and peace, and to give her something in return he played songs for her, the antique music he loved: dances, madrigals, melodies of courtly love, a solstice song two millennia old. She did not make him feel that he had to talk with her, nor did he feel that he had to pretend anything.

With Shen and Theo he pretended, exerting all his strength to appear natural—cheerful, confident, filled with light. But then he would let it slip when he was alone with Lise, and with Lise, he talked. He had promised to teach her to cook, and he used the promise as an excuse to keep her with him in the galley for hours at a time. He meant to teach her more than cooking, and ten days was not long enough. *Love life,* he said, *it is precious no matter what happens.* And, *Don't gamble with money,* he said, *it's not important enough. Gamble with your life, your happiness, your health. They're the only stakes worth gambling for. Remember that,* he said, *repeat it back to me.* And, *Promise you'll remember. Promise. Promise,* until she promised, her eyes so troubled that he was forced to check himself, smile, pretend his intensity had been a mistake.

On the last night Hanna woke briefly to see Michael like a shadow at the wall, studying the dim glow of his charts. She slept again and dreamed that Starr Jameson came to see her. At first they were on the *Golden Girl,* but then they were in mountains, in the heart of a D'neeran range Hanna knew well. They were near the top of a peak, but Hanna could not see anything because the morning was filled with mist. Water dripped from shrubs to the ground, and the fog was so low it barely cleared Jameson's head. He wore an expression she had never seen on his face before; he looked both hurt and outraged.

I can't help it, she said, *you knew there must be someone else one day.*

I knew, and it comforted me. But why this man?

Can't you see how beautiful he is?

Since when has a beautiful face meant anything?

There's more to it than that. He gives, he gives with every breath.

Why should that matter to you? You are cold, as cold as you need to be. I was able to give you that. Now you can think—at least, until now, I thought you could.

But I don't want to think.

Then what in heaven's name do you want?

She told him explicitly what she wanted to do, and that she wanted to keep doing it with Michael. Jameson was not jealous. But he said: *You wouldn't be able to keep him. He came from nowhere and that's where he'll go. He has no center—love, you'll say, but love is wayward; you need law and custom as well. You could have kept me, were it not for your pride. But you won't be able to keep him.*

You go to hell, she said.

In the morning Hanna saw Theo, and he talked with some tension of what would happen on D'neera. Hanna thought again of *GeeGee* racing through the sky, carrying only Michael, going out and out. The charts of nothing rose up before her. They came together with Michael's silence and with something she had guessed without explicit awareness. She knew.

Theo spluttered at her; her face must be bleached.

She brushed him away and went in search of Michael. He was in the galley with Lise, who sat on a high stool and dropped pellets of produce into a very large pot set on a very small cooking flat. Lise giggled as the pellets expanded, resuming vegetable shapes. Michael stood beside her, talking of spices.

Hanna thought she was going to be sick. She rocked on a wave of panic, the first she had felt in years.

I have to talk to you, she said, not in words but on a gust of fear. There was a clatter on the polished floor. The ladle he had dropped dribbled streamlets of aromatic broth.

He got the ladle back and gave it to Lise. "Just keep stirring," he said.

Hanna led him to his own room in silence. She felt fragile, breakable; her hand sliding the door shut was not steady.

"I know what you're going to do," she said.

He had no answer. He was silent, watching her.

"You've lied to all of us. You're going Outside, aren't you?"

"It'll be all right," he said.

"Oh, you're mad!" she said, and he moved toward her and touched her, stroked her face and hands, was concentrated on her comfort; she saw abruptly, with the force of revelation, what he was. Time came and went, the Master's hand was light or heavy, and always it was all right. He believed it; that was how he convinced others it was true. And if it were not all right he would make it so, if he could, asking nothing in return. She looked at him with a kind of terror. She had never known anyone like him before. She did not think she would know anyone like him again.

"Why?" she said. "Why?"

"Hanna, there's nothing left for me here. There is absolutely nothing for me here."

"There's nothing out there either!"

He said gently, "There's something I'll try to find. I've been looking for it for a long time."

"What?"

He shook his head, smiling.

"Listen, oh, listen," she said. "I might still be able to keep them from changing you, from Adjusting you. And I might, I could still, D'neera would be sanctuary, I only have to ask. Koroth would take you in, you could stay there, you could be at the House or at my home—" She hardly knew what she said. She was thinking: *You can't go, I don't know you!*

"Think what it would be like," he said. "Could you guarantee Polity treachery wouldn't extend even to D'neera? You could get Koroth to shelter me, but I'd never be safe. I've looked over my shoulder for twenty years. I won't do it again. And think what it would be like for you. D'neera would be the only place where I'd have even a margin of safety, small as it was, and I'd never be able to leave. Can you see me there, an outsider in a telepaths' society, dependent on you? Going slowly crazy, I'd think, and following you around. No, I'll do it this way. Maybe someday I'll come back."

"You won't."

He could not console her. He smoothed the hair at her temples, and she felt a great tenderness in him.

"Hanna, nothing lasts," he said. "Nothing lasts."

She shook her head, but it was hardly a denial at all, so great was his conviction. It had always been true for him. And he might have been a madman—she thought then that he was—but he was not bitter or cynical or in search of pity. Instead she felt only his compassion—for Hanna, looking toward loss she could not even gauge accurately yet; and for all the others who had hoped for shelter, and when they had found it, saw it blow away.

There was no formal countdown. There was only, as the time neared, a slow move toward Control; Hanna joined it. *GeeGee* Jumped just as she entered Control. The stars outside were achingly familiar. Dead ahead, brilliant but not yet a naked-eye disc, was Hanna's own sun.

"One more Jump," Theo said. He fell silent as a strange voice sounded in Control, calling for identification. No one answered. Soon the air rippled with D'neeran voices, first startled at this unscheduled arrival, then impatient at the absence of response, and at last exceedingly cold.

Michael talked over the murmur, running through the plan one last time.

"At ten minutes before landfall, Theo and Lise go down to the main passenger hatch. Theo, you use manual override to open the inner seal so there'll be no delay on the ground. At five minutes, you two—" he looked at Shen and Hanna, "—get Mencken and take him down. Don't take any chances with him. Pick up stunners on your way and drag him out feet first if you have to. I'll pop the outer hatch from up here when we're down. Don't waste a second. Get out and run like hell. I'll be monitoring you and I can't take off till you're clear, understand?"

Hanna was bitter with resentment. That last was unnecessary; he did not need to play on their anxiety for his clean escape to make them move fast. But perhaps he had said it because of Lise, who was already in tears at a parting she thought temporary. Theo stayed close to Lise; Hanna thought he was assigned to keep her under control.

Shen said, "You're at optimum for atmospheric moves. The landside program's laid in."

"Jump her, then."

And there, without a whisper or sensation of movement, was the world of Hanna's birth. The light of its sun, a near-twin to Sol, shone into Control. D'neera was between the ship and the star so that they saw the planet's nightside, the great black circle rimmed with light. Hanna was coming home. To blue and lavender, dew-washed meadows, the horses on the fields of morning, the duties of her House —

(—*and the voices,* said a whisper, *that send you here and there; submitting to the Polity, treading amongst its rules; what else is there? See what happens to those who step outside, oh yes Outside indeed—*)

GeeGee started her preprogrammed descent, an arc of wild speed that would take her round the planet fully three times before she braked for landfall on the day-side. "Start talking," Michael said to Hanna urgently, she remembered what she had to do and heard the shocked voices now, the men and women wondering if they would have to shoot. She identified herself, stumbling over the words, unreasonably giving the birth-name unused since childhood instead of her name in Koroth's House, by which she was better known: "It's H'ana Bassanio, don't fire, I'm just coming—"

Home. She could not say the word.

GeeGee skidded through the terminator and leapt into full light. Below there was dazzling white cloud. Hanna heard herself talking, making sense maybe to someone but not to herself. Because there were other voices at her back and she heard them as if they were the only sounds in the silence of deep space.

Lise said, "But can you fly *Gee* by yourself?"

"You could fly *Gee* by yourself."

"If they shoot at you, they'll only make you land? Sure?"

"I'm sure. Go on, little puss. It's time to go."

"But what if they hit something else?"

"They won't. They're good."

"But if they do, you'll *crash.*"

Hanna's head jerked right around. She said brutally, "He doesn't care if he does."

GeeGee flashed into the dark again. Control was full of shadows. Michael walked purposefully toward Hanna. She saw the gold-flecked eyes with clarity in the half-dark, as if they had a light of their own. It took him perhaps two seconds to reach her, but for Hanna time slowed and stopped and the world she had always known turned over. She heard his intent to shut her up, and his rapid calculation of the changes in plan that must be made to offload an unconscious Hanna.

In the last split second, in a single devastating pulse of thought, she told the others exactly what Michael meant to do.

He heard it, too; he knew what she had done and what it meant. They would revolt as soon as they grasped it. They would not let him set them free.

And here it was: the rage she had forgotten burst out like an oily cloud with screams in it. His face changed. *Not Mike. I don't know who this is but not Mike.* A creature hardly human leapt for Hanna's throat. She dived and rolled. Her mind ticked over in an endless second, analyzing. If he knew anything about fighting, the fury had wiped it out. He was fast, though, and she barely got out of the way of the next lunge. Time still was slowed and everything in it was preternaturally clear. Lise wailed, paralyzed with a terror that was half longing to help Michael and half animal recognition that this was no longer Michael but a thing that ought not be helped, a thing he would not wish her to help. Theo was white as a corpse. Shen was busy with *GeeGee,* looking over her shoulder as often as she dared.

She was going to have to hurt him to stop him; if she could; before he caught her and killed her with his hands.

She picked a direction. Two more lunges; two more calculated, dangerous dodges that brought her up with her back to the swiveling seats before an auxiliary control console. When he came at her again, she caught the outstretched arm, bent, shifted—and heaved him over her shoulder headfirst. She spun and pounced like a cat. He was wedged between two seats, struggling to get up, all coordination gone in the passion to destroy. She kicked him on the jaw without compunction and it had no effect at all; so she sprang to the top of the console and crouched and waited. When he came up at last, back half-turned to her, she hit him at the base of the skull

with the edge of her hand. She had to do it twice more before
he went down. Then he was still.

GeeGee skimmed back into the light. Shen swore, hissing.

"Gotta pull out," she said. "Theo. Come help."

Hanna slipped from the console to the floor. She pulled
at Michael to turn him over, and Lise helped her; when he
was on his back, she got his head into her lap and held him.
His mouth bled where her foot had smashed it. The pulse in
his throat faltered under her fingers and her own heart
nearly stopped; then the beat steadied to a slow but strong
rhythm. She nearly wept with relief. Control was full of
voices, it seemed that all of D'neera and the Polity were
shouting at her. It was dark again, and then light as *GeeGee,*
no longer on her programmed course, broke out over one
planetary pole; whether north or south the disoriented
Hanna could not tell. "H'ana!" said a woman's voice, she
knew the sound of it, the Lady of Koroth called her. Shen's
lips were drawn back from her teeth; that was, Hanna saw
with astonishment, a smile of sorts. Shen fed *GeeGee* a
Jump order; they were nearly away. All the Polity's gunboats had been plunging for projected landing sites, and the
change in course had taken them by surprise.

Michael's eyes opened, their color strangely faded; all
Hanna saw was the gold. Almost at once he looked up at
her with knowledge. She smoothed his hair and it felt like
silk to her hand.

He pulled himself to his feet just as *GeeGee* Jumped.
Hanna gave him her shoulder to lean on. He did not reject
it; he needed support and so he accepted it, eternally the
realist. He whispered, "Stay here," and she let him go. The
tall figure staggered and she thought of the spiral stairs.
Theo started after him and she said: *No. He'll be all right.*
She added aloud before Theo could respond, "How is he
after that happens to him?"

"After what happens?" Theo was puzzled. "Getting beat
up by a girl half his size?"

Shen muttered, "Told him he'd got soft."

"The fit, I mean. The craziness. When he turns into somebody else."

Theo looked as if he wanted to deny that anything had
happened. He said, "I never saw it before."

"I saw the start of it once and I haven't been around very long. You must know what I mean."

"All right. All right. I guess I've seen the start of it, too. But I never saw him lose control before. I mean, he could always stop it. He told me, once he told me there were times before when he didn't. But I never saw the whole thing before."

Shen looked at a scanner and said, "We're clear. Nobody around." She made an evil noise that Hanna recognized, after a moment, as a chuckle.

"I have to look at his head," Theo said.

"Not yet. Unless you want to handle him if he starts up again."

"No," Theo said with alarm. "No, I don't."

Shen said abruptly, "Good thing you did that, told us what you did. Outside, huh? If he wasn't shot down first?"

"That's right." Reaction was setting in. He could have crushed her skull between his hands; the thought made her weak. The silver chain bound for Uskos was chokingly tight.

"Can't get rid of us that easy," Shen said. "You're all right."

Hanna did not say anything to that. Shen would not expect it.

She made herself wait a little longer. When five minutes had gone by, she passed through *GeeGee* to Michael's room, stopping on the way to take a stunner from the cabinet where *GeeGee*'s small store of arms was kept. But she knew at once, when she went through his door, that she would not need it. The room was dark except for the glow of starlight; he lay on the bed looking up into the dark. She came to him and touched him, and found that his hair and face and shoulders were wet. He had put his head under cold water.

She stretched out at his side, but he did not speak. Hanna ached as if it were she who had been hit.

"Michael," she said, but there was no answer. She turned and leaned over him in the dark. She put her hands on him and his body was foreign to her as an alien substance. In his rage he had fallen into a dream; he was in it still, and in Hanna, seeing it, recognition woke. Snow and flame and a blood-red sky. A child crying with pain.

She whispered his name at intervals, until finally he moved, remembering her. She could not say anything about

what she had done. Intead she said as steadily as she could,
and practically: "When did you start having those attacks?"

To her surprise he answered, perhaps because he was so
beaten that it did not matter. But he talked as if speaking
hurt.

"The first time was—the night I got away—onto Alta."

There was a jolt of fear and flight. Castillo.

"Got away from *him?*"

"Yes." The quiet voice was hoarse, as if he had been
screaming. Perhaps he had, down here where no one could
hear.

"How long were you with him?"

"I don't know. Months, I think . . . There were never any
clocks. I guessed about day and night. I got bigger. . . I knew
we'd landed somewhere. He went out and came back drunk.
He forgot to lock the door. It was the first time he ever
forgot and I tried to run out and he caught me. It was always
bad, but it was worse that night . . ."

His voice trailed away. She saw a picture of explicit sexual brutality, an agonized child caught in terror and helpless
rage. She said, her own voice not quite steady, "He gave me
to the others, but he never touched me himself, not once. I
never thought about it. If I had, I'd have thought he only
liked men."

Michael said, "Only when he can't get little boys."

"You must have been an exquisite child."

"That's why he took—" The ragged voice stopped.

"Took you away from where, Mike?"

The silence lengthened in despair. She was whispering
again, and shaking. "You don't know, do you?"

He turned his head away; he was trembling, too. She said
with urgency, as if the quick question let her leap an abyss
without looking down, "How did you get away?"

"He passed out . . ."So faint she heard more thought
than words. "There was something—heavy—I can't remember what it was. I got it—somehow I got it up. I couldn't
hold things, I, my hands—"

She thought he was going to choke. She stroked his
cheek, willing him to breathe. "Your hands were injured.
Did he do that?"

"He saw it done. When he—took me on board—he tried
to fix them. So I could use them for him. On him. He was,

he was satisfied with how they came out. He liked, liked ruining things, I think. And so I dropped it on his head—" He was entirely unaware of a disjuncture. "I didn't remember until later. That was the first time."

"And then you ran out?"

"Yes."

"Got off the ship?"

"Somehow. I don't remember. Hanna, don't you see what you've done?"

Another whisper. "I know what I did . . ."

"I can't take the rest of you Outside." He was trying patiently to explain. "Lise and Theo and Shen, they've got a right to a real life. We can't just fly around forever with no place to land. But they won't let me give myself up. That's why I had to leave them behind . . ." His voice trailed away. *GeeGee* closed in on them, claustrophobic.

Hanna's fingers went to the chain at her throat. The links pressed into her skin. "There's Uskos," she said.

He shook his head, uncomprehending. She said, "I'm a citizen of the nation of Ell. There's a story I promised Rubee I would tell. Would the Polity risk an incident to get us back? I don't know. I don't think so."

She waited while he absorbed it. She knew when he had grasped it, because she felt a little of the laughter revive in him. It was a giant joke on the Polity, and he turned toward her in the dark, almost smiling.

"I'd rather run toward something than away," he said. "But I seem to remember the course was secret."

"They gave it to me, though." She lifted a hand to her throat and spoke a word in Ellsian. The silver chain parted and slid into her hand, shining in the faint starlight. She held it out to him.

"It's in here," she said.

He did not take it at once. He said, "You know what you're doing?"

"Yes. Take it."

"I know what you had back there. You can say goodbye to all of it if you do this."

She was barefoot and wore another woman's clothes. The last thing she possessed was in her hand.

"I know," she said. "Take it."

After a minute he did. He did not speak again. She lay

close beside him and presently he fell into a quiet sleep, still holding the chain. Hanna did not sleep; she looked out at the stars and seemed to hear the blowing of a clear strong wind.

Hiero-volan Mencken was told nothing. He had been told nothing from the moment he woke, tingling and dizzy, in the dark little room he identified as part of the *Golden Girl*'s staff quarters. His shouts did no good, except perhaps to relieve his own feelings, his head hurt and he stopped shouting quickly. There was nothing in the room or on his person that would help him get away. If he ever got his hands on Hanna ril-Koroth—

He did not know what had happened. He thought it was Hanna who had stunned him somehow. But perhaps she had been doped, drained, brainwashed and filled up again, her personality altered; no other explanation was conceivable.

He waited for ten days, subject sometimes to concerts his captors may have considered entertainment, or torture.

> *J'ai trove qui me vent amer;*
> *s'amerai, quant la brunete au vis cler m'a dit,*
> *que s'amour avrai,*
> *bien me doi de li loer . . .*

"What the hell does that mean?" he said when it broke in on his lunch, and got nearly the only piece of information he was given on the *Golden Girl,* for what good it did him. While he drank the excellent soup—the food was good, he had to admit—Michael Kristofik smiled and translated: "I've found one who wants to love me; if I should love, as the dark lady with the bright face told me I'd have her love, I'm to be praised for her."

It made no more sense in Standard than it had in whatever the original language was. Kristofik looked happier than he had any right to be. He had only put off the inevitable, he was a dead man so far as his present antisocial personality was concerned, but he looked as if he'd forgotten that. But Mencken could not take advantage of the lapse because Shen Lo-Yang did not take her eyes off him, she did not even seem to blink, and the stunner she leveled at him was set for full power, which at this range could be fatal.

The next thing Kristofik told him, when he had been there nine days, was that on the morrow he would leave the *Golden Girl*. He was told that someone would come for him when it was time, and he was advised to go quietly. He was told he would then be safe, and free to pursue justice as he chose.

So he waited through the next day, but nothing happened; at any rate not to him. For a time the sounds of the ship changed in a way he recognized as a difficult but slickly accomplished set of maneuvers; the self-contained gravitational field of the spacecraft did not waver, but Mencken thought they were in an atmosphere. This was it, he thought. But then it ended and time went on and on into the night, hour after hour without activity or news; he did not even get any dinner.

Went wrong somehow, whatever they planned. He had mixed feelings about that. Some of it was grim satisfaction; was Hiero-volan Mencken to be shoved off a pirate ship with a gun in his back, while the pirate laughed at him? Never. On the other hand—the other hand was not good to think about. He had a family waiting for him. He did not like thinking of how long they might have to wait.

"What happened?" he said next morning when they brought him breakfast. There was a lot of it, as if they were making up for the meal missed the night before.

Kristofik and Lo-Yang did not answer. They looked at him as if—he saw this acutely—he were a problem. He was by no means a coward and he ate his well-made omelet with deliberation, studying the black-clad man and woman who had his life in their hands. He thought he detected in Shen Lo-Yang a certain pleasure, which was a nasty thought, considering her history. Kristofik was pale and his mouth showed the trace of a shallow cut. Trouble from outside?— but the *Golden Girl* had not landed anywhere or been boarded; he was sure of that. Perhaps Lady Hanna had slipped out of control, a heartening possibility.

Some hours afterward the *Golden Girl* stopped. He had not heard for some time the characteristic stresses and puffs that meant Jumps; instead there were the louder but less abrupt sounds of movement in realspace. Suddenly there was almost silence, as all movement ceased; life support alone did not make much noise. His door opened. In it this time there were three people, not two, and all of them were armed. They wore spacesuits, but their helmets were not in place. Kristofik and Lo-Yang, of course; but the third was Lady Hanna ril-Koroth. She looked beautiful and calm. He said, "Are you sure you're pointing that gun the right way?"

"Come on out," she said.

They marched him toward the tail of the *Golden Girl,* not leading him but telling him where to go, staying a safe distance behind. Michael Kristofik said, "You're getting out of this safe and sound."

"What did you do to Lady Hanna?"

"It's what he *does,*" she said sweetly. "Several times, when he's having a good day."

Mencken glanced around. He did not understand, but Kristofik evidently did, and looked scandalized. Kristofik said, "Your own suit's waiting for you, and your maneuvers pack. We're next door to a relay. I'll tell you the number if you want to know, but it doesn't matter; you can't broadcast from on-site anyway. We'll wait till you've got yourself anchored and then we'll move out. We'll contact Fleet and tell them where you are. You should be picked up in less than twenty-four hours."

"How'd he do it?" Mencken said to Hanna. "Drugs?"

"Is that what they're all going to think?" she said. "Tell them this. Tell Lady Koroth and Commissioner Vickery and Gil Figueiredo and Starr Jameson especially, tell Starr in person, give him this message: I quit."

The suit was outside an air lock whose indicator lights showed ready. Mencken put it on and waited while the others fastened their helmets, one at a time, so two of them always had him covered. There was no haste or confusion; the teamwork reminded him of his colleagues in I&S. They escorted him into the lock and out of it. Free fall caught at his stomach and he fumbled for the maneuvers pack, switching it on. He saw that they were indeed close to an Inspace relay, close enough for a searchlight to pick out the details of its platforms and antennae.

He could not help saying, "I hope you really are going to contact Fleet."

We will, said a voice in his head, so clearly he might have mistaken it for speech, except that he had had contact with telepaths before; also it carried the absolute assurance of truth that speech could never have.

He gave up, having no longer any choice. They stayed where they were while he glided the short distance to the relay. He had no way to tell when the others went back into the ship; the *Golden Girl* did not move and kept the search-light shining while he hooked his utility belt to a steel stanchion. After that the searchlight blinked out. The *Golden Girl* moved away; its other lights became fainter and disappeared.

He only had to wait seven hours. It was not even long enough to get hungry, after the breakfast he had had; it only seemed like an eternity.

Chapter 4

Gaaf the medic, a former physician of Fleet, was trapped in the *Avalon,* and trapped by more than metal. There were the dreams, and waking nightmares, too.

First there was the uproar on Revenge. Gaaf watched it. All of them went to the warehouse to retrieve the treasures stored there, but all the things were gone. Castillo made certain statements about what would be done to the People of the Rose. There would not be much living in the City of the Rose when he was finished. Gaaf would have preferred not believing the threats, but he believed them. Castillo's face was scarlet and he screamed at Suarez to bring him the headman of the town. While he waited he paced and snarled, and then he said more about what he was going to do. Gaaf started to go away but thought: *What if he notices I'm gone? What if he knows I left because of him? What if he gets angry at me?* —and so he stayed. He stood just inside the *Avalon* and watched Castillo interrogate Elder Rann. He saw the D'neeran woman again, walking in front of Juel to her death, and turned away as if that would make it not real and sink it into dream.

And then there was the shocking end of it, he heard the sounds outside and hesitated, thinking he ought to go see, and Castillo came back, running and yelling orders through an intercom to Wales on the flight deck. Gaaf was in his way and was shoved aside. The push was hard enough to knock him into the wall and bruise his shoulder, and the first instant of shock and pain brought tears to his eyes. He collected himself and followed Castillo slowly to the flight deck. But they were taking off when he got there, in a hurry, jabbering. Later he found out Juel was dead.

The *Avalon* left Revenge behind and moved out into space. There was no more talk about the People of the Rose. Instead they talked about the *Golden Girl*. The Avalon had gotten a good look at her: a pretty ship, an expensive, sophisticated toy. A Dru-class yacht. Gaaf had never seen one before. He stared at the pictures and tried to imagine the luxury inside. You had to be born to wealth to have one, he thought. But why would anyone who could own one be on Revenge? What interest could anyone like that have in stealing Castillo's store of trade goods?

Far away from Revenge, in deep space, the *Avalon* waited. The men asked: for what? But Castillo kept his own counsel. Besides Castillo there were five of them now that Juel was dead: Suarez, Wales, Gaaf, Ta, and Bakti. They passed time with gambling and watching the 'beams. What the 'beams had to say was going to be crucial. What was the golden ship going to do with the woman who was the only witness to the aliens' deaths?—it was a mystery. The *Avalon* filled up with the stink of fear. If Oversight had come to Revenge between scheduled visits, if a Fleet representative had been there to warn them off, that would have been one thing. But the golden ship could have nothing to do with Fleet. And nobody knew about Castillo and Revenge. Except—Castillo in those early hours looked at the men of his crew with (it seemed to Gaaf) something new in the ice-blue eyes—

They waited, watching the 'beams. They waited for information about the golden ship. It did not occur to any of them that Hanna might be dead and the secret of their identities gone with her—to any of them except Gaaf, the only one who knew how sick she had been. He did not tell the others, because he did not dare tell Castillo that he had eased her pain and thus, surely, helped her turn on them. But he was haunted, and his dreams were haunted, too, by the swollen brutalized face, the stripped fever-hot body; by knowing he had played God and given her (though he had not known it then) a chance at life. A voice echoed in his mind, fuzzy with fever and drugs. Equally without fear or gratitude she called to him: *Wait!* Still he was afraid that she was dead. But she might get treatment in time. But from whom?

The name of the *Golden Girl*'s owner came finally. Gaaf

was on the flight deck when it came. There was a picture with it, a routine identification shot. Gaaf looked at the face and wondered what it would be like to be handsome and rich. The man in the picture looked gently amused. Castillo barely glanced at it. He knew the name; he did not have to look at the face that went with it. Suarez also knew it, and cursed bitterly. Castillo only said: "Him!"—as he had said once before, laughing then.

"Who is he?" Gaaf asked, but softly, so that Castillo could choose to overlook the question. And he did overlook it, or did not hear it. He looked at the image with cold hate.

The *Avalon* went nowhere for a time. "What are we waiting for?" said the others.

"You'll see," Castillo answered in his soft voice.

Gaaf wondered if that meant Castillo didn't know, had no ideas.

Castillo and Suarez talked together privately a great deal. They did not tell anyone what they talked about.

Twelve hours after Hanna's escape:

Gaaf slept fitfully, an hour at a time. The aliens died over and over in his sleep. Hanna's eyes were blank with shock and blue as meadow grasses in the clear morning light after a night of storms. She threw herself at Castillo and Wales turned the stunner on her and she fell, the distant sleepiness of stun softening her face.

Twenty-four hours:

Castillo was calm. There was nothing on the 'beams. The men gambled and drank. "If he's smart, he'll kill her," Suarez said. "He doesn't need the attention."

"Worst thing he could do," Castillo said. "They're looking for him, not us. She said so. He needs her."

"He might not know that."

A smile of real pleasure. "If he finds out too late, when she's dead—that's best for us. More time."

"They'll drag it out of him, though. That he had her. Where he got her. Us."

That was not a private talk. Gaaf heard it, but it was too complicated for him. Every place in the *Avalon* seemed dark. There was shadow on all the faces. He went once to the room where Hanna had been imprisoned and saw the gold chain on the floor. He saw its provocative gleam against smooth skin—until the skin bruised and bled. He had not been able to watch the beating, but Wales had come to get him to wake her up, and so he had to see what they had done.

He put the chain into his pocket. When he revived her, she had been warm under his hands . . .

Suarez had been with Castillo a long time, longer than any of them except the dead Juel. Gaaf was the new man. He had been on the *Avalon* for six months, buying medical supplies for resale, and this was to have been his first run to the place they called Gadrah. He supposed it was something like Revenge. When they got there, he was to perform some kind of service, act as physician to some vague population of colonists. There was a great deal he had not been told.

He came across Suarez in the common room. Suarez, drinking alone, was talkative. Gaaf asked him who Michael Kristofik was.

"A mistake," Suarez said. "That's what he is, a mistake."

"What kind of mistake?"

"I remember," Suarez said in a confiding voice. His eyes had a secretive look.

"What do you remember?" Gaaf said, bolder.

"Prettiest little boy you ever saw. Got away one night on Alta."

A nightmare that was not a dream swept over Gaaf. Cries in the night months ago, no dream; in space near Colony One, which they had left in a hurry for no reason Gaaf could see. They were a child's cries, but in the morning no child was aboard. Later, on Willow, he watched Castillo watch a fresh baby-fat boy, maybe ten years old; the dilated eyes came out of a bad dream. The boy was with a crowd of family. He left with them, safe, out of reach. You could not forget nightmares when the pieces added up by day. Castillo's expression. Cries in the night. The pretty boy who got away.

"Mikhail," Suarez said.

"What?"

"That's his name. Wonder if he remembers."

Gaaf thought about something else, retreating. He put his hand in his pocket, and the chain rubbed against his fingers.

Slight as the wisp of a dream and with burning flesh. The black bone-deep bruises on her thighs. *I couldn't do what they did,* Gaaf thought. *I'd be gentle. So careful—*

He dreamed about it, smiling a little. But Suarez said, "He went to whoring on Valentine. Then he pulled off a big one. I mean big."

The lights in the common room seemed dim. It was darker and darker. Chairs, tables, everyday objects thickened; they had sharp angles in the dark, were unrelieved cubes.

"What's the mistake?" Gaaf asked.

"He's still alive," Suarez said.

Thirty-six hours:

He slept again, a little. Hard fists on soft skin. She cried out, tears of agony stood in her eyes, burst out, coursed down the discoloring cheeks.

"Oh no. Oh no—" He woke again and stumbled to the common room. They were listening to the 'beams. The hunt was up. Not for them. But only not yet.

"We have to go," Suarez said.

He sat at Castillo's right hand. Castillo sat at the head of a long table. He had something in his hands. Gaaf had seen it before: a cylinder of densely engraved gold. At one end there was a rim of flashing jewels round a circle of blackness. Castillo turned it over and over.

"Go where?" said Ta. His nails were badly bitten; he was subject in some moods to something like remorse.

"Gadrah," Castillo said. "As planned."

"They'll get us there, too!" Ta said with violence.

"They won't," Castillo said. The faint smile covered his whole face. *I know something you don't,* it said.

"Fleet'll be everywhere for this. There's no place they won't go."

"Not Gadrah," Castillo said, and he said it with absolute certainty.

"Why not?" Ta said.

"You'll see. But our cargo's incomplete. We were robbed," Castillo said without irony. "This is the last run. We're trading for more than payload this time. There's not enough to trade."

The things stored on Revenge had been purchased legitimately. There was no chance of replacing them.

Wales said, "You're not thinking of another raid some-place."

"We might not need one." The smile stayed in place. "We might be able to get somebody to give us what we need."

"How?" Wales said.

Castillo explained. He kept turning the golden cylinder in his hands. The engraved letters on it, the ones in Standard, said plainly where it could take them.

Space fled away behind them. Now they had an itinerary, and the first place they would go was Outside. Gaaf, though ten years with the Interworld Fleet, shrank from it. In Colonial Oversight the stops had been far apart, the isolation profound; each tour of duty was like being Outside, or so he had always thought, and he had never been sure the Fleet would return. To avoid thinking of it he made his head be full of Gadrah: a simple puzzle, a place an Oversight veteran should know.

Suarez showed him pictures of two children of Gadrah and their mother. He said they were his children and their mother's name was Nekotym. She was a plump creature with bad teeth and extraordinary eyes of warm amber flecked with gold.

"I never heard of the place," Gaaf said. "Is it called something else?"

"Maybe."

"What's it called?"

Suarez grinned. Gaaf persisted. "Why's he so sure Fleet won't pick us up there?"

"You'll see when you get there," Suarez said, sounding like Castillo.

Gaaf spent a long time ciphering it out. At least he evolved a satisfactory explanation: that wherever Gadrah was, Castillo's cover there was impenetrable. It was the only possible explanation.

Still Gaaf ought to know about the place; ought to have heard of it, at least, by whatever name.

He tossed and turned in the dark nights, doping himself to sleep when he was desperate for rest. The rags of his life flapped around him in the dark. He had not meant to come

to this. He had not meant to witness murder and break
bread with murderers. Yet inexorably he had come here. He
had never made one single right choice, had not even been
a very good physician. There had been too many deaths in
the backwaters of a star-spanning culture, and too many of
the bereaved had shaken his hand and thanked him, like
God, for his failures. His progress from a failing farm on
Co-op to greater failures on lesser worlds had been—no
progress at all. Increasingly furtive, increasingly alone, he
had garnered no good memories to take along on the longest journey he had ever made. He had done one brave
thing in his life, and only one: in a sudden access of good
taste where a woman was concerned, he had tried to make
dying easier for Hanna ril-Koroth. The pathetic inadequacy
of it ground at him and gnawed his dreams. There had been
a stunner in his hands. A brave man with a stunner could
have saved her. But he was not used to saving people; he
was only used to helping them die.

And yet she had survived. They heard it on the 'beams as
they hurtled toward Omega. The news came out of D'neera
somehow, on the heels of the news of the hunt for Michael
Kristofik. No one was surprised, except Gaaf. He had to
stay away from them, he could not let them see it. Someone
else had saved her. The bruises and fever must be gone. She
must look as she had when he saw her first, seated between
two lumps of alien flesh, holding one by its thready hand.
Steady sapphire eyes: *she* knew what she was doing. Gaaf
did not even know where he was going, he did not even
know what Gadrah was. But first he was going to the planet
of the aliens. He did not know anything about aliens either,
except that he did not like them. *She* knew about aliens. *She*
was not afraid of the Outside. She was supposed to have
gone there. He was going in her place, and someone else
had saved her; a criminal, it seemed; a braver one than Gaaf.
   They passed beyond Omega and heard nothing more.

It started to seem as if pieces of the *Avalon* were missing. In
the dark; it was always dark. Sometimes what the other men
said made no sense, as if they spoke an alien tongue. They
gave Gaaf peculiar looks at times. He stayed in his cabin,

but it was dark there, too. The nightmare went on without end. But when it ended, they would be where the aliens were. After that—Gaaf's mind skipped ahead, passing over the aliens. After that it would be Gadrah, where there were people.

Sometimes, when he had the energy, when the men of the *Avalon* looked like people, he tried to find out about Gadrah.

He was afraid to question Castillo, and Wales was as secretive as Suarez. So he approached Ta, but Ta had made only one trip to Gadrah in three years. He said Castillo and the men of the *Avalon* were important at Gadrah, that Castillo was a powerful man. Ta said there was a city of white stone that shone in daylight, but the sky always looked cloudy at night. The inhabitants of the city dressed in fine garments and jewels, the finest the Polity could provide. The girls were lubricious, the liquor strong.

It did not sound like any place Gaaf had seen or heard of in his years with Oversight. But after a while it was plain that Ta was nearly as ignorant as Gaaf; that at Gadrah he had been too preoccupied with spirits and girls to look around much, and the memories he had were unreliable.

Gaaf wanted to ask if Ta had ever heard the others talk about the way to get there, but he was afraid to. He was afraid Castillo would find out about his questions.

The other man on the *Avalon* was Bakti. In ten years he had been to Gadrah three times. He did not know much more about it than Ta. But one night, hunkered in the dim corridor near the black room where Hanna had been held (her blood still spotted the floor), he said to Gaaf, "I don't think we're going back."

"Back where?"

"Civilization," Bakti said. He talked as if he knew what it meant.

"What do you mean, civilization? Gadrah's civilized, isn't it?"

The other man's face was uneasy in the shadow. "It's a long way out."

"So?"

"A *long* way."

Bakti looked at Gaaf emphatically. Gaaf shook his head and Bakti hunched closer.

"Listen," he said, "I don't think anybody else knows where it is. It's out past Heartworld, I know that. And there's no charted settlements out there. I looked it up. I don't think anybody knows except *him*. And maybe Suarez. Juel knew. The other trips I made, they didn't let anybody else onto flight deck. You couldn't pick up a relay transmission. It was like it is out here. They said it was us that was shut down for security. I don't think so. I don't think there was anything to pick up. It was a lot like this. A long, long trip. And there wasn't anybody else out there."

Gaaf looked at Bakti blankly. Bakti was hinting the impossible, a trap for the credulous. An Oversight veteran would know. The disbelief showed on his face.

Bakti said, "Listen. Most of the people there, they don't even speak Standard. Most of 'em don't read it. Most of 'em can't read at all."

Gaaf grunted. That was unusual even for an isolate like Revenge.

"And they keep slaves. Would the Polity put up with that if they knew?"

Gaaf refused to take the statement literally. "It's not much better on Nestor. They've never done anything about Nestor."

"Nestor's got a fleet of its own. This place doesn't. Even on Nestor there's Polity observers walking around. I never saw anybody from the Polity on Gadrah but us. They talk like nobody ever comes there but us."

"Oversight does," Gaaf said. What Bakti proposed was unbelievable, so Gaaf did not believe it.

He would see it for himself, and in the meantime he was going to see the aliens.

Hanna's face when the aliens died was painted on his dreams. She had tried to save them. She had suffered for them. Nobody had ever done any of that for Gaaf. Nobody had ever looked at him like that. He did not think anyone ever would.

The journey of the *Avalon* went on for four weeks, which was as long as any point-to-point journey inside human space ever had to last. Then it went on for another week, and another. After that it was impossible for Gaaf to disregard the truth that he was really Outside, and he stopped counting. The others had, perhaps, less imagination; they were not as disturbed as he. Or maybe they were reassured by Castillo's calmness. The red-haired man was as tranquil as if he were native to Outside, as if the dangers of the flight were insignificant. To be so he must be a masterful pilot. Whenever Gaaf saw him, the empty half-smile was in place on his lips, and his eyes were calm to the point of vacancy. Their light blue was transparent at times. But Gaaf, when he looked into that window (when he dared), looked through it, saw nothing: blank vacuum.

He seldom saw Castillo, or any of the others. They lived on packaged rations and did not come together to eat, only to drink or gamble or watch dramas of human lives from standard recreational programming play out in the walls of the common room for hours on end. Otherwise they moved in separate orbits, colliding accidentally and not often.

The *Avalon* seemed more dark each day. Gaaf secretly brought more lights to his room from other places, and tried to make the shadows flee. But they lurked at the corners of his eyes even when the room was bright as a star. So in the glare of light he closed his eyes and thought of Hanna to keep from thinking of other things. Old habits reasserted themselves and he stopped thinking of the reality of pain which he had witnessed, and remembered the beauty she had been at the very start, an untouchable ideal, like all beautiful women. But they were not untouchable in fantasy, and so she played a part in the limited reach of his sweaty imaginings. There was not much to do on the *Avalon*, and it was a long voyage.

One day when he had gone straight from fantasy into sleep, he woke with a sense of alarm. He knew immediately what had caused it: a change in the background noises of the *Avalon*. It took him a minute longer to realize that the ship had stopped. He went into the corridor with dread. Ta and Bakti huddled in a dark corner and talked in low voices. They fell silent when he came close.

"What happened?" he said.

It was Bakti who answered. "We're there."

"Where?"—for a minute he thought they meant Gadrah. That was how little he wanted to go to Uskos.

"Alien country," Ta said.

Gaaf went to the flight deck. He had been there frequently throughout the flight, and so had all the others; on this trip it did not appear to be, as Bakti had said of other journeys, forbidden. Castillo and Wales and Suarez were there. Castillo talked. His voice was strange and what he said was a rasping gabble. Then Gaaf saw the transparent shield of an automatic translator in front of his mouth, which damped the vibrations of his voice, twisted them around, and turned them into another language.

Almost as soon as Gaaf came in, Castillo switched off the translator and looked around. "We're landing," he said.

The *Avalon* was guided to a city of great stone buildings, all identical and so massive they seemed monolithic. Gaaf was on the flight deck for the landing. The *Avalon,* accompanied by (or strategically surrounded by) an escort, glided over the city for a long time. It went on and on, the truncated tops of stepped piles of masonry all alike ticking away beneath them. This was the City of the Center, by which was meant it was treaty ground, and here came the beings of Ell and Sa, of Ree and Naa and other lands, to settle their differences and have peace. Gaaf looked out on the City of the Center with blank eyes. Before the landing Castillo turned off the translator again. He said, "We'll be traveling a lot. I told them we want to. Look out for what we need."

Gaaf thought that meant there had been a promise, and whatever was asked for would be given. So maybe the crazy scheme would work and Castillo would get what he wanted from the ignorant aliens. He trembled with relief, hoping no one would notice. Quite apart from other dreadful suspicions, after what had happened to the aliens and Hanna, Gaaf had come to understand that Castillo dealt out death casually and apparently without fear. It meant nothing. It only meant something had gotten in his way. Gaaf did not want to see any more of it. He had never thought himself a violent man, and now he knew he could not strike or wound or risk his life even to save someone else's more valuable life. That was why, when they needed him to wake up Hanna, they had had to come and get him after his flight from what the others did, and why his hands had trembled when he lifted her bleeding head.

There was a great commotion at landing. There were translators enough to go around, both ear- and mouthpieces and the processing modules for the hand or belt. What was the *Avalon* doing with all these translator units? —nobody used them in human space, they were only used by people who had business in places where Standard was unknown. No one on the *Avalon* asked Castillo about that, but Ta said, "How'd we get the program?"

Castillo gave him an amused look, but he did not answer. It was Suarez who said, "Got it soon as we decided. Hook into any relay and tie in with D'neera. Ask for D'vornan library. That's all."

"They just give it to you?"

"Anything you want."

They came off the ship all together. They were armed. Just before they went out Castillo said, "Don't answer any questions. Not now, not later. I answer the questions."

Outside the air was stunning in its brightness and clarity. Gaaf was blinded; he put his hands to his eyes, shielding them from the light of the star. Nothing shielded him from the heat. Yet he was only in the sub-tropics, and they were only a little more hot and more brilliant than comparable latitudes of Earth. But the *Avalon* had been very dark, and Gaaf had sprung from a cool climate.

Finally he took his hands from his face. Eyes blinking and watering, he saw Castillo hand the golden cylinder to the aliens. He called it a token of faith. He said Rubee and Awnlee of Ell would not return, but men who would have been their friends, though too late to save them from beings alien to humans as well as Uskosians, had made this journey in their place and come to initiate friendship. After that they climbed into wheeled vehicles and were taken through the towering city. But Gaaf's eyes kept watering, so that he did not see anything.

It was not so bright in the chambers of Norsa. Norsa, a personage of indeterminate position and age, appeared to be in charge. Gaaf knew that was his name because he said "I am Norsa," but his description of his function was beyond the capability of the translator. He wore a garment that looked like a brilliant, lavishly embroidered blue barrel. Other Uskosians were there also. They talked with Castillo. At first Gaaf did not listen, but looked in horror at the aliens. They were unutterably ugly. Their skin was dank and leathery, in color a dirty brown. The depressions of their eyespots were filled with an unstable colloid that made him want to retch, and the agitated cilia round their mouths made his skin crawl. Their hands were variable and blunt; he looked for the long thin strings of fingers that had been wrapped around Hanna ril-Koroth's small human hands, but he did not see any. And they stank. The whole place stank. The walls of Norsa's chambers were golden, except where they were streaked with bands of other colors, some bright and some subtle. The bands were horizontal and strapped them into the room, which seemed to shrink.

Gaaf began to hear the conversation. Norsa said: "It is a strange tale you tell."

"Your emissaries indeed met with misfortune," Castillo answered.

"Is it possible to obtain their bodies?"

"We could not find them. They were put into the sea."

Gaaf's eyes wandered to a sweeping window on the city. It was as impressive from here as it had been from the air. The gleaming towers marched away into the sky, making him small.

He heard a name he recognized and his attention sharpened:

"—and this creature of another people, to whom this gift was made—this Hanna ril-Koroth—betrayed honored Rubee and his steadfast selfing?"

"That is what we learned."

"But why?" Norsa said, and even in the mechanical impersonality of the Standard words fed into Gaaf's ears, there was a tone of perplexity.

"Zeigans are not like humans," Castillo said. "They hate those of other species, even humans. Humans do not often go there. Humans went there this time only because there was word of your envoys landing there. But we were too late for anything except vengeance."

When Castillo finished talking there was silence. But after a time Norsa said, "Your people will have the gratitude of mine for the vengeance you took. Also we must have gratitude that it is you, the human beings, who have come to seek us; rather than those others who would wish us only to die. It was too much to think that we would find only peace in the stars. Yet that was our hope."

They were given a spacious place to stay, which, however, was well guarded. Surrounding it was a garden. Many of the flowers were tall, coming higher than Gaaf's waist; they had great blossoms made of flat petals; they were in color bright yellow, deep gold, and vivid pink, and glowed so brightly, and were so perfect, that at first he thought they were artificial. Before the first evening was over there would be more meetings, but for a short while they were alone. They left the house and went to the garden, "In case the walls have ears," Castillo said, and they walked among the flowers.

"All of you listen," Castillo said. He looked around, shepherding them with his eyes. Some of them were nervous. The reality of their presence on an alien world getting its first sight of humans was sinking in.

"Don't answer any questions unless you have to," Castillo said. "If you have to, say as little as you can. Don't even talk about it among yourselves, in case they're listening. If you have to talk, keep the story straight. Their envoys first made contact with Zeig-Daru. They got killed there, Fleet heard about it, that's how we got the course and why we're here. They were killed by Zeigans. Remember that."

"What about the D'neeran woman?" Ta said.

"The name's right on the course module, says she was their friend. I had to bring it up. They think she was a Zeigan and we executed her for what they did."

"They won't swallow it," Ta said, "the Zeigans are telepaths, they can't pretend to make friends first and kill you later, they just kill you right away."

Castillo said, "They don't know that here. So forget you ever knew it."

Later there was a banquet at which the food looked terrible and tasted worse. Suarez and Wales went back to the *Avalon* and returned with real food, but Gaaf did not eat; the drinks had been all right, and he was asleep. Only in his dreams Hanna protested bitterly, as she had not protested, not once, aboard the *Avalon*.

They began traveling at once. Despite Castillo's strictures the men talked among themselves. "He said we don't have much time before the Polity comes," Bakti told Gaaf.

"He told *them* that?"

"No, no, I don't know what he told *them*. That's what he told Suarez."

"You heard Suarez say that?"

"No, that's what Ta said Suarez said."

So it was impossible to know what could be believed. That did not stop the men from talking, and it did not keep Gaaf from listening.

They did their traveling in the *Avalon,* though transport was courteously offered. What explanation could Castillo have given the aliens for this? How did he explain their going armed—and why did he want them to be armed? How did he justify keeping their hosts off the *Avalon?* Why did he keep them off?—Gaaf did not hear all the lies and so he never knew if a lie were at issue, or an omission. It crossed his mind that the same thing was precisely true of what Castillo told/lied about/did not tell the men of the *Avalon.* There was no use listening to words at all. The range of certainties shrank from hour to hour. To: food and drink to go into the mouth. A smelly cubicle on the *Avalon.* The physical existence of the other men of Castillo's crew. Gaaf's own body was less certain than it ought to be; it had tics, twitches, moments when it seemed to fade. As for the outside world, the alien world, it was all a single shining piece, like a peculiar dream to the meaning of which there was no point of entry.

Two beings were assigned to him, him personally, to assist him (or maybe to watch him or both). He was nearly afraid to speak to them at all. Their names were Biru and Brinee, and whenever the *Avalon* landed in its travels they were there, like personal demons. Gaaf dreaded stepping off the ship and seeing them, inescapable. The other members of the crew had their personal devils, too, and Castillo had several. But Castillo's face, unlike Gaaf's, never altered at the sight of them. In their presence he was impassive, and at other times he never spoke of them except to make coarse jokes about the presumed sexual practices of this species.

All time was a single piece to Gaaf, a seamless tissue. There were events, but it did not seem to him that they marked a progression. The events might as well have coexisted all together: until the very end.

There was:

A day of rain like the rain Gaaf remembered from the poor fields of Tarim on Co-op, the water coming down in a curtain like a solid substance. Without being able to see anything because of this cataract, he entered, with the others, a building that grew out of the rain. The water poured down with such power that inside it could be heard pounding the structure's roof, though the building was substantial. Gaaf was dizzy with the stench of the aliens. There were hundreds of them here, spots of gaudy color in their overdecorated garments, though they sat in shadow on long benches. Only the foremost portion of the great chamber was brightly lit, and there, set well to the back of a deep platform, were two black cubes. The human beings were taken to the front of the hall and given cushioned seats. A being dressed in scarlet came to the edge of the platform.

"I am Balee of Ell," he said, and began to speak or to declaim, and presently Gaaf realized that he was attending some kind of memorial service for Rubee and Awnlee of Ell. When Balee was done, music began: a kind of irregular drone punctuated by scrapes and squawks. More beings came onto the platform, until it was filled with them. They were masked, and they glittered and dripped with jewels.

Suarez sat at Gaaf's right, and Castillo beyond Suarez. Gaaf heard Suarez whisper, "Those stones real?"

Castillo breathed, "Find out."

Balee of Ell said, "And this is the story of the Fate of Relell."

Gongs sounded, setting up vibrations in the walls, the furnishings, the bones. The beings on the platform moved in the stately ritual of the Fate of Relell.

"On a day," said Balee, "Relell of the tribe of Relell in the land of Ell set forth with his selfings and all his kinsmen to settle on the far shore of the land of Naa. For in that time the coast of Ell was torn by great storms, and against those storms the Master of Chaos aided none, but watched.

"And Relell and his selfings and all the people went forth in fair ships well made, yet scarcely were they out of sight of land when the ship of Relell's selfing Uprell foundered, and all who traveled in it were lost. Yet when the people looked behind they saw that the storms were worse than before, and so they could not go back; yet when they

looked before them they saw the Master of Chaos. Therefore they went on."

There was a good deal of noise on the platform-stage.
Balee's voice was amplified, the stiff robes of the players
crackled and swished, they chanted and cried out, and the
droning went on, too, interrupted by other raucous noises.
Under cover of all this Castillo and Suarez talked softly
together. Gaaf leaned toward them, trying to appear as if he
did not.

"Where do they keep it?"

"We'll find out."

"Find out where it is from the air."

"It won't be enough."

"Mark one, though."

"And they came after great peril and loss to the shore of
the land of Naa, and it was summer. Yet the Master of
Chaos had caused the season to sicken, and though summer
it was cold, and nothing grew in all that fair land. And so
when the people sought to plant the seeds they had brought,
the seeds died in the ground, and nothing lived and all the
land was barren. And there was an end to the food that had
come on the ships, and there was great suffering. And the
Master of Chaos walked among the people of Relell and
watched, yet he did not signify amusement, but was grim
and did not answer those who cried to him.

"The winter came, and Relell, though starving, was
gravid, and his time came upon him and he brought forth a
selfing whom he named Senu; for he wished the Master to
be unaware that the youngling was of the land of Ell or the
tribe of Relell or that he was the selfing of Relell, and thus
he hoped that Senu would be spared. But the Master came
to him as he suckled the babe, and it died at Relell's teat,
and the Master watched. And Relell cried out to him, but
the Master did not answer, and disappeared.

"At length the winter passed and spring came, and of
those who had set forth from the land of Ell, only the twen-
tieth part remained, and they had scarcely strength to hunt
or fish. Yet they did, for they said to one another, 'Now at
last the winter is past, and surely now the Master will cease
to discourage our endeavor.' And they grew stronger; but
one day there came storms and wind. The wind blew down
their huts and blew away their ships and weapons, and they

ran from the waves that came onto the shore. And Relell with his last strength tied himself to a tree so that he might not be washed away.

"But then he looked out to sea, and on the sea he saw a wave as big as a mountain, and he knew that his end had come. And in the wave he saw the lineaments of the Master of Chaos, and he cried out to the Master of Chaos, 'Why? It was a brave undertaking done correctly. What is the reason for these things?'

"But the wave overcame him and he was swept away and drowned, along with all the people. And when all of them were gone the Master of Chaos looked down and said, 'There was no reason.' Yet he did not signify amusement.

"And so," said Balee abruptly, "it is until this moment," and everything stopped.

After that the players went one by one to the black cubes and took off their jewels and laid them on the cubes. They grew into blazing heaps which Castillo watched with concentration; Suarez's mouth was open. Then it was over.

There was:

One more standardized tour of a manufacturing facility. Gaaf was on the flight deck again when the *Avalon* landed near it. Castillo and Suarez talked. Gaaf listened, and as he listened there filtered into his comprehension, too slowly for alarm, the reasons Castillo used the *Avalon* for local transport rather than accept the transportation the aliens offered. One reason was that here they could talk among themselves. Another was that this way they could build up detailed maps of where they had been so that, if they wished, they could come back to a place quickly.

Gaaf was not sure what that meant.

They got off the ship and there were greetings. Here were Biru and Brinee, and here also were the other beings of the official party of escorts, the devils who shadowed Castillo and the others. Here were the beings who managed this particular facility, and at their heels something else: a small furred bright-eyed creature on all fours, with a kind of embroidered saddle on its back. It made ambiguous noises the translator could not render into Standard.

The factory was built in a brown countryside. There was warmth in the sunlight, and Gaaf did not know if this country was always brown, or if it was only not the season of growth. The factory made no pretense of fitting into its surroundings. It had cupolas, and its enameled facade was indigo and maroon. Gaaf's bitter youth on Co-op had convinced him that all factories ought to be underground. The Uskosians were proud of this one, though; it pleased them; they talked as if they were amused by its effrontery.

Castillo acted amused.

They went through the factory and the thing with the saddle got interested in Gaaf. It sidled up to him, pranced around his feet, tripped him up. He kept thinking it would bite him, he dodged it, he made tentative kicking movements, and finally he ducked into a dark passageway to escape it. It followed him. So did Brinee, who found him leaning against a wall, sweating, trembling, and cursing the beast in a whisper. His agitation was apparent even to non-human eyes, and Brinee shooed the thing away.

Brinee said, "I am sorry. It is only a pet."

Brinee stood between Gaaf and the end of the passage. Gaaf looked past him longingly. Where were the other human beings?—he had to catch up with them. But he could not bring himself to walk toward Brinee in the dark.

Brinee said after a while, "My far-kin Awnlee had such a one as a child. He loved it dearly."

Gaaf knew which of the dead aliens was Awnlee. Hanna's mental cry of anguish at his death had been perceptible to all of them.

The passageway was murky as the middle of a night. Something seemed to tug at the leg of Gaaf's trousers; he looked down in a frenzy, kicking. But there was nothing there.

"Are you well?" Brinee said.

Gaaf passed a shaking hand over his face and said, "This is hell."

The word came out of the translator in unadorned Standard. Neither Ell nor any other Uskosian land had an equivalent concept or a comparable word.

"Ell?" said Brinee. "No, today we are in the land of Ree. Let us join the others."

Throughout the rest of the tour, Gaaf felt animals snapping at his ankles. There were never any animals there, though.

The factory produced fine liqueurs the color of ripe

grain. There were jars and jars of them stacked, shelved, crated, awaiting shipment.

Castillo tasted the liqueurs and nodded. He said to Suarez, with no attempt at concealment, "Mark two."

The aliens had no idea what he meant. Gaaf was beginning to guess.

They were given certain gifts, as Castillo had predicted. Half a dozen jars of the exotic liqueur; a pyramid of spun-crystal many-colored balls that made sweet sounds when the wind blew over them; stiff ceremonial gowns and masks in primary colors; a handful of other things; not much.

"They took a fortune in presents to Earth," Ta complained aboard the *Avalon*.

"They expect a return before they do that again," Castillo answered.

That was enough to satisfy Ta, but Gaaf, emboldened by this rare communicativeness in Castillo, said, "Did they come out and say that?"

"Hinted."

"That's a hell of an attitude," Ta said, aggrieved.

Wales said, "The funny thing is we've got what the Polity was going to give them right down in the holds."

Some of them chuckled, but Gaaf did not see the humor in it.

"Don't say so when they're around," Castillo said. "Not a word."

They were traveling toward a city in the heart of Ell where they would be welcomed by an agrarian guild. Suarez said before they landed, "Won't be much here, I guess."

"You never know," Castillo said. "There's something they want us to see later, some kind of museum. Might round us out, if it's as good as I think it is. It's time we went. Long way to Gadrah. Back to Omega, a good six weeks; a week to Heartworld sector; then another five. Three months. We might pass the Polity on the way, I guess," he said, and the smile came again.

They had now been on Uskos for two Standard weeks, and Gaaf had thought himself adjusting to it. By that he meant that he had learned to blank out the nonhuman landscapes, beings, language, and artifacts. He clung instead

to the interludes on the *Avalon* as if they were life, and all
the rest a dream to be endured. In this life a single image
suddenly stood out, clear if not technically accurate. It was
the course Castillo projected: a course through the waste of
Outside, then into and out the other side of human space to
another void. In the middle—to be crossed with casual
haste, touching nothing—was all the space Gaaf had ever
known before: Earth and Fleet's headquarters at Admin,
the amusements of Valentine, the roiling network of Polity
culture, even the outposts to which Oversight ministered,
even (God help him) Co-op. And everything outside that
was barren: a few alien civilization that were patches of terrifying light; and Gadrah, the unknown.

He put his head down on his knees because he felt faint.
"You sick?" Bakti said.

He mumbled, "I don't feel so good."

"That's a joke," Suarez said. "The doctor gets sick."

He thought of saying: *Maybe we can catch what they have
here.* But he did not, because he suddenly did not want
them to have an overriding reason for wanting a physician
aboard.

He still had his head down at the landing. He said, "I
have to stay here. I can't sit through one of those God damn
shows the way I feel."

"I don't know if I can get through another one either,"
Wales said, but they were indifferent.

Castillo said, "If somebody's here, at least we don't have
to secure the ship. Just keep your eyes open."

"Yes," Gaaf said.

They were down and the others filed out to the farmers'
guildhall and a dignified spectacle of sowing and reaping, to
the some-kind-of-museum which might be—what? Mark
five? Mark six? Mark the last, anyway.

Gaaf did not raise his head until they were gone. When
he did he had real difficulty doing it, because of the fatigue
that dragged at his bones all the time. From the flight deck
he saw that the sky outside was gray. The town of Elenstap
was spread out before him on a series of gracefully folded
hills. Many of the structures in it were brightly colored, so
that it presented a festive air. But the colors all ran together,
and it was not a human spectacle, and Gaaf shrank away
from it, back into the dimness of the *Avalon*.

The unknown. He chewed the palm of one hand. His head ached.

He thought: *I can't do it.*

He thought of what would happen if he begged Castillo to leave him somewhere, anywhere, in human space.

He would be killed. That's what would happen.

He looked toward the controls of the *Avalon.* He had been in Fleet too long not to know something about them. For centuries the human species' desire for many spacecraft had run head-on into the complexity of interstellar flight, and the result had been standardization. A brave man would hijack the *Avalon* and—

But Gaaf was not a brave man.

The Fleet would come eventually to this world of aliens. They would take him and probe him and punish him for his part in what had happened to the *Far-Flying Bird.*

Unless. There was his Fleet record: adequate if not outstanding. There was what he had done for Hanna.

And if the impossible was true? Then there might be more. If it was true.

Desperation gave him a small cunning. He crept toward the controls after all. Trembling, looking over his shoulder, he researched the course to Gadrah.

And there it was, as he had feared but not quite, not really, believed until now: a lonely track past the limits of known space, bumped off the inner edge of the spiral arm that had in it not only Earth and her offspring, but all the habitable worlds supposedly known to any human beings.

Aboard the *Avalon,* standardized, were data storage modules no longer than a finger and a centimeter thick. Gaaf knew where to find them. He put onto one what he wanted to take, and ordered the *Avalon* to forget his tampering.

Then he sat back, quaking and twitching, to wait.

The Treasure Store of Elenstap in the Land of Ell was a fair, proud structure three stories high, with two wings set at angles to the main bulk of the building, which was the older portion. Ell had been essentially at peace for a thousand years, and its people's lively interest in the arts for those thousand years and longer was reflected in the land's Treasure Stores, by which name was meant public treasures that belonged to all the people who came to admire them. The newer wings of the Store of Elenstap had been constructed to complement the Old Store. They were made of white marble streaked with russet, the marble having come from the same quarry that had supplied the stone for the Old Store. Set into the exterior walls at intervals were palimpsests representing the most important works within, and the representations, though stylized, were masterpieces in their own right. Also the cartouches had been treated with a substance, invisible by day, that absorbed the daylight and shone at night. The Store stood by itself in a grove outside the city, and visitors to Elenstap came there at night to regard a sight no visitor should miss: the radiant images floating in the dark, seemingly unsupported, a catalog in light of the chief treasures of that place.

The *Avalon* remained at Elenstap that night. The crew rejected the hospitality of Elenstap and stayed on board. If the townsfolk or the official party from the City of the Center were offended, they did not say so, and the humans could not read the nonhuman faces or tell what the movements of the heavy bodies said.

At twilight it began to rain. There was a sharp burst of wind and water which declined to a settled drizzle. No one would come to stand outside the Treasure Store that night, though it glowed brightly as ever in the rain.

Before dusk changed fully to night, Castillo began to detail certain plans he had been formulating since the *Avalon's* arrival. Not even Gaaf was surprised by them. But his lack of surprise was of a different order from that of the others. He had made a vague guess at what would be done, deducing it from what Castillo said. The others had not had to guess. There was something that they needed on this world, and it had not been given to them. Therefore they would take it.

Gaaf listened to them talk and they turned into aliens — strange smooth-skinned beings with flexible mouths. This terrified him, and the *Avalon* was very dark. His simple plan for escaping them seemed a hopeless thread. He was afraid they could read his mind, that someone had read it all along, like the woman who ought to have died on the *Avalon*. He even thought he saw her at a corner of the dark room.

Don't give me away! he begged, but she did not hear him;

she disappeared. He knew she had not really been there, he
was not crazy. All the same his body twitched. The Uskosians were no good either, anatomical freaks with muscle
in the wrong places. They were the only link he had left to
the Polity, though; to real human beings.

The briefing was over and he had not heard a word of it.

In the middle of the night the *Avalon* lifted into the air.
It flew straight over Elenstap and came to the Treasure
Store, and it pushed fire before it. The end of the new west
wing blew away. The *Avalon* hovered at the broken end and
the men threw down a ramp to bridge the gap between the
ship and the smoky second floor of the Store. Gaaf shoved
through the men at the end of the ramp. He did not remember going there. Wales yelled, "You're supposed to be up
with Suarez!" but they were in a hurry, they did not have a
second to spare, and no one else questioned Gaaf. Castillo
looked at him and the pale blue gaze looked through him;
then Castillo turned away.

Gaaf prayed to something and ran after the others,
across the ramp, fleeing from darkness into the dark.

The others had lights and wore masks to protect them
from the dust and smoke. Gaaf had no equipment. He ran
in the dark, tripping over broken stones, falling. His clothes
ripped, his hands bled; he got up again and ran into a wall.
But he fell on it weeping with relief. He fumbled through
the dark with his hands on the wall, bumping into things
and knocking them over, or bruising himself against heavier
objects that would not move. A door opened under his
hands and he fell inward into a blacker darkness and the
door snapped shut behind him; the air was cleaner here, but
he could see nothing and crawled in the blackness, clawing
for the door. He found it and crawled out into the smoke
again—and saw a light bob as a man ran back toward the
ship with something in his hands.

He kept dragging himself along the wall, stumbling and
choking. He was dazed, he had forgotten why he was doing
this (but he knew he could not go back); it was blind flight
propelled by blind hope, but the hope was light years distant where there were human beings. Another door opened,
on light this time, and fresher air; Gaaf saw a staircase, and
he half-fell down it. The stairs were painted like the rainbow and gracefully railed, lit by lamps shaped like minia-

ture starbursts, though this way was for emergencies and seldom used. It was pretty, for a nightmare.

He could not read the strange alien signs. But the aliens left nothing to chance, not on a route designed for frightened beings trying to get out. The door that led outside was transparent, the blessed wet night showed through it, and it opened outward as soon as Gaaf fell on it. He stumbled out into the rain. There was a terrible howling somewhere, horrible screams far away but surely louder than any normal throat could make—he did not recognize it as machine noise, fire or disaster control devices racing to the Store of Elenstap and making their ordinary sounds. It seemed that something living and huge and ravening was coming for *him*—

A dark shape passed overhead, accelerating to another target. If Gaaf had been missed from the *Avalon,* no one had bothered looking for him.

He stumbled through the grove of trees with wet branches lashing at his head, and out into the soggy fields.

In the night Gaaf began to understand about the Master of Chaos. Rain pattered on trees he could not see in the dark, and the wind moaned through them. He walked zigzag and blind, falling when stones and other objects turned under his feet, capricious and malevolent. The ground kept falling away or rising up in front of him, so that he moved in a drunken lurch. He could not see anything. He could not even see the lights of Elenstap reflected from the clouds. He did not know if he were walking away from the town or toward it, he went in no direction but randomness.

He kept his right hand in his pocket much of the time, clutching the precious wafer that might buy his life from the Polity. The gold chain was there, too. And maybe she would plead for his freedom as she had pleaded for the aliens' lives. And when she learned of his flight from Castillo and learned of this journey in the dark she would say, *How brave you are, Henrik Gaaf.* The blue eyes would rest on him gently and—

He talked to her in the dark. He talked to his sisters on Co-op also. But they said, *Quite whining, Henrik, shut up and work.*

The rain slackened and stopped. After that there were

new noises in the dark as nightbeasts crept from hiding and set about the hunt. There were not so many trees, and then none. The ground was more even and things grew in it in rows which Gaaf followed because it was easier walking that way. Sometimes there were no rows, but solid masses of vegetation that caught at his legs and feet like snapping animals. He stumbled on, wet to the skin, cold and hungry and very tired.

When he could go no farther, he sat down on the ground. He tried to imagine Hanna beside him, the warmth, but he could not. He was too cold.

He fell asleep without knowing it, and when he woke up it was light and an alien bent over him. He yelled and squirmed away from the touch and then he saw that he was surrounded by a ring of them. He began to weep. He wept all the rest of the day; they looked at him without comprehension. There were no translators and they could not talk to him, though they tried; they tried very hard. And they took him back to the City of the Center and put him in a bare locked place, he had not expected anything else, he had not expected anything, and he was passive and only wept; but when they took the wafer of data away from him, he howled so desperately that they gave it back to him again.

Chapter 5

A long space voyage is the ultimate reach of boredom; any Fleet cadet will attest to that. The leaps of starflight pall after a time, the dark outside has no end, and all parts of the universe look the same. Library terminals and holo-shows are finite resources; one's companions rub on one's nerves. The journey is not an end, but only a means toward one. Getting there is a state of stasis to be endured, and it seems as if the end will never come.

But there are also people who seek space with passion. With freedom from planets and solid ground comes a freedom like that of the sea. For these persons, where there are no other beings, there can be no obligations. Time is measured not by the tyranny of regulated clocks, but by Jumps; a very different matter, since no two are of the same length, and the exact point of terminus is increasingly hard to predict as routine paths are left behind. For those who absent themselves further from the human race, avoiding use of the relay system, a season in space can be as close to perfect freedom as any human being will get.

In order to take up the course to Uskos, the *Golden Girl* first had to go to Omega.

That was the hard part. Humankind was universally unfriendly, and the sense that it was so grated on everyone but Michael, and the others grated on him.

Theo spent too much time with the newsbeams, helping no one's mood. There was nothing to be heard about Mencken, but there was news from D'neera, since D'neerans talk profusely about everything they know or think they know. The magistrates of D'neera clearly had been lied to. Hanna's message had not been delivered to Lady Koroth, and the magistrates, in ignorance of the facts, clamored for Hanna. A flower of their civilization, beloved, needed and missed, Lady-Koroth-to-be, dutiful daughter of her House, she could not be spared: the magistrates appealed at large to the Polity and the man it sought. They said Polity clumsiness in trying to trap Michael had caused him to abort, what other reason could there be?—they wanted Hanna too badly to engage in games or duels, there would be no more traps, if only Michael would bring her home where she belonged.

Theo told Michael about this, and told Hanna, too; she got a pinched look around the mouth and disappeared into the room of mirrors. She would not come to Michael's bed and she would not talk about it. He did not know what to do for her and she would not tell him.

One living D'neeran who can keep her mouth shut, and that's the one I get—

Lise was pale and quiet. She had not understood the events at D'neera when they happened, but Theo of the flapping tongue explained. She was outraged. Michael tried for hours to tease the reproach from her eyes. She forgave him finally for trying to abandon her, but in a flood of tears. "Don't do it again!" she cried, and charged into a full-blown tantrum in which he saw, to his horror, imitated elements of the display he had put on three days before. At the height of it Hanna flew out of hiding, cheeks burning, her sensitivity to emotion exacerbated past bearing. She pounced on Lise and shook her; Lise retaliated with fingernails; Michael at the risk of life and limb was about to dive into the melee when Shen, watching with calm interest, caught his arm.

"No harm done," Shen said.

"What the hell are you saying!"—they rolled on the floor now, spitting.

"See what she's doing. Look."

And when he made himself be still and look, he saw that Hanna, though her hair nearly stood on end, did nothing more than passively defend herself, blocking blows and guarding the hair Lise pulled.

It did not last long. Lise went limp and cried again and Hanna held her. Michael came up to them cautiously; they paid no attention to him. "I know," Hanna was saying, "I know, I know, it hurts so much ..." She laid her cheek

against Lise's and they cried together. Michael did not
know which of too many kinds of abandonment Hanna
grieved for—what she had just done to D'neera? What had
been done to her in the past?—or Lise either, for that matter. The range of possibilities was chilling. He thought of
Claire, Emma, Kareem, the dogs, the cats, the tourmaline
faded and dead by now; he was sick. Hanna lifted her tear-
stained face. "Come here," she said, and held out her hand.
He sank to the floor with them and they drew him in, and
he bowed his head and wept, too, for a good life made at
great cost and senselessly destroyed. Whatever happened
now, he would not have it again.

In the hours before they came to Omega, Hanna, sleeping
in the arbitrary predawn, slipped in and out of slumber. She
had discovered that some of the mirrors could be made
transparent, and she could look out from this room as she
could from Michael's next door. In the absence of artificial
light, stars reflected jaggedly everywhere. Each time she
opened her eyes that night, she floated in a bath of diamond-
dust. It was beautiful, but not restful. It seemed that somewhere another Hanna moved parallel to this same track,
approaching Omega with Rubee and Awnlee once more.
The voices channeled through Omega bounced off the cradling stars. Nearby was a ship of the Polity; on cue it would
come sailing to the ravaged *Bird*.

The sense of time slightly askew was very strong. Hours
later at Omega it still wrapped her in dream—the kind of
dream which makes waking welcome. But this time there
was no wait at Omega, no systems checks with Fleet cooperation. "Ready as she'll ever be," Shen said briefly, when
GeeGee was on the edge of the long Jump that had marked
the *Bird*'s end.

"Let's go," Michael said, and they went, *GeeGee* making
the Jump without the histrionics in which Uskosian spacecraft indulged. There was a certain tension in Michael and
Shen. It was possible that the *Bird* was still out here somewhere, with official company. She was not; she must have
been taken away. There was nothing out here: no people, no
relays, no voices, no habitats. Nothing.

GeeGee clucked away at the calculations preceding the
next Jump. Lise, curled against the wall, returned to her ab-

sorption in a doll. She ought to be outgrowing dolls, but this was one of the sort whose appearance could be manipulated in detail. Not long ago it had looked like the pseudo-Zeigans of Hanna's hallucinations, and had suffered a good deal as Lise avenged the fright she had gotten. Now it had human features, light brown skin, and long black hair. Lise worked on making it beautiful, and on making its blue eyes exactly the shade of Hanna's. Shen put her feet up on a control panel and almost smiled. Michael and Theo talked seriously together. Hanna thought that was a good thing; someone had better be serious about this great step into silence. She went closer; they were discussing what to have for dinner.

The dream-cloud of threat vanished from her mind quite suddenly. She went to Michael and waited until Theo went away. Then she said, "I suppose I ought to move in with you."

"Of course you should," he said, and that was that.

The beings on the *Far-Flying Bird* had expected to reach Uskos from Omega in approximately five Standard weeks. The *Golden Girl*'s capacity for data manipulation was not as great, and for *GeeGee* the trip would take seven weeks. It was a long time to live between the dubious past and the uncertain future.

Michael did not think much about what he had lost. There was nothing he could do about it.

The future was a different matter, but he could do nothing about that either, yet. It would come as it would come. You took the opportunities you had and made more when you could. That was the deal the universe handed you. It was the only one you got.

He liked hearing Hanna talk about futures. They were not futures you would expect from a woman who had tried to kill you with a colloidal disruptor at first sight.

"Before the Polity comes," she said, "we can move on. There are places out there like D'neera before the Founders came. We could find one and start all over."

"Inventing fire," he said wryly, "unless you can recreate technology."

"I'm a technological idiot. I only know how to make

things work if other beings put them together right. I'm a specialist, you know."

"How do we start over, then?"

"With babies, of course. What else do you need to start over? Yours and mine. Theo's and Lise's. And Shen— Shen—"

"Shen as a mother doesn't quite—"

"No. No, it doesn't compute. Are you sterile?"

"Not for much longer."

"Me either. That's all right, then."

Lise wanted to pilot the *Golden Girl.*

"You said even I could fly her alone. You said that."

"It was true."

"Teach me, then. You're teaching Hanna."

"You can't read well enough."

"But all you do is talk to *Gee!*"

"Not quite. That's not quite enough."

She said that she would learn to read better if he would teach her about *GeeGee.* At that time she had become interested in remarks Hanna had dropped about the place where they were going. Hanna, to encourage Lise, wrote a lively synopsis of what she had learned about Uskos from Rubee and Awnlee. It began as a primer, but because part of Hanna was a scholar, it was comprehensive. The others read it, too, and talked about it a good deal.

Hanna instructed them: "The first thing to remember is that Uskosians are friendly."

But Shen said, "Never seen human beings. No reports. First thing we tell 'em is the envoys got murdered. Second thing, we're in a stolen ship, hope Contact never shows up. Stay friendly? Huh."

"Well. When you put it like that—"

There was a past, too. It could not be excised from the future.

Hanna whispered endearments in four languages, panting. The small fists dug into his back, the little claws of her fingernails nearly pierced his skin. She treated his mouth as her personal property. These moods were like an exorcism, as if past and future could be made to disappear if only the present was narrowed to sensation. "Darling Michael, sweet Mike—" He kissed her throat and she trembled; he licked droplets of moisture from her breasts and she shivered and sighed, an animal with swollen blank eyes. "Mikhail," she cried, "Mikhail—!"

He froze so sharply she must feel it, then thought she had not noticed; she closed around him like a vise, strong arms wrapped around his neck, strong legs pinning his hips. The name echoed in his head.

"Never mind," she said clearly. "Let it go."

"But—"

The shock got worse as it sank in. She felt him soften, and remarked on his failure coarsely.

"I'm not made of stone," he said, distracted.

One hand tangled in his hair; the other slipped between them and took up a purposeful caress.

"Where did it come from?" he said.

"I don't know. Not now, darling."

His cultivated detachment slipped under her slippery hand. "That's right," she said. "Oh, yes."

"Right," he said, it was the last articulate sound he made for some time; he could worry later about the pitfalls of loving a telepath.

Theo studied medical texts. Sometimes he had questions, and each time he started for Control. The first time he went all the way there before he remembered there was nobody to call, and the only library to which he had access was the *Golden Girl*'s own. After that he never got out of his seat; but he half-rose, a reader clutched in his hand, more than once.

He also haunted the medlab, which since Michael's purchase of the *Golden Girl* had been used only for analyzing Hanna's blood. He spent hours becoming familiar with the equipment, going back and forth between the electronic instruction manuals and the mechanical and computer controls. After a while, at times, he thought he could use some of it; at other times the equipment laughed at him, if crystal and metal could be said to laugh.

His chief comfort was that all *GeeGee*'s passengers were healthy. He had even reimmunized Hanna against Dawkin's fever—though that might have been the worst thing he could do. Who knew what was waiting on Uskos?

"Nothing," Hanna said with finality, finding him one day in the medlab; she wandered about, touching polished chrome.

"Why'd the Polity go to so much trouble with you, then?"

"They always overdo the wrong things. Can you deliver babies, Theo?"

He stared at her in disgust. They were at this time approximately halfway through the time to Uskos (rather more than half the distance), and there were long intervals when Hanna and Michael disappeared from the life of the *Golden Girl,* to reappear softened, blurred, and shamelessly devoted. In six years Theo had seen Michael through half a dozen affairs, but nothing like this. There had always been a trace of unwillingness in his surrender before, something withheld; but this woman was affecting his brain, there was more than gonads involved.

She looked at him and he thought she had felt his disgust, but she only smiled in an absentminded way.

"It was because of something that happened with Zeig-Daru," she said. "There was a cut on my arm. Here." She showed him the inside of her right forearm. It was smooth and glossy; her skin glowed, these days.

She said, "They finally found out what the infection was, but they never could cure it. They ended up cutting out the whole chunk and regenerating down to the bone. So they decided, when the Uskosians made contact, to be extra careful. But they admitted we're not likely to trade diseases."

He was relieved to hear her talking in practical terms.

"How'd you get the cut?" he said.

"It was a knife wound," she said. "But I won. Killed 'em all."

She smiled at him again and walked out, leaving him gaping.

He pulled himself together and got back to work. If anybody got hurt or sick, he was all they had. That went for all of them, even a bubblebrain who talked in one breath of babies and killing.

They kept a sort of erratic Standard time, and erratic half-regular watches in Control. Michael, as the paid companion of some traveler in the past, had picked up enough knowledge of spaceflight to obtain pilot's certification for most ships of *GeeGee*'s class. Shen had a sound background in military training, and had refreshed her skills with *GeeGee;* she and Michael between them had browbeaten Theo into learning enough to follow *GeeGee*'s own precise instructions. That was good enough for the common routes of human space. What *GeeGee* did now was not so easy. There were questions to be answered and decisions to be made. There was also, fortunately, Hanna. She had begun intensive spaceflight training in her teens, she had been a pilot before she was anything else, and she could fly (she said once, casually) anything. The result was that in practice her watch was flexible; it began whenever there was a question and ended when the hard parts were over. She was the acknowledged authority on the journey, and on call all the time.

Her "watch" ended one night near the middle of the night. Theo had taken over in Control, and Shen and Lise were asleep. Hanna rested with Michael in the smaller lounge, which was quite dark. Even the ports were dimmed, so little light entered from the field of stars. Hanna sat at one end of the small room, Michael at the other but not far away. Each was visible to the other only as a shadow. Michael had said something about Uskos, and then they had been silent for a time. As if a couple of meters between them made a difference, Hanna began to think of Michael as she had never thought of him: objectively. He had essentially relinquished command of the *Golden Girl* to her. In the timeless round of their days and nights he was almost a passive presence, anticipating her wishes and meeting all her desires. He was sunlight uncomplicated by shadows; a pattern of simplicity, all surface. It would be easy to think of him as weak.

And yet. Her very first perception of him had been as a presence of shadow crouched beside the *Avalon*. He had been in grave danger; but there had been no anxiety or fear in his thought. Afterward there had been that night of intense emotional union. Most true-humans could not have done what Michael had done. Most true-humans, fearing dissolution in her madness, would have knocked her out with drugs or otherwise, and almost certainly killed her.

And then there was the rendezvous with the Polity and what he had done to meet it, and the decision to flee Outside to nothing less than death.

She thought of water, sunlit, dappled with the shapes of leaves. If you slammed into it, it slammed back and broke bones and broke skulls. If you came to it gently it shifted, accommodating. It crept into corners, changed shape silently; it sank through sand and found crevices invisible to eyes. In heat it evaporated into gas and dissipated; in cold it froze to crystalline solids of great beauty. It adapted infallibly to circumstance; but it was very strong.

But the metaphor did not hold up indefinitely, because in Michael there was also a black place where Hanna could not go. Michael could not either, not at will. He only endured it, when he had to. It had nothing to do with sunlit water. "I guess," he said into the dark, very quietly, "we ought to learn how to be polite to the Uskosians."

"Polite?"

"To say 'please' and 'thank you' and so on. In Uskosian."

"Ellsian . . . That's not a bad idea."

"It's a little late to start learning the whole language. Is it hard?"

"Not very. Not like F'thalian. These beings think in the same patterns we do, at least, and the linguistic structure — of Ellsian, anyway — is comprehensible." She thought unwillingly that she was going to have to start working again. "We could have tapped into D'vornan and picked up the language programs."

"Could we? But we don't have any translators to use when we get there."

"It would have helped, though. My accent's not perfect; human throats and tongues aren't made like theirs. The Polity translators were programmed with Awnlee's help, and I can't duplicate what he did. I can make a basic phrasebook for the rest of you, though."

"Have to do."

"Yes. I guess it will."

Once or twice she used the name again: "Mikhail." She did not mean to do it, and knew what she had done only after she had said it. The first time she paused, surprised at herself; she looked quickly at Michael for his reaction. There was also a certain invitation in her eyes. If he wanted to say more, she was ready to hear it. But he smiled and shook his head, and she picked up a cushion and threw it at him. "All right," she said. "Who needs to know anyway?"

The second time she did not even hear herself say it. He did not know where it had come from, how she had dredged it from his memory, why it had slipped from the end of her tongue. She said it half in her sleep as she drifted away. Michael could not follow her; he was immediately awake. He lay with his head on her breast, so restful, such a restful place. What was he going to tell her, how much, when, and what did it matter now, the little he knew? B was gone, must be gone forever. The hopeless quest into dust was postponed, at the very least; he would not pursue that path if Hanna could produce, magically, another life for him. He was entirely in her hands, hers and the hands of chance. The hands of the Master of Chaos.

He sighed and turned his mouth to her skin. She woke a little; her fingers ruffled his hair.

"But if you'd told the Polity," she said, "they would have searched."

He stopped breathing. She was more than half asleep; not even half awake. The compulsion to speak to her dream was strong.

Why not? She would find out anyway—

And so he answered, and relief, like the release of a long tension, made him weak, and his speech was slurred.

"They wouldn't have believed it. Not without a probe. With one they'd have had me."

"Then you didn't know yourself ... until after the *Queen.*"

She was a sleepwalker, an oracle, and he was not sure he heard her words with his ears.

"It was hard," he said. "Nobody knows how hard. A kid in the dark ... Didn't know there was anyplace else. Thought Alta was part of the same world. Later I knew there were more, but then I thought it was someplace like Revenge. Didn't dare ask questions. Afraid they'd send me back. Thinking they could. Didn't guess the truth till long after the *Queen.* Too late."

"Yes," she said. She was awake now. Her arms tightened around him, or around the lost child he had been. She did

not ask any more questions. But he thought that for the first
time in his life there was a certainty in it: Hanna's flesh and
blood, the beating of her heart.

Hanna lay still. The words bubbling up to consciousness
stung her, connecting. With the speculations of an aged
monk; with a vision of flame in a silver-shot sky. The questions she did not ask trembled in her mouth. Who should
know more about Lost Worlds than she? It was Hanna who
had brought back the news of one Lost World in the first
terrible weeks of contact with Zeig-Daru: a message of destruction, a tale of a colony long dead. Almost, in this moment, she believed the old abbot had been right.

Then sense asserted itself. *"If he got to Alta from a Lost
World, it couldn't be considered lost . . ."* The voice of ultimate common sense; Jameson's voice. The fire had to have
been on Nestor where such things could happen at the
hands of the so-called law; or maybe, even, on Co-op, in the
great riots a few years before Hanna was born. It was easier
to believe that this strange, exquisite man lived with one
great delusion than to believe in Lost Worlds.

Finally she said softly, "Mike? Where could it have been
really?"

But now he was asleep, at peace, and she would not
rouse him to talk about yesterday.

Then they were there, a new world broad before them: *Like
a feast,* Michael thought, watching Hanna's intent face. And
he stood by her place in Control and felt regret for what
would be finished today, the honeymoon. Past now.

Hanna had no time for regret. She was worried.

GeeGee had moved in slowly, broadcasting a simple
speech Hanna had recorded in Ellsian. It said: "I am the
friend of Rubee and Awnlee of Ell, she who traveled with
them: an alien, a visitor, a guest. As gifting I bear the story
of the Journey of Rubee. I will have great honor if you will
speak with me."

Hanna liked this speech. It was dramatic, it was designed
to provoke curiosity (a fact the Uskosians would recognize
and approve), and it was courteous. Hanna had spent some
time concocting it. Uskos should fall at once into a frenzy
of welcoming.

Instead there were flat acknowledgments in harsh-sounding voices that had the half-familiarity of a dream, followed by a command for the travelers to do exactly as they were instructed. There was no threat, but also there was no welcome, not even the most formal of courtesies. When *GeeGee* landed at last—it took a long time to get permission to land—they were directed to a desert, a place of dried watercourses in a red-brown land. And an escort of Uskosian vessels landed with them, gently as a fleet of butterflies, surrounding the *Golden Girl*.

They went through *GeeGee* to the starboard lock, and Hanna went out with the others behind her. The sky was vast and opalescent and a cold wind came from it. There were sharp stones on the rusty soil, splintered by heat and cold, and scrubby plants that bent in the wind. Five stream-lined vessels flaunted gaudy insignia in an arc in front of Hanna; the others had landed behind her, to *GeeGee*'s port side, completing a precise circle with *GeeGee* small and impotent at the center. Between *GeeGee* and the ring of aircraft a single Uskosian waited, a spot of vivid color in the gray wind. Hanna led her little party toward him. He stood without moving; even the stiff fabric of his bright blue uniform did not sway in the wind.

The humans came up to him and stopped. When they did, other Uskosians came out of the other vessels, so colorfully garbed they might have been sifted through a prism. Hanna looked around and saw that her party was surrounded.

She said to the blue-clad being in Ellsian, with all the courtesy Uskos had taught her: "I am she who was the companion of Rubee and Awnlee of Ell, and was present at the end of their journey. I have news of them, though grievous news."

The being did not answer at once. There were pouches and a slackness in his face that showed he was about Rubee's age, and there was something of Rubee's stateliness in him. The advancing Uskosians in their bright uniforms stopped. It was wrong, all wrong; a Polity mission must have gotten here first, and at any moment humans must show themselves and seize Michael and Hanna, too. Yet she sensed no human presences except those she knew, and though she did not probe the thought of the being before her, there was no hint that he acted on behalf of humans.

At last he said, "I am Norsa of Ell, a maker of agreements."

Hanna answered politely, "I am 'Anarilporot. My companions are named—"

She stopped. At the sound of her name—which she had rendered as an Uskosian would say it—Norsa had lifted his hand. The aliens converged, each holding at ready a glossy shaft of metal. The weapons were not stunners. They could release a force that punched holes in flesh.

She had not meant to shock Uskos with telepathy at once. But she used it to say unhappily to Norsa, because it carried conviction more powerfully than speech: *I did not expect this greeting for the friend of Rubee and Awnlee, Rubee's selfing in the second degree of adoption, Awnlee's nearkin!*

Norsa was sufficiently shocked, the tendrils round his mouth squirmed with it, but he took Hanna away anyway. The other humans also were removed, separately, except that Lise and Michael were permitted to remain together; that was because the child shrieked and clung to Michael, and Hanna, seeing weapons leveled, said to Norsa, "But they are sire and selfing!"

Shen who had made a sharp movement toward Michael also was in danger. "No!" he said, and Shen stopped in midstride. "Hanna will fix it," he said, but his voice was strange.

Hanna was led away. She got a last glimpse of Michael standing in the waste, looking at her over Lise's curls. Shen and Theo also watched her go, and they looked after her mistrustfully. But Michael's eyes were as strange as his voice: without hope. She could not do anything about it then, she could not even stop to comfort him, and had to walk away.

On a day (said Hanna), *Rubee of Ell set forth with his selfing Awnlee to seek the persons of other stars; and the vessel which bore Rubee and his selfing outward was the* Far-Flying Bird, *which was the pride and flower of the land of Ell and of all Uskos. And Rubee and Awnlee sailed on and on, and the years went by; for space was dark and empty, and it*

seemed there were no other persons among the stars. Yet they did not fear, but felt themselves better acquainted with the Master of Chaos than they had been before.

They came at last to a place among the stars where other persons were, and these persons called themselves Humans, which Rubee and Awnlee rendered "'Unans," and this meant in the tongue of the 'Unans, "persons." And the 'Unans sent to Rubee and Awnlee one 'Anarilporot to be their friend and guide, and they were feasted and made welcome, and they made gifts to the 'Unans and were given fine presents in return, and they traveled widely among 'Unans, and always they were welcome.

Yet one day Rubee said to 'Anarilporot, "The hour approaches when we must leave, for we wish to come to our home on the fourteenth day of Strrrl." But certain wise 'Unans sought to discourage the departure, for they had heard the whisper of the Master of Chaos. But Rubee was firm, and set forth as he had decided, and he was accompanied not only by his selfing Awnlee but by 'Anarilporot, even as in past times Erell and Awtell were accompanied by Porsa of Sa. And there was great friendship among these three, and especially between 'Anarilporot and Awnlee, so that Rubee claimed 'Anarilporot as his selfing in the second degree of adoption. And Rubee made the beginning of the story of the Friendship of Awnlee, which now is lost; yet in truth it is the same as the story of the Journey of Rubee.

And when the Far-Flying Bird *had been on its journey only shortly, certain 'Unans came and took away the gifts made to Rubee and Awnlee, and they killed Rubee and Awnlee in the sight of 'Anarilporot, who grieved for them and grieves for them and will always grieve for them. And 'Anarilporot also would have died, except that the Master of Chaos was present, and because of certain things 'Anarilporot said to the 'Unans with the Master's encouragement, they did not kill her, but took her away from the* Far-Flying Bird. *And nonetheless she would have died, but she was saved by certain other 'Unans who were enemies of those who had killed Rubee and Awnlee.*

In time 'Anarilporot came to Uskos without Rubee and Awnlee, but with the 'Unans who had saved her, and also with gifts which the Master had placed ready to her hand. Yet when she came to the land of Ell, 'Anarilporot was received

*without courtesy, and concluded therefore that the Master of
Chaos had come before her; yet where is the Master not present? And so the story of the Journey of Rubee, which is also
the story of the Friendship of Awnlee, and yet also the story
of the Fate of 'Anarilporot, is not ended; for its ending lies in
the hand of the Master of Chaos, which even now moves to
write it.*

Past Norsa and the other beings who examined Hanna,
there was a window. While daylight remained she could see
the towers of the City of the Center through it. Later, when
it became dark, the tops of the towers were still visible; they
were illuminated at night, and hung in the black sky like a
fleet holding steadfast over the city.

She answered every question that was put to her without
hesitation or evasion. She was not allowed to ask any in
return. "Later, perhaps," Norsa said, "if we are satisfied." He
asked most of the questions, but the others also participated; they were, Hanna recognized, a committee.

Night deepened, came to its turning, and began the slow
progress toward morning. The persons of the committee
melted away one by one. Hanna was given food and drink,
but they did not interest her. She began to feel the weight
of exhaustion in every muscle; she kept her head upright
with conscious effort. There was weariness in Norsa's face
as well. At last there were pauses between questions, and
the pauses grew longer—and in them Hanna saw that the
tension attending her presence had eased. Therefore during
one halt she said, "I wish to offer only cooperation; yet I do
not understand the reason for this sparse welcome. Since
first we met in the wildlands I have known there is in you
hostility and mistrust. This was not what Rubee gave me to
expect, and therefore I knew that the Master had come here
before me; but the shape of this occurrence is not clear."

Norsa regarded her with caution. He answered, however,
"Other 'Unans came here before you."

She let out breath in a little puff. Now that her fear was
confirmed she was nearly too tired to react. Yet she must
start now, with Norsa and the Polity's representatives, to
insist on her rights of kinship—though in the face of this
reception, they seemed dubious.

"Where are the other 'Unans?" she said. "It is necessary that I speak with them." Absurd that they had not come seeking her!

"They are gone," Norsa said. "I do not know where they have gone."

"Gone?" She did not understand him. "When will they return?"

"I do not think they will return," he said in a curious tone.

Of course they would. "Why did they go?" she said.

"Their reasons were excellent."

Hanna said, "I feel that I play the Game of Scant Deduction. Will you speak to me plainly? I have made it clear that we are not the official representatives of our people, and I have had the thought that those representatives might have preceded us here; yet you have asked many questions which those persons would have answered fully, and in your description of their actions I perceive anomalies."

"Those who came *said* they were official representatives," Norsa said doubtfully. "Yet they did not behave as we expected such representatives to behave. Also they said that 'Anarilporot was dead."

He rose and went out of the room, leaving Hanna to the care of guards. She was groggy with fatigue and was not sure she had heard his last words right; what she thought he had said made no sense.

All the other persons of the committee had gone away to bed. Two silent guards were left; perhaps they always worked at night, because they did not seem tired, but regarded Hanna with lively interest. If she moved aggressively, though, no doubt they would react quickly enough.

Norsa came back with a small enameled box in his changing hands. He put the box down in front of Hanna and opened it and took something out. "Do you know what this is?" he asked.

She stared at the golden cylinder with its ring of jewels at the top. She knew what it was but rejected the notion; it was preposterous. She put out her hand and Norsa gave the thing to her. She looked at the engraving and saw that she had been right in the first place.

"But this is mine! Rubee gave it to me! How did you—? It must have been the official party who came and—"

An explosive memory rose into her mind, shocking her so that she transmitted it to Norsa without warning. *Half unconscious, she lay stunned with loss while a thin man reached for the circlet of jewels—*

"*They* came?" She was incredulous. "Those who murdered Rubee and Awnlee?"

"That is how it appears," Norsa said. He added, "Please do not startle me like that!"

"I regret ..." The words of apology came by themselves; it was hard to absorb the truth. Norsa regarded her calmly, though with some wariness, as if he expected her to fling another memory of violence at his head.

She said, "This gives me great amazement, Norsa. Now I know why you did not give us any welcome. These persons may have behaved grievously. Will you tell me of their acts?"

Norsa debated within himself, and Hanna saw that he was about to embark on a catalog of grievances. She waited with considerable apprehension.

Norsa said at last, "We made them welcome. There were doubts from the first. They did not ask the questions that would be expected of beings come first to a new world; yet we had no experience with such beings, and thought our expectations perhaps were wrong. Nor did they wish to answer questions; I have learned more in this night with you than in many days with them. And when they had been here for a time, at the end, they set about destruction. They took precious goods from Ell and also from other lands. In this endeavor they destroyed all that was in their way; and at the last, in the burning of a great costumerie, several hapless persons who labored in that place were killed."

Norsa had seen some of the destruction at first hand. Hanna saw it now in his thoughts. She bowed her head.

"After they did those things ..." Norsa looked at the object in Hanna's hands. "There is the course," he said. "It was evident that we must set forth and follow it, and at the end find out their reasons. But we have not yet done anything, because there has been much discussion of what we might find. Some among us have said: 'Withdraw; give up space; stay at home!' Others have said: 'We must have vengeance, and assert our honor and vigor!' And others have said, 'These persons in the depths of space know of our existence, and also our whereabouts; and so, if we do not seek them out, they will continue to seek us.' And still others have answered, 'Indeed that is true, and they will prey on us.' And so we have debated, and done nothing. Yet perhaps now that you have come, you can tell us the motive for these events, which we do not understand."

Hanna was vividly reminded of Rubee. She could have wept.

She said, "I do not know the reason. Perhaps they wish to sell the precious things they took, as surely they meant to do with the gifts which were taken from the *Far-Flying Bird*. I do not know how they could sell them, or where, for already they are hunted by the true representatives of human beings for their actions on the *Far-Flying Bird*. They would have to go to a far place indeed, far from law; and there is no place so far as to evade human law, not in a matter such as this. There can be no escape for them, Norsa. It must seem to you that humans have little regard for law; do not even my own actions, as I have described them to you, indicate so? But indeed there is in humans a great impulse toward law, and the humans who did these things will be found and, at the least, confined. But I cannot tell you more than that, because I do not know any more."

She spoke with her thought as well as her tongue, and when she was finished she saw that her simple honesty had convinced Norsa. They had come to an understanding at last. There were no more difficulties in the way.

But Norsa said, incredibly, "One of those who came before is still here."

"Still here?" she repeated.

"One of those who came remained behind. Was it by his choice? Was it by the will of another? I do not know. I have been unable to determine the truth. None of those persons spoke any Uskosian tongue, but used devices which translated their words into those of Ell, and the language of Ell into words they understood. They took all the devices away with them, and we have not been able to ask questions of the one who remained behind."

"I must see him," said Hanna in a dream.

"Immediately."

They went out into the night. The guards accompanied them; Norsa might be softening, but he was not a fool. It was summer in the City of the Center, and night closed around Hanna like warm water. The air was clean and before she got into a shiny vehicle with Norsa and her guards, she stopped and breathed deeply. She had been in space too long. The air of a living world caressed her cheeks. In her weariness she could have fallen asleep in the gentle night, floating in it.

Yet as they rode through the quiet streets, and she thought about what she was doing, her chest was tight. Which of the men of the *Avalon* would it be? Not Castillo, surely; more likely a man he had deliberately abandoned. It could not be Juel, whom she had killed. *One down:* the palm of her hand itched. She wished for a weapon. Not a stunner; something deadly.

They drew up before a great building which looked just like the one they had left, and walked through its spacious galleries. Norsa spoke and Hanna answered at random, until they stopped before a door and he said, "Have you too much weariness? You do not hear all I say."

"It is not weariness."

"Ah?"

"It is rage."

"Rage? Why?"

"It is because of a thing that was done to me. I wish to kill," she said honestly. "I may kill this human, Norsa."

Norsa said, "We will not let you kill this creature. If that is your desire, I will not even let you see him."

She wondered where her sense of civilized behavior had gone. Then she thought: *I will be civilized. I will not kill him now, whichever it is. That would be an insult to Norsa. I will kill him later.*

"Let us go in," she said. "You may observe me. If I do something that causes you agitation, you will stop me."

They went into an antechamber where they waited for some minutes while the nightwatch went to wake up the man in a farther room. But presently the watchman came back and said, "He will not come out."

"Then we will go in," Norsa said, and they went into the next room and Hanna saw Henrik Gaaf.

She was startled. He was not. He was far past ordinary surprise.

The room was sparsely furnished and there was a pallet

which might have served as a bed, but Gaaf huddled in a pile of coverlets on the floor. He had his back to a corner. He was emaciated and pale, and he blinked at her and a slow smile spread over his face.

Hanna took a step toward him. Norsa said quietly, "Anarilporot!"

"I will not harm him," Hanna said. "This one gave me a kindness. The Master encouraged him to do so and therefore I lived, though it was meant for me to die as Rubee and Awnlee died. I will not harm this one."

She took another step, though with reluctance. It seemed that something was going to happen that she would not like. It did. Gaaf came up out of his swaddling and threw himself on her feet. She backed away and he caught at her legs so that she lost her balance and sat down abruptly face to face with him. She had looked once into a lava lake that seethed and boiled. It came back to her because that was what she saw inside Gaaf. He pawed at her face and hair and she wanted to hit him and escape—but she did not, though her skin crawled. She ground her teeth and set herself to endure him; she studied him through her revulsion. He smiled and crooned and his eyes had an expression she had never seen before. He patted her shoulders and then her breasts; she twitched violently and caught his hands to keep them off her. He was content with holding her hands. He whispered and whispered and she sorted out the words that ran together. "Came for me, you, you...! Not alone. Not alone here any more..."

His hands twisted out of hers and caressed her arms. She shuddered. A longing for Michael possessed her, for the touch of his clean hands. She made herself keep still and listen.

"...home take me home...See? See what I've got."

He fumbled in a pocket; when he let go of her to do it, she crept away. "...see...see..." She looked with disbelief at the broken gold chain; recognized it, and shuddered again. And here was something else. "Here...seeseesee!"

Norsa squatted beside her. "Do you know that that is?"

She had to try twice before she could answer. "It is an ordinary data storage module."

"What is its significance to him?"

"I do not know. I have to get out," she said suddenly in

Standard. She jerked away from Gaaf, evading the clutching hands; she got to her feet and walked out quickly, though her knees trembled. The ubiquitous guards followed her into the gallery outside Gaaf's rooms. She stood shaking until Norsa came out.

He said with interest, "There is water coming from your eyespots."

"Yes. It will stop by itself in a little while."

Norsa said, "Is that person deranged?"

"I think so."

"We thought it possible, but we could not know. We did not know what to do, and were afraid in our ignorance to attempt any help. We have fed him as best we could, by force, despite the risk; there was nothing else we dared to do. Is there help you can give?"

"I do not know. There is one among my companions who has some skill in healing sickness of the body. I do not know about sickness of the spirit. Perhaps there is help he can give."

"Tell me which it is, and I will send for him at once."

"No. I mean—as you wish, Norsa. But I cannot explain to him tonight. I can give no more help to anyone any more in this night which grows old so that morning has almost come. I must have rest."

"Then you will have rest. Is there anything with which I can provide you for your comfort?"

The tears had stopped, but they started up again. "You can provide my companion Michael," she said. "He is my shelter in the night. I am grieved by lacking him. Surely you know we will cause you no harm. Is it necessary that we be parted?"

"Perhaps not," Norsa said after a pause. "Yet it must be so in what is left of this night, for he is far away. Yet tomorrow perhaps this will change."

"I have gratitude."

She wiped her eyes and followed Norsa back to the street. Tomorrow he would bring Michael to her. Tomorrow also they would have to do something about Gaaf, if they could, if Theo could, but she could not think of it tonight; she was dizzy and her eyes were full of fog. When they came to her quarters she was already asleep and Norsa had to wake her before she could go in. When he touched her to rouse her, she said sleepily, "Mike?" and Norsa looked at her curiously and thought of questions that had to do with this odd bonding. But he was too polite to ask them then; a weary guest must first be given sleep.

Michael spent the first night in a nightmare of pacing through the rooms of a place that he took to be a luxurious prison; later he learned it was a private home. But it was a prison all the same, because he was guarded. The guards did not try to stop him in his restlessness, but they stood at each doorway that led out into the night. He paced because he was trembling on the edge of the terrible rage, which he finally knew had to do with being impotent and trapped. But he could not give into it because of Lise; because of her he fought it back. She held him there with her frightened eyes: she sensed what the pacing meant, and feared abandonment. And it was because she would not close her eyes, because she would not look away from him even when her face was gray with exhaustion, that he finally stopped moving. He saw that as long as she touched him, she could rest; so he forced himself to join her on a pallet meant (his guards made him understand) for sleeping, and with both Lise's hands clutching his arm, he, too, slept. But even in sleep he waited for the Polity to come, waited to be led away in chains.

In the morning they were taken away again. He thought the next thing he saw would be the face of a human being from I&S. Instead, after a journey of several hours, the vehicle that carried him and Lise and their guards drew up before a labyrinth of a cream-colored house in the center of a garden, and Hanna came out to meet him. She said that Shen was already there, and that Theo would come soon but had been called away to see another human. She told him about Castillo—in shock, he scarcely understood her—and about Henrik Gaaf. She put her arms around his neck and talked to him gently.

"It's going to be all right," she said. "But it's not all right, is it? What's wrong?"

"I don't know . . ." He detached himself from her and passed his hands over his face. He looked beyond her to the house the Uskosians had loaned their honored guests. The roof shone like copper, the eaves were loaded with gingerbread fancywork. Wide doors stood open to the summer wind, and the interior looked, from here, dim and cool. It was a dream waiting to suck him in. It was the wrong dream, he thought. He had to run, he had to get away, he could not wait on fate though it might come after him anyway.

But Lise had already run down the path to the central door, where Shen had appeared. Hanna took his hand and drew him toward the house, and he followed her into a dream of summer.

By the end of the next day they had begun to fall into natural orbits; at the end of seven days, a Standard week, the process was complete.

Hanna was the first to leave. If she had come to Uskos for sanctuary, she forgot the fact immediately; she was still, and first, a scholar. Norsa gave her workrooms in the city, a vehicle, a chauffeur, and she left Michael each morning and returned at night. Though she saw that a cold hand lay on his heart, it seemed to her that he had strayed into precisely the right dream. If he disagreed, that was his business. So she talked to Uskosians and made notes. "I suspect," she wrote, "that the unusually high rate of mutation on Uskos, which has promoted evolution despite the asexuality of life here, was the origin of the concept of the Master of Chaos; while the identity of generations (though modified by environmental factors and the occasional successful mutation) most likely is linked to the conservative world view expressed in the tales . . . Uskosians handle the physical universe much as we do, but in their attitude toward it there is something else: a perpetual suspense. They do not say only, 'What will happen *if we do this?*' They also say, 'What will *happen to us?*' . . . The Uskosians with whom I talk are becoming aware of this difference between their perspective and ours and, curiously, feel this makes us far more vulnerable than they are. Several have used a phrase I had not heard before. I'm not sure if the best translation is 'children of chaos' or 'the Master's children.' But they meant human beings. I'm sure of that."

Hanna finished this passage late at night in a room she had commandeered for work in the humans' maze of a house. When she was done, she showed it to Michael. He looked at the last lines for a long time. Then he said, "Oh, hell, I could've told you that."

Lise was the next to go. A friendly neighbor's selfing came, then brought other younglings; they enticed Lise from the garden and soon she was running about the town with them in torrents of noise, her slim legs flashing golden among their square brown bodies. Uskosians were indulgent with their offspring, and no one thought it odd that Lise was allowed to run free as she wished. She even followed her new companions to their study groups, the instructors encouraging her visits as highly educational, and her Ellsian improved rapidly.

She came home in tears one day, however; the younglings played many games which required infinitely flexible hands, and Lise could not keep up.

"It can't be helped," Michael said. "I'm sorry, little puss. It can't be helped. You have pretty hands"—they were very grimy—"but they're human hands."

"Then I don't want them!" she cried.

"Yes you do!" His voice was harsh and she looked up in surprise; he held her dirty paws tightly.

"Mike?" she said.

Instead of answering, he bent and gently kissed the backs of her hands. She turned them over and looked at them with greater approval.

"I can run faster than they can," she said.

"I know. You run like the wind. Don't show off too much, though. Now run back and watch them so you can tell Hanna what they do. And then when they have a different game, you can play with them."

She darted out through the garden, brilliant as the flowers. Michael watched her go and thought that she had grown, and at any time now would sprout breasts. Lise had no idea how old she was. This seemed ordinary to Michael, who thought his age in Standard years was somewhere in the early forties. And when her body did change, and her mind? He was afraid it would be hard for her, as it had been for him. When the world turned out to be different from everything you thought it was beforehand, you could withdraw from it—or run at it head-on, no matter how ill-informed you were. Either course was disastrous. But he

would be there to help her—he hoped—and so would
Hanna—

Oh? said a ghostly chuckle in his head. *What have you
ever saved from the sucking dark? Or whom?*

He shook his head, blinking. A cloud must have passed
over the sun.

Think of something else—

—and here in the sunlight Lise was granted an Indian
summer of childhood, among children so alien that her
queer combination of ignorance and sophistication went
unnoticed. The longer it lasted, the better.

That was the last time she came back during the day
except to eat or entertain her lively friends, and she reported dutifully to Hanna on the younglings' games.

Next Theo went. On the fourth night Hanna came in and
said to him, "You have to talk to them about biology. I don't
know enough. Medicine, physiology, genetics—I need a
whole Contact team. I don't have one. You're it."

"I don't know enough either," Theo said. He had not
ventured into the city. He spent his days sleeping or loung-
ing in the garden, staring out at the skyline beyond the
trees. He avoided the others, and reminded Hanna of a man
about to leap into a lake of cold water and hesitating on the
edge.

Hanna was hot and tired, and she had rarely refrained
from leaping into anything.

"You know more than I do. You're an expert, compared
to me. Take them to *GeeGee* and open up the medlab."

"I don't know enough," he repeated.

Hanna looked at Michael, but Michael said, "I'd better
see about dinner," and left.

Hanna said to Theo, "Look what you did for me. Look
what you're doing for Henrik."

Theo snorted. Henrik Gaaf was present at this conversation: piled in a corner, gazing blankly ahead.

"But he said something today, Theo. He actually said
good morning to me."

Theo said, "I haven't heard him say anything."

"Well, I have. Whatever you're doing is working. You
know enough, Theo—you just don't believe you do."

He shook his head. Hanna went to where he perched on

a shapeless mass supposed to be a chair, and sank to her knees so that she was looking up at him.

"Theo," she said, "where would Mike be without me?"

He did not speak. She went on, "You know the answer. I don't know if you think it means you owe me anything. If you do, please do this for me. For me and for Mike and for the beings who might save him before it's all over. I'll never ask you for another favor. Please."

She had invested the words with an urgency that was more than verbal. He thought about it for a while. Finally he muttered, "I'll try."

"Thank you. Anyway, Theo, you can't know less about humans than the Uskosians do. They won't know when you're wrong!"

So Theo left next day to do his best with a committee of physicians from the nations of Uskos. It was more interesting than he expected, his curiosity was aroused, and he went back the day after that. Soon he only came back at night, too.

Shen got bored and just walked out. She found her way unerringly to a raucous section of the city the Uskosians had not talked about. Somebody bought her a drink, and she liked it so well that she persuaded Hanna to get Norsa to give her some money. He was pleased to do it, but she rarely had to spend anything. She became very popular in certain quarters, and stayed out till dawn some nights, and came home singing, even when she was carried home.

So they were all gone, settling into courses that circled Michael, the still point around which they swung and revolved, the home, more than the house, to which they came back. He watched them go and come as people had come and gone for years, so sure of his care that they scarcely noticed it. Now in the mornings the house was silent. On the eighth morning Michael stood in it and listened. To silence, except for the quiet wind blowing through the garden trees. Inside the house it was dim and, at this hour, still cool, and outdoors the light poured down.

There were street musicians in the City of the Center. Michael had heard what they played, and though it was strange and harsh to his ears, the games they played with pitch and rhythm had possibilities.

He got his flute and went into the garden, because one still was left, and never would leave by himself. Gaaf sat among the flowers and stared at nothing.

Michael said quietly, "Let's go for a walk."

Gaaf was by no means normal, but he was more responsive than he had been when Theo brought him home. He looked up and mumbled, "Where?"

"I don't know. Anywhere. Come on."

Gaaf climbed to his feet, small and vague beside Michael. They went out together, Gaaf treading close on Michael's heels.

Summer closed over them. The flowers in the garden, instead of fading, grew taller and more brilliant until they were a blaze of colored light. The humans seemed to see them even in the dark, as if some afterimage were imprinted on the retinas of their eyes. The flowers worried Theo. Like flowers everywhere they attracted insects: why? There was no need for pollination.

"Think," Hanna urged.

"I'll ask Ritee and the others."

"No, don't. Think about it."

"You know?"

"I know. I knew before someone told me. Think. Use your eyes."

So he walked in the garden hour after hour, thinking — until he saw it: saw a flower close over an insect, and when it opened later there was nothing left but a little debris.

"I swear I heard it burp," he said to Hanna, and she laughed.

She laughed often in those days, which fell into one another in a golden cascade like the notes from Michael's flute. All the days were alike, so that time seemed to have stopped, frozen at high summer in a great gout of light. The flood of sunlight changed them. Hanna and Michael and Shen turned very dark, and their eyes, blue and amber and green, were startling. Lise was dusted with gold all over, and even Henrik Gaaf turned nut-brown. But the best Theo could do for his own transparent skin was keep it from broiling.

It was the dry season, and there were seldom clouds. The

heat was unremitting but not unpleasant, they were dazed with it, in the dusk they sat on a veranda and talked in lazy tones until they straggled off to bed. It was a civilized kind of heat, like their hosts: courteous, attentive to the comfort of a guest. They lived in the safest of sanctuaries—safe in its comfort, safe in its dreamlike separation from any world that had ever been real to them before, and safe in fact—for a time.

No one thought of it explicitly as refuge except Michael, but he thought of it that way less and less. Someday the Polity would come, of course. But if he was only waiting for an end to this world Hanna had given him, he ought to be looking at the sky, and he was not. He looked over his shoulder instead, he looked at the ground at his feet; he did not wait for something from the sky; he waited for the world to be rent and for a look at something deep in an abyss.

Yet his days were as quiet as those of the others. When the morning began to grow hot, he would leave the house with Gaaf tagging behind him, climb into one of the chauffeured vehicles placed at the humans' disposal, and be carried through the city to the place where musicians gathered. Monolithic the city might be, but there were crevices and crannies where gardens had been planted, fountains set to soaring, and parks laid out, each lovely and unique. Through the middle of the day he sat cross-legged and nearly naked in the sun, burning blacker and blacker, in time not a novelty but a colleague. He searched *GeeGee*'s library for works on music theory that did not rely on the written word. The leathery beings who played impossible instruments with inhuman hands learned human musical notation quickly, and Michael quickly learned theirs. His Ellsian got better, if somewhat specialized, and he talked fluently of greater and lesser scales. Sometimes he played dances from the Renaissance of Earth's western world, tunes a thousand and more years old, and the beings of Uskos came near and danced, stumping solemnly and rhythmically in circles round the alien with his shining instrument, while one of their number accompanied him on a drum. Sometimes the man and the other musicians played together, the notes of the flute darting silver and gold through the deeper chords. There were strange duets, and when Michael sang he collected crowds who threw money into hollow pots that rang when the coins fell inside. The days together were a timeless dream made of nothing but music; they were rich heavy drops that fell into still water, pregnant with light.

"Indeed all is chaos," said the aliens in their soft growly voices, "yet we of the Musicians Guild impose order on it. It is transitory indeed; all order is transitory. Thus our assertion of sentient being lies in art, which patterns time in beauty."

At the height of each day's heat the crowds dispersed. The musicians drifted away as they had each summer for a hundred years, as they would for a hundred more. Occasionally Michael and Gaaf accompanied individuals to their homes or customary haunts (in one of which, once, they met Shen). More often they sought a shady spot and were quiet under the weight of the heat. Michael talked to Gaaf, dutifully following Theo's instructions: *Let him hear human voices. Talk to him.* Gaaf was a good listener; he never interrupted, never contradicted, never asked difficult questions; he never made a sound. He was motionless, a brown statue with eyes that shifted now and then but never met Michael's. And an extraordinary thing occurred. Michael found there were things he could not talk about. He could talk about now, about quiet, neutral things: how to make a stew, how long the flowers in the garden would grow, a new game Lise had learned; present things. But he tried to speak of the estate left behind on Valentine, how the sea sounded distantly all night and all day, how the peace of it was enlivened by companions of one's choice, and he could not; he tried to talk of how he had bought and fitted *GeeGee,* the pleasure he had felt as the ship became his before his eyes, but the words caught and choked in his throat. Those had been dreams, too, and he was filled with a sense that they had been incomplete, that something was missing and they were unreal. He began to think he had made a wrong choice. Flight and search might have been the better one. He might have found what he sought; then everything would be real again.

Once, though, he spoke of the past, but of a more distant past. It happened on the first day on which he was offered a portion of the morning's proceeds before the musicians took their pay away to eat and drink it up. He nearly refused his share, then remembered just in time that that would be impolite. Later, sitting under a tree whose every branch burst with miniature duplicates of itself which would drop and seek anchor in the soil when the days shortened, he pulled the coins from his pocket and looked at them. They were bright gold and heavy and closely engraved with text that for all he knew might be (and probably was) a legend of the beginning of money.

Suddenly he laughed. So all the riches had come to this, begging to begging, and once more he sang for his bread. He said so to Gaaf, laughing.

"It's easier now, though. Easier . . ." The laughter faded; he talked on; the words came of their own accord. He had never said them to anyone before, not even Hanna. But this was like talking to no one.

"Easier than saying yes yes yes . . . 'Yes, ma'am, I can do that to you, but it costs a little more . . .' 'Yes-sir, you can do that to me, it doesn't matter if it hurts as long as you pay enough, the docs are good at fixing us up.' 'Yes, Brother, I have spent the requisite hours on my knees contemplating the sin of aggression, only there's some other people I wish you'd told that to, but you wouldn't know them . . .' I would've had to do it twenty years to get as rich as I wanted to be. So I did something else. I invested it. You know how I invested it, don't you? Everybody knows. After that it was easy. The women, all I had to do was look at 'em. Snapped my fingers and down they went. The money had a lot to do with it. So I got radar in my head. Learned to see the ones who looked past the money and the face. Not," he said, scrupulously honest, "that it didn't have advantages. It just wasn't enough. You know what I mean?"

Gaaf did not answer. He did not appear to have heard. Michael looked at him doubtfully and said, "No, I guess you don't."

Clouds had settled over the sun; the sky was gray. There was a roll of thunder and raindrops splattered the pavement.

Gaaf lifted his head with an expression of deadly fear. The flute rolled over the pavement with a *ping;* Michael kicked it in his scramble to get to Gaaf. He laid one hand on the man's shoulder, the other on his head.

"It's all right. It's all right. Nobody's going to hurt you. Henrik! It's all right!"

Gaaf breathed noisily. He looked around as if he did not know where he was.

He began to talk. It was the first time he had said more than two consecutive words. He talked disjointedly of the Treasure Store of Elenstap and the night of stumbling through the farmlands. He talked about the morning when the aliens found him, but he was hazy about it. All he could remember was being afraid. He thought they would blame him for what the men of Castillo's crew had done in the night; he thought they would do something to him. He thought that all the time until Hanna came, he expected to be tortured or put to death, he thought they only put it off to torment him. He said all this with surprising clarity.

At the end Michael said, "It's over now."

"Until they come," Gaaf said, meaning the Polity.

"Yeah, well, we've all got that to worry about."

A smile snaked across Gaaf's mouth, a trailing thing of remarkable nastiness.

"Not me," he said. "Everything's been easy for you. It's my turn."

Michael shook his head. "What the hell are you talking about?" he said, but his mind shot on to something else. Gaaf was talking, Gaaf remembered; Michael crouched in front of him; a tremor ran through him, wraiths shifted under his feet.

"Henrik," he said, "where were they going? When they left here?"

Gaaf's eyes settled on his face. He must have heard the plea in Michael's voice, and God knew what was in his too-transparent eyes; Gaaf shrank away.

"Do you know? Do you remember? Henrik. . . !"

But the animation drained from Gaaf's eyes. He fondled something in his pocket, and sank back into silence.

The time sense of a dream is skewed, but Hanna always knew how long she had been on Uskos. When it got to be half a summer, she looked at the sky more often. Where was the Polity mission? Clouds came into the sky, a harbinger of wet autumn. Henrik was getting better.

What time is it? Time. What day? The day was frozen in miniature, as if everything within view was very small but perfectly clear. Not for the first time, not quite; but for the first time Henrik could question what he saw. Directly in front of him, the rangy man with the face carved by an angel. The gentle hands. On his shoulders. *"Here, this way. Don't fall. There's a step."* The music. The man's eyes were closed, he communicated only with the pipe at his mouth. Piercing fantastic rills. Overhead a gray sky. On every side, an appreciative circle, the others. The aliens. *Oh no. Oh no.*

He shrank, hiding. No one noticed. *What day is it? When will they come?* They would come to take him home. And they would take the musician away; he was sure they would do that, without knowing why he was sure.

The wind was cooler today. Cooler than when? — he did not know. He could not remember. He thought of the woman, remembering, hand in his pocket, fondling the chain. And the other thing, the slip of metal. Only now he remembered something more, without detail. The woman wasn't alone, she didn't sleep alone; she lived with the dark musician. There were details now, disjointed and unplaced in time, but very clear. Blue eyes distant and cool on poor Henrik's face, turning and warming to: *Mike. That's his name. I hate him. I hate him. Who is he? Poor Henrik can't quite remember. Poor Henrik's not quite himself.*

Hanna confided in Norsa. Telling her troubles to an alien did not strike her as an unusual thing to do.

She told him: "My companion Michael has a troubled heart, and I do not know how to give him aid."

"What trouble could he have? For he is well-mated and also has the love of other companions, nor is he hungry or ill or enslaved. And by all that you have told me of 'Unans, he ought therefore to be happy."

"That is correct, and therefore it is all the more difficult to give help to him in his distress."

"Does he fear the law of 'Unans, when other 'Unans come here? For the gentle hints of my colleagues and myself ought to suffice in sealing his freedom, if all that you say is right; and even if we wished, we could not now withhold them. Else the persons of the Physicians Guild, and those of the Musicians Guild, will spring, as you have taught me to say, 'on our backs.' We do not want that to happen!'"

"That is true, and so I have told Michael. Yet it is not enough, Norsa. And I do not know what to do, for he continues to grow worse."

The clouds had moved in all the morning, and the wind was fresh, lifting Michael's hair and chilling his bare shoulders. The musicians of the city looked at the sky and tested the wind with dampened fingers. They gave Michael small pieces of paper on which they had written names, places, contact codes: "In the event we do not return," they said, "for autumn is early; yet song flourishes even in winter in warmer climes."

So he sang a troubadour's song for them:

Adieu, mes amours, adieu vous comment,
Adieu, mes amours, jusque au printemps!

"What does that mean?" they asked when he was done, and he translated loosely:

"Good-bye my companions, good-bye until spring; I have naught to live on, not a thing; only air unless I get the favor of a king!"

"Ah, that is a good song," they said, and went away singing it.

The tiny trees still clung to the branches of their sires, stubborn in the gusting wind. There was dampness in it. The vehicle which had brought Michael and Gaaf had gone home, according to custom. They would have to walk whether the rain caught them or not. So they set out through the city with the wind blowing about their ears, for once without the interested participation of spectators who had all withdrawn to await the storm; and they walked through the back ways, the lesser-known paths Michael discovered instinctively. Presently they were walking through a part of the town they had not seen before: by the side of a moss-choked stream that waited for the cataracts of autumn storms.

The heavy vegetable smell of the moss was familiar. Michael had not smelled it for a long time. He avoided the places where it might assault him.

Haven, supposed to be, like this; from myself that time, though. Wasted, worthless human being: what did it? The girl I didn't know in the morning, that last night on Colony One? Crying all night on my pillow, didn't know till I climbed up in the morning from the dead. What I wanted was dope; what was I using then? Saw the bruises on her face, said what the hell did you do. She said: You did it. You did it. You.

He wanted to get away from the stream, but they had followed it into a cut between high banks, smoothly made of concrete and offering no way out. The wind played above, outside this narrow gorge where the air sat heavy and sullen over the dwindling, stinking thread of water.

Find me a place, Kareem. A place to go. Please. No people. No dope . . . And he did, but he hadn't seen it. Hot and dry and the stream drying up so the smell came in—

"Here," he said quietly. "This way, Henrik." Steps cut into the wall led straight up, a hard climb though the bank was lower; near the top a burst of wind shook them. Gaaf swayed and Michael put out a hand to steady him. At the top the monumental buildings of the city stood over them, perpetually falling if you looked up too long. The wind slapped their faces, and then the rain; only a few drops, so far.

Henrick Gaaf said clearly, "We're going to get wet."

Michael was silent with surprise. He stole a look at Gaaf's face. It was different, intelligent, *like a bright rat,* Michael thought, and disliked himself for it.

"It's a long way home," he said.

"Home," Gaaf said in a curious tone.

They walked up the broad street in the wind, in silence. The moss smell was gone, and the memories that had threatened to come into the light had diminished. *This is what I get for not running,* he thought, and put the memories back where they belonged, with an effort.

Think of something else—

Hanna had gone home early to avoid the rain, to her chauffeur's relief. She went to the room where she worked each evening, distilling the observations of the day, and settled to work. The first patter of raindrops swelled to a steady susurration. Thunder growled, but she did not hear it. The room had been dim when she came in, and slowly it got darker.

The self-contained processing unit shone with its own light, and she did not stop to illuminate the room. A smell of damp earth came in through the windows.

"Today," she wrote, "I learned through debate with the Philosophers Guild that there is already a movement toward consensus on the significance of this world's very first contact with humans, meaning not Rubee's and Awnlee's journey to our space, but the visit Castillo and his men made here in the *Avalon*. 'That's easy,' they said. 'That was obviously the Master's hand.'

"I asked how they knew. The explanation was complicated, but in essence it seemed to be that this visit was of the same order as natural disaster. It is clear that at the deepest level, Uskos is less concerned with cause than with effect, and the stance, in short, is phenomenological. Still, this is only an explicit, intellectual acceptance of common experience, a shift in emphasis from the human view, which is inclined to subordinate the event to its explanation. There is less detachment from primal experience—"

Hanna had been concentrating intently. Something like a prick between her shoulder blades distracted her. As soon as she was aware of it, it drilled into her back. She leapt up, spun around: pure reflex.

"Henrik . . ." She sighed, relaxing. "I didn't know you'd come home. You startled me."

Gaaf did not answer. He stood and looked at her. She thought suddenly that he had been there for some time, staring at her head framed in light. *A fine target,* she thought absurdly, but it was not so absurd. She had a faint vision of what he saw now. The light fell on her weakly; the curves of her body in its scanty summer clothing were pronounced to his eyes.

He walked toward her, his purpose clear. She took a step backward and bumped into the wall. He reached for her and she said, "Henrik, don't," and called, worried: *Mike!* She was not afraid of Gaaf, she could extricate herself from the unfortunate scene easily enough, but she might not be able to do it without injuring him. Gaaf's hands were soft and sticky as slugs and not very strong. He pressed and smothered her against the wall, yet there was no threat in him. He embraced her without violence nor any understanding of her reluctance. Blind compulsion propelled him, some semblance of love, and she did not want to hurt him either physically or in thought. She managed to keep her mouth away from his, managed to reasonably confine his hands. "No, no," she said, "I don't like this, Henrik, I don't want to do this. Please stop, Henrik. Please stop!" *Mike!* she said again, urgently; Gaaf slobbered at her neck; she felt sick. "Please, Henrik, stop. I don't want to hurt you. Please!"

Michael came into the room in a hurry, heard Gaaf's breathing, saw the shapes struggling in the dark. "No, please!" he heard Hanna say. He crossed the room, got hold of Gaaf's right arm, lifted him without effort, and threw him at a blank spot on the wall. Gaaf hit it with a thud, slid down it, and was still.

Hanna cried, "Why did you do that!" and plunged past Michael before he could answer. She flew to Gaaf and knelt beside him, feeling his pulse, running her hands over him, testing for broken bones.

Michael said stupidly, "Huh?"

"If I'd wanted to break his neck, I could've done that myself!"

"But—"

"Did you have to be so rough?"

He swore softly at her back, at the unfairness. Gaaf was conscious and she cradled his head against her breast, no doubt, Michael thought, to Henrik's entire satisfaction. He went to them and squatted beside Hanna to apologize and help Gaaf up. But when he put out his hand, Gaaf whimpered and cringed away.

"Don't hurt me," he wept, "don't hurt me, I won't do it, I won't do anything—"

The sound, the shadow-man, the weak movement in the dark came together; Michael was somewhere else.

I beg you, said the body in the dark at his feet, bereft of pride, bereft of triumph; *I won't do it, I swear! Don't hurt me, don't do it, I beg, let me live—!*

Hands grabbed his feet and he kicked them. Another grasped his arm; he threw it off. He did not remember getting through the dark house. But he was in the garden, standing shaking among the drenched flowers. The rain fell and fell, whispering old pleas.

Hanna came after him at once. She came up behind him

and put her arms around him, and set her face against his back.

She said softly, "I saw that."

The warmth at his back soaked into his spine, but he was rigid. She felt for his hands and he let her have them.

She said dreamily, "It was dark. Dark and lonely. It was a long time ago. But it was you. Not a child. You."

He shook his head as if he could deny it, and rain ran from his hair into his eyes.

"I didn't want to hurt him," he said in someone else's voice, and Hanna answered in a sleepy trance-tone, the oracle's voice: "Who?"

His voice shook. "This is all for nothing, because of what I did. All you've done won't be enough. But I had to do it. I did what I had to do."

"I know. I know . . ."

The voice was infinitely tender. The softness underfoot, the universal grasses that held worlds together, gave way. He closed his eyes to stop this world from heaving and threatening to crack. But waves ran through the ground as if something alive writhed underneath it. Nothing was solid: nothing except the arms around his waist.

She said, "You are the most gentle human being I have ever known."

It seemed to him mockery. But presently he detached himself from Hanna and turned to face her.

"C'mon," he said. "They think we don't have the sense to come in out of the rain. Maybe they're right."

In the gray light her face was remote and beautiful. "When was it?" she said.

"A long time ago," he said. "When I was somebody else."

They walked back toward the house together, and he began to tell her about it.

The planning and execution of the robbery of the *Pavonis Queen* had not been easy. Toward the end the details took so much time that there was no time for sleep. Afterward Michael personally dumped the body of the single casualty into space. In those days his face seldom showed what he really thought, and he performed the task without visible emotion. But when it was all over he was very tired. He was (best guess) twenty-three or twenty-four, and he had never been tired before.

It didn't matter, because there was nothing he had to do. For the first time in his life he had nothing to reach for. He hired Kareem to look after the money and make it grow—and was lucky, luckier than his ignorance deserved and luckier than he knew at the time, because Kareem was an honest man.

There was plenty of money to start with, even after the others were paid off, and Kareem started making it increase at once.

Michael had nothing to do but spend it. At first he did not know what to spend it on, but he found out quickly what to buy: any damn thing he wanted.

But it wasn't the way he had thought it would be. He bought fine clothes—and did not recognize himself in them. He was not vain, having come to regard his looks only as a marketable commodity, but he was a realist, and he knew he required no adornment. He gave that up and bought meals that would cost an ordinary workman a week's wages; but they didn't fill him up any better or longer than plain food. He bought places to live and didn't live in them because they always seemed empty no matter how many people came to them (and people came, all right, but he looked around sometimes and saw that they were strangers). Inevitably he tired of the fine homes, and they went on the block. Kareem saw to it that they went for a profit. And Michael bought expensive machines and abandoned them, bought expensive women and abandoned them, bought expensive art—and kept that longer, at least, though years later, acting from an obscure desire for simplicity, he began to rid himself even of that. At a profit.

He didn't buy friends. He bought companions, but he always knew exactly what he was getting for his cash.

He got tired of buying things. There had to be more to freedom that that. So he behaved like a free man; he traveled. He went to all the worlds of the Polity, no longer a smiling guest, someone's pampered toy, but alone (except when he bought a woman to take along). He went to all the great capitals. He found nothing in them except more things to buy.

But that ceased to concern him because he came to see

all things through a thickening haze. He drank a good deal, and became indifferent to the quality of what he drank. He was young and strong and the drink was of little consequence. But the mainstream of Polity culture had been notoriously drug-soaked for the last century, and that was a different matter. There was a dizzying spectrum of choices, and Michael, who could afford anything he wanted, started at one end of it and worked his way steadily toward the other. He didn't know what he would do after he got there. But probably he would never get there. He mixed compounds with abandon, for one thing. For another, he developed a penchant for the illegal, which made it a risky business not only from the point of view of the law wherever he happened to be, but also because of the unpredictability of what he injected, ingested, or otherwise absorbed. And then when he was spaced, he got into fights. Somebody would kill him someday, or he would kill somebody else, and that would be the end of it.

The end didn't come and didn't come and didn't come, and he lived that way for five years.

Through all of it he clung to music. The flute went with him everywhere. He had always taken lessons, and now, with the quiet exchange of a great deal of money, he took them from the masters of his time. Not necessarily those he would have chosen; some would not have him as a pupil at any price. He did not resent their refusal, but acknowledged their judgment, which had to do with character not talent. After all, there were days when his hands shook too hard to hold the instrument. But as soon as they were steadier he would pick it up again. And he carried a collection of music cubes, too, compulsively. Here was order, when there was no order anywhere else. Also his inclination led him deeper and deeper into the past, so that he learned, in his pursuit of essential harmonies, ancient history and archaic tongues. He had educated himself with fierce determination and he did not care who knew it, but though he acquired a stunning expertise in this one esoteric area, he kept his mouth shut about it. In all human space he shared this part of him only with a handful of other musicians and scholars. He played sometimes for them, but usually for himself, and never for anyone else, clutching music to himself in solitude—as if it could be taken away from him, if people knew it was precious.

Toward the end he stopped playing. Toward the end he acknowledged that he was not worthy of the music. And so he had been right, it could be taken away. Toward the end he could not even hear it in his head.

He was trying to kill himself. Exactly how the fact came to his attention was unclear, though it had something to do with the girl in his bed on Colony One. He did not know what she had done to trigger the rage in him, and he never found out. It happened at the end of a week he scarcely remembered. He was very sick from doping, he could not think, and so he acted entirely from instinct. He got from her the name of a medic who would not ask embarrassing questions, and he went to get the man and brought him back to take care of her. He was filled with bewildering compassion, he promised to stay with her until she was well, he left her only to obtain some things she needed for the time it would take for the bruises to heal, and he bought presents for her, too; and when he came back she was gone.

This happened in luxurious lodgings in a town whose name he could not remember. The rooms the girl had left (his rational mind insisted) were bright, clean, and comfortable: worth the high cost of a few days' stay. But in memory they were dim and grimy. He stood in them knowing he was alone.

By merciful coincidence an express flight for Valentine would leave in a few hours. He booked passage and left with nothing but his silent flute, leaving everything else behind.

He knew before he got to Valentine that this time he was really ill. He couldn't sleep, couldn't keep food down, got weaker instead of stronger even though he had left behind his stock of dope. But he was not suffering from the interruption of any addiction. He was not seriously addicted to anything, and he had altered his habits before when his body became insistent. He had never felt this bad. It came to him that he could not go back to his customary pursuits on Valentine, at least not right away, and so he contacted Kareem from space and arranged for Kareem to find a place where he could stay until his strength returned. Kareem agreed, his face expressionless. Years later Michael still would not know what Kareem thought of him in those days. He did not ask; the answer might be too painful to hear.

In the remainder of the passage to Valentine, he began to want certain things he had never valued before: simple food, peaceful sleep, solitude, silence. He wanted them very badly and did not look past them, because it seemed to him a given, inescapable, that when he left the sanctuary Kareem had prepared for him, he would return to living just as he had lived until then. Even when he disembarked at Port of Shoreground (moving carefully because his head was light and his limbs treacherous) and climbed into the pre-programmed aircar Kareem had sent for him, he could not read the future in his overwhelming sense of escape.

The car took him north along the coast and then inland— as he discovered only when it had landed and he asked it where he was; during the first minutes of the flight he had fallen into the first real sleep he had had in weeks.

The place was a lodge by the edge of a stream that flowed north to join the network of tributaries of the Black River, which eventually, much farther north, poured into the sea. He had an idea that this was sportsmen's territory, and the lodge one of a string of similar facilities that dotted the area, but he did not realize until later that he knew that because once he had been told he owned some of them. Later, when he took an interest in what he owned, and went back to see if there were ghosts there (there were), he learned that this was the smallest of them. It had few amenities and was intended for the serious hunter who only wanted a base to come back to at night. It had a single mirror that showed him a stranger with heavy eyes and a thickening middle. The cabin did not talk to him; its intelligence was on the most basic level. It was as isolated as it was possible to be, and as primitive as it could be without being a thatched hut, and no one came there without a reason.

So for a little while he had what he wanted. Solitude: which meant that he could not hurt anyone else. Food, sleep: the absolute foundations of existence, as he discovered in his gratitude for being able to eat and sleep again. And silence: but why did he want that, when he was used to the din of voices and machines?

He found out why. It was so he could hear himself.

The weather was dry and hot and Michael looked at the

forest and thought of walking in it, but he was weak, and too many other things screamed for his attention, so he sat on the porch and watched the shadows travel like a compass of the day, pointing west in the morning and east at night. It seemed important to be very still because the ground pitched and yawed whenever he got up. He thought he might be going mad—because though he was alone, somebody asked him questions. Michael thought he knew this stranger, or had known him once, before the dark closed in. He had lived in Michael's head for a long time, but he had been silent or, more likely, drowned out. Now he could be heard. He insisted on a dialogue, and the long conversation went on and on. Michael remembered parts of it word for word for the rest of his life.

"Do you think," said the stranger, "you're any better than the animals who started you out this way?"

"Sure I am. Look at the *Queen*. I said I wouldn't hurt anybody, and I didn't, did I?"

"Oh, come on. What about the spacer who lost an eye in that bar on Co-op? The one whose head you bashed in at Shoreground last year? Not to mention that girl—"

"They're all right. I made sure they were all right."

"So your bones wouldn't rot in jail—"

The voice took him through every remembered incident of his life. It weighed up, evaluated, and interpreted. He began to learn about accountability, though he grasped the concept only dimly; he also began to learn about possibilities he had never considered before. One of the things you could do with money was give it away. One thing you could do if women fell all over you was take a closer look at the ones who did not; it was even possible that pleasing a woman worth pleasing went beyond what happened in bed. It was possible that the mind that had mastered the *Pavonis Queen* puzzle was good for other things as well. The possibilities might mean there were other ways to live, and maybe even that there were things to live for.

These were new ideas. He grasped them, however, eagerly and easily. He did not attribute his quickness to any special virtue on his part. It was only that he had gotten what he thought he wanted, and it was not worth having. And all he felt, when he thought that he might be able to change, was relief so great there was no room for righteousness—or guilt.

The days ran into each other, and when he came to this point where he began to see the astonishing possibilities, he was not sure how long he had been in the forest. He was not in a hurry to leave. It was taking some time to get acquainted with this person in his head, whose name, oddly enough, was Michael, too. He was likable, not bad company at all; he couldn't do anything about the chasm Michael saw sometimes, but he said *What did you expect anyway?* At least he was a thoroughgoing realist who admitted without hesitation that there were more questions than answers.

But finally Michael knew he could not stay there any longer. It was time to do something else. Get a new place to live, only for a long time this time: on the Carnivaltown dome, maybe, close to where he had started from, close enough to see it, but a little distance away. He would buy it empty, furnish it with absolute basics, and take his time filling it up. He would give some thought to what he filled it up with. And he would find out what Kareem was doing with his fortune, and see if he could learn how to do some of it himself, though starting as the most ignorant of pupils.

He had a vague notion of fishing for his dinner on the last night, and went to look at the stream. But it had fallen much lower than when he arrived, and even in the deeper pools downstream there were thick pads of moss on the stones in the shallows, and a smell of decay in the mud at the margins. He wasn't hungry anyway. He walked back to the cabin in the dusk thinking that he might, tonight, take up the flute again, and see if it would let him play it. And he thought he heard a whine high above as he walked, as if an aircar crossed the sky, but that was unlikely, and he was preoccupied, and dismissed the notion.

He went into the cabin and a man was waiting for him.

He thought the man was someone Kareem had sent to get him, or to tell him something. Not that Kareem had ever done anything of the kind before, Michael being unnecessary to anything Kareem did, but he could not think of any other reason for this stranger to be here.

The man did not say anything, so Michael made some polite, questioning remark.

The man said, "You don't recognize me, do you?"

To the best of Michael's knowledge he had never seen the man before. He said, "Should I?"

"I hope not. Ivo Tonson. Remember me?"

Michael said incredulously, "Ivo?" and the other man laughed. Not even the laugh was familiar.

"They did a good job, didn't they? Know what I did a couple years ago? Went back to Earth and looked up my wife. Walked up and asked for directions. She didn't even blink. So how are you, my boy?"

Michael put his hands in his pockets and looked at Ivo Tonson without answering. It was now nearly five Standard years since the *Pavonis Queen* incident. There had never been any repercussions, and he had gradually left behind the paranoia that had, of necessity, affected every breath he took through every stage of preparation for the crime. But now he felt its old familiar touch. There was no good reason, not one, for Tonson to seek him out after all this time.

He said, "How did you find me here?"

"Oh, that was easy. I called up your headman and told him you'd tried to contact me, left a message saying I was to join you, but neglected to say where you were. I may have suggested there was a party getting ready to happen. He didn't ask any questions. I don't think," Tonson said, "he entirely approves of you, dear boy."

"That's no news . . ."

The air stirred a little, sluggishly. Michael had bypassed the cabin's climate control and opened all the windows, thinking the night would turn cool, but the heat of the day still lingered. The thick smell of the parched stream came in, and the smell of danger with it.

He said, "What do you want?"

"Why, the renewal of old ties, of course. Let me tell you what I've been doing."

"I don't want to know," Michael said.

"Well, you're going to hear it anyway. We'll do this my way, my boy. We always did, didn't we? And so cooperative you always were. Always pleasant. Always smiling. Even when I hurt you. I always thought you liked it, my dear."

Tonson looked around and sat down, making himself at home. He had not had his body structure tampered with, whatever had been done to change the rest of him. He was still a little man with no muscle to speak of. He would be easy to handle; but Michael suspected he was armed.

He stood where he was and no doubt appeared to listen,

but he took in little of the talk, which had to do with a series of disastrous investments. Instead of listening, Michael thought of what he had gone through to get this roly-poly sadist's cooperation, the information that was the key to the one big coup he needed to start life over again. It had gotten so he winced whenever he heard the cheery voice across space: "Be in Shoreground in a few days, my dear. You'll be ready, won't you?"

Tonson said something again about renewing old ties, only this time he was explicit about what he meant.

Michael said softly, "I don't do that any more. I'm not for sale any more."

"A pity. Truly a pity. You look just as fine as you ever did, although," Tonson said judiciously, "you seem a little unwell. Not due to this unexpected visit, I hope. Still, if old friendships mean nothing to you, I'm prepared to deal on a businesslike basis."

"I told you, I'm not—"

"Oh, I don't mean that. I don't mean that at all. I came about money. Mostly."

"Oh, yes?" said Michael, and it was as if a string that ran all through his body, out to the ends of his fingers and toes, drew taut. He knew what was happening now. It only remained to hear the details.

He listened. It was worse than he expected. He heard about the hint already lodged with I&S, the promise of more information to come. "It all depends on you, dear boy. I looked for you on Colony One, to tell you it wasn't safe for you there any more, but I missed you. You'd left in rather a hurry." He wanted nothing as simple as cash. He wanted a partnership in Michael's growing network of interests.

Michael considered it. There was enough, God knew, to go around. If it were as simple as that—

But it was not. The man who wanted a partnership today could want control tomorrow. And Tonson suggested, more delicately this time, that there were other things he might want. So Michael still was for sale after all, only now the payoff was silence.

He shrugged and said, "I'll think about it. Want a drink?"

"Delighted. Delighted you're being reasonable, but I

knew you would ..." The man's eyes said: *What else could you do?* "We'll drink to our new relationship, my boy."

Michael nodded, walked past Tonson without looking at him—and turned on his heel and struck. Tonson slumped where he sat, unconscious.

It was the start of another nightmare, the kind he had thought he would never have to live through again. There were enough of them already, more than any human being should have. Unless he were being punished by some ruthless god for unspeakable crimes, though he could not remember committing any that bad: until now. The voice in his head, now when it might have been helpful, was gone. He had been right, Tonson was armed, and with a laser pistol, nothing as harmless as a stungun. Michael took it away, poured water over Tonson's head to wake him, and asked questions. Tonson did not want to answer them. But Michael had to know the answers, the extent of his danger, whether it stretched beyond this one man. To find out he used the pistol, setting the output low, not intense enough to burn through metal but easily hot enough to cook meat. It was (until then) the hardest thing he had ever done and the smell of scorched flesh gagged him, but there was, fortunately, little courage in Ivo Tonson, and not much pain was required to force him to answer. And perhaps in his terror he was not capable of understanding that fortitude, or lies at least, might mean he might keep on living. But he did not even lie, though the truth condemned him. He had not insured his life by leaving his dangerous information with anyone else, and he had relied on the weapon for protection. He had not had anything to do directly with the *Pavonis Queen* and had not seen Michael's cold efficiency there. He had only known Michael in Carnivaltown, and he had not really expected resistance from the compliant, uncomplaining boy he remembered. No one had known he was coming to Valentine, and he had come using another new name. He had flown from Shoreground in an autocab and sent it back to its base, having expended (the terrified Tonson said) the last of his cash on the long ride, converted from the last of his credit; so he could not even be traced that way. It was possible (he admitted toward the end, with the little breath screaming left) he would not even be missed.

"You're making it easy," Michael said. He was hunched against the wall next to Tonson then. Except that Tonson's hands and legs were bound, an observer would have had a hard time deciding which of the two sweating, wretched men was the victim.

"I won't do it, won't do anything, it's a mistake, all a mistake, you know I couldn't do it, I care for you too much, dear boy, I swear I won't—"

The short night moved on, the sullen air hardly moving. The hollowness under the world was unmistakable, and the lights in the cabin were yellow and dim and resembled eyes. Michael knew what he was going to do. But not just yet, because he could not. And he thought of finding something to use to soothe Tonson's burns, but that was ludicrous, in view of what he was going to do, and maybe (he thought) the pain even was a blessing, because Tonson knew what was going to happen, too, and pain might distract him from the worse agony of fear.

Finally—hours had gone by—he got up, because one thing he had to do was best done in darkness, and the ocean was far away, and morning dangerously near. He got the pistol, which he had put well out of the bound man's reach, and came back and stood over him. Ivo Tonson began to plead. Michael stood there for a long time. The delay was the worst torture he could have inflicted on Tonson, but that was not why he waited. He waited because he could not make himself do the necessary next thing. Where was the murderous rage when he needed it? He listened to the sobs and whispers until they ran into one another and turned into a meaningless babble. He waited until he had convinced himself that the thing at his feet was not human, not even alive, was a bundle of old clothes that did not even move of their own accord but only rocked with the floor, which seemed to move in sickening waves.

Then he knelt on the uneasy floor, put the pistol to the base of Tonson's skull, and burned out his brain. It was a quick business, and very clean.

He loaded the body into the aircar that had brought him here. He would not come back, had brought nothing with him but his flute, and he took that away, too. He also took heavy stones from the bed of the stream. He flew out to sea and just before dawn threw the weighted body into the water, now really a bunch of old clothes, as limp and as tousled. Then he flew back to Shoreground and got rooms at an inn, because he could not remember if he still owned anything that might pass for a home. He had to sleep, but before he did, he took up the flute. To his surprise, it allowed him to play it; or, more accurately, it played itself. He did not think about what to play. The melodies came by themselves, the gentlest and most peaceful tunes he had heard in all his years, and they came for hours. After a while the music began to talk to him. It said that this was just like everything else, one more thing to be left in the past. It said there was now no reason, none at all, not to act on possibilities, because there were no worse places to go than he had gone, no worse things to do than he had done, no worse man to be than he was. And what was done was finally, irretrievably done, and the future would be better because it had to be, because if it were not there was no justification, never would be, never, for the things he had done, especially this last act. But the music was forgiving, and held out hopes of penance. When it finished talking he put down the flute and slept for two days; after which he began to live, but not to live again because that was not what he had been doing before; he only started, for the first time, to live.

It took Michael a long time to tell this story. Hanna listened to the words, and also to the memories that went along with them. She knew that he had never told anyone about it before, and she knew he was not sure that when she had heard it, she would continue to love him. But it made no difference to her in that respect.

At the end, when he talked of sleep and was so exhausted that he finished the tale hardly awake, she went to the pallet where he lay—they had returned to their own rooms—and sat down beside him. She took his hand, and told him it made no difference. But he wanted to be sure she knew she could not save him, never could have saved him. "Amnesty for robbery's one thing. The Uskosians don't know about this because you didn't know. This is something else."

"Not if the Polity doesn't know either."

"But how can you know they don't know?"

The forgotten chill of the rain penetrated to her bones. She heard a voice from a summer on Earth: *Don't forget the man he's believed to have killed . . .*

Michael had one more thing to say. She bent over him to hear it. "I hate pain," he said quietly, and it was not only his own pain that he meant; and he turned his head away from her and escaped into sleep.

By next day the rain had begun in earnest. It fell in sheets for hours, sometimes with thunder and lightning and sometimes not. The reason the city was sited on high ground became apparent. The streams that wound through it were not entirely decorative; they were a necessity at this season, supplementing the underground storm sewers which were inadequate for the coming of autumn. The waters were full of miniature shrubs and trees that washed down and down to fetch up at last at high-water mark somewhere else, fresh and healthy after their journey in the nutrient-laden waters. The water also spurred the growth of fine rootlets that would cling to damp soil long enough for taproots to strike into the soil hard and fast.

So the rain was useful and necessary, and it was accepted with such fatalism that the City of the Center essentially shut down. Many inhabitants removed to drier places. Those who did not stayed in their homes. Only indispensable personnel were expected to be at their places of work at this season. The storms were early this year, however, and adjustments had to be made for a day or two. By pleading the suddenness of the onset of the storms, Hanna even got her chauffeur to take her to Norsa's offices one more time. The chauffeur was depressed about it; he would have been more depressed if he had known that she went only to ask Norsa to arrange a journey for Michael and herself. "I wish to see a place of which Awnlee told me," she said. "I wish to travel to the Red Forest of Ree."

Norsa had been looking out the window and twiddling his fingers, a sight in itself worth the trip.

"But why?" he said. "For the weather in Ree is even worse."

"Nonetheless I must go, and immediately."

"Then we will all go tomorrow," Norsa said, "and, at the least, will be over the rain for a time and not under it."

So Hanna went home through the rain, hoping that tonight would be better than the night before, that Michael would not wake again and again tense as a beast of prey that feels the hunter closing in, and that, with luck, the excursion to Ree would shake him from his despair.

Heavy cloud brought the evening on them early. After dinner Shen disappeared into the thickening night, clad in an Uskosian rain garment that made her look like a shiny robot not even of human shape. Lise prevailed on Theo to take her to the home of a friend who lived farther away than most. When they, too, had gone, Hanna packed a few necessities for the journey to Ree and afterward tried to settle to work; but she could not work. She gave up and wandered through the enormous house and thought of the Red Forest of Ree, its great plumes sodden and drooping to the ground. That was not how Awnlee had wanted her to see it. In his mind, when he spoke of it, there had been sunlight.

I must get Michael away from here altogether, she thought; she thought it often. But each time there came another thought: *There is nowhere left to go.*

Presently the house warbled over the noises of the storm, startling her: someone was calling in. Henrik would not answer. Michael would, but he did not, at least not before Hanna had hunted down the warble in a nearby room where the utility panel was concealed behind a bronze plaque more or less in the form of a being of Uskos. *Aliore as Pure Art,* said an explanatory legend on the side, which she had to press to open the panel. She fumbled with the tiny dials behind the plaque.

Theo's voice roared at her; she jumped and got the volume down. "What? What?" she said.

"Can't you hear me? I said, young Binell's sire wants us to stay the night. He thinks it's crazy to try going home. I think he's right. Listen, if the power goes out, don't worry. I hear they're putting skeleton crews on infrastructure and sending everybody else home."

"What? All right. Is it getting worse?"

"This is only the start. Listen, you'll be all right without the Box, won't you?"

That was what they called the vehicle Theo had taken; Shen had left in the one they called the Little Box. They had all learned to drive them, more or less.

"We're not going anywhere."

"All right. You know where we are, if you need us."

"I'll see you tomorrow, then."

But the last words echoed back at her, a yellow light twinkled from the panel, and the lights in the room at her back dimmed suddenly. She leaned over and found that her Uskosian tutors had taught her enough so that she could just read the engraving. It said: *At present there can be no connection save with the Emergency Contact Locus nearest this site.*

What was left of the light began to fade. Spurred by a memory of something that had not seemed important when she was shown it, she flew through the house to an alcove under a stair. She got her hands on an emergency lantern just as the lights went out altogether, and turned it on with relief. It was shaped like a candle, and the light at its tip even acted like flame, bending and wavering and casting swooping shadows; but the light was cold.

She stood cupping the light as if it were a real candle, and listened to the rumor of the wind. The air was cooler in the storm, and she shivered, but not with cold; there was a primeval strength to winds like this which demanded notice. And she remembered, fishing it from a dialogue on a long summer day far off on Earth, the reason power was cut off and ordinary pursuits put aside during storms like this. It was not (as Theo had thought) a necessity or even a precaution, but a ritual. In some households there would be talk of the Master's hand, and the younglings would be instructed by the storm. In others there would be no talk—but everyone would stop, and acknowledge the wind and the flood.

She went slowly to the room where Michael was, thinking that perhaps he would be watching the storm, too, his eyes clear with fascination. And she found him in a room adjoining the veranda, and the wide doors were open so that the tumult of the storm came in on a spray of rain; but he was asleep, and did not see any of it. He lay just outside the range of the spray on a lounge that was poorly formed for the human body, so that he sprawled across it like a broken child. There was a music cube at his head, and Hanna came near and heard a shout of summer and sunlight. But outside the night was pitch-dark, and she did not see but heard the thrashing of the garden trees.

Henrik sat in a corner on a pile of rugs. He had been watching Michael in the dark.

Hanna knew it; she was revolted. There had been a change in Henrik, as if the moment of violence the day before had waked him from a deep sleep. His new attention was fixed on Michael, and it was inimical.

She sat down at Michael's head as if to shield him from Gaaf's eyes with her body and her light. Patches of the sky lit up from time to time with lightning, and were followed by rumbles of thunder from other places in the city.

Her tension increased. But it was not because of the storm; it was because of Henrik.

Does he think I can't feel his hatred? What if he tries to do something about it?

And if she could see into his head a little? She ought not make the attempt. *Ought* not: a social prohibition against the invasion of the ultimate fortress of privacy. But it was a prohibition that had ceased to trouble Hanna much in these last years, and she might never have so good an opportunity. There was no one near to distract her, and Michael slept deeply. She put her free hand on his forehead and he did not feel it.

And so she made her mind empty in something that was kin to the satya trance, though not so complete or difficult; she made herself hollow, a gong that would resonate to whatever touched it. First the room and then the wind and rain became remote, and she entered a shell of silence; and into this focusing of perception she admitted the point of life that was Henrik.

Thus it was that as the storm thundered on she saw herself, and what poor Henrik thought of her: not much. She was hardly present in his head at all. She was tiny in the map he had made of the world, an appendage to something larger than life that loomed like a threat. It was powerful, detestable, and malignant. It was Michael.

Somewhere far outside the trance she was horrified. Inside it, cool logic operated. It said that under the blankness of the past weeks, an obsession had grown in Gaaf. The burden of uncounted humiliations, the weight of his life, must have a focus; and here, where humankind was concentrated in a handful of personalities, here in a place he did not want to acknowledge as real, Michael had become the focus.

She ceased to hear the storm. Without emotion and therefore unrecognized by Gaaf, she slipped through the perpetual panic of his thought.

Fortune's favored child: that was how he saw Michael. Had Hanna been herself she might have laughed, though bitterly. *How is that?* she asked, but he thought the question came from inside himself, so skillful was Hanna and so (still) befuddled was Gaaf, and inexperienced in this way of communication; so he answered, and he answered with envy.

She murmured agreement in Gaaf's brain. *He has so much . . .* But she could not have done it if she had not made herself an echo.

The women and the money, the money and the women . . .

There was not much distinction between the two. In Gaaf's eyes they fell into Michael's hands, into his arms, coins and great gouts of credit, a procession of women who offered themselves like shameless animals—

Somewhere outside the half-trance Hanna laughed to herself. Had she been that bad about it? No doubt.

He will pay for it! Gaaf said (he supposed) to himself, with such clarity and certainty that Hanna for an instant lost control, and heard the storm again, and the shadow in the corner stirred, alerted.

Outside the trance she was deeply alarmed. But she could not afford alarm; if Gaaf felt it, even he would know what she was doing. She wrapped herself in trance like a shield of silence, purposeful and irresistible. She engaged in no casual inquiry now. It was essential to find out what Henrik meant by his smug conviction. And she crept up on him as stealthily as if it meant Michael's life; as it might, if the satisfaction she had read in Gaaf, the sureness of coming revenge, had a foundation in fact.

. . . satisfying! she breathed in the corners of his mind, a vengeful echo.

He gloated: *They will take him away.*

And, . . . *power!* Hanna purred, catching at the knowledge of power in his hand, and there were quick little flashes of events and the burden of all that power:

Michael looking at bright alien coins in his hand, talking of pain.

Michael on his knees, begging.

For what?

The answer was an image of distance and utter isolation.

And I have it! Gaaf thought, triumphant, and she saw that he had something, she even felt it as he felt in his pocket.

And its name? said the echo in his head, his own thought (he believed), and he answered, thought the word, said it, even said it half–out loud.

She pulled out of him then, wrenching herself away from trance. As soon as she did, her stomach revolted; she put her head on her knees to keep from being sick. When she looked up, Gaaf was upright and staring at her. Suspecting. In fact he should know perfectly well what she had done; only he could not believe it.

She ignored him. She turned to Michael and touched him until he woke. He smiled at her as he always did when he woke and found her there.

It did not seem to Hanna that what she had learned could be of any significance, yet it seemed so important to Gaaf, this thing Michael had begged for and Gaaf had withheld. She said hesitantly, even shyly, because she felt ridiculous, "Does the name 'Gadrah' mean anything to you?"

He almost fainted.

When she told him about the module, he took it away from Gaaf. Gaaf resisted, desperate. Hanna was paralyzed with his fury, his fear, her own confusion. She did not recognize Michael. He had gone into shock, the man she knew, and come out someone else. His shadow leapt on the ceiling as he moved on Gaaf. Hanna was afraid he would kill, though this was not what she had seen before, the passion to hurt, he was only consumed by a single goal; but he might kill to get it. She called to him out loud and in thought and he did not hear, she clutched his arm and he flung her away, she had dropped the light, could see nothing, the tumult in the corner was a melee of violence and noise. But all the noise was Gaaf's. Michael did not utter a sound.

He had what he wanted and ran out into the storm.

Gaaf was conscious and essentially unhurt. Hanna did not waste time with him. She picked herself off the floor where Michael had thrown her and ran after him, pursued by a blast of hatred from Gaaf. The wind hit her like a wall when she came onto the veranda. *Hurricane!* she thought, staggering backward, but it was only a gust, and she got back the breath the wind had taken, and pushed away from the house.

She did not think about where to go, she ran without thinking. But when she rounded a corner against the wind, and struck off without thought down a path slippery with rain that led to the street, she knew what her destination was, what Michael's must be: *GeeGee.*

As soon as she knew it, she lost her head. Michael would lift off, he would be gone, no one would know where he had gone and she would never see him again. She could not even keep up with him, much less catch up; sheer weight made a difference in this storm, where the wind shoved her backward and knocked her from side to side. She called his name, but the wind blew it away, so she cried out to him in thought, too. Her feet slipped on the tiles of the path and she fell with a splash; it did not matter, she had been soaked as soon as she got to the door, and now the wind whipped her dripping hair against her face with a force that stung.

The street was not quite dark. Its margins were edged with lines of light which the curbs took up in daylight and released at night. But nothing moved in the street except water, which made it a stream.

Hopeless, hopeless— The wind slackened and she ran more easily, though there were gusts that unbalanced her. She put her head down and threw herself against it. *Hopeless—* She would (beginning to think again) go back. She would call that Emergency Contact Locus and somehow get through to Norsa. There were guards around *GeeGee* and he would see to it that they would not let Michael board.

The wind blew her around a corner and she bumped head-on into Michael.

She wrapped her arms around his neck and pushed against him as if she could merge her body into his.

"What the hell do you think you're doing!" He shouted into her ear. "I was coming back. I heard you. I felt you fall, I was afraid you'd get hurt."

"Oh yes yes yes," Hanna said, not interested in anything but holding him. He looked around; he had to lift his head to do it, and she clutched him. "Come here," he said. She seized his hand as hard as Lise ever had, and he led her to a wall she had not seen in the dark. There was a gate in it. He struggled with it in the wind, got it open, pulled her through it, and crouched with her in the shelter of the wall. It was cold and black, the rain streamed down the wall and down their backs, and the wind still pulled at them, but it was no longer like being beaten.

Michael tried to speak and Hanna interrupted.

"How could you! How could you do that to Henrik? How could you do this to *me*? You can't run away, I won't let you, you're *mine*—!"

She was seized with a possessiveness she had not known was in her. At some time when she was not looking, it had become a law of nature that Michael could not leave her. She shouted at him, cried, pounded his chest with her fists. He let her rave, listening seriously until she ran down; by then the water had formed a puddle around them.

Hanna subsided at last into sobs. "You can't!" had become "You won't, will you? Please?" And she knew she had made a spectacle of herself, fallen into a patch of pure hysteria. She was ridiculous—and wet; a marine creature whose tears were lost in the water it breathed.

Michael leaned forward, put his mouth against her ear, and began to talk.

"I wasn't going to leave you. I wasn't going to take off. I just wanted to take it to *GeeGee* and see. I couldn't think of anything else. I heard you call and turned back. I always would. I always will. Don't you know that by now? Listen to me. Listen. I will never leave you. Never."

But there was something in the hand which caressed her; she felt it burn into his palm.

"That's it," she said, "isn't it. The place."

"I don't know."

"But you have to find out."

"Yes."

She had stopped crying. Her anger was gone; the weariness it left behind slowed her speech. "Wait until morning," she said.

"In the morning we go to Ree. We won't come back until the day after tomorrow. Do you think I can wait that long? I'll take you back to the house, and I promise to come back. I solemnly swear it. But I'm going to *GeeGee* tonight."

"I'll go with you."

"I don't think—"

"I will. I will."

GeeGee, having been moved near the city for the travelers' convenience, was not far away as distances went: an hour's pleasant walk. Tonight it would be two hours or more, none of it pleasant. In the last years of Hanna's life she had leapt solar systems with ease. Now all her journeys had come down to this: a few kilometers of hard going in the rain.

"You think that's the place," she said.

"I don't know." He was part of the darkness, indistinguishable. Only his hands proved he was there. They had been quiet on Hanna's shoulders, but suddenly they were restless, brushing water from her hair, wiping it from her face; they felt for her substance in the dark.

"What else do you think it could be?"

"I'm afraid to think."

"Does Henrik know?"

"Maybe. Hanna, I don't know anything!"

"Let's go back and ask him," she said craftily.

"No. Why? When we can plug it into *GeeGee* and see?"

She gave up. "I always liked walking in the rain," she said.

The irony was lost on him. "All right. Hold tight to my arm. If the lightning comes too close, we'll lie low in a ditch."

"And drown!"

"C'mon," he said.

◆

The wind and rain diminished, though there were periods when the downpour was as hard as ever. The lightning stayed far away. Once Hanna looked toward the city and saw it strike repeatedly at the top of one of the great towers. The glow rimming the streets was subdued in the rain, and they walked in the middle to avoid the rushing, flooded gutters. Time slowed to an endless moment of wet and cold in which Hanna had leisure to be astounded by her panic. She held to herself the thought, like a magical charm, that her fear had found Michael in the storm, that it had broken through the armor of his obsession and that he had turned back, desiring her safety more than this other thing he wanted. But still he had surprised her again. Nothing she knew about him had prepared her for the unforgiving passion he had shown Gaaf. And she was afraid of where it could take him next.

Toward midnight they reached the *Golden Girl*. There were no guards around *GeeGee* after all. But they appeared as soon as Hanna and Michael came into the welcome, familiar dryness, where even the lights were the color of an old friend; they came running from somewhere inside and stopped in consternation when they saw the humans.

Hanna said to them understandingly, "Indeed it is a very wet night."

"Very," agreed their captain. He raised a hand and with great dignity led his crew out to their proper posts; not without some regretful looks backward.

Control had an abandoned look. Michael sat in the master's place, which had been his until Hanna's greater skill supplanted him. In the last hour Hanna had felt a great purposefulness crystallize in him, and he had hardly been aware of her company. Yet above all there was a great restraint. He did not know what he had, and kept speculation to himself.

He slipped the module into a notch and told *GeeGee*: "Read and store." His face and voice were blank. They waited, Hanna as still as Michael. It seemed to be a very long time before *GeeGee* said, "Done."

"What is it?" Michael asked.

"A course in standard format," *GeeGee* said indifferently.

"What's the destination? Compare with what you've got in memory."

This time the pause was unquestionably very long. At the end of it *GeeGee* said, "The destination is not in my memory."

Michael said so quietly that Hanna scarcely heard him,

"Give me a schematic." But *GeeGee* said, "I cannot produce visual data from this source. Terminal point lies outside my visual matrix."

Hanna said, "We can get a projection." She leaned over Michael's shoulder, pulled a keyboard into position, and slowly, stopping often to consult *GeeGee*, entered a series of commands. She scaled the display so that *GeeGee*'s terminal course referent would be at one side and the unknown destination at the other, and instructed *GeeGee* to superimpose the whole on a map of whatever lay between. The map ought to be accurate enough; it was based on centuries of observation, even though no one had gone out there to look first hand.

The picture that finally came was a fantasy. The prime referent at the left of the screen was Heartworld, but the star at the other edge was, by *GeeGee*'s scale, fully five hundred light-years away. Hanna did not have to ask *GeeGee* to know what that meant. That was unexplored space out there. No one had gone there, not ever—or so all the records said. But here was a course, plain and straight.

Michael did not move. His hair and clothes were partially dry, but only partly, so that he looked half finished. He was very pale and he looked—Hanna blinked at him—terrified.

"But what is it?" she said.

He said, "That's Gadrah." His voice cracked on the second word. He put his head down on the console so she could not see his face.

They spent what was left of the night on the *Golden Girl*. Michael did not sleep. He lay on the bed in his old room and stared upward as if he would see some kind of path emblazoned in the tracery of leaves at the top of the room. Hanna slept, but fitfully. Each time she woke it was with a start, and with heavier eyes. Once she said when she woke, "You didn't believe it existed, did you?"

That was what he had been thinking about. He was used to Hanna; he was not even surprised.

He said, "That's not quite it. I believed it existed, but somehow it wasn't real. Not if nobody else thought it was."

"Except him."

"B. Yes."

"That's really why you needed to find him," she said. This time she did not sound like an oracle, but she might have been the model for one, with her tousled hair and pale cheeks and sleep-haunted eyes.

"It seemed like a good idea at the time," Michael said. He could not interpret her expression. She rolled over and slept again.

Fantasies. They got in the way on Alta, between him and his schooling. Not at first. At first there were only the nightmares, dreadful dreams of noise and screaming and flame, and then, like their extension, the only life he could remember with certainty: the endless time with B, its passing divided into the times when he was locked into a room by himself, and locked into it with B. And the first clear memory that came later was of the Post, and it was no fit medium for fantasy. He would not wish to go there, to that stone-guarded place. Then he remembered a little more, not clearly, without definition. And thought—dreaming over his lessons, washed with sweetness, awash in longing—*When I grow up I will go there.* "There" was a dreambrew of mountains and meadows far from the Post. They would be clean and safe, as they had been before some great event which he thought of one day, inexplicably, as "the relocation." And then—

But he had never gone on from "and then." He only dreamed of the sweet-scented meadows, as if, once there, he could get back everything else still hidden in cloud.

"That's nice," said Hanna, meaning the meadows. He had not known she was awake. "I didn't know there was anything good," she said.

"There was. Before they noticed us."

"Who were 'they'? Who were 'us'?"

"It was so quiet," he said softly, he remembered that, a piece of memory painfully retrieved. He showed her more pieces. "They must have let us alone for a long time, a generation at least. There was music."

"A village." She put a name to something taken from his thought.

"Primitive. But the summers. Oh, the summers!"

The deep shadows of the forest. The cold spray of water on hot days cascading down living rock.

They lay together thinking about summer until Hanna

fell asleep again. She nearly pulled him down into it with her.

Flight. From the truth of what it was, forever out of reach. From Alta. From poverty. From memory. From himself.

"But you did stop," Hanna said drowsily.

"No." The quiet space on *GeeGee* was a world in itself, removed from every place he had ever been. Even time stopped in it. "I kept moving farther and farther out of Shoreground," he said. "I worked harder than I had to, for a long time. Thinking it would make a miracle happen."

"What miracle?"

"I didn't know."

"No miracles," Hanna said, and fell asleep.

After a while he answered her anyway. "No miracles."

Compulsion. The history of the Explosion was a nice hobby for an amateur scholar. He even went to all the places it could possibly be. As a dilettante; so he said.

Then a woman named Hanna ril-Koroth met the People of Zeig-Daru. It was an important meeting. But for Michael all its importance lay in the history of the People, who had once-upon-a-time destroyed a human colony of which humans had no record. Always in his search he had rejected speculation, though rumors of Lost Worlds circled his head like bees as he studied the history of colonization. He had not heeded the tales, fixed on what he thought was real. Until Hanna came back, was carried back, in pieces, talking of lost worlds. Then finally he knew, clearly as if he had always known: no study of what was known would show him what he sought.

And he dragged from his memory a memory of dark night skies. A few dim lanterns of stars shone sparsely in it; they were either very close or very hot. Somewhere in the dust was a Sol-type star with the world he knew going around it. And he went back to the history of the Explosion, and turned his attention to the ships that had disappeared, the shiploads of emigrants cheated or unlucky or otherwise lost in oblivion.

That was all he had meant to do, but control passed out of his hands. There were the first steps of the search for B. The narrowed vision, the subtle changes in his life, like buying *GeeGee,* that meant more than he knew at the time. It was only in the end that it crystallized.

"I wonder you stayed sane," Hanna said.

"Did I stay sane?"

Hanna sat up once more. She said, "Do you know what you are? There's a toy. I've seen it on D'neera, I've seen it in the Polity, I've seen it on F'thal and even on Girritt. It's a little thing with a round bottom. On top there's a torso of a human being or a F'thalian or a Girrian. The bottom's weighted, and every time you give it a push it falls over and then, because the bottom's round, you see, and heavy, it jumps right back up again. That's what you are."

It was not a flattering image, but he took the sense and let go of the picture.

"But is that sane?" he said.

"I don't know."

She slept some more.

Reality.

Hanna woke up for good.

"What are you going to do?" she said.

"Why, go there, of course. Do you need to ask? You already thought of that, earlier tonight."

"But that's only because I was so afraid that's what you would do," Hanna said. She was even paler now. She was not hysterical this time; but he saw that she was, again, afraid.

Norsa fished them out of the *Golden Girl* in the gray morning, complaining mildly because they had not been where they were supposed to be at the appointed time. Outside *GeeGee* the day was dim and everything was wet. It was not raining, but the clouds had turned the morning into dusk. Hanna was very tired, the tiresome morning a dream which felt as if it could turn into a nightmare in a moment. Everything she saw seemed new, even before they departed from the City of the Center. The identical towers seemed—not only inhuman, the nonhuman did not trouble her—but inhumane. The wet streets had a sullen look. Insignificant details sprang to her eyes: a flaw in the paving, a wind-battered flower. The field from which they would begin their journey was a wasteland made for machinery.

They rose through the clouds and flew over their white billows, up in the sunlight Ell would not see for days, and sped toward the northwest. It was a flight of several hours, and Michael spent it looking absently toward the clouds, or toward Hanna and Norsa, but not as if he saw anything. He did not speak. He was silent as Henrik Gaaf had been for so long.

After the flight, and after a further journey made in a Foresters Guild vehicle, and after, finally, a long, wet walk under great green umbrellas, they came to the Scarlet Glades. "Behold the Red Forest!" Norsa said.

Hanna looked and looked again, but saw no Red Forest. They were surrounded by tall trees that did indeed resemble gigantic plumes, but their color was predominantly bronze-green; and though the color shaded at the edges toward red, the place did not look like anything Hanna had seen in Awnlee's thought.

She said, "Norsa, are you sure this is the correct site?"

"I fear Awnlee exaggerated," he said.

"Beyond doubt . . ." Under other circumstances Hanna might have laughed. Now it was all she could do to arrange her face in a facsimile of a smile.

She said, "Awnlee told me there were ruminants large as my house. I suppose the ruminants also are somewhat smaller than he gave me to believe."

"I do not know," Norsa confessed, "because I cannot comprehend what was in his mind. Thus may expectation outpace reality!"

"You do not know how truly you speak," Hanna said, staring at Michael. He did not even hear her.

They left after staying only a little while. Just before they passed out of the forest glade, Hanna turned once more. The glades had not gotten their name without a reason. She pictured the place in sunlight, early in the morning or at sundown, when the light was rich and the bronze leaves came to life. It would not take much imagination to infuse the scene with cinnabar and see all it was in red. That was what Awnlee had chosen to do, and how he had chosen to remember it; and so he had made Hanna a gift of his imagination, and with it, beauty.

"Farewell," she said softly, and Michael finally turned his head, drawn from his preoccupation. But she had said the word for her friend Awnlee. She had no intention at all of saying it to Michael.

*   *   *

It was necessary to exchange courtesies with a committee of the Foresters Guild, and after that they went to a lodge where they were to spend the night, first dining with the committee. Michael was entranced, and smiled at things no one else could see. *A sun shone, and flowers shone at night like the light-storing alloys of Uskos, brighter than the flares of meteorites. Iridescent winged creatures no bigger than his thumb flew to perch on his hand and peer at him with faceted eyes, their fine scales light and dry to the touch. The sound of running water filled the nights, and with it music: an old man with a bow. The voices in the next room talked until he fell asleep, and steered him through shoals of dream.*

He scarcely touched his meal. When the persons of the committee departed, he sat over wine with Hanna and Norsa and heard the rain fall. Few visitors came here during the rains, and except for a reduced staff, the travelers from Ell had the lodge to themselves. The refectory was brightly lit, but there were also festive candles, and Hanna had the other lights extinguished so that they sat in the mellow candlelight. Michael watched Hanna and thought: *How beautiful she is.*

When all the correct formalities had been observed, she spoke his name and he followed her to a sleeping room. Once inside, she began to talk to him. She used Standard words and Ellsian, she used terms he had come to recognize as Girrian and F'thalian, and they meant in their various modes the same things: treasure of my soul, thou finest-furred darling, mate desired above all inferiors, more beloved than self; and she called him by his name: *Mikhail.*

"Wait, oh, wait!" she said.

"I will not wait."

She had an unfair advantage if she chose to use it. If she was afraid for him, angry with him, afraid for herself without him, she could batter him with raw emotion and force him to suffer with her. She did not do it, and all he could think was: *How beautiful she is.*

"You have always done everything alone." She had reduced the light here, too, to candlelight, and shadows were caught in her hair. Trickles of water reflected the flickering light, and flame ran down the windowpanes.

"You do not have to do this alone," she said. "You must not."

"If the others want to come, they can."

"I don't mean that. Mikhail, there is a time and place for governments. Don't think of going alone. Wait for the Polity. They'll go at once, and how could they go without you? They'll need you. And you'll have all your wishes that way. Those people, the ones you called 'they,' who did terrible things—they'll be brought down. All your pain will be revenged. Don't you understand that things must have been as they were because of isolation? When the isolation ends, there'll be light there. It will be a new age. Only be patient, a little patient. Wait. Wait with me, and we'll go together."

The logic could not be argued. "I'm going all the same," he said, "whether the rest of you do or not."

"It's you I don't want going there. Not like this. I would do it a different way. A better way. This is a world, Michael! A whole world, a strange one! How do you think you can have it on your terms? You need authority at your back."

He did not know what she was talking about. She watched him try to understand it. But something had been left out of him, or maybe taken out, and he could not understand. Authority was only something to be gotten over or around or past, a part of the environment, to be dealt with when necessary and otherwise ignored: a concrete, null-value thing, not an abstraction, and certainly disconnected from justice. Once he had told her that Alta had seemed like an alien planet with strange gods. So it was, she now saw, with every place. She would never have to wonder how it happened that Michael had moved easily among aliens in these weeks. He had been among aliens all his life.

She came close and touched him. The shadows round her eyes were dark in the candlelight; she looked bruised.

"Is this how you were in the years before?"

"How I was . . . ?"

"Fixed. Immovable."

He looked at her without comprehension.

"Stubborn!" she said.

"I don't know . . ."

It seemed odd that Hanna who understood so much should not understand that all considerations were irrelevant beside the course in the module next to his skin; that on the threshold of this last journey, for the first time in his conscious memory, the sense of being in flight had left him. He would stand here and listen to her all night, if that was what she wanted, but it would not make any difference.

She saw that finally. Her hands fell away from him. She looked up at him from those shadowed eyes and he said, "It will be all right."

"It won't."

"You don't have to come."

"Do you want me to?"

"No. It could be dangerous," he said with no sense of incongruity, and her mouth tightened; but whatever the temptation might have been, she did not let him feel her anger.

"Is there nothing I can do to bring you to your senses?"

He considered the question carefully and answered, "No."

She did not talk to him any more. She blew out the candles and they undressed in the dark, silently. Angry or not, she turned to to him with caresses, and maybe that was supposed to remind him in another way that he need not go by solitary ways any longer; but the dreams were too strong, he could not accomplish the act of love, and though Hanna stayed beside him through the night, he was alone.

She had to tell Norsa that they were going away. It took a long time, and it was evident to Norsa (Hanna did not try to hide it) that she did not want to start on this journey. They sat together in the Scarlet Glades and he made her a remarkable proposal.

"At one time," he said, "upon your arrival, yours and that of your companions, you said to me that 'Unans must appear to have little regard for law; and to support that statement, you adduced the actions of yourself and your companions up to that time. Yet you told me also that 'Unans have a great impulse toward law. And it seems to me that what your companion Nikell now proposes, though not (as clearly as I can determine) unlawful, does not fall precisely within the bounds of law. Is it for this reason you have distress? For I have come to know you well in the fine days of our association, and it seems to me that in yourself, at least, there is great respect for law."

She answered, "Indeed, Norsa, I believe that what you

have said of me is correct; and in regard to my companion
Michael, it is not so much that he rejects law, as that he acknowledges none. In these last many years he has had no
conflict with law, except as he nearly became its victim,
which is why, as you know, we are here; for except in that
matter only, the goodness of his heart protected him. Yet it
is not law I now fear, but folly. In this matter I would seek
the protection of law and the civilization of humans; yet just
as this human does not consider law's constraint, equally he
does not seek its protection. Therefore he goes forth, I fear,
to great peril, and I cannot restrain him."

Norsa's answer was rash, but its source was the pure impulse of friendship.

"It is possible that he could be restrained, and made to
wait until the other 'Unans arrive."

"Restrained?" she said, faltering.

"Immediately, at your word. You are kin to the citizens
of Ell, and like us a citizen. He is not, however precious he
is to you. If that is what you wish . . ."

After a long pause she said, "No. I have deep gratitude,
Norsa, but I cannot do that. That betrayal would destroy the
affection between us, between Michael and myself, forever."

"Yet you fear for his life, and there can be no greater
destroyer of affection than death, which is the end of all
sharing and exchange."

"That is correct, Norsa. And yet," she said more firmly, "I
cannot do it. I could do it if I knew his death awaited at the
end of this path, but I do not know that. I do not know the
future. And so I can only seek to persuade. I will not exert
force."

"I judge that you choose rightly," Norsa said, "though I
share your concern, and always will share it until I know
that you are safe. For surely you know the story of the Journey of Nlatee, wherein great benefit came to Uskos, though
Nlatee was disobedient and followed a discouraged path."

"Then why did you give me such an offer?"

"It is necessary at times to choose between friendship
and right, and right is not always the correct choice. Likewise, in a matter of affection, as between sire and selfing,
some small betrayal may be useful, where a greater runs
only counter to the desired end."

Norsa's cilia and fingers had stopped moving; even his eyes were still. Hanna eyed him cautiously and said, "I do not know your meaning, Norsa. But it is impossible for me to plan betrayal, however small it may be, at least plan betrayal that must remain secret. I could not, in the long term, hide anything from Michael. I am a telepath, he is accustomed to my free exercise of that faculty, and I could not refrain from the use of it, even if I wished, without his knowledge of my withdrawing. And then I would have to speak truth to him in any case, or watch affection die as surely as in the other instances we have discussed."

"Yet there may be a course around this obstacle, if you wish the aid of a friend, even though you do not know until the moment it shows itself what it is."

"Indeed such aid could be of the greatest value," Hanna said.

"That is all I wished to know. Let us speak of it no more, lest you see what I contemplate without even desiring to see it, as I know sometimes occurs. Instead we will talk of leavetaking, which I know must be soon; yet I, too, shall have many answers to produce both for the populace and its leaders, who do not expect this departure."

As soon as they returned to the city, the objects brought from the *Golden Girl* began to march back to the ship in a steady stream. Theo and Lise and Shen would follow Michael anywhere, but it became necessary to deal with Henrik Gaaf, who might have some useful knowledge of Gadrah. Gaaf had been wandering somewhere when Hanna and Michael returned, and he came into the house to find all the common rooms turned upside down as the others ferreted for personal possessions that seemed, now that they had to be collected, to be everywhere.

Hanna had asked Michael, "How are you going to get Henrik onto *GeeGee*?"

"Any way I have to," he had said. And she was present when Gaaf joined them in the room just off the veranda. This room, spacious and tiled, had remained cool even on the hottest days, and it had been a favorite place for all of them. Now the tiles were dirty with the water they tracked in and out, the baggy lounges looked deflated, and scraps of their summer lives lay everywhere.

Henrik blinked at them and licked his lips. He said, "What are you doing?"

"Leaving," Michael said. He juggled a pair of music cubes and looked at Gaaf dispassionately.

Henrik focused sharply on Michael. He had given up all pretense of vacuity since Hanna's dissection of his brain. "Where to?" he said.

"Where do you think?" Michael said, not unkindly.

Hanna was near the door with Theo; she had been helping him guide a pallet loaded with foodstuffs toward the veranda. She stopped to watch. She did not see the necessity of abducting Gaaf and strongly disapproved.

Gaaf's eyes flickered in her direction. Whatever confidence he had once placed in her was gone, but still he thought of her vaguely as more sympathetic than Michael. He thought about what Michael had said. He knew the answer, but what he said next was what he wanted to hear.

"You're going back to the Polity?"

"No." Michael drifted nearer, relaxed, unthreatening. Gaaf backed away anyway. Theo moved silently into position behind him, something in his hand; now Hanna knew what would happen.

Michael said, "Will you come with us? I need to know what you know. Everything about the man you call Castillo, everything about the men with him. They'll be there. We might have to do something about them."

"No." Gaaf backed up some more, just beginning to grasp it, and torn. The prospect of remaining on Uskos, alone among the aliens, was dreadful. But Gadrah was no better, and Castillo was there.

Michael nodded to Theo, and Theo put one hand on Gaaf's shoulder and jabbed at his back with the other. Gaaf jerked, started to protest, and went down, Theo breaking his fall.

Hanna said quietly, "You didn't try very hard to persuade him."

"Would it have worked?"

She shrugged, chilled. She wondered how safe it would be to defy Michael now — how safe it would be even for her.

They took Henrik to *GeeGee* on a pallet already loaded with bedding, and put him away in the mirrored room

Hanna had once occupied. She sat with him for a time. Just before *GeeGee* took off, Shen looked in, saw Hanna's gloomy face, and said, "You expected something else?"

"What?"

"Just like a man. Thought you'd know."

"What?"

"How they are. Not practical," Shen said, and walked out with no consciousness of having said anything surprising at all.

Chapter 6

When the journey had barely begun, Hanna said to Michael, "What is your plan?"

"How can there be a plan," he said, "when we don't know what's waiting?"

He waited for her answer, laughing at her, expecting a diatribe.

She said frigidly, "We could improve the odds."

He stopped laughing. "I wouldn't object to that."

"Tell us what we're going to. How much do Shen and Theo know? I don't know anything. Teach us geography. Tell us about the culture. You know what to expect. I don't. Teach us the language."

"I don't know it," he said. He was ice. He had gotten there from mirth in half a minute.

She said, "How much do you remember?"

"Not much. I think you know already everything, everything I remember." It was becoming difficult for him to talk. "The end is the only thing that's clear. Before that, I lost nearly everything before that. I don't know why. There were things I remembered later, little things, that I saw like pictures. But I don't know how they fit together. What came in between is gone. I—don't—have—"

Hanna passed her hands over her hair, self-soothing. Life in a broken mirror, shattered and refracted—

"—it clear," he was saying. "Nothing logical, nothing to teach—not any of what you'd call facts. Half of what I think I know, I think I made up. I was Lise's age when they took me away. Maybe younger. It was thirty years ago. The language—nothing. Not a word."

Her hands settled on her chest, to ease the constriction

round her heart. So they were not only going to Gadrah in defiance of sane judgment, they were going without anyone who knew anything about the place, not even Michael, unless Henrik did.

She said, "It's all there."

"I don't know what you mean . . ." He had turned away.

"Everything gets stored," she said. "No memory is completely lost. D'neeran mindhealers are trained to retrieve what seems forgotten. I myself, when it was necessary to find what I knew about the People of Zeig-Daru that I did not remember, was linked with a healer. It didn't work—but that's because the People are—different. And had done certain things no human had heard of, to ensure it wouldn't work. Otherwise I have never known it to fail."

"There are no healers here."

"I'm not a healer. But I'm an Adept, as a healer must be."

"Meaning?"

"It's the trance that makes it possible."

She had told him about the satya trance, how she had used it on the *Avalon*. Slowly he looked around. "A useful thing, that trance . . ."

His voice was low and rough. He was shaken with hope.

"I could take you into it with me. Do you want to do it?"

He was silent for some time. Hanna did not press him. She knew that between the moment of decision and the moment of action, it was sometimes necessary to stand for a little on the brink, to possess for a minute longer the freedom to retreat.

He said, "When can we start?"

They lay on Michael's bed, side by side and relaxed. The room was almost dark.

They had not said anything since taking this position. From that point onward Michael had been more vividly aware of Hanna's personality than at any time before. There had been telepathic contacts like this every day, but they had been fleeting, like a word or a touch or a smile. Now it was as though she uncovered a hidden light. He had thought it would feel like a current flowing between them, but it did not. It was not even like Hanna's hallucinations. Those had been full of movement, rapid changes, a kaleidoscope of memories; this was very still. The only word he could think of to describe it was *there-ness,* and what was there was Hanna.

He knew she had begun to enter the trance, though in an odd way, as if it were not a goal to be reached but already in existence, needing only to be acknowledged; as if getting to it were not a matter of trying, but the relinquishing of effort.

It did not seem very potent. It did not seem strong enough to draw him back through the years, past the barrier of darkness. But suggestions flowed from Hanna, instructions to let go, to float, to drift back and back . . .

We will begin at the ending . . .

Even in trance, he revolted.

Let go. Let go. The beginning, then. Back. Back. And look. What do you see?

The meadow was misty with the distance of years. But flowers grew in it.

Focus.

White flowers. The stamens brushed with velvety gold, petals defined by lines finer than a hair in pink shading to lavender.

And focus.

The soft colors filled his vision. The shapes were new as each heartbeat, older than his life. The plants were tall, their slender stems bending gently in the wind. Long slim serrated leaves, bumpy and a little sticky. *The sap is toxic. I remember.*

Good. Good.

He looked up and the mist was gone. The sky was cloudless, the sun high. Mountains rose to his left, toward the east; westward the land sloped more gently to the valley with its cluster of barns and cottages set on a great stretch of cultivated fields. The vision was clear as the crystalline air. It was real, and surrounded him; the taste of herbal wine filled his mouth. The smell, the dazzling sunlight of a summer day that would never end as long as Michael lived, thrust at him and wounded him; even before the scene was fully formed he sank to his knees on the turf, clutching his belly with a crazy conviction that he had been opened and his insides would fall out. Hanna's soft hands held him together until the transition was over. The feeling passed. He sighed and lifted his eyes to the summer.

"A long summer," Hanna said at his side.

"All the summers everyplace else—summer's always seemed short. I know why, now. They were longer here."

"I see," said her thought: impersonal. Remote.

The air was pure, untainted by a few lazy columns of smoke that rose from the valley floor. Down there a broad river meandered across the basin, folding in on itself in convoluted curves, but the meadow was so high that the forest stretched out on every side looked, from this altitude, more like thick bumpy fabric on the cushions of the mountains, or like thick moss, than what it was.

He said, remembering, "I used to think, if you could jump off the mountain, you'd bounce." And he looked at his shadow and it shrank, because for a moment he was a boy.

Hanna turned for the valley. He followed, not walking so much as floating. At the top of the first steep slope, he paused. The desire to stay in the radiant meadow, where it was safe, was almost unconquerable.

Hanna waited for him at the edge of the meadow. She did not speak or even make a gesture of encouragement. He waited in suspense to find out what he would decide. Then he slipped over the edge.

The end of the meadow turned precipitously into an acute drop, and they slid and scrambled down and down into the forest. The world changed. The trees which had looked to be all of a piece were individuals now. He had not seen trees like them anywhere else. The stems did not grow to great girth, and the branches were sinuous arms that reached for the sky and, through each day, stretched toward the sun in its path, so that in the morning all the forest seemed to lean one way, and in the evening another

Down and down he went, Hanna following easily. What difficulties could there be in this journey they made only in thought? Yet the descent was a strange blend of past and present. There were drops that had been heart-stopping thrills for a boy, and he felt the ghost of that old challenge when he took them, but now they scarcely stretched his long legs. At steppingstone rocks across a chattering stream he stopped to gauge the leap—and then walked over, crossing the gap easily, accepting adulthood and the passage of years, even though nothing had changed. Invisible bird-things called in the quiet of the day. That was the only sound; there was not even wind to stir the trees, and nothing made by man crossed the sky. He took Hanna along trails made by wild things near the little stream, and the trails were just as they had been thirty years before. The peace of the place sank into him. It might have been the morning of creation here, before any strife or evil was made.

Soon they were close to the foot of the mountain. They could not possibly have come so far so rapidly. But trance-time was not realtime.

From a rock ledge they looked down on a pool in the stream, the first pool of any size they had seen. Michael dropped cross-legged on the ledge and smiled at the water. He said, "It's good to swim in. But cold!"

They stayed by the water for a long time. The sun did not move. *A useful thing, that trance.* The music of the invisible birds blended with the song of the water, and never altered. Hanna noticed; she said, "It doesn't change because it's not real. None of this is real."

"It's real somewhere."

"In you."

"It's always been there," he said, smiling. He was back where all smiles had begun.

Hanna said, "We must move on to the village."

There was a burst of cold wind. He said quickly, "No. We can't. It's a long way. I'm tired."

She said objectively, "That is a lie. You half-know yourself that you lie. You are not tired."

He said after a pause, "I'm afraid."

"That is the truth."

Without warning it was twilight. The shadows under the trees were impenetrable; the bird-things stopped singing, and there were ominous rustles deep in the wood. He looked downstream, steeling himself to go on.

Hanna said, "Not today."

"Are you sure?" he said, although he was relieved.

"I'm sure. Hold my hand. We're coming out of it."

Now the star of Uskos was indistinguishable from others in its field. The *Golden Girl*'s journey of some one hundred days was begun. Hanna had taken a longer voyage, she had spent a full year on the exploration ship *Endeavor*; but the *Endeavor* had not covered nearly so great a distance. There was nothing slow and patient about this. *GeeGee*'s course would be essentially parabolic: straight to Omega, where she would veer up and in not toward the heart of human space but toward Heartworld, and not even directly for that world itself but for the equivalent of Omega in that sector, another end-point. Only it was not an end, not for the *Avalon* or for the *Golden Girl* either. Like Omega, the end had become a starting place.

They had come from summer, but all *GeeGee*'s chronometers said bewilderingly that it was midwinter. Midwinter in Standard time, midwinter at Polity Admin —

Hanna stood in Control and looked at the chronometers. She had left Admin more or less at the season she now left Ell, escaping winter once more. Where was Gadrah in its orbit? What would the season be where *GeeGee* landed? Where would she land?

When she asked him, Michael said, "I don't know."

"Do you think there's a landing program included with the course?"

"There isn't. There's orbital compensation based on Standard chronology, though. The usual thing."

"*GeeGee* could work out the year length from that, anyway."

"She did." He smiled up at Hanna's surprised face. "Shen and I did it last night while you were asleep. Jumped the data through every ring we could think of. It's a singleton—"

"What?" The rarity surprised her.

"—and the star's hotter than Sol, but Gadrah's not as far out as you'd expect. The year's only about twice Standard length."

It would make for well defined seasons. Hanna said so.

"They're long, all right. But there's not much axial tilt, and the orbit's more regular than most," he said.

"That would modify the extremes, then. What an odd place, Mike. A singleton? A clear shot in, no gas giants, no big gravity wells, nothing to worry about?"

"But a lot of junk," he said. "A lot of junk! Rocks. Ice. Comets. Lots of comets. There's a warning in the program: most orbits unknown."

"Then how—we can't Jump through it, can we?"

"No. Realspace and radar."

"The best natural defenses I've ever heard of." She was baffled. "Why did they go in in the first place? The original expedition, I mean. Why did they choose that direction, anyhow, when space was open everywhere?"

He leaned back in his place. His brown hands, very dark from the Uskosian sun, rested quietly on the console. He said, "I did a lot of research at one time. I think I know where that expedition originated. I think I know who led it. I know the colonists' names on the manifest—my ancestors' names—but I don't know why they went where they went. The records don't say that."

"You never told me that. Wait."

She was suddenly on overload. She took the seat next to him and put her head down on the console just as he had done a few nights before when Gadrah looked back at him from *GeeGee*'s displays.

"What is it?" he said; a comforting hand touched her back.

She said without lifting her head, "Was this what you were going to try to find on your own? After you left the rest of us on D'neera?"

"Yes. It would have been a disaster. This is one of the regions where I thought it could be, but it wasn't the one I'd picked. I guessed wrong."

"Oh, God."

She kept her face on her folded arms. It would have been a flight with no end, certain death because of the wrong guess. Hanna shivered, and he rubbed her back.

He said, "Maybe I'll find out more there."

"Surely. Yes." She straightened. There was another question. It was enormous; she did not see how she could have overlooked it even for a few days.

She said, "Starr said to me once that if you got to Alta from a Lost World, it couldn't be considered lost. It's not lost. That man knows about it, that B. How?"

"I don't know. I mean to find out."

Stone. Twilight.

The figure at Hanna's side wavered; took courage from

her detachment, and stood firm. The scene became lighter. A dusty, unpaved track wound away among a cluster of structures. All were black in the scanty light, but hardly darker than the sky. Water sounded faintly nearby, a river near at hand, but otherwise the night was silent, with no sound of wind or insect or night-hunting beast. Hanna squinted at the shadowy buildings. They were well made, and did not look as primitive as she had expected them to be. Stone kept them cool in summer, kept the fires' warmth inside in winter. Wells tapped the abundant groundwater. The building stones fit together well, without gaps.

"Craftsmen here," she murmured.

"It was all here before I was born."

He didn't know how he had known that. He sweated with the effort to remember, though there was no heat in the dim light.

"We need light . . . a fire?" she said. "On a hearth?"

"Oh, not fire!"

"All right. All right—"

For an instant it seemed that he vanished. It was not good to let go of trance too quickly, but Hanna did it, falling into the intense, brief confusion that accompanied the wrench. When she came out of that, too, she was leaning over him. She kissed him and lay touching him for a long time. He was calm again. But there was an aching loneliness on the other side of the dark.

She said, "I think remembering is even more important than I thought."

"Why?"

"If you don't do it now, how will it be if you get there and it happens all at once?"

"Oh, but—" He turned his face away from her. It was a gesture she was beginning to know. But he would always turn back again. *Cut out your heart and show it to me,* she would say with each step toward the past. And each time she said it he would wince and turn away. And then turn back, and do it as well as he could. But it was going to take longer than she had thought.

Everything took longer. Hanna had expected Henrik to appear within a day or two, driven by the need for human contact. He did not seem to need it or want it. He slipped out of his room in the middle of *GeeGee*'s nights and raided the galley, usually when Shen was in Control and everyone else was asleep. Hanna ran into him once or twice and he glared at her with hatred. Her liking for him did not increase. In the face of the unexpected difficulty in prying information from Michael, she thought of starting in on Henrik. That would be much simpler than recovering the deeply buried dead. Michael slept poorly, there were bad dreams, he was tired—and they had hardly begun, the trip was only a week old, what would happen to him before the end? Maybe they would have to stop the travels in Michael's mind, maybe the dark years would have to stay dark. If so there would be plenty of time to work on Henrik, to take the practical approach (as Hanna thought of it) to foreknowledge of Gadrah—for she had started to doubt the practicality of what she so cruelly attempted to do with Michael.

Try flowers again. Show me flowers. In the dark, if necessary.

And it was very dark. Twilight here always? Couldn't have been.

It wasn't—

Then he remembered: *Light in the dark like a moon I'd never heard of, never seen—*

Something glimmered at the edge of sight. It waxed brighter and brighter, and exuberant radiance, clumps of light climbing fences, stones, stone walls, exuding a sweet perfume. Flowers. Flowers that shone in the dark.

The wraith beside him asked questions. He didn't know the answers. But his heart trembled with the beauty of the flowers.

"It only happened a few days out of the year. I couldn't have seen it more than a few times."

"Evidently it made an impression."

He felt a great gratitude for her objectivity. It was like having a sound wall at your back. The light of the flowers was cold, and objects near the largest clusters cast shadows.

"Are they cultivated?" said Hanna's wraith.

"In a way. Casually."

Not cut till they go to seed. So they'll grow again. Sometimes we barter the seeds—

"For what?"

"Cloth. Metal. Things we didn't make ourselves—"

A burst of light crawled up the side of the nearest cottage. He looked at it. Hanna took his arm and said, "Home. I know."

He tried to repeat the word, but it died on his tongue. Nonetheless he moved inexorably toward the structure, not walking but effortlessly gliding, as in a dream.

"Where are the people?" she said, but he couldn't think about that.

He tried to stop at the door but slid through it. They were inside. It was very dark.

"Did it happen in the summer?" she asked. "What you said once? When they noticed you?"

"No. It was at the end, the end of—"

Everything: the bronze ceiling of the *Golden Girl* met his eyes, but he plunged back into the dark. There was a shelf ... Here ... He reached upward from habit—habit!—then remembered he was tall. His shadow-hands fell on familiar shapes. An old, old ritual asserted itself. He did not have to think about it.

There was light. Hanna blinked at the small metal lamp in his hands.

"Was that made here?"

"No. No metalworking here. Other places."

"What does it burn?"

"Animal fats."

"How did you light it?"

"Flint."

She was an uncomprehending savage. How did she think you started a fire, anyway?

"Laser matches," she said.

Outside the radius of lamplight the dark was thick. Michael walked into the shadow, hands spilling light. The familiar outlines around him settled into some pattern they had worn into his soul long before, a poignant fit that overpowered for a while the prospect of pain. Hanna wanted information, he could give her some now, while he remembered: "The Post is a twelve-day journey on foot. But at the Post they have machines. They can come here in a day, in the atoes they use."

"Atoes ..."

A picture formed: wheeled vehicles, self-propelled and nearly silent. He had never known how they were powered. Now he guessed, from the vantage of the present. Or the future: "Electric, I think." *Willow manufacture. At Newtown, the Spectator works—*

The prick of astonishment at what his present self knew threatened to balloon. Hanna said, "Don't think about it. Do they have aircraft?"

"I never saw one. No, only one. But it was a spacecraft—"

The light wavered. Something started to grow, snow and fire; he would run. Hanna said, calming him, "The atoes. How many did they have?"

He was silent. She felt the effort he made, and then he answered: "I saw maybe a dozen altogether."

"And the population? And the size of the Post?" she said, because now, she knew, they talked of the Post.

"I don't know—"

"Here, then?" She let him retreat; the village was safer. "Do you know how many people were here?"

"Ninety? Eighty-five?" *Births. A death—*

Instinctively she steered away from the death. "You must have been related to all of them."

"No. I wasn't. Mirrah and Pavah, they used to live somewhere else. They came here to get away—"

The circle of light expanded. They had been pacing through the dark without being able to see anything; now some things were visible. The stone walls had an air of friendliness and safety, the austerity of the interior a grace counterpointing the lush summer outside. The stone was very clean. It had been polished to a warm glow with sand. There were furnishings well made from the region's light wood, each component made of strips bound together for strength. He saw a simple chair with double vision. One: an old friend. Two: a folk artifact, a collector's piece. Rugs braided by dark slender hands. A spray of dried flowers bright in black hair. And here in the deep well of a window cut through stone, a doll, his mother's treasure, the head of crudely glazed ceramic, the body stuffed with rag. And here: the picture she had sewn from colored scraps—

❖

THE MASTER OF CHAOS   691

—borrowed a steel needle from Padma, she'd lost her own. A crowd of tiny figures. "They don't look much like people," I said, teasing her; she was different that spring, soft and round, and bigger day by day. There weren't many children born there, they'd thought I was all they'd have. Now here was another coming. They were happy, and I was, too.

The work pinned in the heavy frame Pavah had made was so bright the colors jumped out. "Look, Mikki, look at the gown this one wears, just like the color of the sky. Oh, if I could make it shiny, like the gown was! If I could show you how it was! And the stones the great lady wore round her neck!"

"Where, Mirrah?"

"At the Post, before you were born."

"I didn't know you'd been to the Post."

Her fingers moved quick and nervous; they were worn, but they looked just like mine. "I don't like to talk about it, Mikki."

"Why?"

She laughed at all my "why's," she always laughed, but she answered when she could. That time she didn't laugh. Her eyes weren't like mine, I had Pavah's eyes, hers were dark, she hid things in them—

It was full night again, this was Hanna at his side, her hand on his arm in reality and in dream. She said softly, "Was Mirrah her name?"

"No. No. It just means, Mother—"

He longed deeply for the *Golden Girl*.

There were voices outside. The people of the place were coming back. But he could not face them yet.

The flute was silent and neglected. Michael slept during much of the day to make up for the sleep he did not get at night. He rarely remembered the dreams that woke him each night, once with a scream. Hanna talked of ending the experiment. It was going too slowly, she said. For every day when she saw a mountainside or a stone house clearly, there were two or three when he could not or would not go farther into the dark, when he stood on the edge of it and the

light would not come and there were no words in the sounds
of the voices there, though he came closer and closer to giving them names, closer to knowing what they said. In the
nights, after the dreams woke him and left him unable to
sleep, he roamed *GeeGee.* Sometimes he met Henrik. He
told Henrik what he knew about their destination, what he
could remember, hoping to jar Henrik into speech. But
Henrik only grunted. There was no doubt that he was sane.
Nor did he seem to be afraid any more. Hanna, when Michael told her about those one-sided conversations, said
Henrik was angry.

"You can tell from what I say?"

"I can tell without that. I feel him sometimes."

"I guess that's better than the way he was. Sometimes
when I talk to him he seems, oh—I don't know. Satisfied."

"Satisfied? Do you tell him how much it hurts to do what
you're doing?"

"I think it shows, when I talk about it."

"So he's satisfied. Because you're suffering?"

"That would be my guess."

"Ugh. Let's stop it. For a while, anyway."

"We're not going fast enough as it is. We could get there
before I remember anything useful."

"Oh, crazy man—!" Hanna did not know she echoed
Shen.

"Not as crazy as I'm likely to get."

"I know. I know. I know."

Hanna did not walk through Michael's memories any more,
she only stood at the edge of them and watched—

—Pavah didn't talk much more than Mirrah did. He had a
smile—I see it in mirrors sometimes. He talked some about
space. Told me the sun was a star, showed me other stars,
what you could see. Said we were on a planet, told me there
were more, with people on them, he said . . .

The night Carmina came, he talked then. Anittas the
midwife shooed us out when the pains got close together.
We both kissed Mirrah before we went and I was scared.
The animals, I'd seen animals get born, this wasn't the same.
And Mirrah who always knew what to do was helpless,

there was no way to stop this, no way to hurry or change it. But she wasn't scared; just busy, working hard.

We went to sit in Firmin's house. Other men kept the vigil, too, while the women stayed with Mirrah. They drank ale, Pavah let me have some, and he and all the others, they treated me different that night, more like a man. Pavah I could tell was listening, I did, too, but you couldn't hear anything through the stone. I didn't listen much to the talk of crops and herds, but after a while they started in on Otto, Otto who slipped away whenever he could to Sutherland where Marlie lived. "Your turn next," they said.

"I remember," Ugo said, "when Otto couldn't see it; couldn't see bringing children into the world. I told him then a girl would change his mind."

"I still don't know it's a good idea," Otto said.

"Maybe not in the east," Firmin said. "Here it's different."

"Only as long as they let us be," Otto said.

"What could they want with us? Some grain sometimes; they're better off letting us alone."

"So far," Pavah said, trying to hear through stone. "No reason to think it'll change. But I didn't like what I saw, when I went east two years ago."

Pavah was what they called the outside man. When there was business with another town, he did it; all the towns had somebody like that. So he usually was the first to get news.

"What did you see?" Abram said. The others all knew, Abram must have known, too, but he was old, sometimes he forgot things, though his fingers never forgot a tune the old fiddle had known. It was there that night between his feet, ready to celebrate.

"Orchards dying, for one thing," Pavah said. "And at Sutherland last summer, Joan, you know, went east to negotiate a new harvest machine. She got it without much need to bargain—because, she said, the blight's spread to the grain, they don't need all the machines they have, there's nothing for them to do."

"It's nothing to do with us," Ugo said. "That's far away."

"They're finally converting," Pavah said. "The native varieties are resistant, that's true. But when the conversion's complete, then what? Native strains follow the seasons, like you'd expect. One crop a year. With the imports they get three. Now they've gone over there's a third as much food. Stockpiles don't last forever. They'll run short. Then what?"

I never heard the answer; there was a stirring at the door and Abram's daughter Padma came in smiling.

"A girl," she said to Pavah. "Pretty as her mother, healthy, too. They're both well."

Pavah's face lit up. "Let's go see your sister, Mikki," he said. We went out, the other men trailed out, too, Abram with his fiddle, and the music followed us to where Mirrah suckled Carmina. She didn't look pretty to me, all purple and squashed! But it was a good night all the same. After a while I went out where the music was and danced, we all danced half the night. We lit a fire for dancing, but later it died, there was light enough from the flowers and the sky was alive, the arc of the Ring looked close enough to touch and the fires Pavah said were burning stones flew from end to end of the sky, even the moons looked solid not just points of light running, running, and Abram made me recite all their names. And before I went to sleep I saw Carmina again, she and Mirrah and Pavah were all asleep together and I thought: when I was born it was like this, too. And now it's all of us together and this funny-looking babe is part of us. I'm somebody's brother. She's their daughter. My sister. Ours.

Remembering was hard work, draining. When something came out of him it stayed out, and not by itself, but surrounded by a net of related memories to be examined one by one. Sometimes they triggered other things, details like electrical shocks. He could begin to sketch an outline for Hanna. The villages like a string of jewels at the base of the mountains—

"—Croft to Dunhill to Sutherland and then south," the peddler said. "Not last year, though. Not last year."

Mirrah hefted a skillet, testing its weight with her fragile wrist. Carmina on her shoulder babbled and peered around with bright bright eyes.

"Where were you last year?"

"East of here. A long way east."

Mirrah laid the skillet in the midsummer dust. She'd heard the new sound in his voice. So had I. Mirrah wasn't going to say any more and I didn't know what to ask. The other women, they were bolder. They got him to say it: Fairfield. He didn't try to hold out, didn't want to—he said: "Fairfield. I was at Fairfield."

It was quieter. The women still handled the cloth and the pots. There was a ring they handed round, it had red stones, Otto came later and bought it for Marlie, for when they married. The women kept looking at the ring. Their minds weren't on it, though. They started to use the kind of talk grown-ups used, not like they didn't want children to understand, it was just that there was so much they didn't have to say, things they knew and kids didn't. They looked grim. Most everybody that day was in the fields, just a few old women were there when the peddler came over the dusty road, not really a road, a dirt track. And Mirrah and me; I'd been sick.

"Fairfield's still there," he said. "But it's not what it was. Half the able-bodied men gone."

"Dead," someone said.

"Who knows? They took them away in the night, the ones they didn't kill on the square the first day—"

"Mikki," Mirrah said, "go look in the cart. Look for the knives."

I didn't want to go, he'd be there a couple of days, there was no hurry.

But Mirrah pushed me away, toward the cart. "You'll be trapping with Pavah, come winter. You'll need a good knife. Go look. Go look!"

Another night, this one arbitrary, a night in space. They all ran together, all the nights, the lamps of the flowers, warm summer nights in Ell, the storm with the lighting flaring, Ree with rain lashing the windowpanes, night after night on the *Golden Girl*—

Michael's head lay in Hanna's lap. Her hands were soft on his face and scarcely moved.

"Tell me the beginning," said her soft voice.

The beginning was in *GeeGee*'s memory, but he did not need to refer to it. He said, "The Hobbes Settlement Corporation was founded in the year 2398 by Richard Hobbes and Thomas Shadhili. Hobbes lived in the former nation of United States, in Namerica. I couldn't trace Shadhili. There was a list of nineteen hundred and four investors. Counting whole families, they represented maybe eight thousand people. The philosophical basis of the venture was isolationist. You know what Earth was like then."

Hanna said guiltily, "Refresh my memory."

"Taxes were high everywhere, higher than any time anywhere on Earth, to support the new colonies. These people had money. They hated the taxes. And the idea of the Polity was in the air. This was before the Plague Years, which was when the idea of a central authority— what turned into the Polity—really took hold. But it was coming, and it wasn't a popular idea. The people who signed up with Hobbes and Shadhili, they didn't want to be around when it happened. They didn't want their descendants to be around. That was one of the reasons for the whole Explosion. One of the many reasons."

"Yes. I knew that," she said with some complacency. "And then?"

"They thought it out well. They equipped the expedition well. But they needed a labor force, so they took twenty thousand other people with them, people who couldn't afford to invest, who were indigent, as far as I could tell. Desperate people. They called it, the investors called it, benevolence. I never ran across any criticism of it. Maybe there wasn't any. There was too much going on then, too much to criticize, too much even to keep up with. What were twenty thousand people, with the millions pouring out? But I've seen the manifests. If you read between the lines, look at the names, look at the places of origin, you can see where the labor force came from. The places that developed last, mostly. The people with dark skin. In Croft—"

It was the first time he had used the name of the village, and it stopped him. After a minute he said, "In Croft, almost everybody was darker than Pavah and me—"

He stopped again, suddenly. Then he said in a different voice, "Why?"

Her hands moved on his face. "There must have been mingling, over the years. On D'neera we're all more or less brown."

He stored the question, let it drop.

"There isn't much more. They left. Nobody ever heard of them again. As far as I know."

"Somebody did."

Hanna tried to match it up with his memories in the dark. The pieces did not quite fit. Time had nibbled away the edges on both sides. But it was possible to make a first approximation of what had happened.

"There was a distinct class system from the start," she said. "Did they know where they were going?"

"Only in the most general way, I think. Remember: there was a wave of optimism all through the Explosion. The universe was full of Earths, they thought. It is, I guess. They're just harder to find than it seemed at first. The prospectus just said, they'd establish a settlement on a planet where a high quality of life could reasonably be expected to be maintained. It said which direction they'd take, but it didn't spot any candidates, and anybody who read it, I think, would assume they never meant to go as far as they did. But maybe they meant to all along, meant to disappear, meant to sever the connection from the start. Or maybe they didn't. Maybe it happened later, for some other reason."

They were silent. She bent to kiss his forehead. He was drifting away again. Remembering—

—Otto was distracted that harvest time, but happy all the time. Otto had a harvest of his own on the way.

"They'd best hurry up and marry," Mirrah said, but nobody could take time for a wedding during harvest, not in Croft or Sutherland either. It didn't much matter; the ribald teasing was just the same as it would be if they'd married before starting the baby, the only difference was that Marlie hadn't left her mother's house yet, still lived in Sutherland instead of in Croft with Otto. Even at harvest the men found time to work on building Otto's house. The women through the summer, when the peddlers came around, had bought household goods for Marlie as well as for themselves; now they sorted through outgrown infants' gear, sewed soft blankets. Mirrah had a special reason to be pleased; Carmina would have a playmate almost her own age.

Marlie held out till after harvest, but only just. The day
before the wedding half of Croft packed up and went to
Sutherland, oxen pulling the carts. It was a fine day, we left
early in the morning when the nip of fall was sharp in the
air and frost made the grasses by the roadside sparkle, and
the stubble in the fields was bright as broken glass. Later it
got warm; we sang all the way. Otto wanted to walk, but
they made him ride in the cart. "You need to rest up," they
said. I didn't ride either; I ran ahead with Pehr, we had con-
tests throwing stones. He was older than me and he always
won, but I thought I would be bigger than him someday,
Pavah was a big man. In Sutherland there was a feast that
started as soon as we got there. Marlie was as big around as
the oxen, she was a little thing and now she looked just like
a ball. Otto shouted when he saw her and picked her up,
grunting, though even carrying the baby she couldn't have
been heavy; she beat at his shoulders to make him put her
down, big rough Otto who'd had this silly grin on his face
ever since he started courting Marlie.

"I'll never act that dumb," Pehr whispered in my ear, but
then I caught him looking at Ader, Joan's girl; I hadn't seen
her for half a year, and she wasn't the same little kid any
more.

It went on all night and half the next day. There was
plenty of food and plenty of ale and drink made from the
sweet berries that grew along the river. Abram had come
riding in a cart with his fiddle. Sutherland had a piper, Kimon his name was; he played with Abram and I fell in love
with the pipe. He let me use it a little, and when he saw how
much I wanted it, he said he'd make me one. People came
in and out all night, they'd sleep for a while in someone's
house and then come back to eat and drink and dance and
talk some more. Toward morning it got quiet; more people
had gone out to sleep for good. Mirrah and Carmina went
to Joan's and went to bed, but Pavah and I stayed up. I was
sleepy, but I didn't want to miss anything. The talk was
softer, Abram dozed off in a corner with the fiddle on his
knees, and I sat by Pavah and tried to keep awake while he
talked with Ugo and Joan and Elot. Joan did for Sutherland
what Pavah did for Croft, carried on outside business. Elot
her husband did what Ugo did, organized work in the fields,
settled disagreements; it was Elot who'd marry Otto and

Marlie the next day. In the middle of the night it was cold outside. Inside the moothall— bigger than Croft's, Sutherland had more people—it was warm, there were three big hearths and fires burned in all of them. The ale went around, but Joan talked about a man who'd come to Sutherland from the Post in one of the metal wagons that ran by themselves. Nobody laughed any more. She didn't like what he'd come for, didn't like what he'd said.

"As if we'd want to move to the flats!" she said.

"Why did he bring it up?" Ugo said.

"He said more farmland has to be cleared, they've got to get more under cultivation than they've had."

"There's not enough of us to make a difference," Ugo said.

But Joan said, "They've more machines there. You can cover six times as much ground, ten times, maybe more."

"We called a moot," Elot said. "Even in the middle of harvest we met on it. Nobody wants to go."

Ugo asked, "Did he say anything about Croft?"

"He said he'd been other places, had more to go to," Joan said. "Told me plenty of people were going. I said, then what do you need us for? He didn't answer, he looked angry, I think he'd lied. I don't think people in other towns wanted to go either."

Pavah hadn't said anything. Joan said, "You're quiet, Alek."

"Too much ale," he said, though that was a lie; his hands were steady as they always were.

We split up and went off to sleep then. Next day after the wedding, after more eating and drinking and dancing, we carried Otto and Marlie home, Marlie with her bulk in a cart and Otto walking alongside, proud as one of his own bullocks. A few days after that Ugo called us to the moothall, he talked about what he'd heard from Joan and Elot. Everybody had already heard about it and their minds were made up; they didn't want to go anywhere. If the man came to Croft from the Post, Pavah would tell him that. Pavah was quiet then, too. We walked home in a light snowfall, the first of the autumn, Pavah and Mirrah and me. I carried Carmina; she couldn't walk yet, though she pulled herself up on anything handy, fences, furniture, legs; she didn't really talk yet either, but she knew how to say "Mirrah" and "Pavah" and got "Mikki" almost right.

Mirrah said to Pavah, "I thought you'd speak the thoughts you've been thinking."

"Why frighten them? Nobody likes to think of the worst. Why frighten friends and neighbors, when nothing's happened yet, and may not happen? The Post has sent no one here, nor back to Sutherland either; Joan said she'll send a message if that happens."

I was getting older, they talked to me sometimes like I was grown up, so I said, "What are you talking about?"

Pavah said, "If they need more people in the fields near the Post, what's to stop them from using force? How much good would it do to say we won't go?"

"They wouldn't have anyplace to put us," I said.

"There aren't many of us," he said.

"Everybody in Croft? And Sutherland, too?"

"That's not many people," he said, smiling. "There's more people at the Post than you can imagine, and room for all of them."

"Barracks," Mirrah said softly.

"What's that?" I said.

"Big, big buildings where everybody lives all together." She and Pavah looked at each other over my head. She said strongly, "I don't want to go back to that, Alek."

They'd been walking with me between them, but Pavah moved around so that he was in the middle, one arm around Mirrah, the other on my shoulder; only he lifted his hand to muss Carmina's hair. The snow floated down; the long winter was almost here. But the barns were heavy with grain, the smokehouses with meat, the cellars and stone barrels with the gardens' and orchards' yield. We wouldn't be hungry, there was nothing to fear, there had never been anything to fear so I didn't know how to be afraid of a guess, a dim threat, something that was just in my father's mind—

Night in the middle of the day. Light enough elsewhere on *GeeGee,* but dark in Michael's room. Head on Hanna's lap again. She stroked his face and worried, she would make herself sick with worry. It seemed to her that Michael was dissolving, breaking up into pieces and floating away.

He was unaware of her anxiety. All he felt was the softness under his head; he might have taken root. Those soft soft hands on his cheeks: part of his own flesh.

"Not as primitive as all that," the soft voice said.

"How do you get that?"

"They speak of machines with accuracy and without fear. They distinguish between native crops and imports. Your father told you of other planets, other people; do they know that's where they came from? And the imports? And the machines?"

He struggled to remember. "It's all so far away," he said.

"Well, did they think the machines were made at the Post?"

"Some were. But—no. They thought others had always been there. A finite number. That the Post was a great treasure house, and the masters released from it what they would, gave us what they wanted to give."

"How do you know this, Mikhail? Is it something you were told?"

"Maybe." He was certain that he had spoken truth, and it was the first thing he had been sure of that did not come from the relived past of the trance, but from some store of general knowledge.

"The beasts that pulled the carts—you called them oxen, but they weren't. Were they native?"

"I guess so. I think so. Yes. They must have been. Sometimes they were hard to manage. We were careful about breeding. It must have gone back years, breeding to make them docile."

"So isolated," she murmured. "So terribly isolated."

"But *it* was good." His eyes stung. "Is it bad to be isolated? When life is so good? The peace."

"It made you too vulnerable. The community, I mean. Tell me about the relocation," she said.

After a minute he turned his head to press his cheek against Hanna's flesh. "I can't," he said. He was dizzy with the effort of remembering—or the fear of it.

"We must know."

"Why? If we only go to what used to be Croft, if I only look at it and leave—"

"Oh, Michael, Michael . . ." There were tears in her voice. "Can you be satisfied with that? Did all of them die, without exception?"

"I don't suppose so—" His hand tightened on her knee.

"Your baby sister?"

He whispered, "I don't know."

"What did she look like, Mike?"

"Dark," he said, "and round, with my eyes, Pavah's eyes. Maybe she's dead. Maybe they killed her, too."

Now his voice was high and tight, his shoulders tense with held-back tears. She said with compassion, "We can stop. Do what you just said: go look at Croft, and leave."

"Without word? I see now what you meant. Can I be there, where Carmina might be, without trying to find out? We'll have to go on," he said, and knew as he said it that there had never been a choice from the beginning. If he had thought so, he had only been deceiving himself. He moved in the dark and drew an uneven breath. He felt Hanna's warmth under his head, and the soft hands, but suddenly their touch was nervous and uncertain; she felt what he felt, the abyss trembling beneath him once more, only now it was going to crack wide open.

"Mike—?"

Not even her hands could hold him up anymore. He took hold of them and pulled her down beside him, smiling in the dark. She said his name uneasily and he kissed her to quiet her, caressed her mechanically, forgot who she was; she was rigid and doubting, but he forgot to care. On the edge of annihilation he had no room to care about anything except one primal act that had nothing to do with mind or even being human, but with living forever in the face of death. Maybe she understood, because she let him do what he wanted, did not protest or push him away, even though at the end he forgot himself altogether and drove into her so violently that she cried out, more startled than hurt. When the spasm was over, he lifted his head and was full of fear as a moment before of desire, a man lost and unmade. He looked into Hanna's eyes and knew how greatly he was loved; but knew also that Hanna saw a stranger, no one she had ever known before.

On the edge of the precipice he said, "What's happening to me?"—and let go and plummeted down and down, and did not hear her start to cry.

Theo, finding Lise in tears one morning, extracted from her the admission that she was lonely for Michael, decided that he would talk to Michael, and set off to find him. But at the door to Michael's room he hesitated; probably both Michael and Hanna were asleep. While he waited, unwilling to ring, the door opened anyhow. Hanna had sensed his presence and his wish; she stood blocking the door and looking at Theo with hard weary eyes. She had not been asleep. The room was dark, however, and Michael was an unmoving lump on the bed up against the wall of stars.

"You can't talk to him now," Hanna said.

"When?" He was exasperated; Hanna was a usurper, she had no right to tell him when he could or could not see Michael.

The short, soft dialogue had waked Michael, though, and behind Hanna he sat up and said, voice dragging, "What is it? What's wrong?"

Theo started forward. Hanna after a moment stood aside. It had seemed that she might not; he was desperately uneasy.

"I have to talk to you about Lise," he said.

"All right." A light came on. Michael blinked in it, half-dazed. He looked so tired and tense that Theo was shocked.

He hid it as best he could and explained his errand. Michael listened, but it was not the old Michael; only half his attention was in this room; he met Theo's eyes only once or twice, and his gaze was bleary. At the end there was a silence. Theo was going to ask if Michael had heard, had understood, but then Michael said, "I can't do anything about it."

It was a wounding blow, but Theo did not know that at once because he could not believe that what it sounded like was what Michael really meant. He said, "You don't have to *do* anything. Just spend a little time with her."

"I can't," Michael said, not looking at Theo. "I don't have anything left."

Theo turned without another word and started out. Hanna still waited by the door. He said tightly, "Now I want to talk to you."

She said indifferently, "All right."

"Not here."

"All right."

She followed him out and shut the door. There was no further sound from inside the room. Theo said, shaking with anger, "What are you doing to him?"

"He's doing it to himself. And to me."

"What is it? What is it, then?"

"Memory." An odd expression flickered across her face. If this had been anybody but Hanna, he would have thought it was helplessness.

"Why don't you stop it? Does he want to go on?"

"Sometimes he does. Sometimes he doesn't. Sometimes I want to stop. Sometimes I don't. What I want doesn't matter anyway. He doesn't need the trance any more, he doesn't need me. He's half in it all the time. What do you want me to do? I can't do anything."

Theo began to pound the wall with his fist, slowly and not very hard, though he wanted to strike hard enough to put his hand through it. Hanna must know how angry he was, but she watched him impassively, indifferently.

"You have to stop him," Theo said. "Can't you see what it's doing to him?"

She said, "I see it. But he believes he is being made whole. It cannot happen without great pain. But he is grateful. Even in his pain he is grateful."

"Gratitude for pain—there are words for that. Sick words. Why can't you let him be what he was?" Theo spoke with anguish. "You loved what he was."

"What he was?" she said. "It was an artificial construct. Not wholly. He could not have made himself what he was without a foundation. But he did not remember the foundation. Now he does. Having remembered so much he will remember the ending: all the grief. It will get worse before it gets better."

"You're both crazy," Theo said, convinced of it. "I don't know who got crazy first, but you spend all your time in each other's heads and you've both got it. You make Henrik look good. I'm not going to let you keep doing it."

"I would stop him. If I could. If he would."

There was that look again; now he was sure it was helplessness, that Hanna had lost control of the situation.

He cursed her for starting it. "I'll stop him, then," he said.

"How?" said Hanna. Her eyes and voice were empty of feeling.

He did not know. Possibilities of violence and treachery went through his mind. But he knew that Hanna saw them, and his own thoughts sickened him.

Hanna turned her back on him and went into Michael's room without speaking. Theo, with nothing else left to do, returned to Lise and consoled her as well as he could.

—the man who came from the Post at the end of fall, he had the lightest skin I'd ever seen—

(Michael had begun to tremble, his face was slick with sweat, his whole body soaked.

"No," Hanna said. "No. Come out of it."

He wouldn't. He had learned more from Hanna than either of them had thought he could at the start. He could stay in this state without her, and he would not come out.)

—came to our house, it was Pavah he had to talk to. Greeted him as if they knew each other, "Alex" he called Pavah, Pavah must have dealt with him before. There were two other men in the wagon outside. They got out and walked around, stamping their feet to keep warm. But there wasn't anything for them to see, it was a cold day and most everybody was inside, those who hadn't been had gone in when they saw the wagon come. It was long as our house, much too big for three men, but most of it was made to carry goods. The man who came in, I never heard what he was called. They met in the room at the front of the house, and Mirrah took Carmina to another room and they stayed there, Mirrah not saying anything; but Pavah didn't send me to join them.

The man didn't talk very long. It was the same thing Joan had said. They needed to open up more land, they needed farmers to work it. It didn't sound so bad. There was money to be made, the man said; there would be gold. Croft never had much of that, only from grain we sold outside the village, passing through so many hands that not much gold filtered back.

"Who would own the land?" Pavah said.

"Who owns it here? No one. Everyone. What's the difference?"

"It's a good life here," Pavah said.

"No difference," the man said. "Maybe better for you, as middleman. You've got the blood. That could make it profitable for you."

"It never did me much good before. It doesn't matter; it's

Croft I speak for. And Croft's decided. We have no wish to go. We will not go."

"Winter's hard here," the man said. "You spend it cutting wood just to keep warm. In the east there are easier ways."

"I know," Pavah said. "I smell it sometimes. But only in bad dreams. Give me woodsmoke. Keep the gas."

In the other room Carmina began to cry. She hardly ever did that, and not for long; she'd wanted to come to Pavah, most likely, and Mirrah had held her back. I heard Mirrah talking to her, getting her interested in something else, and the crying stopped. The man said. "You've another, then? Felicitations, Alex. Another fine son? Will this one take your place when you're gone? Who'll speak for Croft when you're gone?"

There was something in his face I didn't understand but Pavah did. Something else came into Pavah's eyes, it took a minute to see what it was, I'd seen him angry so seldom.

"You're a fool if you think it matters who you deal with," he said. "I tell you I speak for Croft. Not only for myself, though my neighbors' wishes are mine, too. We knew you'd been to Sutherland. We decided what to say if you came here. Now you've heard what we say. Be on your way."

"I would see Lillin first, with your permission," said the man; he meant Mirrah.

"I do not tell her who she may see. If she wanted to see you, she would come out. You've outstayed your welcome. This is my house. I'm master here. I bid you go."

The man left then, saying nothing. I thought Pavah had driven him out, and I was proud. But when the wagon had gone and Mirrah came out, Pavah said, "He went too quietly," and Mirrah whispered, "Yes? Why?"

"I must go to Sutherland," Pavah said.

"Now, Alek?"

"As soon as we've met. To carry the news to Joan and Elot, to see if he's been there and what he said."

And so we all went to the moothall, and there was worry enough but no one knew what to do, except wait. Pavah went to Sutherland, and—

In the silence at the end of thought, Hanna struggled from the past in a daze. The memories had never been so powerful before; coming back was like a great Jump between worlds with no sense of transition. Michael had done what Hanna had not been able to do to him: draw her forcibly from that place of the mind. She had to fight to sit up and speak.

"What happened?" she said, meaning what had happened there and then, not now and here.

His gaze was still fixed in that great distance. He scarcely saw *GeeGee,* scarcely saw Hanna even though she was directly before his eyes. She twisted her hands together, all she could think of was the end, there must be an end, it must come sometime. "What happened?" she repeated, unheard; she said it over and over again. What happened? What happened?

He heard the question finally. He was lost in the dark and did not look at her. "I think I went with my father to Sutherland," he said.

He was looking into a cloud. It would be easier to die than go into it; it would be preferable; she saw how thin he had gotten, as if looking on disaster in the first hours after it occurs, when the mind refuses to believe that everything has changed and things will never be as they were.

"Went to Sutherland," she said. "What happened there? What happened?"

"I think I never saw Croft again," he said.

For once Hanna had taken her turn in Control. At least that was what Michael thought when he woke alone, looked at a chronometer, and saw the time.

He sat up slowly, shaky and hungry. It had been some time since he ate, a day or longer. He only ate when Hanna insisted and sometimes refused food then. He did not know what day it was; only he knew that they had been in space a long time. He tried to remember his last meal. And met only mist.

He sat on his bed in the dark for a long time. His mind was not clear, but seemed more clear than it had been; clear enough to know that it was clouded. He remembered—a true, new memory, this—reaching for Hanna—an hour ago? Days ago? She had pulled away. "What's wrong?" he had said.

"Last time you hurt me—"

She had been afraid of him, in her eyes there were recollections of the *Avalon*. He said he could not have hurt
her. She insisted until he thought she had imagined it, had
lost her mind, and then it seemed to him that the only firm
thing in the world had collapsed and gone away from him.
But then she had convinced him that it was true, that he
had betrayed her trust, given her pain not pleasure, re-
tained no slightest memory of the incident—and then he
knew that he was the one who was mad, and with it a monster.

But even that was better than the other thing, than Hanna's clear sanity being lost to him, even if she could not love
him any more. And certainly after that she could not. She
was gone because he had hurt her (he forgot about Control); she was gone because he was a monster.

Another memory crept into his despair: Theo seeking
help for Lise. He had turned Theo away, abandoned Lise.
He got up quickly at the thought, and staggered at a surge
of dizziness. When it cleared he was bending over cold water, splashing it on his face. He lifted his head and saw a
monster in the mirror, a tragic mask, a face that had forgotten how to smile.

He got out of the room somehow and went to look for
Lise. He found her in her cabin, seated at a desk with a
reader before her. She looked up calmly, not at all as if she
were surprised to see him.

He said, "Puss, are you all right?" His voice did not come
out the way he wanted it to.

She nodded. He found a place to sit and then could not
think of anything else to say. He tried to talk anyway, stam-
mering out some apology for his neglect, but she did not let
him finish.

"I know," she said. "Theo told me what you're trying to
do. I know it's hard. You don't have to worry about me."

Tears of weakness blurred his eyes. It was the saddest
thing he had ever heard. He was used to worrying about
Lise, he was used to taking care of people, that was what he
did, that was what he was. Now Lise said he should not do
it. He would have to be a monster.

Lise said critically, "Have you been eating?"

He shook his head.

"I thought Hanna was taking care of you," she said. She

was surprised at Hanna, she disapproved; he heard that in her voice.

He managed to say, "I can still feed myself."

"I don't think you can," Lise said. "Wait."

She slipped out. He did not have the strength to follow.

She came back with bread and butter and cheese and strong, hot tea. He ate and drank automatically. It was hard work getting the bread to his mouth at first, but he was stronger even before he finished, and the mists cleared a little more. He really had been very hungry. He could talk more easily, ask Lise about her studies. She answered with that same calmness, but came to sit beside him and drink tea from his cup, more like herself; still he thought she was subtly older, edging toward maturity.

A picture of a baby named Carmina rose up before his eyes, and he choked on a mouthful of bread. Lise pounded his back, though it wasn't necessary. He wanted to grip her in a tight embrace to keep her safe, forever safe. But he was afraid of what he might do to her. He swung toward tears again. "Where's Hanna?" he said, though she was afraid of him and did not love him any more.

"Control," Lise said.

"Yes, it's her watch."

Lise said doubtfully, "They're all Theo's now, I think, except he makes Shen stay up and do more. But he went to get Hanna. He said he needed her."

There must be something wrong. But not too badly wrong or they would have come to get him. Or would they? Why would they?

He got up and went out, followed by Lise; made it up the spiral stairs and into Control. Hanna and Theo were there, their backs to him. It was blindingly bright. There was a high, regular sound in the room; it was familiar, he ought to know what it was.

He did. It was an audible accompaniment to some contact *GeeGee* had made, carrying no information but providing certain psychological benefits for the novice in space—or for a wanderer long out of reach of human sounds.

"A relay," he said to the pair of backs, so weakly he thought they wouldn't hear him.

They did, though. Hanna said, "It's Omega. We've

crossed over." She glanced around and went very still. She
had not seen him in full light for two or three days. She said
in an ordinary voice—but her eyes studied him sharply—
"It's a complicated course from here. There's no prime
route between here and where we need to go. We'll change
course several times. The interpolations are complex; it will
take nearly four weeks."

Four weeks were nothing to Michael who blundered
through forty years. Theo also turned around; he looked at
Michael narrowly and said, "We can get news now."

Michael looked at him stupidly. Theo said, "We can find
out if the situation's changed. Maybe they've made new offers, public offers. At least we can find out about the mission
to Uskos."

It was too much; he swayed and they came to him, Theo
alerted by his face, Hanna by something more. He clutched
Hanna, trying to talk. He said, or thought he said, "I'm sorry
I hurt you. I'm sorry. I'm so sorry!"

"Satisfied?" Theo said to Hanna savagely, when they had
got him back to bed.

"Shut up," she said.

He heard Theo say he was not diseased and talk about what
had been done for Henrik. He put out a hand and got hold
of Theo's wrist. He was weak, for a man not diseased, but it
was not that his body had failed him; rather, the air here, in
the present, was a thick liquid hard to push through.

But he did not have to talk. Hanna translated to Theo
what he thought.

"He doesn't want to be drugged like Henrik was."

"Am I supposed to just stand here and watch this happen?"

"It has a natural course."

Somehow, through Hanna, he felt Theo's incredulity.

Hanna's voice. "I don't say that. He says it. He says: let
him finish."

They argued. In the end Theo won; won something. Michael knew that because he felt Theo inject something into
his arm. Maybe it was supposed to connect him with some
kind of reality.

He felt it begin to work. And saw reality, all right, only
not the one Theo had wanted him to have.

The sense of Theo's presence faded. But Hanna's was strong.

Stop it, she said to him, *stop!*

He wouldn't; he couldn't. Hanna could not know the favor she had done him, opening the past; nor Theo just now with the stuff he had forced into Michael's veins. He saw like an open door the gate of trance Hanna had shown him long before.

Don't do it. Stop—

—walking in the dark morning, the days were shorter, we left before dawn to reach Sutherland by dark. Bitter cold but we were warm enough with movement and furs. We'd eaten before we left, hot cakes Mirrah baked on the hearth; we had more packed away for mid-day, and meat, fresh-cooked for a journey of only a day and that in the cold; but I always pitied the little caged animals killed for meat, I couldn't do it, couldn't slash the small furred throats, though Pavah said it had to be done, I'd have to learn to do it, praying maybe in apology as many did acknowledging kinship; but he'd never made me do it. *Time enough* he said— Cheese Mirrah had sent, fruit from the winter store, water and strong wine, till Pavah laughed and groaned: "You'll kill us of surfeit, woman! It's only lunch we want!"

"It's hard walking on an empty stomach," she had said. "To be warm you need to eat."

For a long time we talked little, warming with the walking and the rising sun. We did not speak of the Post till almost midday. And Pavah would have said nothing had I not asked, and when I did it was no great question; only, "What do we do at Sutherland, Pavah?"

"Tell them what happened," he said. "Find if they've thoughts on it."

"How much thinking can there be?" I said.

"Thoughts of resistance, perhaps. There might be some. But it would be folly."

"Why?" I said. "Would it be like Fairfield?" But Fairfield wasn't real to me, it was only a name.

"You heard of that? Of course you did," he said, answering himself. "Croft's small, we all hear what the others hear."

"I don't know what they did at Fairfield," I said. "I heard of killing, but how? There are strong men in Croft and Sutherland; Fairfield must have had strong men, too."

"With no weapons but hunters' knives," he said, "or woodsmen's axes."

"Hunters have bows, too, and spears."

"That's not what I speak of." We walked on in silence. I did not break it; I knew he would speak again. He said, "It's time you knew of such things. I thought to wait till you were older, but you grow fast. And maybe you'll age faster still, if—"

He didn't go on from "if"; he started over. "They've weapons that shoot projectiles that pierce to the heart, fired by a burning powder. They've weapons that pour out a light that burns. Those I've seen, in the hunts in the forests beyond the Post. And I've heard of a weapon that seemingly does nothing at all, except when it's pointed at a man, he dies. That I've not seen. Nor have I seen another thing they talk of, a weapon that stops and crumples a man in a step, though later he wakes unharmed. It might be true. It might not."

"The hunts you saw, was it when you went to the Post for Croft?" I said, but I knew it was not.

"They were before you even were, before your Mirrah and I married; when we lived there."

"What did you do there? How did you come away?"

"We were servants of the masters, Lillin and I. It was a hard life, though not as hard as some. When I came to know Lillin, I asked permission to leave, to go away west of the mountains, and it was granted."

"That doesn't sound so bad," I said.

"Well, you ought to know this; maybe you'll need to know it one day. That's not something that happens often, a servant permitted to leave. To leave without permission is against the law. A man can be punished for it, or a woman; they can even be killed. But they let me go because I was an embarrassment."

He grinned, his teeth white as cloud in the winter sky.

"Why an embarrassment?" I said.

"These eyes. Yours and mine and Carmina's. My mirrah, your grandmother you never knew, was a servant, too, and a pretty thing. A son of a master's house took a liking to her.

I was the result. These are known eyes, one family's eyes, though they've spread through intermarriage. When you see them, you know whose blood runs in the veins. And you see them in the fields and factories, too; but they were willing enough to get them out of the house. And so we were allowed to leave. We had to leave behind all we had, though; came to Croft with the clothes on our backs."

I understood about the eyes, all right, having worked with breeding stock since I could walk, but I didn't know what it all meant. He wouldn't talk about it any more; after a while I stopped asking questions.

Then in the afternoon we came to Sutherland. It lay behind a hill, else we'd have seen the trouble before it was too late; but men stepped out of a grove at the side of the road. They wore clothes like the men who'd been to Croft, and they carried things in their hands they pointed at us.

Pavah stopped and pushed me behind him, all in a moment. I didn't want to hide behind his back, but he wanted me there, it was hard to know what I should do. He said a few words to them, and they to him; he told them we weren't of Sutherland; they told us to go on, we were Sutherlanders now. And we went on; because I knew without asking what the things were the men carried, they were weapons like Pavah had told me about, and the men watched us.

When we came around the hill, I saw the streets of Sutherland were full of more of the metal wagons than I'd ever seen before, ever imagined there could be. People were carrying things into the wagons, furniture, clothes, household goods: the houses were being emptied. "So it's come," Pavah said.

The Postmen went away but there were others everywhere, all with weapons, they watched us with the others. Then Joan saw us and came to us. She'd been crying, and by the time she got to us she was crying again. "Alek, you shouldn't have come," she said.

Between sobs she told him how they'd come in the wagons in the morning, made the people come together, told them what to do. While she talked, I looked around and saw many people weeping, but they kept on anyway, carrying things to the wagons.

Pavah said, "Has there been resistance?"

"In the first hours, and two men dead." She named them;

one was Kimon. "Since then, no one. We think of Fairfield. But I was nearly the third. I was nearly the third."

"How was that?" Pavah said.

She stopped crying, still too angry for tears. "One of them put his hands on Ader. He put his hands on her. And I screamed at him and went to kill him, but an officer stopped him, stopped me. 'There'll be none of that,' he said, and the animal went away. Alek, there'll be nothing left. They said they'll come back for the stores and the herds."

"Have they said anything about Croft?" he asked.

"It's next, they said."

Elot came up then; Joan cried and he held her and patted her shoulders, though he was heavy with grief. Pavah started helping the people load their goods, and I did what he did. It was late, the dark began to come; he looked around to make sure none of the Postmen were near and said, "I have to get back to Croft. I must tell them what's coming, tell them not to resist."

I said hotly, "We're to go like oxen where we're driven?"

"Where's there to run to, in winter? They'd be on us in a day. You haven't seen the guns fired yet, Mikhail, but you heard Joan: two men dead. Otto'd be the first to go in Croft, I think."

"When will we go?" I said.

"Soon, in the dusk. Listen. There's a risk. If I don't get clean away at once, they'll shoot. I have to carry back word, I have to be with Mirrah, but you don't. We'll all be taken to the same place. Stay with Joan, and we'll find each other when we get where they take us."

"I don't want to stay," I said.

"But I want you to," he said, and dropped what he was carrying and hugged me hard for a long time. I wanted to cry, but I was too old for that.

"I love you," he said. And he didn't have to go back to Croft at all; only he couldn't bear Mirrah's being without him.

When it was dark, he edged to the edge of the light and then took off, fleet of foot. He underestimated the range of the guns, I think. While a little light still caught him they fired, one, two, three—I think all three bullets found him. He was dead when he hit the ground, he was dead when I got to him, and one of them fired at me, too, but he missed and the others stopped him, knowing I wouldn't run far, only to him. I threw myself on him and cried and cried until Joan came and made me leave him—

Michael cried for an hour altogether, without shame or restraint. Hanna held him in the dark and cried, too. He said, "I could have run the other way, gone first, distracted them, they might not have seen him in time, they might have missed."

"Michael, Mikhail, don't say that, no. He did what you would have done in his place."

"If I had, if I had—"

"There was nothing you could do. There was nothing you could do! It would not have changed anything."

"But he—"

"—did what he had to do. Hush, my love. Hush."

As if he had crossed some dreadful threshold and, having crossed it, was stronger, Michael surprised Hanna by making a partial recovery. Sometimes he was much like himself; was himself. Turned up in Control at his scheduled hours, turned questions aside, took over the running of his ship with relief at its prosaic demands as if he visited another country and was glad for the escape. He was much quieter than before. And whenever he slipped away into the half-trance half-dream, Hanna always knew at once, even if she were as far away from him as it was possible to get on the *Golden Girl*. She went with him each time, flying to his side—

—two days in the damn metal wagons, crowded among the weeping women, a shrieking baby or two. There was hardly air for breath. An old man died and was taken away—for burial the Postmen said but I think not, I think his bones lie scattered still beside the road. His old wife cried all the second day, rocked back and forth in misery. Joan tried to take care of me, stayed at my side until then, but the old woman was her aunt, her dead mother's sister, and needed her, no, needed more than Joan could ever give; but she left me with Ader. We wriggled to a corner and kept it. In the dark Ader gave me what comfort she could; did Joan know? And look

the other way? Thinking, the boy's our own kind, a good
boy, Alek's son? I was too young but near old enough; did
Joan think Ader a mother at, what, fourteen?—would be
safer that way? And then we came to the forests flatter than
the river valley, old seabed it must have been, the sea not
far they said, and under the topsoil, sand. The wind blew all
the time. Sea level: summers were longer there, I heard. All
the same in winter it was dusted with snow, but mud
squelched underfoot after morning frosts. Flocks of water-
fowl darkened the sky and the sky was big with no mountains to close it in. Only forest.

Joan found Mirrah right away. Wouldn't let me see her at
first; told her about Pavah so I needn't. I don't know how
she told her, what words she used. Then Mirrah had to see
me, was frantic to see me, as if I were dead, too, until she
did. I'd never seen her cry before. Shaking with despair in
the night, and Carmina cried, too, not knowing why. And I
wanted to protect them, to save them, but it was too late,
was already done.

They made me stay in one of the men's buildings, there
were six of them, nor was everyone in them from Sutherland
or Croft. Altogether in ten great barracks there were fifteen
hundred men and boys; in twelve more, somewhat a greater
number of women and girls, and the smallest children regardless of sex. Families met in the cold evenings but only outdoors when the day's quota of trees was felled and the smoke
of their burning made a reek round the camp. The land was
more barren each day, each day they marched us farther
away. There was great unhappiness, but not much fear. There
would be towns, they promised; when the land was cleared,
before the spring working of the soil began, families would
be reunited, a town would be built, everything would be as it
had been before only in a different place, there would be
machines so the land could be farmed. They took from each
barracks a few men or women and took them to the Post,
showed them our herds, our goods stored away, waiting for
us; they gave us back our own food to eat. We believed them.
Why not? What else was there to believe?

Face sooty from the smoke, arms aching from the ax, I
worked. If all Croft had been in my work party and barracks, or Croft and Sutherland together, we might have pretended to be a town. But they separated us, I was with few

I knew and many I didn't, and we were all parts of broken things, split and dazed. I heard that Otto and Marlie with their baby boy, they met secretly and walked away one night, out in the cold; were followed, caught, brought back; that was all. Just brought back. "So they mean us no harm," the men said. But Otto had a strong back, was valuable—

Morning, Michael's watch, but Hanna went to Control instead. She had left Michael sleeping after a night in a winter of exile. He was tired as if all night he had really wielded an ax. When she went into Control, she found Henrik. He did not hear her come in.

"Good morning," she said.

He jumped, a violent movement; turned an animal's face to her. His guilt rolled over her like an ocean wave. She gaped. "What the hell are you doing?"

"Nothing," he lied.

He gathered himself for some effort, and she braced herself, amazed and half-afraid. But he only rushed past her, out of the chamber, and she heard him skidding down the spiral stair.

She went to the seat he had left and tried to see what he had been doing. He had wiped the display with a single touch, probably the instant he heard her voice, but he had forgotten to cancel command mode, and there were indicators she could read. He had been preparing to transmit a call from the *Golden Girl;* to whom it was directed she could not tell. He had not made it, though. She had come in time to prevent it.

Not wanting to leave Control unattended, she used internal communications to call Theo. He was not in his quarters, but she found him with Lise. "Come up here," she said.

He came at once, worried.

"Henrik was trying to call out," she said.

"Who to?"

"I don't know. Who could he call? He doesn't have anybody out there. But he doesn't want to be here, he wants us to stop; he must have been trying to reach the Polity."

"We have to make sure he can't. I don't want to lock him up. Can you fix it so *GeeGee* won't transmit without a code we all know but him?"

"Easily."

"Something easy to remember, but something he won't guess."

She used her birth-name, Bassanio, as the code. Theo said when she was done, "Why did you call me and not Mike?"

She blinked at him. "Mike's no good for anything," she said.

He did not say anything, he only looked at her, stunned. The implication was that he, Theo, *was* good for something. He hadn't thought that anyone but Mike would ever think that.

—noise all the time, the axes' thud, the crackle of the fires. A man stumbled and cut off part of his foot; they took him away. He didn't come back. Weeks later we heard he'd bled to death. It wasn't bad, not too bad. Except. A man from Honiton which I'd never heard of till that winter, he'd been there longer building barracks through the fall, one day he put down the ax. "I'm a free man. I won't do this any more," he said. Firmin said, "Think you'd better." Firmin, thank God, was in my barracks, he tried to stay close to me. The other man said, "What's going to happen? We'll see."

After a while the Postmen came, they were never far away, some always in sight. Tried persuasion. Moved to threats. Consulted with each other. Called reinforcements. And beat him. At first there was a move to help him, but they stood in a ring with their guns pointing out, fired once all at once into the air and we stood there. Trying not to watch. I saw tears on Firmin's face. They left the man bleeding in the sharp hard mud, left him to lie there all day, in the middle of the circle of guns. They didn't care if he froze to death, but he didn't. At night they let us carry him back and he groaned all night, breathing hard. In the morning they took him away. He came back in a week or two, but his face didn't look the same, that was why they sent him back, I think, so we'd see him every day and re-member. He worked, he never tried to stop again. None of us did—

Hanna started to have dreams of water. The lake at D'vornan shrouded in autumn fogs, the slow river that rolled through City Koroth; most often the sea at Serewind, where she had grown up. Maybe it was just because she was in space, where every gram of moist vapor was reclaimed and recycled. But sometimes it seemed to her that the sounds of water came to her from Michael's dreams. Sometimes behind his words, behind, even, those memories that had come fully into the light, there was the gray light of a distant sea. And meanwhile he lived half on Gadrah and half here; saw Hanna sometimes clearly, sometimes dimly as a ghost.

One day—they were more than halfway to Heartworld sector, measured in time and not by the twists of their convoluted course—she tried again to help him, to use distance and cool logic to interpret that other world he saw:

"A policy of deliberate terror." Her hands moved on his face. "They fed you well enough, with your own confiscated stores, yes? Housed you warmly. Keeping the labor force healthy. But they split families up, communities. Retaliated harshly at the first sign of rebellion."

"But you can't call it terror, not really. If you did what you were supposed to do nothing happened."

"They weren't capricious, then."

"Not that."

She leaned over him, her hands light and nervous. *Gray water meets gray sky somewhere out there.* He reached up; the graceful fingers touched her face, traced her features as if he were blind and sought to see her.

"I hurt you," he said.

She shrugged. "I could have stopped you. With force, if I'd wanted. But it wouldn't have taken that. Talking would have done it."

"Why did you let me do it?"

She shrugged again. He realized that she had never said it, not once in all the months had she said the most dangerous word her heart could conceive. But she sank down beside him, found his mouth: a cool drink of fresh water. *Salt air on a salt cold wind.*

"I love you," he said. "I want to marry you. I want to have children with you. I want to live with you all our lives."

Hanna said when she got her voice back, "That covers a lot of territory."

"All right. I know it's scary."

"I can't answer. I can't decide."

"My timing might be a little off, I admit—"

So the laughter was coming back and he was becoming himself again. Even if it was not quite the same self—

—and Georg came one day round the middle of the day while we ate, not in the big building where we took it in shifts morning and night, a hundred men at a time and less talk than you'd think because their minds were on the little time there'd be later to seek out those they loved before the lights were extinguished in the cold and the cold dark closed in; no, it was daytime, he came to the dead forest supposed to turn into fields by spring, where the midday meal was carried round by trucks. Women and old men from the barracks served the food—not Mirrah—she'd gotten herself assigned with the women who looked after the young children all day, so she could be with Carmina. There was nothing she could do to be more with me; we met in the courtyards at night.

Ate the bread made from Croft's own good grain but there wasn't much, there was less as the days went by—they said the stores ran short but they lied, there'd been enough and to spare when we left. The Postmen stood off by the unfelled trees with their share, no greater than ours—but what did they eat at night at the Post, when the nightshift came where we were and the others went back? They got no thinner that I could see. I saw the wagon come growling and humming across the waste and paid it no heed, they came and went all the time. Saw the man who went to the Postmen and later they looked toward where I was, but I didn't know they looked at me, till one came and said, "Boy, come with me."

Cold that day, I could see my breath, I followed it to the other men, thinking they'd give me an errand, send me through the wood to another worksite where it wasn't worth driving; they'd done that before. But the Postman took me to Georg with his face like polished stone, like the flint that looked smooth, even oily, but with sharp edges where it was split.

"There's room at the Post for young men like you," he

said in that voice that was smooth like his face, then he said what he meant—could I dance, could I sing, play music, do magic tricks? Could I learn? Could I be taught? Had I gifts?—"It's not enough to look good," he said, and almost gave up, as he told me later. I looked so stupid, knowing nothing of what he meant.

"I'll give you a trial," he said. When I understood he meant me to go to the Post, to live there, I balked. The desert wood wasn't Croft, but I'd been there a time, Mirrah was there, Carmina, everyone I'd ever known. I had no interest in leaving, none. Not even curiosity. I only wanted to be left alone.

Still he talked, dull though he thought me. He was bored, getting cold, but thorough. He said there'd be good living at the Post, I could have gold if I did well. He asked about my mirrah and said if I were apt I could help her—and had me. I didn't know that, but maybe he did.

Firmin came to us then, and the Postmen did nothing and let him come.

"What do you say to the boy?" he said.

"I've told him of opportunities," Georg said. "He's a handsome child. If he has any gifts for pleasing, it could be well for him at the Post."

"He has none," Firmin said. "An ill-tempered, inept child," so that I looked at him in surprise, though a moment's thought told me his aim.

"Are you his father?" Georg said.

"His father's dead. But I've an interest."

"Then you shouldn't wish to keep him here. I offer a chance not many have. I heard of him in passing, through the friend of a friend. A lovely boy, they said, heard singing one night, a lullaby for a little girl. Was it your sister, boy? We'll see if anything can be made of him. If not, he'll return."

Firmin wanted to argue, but I saw the Postmen moving in. Their weapons on that gray day looked not shiny but dead. "It's all right, I want to go," I said, afraid for him—

Hanna kept her watches now, and part of Michael's, too, as he kept part of hers; her presence in Control overlapped his by a considerable margin, so that it was impossible to tell, by merely looking into Control and seeing who was there,

whose watch it formally was. They talked casually and unnecessarily about *GeeGee*'s workings, her faithful pursuit of
the course Hanna had laid in at Omega. The worlds and
stars of human space rose up on monitors, were glittering
beacons for a day or two, and vanished and fell behind. Michael looked nearly himself again, stronger, more active.
But that was a shell and a concealment. His body lived on
GeeGee, and some of his mind, but only enough to make
the proper motions. In front of his eyes, with the substance
of reality, memory played itself out. When he lay down, he
would pass not into sleep but into the trance-state Hanna
had taught him, and more of the veil would be withdrawn.
He no longer plunged toward it, but neither did he avoid it;
it was inevitable, and he was content to let it unfold at its
own pace. In these hours in Control and elsewhere on *Gee-
Gee* when he was nominally normal and awake, what he
had seen in the last hours of trance gained solidity, and took
its place in the context of the whole. His mother's face had
the clarity of a fine portrait now: the liquid eyes, the black
ringlets framing the high forehead furrowed with grief. The
comforts of the *Golden Girl* faded to nothing. Crosslegged
on frozen ground swept roughly clear of snow in the harsh
glare of light that let no one escape or be private, he held
Carmina on his lap and sang to her in a boy's soprano,
strong and clear, however, and true:

> *Baby, sleep: thy pavah watches*
> *thy pavah with infinite care. Baby, dream:*
> *sweet dreams of pretty toys thy pavah gives thee*
> *Baby, sleep: safe in thy pavah's hands, the night holds only*
> *comfort for thee!*

Only sometimes his tears fell on her curly head.
    And meanwhile he said quite ordinary things to Hanna,
touched her sometimes, turned his head to smile when she
touched him, gave *GeeGee* the right orders (prompted by
GeeGee herself); at some imperceptible point the watch
would cease to be officially his and become officially Hanna's, freeing him to leave; and finally he would go, to drift
about *GeeGee* aimlessly as a ghost until it was time to return to his room (as alien now as Uskos) and relive another
event, another day.

Hanna left behind in Control tried to think of other things. It was not good for her or Michael (common sense told her, and Theo told her repeatedly) for Hanna to permit herself to sink altogether into Michael's obsession. Theo always came early, long before it was time for him to relieve Hanna. He planted himself solidly beside her and talked of what he had lately seen on the 'beams, talked of Lise's studies, encouraged Lise to wander in and out, encouraged Hanna to start the lessons promised the girl in *GeeGee*'s operation; he talked of Henrik, speculating on the traits of character or the history that had made Henrik what he was, and on what they might expect of him; when Hanna was more than usually silent he talked of her work in exopsychology (which was in *GeeGee*'s library and which he had read), misinterpreting it so outrageously that Hanna in a fury must correct him, was forced to think of something besides Michael, which was what Theo had intended in the first place.

"You think you're keeping me sane," she said. "If you think I don't see through it, you're the one who's crazy."

"On this ship, who isn't?" Theo said. "Mike's forgotten what year he's supposed to be living in. Henrik's plotting something—I swear that's what he thinks he's doing. Shen, do you ever see Shen? No? I don't either, except when she shows up at the end of my watch. I haven't heard her talk for a week. Sometimes she grunts. You're crazy because you're crazy about Mike. And Lise and me, we've adjusted. Adjusted to all that! So we must be crazy, too."

They were silent for a time—Theo could not talk continuously for hours, he had to stop sometimes—until Hanna said, "Theo, do you ever think of scanning for messages for us? When you're here alone at night?"

Theo said, not answering the question directly—but it was an answer all the same—"We used to scan all the time. When Mike first got *GeeGee,* when we used to cruise around, trying her out, playing with her, we were always in recept mode. We kept Shoreground time so Mike and Kareem could talk a couple times a day. For a while all the calls that went to the house, we had 'em sent to *GeeGee.* My God, was it expensive. We were playing ... In the middle of the night a couple of times, this woman who was after Mike, she'd call up half-spaced and get him out of bed and tell him what she'd like to be doing with him that very minute. He didn't know whether to laugh or cry."

Hanna's nose wrinkled with distaste. "Did she get him?"

"No, but she came close. It was a long dry spell before you came along, you know. That's why I said, sometimes he was ready to cry."

"I didn't know that. He never told me. It couldn't have been because—because there weren't candidates."

"There was never a lack of candidates. But he was funny the last year or two," Theo said thoughtfully. "Like nobody he saw was right, not even just for fun. The last year or so before we headed out for Revenge, I don't think there was anybody. I hated it."

"*You* hated it? Why?"

"Look, pretty women have pretty friends. I was doing all right with the fallout."

He was so wistful that Hanna laughed. The lighter mood stayed with her until her watch was over, but later, when she was settled in the small lounge with a reader in her hand, the words it displayed unseen, her thoughts returned to the question she had asked Theo—the question he had not wanted to answer, as was apparent now.

A simple instruction to *GeeGee* would be enough—and she wrestled more and more with the compulsion to give it. If she did, what might she hear? What message? The Lady of Koroth, perhaps: "I beg you to come home. I will make all pathways smooth. Though you have abandoned your birthright, I have not abandoned you." Or Starr: "Do you think me too small to confess to error? I'll see to it your homecoming will be safe—yes, his, too, even his . . ."

But that is not what he wishes, she said to the imaginary voices. *He would go on, on and on to the end which was his beginning, without reference to your forgiveness or your power. Perhaps my purpose should be his. Perhaps it should remain his.*

And so she would fight her compulsion, see space go by in silence, come always closer to a place where once again the voices would be out of reach. She would listen only to the voices Michael heard—

◆

—was so amazed by what I saw around me, that I had no more homesickness than before. I dreamed of Croft and Pavah each night, but it had been so since that day anyway. I did not know what to call the place, it was bigger than a village like Sutherland or Croft, it was only the Post, and it spread over many hectares of land there by the sea, first on the landward side a great ring of cultivated land, then a circle of factories and warehouses, then one of barracks after barracks, and then the tall white wall with the towers behind. They were not really rings, as I came to see, but half-rings, and the ends of each ended at the sea. Later, too, I came to know there was more to it than my eyes first saw. Not all the barracks were what they seemed, but some were divided into rooms where families might live together; and between those and the wall, there were houses like those I had known in Croft, and in them lived certain people who had earned the right—trusted servants of those who lived behind the wall, who performed their duties at the proper hours and afterward were permitted to leave, passing in and out unquestioned; the soldiers who watched the wall and their families; and also those like Georg, and like Alban and Kia, who took me in. But though there might be a blurring in the purposes of what I saw outside the wall, the meaning of the thing itself was clear, nor was there ever any doubt of its reason: it was to keep the multitude of those outside it, out.

Georg told me nothing more than he had already said on the first day when he carried me to Alban's house. But Kia took pity on my ignorance. She fed me, rations she said, but more than I was used to getting of late, and asked as Georg had asked if I could dance, sing, juggle, entertain? I said I didn't know, I'd never tried.

"Yet you've been heard to sing; so Georg said."

"The songs we sang in Croft," I answered.

"Well, they won't do here! Here they want songs of love, child."

"Like this?—
Pretty Rosie, bouncing Rosie,
Why do you fly so fast?
Stay a while and play a while
With me while summer lasts,
Bouncing Rosie come to play
Upon the summer grass—"

"No, no," said Kia laughing. "Listen!" And she sang in a low voice, so beautifully that I was enthralled, but slowly:

No music sounds sweet as my lover's song.
Song the sea sings to me, alas!
The sea winds have blown away his adoration,
The sea waves have washed me from his heart.
Only in the wind do I hear him sing my name.

She laughed again at my expression; I had never heard so sweet a voice.

"You're too young for that," she said. "Though your voice seems good, and if it survives changing, and your face lives up to its promise as you grow, the young ladies beyond the wall will be sighing for you in a few years' time!"

"What young ladies?" I said. "What's beyond the wall?"

"The masters," Kia said. "You've heard of the masters surely, even west of the mountains."

"I've heard of them, but I don't know what they are."

Kia looked as if she thought I might be playing a joke on her, either that or my ignorance had no limit. Finally she saw the second thing was true and explained, but either she didn't make a very good job of it or I couldn't get my thought around what she said, because still it had no sense, It was a jumble of people who were different, who were rich, who ate without working for it, who had things I'd never heard of before, who did what they liked all the time. But maybe she explained it well enough after all, because even when I learned more about it, I never learned anything to contradict what I thought she'd said.

Then Alban came home, and late though it was, when he found I'd never seen the sea he took me to it. We walked with the wind stirring round our ears through cold cobbled streets, the first I'd ever seen, always curving and curving toward the north with the wall and the soldiers' houses at our right. And there were gates in the wall, with broad roads smoothly paved with stone leading straight to them; but they were closed, and over each one was a kind of little house with windows, and Alban said there were soldiers in them. Then far off I began to hear a sound, which was sometimes like thunder and sometimes like a hiss, and at last we came around a final bulge in the wall—which was not a

perfect half-circle, but in places bulged out or withdrew—
and the wind struck me with a force to take my breath away,
and there was a glimmer of pale sand and beyond that the
sea. The foam that rolled up on the sand was luminous, and
the wind took it and blew it stinging onto my face. But out
past where the waves broke, out to sea, there was nothing
but blackness. It was so cold I shook, though I had still the
warm cloak Mirrah had made for me just before leaving
Croft, laughing and exclaiming on my growth, *Soon I'll have
no time for anything but making clothes for Mikki*— The
salt wind brought wetness to my eyes. Alban said the sea
went on forever. I had to turn my head to see light, and even
the lights of the walled city were set well back from the sea,
and they wavered with the wind and the blurring of my
eyes. It was a bigger world than I had thought, this planet as
Pavah had called it, it did not seem like a place where I
might have been born.

I think Alban talked a little, but I heard nothing of what
he said; not that night. When he was done talking and
thought I should be done looking, he said we must go home
(though it was not my home), and we walked away in the
dark.

I was used to working with my hands, stockherding, stone
cutting, the dirt hot on my arms with the summer sun. The
tricks Georg put me up to didn't seem like work, and each
day it was something different. The dancing-master made
me twist, sway, wanted me to fly through the air, it seemed,
and Kia made me sing; somebody they called the master of
hands came once, tried to teach me an illusion or two but
went away disgusted; still he told Georg there was hope for
me later, when I was over the worst of my growth and the
parts of my body didn't run away from each other any more.
Yet the dancing-master said it was too late, while Kia said
soon it would be the wrong time for my voice, though it
wasn't yet. I couldn't see what they wanted with me, didn't
see why they kept me there. But Kia one night while they
drank wine, she and Alban and Georg and some others of
the performers whose services were not needed behind the
wall that night, she took my chin in her hand and turned my
face to the light: "What a waste it'd be!" she said. Saw the
question in my eyes, I think, and talked about faces and

fortunes. At first it made a nonsense in my head. But I understood something before she was done: "Such a pretty flower to bloom for the countryfolk!" she said, and like a light breaking I knew how I looked through her eyes. It explained much, the exclaimings over me by Mirrah's friends in Sutherland each time we went there as I grew, which went back as far as I could remember; it explained a man weeping with loneliness who had approached me in the barracks one night when the lights were turned out, though my sleepiness and ignorance had turned him away; and Georg, of course, what he had heard. I pondered it while they drank, seeing that in Croft they had been used to me from birth and so no one had ever commented on how I looked, or maybe didn't really see me. I was Pavah's son, Mirrah's son, a hard worker, of easy temper and, I had been told, sweet nature, and those who knew me had not cared about my face.

Then Kia, filled with wine, began to cry. They had taken me from my mirrah, she said, and from that passed into lamenting that she had no child. Alban was silent and grim, having heard it all before. And it was then by accident that they learned what I was good for, because one of the men, Norn by name, had brought with him an instrument, and it leaned in a corner; and as Kia wept, and Alban grew sullen, and it was plain that he felt himself accused and a quarrel was brewing, I crept to the corner to get away and began to play with the instrument. Norn, also wishing to escape, followed me and showed me its principles. Yet it seemed that I knew them and had only to be reminded how to turn my breath into music. Norn became silent, speaking only now and then in a whisper to correct my fingering or give me some other word of advice, and I played a song Kia had taught me, and then the one she had sung on that first night, and then a song I knew from Croft. I paid no attention to the others, only to Norn's whispers, which I heard eagerly and which my breath and fingers translated without further thought. I was happy for the first time since the day of the walk to Sutherland, and more than happy, there was a wholeness I had not imagined before, nor could I name it in any way. And I was not conscious of doing or being anything remarkable, and when I looked up and saw that all of them stared at me, their eyes shining in the dim lamplight, my first thought was that I had done something wrong.

But that was not why they gaped at me, as I learned soon enough.

"Still you must learn other things," Georg said. So once a day the dancing-master came to teach me pliés, pirouettes, and other moves with outlandish names; also Kia kept teaching me songs to sing and telling me where to breathe. Norn also came a day or two to teach the flute, but then desisted. "I am afraid of doing more harm than good," he said. His place was taken by a woman named Portia, who on the first day of her coming crashed into Kia's kitchen crying, "Where is it? Where is this prodigy? I must see it!" And she was not awed as Norn had been, which was good, since I was getting a swelled head; but she listened to me play and said, "You have much to learn, boy!" And proceeded to teach, thereby earning my affection without ever doing anything else to get it. She did not need to do anything else.

So the music was consolation and I needed consoling, yes, needed it. Otherwise when the novelty of being there had worn off, when it ceased to be a visit to a new place and became each day's life, I would not have been able to bear it. Pavah since his death had visited me in dreams each night; now Mirrah came also, carrying Carmina. They smiled at me and told me what a good boy I was, a fine son whom they approved and were glad to have, which in truth was what they had always done; Mirrah was the one to say the words, but I had always known that she spoke for Pavah, too. And so now they were gone, Pavah into the gray country that has no end, and Mirrah might as well have been there, too, for all I saw of her. Yet I did hear a little from time to time, for Kia knew a captain whose men went each day to the camp, the same who had first brought me to the notice of Georg, and she got him to bring news of Mirrah, and carry news back. So I heard that she was well, and that Carmina talked now, really talked, and remembered Mikki. This helped, too; I do not know if music alone would have been enough. I think not. But together, they were enough.

Thus the end of autumn passed away and the winter came in on great storms of wind that filled the air with flying snow. There were fogs that hid even the top of the white

wall if I stood at its foot and looked up; and rains that lasted
three or four days and consisted of a salty soup that did not
so much fall as hover, creeping into houses and garments
and covering everything with damp. But there were also
days when the sky leapt high and blue over my head, and
the Ring was a dagger-stroke across it for the sharp-eyed to
see. In fair weather or foul I went about the town as I could,
though with an easier heart when the day had been light, as
if the sun illuminated my soul. I was not filled with any great
curiosity, no, I was incurious as I had been on the day Georg
first came to the camp, a truth which was not much like me,
who had explored every stone, game trail, streamlet and
grove within a boy's reach around Croft; but I was drawn all
the same, as if one stride led to another, though I thought I
had no wish to walk on. There was little enough time for
exploring, for between dancing and Kia and Portia and the
lessons Portia set me I was busy all the day; but an hour or
two of the dancing-master was not enough to satisfy my
body, used as it was to climbing and running and rough play.
The dark came early, and Kia had some notion I should not
be out in the night, and I sought to obey, my own notion
being that she stood in Mirrah's place, and wanted for me
what Mirrah would want; but the upshot was that I found it
hard to fall asleep, and my legs of their own accord would
kick and twitch, seeking all on their own to run. And after
some days when my eyes were half-closed with lack of rest,
Portia said that she would speak to Kia; and afterward Kia
said I might go out at night, providing I were home an hour
before the curfew, which came about two hours before the
middle of the night.

It was in the dark, then, that I roamed, learning by chance
the names of the streets and alleys, and what kinds of people
lived in them. In the Street of Wheelwrights an old lady took
a fancy to my face and then to what I had to tell her, for she
had never been away from the town and loved to hear about
the mountains, here where she had only ever seen flat sand,
fields, marshes: "And you have to look up to see the tops!"
she said often, marveling. I found the docks from which the
fishermen set forth each day, but hardly ever saw a fisher-
man, for their work began before dawn and was done by
dusk. Still I saw one of the fishers once or twice, working by
lamplight to mend a plank or a net, and he talked of the

storms that might come without warning and take men, boats, and all to the bottom of the sea. And afterward I never had a bite from the sea without thinking of the brave boats going light over the ocean waves.

So through the nights of that winter, while the wind blew cold and sharp, I went around the town. There were few children, which had also been true in Croft and Sutherland, and though those of the part of the town where I lived were friendly enough, it was different among the great buildings where the greater part of the people lived. None there wanted to join my rambles, or invite me into their games, or even talk to me, once they learned where I lived and what I was to be. "We want none of the masters' garbage," one said to me, a boy of about my own age, and another called names and spat at me, and a third heaved a stone at my head. I was no fighter, and was not angry but bewildered; and Kia told me there was jealousy among the mass of people for those who were attached to the masters, and worked for them or guarded or entertained them. But the boy who had thrown the stone, he had not even heard me speak, I had not opened my mouth, and Kia looked at me considering as if about to speak; but then she turned my question away and talked of something else. But she had been looking at my eyes, and I remembered what Pavah had said on the day of his death.

"Whose eyes are these?" I said.

She considered again a longer time, so that I thought still she would not answer. But at last she said, "Saddhi."

"What does that mean?" I said.

"They are one of the great families." She waited again, but this time I saw she had more to say, so I waited, too. "We've talked of your eyes," she said. "Georg did not know when he went for you that you had them. But perhaps they'll be less conspicuous with age. Sometimes they fade."

"My pavah had them," I said. I had never spoken of Pavah there before.

"You'd best hope they're not a pass back to the fields," she said. "We've talked of hiding them."

"Hiding them? How?"

"By way of small things that are put in the eyes, smaller than this." Here she showed me the nail of her little finger. "It doesn't hurt and does no harm."

"But why must they be hidden?"

"It's this way," she said, and set out on a long and unclear explanation which she strung out so long and so confusingly, to suit her delicacy and my age, that I would have been none the wiser, except that when it was rendered out it amounted to the same thing Pavah had said—somebody might be embarrassed by the bastard in the house, or in this case the bastard's son.

Yet no one else in the barracks ever looked twice at my eyes, and though I saw none like them, I remembered what Pavah had said about their being in the factories and fields. And while I did not stop going to that other part of the town, I no longer tried to make friends, and only stood on the edges of groups of men or women and listened to their talk. Much of it was not good to hear. On one night, one night alone, I heard men talking of how rations had been cut again, and wondering what there'd be to eat by winter's end, and women talking of an illness that had swept through a building which had been sealed and remained sealed, trapping those inside. They talked also of a baby which had died, though, they said with bitterness, those behind the wall had medicines which would have saved it. And at another gathering of men I heard that the fishers were being driven to sea even in dangerous weather, and told to bring back greater and greater catches.

I learned nearly all that I learned from these walks in the night, slipping from one knot of men or women to another and seeking not to stand out; for Kia and Alban spoke of the people seldom, and slightingly, and I did not know that their feelings did not match their words, and the words were said as a concealment. But had they spoken to me freely, they could have told me only what I saw with my eyes: that the hunger was growing out there where the favored of the masters did not live, and with it sickness; and the people were not yet starving and so not in despair, but angry.

Finally there came a night of bitter cold when I was taken behind the wall. There was to be an event there, one of the gatherings that went on all year long, though more in the winter when life was confined—for the masters did not stay altogether behind the wall, I was told, and in the warm evenings of summer especially were to be seen walking in the

town. And even in the winter they might go abroad, but I
had never seen any of them. For this occasion Portia re-
hearsed me with the flute in earnest, three songs only, and
simple ones, one as an accompaniment to Kia's singing.
Though they were simple they were no less beautiful—only
I was heartily sick of them in the end! For Portia made me
play them so often that I would wake in the night with fingers moving and mouth puckered, still rehearsing. I was
also required to wear a new suit of clothes of fabric so fine
that the touch of a finger left a mark on it, so sensitive was
the pile; and if I drew my hand across it, I shivered at the
touch. There was a great bloused tunic over a singlet that fit
close, and breeches which came only to the knee and white
stockings under that, and soft crimson boots to the ankle,
hard to walk in, for there was a stilt at each heel, which
made me taller and tilted me forward; and Kia watched me
learn to walk in those boots and laughed.

"This is harder than the music," I said, but practiced dutifully, until I could move in the things without stumbling;
because it seemed important to Kia who stood in my mirrah's place. And nothing was the same as it had been before,
and already, first in the barracks at the woodland camp
where the wind howled and Pavah smiled behind my closed
eyes, and then in the dark streets of the town about the Post,
I had concluded though not without tears and struggle, that
it was not the part of a man to pine for yesterday, which
seemed senseless as wishing in autumn for spring. If winter
had come to me, then so it must be.

So dressed in my crimson boots and dressed in gold and
swathed in a cloak much less fine, for the protection of the
richer garments, I passed through the wall at last through
one of the gates which I had never seen open, and inside the
gate there was a cobbled court where there burned enough
lights to turn the winter night into day. But snow fell and
had been falling since daylight and the snow stopped and
dimmed the light; and the little fires that burned in their
coverings of glass melted the snow that fell on them, and
the snowmelt blurred and ran down the glass like yellow
tears, to fall on the stones, where it froze. But I forgot the
cold soon enough; for everywhere I looked, behind that
bright wall, were so many new things that it seemed I had
been transported altogether to a new place, which had

never even heard of Croft, could not even be a part of the Post I was coming to know.

The plain size of it astonished me at the beginning, for the structures whose towers I had seen from the other side of the wall were lofty indeed, and stood not separate but connected by walkways, archways, passages and tunnels, so that it was all a single thing, yet so large that an hour's walk might be required to go from one end of it to another, and the stones of which it was made everywhere had been carved and tormented into ornament. I glimpsed many courtyards, too, and each had its fountain (though now they held strange shapes of ice, not flowing water).

And when we had passed inside there were countless hallways, and such twists and turns and changes of direction that I was bewildered; and a kitchen that had in it a dozen cooks, who gave us mugs of a hot drink that went to my head and made me dizzy; and large rooms so full of wonders that I could hardly take anything in. There were pictures that moved and made me stare, for I thought them real at first, and then was shamed by my stupidity; there was music that came from nowhere, played on instruments I had never heard, or sung by voices like none I had heard before, and rendered in words the sense of which I could not make out, not one. There were shapes and colors like a festival wilder than any dream I had ever had (but they filled my dreams for a long time after); yet in all that riot of strange new things, one stood out, a simple thing in itself: a small table of a wood I had never seen or heard of. It seemed heavier than the woods I had known in Croft or even at the camp, and it was so dark that my eyes took it to be black; only when I looked closer, under the darkness there was light trying to get out, shifting as my eyes moved, and drawing me in with the promise of gold. And its shape was simple, a matter of curves it seemed any child could think up; but the lines together moved my heart, so that I stood and looked at it as if no other table had ever been made before, and there was no other proper shape for such a thing.

Now with looking at this thing I had fallen behind, so that Kia, turning in impatience, came to fetch me, and she looked at me and laughed, for tears had come to my eyes.

"It is like the music," I said, because music sometimes

touched me as this object did, and Kia did not laugh when it was music that moved me.

"Be glad you have music," she answered. "It is all you will ever have. I can show you the man who made this, I can show you his house, and you can look all over it without finding any such thing. He cannot keep his own work, it is too precious; the masters send him wood, it comes from far away, and all that he makes with it, comes here. How else can he eat? Be glad your gift is for music, Mikhail. It does not take as long to make as a piece like this, and it cannot be taken away as this can. No matter how much you make there is music left, there is more than when you began."

And Kia laughed again, but as if the light that rested within the wood had put a different face on all I saw, it was plain that her laughter was a covering for some pain that lay within.

"If your eyes did not name your fathers, your tastes would," she said.

And who might my fathers be? —the question lay on my tongue, but I did not speak it, I knew the answer: my fathers were also the fathers of those who held this inner city, and it might be that a cousin of mine, of my age, with these same eyes, lived behind the wall always in the presence of beauty.

This thought took all my attention, so that Kia was able to take me on through the endless halls without my protesting, for I hardly saw where we went, and at last we came to rest in a small room behind a figured curtain.

Here the instruments were given their final tuning and the singers hummed, their voices running up and down the scales which in this place did not seem familiar but mysterious, as if we prepared for some great event. Here also Kia told me to open my eyes, and she held them open one by one, and put into them the objects she had told me about, which I had tried already on the day before and so knew would not hurt me, would only feel strange going in and then be forgotten. But I knew, because I had looked in a mirror on the first trial, that they made my eyes appear as black as Mirrah's.

After which, a little later, one put his head through the curtain and nodded at Kia, and we filed through the opening and the music began.

It was good that I had little to play; I was full of looking that night, though what I saw did not live up to my expectations, those having become so great, and the greater for having no clear notion of what I was to see. Did I think the masters would have two heads apiece? That all their garments would be made of gold? When they entered they were different indeed, magnificent to my eyes. They seated themselves at a long table some distance from the dais where the musicians were staioned, and there were jewels and fine fabrics all new to me, and gold, yes, more gold than I had imagined being in the whole world. And I told myself that under all this splendor there were men and women neither larger nor more fair than any others I had seen, and maybe no more wise—yet they were different all the same, and it seemed to me that the difference was this: they had no eyes. Oh, eyes they had, and in the proper places, but their use was reserved for each other, for their jewels and gowns and the delicacies before them. They did not see the musicians, no, we were invisible, and even when those eyes strayed in our direction they looked through us as if to the wall, and it was the same with the men and women who served at table. And there were more who served than who ate, so that if the musicians also were counted, and the cooks in the great kitchen, and the Postmen who guarded the entrance through which we had come, there might be three or four persons who lived, on this night, only to make an hour or two pleasant for each of these folk; and I looked at them with attention, trying to understand why this was.

There was one at the end of the table who would be the host, for those who served at table deferred to him, and to the woman at its other end; and both of these were old, the man with white hair and a great white beard, the woman with hair gray as the winter's cloud, and wrinkled skin beneath the collar of jewels at her throat. There were also several others, among them a man who drew my eyes because of his coloring, like none I had ever seen: pale, with eyes so light I wondered (at that distance) if they had any color or were transparent as clear ice, and on his head a stiff brush of hair that shifted color in the candlelight and sometimes showed the hue of flame. And this man was different from the others, because he saw us; or at least he saw me, when the time for my part in the music came. Though I played well, first the two songs I had learned for unaccompanied flute, and the other with Kia's voice, there was nothing to set off this part of the music to make it special; but at the end I looked up to see that this man looked at me closely. And Kia beside me set her hand on my back, and I knew that she also had seen that he looked at me; but why that should move her to touch me, I did not know.

I was done and my reason for being there fulfilled, and I continued to listen to the players, but more to the talk at table, and especially, now, to the man who had looked at me. He spoke softly, so that it was hard to hear what he said; but soon it was evident that he was a traveler, would leave this place at some time and go on, though I did not know where there was to go.

"And how many years will pass before you come again?" asked the wife of the host, and he answered, "I cannot say. It's not that I would not come more often, as you know."

"I know," she answered, sighing. "We know what you bring is not given you as gift. But what can we do, how pay?—the mines are empty, all the workers have had to turn to the fields. A nostrum for the blight—that's what you should bring!"

"And maybe I will next time," he said. "But the difficulty lies in obtaining it without stirring the curiosity you must avoid. I'll take the samples with me, the grain, the seeds and leaves, the spoiled fruit; those are all imports, and at first look no one will see anything to surprise. And if the blight should also be imported, something lain dormant these many years, then the remedy might be easy to find. But more likely it is not. More likely it is native, something never seen there before, and the business will be harder. All you've paid me may not be enough for the bribes and the mouths to be closed."

"Yet all we have may depend on you," said another man.

"A heavy responsibility," the traveler said. "But there is another thing I might do for you: carry word."

There was silence, but I saw them shake their heads; and the youngest of the women said, "Then we would lose all we have."

"A hard choice," the traveler said. "You know what

Oversight's meddling would do; but it may be that only hunger lies at the end of the path you walk now."

All this puzzled me, and I thought I would ask Kia later what it meant, and that the time would come soon because the meal was ending—and I had wondered for some time if it ever would—there were such processions of platters, changes of plate, so many flagons of drink! And I was hungry from watching all those others eat, and also tired of sitting still, so that Kia already had whispered to me that I must not fidget. But finally it did end, and those at the table rose to go out; only the traveler did not go out right away, but turned aside to the dais where we were.

And Kia stiffened at my side when she saw that his attention was for me, though I did not know why, for there was nothing out of the way in what he said to me. He wanted to know my name and age, and how long I had been among the players, and why he had not seen me before; and also, when he learned that I had only this season come to the town, he asked whether I liked it there. Then he gave me a coin and went out (so it was true what Georg had said, I could get gold here); but when I looked at Kia she was breathing hard and quick, and I saw that she was angry.

Now the servants of the house began to clear away the remains of the feast, and I understood from some words that passed that we were to return to the kitchens, and find a place in our bellies for whatever good things might be left. But Kia's anger burst forth, so that as we walked to the kitchens I saw nothing, but only listened to Kia; and she talked of the traveler, warning me against him.

"I will speak to the Mistress Ehr," she said. "I will not have it happen, what might happen!"

But one of the players said, "They all have their toys, Kia. You said nothing to Coro when the Saddhi lad attached her to his house, nor to Yav when the Mistress Conneril's husband lost his powers and she looked about and Yav took her eyes."

"Coro was not a child, and Yav was a full-grown man," Kia answered. "Such things happen; how would they not, when we live by favor of men like the Saddhi lad, and women like the Mistress Conneril? But this man Tistou is another thing. Well, maybe he will bring a remedy for the blight and maybe not—and maybe when he comes again, he will not find what he expects."

Then she said she would not bring me behind the wall again until the traveler Tistou was gone, so that he should not see me and be reminded of me. But it came upon me that I had understood nothing that night, nothing but the music which my very bones understood; and my ignorance made me sad and weary, and it took all the good tidbits the cooks could give me to cheer me again.

Now I ceased to go to the greater town, for the nights were even colder than before, and it was more pleasant to do my roaming in the streets by the wall, where I knew many and had only to rap on a door at the need to get warm. In this way, too, I met Kia's neighbors, and soon I saw that these neighbors were of two sorts, and divided by the way in which Kia talked with them, or before them. With most all her talk was small gossip of the neighborhood, of the scarcity of food in the marketplace, and other matters such as these. But with some she talked with passion of the greater town, and there were conferences from which I was excluded, and sent to stand outside the door shivering and warn Kia if anyone approached; and when this happened, then like masks the faces of those inside would change, and when the newcomer entered the talk again would be unimportant. I begged Kia to tell me the reason for these strange proceedings, but she would not tell me. So I was left to guess, and my guesses brought me no comfort; and often at night after one of these conferences, I would dream of Pavah again, and not as if he visited me with smiles; no, I would see him run, hear the guns, see him fall, and wake with a cold fist clutching the heart in my chest.

Now, what Kia would not tell me, I thought to find out in another way, and for this purpose attached myself to one of those who shared her secrets, a man called Leren who lived some distance away, but still in the closer ring. But there was more than purpose in the companionship that sprang up between us, for Leren took to me and I to him, and all the more because he reminded me of Otto in his plain blunt ways, though in stature and face they were nothing like.

This Leren was a single man, black-bearded and young, and was a handyman for the upkeep of that beyond the wall, all parts of which he knew well, though to me it was a mystery. He had a tale to tell of a summer's day when he pointed the stones of that city's highest tower, where only a scarce skyfowl might come once a year, it was so high above the waters where the seabirds found their meals; and on that day he looked out to the edge of the sea where it curved to the world's other side, the wind tearing his beard, dizzy with the sun and alone above the Post, and saw it spread small at his feet. He had a tale also of a maiden who did not acknowledge his presence at her window, where he had come to mend a casement, and whom he watched as she removed her garments, supple as a fish and white as the silver band of the Ring on a cloudless night in spring—this tale he told with humor, swearing that he had seen her eyes shift at the start toward where he stood, and wondering how she would have greeted him, had he come in. He had many stories like these and I listened to them all, and listened also to the men who came to drink ale by his fire, for the speech here was less guarded. They said that each day there were more deaths in the town, and the masters heeded them not and were sleek and fat and did no rationing for themselves, but only ordered it for others. There was anger among these men, who talked of the guardhouses over the gates like men who had studied them well. And though they said no word of plans before me, still it was plain there was a plan; for they spoke of the traveler as well, and there was something they wished to do, but would not do until he was gone, and it worried them that he tarried.

"If the sickness takes us first, there will be no hope," they said.

"It is the old for the most part so far," Leren said, and though he was a noisy man full of loud laughter, his voice was soft and sad.

"And babes," said another man, "and those already sick from some other cause: the weak. But the strong will begin dying soon."

"The masters will sicken of it, too," said still another, a man named Willem.

"They will not," said a fourth man. "He brings them medicines, the man Tistou."

"The undying," Willem said, and spat into the fire.

"No one is undying," Leren said.

"He came in my grandfather's time," Willem said. "And I have grown from child to man, and seen him at the start and end of that time, and he has not changed one jot. Where he comes from, things are different. Who knows what is possible there?"

The others said, "We have heard that he comes from the other side of the world. It might be worth seeking that side."

Leren laughed and said, "So you believe that story? They want us to believe it; they do not want us to think far. Other places! The one that spawned him is farther away than you can imagine. The sons of the masters admit it, when the time is right. There are things they will say in secret to one of their own age, swearing him to silence, which they are not supposed to tell. But some say also that this is not the man who came when our grandfathers were young. This Tistou had a grandfather, too."

"I would not care what he had," Willem said, "if he would take the flying machine and go away. We cannot fight that. But when he comes again, I will see him dead."

"Some father will kill him someday," Leren said, "or a mother holding onto her child with one hand and a knife with the other."

Here Willem looked at me with thoughtful eyes and said, "Animals can be trapped. Maybe we have the bait to trap that one, if we are willing to use it."

But Leren laughed out loud and said, "Only if you wish to die, too, by Kia's hand!" And they spoke of it no more.

Now for a time I ceased to go to Leren's house, because something happened that drove everything else from my mind. Kia, and the captain of the Postmen who went to the camp, did a great kindness for me; and one day when a light snow fell, a wagon of the Postmen stopped at our door, and from it came Mirrah, Carmina clinging to her. I did not know how Kia had done it, what promises or payments she had made, or what might have passed between her and the captain then or another time. She would not say, she would not tell me when the excess of my joy was spent and I could ask questions. But I did not spend a long time asking them. How this thing had come about was nothing next to Mirrah's presence, though she was not the Mirrah of all my years before, but a woman who did not smile, not even at my teasing. Yet I saw in her tears at our meeting that being with me lifted a great care from her soul, and in her way of looking at me, that in me she had all of Pavah she would ever have again. She did not speak of him, though a time had come when I wanted to talk of him, but I saw that I must wait. And so I let words go, and instead made music for her, sitting at her feet for hours at a time with no sound to be heard except the crackle of the fire, and the wind moaning outside, and the melodies I made with my flute.

Yet this peace did not last long. The rumors of sickness grew more and more loud, until it seemed like the ocean tide rising over the town, and one day the Postmen came from door to door, shouting and giving orders, and saying that beginning on the next day, no man would be allowed to leave his house, not even to take his needs and his money to the marketplace, but rations of fish and grain would be taken from house to house; and also the servants of the masters would be locked behind the wall, so they might not carry contagion with passing back and forth. And when Kia heard this she said she must go to the market at once, and Mirrah went with her; and when they had gone, and I thought of the confinement ahead, I ran out the door to have freedom while I could.

I went to Leren's without thought, my feet slipping over the cobbles in that direction from habit. And when I came to his house he was leaving it, brooding behind his beard as he closed the door. He was bound for the greater town, and at first he did not want my company. His hard hands were nervous, his eyes kept straying toward the town; I thought he had a burden on his back, but looked again, and saw that if he bore a weight it must be of the mind. "This is no stroll for pleasure!" he said, but my eagerness to follow him was great, and in the end he gave in to stop my begging.

So we set out at a quick pace, and soon left behind all the streets of small houses, and came to the first rows of giant barracks, where families lived crammed together in single rooms, and ate and bathed together in a crowd. These were a larger and permanent version of the forest camp I had come from, and I told Leren that had been worse, for here those who loved one another lived together. But Leren said I was wrong, he said it roughly; his mood that day was grim.

"It's maybe no better there," he said, "but no worse ei-

ther, as you'd find soon enough if you tried living in one of
those—" He pointed at a structure we passed: a heap of
dirty brick with a few scant windows like clouded eyes.
"There's no love in there," he said. "It dies with the crowding. Take a man and a maid young enough for the juices to
flow in spite of the work: they find a way to get out of the
reach of eyes, and he gets her with child. Then they get a
room; it's the only way to get one, to get out of the men's
barracks, or the women's. So far it's a change for the better.
The child comes, and maybe it lives and maybe not, and
maybe the mother lives and maybe not. There's little
enough care beforehand, and she works right up to her
time, unless she's sick near death. Now there's three of them
there. The child gets bigger and the room gets smaller.
They're tired with work and maybe the mother's mother
gets too old to work, or too sick—well, the old one comes
to that room, too, and the care of her is visited on the family's head. There's no quiet, no room or time for thought,
and any love there might have been gets trodden underfoot
until it dies. A man raises his hand 'gainst his wife, both
raise their hands 'gainst the child, and maybe the poor old
grandmother is beaten, too. You know nothing about it.
What could you know, coming from the freedom of the
fields?"

My heart shrank, and now there was no talking as we
walked on, and I tried to imagine how it would have been,
Pavah and Mirrah and Carmina and me all together in one
tiny room, but I could not, nor could I think of Pavah striking me, I could not imagine it at all. And while I thought, we
passed through the ring of barracks, not in a straight line
but zigzagging toward the north, passing those places one
by one and passing between pairs of them—they rose up
more sheer than the mountains and were dark against the
sky, which was gray with snow, and I tried not to look at
them, for it seemed they might fall on me. And when at last
we broke out of them, I was glad—only where we went
then, was worse, for we plunged into the ring of factories
and warehouses. I had never been there before, for that part
of the town was silent and deserted at night, when I did my
wandering; but sometimes in the days I had seen clouds of
black smoke rising over it, to be blown away inland by the
wind from the sea. I followed Leren in silence, my eyes being

busy enough without making work for my mouth. The structures here did not all look alike; most were made of brick, but here and there was metal, and there were turrets, troughs, wires, and pipes in great variety and abundance. After its fashion it was not even ugly, but looked as if a giant had gone mad and thrown his toys about—and then set them afire, for some of these places spouted smoke. It was not beautiful, no, not that, unless there be a kind of beauty in desolation, for desolate it was: the ground was covered with grit, and nothing grew there, nor did it seem that anything could grow there again. But also it seemed that words like "beauty" and "ugliness" did not apply here, that this place was a thing in itself and like nothing else, and so could not be compared with anything.

Now Leren turned into one of these places, still moving swiftly, and we plunged into a maze of hallways and chambers, all dirty and dark; but there was no one inside, and it was silent, though I had expected the place to be filled with noise and machines and men working.

"Where is everybody?" I asked, and Leren answered: "Many of the factories are idle. They have little to work with; the mines were at half-strength all autumn long, and spring and summer, too. But this one has had work, until now. It was working yesterday, and there was no plan to close it."

"What do they make here?" I said.

"Plate," he said with loathing. "Plate for the masters' tables, finer than my bread will ever see! Well, they'd best take care not to break any more; there's none new being made."

He stood in one place and shouted a name, but no one answered his call, and the sounds of his voice echoed in the dark. "Gordon!" he cried out. "Gordon! Are you here? Is anybody here?" And at length he gave over shouting and stood silent in that dim place where I could hardly see his eyes, and I wished to ask who Gordon was, but I did not. I thought Leren had forgotten I was there. And he turned and plunged through the dark to where we had come in without a word to me, though he mumbled to himself, and once more in a frozen lane with that tangle of pipes in the sky he walked on ever faster, and I went beside him, half-running to keep up. "The infirmary," he said, "they must have taken him to the infirmary." And back we went into the ring of barracks, but through a part I had never seen before, until we turned down another street, at the end of which there was a structure much smaller than most, and all on one level not climbing toward the sky. I saw nothing of the place save the outer door; for a woman came out to greet us, and said the man Leren sought was not there.

"He must be there," Leren said, "he was taken ill yesterday, word came to me last night, and I would have come then, but curfew was too near."

"There are other infirmaries," the woman said. Her skin was dark, but there were blacker pouches under her eyes.

"There are no others near Millside."

"Millside?" said the woman. "Yes, there are men here from Millside. But none of that name, and none who came as late as yesterday."

Leren fell silent and stared. And at length the woman made as if to turn away, but he put out his hand and said entreating her, "What is wrong at Millside?"

She answered, "What is wrong everywhere? They have the fever. That is all we do here now: nurse those who have it to recovery or death, and keep them isolated from all others. All the infirmaries are full. Soon the sick must go elsewhere; to the forest, I think." And she said that all the infirmaries, on the day before, had been ordered to turn out all who were not sick of the new fever; and they were by no means empty, but overflowed.

"But how can they go to the forest?" Leren said. "Will they lie on the ground in the snow?"

"I do not know," the woman said, the words were slurred and indistinct, and I saw that she was desperately tired. "There is a place, not far, where land is being cleared, and so there are places for the workers to live. It's said they may be sent there."

"But there are people there already!" I said, for I knew the place she meant.

The woman gave me hardly a glance. "There are people here, too," she said. "If it must burn itself out, better there than here, where there are so many more to die. As for me, I do not care where I go. All the nurses have run away, and only I and two others are left. I will die of this fever, I think. I do not care whether I die there or here."

Now Leren had wildness in his eyes. He said, "Is that where they of Millside have gone?"

"They have not," the woman said. She looked at Leren, and I saw that she would have had pity for him, had there been any pity left, but it was all burned and worn out of her. "There were too many," she said. "They brought us a sick man from Millside, then five, then fifteen. Then there was no room. We have babes here, children, mothers. I will not turn out a child so a man full of life may take its place."

But Leren had another question, only he could not ask it. I saw it tremble on his lips, but he could not get it out. And the woman looked at him with the last shard of her pity, which had come up from some unknown place, and answered it: "They have sealed Millside up. Those who live will come out."

But that was the last thing I heard her say, for Leren gave a great cry and turned and ran toward the north, I following and soon out of breath, remembering what I had heard before when a place had been sealed. On either hand the rows of brick stood up and were silent and full of pain, and what could it be like closed into those walls in the deadly air without escape?

Leren could not run forever, he had to slow, so I could, too; I walked with him, panting as he panted. And when my breath returned I longed to ask who Gordon was, but I looked at Leren's face and did not; for it looked like Mirrah's on the night she learned of Pavah's death, only Leren did not cry as Mirrah had, but the pain inside was the same, the clawing and eating alive.

At last at noon (but the clouds were thickening and there were no shadows in the gray light), we came to Millside, which stood by itself at a low place in the ground and near a frozen stream; also it was close to the sea. And already when we first saw it, Leren slowed, and slowed and slowed again as we came nearer, for at each of the small mingy doors stood a man in the uniform of the guards of the Post, and they had guns like the one which had killed Pavah. And Leren slowed still more, like a man in a bad dream where the earth turns to water and he cannot make his way through it; for he knew it was no use to approach that place, but was driven all the same. And there seemed no threat in the Postmen who watched us come, they stood at first with their weapons on their backs—and when, as we came close, they took them from their backs, even then they held them loosely in their arms. Only when we came to a certain distance of one of them, then he gripped the weapon more firmly, and so did those on either side of him; then Leren stopped.

He did not speak immediately, as if he were trying to think of what to say. He only looked at the Postman, and the Postman looked at him. But finally he said—it was a voice I had not heard from him before, a low yearning voice without hope—"My brother is inside."

Now the Postmen were of many sorts, as I had found at the camp, some being cold and others more or less kind, within the limits of their duties, and this one maybe was less unkind than unnerved by Leren's aspect, which was that of a man in despair—"Go," he said, bringing up his weapon. "No one can go in. No one can come out."

And Leren looked up at the Postman some more, and then he lifted his eyes up the side of the building, to the very top, as if he would see Gordon there; but no one was there. He stood there long, looking up at the bricks and then at the Postman and up at the bricks again, seeking as I thought for a face at a window, but in his misery he was dumb. And at last the Postman pointed his gun at Leren's breast, and the memory of what I had seen happen to Pavah took me, and I pulled at Leren's arm and called his name, near weeping; at which he looked at the gun for so long that I thought he contemplated taking it away. And he had made no move that might be taken as threat, nor had any but those few words been exchanged, yet the day stretched out like a thread taut and ready to break, and others of the Postmen began to come toward us.

Then Leren walked away. He turned often to look over his shoulder until the place was out of sight and hidden by other barracks that came between, and he was silent; but after a time, as we came near his house, the tears began to run down his face and into his beard, and his shoulders shook with them. I could not comfort him, there was no comfort to give, but when finally he talked I could listen; still what he said had little to do with Gordon.

"It cannot last forever. There must be an end. There are stores enough of guns, and men to fire them, yes, willing men enough, and only a matter of getting the guns. It's talked of, did you know that? It has been talked of, there is more talk each day, even in Millside, especially there, and close to the wall and even behind it, too. It started at Millside. It started there. But if Millside dies, it will start again somewhere else. Do you hear?" Here he stopped in the street and seized my arm, and stared into my face with the tears still in his eyes and said, "It will start somewhere else!"

"Yes," I whispered, but he went on without hearing me: "Remember this, remember what you saw, if you live through what comes on us all. Don't let them buy you. Remember!"

"I will remember," I said.

He let go of me and gave me a push: "Go home," he said. "Go home and wait for the fever." And I looked about and saw that the street was empty.

"I will go," I said, "but I will come to see you again. And maybe your brother will live."

"Yes, and maybe the Ring will fall. Go!"

With that he turned for home, and so did I, our ways parting; and I saw no one else until I came to Kia's door.

Now the days drew near to the shortest of the year and the hardest of the cold came on us early. There was no more dancing-master, nor did Portia come, and the players ceased their trade. The snow fell, and the world stopped. We did not go anywhere and what we needed was brought to us, though scanty enough, and brought in half-empty carts; but the seeming end of time had more to do with lack of news, which we could not get any more, except sometimes when a neighbor ducked through our door looking over her shoulder to make sure she was not seen. So we heard, but as if at a great distance, of death swelling in the town; how the newly sick might disappear, no one knowing where they were taken; we heard of the sealing of more of the great barracks, and how the inhabitants of one set it afire but were shot as they ran from the flames or forced back to burn alive; and we heard of empty factories, and how fuel might soon be short, as food already was. But these whispers were like tales of events that had happened far away. The Postmen who came with food and fuel would say nothing, and we heard nothing of how things were behind the wall. There might have been no one there, all might have fled from the sickness—yet clearly someone remained to give the orders that kept us in isolation, and other orders that reduced the food the Postmen brought day by day—and our neighbors said the numbers of the fishers, too, had shrunk, so that there were fewer to bring food from the sea. And we weakened, and were often hungry, except Carmina who got shares of all our portions; and I began to think of how it might end.

But one night when I had only begun to think of the end, there came a rattle at the door, and a man put his face into it, and I saw that it was Willem. He spoke a few quick words to Kia which I could not hear, and then was gone without acknowledging my presence. Alban hurried to Kia's side and she whispered to him, and he said so that I could hear, seeming astounded, "He is running away? Where can he go? Can it be so bad?"

"His head is light with hunger," Kia said, but she twisted her hands in her skirt, and her brow twisted, too.

She looked at Alban and he said, "In the morning we will try to find out more."

"Morning will be too late," she said.

And they began to argue the wisdom of going that same night for news of some kind—of the sickness, I thought, for what else could it be?—and then they spoke of Leren and of streets and passages that led out of sight, with luck, to his house; and I said I knew all the ways there were to get there.

So they sent me out into the cold with a question: I was to ask Leren what had happened (though I still did not know what they thought that was). I made the journey safely, treading ice in the dark, for the streets were not lighted, and came safely to Leren's house and asked my question—I did not even go in, he was in no way glad to see me, his mind was on other things, and he stood in the door looking into the dark with fear in his face.

He said, "One of those at Millside wanted to get out. To get out he betrayed us all. He was not satisfied with giving the names of Millside men already doomed with fever; no, he has given them every name he ever heard. I have it from a guard who was one of those named and now runs for his life. I cannot make up my mind to run. It is winter, there is nothing but snow. It will be dying all the same; only the means will be different."

Then he turned into the room and took a scrap of paper, and wrote some lines and gave them to me for Kia.

"What does it say?" I said.

"It says get out. Get out. Get out."

"What does this mean?" I said.

"Do you know what they had at Millside?" he said. "There was a map of the wall that showed each place where weapons are stored. The locks are strange things, they are worked with numbers that are pushed with the hand. For some of them we had the numbers."

I began to understand, and not all the ice in my back came from the winter.

"If we go, where can we go?" I said. But he did not answer, and shut the door in my face.

I did not know what it all meant, but I knew enough to be afraid as I ran back through the dark, though it was only the beginning of fear, born less of understanding than of what I had seen in Kia's face and heard in Leren's voice. So I hurried, scarcely heeding the ice underfoot; only as I came close to Kia's street, I saw light shining over the roofs; I saw, as I came closer still, light filtering between houses and other small buildings that lay between; and I heard voices on the wind, men's voices, some shouting to others. I did not feel any fear, did not feel anything, except an urgency to get to Mirrah and to Kia's house, and this carried me over the ice. But I ran without looking at the ground. My eyes were all for the sky. For when I had gone only a little distance, not far from Leren's house, I had seen a thing that hung in the sky not much higher than rooftop-level, a thing big as many houses put together. I could not make out what it was, I saw only one piece of it at a time, as the roofs between cut one part or another from my sight, but it was long and slender like a needle in the sky, and shafts of light shone downward from its belly. *They are not directed at Kia's house,* I said to myself. *They will not touch me.* And I continued to say this until I came around the last corner and saw all of it at once: the air and the street filled with light from the thing in the sky, the street filled with Postmen, too, all carrying weapons and looking about and shouting to each other, and Kia's door wide open, and then, tearing from that door greater than the noise of the crowd, a woman's screams.

I did not know if it were Mirrah or Kia I heard, I did not know or feel anything, I only ran on blind to the Postmen and the thing in the sky. I was seized and hurled to the ground, though I fought, knowing for the first time what it was to wish to hurt men with my hands; for they stood between me and Mirrah. And a time passed which I could not measure. I felt no cold, though I lay bound on the ice and bound also to one of the Postmen's wagons; for I had continued to struggle and seek to drag myself toward the house after my hands and feet were tied, until they attached me to something that would not move. I wept and bit at the ropes and when anyone came near me, screamed curses, and the men, well-armed as they were, and helpless as I was, stood away from me with amazement in their eyes, as if I were a wild beast. And the sounds came from Kia's house in broken fragments, there would be a silence and then another scream, at each of which I thought my whole body would shatter; until there came the sound of guns, and after that, from that house, a silence that did not end.

At that the strength went out of me, to fight or do anything else. The street remained bright, but I saw all else that happened in colors of black. Men came from the house, the first of them being the traveler Tistou. And he waved the Postmen back, and as they removed to the farther side of the street they released me from the wagon and took me with them, dragging me across the ice; and the traveler spoke into something he carried, and a greater shaft of light came from the thing over my head, and Kia's house was not there any more. There was only fire where it had been.

Now none of Kia's neighbors had shown themselves, but the Postmen went from house to house ordering them into the street until it was filled with bodies and moving limbs edging away from the fire, and one shouted at them, a man dressed in clothes so fine that I knew he came from behind the wall; and he told them to look on what had been done and learn from it. After that for a further lesson he broke my hands. And I knew nothing for a little time after, but the cold woke me and in my pain I saw that the traveler knelt over me. He took my chin in his large cold hand just as Kia had once done; only when he looked into my eyes, which he had not seen before in their natural state, he laughed and spoke to the man who stood by in his rich garments.

"They will not soon forget this night," the traveler said. "I am glad to have been of help. No reward is necessary. But if you insist, then I will take this—"

And his mouth smiled at me. But his eyes were transparent, as I had suspected, and there was nothing behind them but a great emptiness. And how could anything else have been there? Because where Mirrah and Carmina had been, and Kia and Alban, and no doubt Leren, too, and their homes and their lives, now there was nothing, what marked his path was emptiness and absence and lack, where there had been life. And I knew in some way what he would do to me, how it would be done, what living would be like, such living as I had left, and I knew that when he was done he would kill me; but I knew also that if he did not I would never know fear again. There would not be anything worse that could happen to me than what had happened in this season, along with what this traveler would cause to happen in the waste he prepared for me. But not all of it had happened yet, and the agony of my hands filled all my body and mind, and I could still be afraid, because I was.

"Take him," said the man from behind the wall. And the traveler took me away.

During the days it took for the last memories to come forward into light, Hanna did not leave Michael in body or in thought. She was a silent spectator (as he wished), and at the end of it he evicted her. Not forcibly, but by way of something that was half request and half order; in either case, she could not refuse it.

She told the others, "He is very sick." But she was not sure how true that was, though he did not talk to her. He lay on his bed and it was difficult to tell whether he was awake or asleep, even when his eyes were open. But he ate, when Hanna brought food to the room. And as before, in the middle of the night he left it and wandered around the *Golden Girl* with an uncanny knack for avoiding anyone else who might be abroad in the night.

GeeGee came to Heartworld, then left it far behind. They were nearly at the point of decision. Soon they must turn back, or entrust themselves to a course known, in all the universe, only to the man who had as many names as there were stars.

Hanna always knew precisely where the *Golden Girl* was. She spent a third of her time in Control, dividing up each twenty-four hours into pieces with Theo and Shen. She did the slight work automatically and otherwise listened anxiously for Michael's voice, footsteps, even a thought. She did not hear any of those things. And once or twice she whispered her birthname to *GeeGee,* the code that would permit her to reach across space and establish a connection with her own past life—but she never went any further than saying the word. If Theo did it, too, in his own hours on watch, she did not know about it.

This half-a-life continued without change until they were a few hours from the relay which they had begun to call Theta, to mark its distance from Omega on the other side of space. In the early morning hours, not long after midnight, Shen watched *GeeGee* measure the distance to that endpoint. Theo could not sleep; he came to watch, too, not saying anything. Lise woke from a nightmare and joined them, seeking what comfort she could get from their presence. And Henrik, wide awake, got the notion that the walls of mirrors were looking at him with some purpose, and went out to escape. He did not mean to go to the others in Control, he wanted to keep away from them, but he couldn't shake the thought of the mirrors, the mirrors might follow him; so he went to Control, just in case.

Hanna woke up, too. Michael was gone. She went out shivering (she had been dreaming of winter) to look for him. *GeeGee* was waiting and silent. Hanna went into Control, into the middle of the waiting, and Theo looked around and said, "What next?"

How the hell do I know?

She was standing in the door, and she did not know the answer even when the footsteps finally came up behind her. Hands fell on her shoulders. She waited to find out whose they were.

"It's time to start feeding the course to *GeeGee,*" Michael said. So if she turned around, it would not be a twelve-year-old boy she saw, a poor fit in the man's body. But maybe it would not be Michael either.

Shen asked no questions; she began talking to *GeeGee,* preparing the ship for the new course. Michael said, "The language won't be hard. It's got a lot in common with Standard. If you could learn Ellsian, you can learn this."

He turned Hanna around and spoke to her. The others didn't know enough to understand his next words; not yet. "I don't think what we're going to find is what I left. When I left, there was the blight, the epidemic, the start of a revolution. We don't know how they turned out. But I don't think anything's gotten better."

Hanna said, "You mean to do something about it."

"Something."

"You would. But what?"

He shrugged. He looked just as he had always looked, except that he was very thin. He said, "B made a lot of difference. We could make a difference, too. You can let things happen, or you can make them happen."

"What kinds of things?" she said.

"We won't know till we get there," he said.

Chapter 7

With a kind of jolt, a thump Hanna later swore she heard, the small world of the *Golden Girl* returned to normal. Lise began to smile again. Shen told Michael daily that he had gotten too soft to be a revolutionary. Even Henrik came out of his hole, drawn by the general atmosphere of well-being, and some of his furtiveness dissipated. He said he would tell them everything he could, but except for what he knew about the men of the *Avalon,* he had no useful information. "So all that was for nothing," Michael said, meaning Henrik's abduction, but he forgot to apologize for it.

There was nothing to do but spend the remaining weeks teaching the others how to get along in his native tongue. He taught them everything else he remembered, too, warning them that information thirty years out of date might be more dangerous than none. Instead of the caution he meant them to learn, they developed a lively curiosity about what they would find. The holiday atmosphere of Uskos returned, the journey became an excursion, and at times they left *GeeGee* to run herself and played games in the lounge, shouting with laughter.

Hanna should have known better. She knew it, too, but her fear for Michael had gone on too long and gone too deep. It was enough to see him whole, enough to be loved again. He was back. It was enough.

A thread of black ahead of them got bigger, turned into a cloud, grew until it covered everything before them. When they passed into its tenuous fringe, it looked as if nothing was there, as if they plunged into black emptiness. Not even that troubled them. They sailed through the dust in a capsule of light, and the only acknowledgment they gave the dark was to agree that it was boring. They came to the stellar system of Gadrah, took a week to get through its shoals, hunted down the place itself, and finally saw it: blue and rich with water, dappled with cloud, magnificently ringed.

Hanna had taken care to time the arrival for the middle of the night, and lied about when it would happen. She did not want anyone but Michaël in Control when the time came. When it did, he stood without moving, not taking his eyes off the sight. Even if the others had been there, he would not have noticed them. Hanna stayed out of his head, out of his way, for a full hour. But finally she went to him and touched him, and he smiled at her. She had never seen so much peace in his eyes.

"I'm all right," he said.

"I'll get some sleep, then."

"Do."

She was nearly at the door when he said, "Thank you."

Hanna added up everything that had happened since her last sight of Earth.

"Don't mention it," she said, and went to bed.

Cruising coastlines: at high magnification each coast was the track of a demented snake. They stayed high, out of reach of the naked eye. It was amazing how many shores were backed by mountains close enough and tall enough to suggest that the Post might be there.

It would have been faster to look for heat, but *GeeGee* was not seeing so well in infrared. She was considerably overdue for maintenance.

It took longer to explore a coastline than Hanna had ever dreamed. They limited the search to the eastern edges of continental bodies, and to temperate latitudes. Even with those restrictions there was a lot of coastline, and it was deserted, not counting the profusion of animal life. Hanna looked at the animals and shuddered. Not because these animals were especially frightening—they were not, they came in an ordinary range of shapes and habits—but because there were no humans, nothing had been tamed. *There weren't many children born here,* he had said. There had never been many children. Something on Gadrah wouldn't let humans breed.

After three days they had narrowed the search to a coast which had been masked by cloud for all of those days. The clouds were not local, but part of an immense funnel that spread over half a continent, and the funnel was not moving. "It would be a long hurricane season," Hanna said, thinking of the length of all seasons here, and Michael looked at her blankly. Hurricanes had not come to the mountains. "Radio," she said suddenly (it had nothing to do with hurricanes), and his face was more blank still.

But Lise—who sometimes still nestled against the wall, but today, prim and upright, had taken a seat—said, "They would want radio. To keep in touch with the people who ran the mines. And the soldiers, when they went places."

"I never heard of one or saw one," Michael said. And when Hanna set *GeeGee* to scanning, they heard nothing.

This part of the world was turning away from the sun, and *GeeGee* with it. It was getting dark under the clouds down there. Aboard *GeeGee,* however, it was morning.

"We'll have to wait for the clouds to clear," Hanna said.

"It's fall there," Michael said.

"Hurricane season."

"All right, but I mean, in the fall there were weeks of cloud. If we want to see anything we'll have to get under them."

"They're *low* clouds. If we get under them, anybody down there can see us, too."

"Not at night."

"*GeeGee* is not soundless in atmosphere," Hanna pointed out. "Do want him to hear us and look up? Castillo? 'B'? Why do you call him B anyway? When here they called him Tistou?"

"They called him that, B, on the ship."

There was a warning in his tone. Michael did not need to be in trance to remember what had happened on the proto-*Avalon.* But he did not talk about it.

Hanna took the warning and retreated. "Wait till it clears."

A lifetime of patience told Michael to listen. He thought about it. He said finally, "We'll wait another day or two. But not weeks."

The morning went on; under *GeeGee,* in geosynchronous orbit, evening progressed. The night would be very dark on the ground. Michael disappeared, leaving Hanna in Control; he roamed the ship, a big cat prowling a cage. Hanna tracked him without effort from her place in Control. She hardly needed to be a telepath to know what he was doing at each moment.

When she heard a voice she said automatically, "What?" and looked around, thinking someone had come in and spoken. But Lise pointed silently at a communications panel, and another voice said incomprehensible words.

Lise said softly, "*GeeGee*'s got something on radio. They said: It's a false alarm. Nobody sick here."

"They? Oh!"

"It was something like that."

Mike! Hanna called, and strained to hear more. It was tantalizing, the words had a familiar sound, and at each syllable she felt herself on the point of understanding. Lise was quicker; she translated the next phrases aloud while Hanna still fumbled for their meaning.

"They say there's no use leaving tonight. They don't want to ride back in the rain."

"From where? Have they said from where? Or where to?"

"Not yet . . ."

"*Morning,*" somebody said, she knew that word. Michael came in and stood still. "*But it will be wet, all the same.*"

"*If it is, it is.*"

"*Well, it has rained for a week. Why should tomorrow be different?*"

Two men laughed together.

"*We'll swim back soon as we can.*"

"*Luck!*"

The radio burped, went on with a quiet hiss; there were no more voices.

"So it's down there," Hanna said. "Under the clouds. Somewhere."

Time to go. Michael would not wait any longer. "We'll fly over sooner or later," he said, "at night, too. Why not in the rain?" And they fell through the clouds into darkness and wet. "No one's going to spot us," Michael said. "The Post won't have radar; what for? The *Avalon*'s shut down. Guaranteed. Conserving power. When what she's got is gone, there won't be any more."

More coastline. It was dark, but *GeeGee* built up pictures from contrast, mimicking the human eye. Sand dunes made into islands by stands of patchy grass. Bays and inlets and slow-moving creeks like the one by Millside. Marshlands turned to lakes by the rain. Finally—there was silence when they saw this—the regular outlines of cultivated fields. All of it was in tones of gray and black.

Then buildings. There was a sound at Hanna's side, it was Michael; she heard him before she saw the heaps of stone just barely in view.

GeeGee moved on slowly, recording. The humans were silent. Hanna recognized what she saw from the air, as if all along, while she read Michael's memories, she had known how it would look from above. It was all there, the irregular half-circles, the pale wall, inside it the enclave up against the sea.

Michael murmured, "There's no light."

"Some." *GeeGee*'s rendering showed bright spots that had to be lights.

"Not enough."

"It was a dark town."

"Not this dark. And not inside the wall."

He was going to tell *GeeGee* to stop, but Hanna put a hand on his arm. "We're defenseless," she said, and Shen looked around and nodded.

"We keep moving, then," he said.

There wasn't much of it. There were fields again, and the whole thing faded behind them. Hanna had expected something bigger—but what they had seen would look big to a child. They flew on toward the north, still slowly. Hanna said, "What now?"

She did not mention Croft. There was a road that went to Croft. But first they would have to find it.

"I want to find out what's wrong," he said.

"You're sure something's wrong?"

"There weren't any lights on the walls."

"No." The dark winter and the sickness and the blight came to her mind. But that had been thirty years ago.

"It was all right a few years ago," she said. "That's what they told Henrik."

He took a deep breath and seemed to shake himself. "We won't find out any more from up here."

"Who goes? You and me and Shen," she added, answering herself. "You don't go alone!"

"Then find some hills to hide *GeeGee* in," he said. "And get ready to get wet."

There were no appreciable hills within three days' walk from the town. And *GeeGee* would stand out like a nova to anything looking down from the air.

After they had thought about it for some time, Michael said, "There won't be anything in the air."

The others were not of his opinion. None of them had ever lived in a place where nothing but birds flew.

"What about *Avalon?*" Shen said.

"Flying where? Looking for what? We'll chance it," he said, he smiled at them, he liked taking risks, risk had made him. Hanna was worried, Shen glum.

They would take stunners with them. Hanna thought: *At the first opportunity we must steal something better. Something fatal.* And heard Shen's identical thought. They put the stunners in the pockets of warmcoats unused since Revenge. The coats were waterproof and would be useful if the weather turned really cold. Hanna thought the coats inadequate, too. She would have liked body armor better.

They spent some hours selecting a landing site. It had to be open land but not marsh, solid ground but not forest, near a road but too far away to be seen from it. They settled on a patch that had been cultivated once—the remains of a fence still edged it—but now was overgrown with grasses and slim seedlings of native trees. There was nothing like it nearby; it was an island in virgin woodland, and Hanna puzzled over the anomaly. But it suited their purpose.

She and Michael and Shen stepped out of *GeeGee* into a wet dawn. They walked through woods at first, and it was hard to know when the rain stopped, if it ever stopped, because every step brought down water from the trees. Hanna thought nostalgically of the Red Forest of Ree, where travelers could command umbrellas. There were no umbrellas here; only water.

In an hour, however, they reached the road. Rain fell from the open sky, and when they came from under the trees it was full light. The road was lightly paved, but in poor condition; there were holes and scattered blocks of paving matter.

"Kept up until lately," Shen said.

"I wonder," Michael said. He looked at Hanna. "Think something did happen, since B was last here?"

"That field where we landed, that hasn't been fallow very long, either."

He looked up the road, not in the direction they meant to take, toward the sea, but landward. "The road from Sutherland was paved," he said, remembering how it had felt in the stifling truck. "We didn't spot many paved roads from the air." But he turned and started walking the right way.

They planned to walk all day. They carried no weight, except for communicators and the stunners; by evening they would be at the town, would look for a place to sleep but go without if necessary. They did not hurry. They did not want to come to the Post before dark. Hanna resigned herself to hunger, being wet, getting tired. But when the walking had established its own rhythm, and discomfort had come to seem the norm, she began to feel something else: the loneliness of the place. There was no sign of habitation except for the road, and they walked hour after hour without seeing anyone on it. There was no sound of machines; only wind and rain and, rarely, a rustle at the roadside when a small animal ran from their passage. They spoke seldom, and when they did their voices were loud. Soon even the slight noise of their footsteps was like thunder. And when they rounded a curve in the road and saw a structure built by hands, Hanna stood and stared, might have stared all day—except that Michael, diving for cover, turned back to pull her after him into the bush.

Shen was already there. She looked at Hanna with disapproval.

Here the soil had encroached on the road, and a tangle of grasses and scraggly shrubs rose up at the edge of the trees nearest the road. To the right and ahead there was a clearing, and the building nestled against the forest at the rear of this space, the setback having kept them from seeing it until they reached the clearing itself. Michael peered from behind the screen of brush. The clearing was in the same condition as *GeeGee*'s landing site. The house was built of dressed stone and was structurally intact, but some of the glazed windows were broken, and no light came from any of them in the dark afternoon. A few tiles had fallen from the roof, the gutters were thick with debris; it was the picture of desertion. But it was not deserted. There were chimneys at each of the three corners in sight—and over the roof, from the place where a fourth chimney ought to be, a stream of smoke rose sadly into the drizzle.

Hanna whispered, "What is it?"

"I don't know." He racked his newfound memory. There was nothing. "It looks like one of *their* places. But we must be a long way from the Post."

"Five or six hours on foot," Shen said. "In a landcar, half an hour's ride."

She added, "Start here."

"Start what?"

"Questions."

Hanna nodded. Michael was slower. Then he saw what they did, the advantages. If there were people here there would only be a few, isolated from the city. They would not have to be entirely ignorant when they reached the Post; they could find out something about it here.

"All right," he said. "We'll knock on the front door."

"Wait," Hanna said. "Stop thinking."

A ridiculous request—but he tried; could stop thinking in words, anyway. Shen became quiet as a stone. Hanna bowed her head, eyes closed. Listening for what? The afternoon was darker. Michael felt himself slip some mooring and float, as if he might take leave of his body. The absoluteness of time slipped; he was back in trance. He was suddenly certain that there were three people in that dying building. Two males, one female. *They think of the past and what might be and what might never be. One with hope and one without and one whose hope is soured . . .*

Hanna lifted her head. "They're not on guard," she said. "I could find out more, if we waited. But I think some other people might be here before dark."

"I didn't catch that." He looked at her in wonder. "I saw some of it, though. Did you make that happen?"

"What?"

He looked at Shen. "Did you see it?"

She gave him a dubious look and shook her head.

"Never mind," Hanna said. "You're not turning into a telepath. It'll only happen when we're together."

"Right. Come on," he said, shaken, and stepped out of the brush.

They crossed the dreary clearing, mounted a shallow flight of stone steps, and passed over the colonnaded porch without hearing a challenge. Shen's eyes darted everywhere, but Hanna's were distant; she watched for threat with another sense. They did not knock. The door opened with a creak, but nothing met them in the dark passage beyond. There were doors on either side of the hallway, some open and some not; they looked into all the rooms and found no one. The rooms were furnished, but in most the dust lay thick.

Hanna said to Michael's thought, with conviction: *There are ghosts here. Living or not, they are ghosts.*

He didn't like that. He walked more quickly, found a passage that seemed to lead toward the corner of the house where a fire must burn, and started into it. Near the end there was a door that promised revelations. But there was a staircase, too, and before he had taken three steps there was a flicker of light at the top of it.

He was flat on his belly with the stunner drawn before he thought about what to do. Behind him Hanna and Shen had dropped, too.

The top of the stair disappeared into shadow. A figure came out of the shadow and stopped with a gasp. A girl no more than eighteen stood shrinking in fright from the muzzles pointed in her direction. She held a lamp in both shaking hands.

Michael got up with a sigh and put the gun away. "I greet you," he said, the first words he had spoken to a native of this place in more than thirty years. But the girl only stared; perhaps he had gotten the language wrong after all.

Hanna had risen, too. She said quietly in the same tongue, "I am sorry; you surprised us. We will not hurt you. Please come down. We would like to talk to you." *If she doesn't come down, we'll go after her,* she added, but no one but Michael heard that.

But the girl started down the staircase. They did not move; their stillness calmed her. When she came near, the light showed a pale oval face, brown hair exquisitely dressed, soft blue eyes; she wore a richly figured blue gown that was a little large for her and looked as if it had been made for someone else. She looked from one to another and stopped in front of Michael and looked up—and stared, discomfiting him; started to speak, was silent, stared some more.

"Eyes," Hanna muttered in Standard.

"What—oh. My name is Mikhail," he said to the girl. "Who did you think I was?"

"You are a Saddhi, that is plain," she answered. "But I have never seen you before."

"What is your name?"

"Marin—of the Saddhis. Why do I not know you? Why have I not heard of you?"

He could not answer. The words took their time sinking in. Nowhere else in the universe would his eyes say who he was.

There was a sound beyond the door at the end of the passage. Hanna whispered to Shen and the two women, practical, flawless, slipped by Michael and Marin and took up positions of guard, Shen on the staircase, Hanna in the angle the door would make when it opened.

"What do they want?" said Marin, voice rising. He thought she might flee and put a hand on her shoulder. She looked up again and was still.

The door opened and a man came in. He was clearly a near relative of the girl; his face declared it. He said sharply, "Who are you? What do you do here?" Then he saw Shen and her stunner and froze. He had not seen Hanna, who waited as if expecting someone else to come in.

Michael felt a lurch, a great compulsion to tell the truth, to reveal himself. Instead he said a half-truth, with difficulty: "We are travelers."

"Well, what of it? Where from? Why intrude on my home with weapons? Come here, Marin."

She did not obey. She said, "He is of the family, Pavah. But he is called Mikhail, and I have never heard of one so named."

"There is no one," said the man; he was irritated, not afraid. He went forward to fetch his daughter and also saw Michael's eyes. He said, "Marin, go. Get your uncle." And to Michael, savagely, "What do you want? There is nothing here to steal. There is nothing here for you."

He talked like a man who was used to being robbed, with more bitterness than fear. *Saddhi,* said the echo of Marin's voice. Shadhili? Michael could not say a word. Centuries ticked away while he looked at his kinsman with a bastard's eyes, disowned. The chill of the place got colder. He still held Marin's shoulder; that alone was warm. He let go and she moved for the first time since he had touched her. The silence had lasted too long.

Hanna came forward then. "We will not take anything," she said. "We are travelers, as Mikhail said. We need knowledge of this land. Do our weapons trouble you? We have them because we did not know what we would find. We will put them away—if you give your word that we are safe."

"Why, as to that . . ." The man half-smiled. "How can any man pledge to another that he will be safe at all times and in all ways? But I will not try to harm you. Is that enough?"

"It will suffice," Hanna said.

They made a strange picture on that wet afternoon, the three men, three women, two sets of flotsam thrown up by the sea. They talked by the fire in a high square room that appeared at first glance well-kept. But the fire scarcely touched the damp, and it flared up sometimes, and showed details of disintegration: spreading cracks in window cornices, water-stained walls, fragments of tile underfoot. The lamps shed no light; they only thickened the shadows in the room. The man Marin called father was Orne. The uncle who had not stirred from the fire was Hyde. Orne called him brother, but they did not look much alike. Instead when Michael looked into Hyde's face, he looked into a distorting mirror. It was not only that Hyde had the Saddhi eyes; there were other resemblances, too. They kept Michael silent— silent as Hyde, who acknowledged their presence with an indifferent nod and went on staring at the fire.

They sat in a semicircle before the fire, their backs to the door. But Hanna had turned her seat so that she could see most of the room, and Shen was openly on guard in a corner from which she could see all the rest. Hanna did most of the talking, too. Did she think Michael too simple to spin a convincing lie?—but he knew what she was doing before she was half-done. She plucked Orne's own conjectures from his thoughts, let him make up a tale that suited him; then she confirmed his guesses. She said the travelers had come from a settlement so far away that there had been no news of the Post in some time, and they had come to get some, guessing as they came that much was awry, finding nearer settlements abandoned. They had gotten clothes and weapons in one of these, Hanna said. (Had some question crossed Orne's mind about their gear? Hanna's eyes were not guileless. But they said: *Prove that I lie.*)

"One of the lost hamlets to the south, no doubt," Orne said, and his eyes were sharp, but Hanna answered, "No, far to the north. I did not know anyone lived to the south." She must have seen a map in Orne's head, and slipped past a trap.

"There were towns at the end of this road," the girl Marin said. "I have heard that people live there again. Is it true?"

"We saw no one, but we did not go to all of them. What towns were they?" Hanna said. Michael lifted his head, listening for a name.

"What does it matter?" Orne said. "They rot with the rest. Leave the dead in peace!"

"How many dead?" Hanna said. "Of what cause?"

"Did it not come to your little godforsaken town? Well, it was the sickness. You'd best hope you don't take it home with you; it is not dead yet. Not quite."

Michael said, "There was a great sickness long ago, when I was a child. But it passed. Was this the same?"

"It might have been. The leeches talk of cycles of the thing. Where do you live, that you do not know this, and your speech has come to sound strange?"

Michael stirred a little. He had worried about the accent that was heavy on Hanna's tongue, and Shen's, and even his, though not so thick. But Hanna ignored the question. She said, "We have heard that the great families were spared in that earlier time. I do not think you have been spared."

"No, as you can see. Birds nest in the tower that was my wife's chamber, and worms crawl in the cradle of my brother's child. His wife also died, and our father and mother, though we fled here at the first, to this summer lodge. No great loss, you might think, the old being anyhow in sight of death; but their old age had promised to be hale. That was how it was. Few families lost less than two parts of their folk—this time."

"And the rest of the people?" Michael said. His tongue did not want to move. The words on it weighed it down. "The people who, I heard, lived crowded close outside the wall?"

"Worse," Orne said. "Hardly any are left. There is no help to be gotten anywhere, no one to farm, no one to work."

"How do you live?" Hanna said.

"Well, there are the fields we used to own, when owning them meant something. There are still the tithes, though so few folk remain that tithes do no more than fill our mouths."

Hyde spoke for the first time, rumbling: "It will not come again."

Orne would have gone on without giving any attention to his brother, but Hanna said, "What will not come again?"

Hyde said, "Life. Now we die. Only a fool denies it."

Marin leaned closer to the fire; Michael could not see her face. Orne said, "My brother's mind was turned by grief. He would have it that all who live now are doomed."

"I am not a fool," Hyde said. "I remember the old days, before sickness and want. It began to break then, yes, when we were boys. Now it is broken. I will see the end of the world."

There was silence, except for the sound of the rain, which began to form itself into a sad melody. At last Michael said, "Is there no more music, then?"

Orne looked at him curiously. "No, no more. I don't think there are any musicians left. If you find one, don't send him here, unless he can feed himself. And what musician ever could?"

They had stayed too long. The dark was rolling in, and they could not go on tonight. The servants of the house had gone to town for stores and might return tonight, tomorrow, next week. Their places were the empty ones Hanna had sensed; they were the others who belonged here and would come home. If they had been there, Michael thought, the travelers would have been relegated to their company. Since they were not, certain distinctions were blurred. Orne gave them a hot porridge he made himself, and bitter beer to go with it, and the parties ate and drank together. But later he told them to sleep on the floor before the fire and told them where to find bedding; then he and Hyde and Marin disappeared into the upper regions of the house, where there were beds.

They got through to Theo and took turns whispering to him, and afterward went to sleep. Only one thing more happened that night, in that house. Michael woke to find the fire dead; he was cold. It was very dark, and he got up to look for more blankets. He was coming back through the hall with his arms full when he saw a light at the head of the stairs, just where he had seen it in the afternoon. It was Marin again. She came down on soft bare feet and stood there and looked at him in silence.

He said something to her, a nothing-meaning courtesy. But she said after a further silence, "It is lonely here."

"Yes," he said. "I see it must be."

"I am young," she said in a low voice. "I have no one. I see no one. I see no one like you."

It was an invitation, the saddest he had ever heard. He hesitated, trying to find words, and she must have thought he had not understood, because she made it clear. "Will you come with me to my room?"

"I can't," he said. "I'm very sorry."

"My father sleeps soundly, my uncle, too. I walk in the night and they do not hear. I look out and see nothing. I hear nothing. There is nothing to hear." Her eyes filled with tears. "My father talks only of getting enough to eat, my uncle of how everything will end. Nothing changes, each day is like the day before, and always tomorrow will be like today, until I am old. I was to be married, but now he is dead, my cousin who was my betrothed. You are my cousin, too, though my father will not say it. I do not know why. The old ways are dead. Will you give me at least a memory to hold?"

She stepped closer and he repeated, "I can't."

"Is it because of the woman who is with you?" she said. "I saw how you look at her, but I am prettier than she is."

He remembered the jewels and soft gowns of the Mistresses of the Post, and beside them set Hanna with her dangerous hands. There was a hardness and strength in Hanna that Marin could not have seen in the women she had known.

"I'm sorry," he said again.

The girl turned away without another word, taking the

light with her. He found his way back to Hanna with relief
and spread another blanket over her.

They woke early and left before the household stirred;
he did not want to see Marin again.

He had not slept well. All night he had been troubled by
visions of sad broken windows, darkness where there ought
to be light. The rooms behind the windows were empty. The
dreams did not leave him with the dawn. The rain kept coming down, soaking his bare head, trickling down his neck.
Beside him Hanna and Shen plodded on, heads down, not
very fast, talking softly of how far there was to go.

"We still don't want to get there in the light," Hanna said.

"Sooner I see a fire the better," Shen said.

"We're not going in daylight unless we know where *he* is.
They didn't say anything about him. I couldn't ask. We
shouldn't know anything about him, if we were what I said.
They would have had to give me an opening, and they
didn't."

She glanced at Michael, inviting his comment, but he
didn't have one. B did not seem real—nor did the misty
morning, nor the wraiths they had left behind. All the things
he had finally remembered, a world of them, had vanished
during the years of his forgetfulness. Nothing was the way
he had thought it would be. *My father talks only of getting
enough to eat, my uncle of how everything will end . . .*

They went on quietly for a while. Shen said, "Think we
could get sick?"

Hanna paused a moment, lifted her head and looked at
the rain as if it were an enemy. It might be; every breath
they took was loaded with microbes.

"People have survived here for centuries," she said.
"That suggests there's nothing here that could kill us before
we could get help, no alien bug we've no defenses against.
But something's been happening."

"The same thing," Michael said. "That's what Orne said.
But they called it the new fever, when I heard of it before.
Something the settlers brought with them might have mu-
tated."

"So we could get sick," Shen said. "Real good news."

But Hanna said, "There's another possibility. I'd like to
plot these cycles against B's visits."

Shen said, "A carrier?" but Michael said simultaneously, "No. They would have had it behind the wall. It would have spread out from there."

Hanna gave him another look, but she did not try to refute him.

Toward midday the forest gave way to open grassland which once had been farmed. Before the trees thinned too much they sat at the roadside and chewed on nutrient tablets. The road was very straight, and they could have seen to its vanishing point on a clear day; today it disappeared into rain. But they saw the darker shape that began to emerge from the mist, and slipped into the scant cover of the trees. What came out of the rain was a truck straight out of Michael's memories— and this one was so battered, so noisy, so old, that he might have seen this very one as a child. There were people in the cab, and a dozen bundles bounced around in the back.

They stayed out of sight until it was gone. Hanna said, "They're going to where we spent the night, I think. They're Orne's servants going home."

Shen looked into the rain where the truck had vanished. A last faint squeak-and-rattle sounded through the patter of the rain.

"Why do they go back?" she said.

"Habit," Hanna answered.

"Home," Michael said.

On the *Golden Girl,* Theo dozed uneasily in Control. He was trying to get adjusted to the cycle of daylight here, and it was hard going. There was a local-time chronometer keyed to Gadrah's roation, and another that kept Standard time. Theo had started to think Standard time was an aberration, there wasn't any such thing, Standard didn't mean standard at all. But his body didn't like this new kind of time, and today he could neither sleep soundly nor wake completely.

He came out of this twilight state for the second or third time in a Standard hour and straightened groggily in his seat. He thought of coffee and then, with lust, of his bed. If he could lie down in the dark, he might get some real sleep. But Michael might call again, and what if something happened, what if the three outside needed him fast?

He remembered then that he wasn't the only person with ears left on *GeeGee*.

He went to Lise's room, but she was sound asleep, the picture of peace. She wasn't worried about Michael out there in the rain; she thought nothing could hurt him, he could do anything.

Theo couldn't bring himself to wake her. He went to Henrik's room, found no Henrik, and set off on a tour of *GeeGee*, resolved that Henrik would do something for his keep for a change. What he found, instead of Henrik, was an open locker spilling out their winter gear. More was missing than Michael and Shen and Hanna had taken.

He went outdoors, stood in the rain, called Henrik's name, walked in circles around *GeeGee*, shouting. Maybe Henrik had only gone for a walk; it had been a long time since any of them touched ground. But he got no answer, and finally, because he didn't know what to make of it but was sure it meant nothing good, he called Michael.

"Now we don't know where Henrik is either," Hanna said.

Night falling again. They had dawdled through the last few kilometers, where the road was bordered by fields farmed only last summer. Rain had fallen all day, rarely hard but never stopping, and it had slipped through every crevice it could find and made layers of damp next to the skin. Only movement kept them warm. From here the road made a sudden, meaningless curve and turned slightly downhill. Against the dark sky at the limit of sight there was a blur of deeper shadow. It might have some straight edges—or might not; eyes played tricks in the waning light.

After Hanna spoke, they were quiet. Michael thought there was no sense to Henrik's leaving, nowhere for him to go, nothing for him to do. There was only the road to follow, to Orne's ruined summer lodge and then on to the Post. He could not hope to lose himself in the native population; he had been there when they told Theo there was little population left.

Shen said: "Tricks. B."

"Habit," Hanna said. "Home."

Michael said, "No. Oh, no. He hated them. He was afraid of them."

There was a little explosive sound in the dark, Shen's

breath; her hand fell on Michael's and clutched it like a claw.

"What's wrong with you?" she said. "He would've sold them to the Polity, that's what he wanted to do. He tried to call out of *GeeGee,* didn't he? To sell us, just the same. Now what's he got to sell? Us again. To B this time. We could get the Polity here if we wanted, get I&S; if Henrik hasn't thought of it, B will. Wait till he finds out we're here! See how fast he kills us! So Henrik tells him we're here, where *GeeGee* is. Thinks he'll be safe from B that way."

"We have to get B," Hanna said. "Before he gets us."

Michael said, "Wait a minute," and they turned to him. The protest he wanted to make died on his lips. He looked silently at the women in the dark. He could not see their faces clearly; they were shadows, Fates, sisters out of myth. They had guarded his back at every step on this road, deadly enemies to any enemy of his.

"I only want to find Carmina," he said.

"No revolution?" Shen inquired. She sounded disappointed.

"Oh, no," Hanna said. "That's not what this world needs. Not now."

And it was darker still; when he moved, water fell from his shoulders. Which carried something heavy, though he could not look at it yet. It was not necessary, not yet, it could be delayed; there was enough to see in the gap between what he had expected and what he had found. And what they were walking toward was something else to see—that made enough dread to fill up his head and keep it from speculating *what if . . .*

The shadows on the horizon had been rooftops, all right. They were closer than they had appeared, and the travelers were among them quickly. Whatever was wrong with Michael's head got worse. It was not that he didn't see material reality. He walked on real pavement, splashing through puddles and runnels of water that added to the wet in his boots. He saw the stark piles of the factories, the nightmare shapes of the great barracks looming over his head. Superimposed on these, however, were pictures of the way it had been before. The loose stones underfoot reminded him of ice. And there was an unreality that had nothing to do with either now or then. The factories, barracks, streets, all were dark, and nothing moved anywhere, except water. This could not be a real city. Instead it was a bad dream in which the dreamer comes to a familiar town and finds it crumbling and abandoned. The dark was more than night; it was the darkness hidden in the heart that shows itself only in dreams, where no sun has ever come or ever will come. And because the desertion was real, and the city disintegrating in reality, it seemed dreadfully possible that endless darkness could be real, too.

Michael had feared nothing since the day he escaped from the creature B. He was not afraid now. But his vigilance was gone with his sense of what was real. Anything might come out of the dark and he would not know until it was upon him, just as in a dream.

But the women moved smoothly as cats, ears pricked, eyes everywhere. They were silent. He suspected that Hanna communicated with Shen, guarding him.

When he saw the first faint lights, on the lowest floor of one of the barracks, he turned in another direction. There was someone here after all—but he was reluctant to see who or what it was. What might answer the door you knocked on in a dream like this?

They saw more lights; came around a corner and saw other shapes walking in the dark, three or four of them, heads down and moving away. Michael did not hail them.

He did not know where he was headed. He kept going, not thinking, letting his feet carry him on. The cold rain had been falling forever. Together with the black sky it crushed his heart. Why had he come here?—if he had not tried, if he had never tried, he could have gone on with his life where the sun shone.

If he had done that, something whispered, he would never have saved Lise, never known Hanna.

But he would not have known what he lacked. And he would not have heard *what if. What if I had not been—*

They came to the stone houses. Somewhere behind them was the wall. But it was not lighted, and it was only a shadow against the dead black of the sky.

He looked inside the doorway of a house. The door hung from one hinge and water had blown across the threshold. The next house was the same, and the next. Shen produced a tiny light. It was no longer than her finger but gave off an intense narrow beam. The light showed a jumble of sturdy furnishings beginning to show the effects of abandonment and damp. The cupboards built into kitchen walls were open and empty. Their doors swung crazily and crockery was smashed on the floor.

Hanna said, "Somebody was looking for food, I'd bet."

Her voice was not loud, but Michael jumped as at a shout. Until now, in this deserted town, they had heard only furtive rustles which he had identified at once. Rats had come to Gadrah with the original stores of grain, and they had flourished.

Shen said, "The ones we saw walking—nobody else left?"

Michael turned to Hanna with an appeal. He saw her face now in reflected light, and it was intent.

"It's happened," she said. "Colonies have failed. Fertility's depressed here. I'd guess there were less than a hundred thousand people here at the peak—on the whole planet, I mean, not just here."

"Can't all be dead," Shen said.

"We haven't looked everywhere. And listen. Orne's daughter said she'd heard there were people again in some of the small towns. 'Again,' she said; that means they're coming from somewhere."

Michael said, "There wasn't anyplace but here."

"I know. Who's behind the wall now? Why hasn't Orne come back?"

Michael thought of what was behind the wall. He had known too little about what was there; his memory had made it monolithic.

"There would be more comforts there," Hanna said. "Luxuries. Stores of food, at least for a while. The great families ran away, like Orne's. The soldiers would have been sick, too, died or left their posts. It all broke down. So where did the people go?"

"Behind the wall," he said. "Where they couldn't go before. Of course."

When they came closer to the wall, they saw that all the gates were open like cavernous mouths. They walked beside it for a long time, looking through the gates at intervals.

There was only more of the wet dark in there. Michael blessed the rain, which kept people in who might otherwise have come out; but a scene rose up before his eyes, another possibility. That was a fragrant spring evening under clear skies—and still the street was empty, no foot trod it but his, and ghosts grinned from the gates with the faces of skulls.

"We have to go in sometime," Shen said.

Hanna said, "Not without scouting. We're lucky there's no one around."

There isn't anybody anywhere! Michael thought. But Hanna said, "Oh, yes, there are people in there. But where's B? That's what I want to know before I walk in blind. The *Avalon* didn't show up on *GeeGee*'s visuals. Why not? Where'd he put it?"

"They'll be looking for us real soon," Shen said.

Hanna nodded and Michael said, "How do you get that?"

"Henrik," Shen said. "Gone how long? Theo didn't know. Gets to Orne tonight, maybe takes that truck—could be right behind us. Get in, get out before he comes." The last words sounded final. She said to Hanna, ignoring Michael, "Go in now."

Hanna said thoughtfully, "We could wait for him. Go back to the road we came in on and get him when he comes."

"And do what when we have him?" Michael said.

Shen said, "Pointblank stun to the brain."

Hanna said, "If that doesn't do it, bare hands."

He looked at the guardian shadows in disbelief. They looked back and Hanna said, "All right."

"Guess not," Shen said. "Move fast, then."

"Up there," Hanna said, pointing. "That gate."

"Then?" Shen said.

"Straight back, straight east, toward the sea. No, we're near the middle, aren't we? We haven't seen any lights. We'll try a diagonal, then, toward the southeast. We'll cover more territory that way. Does anybody remember how the lights were distributed?"

"On record," Shen said. "Call Theo."

But Michael said, "Never mind. There was a cluster in that direction. That's what we flew over first, coming in. I remember—"

He didn't finish. *Because that's the way Alban took me my first night here.*

Hanna might have heard it anyway, but she said nothing. They walked on to the gate.

Stumbling through courtyards: they did not want to show a light. The sunken gardens were ponds. Hanna walked into one, fell, rose soaked and bruised, knowing she was lucky to have no broken bones. After that they had to risk light.

The dark mansions were all connected. Michael had not forgotten that. But for the first time he knew why, saw the builders, or maybe the image came to him from Hanna. It had been strange and frightening here, a new world unconnected to anything the masters had known before, so they had huddled together, building passages and tunnels so they would never be out of reach or separated from one another—

They found an unlocked door at once. Were there any locked doors left in this place, on this whole world? What was left to guard?

Michael thought he heard a whisper as he stepped inside: *Mikhail!*—a summons. Not Hanna's voice, not her thought. A product of imagination, then.

Now they had to use the light, because the dark inside was so thick that it seemed material, could envelop and smother them, if they wandered out of the circle of light. They were in a great hall, empty except for a thick carpet running its length. Their feet stirred puffs of dust. Hanna led them, light in one hand, weapon in the other. Michael followed blindly, and Shen was at his back. The first hall led into another and another, and that into dark rooms. There was nothing in them to see, they were empty as if no one had ever lived in them. Everything was gone. Here and there an ornament remained, glass or metal or stone; nothing else. Presently Michael realized, without knowing how he reached the conclusion, that everything that could be burned had been taken away for fuel. Even walls not made of stone were gone, even floors; the light saved them from falling into black pits. There was a smell of dust, the air was thick with it, it got into their noses and made them sneeze, so that they abandoned the instinctive attempt to walk in silence. The corners were heavy with cobwebs. And there were sounds. Rats were masters of these rooms. Also the wind had risen; or did he imagine that? He heard it, any-how: howling round rooftops and corners till the howls turned to distant screams, and the scurryings inside walls turned to chuckles.

They might have been going in circles, but Hanna never stopped, or even hesitated. He could not imagine what compass had its home in her head. Or was there no compass at all? Was it only that she trusted her zigzag course would lead them somewhere? Left then right, left, right — she went on steadily. But it was odd that they never were outside, never passed into an open courtyard. They might as well have been underground.

He kept following the steady light while the wind and the rats tore at his ears, the screams got louder, the endless chuckle swelled to laughter, an uproar of mirth. So this was what he had dreamed of, what he had had to find. The pas-sion for freedom was wasted. There were no masters left — save one; Chaos ruled here.

The sunlit place where aliens had told him about that Master was gone. He could not remember the sun.

If I had not been self-seeking, self-protecting —

Hanna stopped suddenly, and he bumped into her. He put his arms around her from behind, holding on. She whis-pered, "I heard something," and turned the light off. Mi-chael only heard screams; they were louder in the dark. But his eyes adjusted and it was not perfectly black. There was a glow ahead.

Hanna stepped out of his arms. She put away the stunner she held and gave the light to Shen. "Wait," she said, and walked toward the light.

The old gaslight fixtures still worked. Gas burned in a fire-place, too, with a steady subliminal roar, in a row of tiny jets that looked like teeth. There were cooking pots at the fire, a pile of blankets in front of it. An old man sat on the blan-kets and looked up from hollow eyes.

Travelers, Hanna said, and spoke her piece; told the old man about Michael, half-truths. *He lived here as a boy and seeks old friends.*

Dead, most like.

His name was Conwy, he told her. Only half her mind

was on what he said. The other half was on B. She did not
know how to ask this Conwy about B, not without rousing
more interest than she wanted to rouse.

Three of us. May we—?

I have little to eat, but it is yours—

She walked back to Michael and Shen and saw that Michael was far away, farther away than he had ever been in
trance or memory. He was in shock, she thought dispassionately. His face, which would be the pattern of beauty for her
all the rest of her life, was bewildered. Shen had seen it, too.
Hanna did not say anything to Shen about what the two of
them must do. Shen already knew. There were two of them
to think; that would have to be enough.

A dream. He remembered feeling like this before sometimes—
when he was saturated with drink or drugs, and nothing that
happened was connected to anything else, and faces were
phantasms that came out of air and went back into it, and
every phrase uttered by every voice was significant, masking a
secret that in a minute, just a minute, he would understand. It
was stupid, not to be able to understand.

Here was a lean old face with sunken cheeks. "I lived in
the barracks in those years," Conwy said, "in Zed-Alpha-
Eight. I had a wife. I had a child. Two other children were
born dead. Now my wife and the child who lived, they are
dead, too."

Croft, Michael heard himself say. *Sutherland,* he said.

Conwy had not heard of them. He had not known a
woman called Kia.

"Dead, so many dead," he said.

"This time?" Michael was learning. The smell of the gas
was strong, it must be full of impurities.

"Every time. This is the fourth, and the worst. Finished,
some say. I don't know. No doubt it will come again."

The shadows in the room jiggled at a draft. They were all
Michael could see. He heard Hanna murmur questions,
Conwy answering. Conwy knew a man, old like himself,
who had been a musician once.

"Take us there," Hanna said.

"He will be sleeping," Conwy said.

"I know." She knelt at Conwy's side and smiled at him.
She was not hard now. She was softened, and the softness

was real, not deceit, and when she smiled even Marin would have thought her beautiful.

"Well, then, we will make him wake up," Conwy said.

And it was not far, and the man at the end of the path was Norn, bald now, with deep eyes under heavy brows. Michael recognized him, and wept.

Hanna squatted side by side with Shen. Shen whispered, "Past the middle of the night."

"I know."

"Where's B?"

"Maybe this one knows."

"Wouldn't count on longer than dawn."

"No."

Shen inched closer. She said, "What's wrong with Mike?"

Hanna said calmly, "He'll be all right."

"Never seen this."

"I have."

"All right. All right. Look, he's different. Not like anybody else. I know that. Think I don't know that? Never seen this, though. Gotta get him out of here."

"In a while."

Shen did not find this satisfactory. She retreated into sullen silence, fingering her stunner. It would not be good enough if B caught up with them.

Norn in rags was enthroned on a magnificent chair. "I was not there, but I heard," he said. "There was nothing left but burnt bones. There were three of them, yes, three piles of smoked bones. I heard they were kind to Kia, that after what they did she would not have walked again, nor sung, and killing her was kind. I heard Alban was there, and died, too, and the visitor, the woman Lillin, your mother. Did you hope she had escaped?"

"No." On the ship without a name Michael had heard too much about Lillin's death. He had never hoped it was a lie. The details had been too cruelly clear.

"The babe lived," Norn said.

"Lived . . ."

"Oh, yes. Snatched out living at the last by one of those who killed her mother. I did not know the man. But evidently there were some things he could not do, and leaving the child in that house, knowing the fire would be next, was a thing he could not stand for. He handed her to the first woman he saw in the street. Ercole; do you remember Ercole? She is dead now."

"I do not—no, perhaps I do. What happened then to the child?"

"Why, I do not know for a certainty. Ercole kept her a time, though the winter was lean. There has not been a winter of such thinness in my lifetime, not even the last, though the one that comes now will starve us all. Ercole kept her until a man and woman came seeking you and your mother and the babe."

"When? Who were they? Where did they go?"

"Slowly, slowly. It was a long time ago. With Kia gone I had no reason to go to that part of the town, you understand? I do not remember what else I heard. It is too long ago. Why did you wait so long to come back? They said Tistou took you away; where have you been?"

"I didn't know the way back," Michael said, but Norn looked at him with mistrust, so he said, "There were people, when I was a boy, who thought Tistou came from another world. Do you remember that?"

"Yes," Norn said. "There are those who think so still. They say he comes from a homeland of which this was to be an outpost. But we are forgotten; that is what they say. When I was younger, I believed the part about the homeland, because surely this world is forgotten, but not that the traveler went back and forth. Now I wonder. He comes and goes, he has the only flying machine ever seen, and he has not grown old, as I have. Did you learn the truth?"

"It is all true. When I escaped from him, I was not here any more. I have tried to find my way back ever since."

Michael waited for Norn to take it in. Norn scowled and was silent. Hanna said gently, "It is hard to understand. But what Mikhail says is true. We will go back, and you will not be forgotten any more. People will come with food and medicines. But now Mikhail must find his sister, if she lives; and the traveler is here now, is he not? We found this place by following him, but he does not know that yet. If he finds out, he will try to kill us before we can bring help. Do you know where he is?"

"No," Norn said. He looked at Michael shrewdly. "If that is true, you must have a flying machine, too. Where is yours?"

Michael's mind was on the piles of bones, the weeping child given to a stranger in the street. Hanna answered, "It is hidden, we hope. We cannot allow Tistou to know we are here."

"Is it warm inside, like his? Is there plenty to eat? That is what they say of his, but he does not give much away. He came in the summer, there was food then, not much but enough. Now there is hardly any. Men have gone to Tistou to beg, and he has sent them away with empty hands. Then he grew tired of beggars, it seems, for the last one who went, he killed. Do you have food?"

"We have food. We will bring it, if we can. But if we are to do that, and if we are to get away to bring help here, we must know where Tistou is. Is there anyone who knows?"

Norn said to Michael, "Do you still play?"

Michael nodded slightly. Hanna saw fire reflected in his eyes, red against the snow. She said, "He has become a master of the instrument. If there is a chance, he will play for you. But you must help him get the chance. Norn, we are in deadly danger from this Tistou. There is a man who came here with us, who knew Tistou from before, and he has disappeared. I think he will betray us, do you understand? We must know where our enemy is. Will you not help us?"

"I have told you I do not know," Norn said, and it was the truth. But then he said, "There is one who may know. I will take you to her."

Deeper into the night, into the maze. Even Hanna was lost now. Norn could not move fast. His spine and the joints of his legs were knobby and inflamed, and every step was painful. Michael supported him. He thought of the medicines on the *Golden Girl;* he thought that where he had grown up, Norn's condition must be a footnote to the history of medicine. And then he wondered about Norn's age. He could not be more than sixty in Standard years.

Hanna murmured, "We take them for granted, the anti-senescence treatments. I've had one. And you?"

"Two."

Norn ought to be still a young man.

Norn talked as he cautiously, painfully moved.

"A bad winter, that. But this one that comes, I will not see its end."

Sometimes there were sounds in the rooms they passed, as sleepers roused at the slow footsteps. But only once did anyone look out.

"By that spring so long ago, many folk were scattered, and the guards too weak to follow."

The years flickered as Norn talked, springs rising and falling. A slow recovery; the next two waves of sickness had not been so bad. The masters had still lived behind their wall.

"All who might have risen up were dead, or fled. There were none fool enough to do what Kia did."

New seedstock appeared, blight-resistant, giving great yields. "Did he bring it?" Hanna said. "The man Tistou?"

"Perhaps," Norn said, and Shen said, "Why?"

Hanna answered, "Why did he do anything? He does not seem to have gotten rich through coming here. How did he come here to begin with? Who is he?"

Now for the first time there was a gust of outside air. They turned into a hall where arched windows made up one side. Some were open and others broken, and a strong breeze blew through them. The sound of the sea was audible. Hanna turned to one of the windows. She had been born near an ocean, and could not resist the sound of any sea. But the night was so dark that the waves, however close, were invisible.

"This way," Norn said, not pointing but shifting his weight on Michael's arm to indicate the path. They went through an arched door opposite the windows and stood in the dark. "Darya! Daryeva!" called Norn, and Hanna's light picked out a figure on the floor.

She was Norn's granddaughter. She was perhaps sixteen, with a little pointed brown face and large eyes. She looked at all of them, even Norn, with fear, and Norn stood there and told them her history: how in the first weeks after Tistou had come, in the summer, one of his companions had seen Daryeva, and liked what he saw; how Daryeva had not stayed out of sight but sought out the man, and lived for a time now and then on the flying machine; how she had started a child, and lost it, and then seemingly lost her power to charm the big fair-haired man, because he rarely came to see her now; how her own folk, virtuous, would have nothing to do with her.

Not calculated to gain her confidence, Hanna said to Michael's head. But the girl said to Norn: "When you thought I could get food for you, you were not so quick to cry punishment! What do you do here, old man? Will you sell me for the night for half a loaf, as before?"

Norn began to shout. Hanna said quickly, "Get him out of here," and Shen did it without much trouble, marching the old man out with an arm locked behind his back. They heard him cursing in the hall, in a burst of wind that blew in.

Hanna and Michael sat down uninvited, but with a common impulse. There was no point in scaring the child with shadows twice her size.

"You do it," Hanna said to Michael; he read the meaning in her eyes. *You can gain anyone's trust.*

But he asked his own questions, not the ones Hanna wanted him to ask. *Did you ever hear of a woman called Kia? The name Lillin? A girl, no, woman, Carmina, now twice your age?* Daryeva thought him mad; harmless, though; his eyes were so hurt, his voice so gentle. She developed a small frightened coyness, a poor residue of her liaison with the man Wales. Hanna moved at Michael's side, said impatiently in his head, *Ask her about the* Avalon! He only thought: *Poor little Darya.* "Soft," Hanna muttered in Standard, "you're too damn soft. Shen was right." She shifted languages. "Where have they gone to, girl, the man who got you with child, and the others, and the machine that flies?"

"It does not only fly," the girl said. "It is a spaceship." She said the Standard word well, with little accent.

"Well, and where has it gone? Where is it hidden?"

Defiance flared in the great eyes. Michael touched her arm and said gently, "Please answer."

She would answer for him. She said, ignoring Hanna, "It has gone away to the south where it is warm. Once before it went, and I went, too. He did not take me this time. But he will come back."

"Do you want to wait for him?" Michael said. "You could come with us instead."

The defiance melted. Her eyes became luminous; she was a child, reminding him painfully of Lise.

Hanna said, "We can't take her now. We'll come back for her if we can."

She was exasperated. There was nervousness in her voice, in every quick movement.

"He's not even in this part of the world," Michael said. "We don't have to hurry any more."

"Just how long do you think it will take us to question every old man and woman in the place?"

"Not long. When it gets light, not long."

They waited for dawn in Daryeva's little room. It was scarcely more than a closet, but she had made it her own. There were shells from a southern sea, a bracelet of Polity manufacture—part of the *Far-Flying Bird*'s stolen trove, Hanna guessed. There were dried native flowers in a Polity vase, a music cube made on Willow, a head clumsily carved of highland wood. It was supposed to resemble Daryeva; Wales had made it for her.

Hanna and Shen wandered in and out. One of them was always in the hall, listening, watching. Michael stayed with Daryeva. She told him the story of her short life. She was young and resilient and she did not know how sad it was. He put his arm around her, half-blinded—sometimes she was Lise, sometimes himself. He was too torn with pity to see clearly. But it seemed to him that none of what had happened to Daryeva needed to have happened.

If I had not been so self-protecting I would have, could have—

Morning finally came. The rain had stopped. Hanna and Shen looked through the broken arches uncertainly, as if, deprived of rain, they might no longer be on the same world. Outside the arches was a broad stone esplanade set two meters above the wet sand, which stretched a considerable distance to the receding tide. Sea and sky alike were gray.

When it was full light, Michael had Daryeva take them to a courtyard she had told him about in the night. It was almost in the center of the occupied portion of the maze, and it was all the marketplace of which the Post could now boast. In the early morning people straggled in. Some brought food from outside, not much; those fortunate enough to have food grown and stored against the winter begrudged it. But there were still warm clothes and blankets to be looted from the ruined mansions, and a certain trade was carried out that way, food for warmth.

Michael moved from person to person, group to group. His questions were thrown back at him unanswered. He might as well have been on the wrong world. *I knew no one of that name. Nor that.* He was an antic figure here, too well fed, too well clothed, with the dark women dogging his heels and the pariah Daryeva following. *How old do you think I am, to remember those days? Why, I was not even born!* There was no body of shared knowledge, no collective memory, it had died with the old and with displacement, or what was left was crippled and incomplete. *I have never heard of such a town. Never. Never.* "Every old man and woman in the place," Hanna had said; but the old were rare. The look of age was deceiving. The "old," like Norn, might be only of an age that elsewhere would be the beginning of life's prime. Shen thought little of it, Michael nothing. But Hanna that morning felt stifling horror for a while. It was unnatural and obscene for death to come after so few years. She told herself anti-senescence was really the unnatural thing, but it didn't help; she was horrified still. The specter of early death made ghosts even of the young.

It was in the center of the circles of the doomed, then, that Michael stood and shouted, reckless. He threw names into the gray wind and they blew back to his mouth. Shen grumbled without ceasing, watched the crowd with slitted eyes; Hanna watched the sky. Both missed at first the man — a young man—who finally came forward and tugged Michael's arm. But they saw Michael bend his head to the other's, and started forward, hands on their hidden weapons.

The man slipped away before they got to him. But Michael came to meet them. His eyes glittered.

"That was the road to Croft, the one we came in on," he said.

Hanna looked at the circles of murmuring men and women, but she could not see where the man had gone.

"It is dead," she said. "Marin said so."

"No, no. People have come back, she said."

"And what does that mean, when the people who once lived there are dead? They were all taken from the town when you were. Does it matter who lives there now?"

"It might. Do you remember what Norn said? The man and woman who took Carmina, knew us. They must have come from Croft or Sutherland. And later, he said, the people scattered. They could have gone home."

"All right. All right." She pulled the communicator from her pocket. "We'll get *GeeGee* in. Follow the road to its end." She looked at the sky as she thumbed the transmittal switch. If *GeeGee* could monitor ground transmissions from the air, the *Avalon* could, too. But the gray sky was empty.

GeeGee was ready for quick flight, as she had been everywhere. A very sleepy Theo landed her at the Post thirty minutes after Hanna's call. "I'm going to bed now," he said, but he didn't. He waited in Control with the others, watching the land unroll beneath the *Golden Girl*. They passed over Orne's house in minutes and flew steadily north over the deserted lands.

"It's not paved all the way," Michael said.

"You remember?"

"I remember—" *The dusty track through Croft.* For all he had ever known it was dust all the way to its unknown end. He closed his eyes briefly, remembering, and constructed a map in his head. The paving stretched to Sutherland. Croft lay a little to the southwest, with the dirt track (how deep in mud today?) curving through its tiny heart. One end went to Sutherland; the other must keep up the curve, and come around to join the main road to the Post.

When he looked again, they were flashing over *GeeGee*'s first landing site, that abandoned clearing in the wilderness. He might never know why it was there. Orne's summer lodge had surprised him, too. He had not known the masters ever left their walls, except to walk in the town like gods. There was so much he did not know, might have learned long ago—if he had told the truth at the start on Alta. Instead he had allowed the last, the only memories to seal his lips, had turned away all questions, until it was too late and the *Pavonis Queen* separated him for good from any power that might have tracked down B and uncovered the secrets of this place. While here the people died in waves of sickness, their brutal unbalanced civilization toppling.

I could have stopped it. I let it happen—

But he had been rattled and shaken like a die in a cup, and the hand that had done it was here somewhere. He thought of that soft white hand with an awe so deep it was nearly terror.

Hanna said softly, "He is only a man."

Maybe.

He was weak, so sick he doubled over. When he recovered enough to straighten, he said, "How could one man get so much power?"

"Why, chance," said the dark woman, an oracle again. He looked into her eyes and thought he saw the ambiguous eyespots of Uskos. "Not much is predictable and not much is just," she said; she might have been Norsa citing a lesson of the Master.

"No," Michael said, rejecting it.

"You knew that," she said. "Every day of your life has proved it."

He felt the others watching him, and felt the burden of their lives, which all of them, even Hanna, owed to him. He felt the futility of it in the face of the desertion below.

"Yes," said Hanna. "But you'll go back for Daryeva all the same, when you can. Won't you?"

The sickness began to pass. "Of course," he said.

The land rose under *GeeGee*. There must be changes in the nature of the forest below, but they were not evident from the air. The road snaked on patiently and the horizon billowed with mountains. They were flying low, under the cloud cover, but before they reached the mountains the clouds changed, were higher and thinner, the air brighter; the great funnel was moving at last. They did not have to slow as much as he had expected to follow the road, which after a tortuous course of preliminary turns made straight for a gap in the last fold of land. Sunlight flashed off *Gee-Gee*'s nose as she emerged from it, the flanks of the mountains fell away, the road swooped down in the sun on a broad plateau and turned north. There was silence in Control.

He saw the dirt track veering west before anybody else. When he told Theo to turn *GeeGee* and follow it, nobody said anything.

The land moved under them dun and green. The mountains threw out a feeler, and the village on its unhurried river nestled up against them. He had seen it from the air before, yes, from that mountain peak. The perspective was different, but he would have known it in spite of worse distortions. Home.

He took the helm and set *GeeGee* down slowly in a barren grain field, wondering if he would have to ask someone to finish the job; his knees and hands were weak. Croft appeared eerily unchanged. Even the field was recently harvested; people lived here, then. *Most likely nobody I knew*, he cautioned himself. And a figure walked across the field toward *GeeGee*, stopping, however, a hundred meters from the nearest structure (Annitas' house), too far from *GeeGee* to make out a face.

"Mike," said Hanna. "Look." He looked, and saw what she indicated: a second figure, this one half-hidden by the corner of the house. It held something. A weapon?

"Covering the other one," Hanna said.

He went alone to meet the man who stood in the field. The brilliant sunlight shone on his head with a trace of autumn warmth, but a strong wind was blowing, pushing the clouds away. The air had the heady wine taste he remembered, had never tasted anywhere else. He walked quickly, but it seemed to take a long time. The man who waited was powerfully built, with a grizzled head and broad familiar face. His eyes got bigger and bigger as Michael came near. Michael stopped in front of him and said, "Otto?"

"A-Alek?" said the other man, hardly getting it out.

"It's Mikhail. I've come back. Looking for my sister; is she alive?"

Otto got his mouth shut. He turned and waved a jerky arm and the other figure, armed, came into the open and came up to them. It was a woman, tall and slender, with a hard lovely face and eyes Michael knew. They were his own. "Greetings, Carmina," he said.

"Somebody has to stay on *GeeGee*," Hanna said to Shen. Lise and Theo were already gone at Michael's beckoning,

Lise tumbling out of *GeeGee* with eager haste, Theo looking stunned.

"You go," Shen said.

"All right." Hanna was nervous. She quivered with alarm;
she had caught some of Michael's superstitious fear in spite
of herself. *B is a real man with real guns,* she told herself, but
she heard Rubee's comfortable voice telling tales all the
same.

Finally she left *GeeGee.* Shen could be trusted, she told
herself. Shen knew what to do.

The wind outside was sharp, the sunlight dizzying. A
faint, luminous streak arced across the high sky: the Ring.
The long slopes tilting up toward the mountains were deserted, but when the wind fell for a moment, she heard the
tinkle of small bells where herd animals clustered in sunny
hollows, gleaning the last sweet mouthfuls of summer
growth. The people who had come out of the stone houses
had all disappeared into one. Hanna went toward it slowly.
Up close, the village did not look whole. Some houses were
deserted and falling, succeeding summers and winters having shifted their stones. But everything was here, on the
whole just as Michael had remembered it. She went into the
house where the others were; it was Otto's, she found.

*That was Marlie and I who came for you. Our son was dead,
the first; later we had another, he lives, here he is. We did not
find you, but we found Carmina. Brought her home.*

Michael could not take his eyes off Carmina. It was
strange to see Alek and Lillin in her face. There was a tran-
quillity in her that he recognized; he had had it, too, sometimes. But rarely, only on the very best days. She had given
him up for dead as soon as she was old enough for Otto to
make her understand what had happened. Her only brother
had been Milo, Otto's living son.

*No one here was ever troubled again. Life went on, and
death; Marlie died last year. But not of that evil, that sickness
brought from outside.*

From outside? Are you sure?

*Yes. Sure. It came only when the traveler came, he brought
it like a gift. Not every time. The last time he came, though, it
followed again. And the masters were not exempt as they had
been before.*

It was what he had feared, the guess Hanna had made, which he had not wanted to face. He looked at her quickly. He saw in her eyes the acknowledgment of his responsibility. But then she looked away, at nothing in particular. She seemed to be listening for something above the chatter. Theo had not registered what Otto said; he was busy trying to be invisible, and failing among these dark people. There were perhaps sixty, most strangers to Michael, and half, he learned, were recent refugees from the Post; they had abandoned it and made their way north at the first report of fever. Life here was lived much as it had been lived before, and the disintegration of the city in the lowlands was a rumor that hardly touched Croft.

Shen waited stolidly on *GeeGee,* ready to take off with an instant's notice or none at all. She was not restless as Hanna would have been in her place, but checked all the indicators with an occasional steady sweep of the eyes. Hanna spoke with her from time to time.

"I don't know when I'll be able to get him out of here. He won't want to go."

"So tell him to bring the sister along."

"It's a thought."

Shen said irritably, "Wouldn't matter if every last body back there didn't know where we are."

"Yes."

And somewhere there was a radio. And somewhere there was Henrik, creeping toward the Post, maybe already there.

"Nowhere to go anyhow," Shen muttered.

"That's not true any more," Hanna said, her voice light and thoughtful. "He'll want to go back now. Just as fast as we can."

"Whatever." Shen went back to studying what *GeeGee* had to say. Ready to run.

The shadows shifted in the clear afternoon. People left Otto's house in twos and threes, going back to their occupations. They cast curious looks at *GeeGee,* but they knew what she was; they were not ignorant.

"We know more than they do on the flats,"Otto said. "That's Carmina's doing."

Carmina smiled and shook her head, disclaiming the

praise, but it was true, Michael found. She had asked questions from the time she could talk, and put the answers together with remarkable accuracy. Nothing Michael said surprised her greatly; only the details fascinated her. She was prepared for days of conversation.

"There can't be days," Hanna said, close to Michael's elbow, touching it impatiently.

"No, I know, that's true."

"Come along with us," said Hanna, addressing Carmina. "We have to get in the air." It was safe in space; safer than here, on the ground and exposed.

"I'll stay. I'll wait for you to come back."

There was a heartbreaking serenity about Carmina, as if she had resigned herself to waiting many years ago with unflagging patience. She was unmarried and childless. It seemed possible that she had never been touched, had held herself always a little apart from life. Not what Michael would have done, here or anywhere; not what he could have done. She was detached even from this exotic brother. Who could be nothing more to her, after all, than a dim memory of song.

"Michael, we have to go!" Hanna said.

"I know." But he did not move. He stayed near Otto's fire, not next to Carmina but placed so that he could look at her without interruption, tracing resemblances.

Hanna jittered, dancing with nerves. "Mike, *please!*"

"It's just that I might not be able to come back again," he said to her in Standard, not wanting to alarm Carmina. "There'll be help from the Polity; I'll make sure of that. But when I turn myself in, it might be the end for me."

"Nonsense," Hanna said. "All you have to do is trade. Information for freedom. I thought you saw that, I thought you knew it. That this was the way out."

"I can't trade with this, I can't take a chance. Enough's happened because I was thinking of myself."

She was unconvinced. Well, she would have all the weeks it took to get back to Theta to try and change his mind. But he did not mean to let it be changed. His survival was not important any more. Gadrah's was.

"Come along, come along, Mike. We have to go."

"In a minute. A few more minutes."

Hanna chewed her fingernails.

*   *   *

The mountains swooped into the great valley and then started up again on the other side, not as high there, but high enough to cut off the sun at a rather early hour. The western shadows crept across the valley and made a final leap; suddenly it was dusk. The gleam of the river faded. Shen got food from the galley and carried it back to Control. There was nothing to see out *GeeGee*'s nose with the naked eye any more, so she adjusted the monitors for night vision and watched them instead. But the radar was more important, the radar searching the sky. Though that, she knew, was terrifyingly limited. The *Avalon* could wind through the mountains low and slow, come up behind that last tall peak, and never be spotted or suspected till she came around the mountain accelerating and spitting fire.

Shen began to think about lifting *GeeGee* into the air, getting above the mountains and scanning exhaustively for an intruder. The only recourse of an unarmed ship facing one with arms was flight. With people on the ground to be picked up, seconds would count.

"Come on," she growled. "Get him out of there. Come on!"

She took the remains of her meal back to the galley and put them away. When she returned to Control, she had made up her mind. She would take *GeeGee* up and look around.

She was reaching for the communications switch to tell Hanna that when the *Avalon* rose up from behind the mountain peak, and radar picked it up and set off a shrill alarm.

The communicator on Hanna's wrist went off frantically. The noises outside were unmistakable, the scream of *Gee-Gee* taking off in a single max-power burst, the thunder of other engines, then a roar that split the night. Hanna flung open the door just in time to see a gout of flame erupt where *GeeGee* had been—but no longer was; she was a flurry of light streaking up the valley and up into the air, headed for space. "She's gone!" Theo said in despair, but Hanna said, "*GeeGee*'s our only chance. Shen's got to keep her safe. And she's drawn them off. We've got some time."

There was another burst of fire, high this time, and far away. Hanna held her breath, but there was no explosion, no fireball. *GeeGee* was still intact, still running hard.

She looked around and saw Michael with relief—the old Michael, to whom danger was a practical problem with concrete solutions.

"They'll come back," he said. "Theo and Lise could stay here. B doesn't know them."

"Henrik does."

"Henrik. Damn him. All right; we've all got to go." He asked Otto, "Have you got anything that would help us get out?"

"Carts," Otto said. "Beasts."

"We'll go on foot, then."

"Where to?" Hanna said.

"Sutherland," Michael said. "Come on."

He had lied, though. As soon as the night hid them from Croft he turned away from the road and led them down the riverbank. "There were too many people back there," he said. "Otto won't tell them what I said, Carmina won't— maybe. What are they going to say when their neighbors are threatened? And there were people there I don't know. Who don't understand what it means, why we have to get away. There used to be a ford here." It was still there. They had to use the light, worrying Michael, but a hillock on the edge of the stream largely hid the ford from Croft. The rocks were slippery underfoot.

"Where's there to go?" Theo said.

"The mountain. Caves there. We've still got food tabs, there's plenty of water; if we're careful we can even use fire. We could hold out for a while."

"They won't stop hunting till they find us," Hanna said.

"If they're looking around Sutherland, though, it'll give Shen a chance to come back and get us."

They ran up the long bare slope of the mountain's foot until Lise lagged behind, her breath coming in painful gasps she had tried to suppress. Michael carried her for a time, and they walked, but they did not stop. It was imperative to get under cover. Even the line of the first trees above was no guarantee of safety; there was no reason to suppose anything was wrong with the *Avalon*'s infrared sensors. They had to get under the earth, into the caves Michael remembered. There was still a long way to go.

Lise said finally, "I can walk." It was the first thing she had said since the crisis began. He put her down and trudged upward. The wind had died with the day, and walking kept them warm. Hanna's face was turned to the sky; she tripped once or twice. But she was no longer looking for the *Avalon,* at least not entirely. She was looking because the sky, clear now, was alive. A tiny moon that cast little light moved across it so quickly the motion was visible; before it disappeared another came, describing a different arc. The Ring was a high distant arch, unchanging; only now that she could see it well, she saw it was really a plurality of rings, a series of delicate-looking bands separated by strips of night. Now and again a meteor flared. It was not the season for any of the great showers. But in one quadrant of the sky a comet shone like a stylized picture of all the comets that had ever existed. All these phenomena stood out prominently in a sky that otherwise was scantily starred. No sky anywhere else was like it.

They came up under the trees, which quickly thickened and cut off the sky. Michael cast the light about, hesitating. His hearing seemed unnaturally sensitive; now he, too, listened for the sounds Hanna strained to hear, the noise of a spacecraft moving across the sky. But there was icy silence on the mountainside. There was only a small cold wind which they had come high enough to feel, a wind that did not touch the valley below. The dying leaves on their malleable trees rattled in the wind; they would not fall until spring.

"This way," he said with more hope than certainty, but when they had wound through a grove where the trees stood close together, he saw he had been right. The game trail he remembered had scarcely shifted. They followed it up.

The *Avalon* was as Henrik had remembered it, only worse in some ways. It was still dark, and it smelled worse than ever, as if no one ever bothered to clean any part of it up, and remnants of food had lain carelessly in corners for months. A bin of foodstuffs had gone bad—as Henrik discovered when he opened it, looking for something to eat, and the stench nearly knocked him over. He closed it quickly, but not before he got a glimpse of what was inside—a writhing heap of something white and wet.

He tried not to think of the *Golden Girl*—the light and the music. But the music would not stay out of his head. *Tambours and sackbuts.* "It's not my fault the bastard got born a thousand years too late," Henrik said, but he only said it to himself. He couldn't say it to anyone here. It was strange to think he could have said that to Theo, or Hanna, or even to Michael Kristofik; Kristofik would only have laughed.

Since there was no one to talk to, he went back to his old cabin and crouched in a corner with his head in his hands, in the dark. Maybe he had done the wrong thing. But it did not seem to him that he had done anything at all. He had watched Michael leave the *Golden Girl* and plunge into the sea of trees and rain, tall and confident, with Hanna and Shen—leaving Henrik behind, like Lise, with Theo to baby-sit for both of them. There was nothing to do but wait, nothing but stay where he was put. He had resented it, and the resentment had grown through a day and a night until it filled him and burst out. He had been carried here against his will, and was he now to be left behind while the others were out in the rain and fresh air? Was he less of a man than the women? At the end of the second day Theo was dozing, Lise invisible. It took only minutes to get what he needed and get outside. He made his way to the road and started down it; maybe he would meet the others coming back. He did not, and the night came, and he meant to turn back, and then realized that he would never see, in the dark, the place where he must leave the road to get back to the ship. And the ship might take off before he reached it; what if it took off? He did not think Theo would wait for him.

The rain came down drearily. The night was colder than he had expected. There was nothing to do but keep following Michael. There was shelter on this road, at least; he had heard the others tell Theo about it the night before. He had to find it. He kept walking.

He did find it; found Orne, his suspicions now fully aroused; woke at dawn with Orne grumbling in his ear, was urged into the ramshackle truck. "I want to find the others, I just want to find them," he said. Orne said, "Well, and this is the way they went." And the town in the cold morning, the curiosity, the talk that went so fast he could not keep up with it. And the pretty brown girl, the radio hidden among her scant belongings, preset for the issuing of warnings. She had not wanted to use it, but her grandfather pushed her aside and took it, plain fear in his eyes. And then the *Avalon* came in across the sky, and it was too late for Henrik to run, too late for him to do anything even if he had been able to think of anything to do.

So now he crouched in the dark, ignored, unimportant, trying to think. B would never go back to the Polity, and Henrik's only chance was to get back to Michael and get away when the others did. Unless they had already gone on the ship B had failed to shoot down.

But B did not think they were all on that ship.

He had asked Henrik: "If some were on the ground, would the others go?"

"No," Henrik had said. He knew them well enough to be sure of that. He had lived with them long enough to know.

He huddled in the dark and waited. No one came near him. No one had spoken to him except B. Ta had not said, "Where you been?" Bakti had not said, "Good to see you." They had not looked the same. There was strained desperation in their faces—and it must have predated the *Golden Girl*'s coming here, it was etched too deep to have sprung up all at once. They looked like men who did not want to be where they were.

The *Avalon* was moving, but no one had told him where. The door opened, the light came on, and he looked up. Maybe someone would tell him something. B stood there, the old empty smile on his lips.

"I think I've got it straight what you did," he said. "Think of anything else I ought to know?"

His voice was toneless. Henrik was reassured. He had told B only what he had to, more than he wanted to; he had not dared to refuse. But he would not offer any more information. He could give Michael that, he could give Hanna that.

"I don't know any more," he said gratefully. "There's nothing more that would help."

"Sure?"

"Sure."

B's hand came around from behind his back. There was something in it, laser pistol or disruptor, Henrik never decided which and there was no time to think about the mistakes he had made; there was an instant of shock, and he was dead.

If the caverns had been too high on the mountain, they could not have made it. Michael was sure of that; sure the *Avalon* would be back in the night, whether it caught up with *GeeGee* or not. If it caught up with *GeeGee* — his first thought was of Shen, but he forced it down. Shen wouldn't like that. She would call him soft. Well, then, even with Shen and *GeeGee* gone there would be a way out, though it would mean getting control of the *Avalon.*

But all they could do now was hide. He urged the others up the mountainside, climbing, climbing. Old landmarks rose up in the dark and fell behind, it was a shorter climb than he remembered; no, his legs were longer, twice as long, an eerie echo of trance. Theo and Hanna went on steadily, breathing hard till the second wind came; then they seemed, as Michael felt, tireless. But it was hard on Lise. She leaned on his arm; he half-carried her.

They came around the edge of a high bluff, and he turned and plunged into the brush at its base.

The opening was still there, and hidden even better than in his childhood; a tree had grown up in front of it. He probed at the undergrowth, using the light openly now, and carefully. Not all the beasts in these mountains were harmless, and some visited caves. He heard Hanna behind him, listening. For bestial near-thought from the cave? For something in the sky? If the latter, there was nothing to hear but Lise gasping and wheezing, desperate for rest.

Hanna said nothing about an animal presence, and there was no sign of a path through the dried grasses underfoot. He got on his knees — the opening was low — and crept in, flashing the light now ahead, now back for the others. His hands and knees sank into mud and scraped on pebbles. Lise objected to the mud, fretful, and he heard Hanna speak to her softly, encouraging, promising sleep.

The mud dried up and faded into rock. A dislodged stone rolled ahead on a gentle downward slope; the ceiling lifted overhead. He got up and walked, crouching, then straightened fully. "Mind your head," Hanna said to Theo or Lise; then they stood beside him in a clutter of loose rocks. The stone underfoot was cool and damp. There was the sound of water nearby, a slow-moving stream; he knew just where it was.

He said, "This is far enough. Somebody's got to be posted at the opening all the time. If Shen calls, we might not pick it up in here."

Theo said, "We can't call *her*. They'd hear."

"Yes. We can only listen, till we know she's close. I'll take the first watch."

Theo looked relieved. He had had even less sleep than the others. He kicked stones away and sat down on the rock without further discussion, leaning against the cave wall. "This feels soft enough," he said. Lise nearly fell next to him. She put her head on his shoulder and he put his arm around her.

Michael turned the light to a dim glow and left it with them. It would shine for months, maybe years; at least they did not have to fear the dark. "The water's just down there," he said, pointing downhill, and made sure they saw where he pointed. "If you need some, for God's sake don't get lost!"

"I'm not that crazy," Theo muttered, and closed his eyes.

Michael crawled back to the mouth of the cave, Hanna following. They laid one of the communicators on a rock in the open and retreated just inside the cave, where they could hear it call but sit upright in some comfort. They swallowed nutrient tablets and took turns going to the stream for water, tiptoeing past Theo and Lise, already sound asleep. When Hanna came back, she had no coat; she had spread it over the other two for warmth. Michael took off his coat, too, and they huddled together under it.

Hanna said, "Oh, God, how I want a bath!"

"There's the stream," he said.

She shivered. "It might come to that."

She leaned against him, still shivering, but not with cold. "Somebody's dead," she said.

"What do you mean? Shen?" he said anxiously.

"I don't think it's Shen. But somebody's died. I felt it on the way up. I would have known if it was Shen. But somebody I know is gone."

Michael held her in silence. He was so accustomed to living with a telepath that she had ceased to seem strange, but sometimes he was reminded that her humanity was of a different order from most, from his.

"It couldn't have been anybody in Croft," he said. "The *Avalon* hasn't come back yet. Somebody at the Post? Somebody on the *Avalon*?"

"I don't think so. I don't know any of those people well enough to feel it if they died. It might not even have been here, it might have been somebody at home. But I think it was here." She paused. "I hope it wasn't Henrik."

He moved involuntarily. He didn't want it to be Henrik. He said as lightly as he could, "What the hell are we going to do about Henrik, anyway?"

"Leave him," she said. "He made his choice. If we get away and get the Polity here, he can go home. To prison, probably."

"I wouldn't like to see that happen."

"No. I guess I wouldn't either. He doesn't really try to be the way he is. He just never knows what he's doing," she said, and Michael laughed.

"I don't either. Do you?"

"Not till it's over," she admitted.

"I stayed too long," he said as if it were the logical sequel. "I couldn't tear myself away."

"I know," she said, forgiving him. She added, "Carmina gave me her gun."

"Is that what you were carrying? Do you know how to use it?"

"I think so." She dug in a pocket and pulled out a bulging pouch; something rattled inside it. "Ammunition," she said.

"That's good. And we've got two stunners. But either way we'll have to be at close range."

"We'll arrange that if we have to," she said.

They sat in silence, waiting. *At the end of the universe,* he thought. Because of the stone overhead and the brush outside, he could not see the sky, not a single star to say there were other places. *Run to ground*—he knew what that meant, now. All the running he had ever done had been only a prelude to this.

But he could not feel despair. Not with Shen out there, faithful; not with Hanna at his side.

He got his hand under her chin, turned her head and kissed her. This night ought to belong to the painful, necessitous nights he had spent dragging himself through memories. But there were all the others, too. Luxury was where you found it, where you made it.

He felt the tension begin to run out of Hanna, melting out like tallow. "I don't want to take too many clothes off," she said.

"We'll see what we can do," he said, and they lay down together on the stony bed, cushioning each other as best they could.

The lights went out one by one in Croft, until the only one left was in the house where Carmina lived with Otto. They had talked for a time, but Carmina was not inclined for conversation, and Otto at length had left her alone. Now as the night wore on, they were silent. Carmina's face was calm but watchful; her eyes moved at every sound. Anyone who knew Michael would have recognized that look.

Her mind was not as quiet as her face and hands. Strangely (but it would not have been strange to anyone who knew Michael) she had no difficulty in accepting what had happened—and might happen. Her brother had come home. That was a fact. He carried the seeds of a revolution; if he got away he would make it happen, and Carmina's life and the lives of everyone she knew would change. That was a fact. Carmina had always dealt in facts, some of them hard. These were better than most.

But the bones of a hard fact, and the richness of the flesh that clothed it, were different things.

Her mind wandered among riches. The man who shared her blood, looking no older than she in spite of the difference in their ages—how little she had learned about him! But much about Gadrah, and much about the worlds outside it. He had seen her thirst for knowledge and ministered to it; she was ashamed, thinking of it; she had not asked what she could give in return. But all he had seemed to want was to look at her.

The candle burned low. The town was silent. There were many who slept, and Otto's gray head drooped and his eyes were half-closed. But no doubt others sat awake in the dark, waiting for a return.

Carmina dreamed, though awake. She dreamed of the worlds of which Mikhail had told her, the busy homeworld, the colonies unlike Gadrah where human life had thrived. She dreamed of governments, too, and law, and what they might do here, where there had never been any law but custom—or the caprices of power.

She had been dreaming this last dream a long time when the sound began. She knew it at once, she had known it when she heard it in the afternoon, and it had brought a stark memory of danger, of screaming and terror and fire.

In the afternoon it had only brought her brother home. But now it was night.

She stood in the open door with the candle behind her, inviting danger. Her view of the landing was clear. One spacecraft looked much like another to inexperienced eyes, but she had studied the *Golden Girl* hungrily while she waited in the day at Otto's back, and even in the dark she was certain this was not the same one. The hunters, then.

She stood unmoving while lights came toward her, drawn by light. Two men came to the door and at last she gave way, backing into the room; there were weapons in their hands, and she knew, by description, what they did. She knew one of the men by description as well. The undying. Tistou.

"Where are they?" he said. He looked at her strangely when the light flashed on her face. Otto had gotten up behind her. Tistou said, "Where are they, old man?"

"Gone," Otto said. "The gold ship came and got them."

The traveler said smiling, "The ship has not come back. It did not turn back soon enough, to have come back. They are here."

"Well, search, then," Otto said.

They did search; they looked in every house and byre, the spaceship hovering overhead and flooding the town with light. The searchers took Carmina with them, and at each cottage, when the householder was roused, they put the end of a weapon to the base of her skull, to show what would happen if there were protests. At each house she smiled, calm and unafraid, and endured it. She even endured (though she did not smile) a clumsy caress from the man with the gun at her head; but Tistou said, "There's no time. Keep your eyes open." After that there was only the gun, better than the heavy hand.

One thing frightened her, though she did not show it.
The ship at the rooftops, the light pouring down—she had
seen that a long time before, her earliest memory.

When they were satisfied Croft hid no fugitives, they
took her back to Otto. They put her against the wall and
pointed the guns at her breast. "Where are they?" Tistou
said.

"I will not tell you," she said, dreaming of law.

"Well, old man?"

"Sutherland," Otto said. "They took the road—" he
pointed—"that way. At least, they said they would go that
way."

"Do you agree?" Tistou asked her, but she would not
move or speak. He looked at her closely again, as if some
memory or moment of knowledge were near.

He stepped back and put the gun in his belt and went
out, followed by the other man, who was very big and fair.
Carmina moved to the door and watched them go. Otto
said, "I had to tell them, child. They would have killed you."

"Yes," she said. "But maybe Mikhail thought of that."

"He was a clever boy," Otto said.

Theo had not looked at the time since nightfall, and he did
not know how long he had slept when Michael woke him.
His chronometer showed Standard time, and it could not
tell him how long it was to dawn. When his eyes were fully
open he saw that Michael was exhausted. Hanna stood
there, too, heavy with sleep.

"Your turn. Wake me in a couple hours," Michael said.

Theo went for water first. On the way back to the mouth
of the cave, passing the others, he saw that Michael and
Hanna were already asleep. Hanna had taken his place and
slept with her arms around Lise, who had hardly stirred,
and Michael held Hanna. The three were very close, very
beautiful—and vulnerable. There was a mountain over
their heads and it could fall and crush them in a moment.

The chill of the cavern reached into Theo's bones. The
only help he could give was to watch, so he did it.

He did not wait inside the cave but just at the opening,
ready to duck inside at the first sign or sound of anything in
the air. He was cold and alone, and even when his eyes adjusted to the dark, even here looking into the open, he felt

smothered; the bluff was a mass of black hung over his head and he faced a tree. On either side of the tree, and at either hand, brush shut out everything except a few patches of starless sky. He longed for a clear line of sight to the valley, for *any* sight of it. Michael had said B would return to the village, but if he did, it would be hard for anyone on the mountainside to know it. The wind rustled gently, and whenever it rose Theo started as if he heard hunters creeping through the wood. Once in a windless moment he thought he heard a spacecraft lift off, and jumped to his feet, ready to run. But as he stood in the dark the sound faded and was gone. He strained his ears and heard only the night, until he was not sure he had heard anything at all.

He sat down and waited again. He was still very tired. But he was on guard, fighting sleep, when the communicator set up a sweet steady signal and an unmistakable voice said, "Mike?"

He had never been so glad to hear anything. He said shakily, "Mike's asleep, I'll get him," and scrambled to wake the others.

They came out to a filament of dawn. It wasn't much, because the mountain blotted out the east. Shen said, "Coming in, where are you?" and they stood in the open and looked up at the lightening sky.

Michael got his communicator back and talked into it, thinking *This is too easy.* "Meet us just under the tree line," he said. "About forty-five degrees south from a straight line up the mountain from Croft. See it?"

"Not yet," she said. There was no sound to indicate *Gee-Gee* was near, and Shen would not tell them where she was, not when someone else might be listening.

They started downhill in a hurry, running and skidding on the steep decline. "What if the other one comes back?" Lise said nervously.

"They'll go after *GeeGee*," Michael answered to reassure her, and saw Hanna nod.

The light strengthened as they went on. Going down was easier than climbing had been, and there was no stopping to peer around in the dark for old, changed landmarks. They were close to the open when they heard *GeeGee,* and a few seconds later saw her gliding in at an altitude not much greater than theirs.

"That's fine," Michael said. "Set her down."

"Hell of a grade," Shen complained. But *GeeGee* stopped in midair and slowly lowered herself toward the ground.

Made it, he thought, and saw Hanna freeze, staring across the valley through the lacy tops of the last trees.

"Tell her to get out!" she cried, there must have been a burst of thought, too, or Shen had seen what Hanna saw, because there was a roar from *GeeGee* and she was gone, leaping into the air as from a catapult. "Back," Michael said, "everybody back!" They did not need to be urged, they all saw the other shape now, a dark blot racing across the valley, and they turned and climbed for their lives. Michael ran behind the others, looking over his shoulder, waiting for an explosion in the air or among them, but there was none. Then the valley was empty and the sound of engines was gone.

They kept running until they tumbled through the mouth of the cave. The dark past the opening was a wall. *I thought I had stopped running,* Michael thought. He had shoved the light into his pocket as the day grew, and now he got it out and turned it on and they wormed their way back to their first resting place. They sat in a circle round the light, panting and sweating in the chill air.

Michael wondered for the first time what would become of them. He looked at Hanna and saw her hunched, head bowed to her knees. He had never seen her like that before.

After a while Theo stretched out on his back on the stone. He said, "They had us. If they'd fired, it would've been over."

"They went for the ship," Michael said. He looked at the stone because otherwise he would look at Hanna, and he did not want to. For once he did not want her reading his thoughts.

She did not have to read them. She had been a soldier and a killer, and she could make out the strategies of violence for herself.

She said without lifting her head, so that her voice was muffled and expressionless, "*GeeGee*'s a lot more important than we are. If he killed us first, there'd be nothing to keep Shen here. So we're bait to keep bringing her back till he shoots her down. Then he can just pick us off . . . He'll come back sooner next time. He was over there waiting. I wonder how long . . . Could you persuade Shen to leave us and carry word home?" She was talking to Michael now, but she still did not raise her head. If Shen did that, a ship of the Fleet would come in a few months' time—but the four left behind would be dead long before then.

She's a realist. Maybe she'd go.

He could not say it. Lise had lain down with her head on Theo's chest, hiding her eyes. How could he tell Shen to go and leave Lise?

"We're tired," he said. "We're not thinking straight. Get some tabs down and get some rest, all of you."

Hanna looked up finally. Her eyes were veiled and she said nothing, only made a one-minute meal of food tabs with the others and afterward said, "Shall I watch?"

"I will. I'll wake you later."

He kissed her quickly and took off for the entrance to the cavern, as if being out of sight meant she could not read his mind.

He waited in the dark and thought about taking a chance.

The first notion had come into his head as he crawled back into the cave, leaving the day behind. He had put it aside as fast as he could, afraid Hanna would see it. He did not think she would like the idea if she knew about it.

The situation was hopeless. The four people on the ground were much less dangerous for B than the *Golden Girl,* which had the course to Gadrah in her data banks. B could not allow her to get away and take that knowledge back to the Polity. But she had to get away—with Hanna and Theo and Lise on board with Shen. He had thought of a way to change things—maybe.

The day had turned bright, and when he looked out from the dark it dazzled him. Time passed, but Hanna did not come out to him, to his relief; she must be asleep; he wanted her to stay asleep. He turned to go where she was—but it was Lise he wanted. And heard someone slither over stone and a moment later saw, to his further relief, that Lise had come out seeking him.

She hunkered down with him between day and night and said, "I couldn't sleep."

"Want to take over on watch?"

"Yes," she said, pleased with his trust.

"Good for you. Wait here a minute."

He crept through the passage of stone for the last time, to the light at the end of it. He meant to steal Hanna's communicator. He was afraid he could not do it without waking her, but she had put it down on the stone beside Carmina's tooled blue-black gun, and he picked it up without disturbing her or making a sound. The disc of light metal was no larger than his palm, and he remembered, incongruously, why he had bought the things in the first place—so he could talk from the great house on Valentine to Theo or Shen on the sand far below at the foot of the cliff, or they could talk to him. Not that anyone going to the beach had ever remembered to take one along. It hadn't mattered; nothing had ever been too urgent to wait.

Then he picked Theo's pocket. Theo muttered and groaned at the light touch, and turned his head back and forth, but he did not wake.

Hanna did not move. He looked at her with longing, but he could not risk a kiss.

He took his booty silently back to Lise. She was in the light now, using the shiny surface of his own communicator as a mirror while she wiped grime from her face with her sleeve.

"Here," he said. "This is Hanna's. I'm taking mine with me. I'm going for a walk and I need it. This is Theo's clock. You keep it. Now, listen. In exactly an hour, if nothing happens sooner, go wake Hanna and Theo up. Tell them I'm going to create a diversion. Do you know what a diversion is?"

"To make those men look the other way?" she said shyly.

"*Very* good. Tell Hanna and Theo that the three of you should go down to the place we were making for this morning. When you get there—this is very important—Hanna's got to get in touch with Shen. Not by voice; telepathically. She has to make Shen understand three things. First, if Shen's not close she's got to come in as close as she dares without being detected. Second, when she's at that point, she's got to let me know. There was a code we used on Revenge, she'll remember it; Hanna should tell her to use it again. And third, when the diversion starts, she's got to pick the three of you up."

He made her repeat it back to him twice. She had it right,

but he had also taken the precaution of recording what he said; Hanna would see the blinking light on her communicator and play it back. He gave it to Lise, and with it the packet of food tabs he carried. Win or lose, he would not need them; the others might.

He got up finally, smiling down at Lise. She had listened to him carefully, too caught up in detail to see any flaw in what he proposed, but a trace of doubt came into her eyes at the last.

"What about you?" she said.

He said readily, "You just wait and see. I haven't come this far to get stopped now. All right?"

"All right . . ."

"Remember, let them sleep for another hour."

Which would give him time to get well away before Hanna woke up and wondered exactly what he meant to do. Maybe it would be all right if she did. She might say grimly: *Yes, someone's got to do something, it might as well be you.* But maybe not. It was better to leave her no choice.

He had come up the mountain once or twice at this time of year to say farewell to summer. The puffball bird-things with their faceted eyes were gone. The forest still tilted in the sunlight, leaning toward morning then evening as the day progressed; all the trees were nearly vertical now. The tenacious leaves made a warm brown roof, and sunlight danced through the spaces between them. The wind had stopped blowing and the silence was so deep as to be a tangible thing. A silence like this was compelling. It warned you to be still and wait and listen, as if the universe had stopped and any sound, however slight, would carry the monumental meaning of its starting up again. His own footsteps made a little noise, but all that did was give him an eerie feeling that he was the only thing in this stasis for which time counted, the only thing that went forward in it, while everything else was frozen in a moment that was, for him, past.

He did not make for the goal he had set the others, the place they had tried to reach at dawn. Instead he crossed the face of the mountain in as straight a line as he could contrive until Croft was directly below him. Then he turned and started down.

He judged that something more than an hour had passed when the trees began to thin and he could see where he was going. He sat down under one of them. Hanna would be awake now, and they should have started for the point that would, he hoped, mark a rendezvous with Shen. They would be moving more slowly than they had in the morning's futile dash for safety; give them half an hour. Then Hanna would have to touch Shen's mind; how long would that take? And then there would be a little more time, or a lot of time, while Shen got into position.

Nothing would happen quickly in any case. No matter how close Shen was now, she would not come in openly. She would creep in behind the mountains, hugging the ground and squeezing *GeeGee* through passages cut by mountain streams. And B would know something was getting ready to happen. He was over there somewhere, watching; maybe he would see the spots of heat on the mountainside, wonder why one had split off, guess it was Michael. He would not do anything about it yet. He would wait for the *Golden Girl.*

Michael settled down under his tree and waited, like B, for the universe to start up again.

Hanna spent the whole way downhill trying to get herself into a condition where entering trance would be possible. She could not even breathe deeply, could not take that first step. *Why, I am afraid,* she thought. She did not know what Michael was going to do. But, *It's too dangerous!* she cried to the indifferent trees. Theo talked gently to Lise, even cheerfully. He did it well; if Hanna had not been a telepath, she would not have guessed that he was afraid, too. But he would not let Lise see it.

The sun had started an imperceptible slide into afternoon when they got to the edge of the trees. The valley was a bowl of light. Croft, to the right and far below, looked as if nothing but peace had ever touched it—except for the charred gouge the *Avalon* had left with a single shot. Smoke rose gently from chimneys and vanished in the transparent air. A few tiny figures moved in and around the village. Harvest was over, the great work of the year was done. They would be mending and repairing, looking after stock, maybe hunting—but no hunters would go abroad today.

Theo warned Lise, "We have to be quiet now. Hanna has to concentrate." Hanna gave him a bitter look. Concentration seemed impossible. All her mind was busy wondering where Michael was; she couldn't think of anything else.

It was necessary, however. She reached for every bit of discipline she had ever learned in her life, and began what she had to do.

This was another mode of being, and the world was a different place. For eyes there were mountain, valley, sky; for Hanna in trance those things, though perceptible, were unimportant and remote. Much closer were the not-voices in her head.

"Think of stones," she had said to Lise and Theo. They had gathered a handful of pebbles and dutifully fixed their eyes, and their thoughts as well as they could, on that object. They had no training in meditation and it was hard. Other things kept breaking in. *Where is Shen, where is Mike? What does Hanna do so silent and still? What's going to happen? Stones. Stones. Stones.* She identified and detached herself from them. There was something like a soft murmur she identified as Croft. There was apprehension there, but no threat. She set that aside, too.

And touched Michael: *Oh, Michael!* she cried; he had been relaxed, but she felt him come to his feet, startled. She was so close to him that his body might have been at her side.

Love, what do you mean to do?

She got a dim picture in answer, dim because he didn't want her to see it. It had something to do with the *Avalon.*

Only the detachment of trance kept her from objecting. In trance it seemed reasonable enough.

There were other presences. She measured them. She had met them before, on the *Avalon.* They had changed, were less confident, and there were not as many as there had been before, but she knew them.

When she had placed all those minds, the men of the *Avalon,* the people of Croft, her own friends, she marked a barrier around them, and reached out for Shen.

Found her at once; saw through her eyes. The warm light in Control, panels blinking as *GeeGee* talked to herself. Shadows of mountains outside the port. Shen was very close, *GeeGee* hidden somehow in a narrow gorge. *Fancy flying to get in!* Shen thought when she was over the first surprise of Hanna's touch.

Excellent indeed, Hanna thought. *Listen now to what comes next—*

Michael sat under the tree, cross-legged, hands folded. The shadows on the mountainside moved slowly, deepening in the hollows that followed the great slopes, trickling into depressions in the valley. The scene took on a texture deep-piled as velvet, and the afternoon light bathed it a rich tinge of gold. He watched it in deep contentment. He looked at the village and put names to the houses. He had not gone to the house where he and Carmina had been born, and he contemplated the unlikelihood that he would ever enter it again. He was calm; he wondered where the old rage had gone. If ever it should appear, surely it should be now, in this trap. But it was gone. Having lost all he had owned, on the point of leaving behind his friends and the love of his life, he was rich—and not alone. He was swimming in gold, the abundant golden light of the valley. The light was the work of a moment. But all moments were filled with gold.

He had lost track of time when the sound came. *Ready,* it had meant on Revenge, and it meant the same thing now. There had been no sight or sound of the *Golden Girl,* and he did not know where she was—but with luck B did not know either.

He did not get up at once. When he did, the universe would start moving again, and he held it back for a minute.

He moved finally; stood up and walked out from the shelter of the trees. The long fall of land before him was smooth, close-cropped by a summer's grazing. He walked down it without haste, his shadow trailing behind. It was silent here, too, as if the land itself was watching.

He reached the valley's edge and veered a little north to pass Croft by without entering it. All the tiny figures had disappeared. He wondered if Carmina watched, and wondered what she thought.

He meant to walk all the way across the valley if he was allowed to get that far. He might not make it—but he went on and on through field and pasture without challenge. He glanced back sometimes and saw pure peace, and Croft was farther away each time. The silence continued undisturbed. Doubt crept into his mind—was he going the wrong way, was B even there?

He is there, said a whisper like a thread of ice, and he faltered for the first time, knowing Hanna on the hillside not only watched him but accompanied him. He had not meant for her to do that.

Go on, she said, *he is waiting for you,* and he recognized the cold voice of trance. She did not ask what he meant to do. Perhaps she knew he had no clear idea. It depended on B.

He came finally to the hills opposite Croft. They were neither as high nor as heavily forested as those on the eastern edge of the valley, but there was plenty of room to hide in them and to hide the *Avalon.* He stopped and looked ahead and to either side without seeing a sign of the ship. There was no whisper in his mind to guide him. Hanna could not know precisely where it was either.

He took the communicator from his pocket and held it in the open. Anyone listening would hear what he said.

He said, "B . . ."

He made a long sound of it, almost a caress. Most likely the creature had not been called by that sound for thirty years.

"B," he said, "let's talk."

The silence was so long that he thought it might not work, even come near working, even make a start. He had nothing to offer and no threat to make. *If I were B, I would kill me now and go right on waiting for* GeeGee. Picking off a leader made good sense. But B might think Hanna the greater threat that way.

Nothing happened. The lovely country spread around him in the same silence as before, until he thought there would be no answer and he must stand here disregarded until he gave up and went back, impotent.

The cold voice split the quiet when he was almost ready to turn. It said: "What's there to talk about?"

"There's questions," Michael said, playing his empty hand. "Questions nobody's asked you before. And there's staying alive. I can't go back either. One minute under probe and I'm a candidate for Adjustment. How about a truce? It could be comfortable here if we get together."

He stood waiting as calmly as if B had a reason to keep him alive. There could not be one. The only question was whether what he said would spark a little curiosity. To come to B like this was an admission of defeat. B would know it, and maybe that would work on him. Maybe confidence would lead him to indulge in some play before he ended it.

The voice said finally: "Talk, then."

Michael said, "Face to face."

He took out the stunner he had, held it out for watching eyes to see, and threw it away from him.

"That's all I've got," he said. "You'll search me anyway. I'm alone and there's four of you. I'll never catch you sleeping like I did the other time."

He waited again. The reminder of what he had done to B one night as a boy was deliberate. It might get him shot down where he stood, but he didn't think so. For this *thing*, he thought (not "man"), that last headache wouldn't matter. Instead B would remember the child and the months of power.

He was right enough for the voice to start up again. It directed him to an opening in the hills to the north, a short walk. When he entered it, long shadows fell over him; it was late. He walked up a grassy cleft, turned into another, followed a winding stream to another. Shadow passed into dusk. A small wind rustled the grasses through which he passed and there were sounds of water. The sky on its way to night was the deep blue of Hanna's eyes. The toneless voice spoke from time to time and told him where to go. In spite of it he was at peace. He was filled with a deep, calm expectation. It was necessary to see the face again, to look into the empty eyes; it had always been necessary. He hardly thought at all. Only he thought, *They are listening over there, Hanna and the rest. They will know where he is. It will help.*

He had not brought the light the others needed, had not expected to have to use it, but his eyes adjusted to the falling night. The sky was clear and the Ring cast some light, maybe as much as Earth's moon, which he had seen once at the full and treasured in memory. He did not stumble.

He crossed, as he was told, a tiny streamlet the width of a stride, and crossed a flat wooded space with a hill rising sharply to the left. That brought him to the bank of a larger stream into which the small one flowed. He turned to the left, downstream, as instructed, and worked his way through the brush. The stream was a barrier to his right, a sheer cliff three times his height to the left. The cliff suddenly cut back, the stream meandered away, and he came round the outcrop of the cliff and saw an open space. It was not large, but it was large enough for the *Avalon*.

The *Avalon* was shut down, or so it looked from here; at least it showed no lights. He wondered how it had tracked him from its place in this creek bottom, how *GeeGee* had been spotted in the morning. He hesitated for a moment, awaiting challenge, but none came, and he went on toward the ship, picking his way among stones cast up by the creek in times of flood.

When he had come nearly to the side of the ship a hatch opened near the ground, falling silently to make a ramp. That was where he had first seen Hanna. There was an oblong of dim light and he walked up the ramp and into the light, and men hidden on either side stepped forward at once and the muzzles of weapons dug into his sides. He held his hands up and open. He did not even look from side to side to see who the men were until they had searched him, which they did thoroughly and not gently. He got by with the communicator, though. It was made to fasten to nearly anything and he had attached it to his coat right over his heart, in plain view, and they did not take it away. He had hoped for that. It might make things easier, if Shen and Hanna heard what was said.

When the men flanking him were done, he looked at them. One was even taller than Michael, and fair; that would be Wales. The other was a smaller brown-eyed man. Michael recognized him from Henrik's description: Bakti.

The weapons shifted away. One moved around, settled in the small of his back, and urged him onward. He kept his hands up and started forward. Wales talked softly, telling him where to go. "Left, all right, now right." They came to a ladder and he stood still while Bakti climbed it; Bakti crouched with a laser pistol while Michael went up. Wales followed. After that they took him through two short corridors at right angles and showed him through a door.

The door took him to the *Avalon*'s equivalent of Control. It did not have *GeeGee*'s plush light and he had not expected it. He had been on other private spacecraft, though, and his flesh tightened fastidiously at this. There might have been a visible movement, because the pistol rammed hard into his spine. There was hardly any illumination besides the *Avalon*'s displays. What there was, was probably Sol-normal, but it was ashen. He looked at a light source and saw the transparent cover deep in dust. Running was taking a toll on the *Avalon,* too.

B waited for him with folded arms. There were lines on his face that had not been there thirty years before, or even twenty, in the glimpse Michael had gotten of him in Shoreground. On Gadrah he was called Undying; but Michael thought: *He is old. Without the treatments he will die soon. Even with them.*

Bakti and Wales still stood behind Michael with weapons at the ready. B took a laser pistol from his own belt and armed it; then he nodded at the other two and they went away. There had been no sign of the fullblood Oriental, Ta, or the one Hanna had called Suarez.

"Back up," B said. "A couple more steps. You can put your hands down now."

Michael let his hands fall. The sense of peace was still with him, and it deepened. In all important respects his objective was accomplished. There was only a moment of distraction to create, and he could pick it. There was no hurry. He had all the time he would ever have, and the last mystery stood in front of him and looked into his eyes.

He said with genuine curiosity, "Why'd you decide to talk to me?"

B answered, "Thought I'd see how you turned out."

"A lot of people have been doing that lately . . . Tell me this," Michael said. "What are you?"

"A traveler," the man said, but the eyes had some expression for once; they were a wolf's. "A merchant," he said.

"I've known a lot of travelers, a lot of merchants. They didn't come here. How did you find out about this place?"

"Luck," B said.

"You weren't just cruising around out here."

"Oh, no," the man said. "There was a record. There was a course. The ship that came here in the Explosion, the first one, went back. One man took it back. He was supposed to sell it, use the money to buy smaller craft. So they could keep the connection, go back and forth. Instead he kept the money and stayed on earth. Kept the course, too. It floated around . . . Never got to a Polity data bank. Not while he was alive, because if anybody came back here they'd find out he was a thief. Not after he died because nobody knew what it was. It was during the Explosion. It was just another course. It got passed down with souvenirs. It was a rich family, thanks to him; they kept their property together. Then they had some hard times. I was trading in curiosities and heard they had some to sell. Looked them over and bought the lot. They didn't know about spacegoing, didn't know what they had, threw it in with the rest for junk. Wasn't anything like it in Polity records. I came to see."

The wolf-look was still there, but there was a new attention in it. Michael knew himself, knew what his transparent face must show: a child's wonder at the tale.

"Then they never meant to stay cut off," he said, as if B ought to have personal knowledge of that time hundreds of years ago, as if he had been alive then.

He is only a man, Hanna whispered in his mind; and as if to confirm it B answered, "Guess not."

"But when you came—didn't they want to make contact then?"

"No," said the man, faint amusement on his face.

"Because they'd have lost what they had. Because Oversight would have come, and they couldn't have kept running things like they did. You told them that. You told them whatever you wanted them to think. But the sickness?" Michael said, not pausing to consider what it meant that the answers came so easily, that this information would not be given to a man who might live.

"It was nothing much," B said. "Dawkins fever. I couldn't get the vaccine, last trip."

"But when you had it, the other trips, you only gave it to the—"

He stopped because he couldn't say the word. *Masters* had never come easily from his tongue. Now he could not say it at all.

B said, "You haven't changed much," and there was a threat in it. He looked at Michael just as he had thirty years ago. Michael knew why. His face and body had grown into mature beauty, but the child who had never been quite lost had returned. All the time in between slipped away, and a child looked at B with clear eyes. This time he was not afraid. There had been wounds inflicted in that earlier captivity, but they were healed. There had been too much kindness given and received since then, too much love. Even the sharp edges of Lillin's death were smoothed since he had seen Carmina, gone with the old rage. There were monsters, all right, real ones, and B was one of them. His monstrosity was his indifference. There were no people where he lived, only objects. He was a sport of nature; there was nothing of him in Michael; he was something that had happened to Michael, and that was all. The monster faced him and held Michael's death in his hands, but he was wrapped in peace, even joy. *I am,* Michael thought, joy rising, *I am Hanna and Theo, Lise and Shen; nothing can change that.* He smiled, and B moved the pistol suddenly, tightening a slackened aim.

"What did you want with Gadrah?" Michael said. "What could they have here you'd possibly need?"

B did not speak. But it was the last question Michael wanted an answer to, and he persisted. "They haven't got much to sell here, they can't buy much. Not enough to make coming out here worth it. Why'd you do it?"

B said with a shrug, "Thought I might need the place. Nobody knows about it, nobody finds me."

"If they started hunting you back there? Because of the children? Or were there other ships like the *Far-Flying Bird?*"

He saw the answer in B's eyes. Private spacecraft disappeared from time to time, luxury craft like *GeeGee,* without a trace. They used common routes and there would be ways to hail them, ways to get aboard with an innocent tale. You would take what you could, jewels, cash, leave no survivors, plunge the dead craft into a sun.

They hadn't done that last thing with the *Bird.* The alien controls would have been beyond them.

He waited a little longer, looking around without being

obvious about it. He was looking for the monitors that had to be here somewhere watching the valley.

"Want to talk truce?" he said, not meaning it, not listening for an answer; only buying time.

The thin smile crossed B's face. "Why not?" he said. He shifted position and Michael saw the screen behind him, hidden by his body until now. There was only one and it was not scanning in infrared, though the picture was enhanced to compensate for the dark. It was coming from the air; there was a mobile spyeye out there, of course. But B had his back to what it showed.

B had seen his eyes move, and looked at him narrowly. Michael thought carefully and deliberately, in words so clear Hanna, if she were with him, could not mistake them: *Get out of my head. The others need you.* He said aloud, "Now, Shen!"

B was not a fool. He guessed. He did not turn to look at the monitor; he moved away from it instead, waving Michael toward it, so he could see monitor and man at the same time. Michael walked in front of it, blocking B's line of sight, counting seconds. He turned his back on the screen and said casually, "What kind of truce would you have in mind?"

B knew what it was about now. He lifted the pistol. There would be no more talk; his eyes were empty as they had always been. Killing was not a pleasure, it was only a task, a permanent, efficient means to an end.

Seconds: Michael charged head down. The last step was a leap. A tremendous shock hit him, a planet fell on him oceans and all; half-conscious, he didn't know where he had been hit till pain started in his shoulder and arm, tentatively at first. It was going to get big and not give him much time. He had bowled B over and the pistol had spun away somewhere and he would never get to it; he tried to use his weight to hold B down and was flung away, strength gone, vision blurring. B yelled for Wales and the smell of burned flesh filled the room. B scrambled for the pistol. *Seconds, more seconds!* B had the pistol and turned, and Michael tried to move his head to look at the monitor but could not do it; the full weight of the pain came down, there wasn't room for anything else, and he blacked out not expecting to wake up again.

*   *   *

Just before *GeeGee* came, Hanna fainted. She had gone suddenly shaky and vague, and Theo, when he saw it, questioned her sharply. "Broke trance too fast," she had said, and then, while Theo watched for the *Golden Girl,* collapsed.

Shen set *GeeGee* down too hard, thinking of nothing but speed. A hatch yawned open on the side and Theo and Lise between them dragged Hanna through it. "We're in!" Theo yelled at an intercom and *GeeGee* lifted. A buzzer went off at the open hatch and Theo could not hear anything else till Shen triggered the closure from Control. The cover lifted into place and sealed itself, and there was quiet again.

Hanna sat up and shook off Theo's hands. Her face was bloodless and her eyes looked bruised. "Oh, God, he's hurt," she said.

"Who? Mike?"

"Yes." She ran trembling hands over her hair. She looked as if she might cry. "How are we ever going to get him out?" she said.

"What did he do?"

"Kept them busy," she said, remembering the weapon in B's hand, and buried her face in her hands.

"Kept them *busy?*" Theo said incredulously.

She did not answer. She got up holding on to Theo, still shaky, but she got steadier on the way to Control. They were skimming over mountains, down low, to Theo's surprise; he had expected Shen to take them into space, dodging the *Avalon.* But there was nothing after them.

"He wanted to keep their attention off the monitor," Hanna said, and repeated, "How do we get him out?"

Theo said, "Look, you're not going to like this. But he must have meant to look after himself. I think he wants us to go."

She was furious—but cut it off; that was more than fear talking. Whatever Michael wanted was what Theo wanted, and he was thinking of Lise. *Get out,* Michael had told her, and she had obeyed blindly; she could not be angry at Theo for doing the same thing.

Theo said persistently, "If he can get off the ship, he'll be all right. He knows the language, the territory—there's Carmina. Maybe he means to go to ground till the Polity comes."

"But he's *hurt*." She realized then that she did not know how badly. She had broken the thin trance-link before it happened, had been pulling herself together from that, and whatever had happened to Michael had come up behind her and knocked her out. She thought for an instant, *Oh God is he dead?* and Lise saw her face and went white.

But if he were dead, she would know it beyond doubt. The best part of her would be dead, too.

Lise said in a trembling voice, "Couldn't you make him stop?"

"I didn't know what was going to happen. It was like he, he knew just what he was doing— Oh," she said in anguish, "God damn him for not being afraid!"

Shen had not said anything. Hanna leaned against the back of Shen's seat. Theo was trying to comfort Lise and *GeeGee*'s normal sounds went on steadily, but there was a great silence, an absent voice. Hanna was weak and could not think.

Shen said, "Theo, you think you could get *GeeGee* home?"

He looked around, his arm around Lise. He was silent for a minute, working it out. "Sure," he said.

"Post." She was talking to Hanna now. "You and me, we steal a truck, see what they've got for guns. Get back there and come in behind, on foot. All right?"

"Wait a minute." Hanna's head started to work again. "They were only at Croft because we were. They'll go back to the Post."

"Yeah. We go, too, then. Get off *GeeGee* farther away. Send Theo back to Theta. Walk in like before, us two. They think nobody's left here, think we went with Theo."

"But if they think that—" There were flaws everywhere Hanna looked. If the *Golden Girl* escaped, B would give up on Gadrah; he would have to make a desperate flight to human space, try to disappear there; nothing else would be left.

Shen said practically, "Find out what he's thinking."

"What? Who?"

"B," Shen said, making a curse of it.

"Oh, but—" She wanted to say she couldn't. Every time she had touched B's thoughts it had been like a breath of the cold of deep space. And she knew, thinking of doing it now, that she was not as competent as she had been before. Because something had happened to Michael, and it was as if it had happened to Hanna herself. Hanna had been wounded, too. Nothing like this had happened to her before; she did not know whether she was diminished or augmented by Michael, but there was no separating one from the other, and the shock of knowing it made her tremble.

Shen looked at her with slanting eyes. "Communicator?" she said, distracting Hanna; what had happened to the communicator Michael carried? It had been broadcasting right up to the end. Shen on *GeeGee,* and the others on the ground, had heard every word of the last dialogue. If it had been destroyed— She turned suddenly so no one could see her face. She had a clear memory of Michael being searched, hoping they would leave the communicator *over his heart—*

If he were dead, she would know it. She clung to the thought.

As if it had been waiting for her to think about it, the communicator she had taken from Lise began to speak.

"Who's in charge?" said the voice like a snake, like a slug; a spider would talk that way. Hanna had the thing in her pocket; she pulled it out as if it were hot. "Where's the D'neeran?" B said.

She kept the shaking out of her voice. "What do you want?" she said without illusions, remembering the *Far-Flying Bird* more clearly than she had in months.

"Want him back?" said the voice.

"I want him back."

"Give me your ship," B said. "Fair trade."

She looked around at the tense faces. But Theo only looked at Lise.

"We have to think about it," she said, the hardest thing she had ever said, and shut off the transmission before B could speak again. Had he been listening to what was said on the *Golden Girl?* No, there had been no sound at all from the other end; the instrument must be shut off.

GeeGee slowed and hovered over forest. Shen said, eyes gleaming, "If we could get back there fast enough Surprise 'em."

"*GeeGee*'s the fastest thing on the planet," Hanna said. "If we take her back, we give her up or get shot down. Or just get shot down. What's he need *GeeGee* for?"

Shen shook her head. "Nothing. Trick," she said.

Not even Michael would recommend this risk, because it was a certainty, not a risk. B would use Michael to entice them to return, and kill them at once; then he would kill Michael, too. And *GeeGee* would never carry news to the Polity, and nothing would change on Gadrah, ever.

It all pointed to one end, the logical thing. If Michael could talk to them now, he would make it clear what he wanted them to do.

But Hanna said, "I can't leave him. Whatever the rest of you do, I can't."

Shen said patiently, "Told you. Find out what they think."

Hanna said without hope, "I'll try."

It took a long time. She retreated to Michael's room, and when she lay down on the bed and tried to clear her mind she was so tired and afraid she did not think she could get up again. She had not known that fear like this would be worse than fearing her own death. Her hand crept out to the empty space at her side, as if she could bring Michael back to it with her yearning. She did not want to touch B's mind. She had touched it before she knew who he was, when he had called the *Far-Flying Bird*. Then she had not even been revolted; her senses had cried *Caution!* but given no more specific warning; there had been no rage or hatred or even madness to trigger recognition. *Evil is cold,* she thought, fumbling. And she thought of what the creature had done, feeling nothing, on Gadrah—bringing death and bringing it finally to his allies, too, indifferent—and of the boy locked in B's quarters, uncomprehending, no mercy given to his sweetness. *He liked, liked ruining things, I think—*

She forgot what she was supposed to do and searched for Michael. She found him, and horror nearly drove her from the dream she had fallen into. He was in shock and in great pain. Nothing had been done for him. The burning light that had made his wound had cauterized it, and there was little bleeding, but every movement started agony up again. He breathed so shallowly that he hardly breathed at all. But then he would have to take a deep breath, and when he did, sometimes it came back out as a cry.

He did not know Hanna was with him. He thought he

had made her up, along with her grief. It did not seem to Hanna that anything could drive her from his side. But the traces of Shen in Michael's thought, Shen's purposefulness, did it.

I will come back, Hanna said. He thought he made that up, too. Pain took his attention again; he did not notice when she left him.

Too weary for discipline, made small by grief, she wandered. It was only luck that took her to B. Like Michael, he did not know she was there, only thought he was thinking about her. He might not like D'neerans (she thought later), but he disliked them without knowing much about what they could do.

Something was missing from his mind; it lacked a part. She wrenched herself away and thought: *He is not a human being.*

Yet by all criteria, he was. He was certainly not an alien, he was not even the Master of Chaos, he was master of nothing.

She opened her eyes and looked at the worked bronze Michael had set overhead. It looked back with the warmth of his eyes. She was so tired that exhaustion itself had shielded her from B, as if, without it, she might have been spattered with filth. She thought back reluctantly. She had learned something, she realized; she had no hope, but she could not say she had come to the end. Not yet.

She got up and went wearily back to Control. *GeeGee* was over ocean now, moving steadily but not fast, just to keep moving. The other three watched the ocean, where reflections of the Ring made a glittering path.

Hanna said without preamble, "He doesn't know we came without telling anybody."

Shen made an impatient movement; Hanna was talking gibberish.

"He's not sure nobody else knows how to get here," Hanna said.

Shen said comprehensively, "Henrik."

"He didn't think about Henrik, maybe he hasn't seen him, maybe Henrik didn't tell him, I don't know. Henrik's dead," she added, sure now. In all the exploration she had done since the morning, there had been no trace of him. Theo started to say something, but Hanna went on talking.

"That means he won't kill us right away. Look, there's more of them and they're armed. I don't know what we can do."

"Find out," Shen said, very pleased.

"Theo?"

"If we put Lise down somewhere safe first."

"No!" Lise said, full of indignation, and Shen said, "Nowhere safe."

After a minute Theo nodded. Hanna said, "Then we all go back."

Michael was left where he had fallen, out of the way and harmless. The chamber was a blur. There were meaningless sounds and he could not move, did not want to. After a long time of pain he could think again. The pain had not gone away, but he was not stupefied any more. But his thoughts followed random paths, and he had no direction to give them. He had not thought of this eventuality, of injury, immobility, captivity. He had expected swift death or a chance to escape, and had gotten neither.

He thought that since he was still alive, he must try to stay that way.

He thought that there were five men in front of him now, all armed; that only if he kept very still was the pain even tolerable; that he could not move without groaning, try to stand without falling, walk without staggering.

There was not much hope of escape. He gave up thinking about it.

Sounds began to fall into words. The blurred edges of the flight deck came into focus. The men stood between Michael and the consoles that housed the controls. Their backs were toward him, but from time to time one or another looked around. To the left was an open locker. He could see some kind of weapon in it; there might be others.

It would do no harm to get closer.

When the five were all turned away from him, he hauled himself up so that he sat with his back to the wall. The cost was blinding pain. They must have turned to look, but he was half-unconscious again, gasping like a dying fish and too weak to move. When the mist cleared, they were looking away.

He started to inch along the wall, using legs and his one good arm, pushing the useless left one ahead. He had looked down once at the black crater the laser had left and absorbed what it meant. If he were trapped on Gadrah he would lose the arm, at the least; without sophisticated medical attention, he would most likely die.

The hand at the end of it, dangling, got in his way. It was turning blue.

The world contracted, all his life contracted, to a simple sequence he would repeat and repeat forever. Hitch and move and brace against the pain and the fog it brought along. Wait for it to ease. He felt no diminution when it did, but his vision would clear, and he would know it must have gotten better.

Watch for another chance. Do it all again.

When he had been doing this for a long time he had moved a meter. The locker was still twice that far away. What was left of his strength was ebbing.

In one of the pauses he thought he heard Hanna's voice. He had imagined it once before, and he thought he must be losing consciousness again. But this time she was not talking to him, and he realized, slowly, that he heard a real voice, and real words, and what they meant.

"You will board, one of you, and we will give you our arms. I understand. If we make any resistance, Michael will be killed. Yes, we all understand."

After all his costly silence, after choking back a scream at every furtive move, he cried out then: "No! No!" He meant it to be a command and a plea for Hanna to hear, but it was a whisper. B heard it, though, and looked at him. He looked at the place Michael had started from, at the locker with the weapon in plain view, and he went to it and picked it up: another laser pistol. He swung it toward Michael and smiled with the faintest amusement, as he had smiled sometimes years ago when he did some unspeakable thing and watched the contorted, tear-stained face like a scientist observing the outcome of an experiment. "You won't need that any more," he said, and aimed for Michael's groin. Michael twisted away and the light burned another crater in his thigh. He made one wretched sound and sank on his face without tears or hope, and the *Avalon* and everything else went away.

The *Golden Girl* skimmed over seaboard, moving quickly but doing nothing like top speed. Shen looked ready to fight; she was the only one who did. A bleak feeling that death was near had come to Hanna. She tried to look back at the path that had led her to it, but she could not see one. *Courses.* Silver necklace of Earth, golden alien treasure, a piece of plain utilitarian metal: exactly what had B found all those years ago? A sheaf of paper? A microchip? She looked for some meaning in the objects, and found none. They had fallen into her life and she had had to make choices about them and that was that. *You choose what you can and the rest is just there.* He had said that to her once. She could not remember when.

Without warning her left leg gave way and she fell on the floor. There was an instant of nothing—she knew that because Theo had been at the other side of Control, and now he was bending over her. Her leg did not hurt; instead she held both hands over her heart. Theo took her pulse, examined her skin; he thought her heart was failing. It was not, but it was breaking. He wanted to know what was wrong with her and she would not tell him. Why hurt him by telling him Michael had been hurt again? But he must know by the tears that ran out of her eyes and down her cheeks. Her will was paralyzed; she could not stop them.

When *GeeGee* got back to Croft's valley, the *Avalon* had moved. It was not hidden but brooding in the open upriver from Croft. Shen brought *GeeGee* in slowly and landed a few meters away from the *Avalon.* She had been told to make the distance between as small as she could. She opened *GeeGee* up and they waited in Control, and Shen looked at Hanna and saw no help. Hanna was broken.

The thing that was supposed to be a man, looked like a man, was biologically a man, crossed the space between the ships. He came quickly. He would not make himself a target any longer that he had to; he thought he might be attacked; he thought they might hurt him though it meant Michael's death. That was how little he knew about them. It was how he thought.

They did nothing. They let him come. He walked into the golden light of Control like a bloated white spider and they only stood there, except Hanna who could not move and did not look up. Close to the door where he stood was a pile of weapons. There were three stunners, all they had left, and

Carmina's well-made, old-fashioned gun. He looked at them as if he did not believe they had gone where they had gone, done what they had done, with a handful of stunners.

He squatted and picked up the stunners one by one and snapped out the power pack from the butt of each. He put the packs and his laser pistol in a pocket, got up holding Carmina's gun, and cocked a finger at Lise. No one had uttered a word. Lise stood still. She was very pale.

"I want to look around," the soft voice said. "You show me."

Theo said to her quietly, "He won't hurt you yet. He wants another hostage."

"That's right," B said, "Listen to your daddy."

Lise took a step forward, shaking. The next step was stronger; she made it the rest of the way a step at a time, haltingly. B put his free hand on her shoulder and pushed her to the door. He said to the others, but mostly to Theo, "You know what happens if you do anything."

Theo said, "You don't need her for that. Unless Mike's already dead."

"Not quite," B said.

Lise looked up, the first time she had dared lift her eyes to his face. "You can kill me," she said. "I don't care. But don't hurt Mike!"

The transparent eyes were impersonal. He watched a performing animal.

"Why do you hate him?" Lise said. Her voice shook. "He never hurt you. He never hurt anybody."

B was not interested. He pushed her again. But Hanna said from the floor, "Earthquake." They looked at her again, even B, but her eyes were empty. She spoke again, with great effort. It was evident that she hardly knew she was speaking, and that she was talking to Lise—for her education. For some reason B listened, too. She said: "Wind. Volcano. Flood." Her eyes met Lise's. They were still empty, but after a moment Lise nodded as if she understood something new. Her face was sad. She was calmer, and she did not look like a little girl.

"People can be like that, too," she said. "Sometimes you don't live through it."

B shoved her then and she went out ahead of him, the gun at her back.

She did just as she was told, though she was slow about it. She had almost stopped thinking. *I used to be afraid like this sometimes before,* she thought, when she did think. But for a year she had forgotten this kind of fear.

B followed her through the galley and the lounges. *Cooking and luscious food, games and conversation.* She wanted those familiar places to mean what they had meant before—she wanted it so badly that she was disoriented, which was why she was slow.

The medlab. "Ever use it?" he said. Theo was a physician, she said with difficulty. The old staff quarters with their alphanumeric locks; they had modified one to lock from outside for the I&S operative, and B looked at it carefully. The cargo hold, and down to the engine rooms, living quarters, Mike's room, Lise's own. *Theo patiently repeating a lesson.* And back to Control.

She wanted to run to Theo, but B held her by the arm. He held her in front of him and poked Carmina's gun into her back. He talked into the air, his voice traveling to the *Avalon.* Who would be killed, who would not be?—it remained an open question, that was the meaning of what he said. There was Polity medical technology here and a Polity-trained doctor. Maybe Theo would be spared. And Lise, as hostage for his good behavior. She got that much out of what B said. But that meant—she shuddered, and the hand was harder on her arm—that Mike wouldn't make it, or Hanna or Shen. There was no use for them.

Hanna's body had forgotten who it belonged to. When she got up it was weak, and twitched. It rose in obedience to some command from outside and let itself be herded out of Control and through *GeeGee* toward the craft's rear, into the room they had made into a cell. The door closed and they were locked in. Lise could finally cling to Theo. Shen stood by the narrow bunk, her face dark with thought, but Hanna sank to the floor again. Her body was numb, especially on the left side, shoulder and thigh. She had never felt anything like it before, she had not know this was possible, this connection of flesh through the spirit. Her efforts at thought did not get anywhere; they spiraled into the pit of Michael's unconsciousness.

Shen came and squatted in front of her. When Hanna did

not look up, Shen took her shoulders and shook her. "Wake up! Pay attention!"

It was too much effort to speak aloud. *I can't,* Hanna said in thought.

Shen shook her again. "What are they all doing?"

I don't know.

"Find out!"

She tried halfheartedly. When she reached out there was only one place she wanted to go, one mind she wanted to see. If she tried hard enough, she could wake him. But only to pain and despair—so she would not do it; but the struggle not to do it, to let go and give him up so his end would be easier, took all the little she had left. She put no name to what she felt, the vast misery. She only knew that Michael's coming death was the most important, the worst thing that had ever happened, and she could not spare thought for her own fate, or Shen's.

Shen felt enough of it to know what was happening in Hanna. Real pain, sharp and stinging, forced its way through Hanna's fog; Shen slapped her methodically, cursing. "Gonna lay down and die? Say where they are. Say it now! Now!"

B's in Control. Doing something.

"Doing what?"

I don't know. The navigational systems. Crippling Gee-Gee. *So we can't go back*—

"What about the rest? They coming over here?"

No. Later. Not yet. She saw through someone's eyes for half a second. The man was on the *Avalon.* There was tension and some kind of suspicion there: dissent inside the wolf pack, directed at B. She couldn't concentrate on it, she couldn't concentrate on the import of what B was doing, exiling them here; she was drawn too hard to the dark shape on the floor at the edge of someone's vision.

Shen got up and roamed the tiny room, furious, thinking. "How bad's Mike hurt?" she said, got no answer, turned to see tears streaming from Hanna's eyes again; went back to her, and went back to slapping her. The wet cheeks were starting to bruise. "Can he walk? *Can he walk!*"

"I don't know, I don't know! I don't think so."

"Gonna have to try. Soon's they leave."

Hanna got a glimpse of what Shen was thinking.

"He can't, it would kill him—"

"You remember before? Broken ribs, fever, you remember what you did?"

"I remember. But—"

"So?"

They stared at each other. Shen shook Hanna again, gently this time. "Gonna die anyway, him, you, everybody. All we got left's one surprise. You're it. You and Mike."

He was conscious of being cold. His body was shutting down. The pain had removed to some distance, was with him and would be there until the end, but hung back for a time like a live thing, a scavenger waiting for an opening. In the half-world of relative peace, images played at random in his head, the mind shutting down, too. He saw the house on Valentine, much too big, ridiculously big, but it had given him the seclusion he wanted. A dark blue-eyed woman lived there, completing his peace. He was not capable of questioning the image. It seemed as if it had been so. It was what he had wanted, and here at nightfall he believed he had had it.

Hanna sat beside him on the beach below the house, dressed in white. The wind gusted hard from the sea and she put up a hand to her frivolous floppy hat, to hold it on. Wisps of hair escaped and stirred softly in the wind. She was smiling, and her eyes were as blue as the sunlit water.

"It won't hurt to get up now," she said. "I'll keep it from hurting."

"Can you?" He did not really doubt her. It was Hanna, he realized now, who kept the pain at bay, so that it made a circle around him but did not quite touch him.

"It's your useful trance," he said, pleased. "All right, then."

The bright white sand dazzled his eyes. If he squinted, he could see other things through the sand. He was somewhere else as well as on the beach, simultaneously. It was too dark to see much of the other place, but he was alone there. There had been other men; they were gone. He had to learn to stand. "Try locking the knee," Hanna said, and it worked. He would never walk normally again, too much muscle was damaged or gone, but if he kept the leg straight and balanced carefully, he could use it as a prop to heave himself along.

The beach was gone, but Hanna walked ahead of him, still in white. One side of the skirt was slit nearly to the hip, and when the wind blew it away, he thought he had never seen anything more lovely than her shapely brown leg. There had been other women, and he remembered them with love and gratitude. They had helped educate him for loving Hanna.

"I didn't tell you often enough how beautiful you are," he said.

"That's all right," she said. "Be careful here. There's a ladder you have to get down."

It helped a lot that he was weightless; or maybe he felt that way because there was, in his undamaged limbs, a strength he had never dreamed he had. Sometimes he hung by his good hand from a rung, supporting his weight one-handed without effort, feeling for a foothold for the usable leg; sometimes, weight on one foot, he leaned precariously inward while he shifted the hand. It was not a long ladder, but it took time all the same. "Don't hurry," Hanna said.

"It would've been good," he said. "Wouldn't it? Nothing else like it for either of us. Once in a lifetime. You couldn't do this with just anybody, could you?"

"I could not." She stood on air beside the ladder. It had gotten very dark, but she was illuminated, and the sea breezes from nowhere stirred her hair and the long white skirt. He looked at her with love.

"I heard of it long ago," she said with the cool objectivity of trance. "It's called a true match, I think. You don't see it often on D'neera or anywhere else—people who go on together for years and years and it only gets stronger. I think that's what we might have been. But there has to be time to find out."

"Why us?" he said. "You and me. We're so different."

"But you have what I need. And I have it for you. Why shouldn't we be different, otherwise?"

"I almost had the rest of what I wanted, once," he said. "Plain peace. I wish I could have found it and given it to you. But we've got more than most people get."

"I know that. I didn't see it at first. Not until this happened, not really. But I know now."

Negotiating the ramp was hard. The ground between the *Avalon* and *GeeGee* was uneven enough to be a worse trial,

and it was dark. There must be an end to the body's resources even in trance, which only permitted them to be
drained far beyond ordinary limits, beyond safety. Michael's
pace, which had not been fast, slowed even more. *GeeGee*
had not come any nearer for some time. Michael wondered
it he had been moving at all, or had only thought so. He
paid close attention to the next awkward step. "I was standing still," he said. "It's not going matter anyway, is it?"

"Probably not," Hanna said, and he looked up and could
not see her any more; only *GeeGee* looming ahead of him
in the night.

They had not bothered to close *GeeGee* up. There was a
ramp here, too, and he dragged himself up it and through
the air lock and into the belly of his ship, which hummed
and showered him with golden light. His own bed was close
at hand, but he turned the other way and saw Hanna at the
top of the spiral stair, her face serene and, now, transparent.
A fragment of lyric came to him, part of the old music he
most loved: *God grant every gentleman such hawks, such
hounds, and such leman!*

"Where are they?" he said. "Do you see anything?"

"I see nothing except what you see. I'm not really there,
Mike."

"Oh, that's right. How am I going to get up the stairs?"

"Pull," she said. And waited without moving, a dimming
figure of light, while he humped awkwardly up the endless
stair, pulling with the good right arm, pushing with right
knee and foot, up one step at a time. Toward the end he had
less strength. He was nearly finished, and when he finally
reached the top, he had to try several times before he could
stand up. *GeeGee*'s light was fading, and to breathe he had
to will his chest to move in and out. He stood wondering
why he had not yet been discovered and stopped, and then
his ears told him why. They had been (he realized) attuned
to a different level of reality altogether. But now when he
paid attention, he heard voices from the direction of Control, angry voices, an argument building. The men were too
busy quarreling about B's erasure of the way home to think
they might have left a threat behind.

He turned and hitched his weary way past the galley,
through the main lounge and the small one, past the medlab. The corridor bent to the left and he took the turn awk-

wardly. In a minute he would turn right again and would
face the door behind which Hanna was shut up. He could
not see her any more. She waited for him where she had
been all the time.

He kept listening to the real world, straining to hear the
voices that had dropped away behind him, and that saved
him, because he heard the sound in the corridor through
which he passed. Just before the second turn there was a
setback, something to do with the mechanical systems, to
his left; he staggered into it and pressed his back flat against
the wall. Someone made the turn he had just made and
came level with him, looking ahead and to the next turn, to
his right therefore, so that Michael had an instant of grace.
It was B, with something in his hand.

Michael saw what it was, Carmina's gun, a deadly thing,
B was going to kill. For an instant, a second in which time
stopped, everything was clear. The riddle of B was simple
after all. Something that might have been a man had said
No! to life some time a long time ago.

Yes! said Michael, and fell on B's back. They went down
together and the gun went off with a great noise. He had no
strength of his own but there was a great inrushing, Hanna's
strength, more. Knee in back, arm around the throat, he
heaved, pulled, felt the straining spine—and heard a crack.
The last air rattled out of B's mouth and he was limp.

It was not Michael but used-up flesh that jerked through
the last few paces, punched the simple sequence that
opened the lock, and held out the gun to Hanna. She took
it, but she never did anything conscious with it. Wales had
come, drawn by the noise, and he fired straight at Michael's
back. The blast took his heart, Hanna felt the heat on her
breast as Michael fell on her, and it was by reflex that she
fired and killed Wales as she fell down with Michael into his
death.

After that Shen went after them, Lise said, *I heard her, she
had that thing that makes the noise and one of them came
and I heard it go off. The others—they're dead, too. She got
them, too. I didn't see that, I was busy. Helping with Mike, till
Shen came, then Theo said go help you, I thought you were
dead, too, you were so still—*

*   *   *

There was something in the medlab which Hanna could not believe had ever been Michael. It was cold in the medlab, icy. Theo had partitioned off the space where Michael's body lay. He and Hanna argued bitterly. They had been arguing for a long time.

You shouldn't be here, he said, *I shouldn't be here, Mike shouldn't. You have to know when to let the dead go, that's what they told me a long time ago. If this was Earth, Willow, maybe Co-op, there'd be a chance, if I'd got him wired in in time, if his brain wasn't dead, but it is—*

Hanna sat in the cold wrapped in blankets Lise had brought. Once, early, she had gone away. Theo left to himself had sat down on the floor and held his head in his hands as if the weight of his own living skull would give him strength to do what he had to do, the last thing he could ever do for Michael. But before he could do it, Hanna had returned. She had found one of the laser pistols and gotten it powered and armed. *You will not let him die,* she had said.

B wiped the course while we were locked up, Shen said, *while the rest were still over there. Been wiped from the Avalon, too. They didn't want to stay, he fixed it so they had to. Did that to their ship then did it to Gee in secret so we're trapped, too. They come and find out, that keeps 'em busy, I guess, while Mike's coming here—*

Theo looked at Hanna's eyes black with madness or grief, he looked at the laser pistol, he grieved, he looked and grieved for hours, hardly comprehending what Shen had said, that they had been robbed of the way home. He looked also at the lines and lights that told him where Michael was and they never changed. Machines kept blood pumping steadily through a cadaver but the brain would never think again, and the sun was gone for good. Between fits of weeping he screamed at Hanna and she screamed back or was silent. *Let me let him go.* He begged abjectly. *Please let me let him go!*

Shen could have taken Hanna from behind with a stunner, and she would have done it if Theo had given her a sign, but he didn't. He thought obscurely that he was doing what Michael would have wanted.

After twenty-four hours of this Hanna collapsed without warning in a silent heap. Theo made sure she was all right and then, weeping, turned off the machines.

*   *   *

Michael was buried in a mountain meadow with Croft's valley spread out below. Hanna spent her days and some of the cold nights in the mountains. She went back to *GeeGee* when hunger drove her, and at those times spoke to no one. In the mountains, though, she talked. She talked to the hills, the streams, and the slanting brown trees, but her words were for ears that were not there, chiefly Rubee's.

"I don't want any more of your stories," she said to Rubee, her hands full of shreds of leaves; she plucked them off the low branches from which they would not fall, still glossy though richly brown, and tore them slowly one by one to bits. She did this all day long. She resented the leaves; they behaved as if they would not give summer up. "What's the use of doing anything? I wish I had never heard of you," she said to dead Rubee.

She got things mixed up. She knew about the deities of a wild mix of human and other cultures, but the only god she clearly remembered was the Master of Chaos, to whom she insisted, at times, that she was not Uskosian, so his rules should not have applied to her. It would have been good to think the Master had a single face—a pale one with transparent eyes—because if that were so, he would be dead. She had felt him die and be killed by joy, she had felt the victory of laughter. But she had also seen the light go out afterward, which proved that horror might take any face, and the twitch of a finger could sweep love and courage away, and it was best to count on the worst and go on free from the illusion of hope.

Crouched by the grave in the early snow like Michael's monument, she "heard" people come up the mountain.

Theo and Lise. And a man and woman not of Croft. Of the Polity.

Her mind took the longest Jump it had ever made.

"There could be help," Norsa had said, "though you will not know until it shows itself what form it will take."

Norsa called them and had them record the course, she thought. *They got onto* GeeGee *while we were in Ree and recorded the course.*

She felt Theo and Lise halt at the meadow's edge. Theo thought approaching Hanna wasn't safe, and he would hold Lise back until it was.

The others came on until they stood beside Hanna, and she looked up at them. They were healthy and fit in their green Fleet uniforms. They looked back at Hanna cautiously. She heard them think that she was not as bad as Theo had said.

"You didn't get him," she said, "he got away," and they changed their minds.

That was all she had to say to the Polity. Two ships had come to Gadrah; one soon went home, and Hanna was on it. In the first weeks of the trip she spoke only once. That was immediately after departure, when she submitted with unexpected docility to medical examination. At the end of it the examining physician said, "Did you know you're pregnant?"

"Yes," Hanna said.

"How long have you known?"

She shrugged.

"Do you want me to end it for you?"

"Try it and I'll kill you," she said.

Chapter 8

So she had decided to live, as was evident from what she had said. She did not feel like living, but she did not feel like dying either; she did not feel much. She was mute at her parting with the others who had been her companions for so many months, and Michael's companions much longer. They would survive. Theo would look after Lise, Lise would give Theo a reason to live, and Shen would tell them both what to do. Someday Hanna would have to finish it with them, they would have to see the child, and Carmina ought to see it too, when Hanna was alive again. But for now she waited for something to bring her to life. Her child was not real yet; it was flesh busily making the structure to be human, but there was no mind that could even sense the echo of her thought. She was still alone, and only on another journey.

And that was your last, she thought to Michael who was not present either, *that was the end of the journey of your life. Why did you take me, if it was the last? And if you took me, why did you let it be the end?*

The physician came back to see her loaded with charts and readouts. He said she would have a boy and talked about genetic analysis. The child would be much like Michael, he said.

When the physician was gone she said to the child who was not present yet, *You'll be a handful, then.*

The Polity's ship came to Theta and crossed into the relay system of human space, and Hanna spoke for the second and last time on that voyage. She asked for and got permission to contact her House, and, not meeting much resistance, resigned what remained of her tenuous position there. Her son would not be a telepath, and D'neera was no place for a true-human.

After that, there was nothing to do but wait for the journey to be done.

It was summer when Hanna got to Earth. The year had come round and started again since she rested under a tree with Rubee and Awnlee. She was put into a medical center and continued to be silent until she was left alone in a room of her own. There were no windows and it was impossible to see the summer. She had acknowledged to herself that she would have to start talking sooner or later; when she tried the door, determined to walk out of the place, and found it locked, she thought she might have waited too long. But it opened suddenly from outside. She stared up in horror; it was too much like what had happened at the end on *GeeGee*, her mind slipped and she thought Michael would be there, his eyes a blaze of gold and sick to death. The vision passed; Starr Jameson stood in front of her. She leaned against him in relief. "Oh, you came," she said.

"Your people at Koroth asked me to. Come on, then," he said.

So she finally came back to his house, the new weight in her belly making her steps nervous, though the swelling was scarcely visible yet. It was not a homecoming, but at least she could talk to Jameson, because it seemed that she had known him all her life, and he was not new as Michael had been, but a constant. All the same, she was slow to find her voice. She had been at Jameson's house for a week before it returned. One evening just at dusk he came to her and suggested they sit in the garden. She went outdoors for the first time since coming here, and was overwhelmed. On spaceships the air had all the life filtered out of it, and no wind ever moved. The garden on this summer evening was fragrant; there were grasses and leaves and flowers to smell. A breeze pressed against her skin, and moonlight made everything silver and black. She was dizzy with the night. Questions crowded to the end of her tongue. She tried to hold them back; to ask them, to be answered, to hear new things, would be to start living again. She had thought herself unready to do it. But she had promised. The child growing under her heart was proof of that.

And then she could not hold it back any longer. "What

happened?" she said. "I don't know anything. What happened to Theo? To Lise? To Shen?"

"It's too early for anything to happen. Nothing's happened," Jameson said. "You nearly cost me Contact; don't you want to hear about that?"

"No. I don't care," Hanna said, feeling an enormous relief. Jameson would not change. Some things remained predictable. "What's going to happen to them, then?"

"Probably nothing," he said. "They're not very important any more, in the view of I&S. They'll soon be free to do whatever they like."

But they'll have to learn to live without Mike, she wanted to say, but instead, as still sometimes happened, a fit of sobbing overtook her, and now that she wanted to talk she could not do it. They were sitting at a table and she put her head down and felt the cool wood against her cheek. Jameson came closer and began to rub her back, and she turned and pressed her face against him. When she could talk, she said, "We could have gotten away. He stayed in Croft and stayed and stayed and I tried to get him to leave. I tried so hard."

"I know," he said.

"You can't know. I didn't tell anybody."

"Jadinow was there. Unlike you, he was willing to tell the story. I heard about it from the reports that came back with you."

"You know everything, then . . ." Because the others had seen everything—except for that last night on the mountainside. She had not been able to think about it consciously, though she had dreamed about it, as if the erotic bond that held her to Michael had reached its flowering then. She supposed her son would be a permanent reminder of that night; she supposed that was when it had happened.

Jameson dropped to the ground by Hanna's chair, an unaccustomed pose. He looked out into the night as if he were waiting to fend off whatever came out of it. There were thoughts she had not let herself think because it had not seemed safe to have them. They came on irresistably as speech, as the smell of the grass.

"I *told* him so," she said. "I told him it was dangerous to go there the way we did. I told him so!"

"I expect he knew," Jameson said. "He was not a stupid man."

"But it was stupid to stay so long in Croft. Stupid!"

Jameson still looked into the dark, though the moonlight must blind him to whatever waited there. "I was not surprised to learn you had gone to Uskos," he said. "I rather thought you would, after the failure at D'neera."

He was starting for some point. Hanna waited.

"You had the necklace," he said. "I worried about it. I mentioned it once or twice. Eventually I&S thought of it themselves, and finally approved the mission to Uskos. By the time it got there, you were gone."

She repeated, "You mentioned the necklace once or twice. That we might go there."

"Yes. Once, I think."

"It's on record, of course. That you did warn them."

"Of course. But they paid no attention. I knew they would not, if they were not reminded often. Daily, perhaps."

"I wondered why no mission came . . ."

They were quiet, watching the moon climb. The silence went on until Hanna said very quietly, the words pushing themselves off her tongue, "Did Mike stay too long in Croft on purpose?"

"I've wondered," Jameson said. "But why would he? His chances were good, after Uskos."

"He never believed that," she said. "He did kill that man so many years ago. In cold blood."

"Did he?" Jameson said. He looked up, but it was hard to make out his expression in the ambiguous light.

"Was he right, then, not to believe?"

"He was probably right," Jameson said. He added, "To wait was understandable, in that case. To seek a final confrontation. I suppose the decision was unconscious, or you would have known. But he risked your life, too. I cannot forgive him for that."

She had no answer. Instead she said, "I dreamed you told me he had no center. It was before I even knew I loved him."

"Well," he said, "you do learn. Slowly, but you learn."

He took her hand and held it, still watching the night, an unshakable guard. "What will you do next?" he asked.

"I don't know. I am truly homeless now."

"You've seen too many deaths," he said.

"I don't want to see any more!" It was awkward to lean

against him, crouched at her side as he was, but she managed it, bending to press her head to his shoulder. He reached around to touch her hair. He said, "I could give you only, some time too soon, another death."

"I know," she said. "That's no reason to withhold all the rest you could give." But her hand rested on her belly, waiting for the quickening.

"You can stay here, you know," he said. "Until you're ready to go."

"I will. For a while."

She had no worries about the means to live; Koroth would take care of its own. But where she should go after the child was born, and what else she should do with living, were different questions.

"I could go to Willow," she said. "Or live on Uskos for a while; I've never met an Uskosian I didn't like. Or I could just travel, or . . ."

Her voice trailed away. It did not matter what she said. Something would come up. Something always came up.

Jameson said, "Your plans seem very uncertain."

"What other kind is there?" she said.

RM Meluch
The Tour of the Merrimack

"This is grand old-fashioned space opera, so toss your disbelief out the nearest airlock and dive in."
—*Publishers Weekly* (starred review)

THE MYRIAD	978-0-7564-0320-1
WOLF STAR	978-0-7564-0383-6
THE SAGITTARIUS COMMAND	978-0-7564-0490-1
STRENGTH AND HONOR	978-0-7564-0578-6
THE NINTH CIRCLE	978-0-7564-0764-3

*Available October and November 2013
in brand new two-in-one omnibus editions!*

Tour of the Merrimack: Volume One
(The Myriad & Wolf Star)
978-0-7564-0954-8

Tour of the Merrimack: Volume Two
(The Sagittarius Command & Strength and Honor)
978-0-7564-0955-5

To Order Call: 1-800-788-6262
www.dawbooks.com